Complete Series Omnibus

The Indigo Reports

CAMERON COOPER

Published by Stories Rule Press Inc.
Edmonton, Alberta, Canada.

Registered offices:
1100-10020 101A Avenue NW
Edmonton AB T5J 3G2

This is an original work by Cameron Cooper
Copyright © 2020

FIRST EDITION: September 2020

This is a work of fiction. Names, characters, places and incidents either are the product of the author's imagination or are used fictitiously, and any resemblance to actual persons, living or dead, business establishments, events, or locales, is entirely coincidental. The publisher does not have any control over and does not assume any responsibility for third-party websites or their content.

A Stories Rule Press publication
All rights reserved
No part of this book may be reproduced, scanned, or distributed in any printed or electronic form without permission. Please do not participate in or encourage piracy of copyrighted materials in violation of the author's rights. Purchase only authorized editions.

Cooper, Cameron
The Indigo Reports/Cameron Cooper—1st Ed.

Science Fiction—Fiction

IngramSpark ISBN: 9781774381908
Amazon KDP Print ISBN: 9781774381854

About *The Indigo Reports*

The Entire Space Opera Series in One Volume

Binge read the full story of Bellona and her Ledanians—a small group of tortured misfits with horrific histories, who struggle to hold back the might of two great empires so that all people everywhere can live freely.

The Indigo Reports is the boxed set of the entire space opera science fiction series by award-winning SF author Cameron Cooper.

In this volume:
0.5 *Flying Blind*
1.0 *New Star Rising*
1.1 *But Now I See*
2.0 *Suns Eclipsed*
3.0 *Worlds Beyond*

Space Opera Science Fiction Omnibus

Praise for *The Indigo Reports*

The story is unpredictable, the horror and pain is real. This is an epic saga!!

The signature intensity and tension of the Indigo series is back!!!

This is epic science fiction at its finest. Realistic far future worlds. Incredible characters and scenarios.

Cameron knows how to tell a story, regardless of whether we are going back in history or forward in time.

Until this book I had forgotten just how much I love good science fiction and Cameron's is not just good, it's exceptional.

This is a complex tale of planetary politics, plotting, spying, scientific marvels, and advanced androids. Plus there is the fascinating floating city of Demos.

The concepts are staggering and intensely interesting.

The Indigo Reports series is far more than I ever anticipated.

This story is terrific! It's intriguing and futuristic and human in its telling.

One of my favorite and most satisfying science fiction series to read. A series to devour.

The Indigo Reports Book 0.5

Flying Blind

CAMERON COOPER

STORIES RULE
EDMONTON • ALBERTA

About *Flying Blind*

Caught between two great enemies.

The freeship *Hathaway* is boarded by the Eriuman navy while smuggling a Karassian, a mortal enemy of the Eriuman. Captain Tatiana Wang must ease her ship and crew to safety.

Flying Blind is the short prequel to the Indigo Reports science fiction series by award-winning SF author Cameron Cooper.

Praise for *Flying Blind*

By the time you get to the end of the story you're sitting on the edge.

An exciting glimpse of what's to come by this author in the SciFi genre.

True SciFi is a magnificent world to enter and this is just the beginning of what I know will be a great series.

Hits all the things that I love about Sci-fi.

So much story!! So much promise!! This will keep my inner nerd happy.

Keeping close tabs on this new Sci-fi series.

This little window into the world of SciFi did not disappoint me, in fact, I think I'm addicted!!

Flying Blind

Freeship Hathaway. Rinat System Provincial Space.

THE APPEARANCE OF THE ERIUMAN patrol surprised everyone, including Tatiana herself. They were in neutral territory, minding their own business. To anyone who looked, they were just a small freeship.

"What in the stars above is Erium doing out here?" she demanded of the whole bridge.

"They're insisting we halt for boarding, Captain!" Ruh called from the communications console.

"Specifics, please," she asked, forcing her voice back to reasonableness. Others would panic if they heard the captain screeching. "And I want our passenger here, right *now*. I have some questions for her."

People moved.

Tatiana ran through possible scenarios, weighing and discarding potential strategies. She didn't have enough information to make a decision, yet. "Ruh?"

Her brother wrinkled his nose as he read the data. "A convoyer. The AI thinks it might be the *Africanus*."

A convoyer. "Scan wide," Tatiana said quickly. "Highest sensitivity. Convoyers don't travel alone." She lifted her voice. "And someone tell me about the *Africanus*!"

There was a murmur of voices by the bridge gate. Three of the crew were hauling their passenger along by her arms. Marisol. As most Karassians did, she had only the one name.

The crewmen holding Marisol let her go. She stood on the decking in front of Tatiana, her arms crossed and her head tilted. She had declared herself an Upgrade, rather than a Standard, but had not specified what category of Upgrade she was. Other Karassians might have insisted on the details. Free citizens just didn't care. At least Marisol *looked* normal. The biocomps and biobots, on the other hand, looked out of place anywhere but central Karassia.

"Why is there a Eriuman patrol demanding to board my ship?" Tatiana asked her.

Marisol shrugged. "When they enter, you can ask them."

"Perhaps I should put you out in front of the welcoming committee," Tatiana said. "They're here for you, aren't they?"

Marisol shook her head. Her hair was perfect Karassian blonde, her lips full and symmetrical and her eyes a flawless brown. She looked much the same as every other Karassian Tatiana had ever met. The standard enhancements every Karassian received before birth made them that way, especially to outsiders. Even her disdain fit the pattern. "They are not here for me," Marisol declared firmly. Too firmly.

"Something you're carrying, then," Tatiana surmised. "Search her."

Marisol tried to struggle. Too many free staters were willing to hold her down. She swore and leaned up on one elbow from her prone position on the deck, as someone handed Tatiana a small, shielded box. It sat on Tatiana's palm, looking innocent.

"A whole patrol for this?" Tatiana moved her hand, examining it from every angle. She made no move to open it, though. Noxious things came in small packages, as well as big, Erium-sized ones.

"Captain, they're calling again!" Ruh said.

Tatiana sighed. "Hide the Karassian."

"How, Captain?" Gelan asked, hauling Marisol to her feet.

"Surprise me," Tatiana told him. "No, wait…" She

looked Marisol over. The Karassian wore the same bored expression she had used since boarding, yesterday. "Here's what you do," she told Galen and outlined the plan swiftly.

Galen grinned, liking it. So did the others. Marisol lost her indifference. Genuine anger flickered in her eyes. She scowled as Galen pulled her away again.

Tatiana hefted the little box once more. Its light weight told her nothing about the contents. The Eriuman patrol hovering above them did, though.

She moved over to the navigation table, bent and tapped the false panel in three corners, in the correct order. The plate popped open, she shoved the box inside and sealed it. "Let them come," she told Ruh. "Not that we can stop them." She tapped her wrist, selecting the wide channel. "Everyone, prep for boarding. The Eriumans are here."

* * * * *

AS THE SHUTTLE ATTACHED ITSELF with a solid thunk and hiss of hydraulics that shuddered and echoed through the bridge, Tatiana reviewed the data on the *Africanus* on Ruh's terminal. Ruh was part of the greeting party as he was the most fluent in Eriuman.

The *Africanus* was one of the oldest of the convoyers in the Eriuman navy. The Karassians would have discarded the old craft a decade ago. The Eriumans considered such practice a waste. The *Africanus* did not bristle with armaments, although she did have a smart canon, which was all she needed against freeships like the *Hathaway*. The *Africanus* had been patrolling Eriuman border states for the last five years, which didn't explain why it was out here in the Rinat system.

Now she wished she had opened the damn box. There was no time, though. The march of boots was already sounding in the access corridor, mixed with the babble of frightened voices.

Tatiana straightened up and turned to the gate. Next to her, Ruh's apprentice, Elmer, gave a shuddering exhalation. Tatiana glanced at his huge, dark eyes. "It will be fine," she assured him.

Elmer swallowed. "I've never seen one before."

"A patrol?"

"An Eriuman." He pressed his lips together for a moment. "Have you?"

Tatiana realized she was stroking her thigh where the long scar lay beneath her trousers and made her hand stop. "Once," she admitted.

"And you lived...."

Only just. She spoke the qualification in her mind, for the boy was unnerved enough. Karassians were crazy. Eriumans were not. They did their killing with cold calculation.

No wonder they hated each other.

The first through the bridge gate was an Eriuman officer, resplendent in purple, the braid and buttons glinting. His black eyes quartered the bridge. His gaze fell on Tatiana...and stayed there. He had correctly identified the most senior officer on the bridge despite their lack of uniforms or pretty rank identifiers like braid and swirls.

Behind the officer, two more junior aides were dragging Ruh along, his arms wrenched behind his back. Ruh looked furious. There was a hand over his mouth, holding in his protests. Ruh had more than a common grasp of language. If he was angry, he tended to use that honed skill.

Tatiana hid her dismay. She lifted her chin, for the officer was much taller than her. He seemed young. His dark olive features were smooth and free of lines—not that such smoothness was a good indicator of age among the Eriuman. Their in-breeding had done more than just purify their bloodlines. From the energetic way he walked to the alertness he was displaying told Tatiana this one was as young as he looked. Yet he had too many buttons and too much braid for a young man. Was he from one of the primary clans, then? It would explain his rank.

She didn't let his youth or possibly privileged rank fool her. No one confronted the Eriuman military, especially their officers, unless it was unavoidable. They were ruthless, disciplined and highly skilled at the art of war and they considered everyone who was not an Eriuman to be inferior and an enemy. Eriuman enemies were dealt with harshly.

Tatiana realized she was rubbing her thigh again. She clenched her fist.

"Captain Tatiana Wang of the freeship *Hathaway*," the officer said. "You will explain your presence in the Rinat system." His Common was flawless. The accent, though, was thick.

All the stories and rumors she had heard in spacer bars across the galaxy whispered to her now. Sometimes, bravado earned respect from the Eriumans, for they appreciated courage.

"Explain to whom, exactly?" Tatiana demanded. "I would prefer to know the name and rank of the officer who boards my ship so presumptuously."

The corner of his mouth quirked upward.

From deeper inside the ship, she could hear more shouting and some screams. There were only three officers standing on the bridge and five soldiers. The soldiers were armed with ghostmakers. The muzzles were all pointing at someone. It left fifteen more of them to comb the ship and one other officer to direct them.

Tatiana tilted her head at the officer and raised a brow. *See?*

"Tribunal Lieutenant Maximilian Cardenas Scordini de Deluca," the officer said.

Tatiana knew enough about their names to pick out the interesting one. He was from the Scordini clan. Privileged, indeed.

"Now, you will explain why you are in Eriuman space without clearance," he added.

"*Eriuman* space?" she repeated, genuinely shocked. "Rinat is free space."

"Not for a standard week now. Have you not been keeping up with news?"

Her heart fell. The Eriumans did not tolerate ignorance. They did not leave warnings marking their territory, nor did they go to any great lengths to explain procedures. If one ventured into their space, it was at one's own risk.

Now they had annexed Rinat. Marisol had failed to mention that when she had been negotiating passage back to Karassia.

Tatiana made herself look as humble as she could manage. Her throat squeezed painfully and her heart, too. "I didn't know," she admitted. "No one on the *Hathaway* went to the surface. We just dropped our passenger and were about to leave. We have another commission, in the Shimshon system."

"You aren't carrying passengers there?" Cardenas asked sharply. "That is economically inefficient."

"Life does not always arrange itself in symmetrical perfection," Tatiana pointed out.

Cardenas considered her. She could hear his men routing out her family, rooting through any nook and cranny. Crashes and the sound of fragile things breaking floated up from the lower decks.

The soldiers barring the gate eased aside, as one of the galley people pushed through, carrying a heavy tray that rattled.

"Perhaps a coffee, Lieutenant?" Tatiana suggested. "While you wait?"

The galley worker came over, cued by Tatiana's suggestion. She held up the tray toward the Lieutenant. He bent over the tray and sniffed. His nose wrinkled and he shook his head. "I will not partake, thank you," he said stiffly.

Tatiana picked up her bowl and filled it. It gave her something to do with her hands. She nodded her thanks at the galley worker, who shuffled over to Elmer, who picked up one of the cups silently. His hand shook.

Tatiana sipped, watching Cardenas.

He turned on his heel, taking in the full extent of the bridge. "You are too relaxed for a freeship caught in Eriuman space."

"Our presence here is quite innocent," she replied as evenly as she could.

"You do not protest over our searching your ship."

"Would a protest halt the search?"

He smiled.

"Search away then," she replied. "You will find nothing. We are a simple family freeship."

"A family ship?" Cardenas looked interested. "There are not many family freeships left."

True. The corporations were stripping the last of the tribal ships from their family holdings. It was an economic fact of life, although she was surprised this Eriuman officer knew that.

"The *Hathaway* has been in my family for four generations," Tatiana told him. "The man your officers are detaining is my younger brother."

Cardenas looked over his shoulder to where Ruh was standing with strained shoulders and a red face. "I have an older sister, too," he said reflectively. He nodded at the officers, who let Ruh loose.

Ruh flexed his shoulders and yanked his jacket back into place. Then, with a scowl at Cardenas, he walked between them, over to Elmer, and served himself coffee, his stiff back toward the Eriumans.

A fourth officer, the one who must have been coordinating the search of the lower decks, hurried onto the bridge, over to Cardenas. He whispered in the lieutenant's ear.

Cardenas nodded and the officer looked toward the gate and waved.

Six more soldiers pushed onto the bridge and circled it, prodding with the points of their guns, pushing with their boots, examining everything.

Tatiana made herself not look at the navigation table.

Cardenas moved in a slow circle around the bridge, following his men. He looked as though he was strolling in a garden. "I suppose it is a coincidence, Captain, that you should be here where we were told we would find a ship trying to smuggle smart crystals into Karassia?" His tone was pleasant. Even friendly.

Tatiana's chest tightened and her wariness grew. She had heard about smart crystals and the AI nanos that built them, but had never seen one. She imagined they would be small. Small enough to fit into a box the size of her hand.

None of her crew so much as twitched in response to Cardenas' probing and Tatiana silently cheered. She schooled her face into pleasant neutral and kept her gaze steady upon Cardenas.

"Yes?" he coaxed.

"I'm not smuggling crystals," she replied as calmly as she could.

"You know what they are, then?"

"I've heard rumors," she admitted. "Something to do with weapons."

"They are the core of intelligent weaponry. Karassians use them. So does Erium. They are rare, though. Difficult to breed." He stopped his slow pacing and looked at her. "Given their solitary purpose, the Eriuman policy is to execute anyone found transporting them, destroy their ship and post warnings to others of the consequences."

Tatiana held her breath. No one spoke. No one moved and again she silently hugged every single one of them.

"We're just a commercial transport, Lieutenant," she told him. "I would not put my whole family in danger for such a risky transaction."

His gaze met hers. "Why should I believe you?"

"Because it is you and your clans who have made it that way," she said flatly. "Of course I would settle my people dirtside, if I could. Only, between you and the Karassian Homogeny, there is nowhere left to go. You enslave a new world every year."

"We extend our protection," he said flatly. "It is your free will to refuse citizenship."

"We do refuse," she said, just as baldly.

Someone snorted, by the gate, drawing their attention.

The soldiers guarding the gate were bending, twisting to look down at their feet.

Zita pushed through their legs, toddling onto the bridge with unsteady steps. She sat down suddenly and looked up at them, her small face curious. She smiled, showing a single tooth.

Another barely smothered laugh sounded.

Tatiana's heart was working too hard for a woman her age. She pressed her hand to her chest as she watched the ghostmaker muzzles wave in Zita's direction.

The little girl got to her feet again and paused, then staggered over to the navigation table, cooing with delight at her own mobility. She gripped the corner of the table, while Cardenas stared down at her with a deep frown.

Zita smiled up at him and took three steps toward him, then sat down again, this time with a small bump.

"More family?" Cardenas asked.

"My great granddaughter," Tatiana said. Her voice was hoarse.

Cardenas crouched. He picked Zita up, his hands looking big and powerful around her middle. She giggled at him, her little fist whacking at his wrist with delight.

Cardenas' mouth curled up at the corner again. "Family…." He was staring at Zita.

Tatiana couldn't stand it anymore. She strode over to him, pulled Zita out of his hands and carried her over to Ruh. Ruh took her. His face was pale, too.

"Keep her quiet," Tatiana murmured.

He nodded and settled the toddler on his hip.

The soldiers at the gate had their ghostmakers back to pointing at people's bellies. Cardenas got back to his feet and brushed off his hands. "Prepare for departure," he said.

Three of the soldiers and one of the officers swiveled and hurried off the bridge, their boots rattling along the access corridor.

Cardenas resettled the folds of his uniform. "You are in Erium space without clearance. In times of war, such as act has natural consequences."

All the ache and tension in her chest froze into a cold, hard pillar mixed of equal parts of fear and anger. She could blame the Karassian woman for putting her family in this position, yet it was really Tatiana's fault. She should have assessed better, stayed on top of the doings of the two vast empires, instead of pretending they and their undeclared war didn't exist. Her ignorance had killed her and her family.

"I understand," she said, her lips stiff and uncooperative.

"I thought you might," Cardenas said. He stepped over to Ruh and chucked Zita's chin.

Tatiana held back her reaction. Sweat prickled under her arms.

Cardenas nodded at her. It was a short, stiff motion of his head that she suspected was possibly some sort of recognition of rank. She didn't understand Eriumans well enough to know for sure.

He left, his shoulders back to square and stiff.

The bridge was silent behind him and the silence and motionlessness held until the outer hatch hissed shut and the shuttle decoupled from the ship with a heavy thud that made the *Hathaway* shudder.

Marisol dropped the heavy coffee tray onto the navigation table with an impact that made the remaining cups and crucibles rattle. "Move!" she cried, tearing off the thick green cap and letting her blonde, distinctive hair drop back around her shoulders. "Get out of here! Before they get back to their ship!"

"Out-run an Eriuman convoyer?" Tatiana replied. "You paid for discretion, not speed. That's what you got."

Marisol shot her hand out, up toward the roof, where the warship would be hanging, well within armament range. "They're going to blow you out of the sky! They're Eriuman. They kill everything that gets in their way!"

"I know," Tatiana said. Calm filled her. There was nothing left to decide or do. "Elmer, track the Erium ship, please."

Elmer wiped the back of his wrist across his eyes and turned back to his console. "Still in position above us."

"Moving, yet?" Tatiana asked.

"They don't have to move!" Marisol shouted. "They can kill us from where they're sitting."

"They won't risk the fallout," Tatiana replied.

"Moving off," Elmer called.

"*Do* something!" Marisol cried.

Tatiana shook her head.

"Coming around," Elmer said.

Marisol screamed. It was a wordless protest.

Everyone else was utterly silent.

Elmer made a choking sound. "They flew over us!" He turned to look at Tatiana. "They're *leaving*!"

Ruh gave a shuddering groan and collapsed on the nearest stool, his arms tightening around Zita. Everyone else gave similar reactions of relief and disbelief. Tatiana didn't indulge herself. Instead, she raced to the navigation table and crouched down next to it.

The hidden panel was open. The little space behind it was empty. The cover hung like a stunted appendage. It had been forced open.

Tatiana realized she was sitting on the deck, her head bowed. Her middle churned with watery sickness.

"You let them *take the crystals?*" Marisol screamed, right next to her. "How *could* you? Do you have any idea what you have done?"

"I do now," Tatiana whispered.

Marisol shook the green cap at Tatiana. "All this *humiliation*, for *nothing*."

"He would have killed you the moment he spotted you. Be thankful they only took the crystals," Tatiana told her.

Ruh sank onto the deck next to her, putting Zita between his knees. "How did you know he wouldn't see her?"

"Because he is an Eriuman," Tatiana said tiredly. "They don't see anyone who isn't of their rank. Workers are invisible to them."

"You know Eriumans so well?" Marisol asked heatedly. "You? A freeshipper?"

Tatiana rubbed her thigh. It was aching. "I knew that much about them. What I didn't know almost got us killed, though. I made a mistake. I thought neutrality meant complacency. I won't make that mistake again." She hauled herself to her feet, using the table as an assist. "Someone get this woman off my ship."

Marisol drew herself upright. "I paid for passage to Karassia!"

"You paid for my ignorance. I'm not ignorant anymore. I would advise you to leave before my compassion fails, Karassian."

* * * * *

THEY DROPPED MARISOL BACK ON Rinat Prime. Ruh came to Tatiana's quarters to give the report. He held out a glittering disk. "And I found Zita playing with this."

Tatiana turned the golden button over and over, examining the crest on the front, the gilding, the detail around the edges and the torn scrap of purple cloth clinging to the back of it.

"He must have given it to Zita when he came over to us, just before he left," Ruh added.

"He chucked her chin as distraction," Tatiana added.

"But why give her a button?" Ruh asked.

Tatiana shook her head. "It's not a button."

"It's not?"

"Do you remember? He said he had a big sister, just as you do."

Ruh grimaced. "Bet his isn't bossy like you."

"Eriumans are patriarchal, so probably not," Tatiana agreed calmly, making Ruh roll his eyes.

"So, if it's not a button, what is it?" he asked.

"A favor." She hefted the shiny disk. "Now I owe him."

Ruh's eyes bulged. "That's…almost cheeky."

"It is," she agreed.

"He wasn't what I expected," Ruh admitted.

"In one way, he was as flawed as all of them. He didn't see what was right under his nose. Neither did I, Ruh. We need to know more about the Eriumans and the Homogeny, both."

Ruh looked a little ill. "Why?" he demanded. "Let them kill each other while the free states live their lives."

"Because that's what we couldn't see," Tatiana told

him. "We keep ourselves deliberately ignorant and pretend their war has nothing to do with us, while they annex and enslave and conquer a system at a time. That is what will kill us. War is coming, Ruh. We need to prepare. We need to get to know our enemies."

The Indigo Reports Book 1.0

New Star Rising

CAMERON COOPER

About *New Star Rising*

Be careful what you ask an android to do…

Bellona Cardenas Scordina de Deluca, daughter of the primary Cardenas family, went missing ten years ago. Reynard Cardenas, Bellona's father and head of the family, receives anonymous, unsubstantiated news that she has been found. He sends the most disposable person in the family to investigate—Sang, the family android.

Sang's investigation trips off chain reactions which shift the generations-old luke-warm war between Erium and Karassia into a galaxy-wide conflagration which will engulf the known worlds, including the neutral, fiercely independent free states…unless a hero can be found who will fight to hold the line against the two colossal forces.

New Star Rising is the first book in the Indigo Reports science fiction series by award-winning SF author Cameron Cooper.

Praise for *New Star Rising*

You won't be disappointed if you're looking for a journey into a never-explored futuristic world before.

It is not a novel that can be skimmed through. Take your time and enjoy the new world that is presented to you.

This novel is fascinating for its rich and complex story line set on multiple planets/worlds.

What an amazing book from start to finish.

What is there not to like? I found myself digging into this book and disappointed at the end of it because I wanted more now rather than having to wait for the next book.

A complex story line that draws you in then keeps you engaged. Nothing formulaic.

Well thought out story. The science fiction components are consistent.

Science fiction with real science! LaGrange points – I am so giddy.

Roller coaster of a story following fabulous characters who move through varying planet and spacecraft environments whilst always dealing with a war that's not a war!

Waring enemies setting each other up to eliminate another enemy. Throw in a "neutral" entity that docs lots of dirty work and this book has all the makings for a great series.

Chapter One

Kachmarain City, Kachmar Sodality, The Karassian Homogeny.

THEY HAD SURVIVED TEN DAYS in the Homogeny, yet Sang still found it difficult to ignore the constant attacks upon their concentration. Screens were everywhere—disposables, transluscents, impermeables for wet conditions, building-sized, thumbnail-sized, embedded in windows, luggage, shopping bags, vehicles and clouds. The spoon they used to eat breakfast had a long, narrow screen running along the handle. The faucets in the ablutions areas featured rosette screens on the activation sensors. Each and every screen offered a different data stream, a unique offering designed to seduce and hold the viewer's attention.

The babble had been overwhelming, at first. After ten days it had evolved into merely distracting, which was why Sang failed to notice they were being observed, until the man made his move. By then it was too late to counter.

Sang held still, on alert. They put their spoon down. Regretfully, they would have to miss breakfast.

The eatery was busy, even this early. Many of the screens were displaying a show featuring a self-confessed biocomp called Chidi who mocked and disparaged the people he met. The Karassians seemed to enjoy the show, enough to train screens to focus on it. Sang did not understand how they could enjoy the derisive negativity. It made Sang uncomfortable.

Therefore, Sang did not watch the screens as so many in the eatery were. They pretended to watch, which allowed them to measure the man's progress toward the far corner where they were sitting. The man would have to move around six long tables, with every stool occupied by noisy Karassians.

The man did not look enhanced. He did not look Karassian, either. He did not have blond hair or the pure, rich brown eyes that Karassians valued. That made him an outsider, as was Sang. Yet he was not Eriuman, either.

Was this the one? Sang waited with tense readiness.

"Will you look at the pretty one, then?" The question came from behind Sang.

"We're going to sit down right next to *you*, sweet one." A different voice. This one, female. Sang was jostled from behind, forcing them to look away from the stranger and up at the pair addressing them.

"You don't look like a Karassian, sweet thing," the woman said. She was native Karassian, visibly enhanced. Her bare arms featured metal sinews that sat on top of her white skin. There were plug-ins at both wrists. She would be strong, then.

The male narrowed his standard brown eyes. He had no chin and a large mouth. "That's a thick lip you have there, little one."

The swollen lip and the bruise on Sang's cheek were courtesy of a scuffle two days ago, when Sang had explained physically why they did not appreciate a hand groping under their skirt when they were trying to board a carriage. Sang had assumed that the disfigurements would deflect interest. They had not.

"Move over, sweet thing," the woman said, bumping Sang's shoulder with her hip. Her metal enhanced hand gripped Sang's arm, tugging them sideways and almost off the stool.

The man was pulling a third stool over to the long bench.

Sang sighed. "I do not wish to keep your company,"

they said.

"We're *good* company," the woman replied. She put her hands around Sang's waist and lifted them, then pushed the stool aside with her foot. She placed Sang on the relocated stool, her hands lingering. "Heavy," she remarked. "You may be enhanced under that odd skin of yours?"

"I believe the lady said she did not want company." The third voice was that of the man who had been watching Sang.

Sang was surprised to feel a sensation of relief trickle through them.

"She's with you?" The woman was irked.

"Told you someone would have her," the man muttered.

Sang looked at the stranger. "I am not with them."

His nod was tiny. "She is with me. Move on."

The woman looked at her partner. "He doesn't look enhanced." Her fingers curled inward, in preparation.

Sang braced for action. They were close enough to the woman, but they would have to turn to get a grip on her. It could be done, even against an enhanced.

The woman shot out her hand toward the stranger. It was very easy to pick her wrist up as she thrust it past Sang. Sang squeezed. Metal tendons bowed. The woman shrieked.

A few heads turned, though not as many as Sang would have expected.

The stranger who was not Karassian gripped Sang's upper arm, not hard, but firmly enough for Sang to know they would not be able to dislodge the grip without causing damage. "Let her go," the man said quietly. "You're drawing attention."

"We are not nearly remarkable enough to do that," Sang said with a confidence built over the last ten days. Only Karassians like Chidi, with their extremes of social behavior, held anyone's attention for long.

The man shook Sang. "Let go."

Sang let the woman go. She snatched her arm back and cradled the wrist. "Freak!" she hissed.

Sang smiled. "If you insist."

The Karassian man pulled the woman away.

Sang got to their feet and moved past the pair. The stranger held on to Sang's arm as they threaded back through the tables. Outside, the sun was dazzling. Sang adjusted their vision.

The man hurried them through the early morning crowds. Karassians did not stay at home if they could find a reason not to. Even though the standard work day did not begin for a while yet, the footpaths were as busy as they would be for the rest of the day.

"Where are you going?" Sang asked the man.

"Somewhere private."

"There is such a place here?"

The man glanced at Sang over his shoulder. "I suggest you not speak again until we reach that place."

Sang remained silent. The man did not remove his hand. Sang didn't protest. It would ward off others, if Sang was seen to be under his control. It simplified things.

The private place was one Sang should have anticipated. The day pod was the third in a row of ten sitting on the edge of the footpath between pedestrians and the occasional ground car. A retreat pod was one place where privacy would be honored, especially if the two of them were seen entering. Karassians liked their pornography, yet they still preferred a closed door for their personal couplings.

The pod accepted the man's scan and opened. He pushed Sang inside and sealed it again.

Sang sat on the wide divan that was the only piece of furniture, while the man turned off all the screens except one. He called up the pod controls.

The sounds of the high street muted. Then the walls turned transparent, allowing bright morning sunlight into the pod.

"It's one way only," the man said. "I need to see if anyone is taking an interest in us."

It was possible to make the walls transparent in both directions. The first time Sang had seen such an arrangement, they had halted, unable to look away from the pair frantically mating on the divan. Others had also stopped to watch the spectacle with mild interest, masking Sang's surprise.

"That is sensible," Sang said, of the man's setting of the walls.

The man sat on the edge of the divan, then swiveled, bringing one knee up onto the thin cushioning. The flowing robe he wore spread over the divan.

"You're an android," he said. "Passing as a woman, which means you're from Erium."

Sang remained silent. This man was not a Karassian. He was not Eriuman, either. There were still too many unknowns for Sang to speak freely.

"You referred to yourself as 'we'," the man pointed out. "You gave yourself away."

Sang was genuinely startled. "I did?" they said carefully. They had been diligent with their references since arriving.

"No one noticed, not with the woman caterwauling about her wrist." The man grinned.

Sang held still, waiting.

His smile faded. He tilted his head, his eyes narrowing. "You're bruised."

"I miscalculated," Sang admitted. "Our study of Karassia told us women were legal equals of men."

"Legally, they are." The man's tone was very dry.

"The objectification of women is of an extreme I had

not anticipated," Sang added. They looked up and around the interior of the pod.

The man rolled his eyes, taking in the pod, too. "Why did you not pass as a man, then? It would have been easier."

"There are reasons why being seen as a woman would be useful." Sang shut up again. There was no need to reveal anything yet.

The man considered Sang. "Two outsiders in Karassia. I have not seen another for days. The last was a convict worker. I have to believe that you being here is not a coincidence." He studied Sang with eyes that were not Karassian brown, but a gray-blue that was flecked with brown, an odd, discordant coloring that marked him as a stranger, as did his black hair and the growth on his chin and cheeks.

"You are not Eriuman," Sang said.

"I am a free citizen." He frowned. "We could circle around each other for days, too cautious to break the silence. One of us needs to speak."

Sang didn't answer.

The man smiled. "You would not voluntarily enter the Homogeny, given how they feel about androids. You were sent. I am hoping you were sent by the man I reached out to, three weeks ago."

Sang drew in a breath and let it out. "Who might that be?"

"Reynard Cardenas."

Sang let their shoulders sag, as if they had relaxed. "What might the message have been?"

"Still cautious. Very well. I told him I thought I might have found his daughter, Bellona."

"Bellona Cardenas has been dead for more than ten standard years," Sang said.

"She's here on Kachmar."

"A member of the Scordini clan here, among rabid

Karassians?" Sang shook their head. "That is not possible. The enraged outcry would have been heard across the galaxy, all the way to Erium."

"Not if they don't know who she was."

"Her genetic markers alone would raise suspicions." Sang curled down their mouth. "Clearly, you have never met an Eriuman."

"I have met more than one," the man replied. "Many times. I realize now that is why the Cardenas sent you. You are different enough to pass as a stranger, not an enemy. As a woman, you can get closer to Bellona without raising suspicions."

"I was sent because my loss would be an acceptable one."

The man frowned. "Reynard Cardenas did not believe my message, then."

"He sent us," Sang pointed out. "Me," they corrected.

"Yet he does not hope."

"No."

The man shook his head. "I have a DNA match."

Sang considered it. "You have seen her." Only someone who had been physically present could have acquired viable DNA for matching. Sang curled their fingers in against the little spurt of excitement and reminded themselves that they held no more hope than Bellona's father did. This was a fool's mission, gladly accepted to serve the Cardenas family.

"I have seen her," the man confirmed.

"It is impossible. Here?"

"She does not look as you remember her. Karassians think her to be one of their own, a very sharp tool in their war chest."

Sang laughed. "Now we *know* you are lying. Bellona would never fight against Erium. If a member of the Scordinii chose to side with the Karassians, the Karassians would have trumpeted it with heralds. They would have trained every screen in the Homogeny to lengthy broadcasts about her deeds. She would be a *cause célèbre,* a crack in the Erium Republic's united front. The Karassians would remind its people of that at every turn."

"You are more right than you know," the man replied. "For that is *exactly* what the Karassians do with her. Only, they do not parade her as a turned Eriuman, for she is not. She is one of their most prized warriors and Karassians everywhere cheer her exploits." The man delivered the rousing litany with a downturned mouth.

"If she is not Eriuman, then…?"

"Bellona Cardenas does not currently exist. The woman you once served is now called Xenia."

Sang shot to their feet. "The *app*?" They shivered and wrapped their arms around themselves.

"Application, appliance, I know not what the proper name for them is, but yes, that is she."

"Apps are androids," Sang replied as calmly as they could manage. "Programmed for destruction, enhanced beyond belief. They fight. When they are not fighting, they are corralled away from Karassians who prefer their intelligent assistants not compete with them for attention."

The man spread his hands in an open gesture. "I do not disagree with you on any of those points bar one. Apps are not androids. They're people, reprogrammed for Karassian use, their natural talents enhanced. When they are not slaving at Karassian orders, they are tucked away and kept harmless and helpless."

Sang rubbed their arms, even though they felt no cold. "If this is even possible, then knowledge of what the Karassians have done would emerge. Rumor, at least, would have trickled out. How could you, a stranger to this place as much as I, possibly know what the rest of the galaxy does not even suspect?"

The man shrugged. "I know, because I was one of them."

* * * * *

Ledan Resort, Ledania, Karassian Homogeny.

XENIA SPOTTED THECLA ON THE other side of the lagoon and gladness touched her. She made her way around the still, green water to where Thecla was limping along in the soft sand, a medic next to her. Thecla was holding her human hand next to her body, as if it was injured.

"Thecla!" Xenia waved to catch her attention and hurried as fast as she could to where Thecla halted, waiting for her. She couldn't walk fast because her quads were sore from a training session. Her back ached, too. She couldn't quite remember the dance movement that might have strained her muscles so much, yet Dana, her coach, assured her that her rehearsal had been excellent and the soreness would soon pass.

Thecla smiled when Xenia got closer.

"You're hurt!" Xenia exclaimed.

"Just my other hand. And my ankle." Thecla held out her human hand to display healing burns. "I spilled lead on it."

Thecla was a sculptor, which was why she had the metal hand. Although Xenia had never seen any of her work, she suspected that Thecla was very good, as she lived here in Ledan. "Did you go away?" Xenia asked. "I didn't know you were gone." It was only now she realized that Thecla had not been around for a while.

That was often true of her other friends here in Ledan. Xenia frowned, staring at the sand. "There was someone else, too…they didn't come back yet."

"Thecla went on tour," the medic said jovially. "To show her work."

Thecla smiled.

"How wonderful!" Xenia exclaimed. "I'm so happy you're such a success, Thecla!"

"Do you two want to have lunch together?" the medic asked.

"Yes, please," Thecla said.

"Yes," Xenia said. She liked having lunch with friends. There were lots of friends…weren't there? Now she was thinking about it, she couldn't recall any of their names.

"Xenia."

She looked up at the medic, uneasy.

"Come and have lunch. Forget about the rest. Food, then a nap and everything will be good again."

Xenia smiled at him. "That sounds nice." She followed them across the sand to the dining hall where lunch would be waiting, wondering if she was hungry.

Chapter Two

Kachmarain City, Kachmar Sodality, The Karassian Homogeny.

THE MAN GLANCED AT THE time and got to his feet. "What is your name?"

Sang hesitated.

"Or should I just call you Indigo?"

Clearly, he knew something of Eriuman ways.

Sang brushed the material of the skirt over their knees, straightening it.

"You can call me Khalil," the man added.

"One name only?" Sang asked cautiously, for that was a Karassian thing.

"Ready," he said. "Khalil Ready."

Reassured, Sang responded. "We are Sang Cardenas Scordini de Indigo."

"The Scordinii," Khalil Ready said. He studied the single screen with the pod settings. "You'd better stick to a gender, Sang. It might prove useful, after all."

"We are female for now. It is not a simple matter to switch."

"You might have breasts, but you're not thinking 'woman'," Ready replied. He glanced over his shoulder. "Trust me on that."

Sang shrugged. "I can remain indistinguishable while I must."

"Not with that hair and those freckles. Although, if you don't scream 'android', it will do." Ready unsealed the pod.

"Where are we going?"

"I have an apartment on the north side of the city,

where we can talk without fear of being overheard. Now I know who you are, it's time to plan."

Sang merely waited.

"No arguments?" Ready asked curiously.

"That is not my function."

"You argued when that pair wanted to play with you," Ready pointed out.

"That was different. They were an obstruction."

"I'm not an obstruction, then?"

"You speak of plans. It is your intent to find Bellona and retrieve her, is it not?"

Khalil Ready narrowed his eyes, considering Sang. "Yes, it is," he said slowly, as if his thoughts were not entirely upon what he was saying.

"That is the task to which I was appointed, too. For as long as our tasks are aligned, you are not an obstruction." Sang nodded toward the door. "Shall we?"

* * * * *

Kachmarain City, Kachmar Sodality, The Karassian Homogeny.

A SENSE OF DIRECTION WAS built into Sang's biological functions, so when Khalil Ready back-tracked and crossed their trail three times, they did not become confused. "We should head farther north if your apartment is indeed in the northern area of the city," Sang said as they climbed down from the sky train platform.

Ready glanced at Sang. "In time."

"Where is the apartment, really?"

Ready didn't respond.

"There is no one following us."

"There are screens everywhere," Ready reminded them.

"Making it impossible to avoid being tracked, in which

case, why try and simply draw attention to ourselves? To anyone watching casually, we are returning to your apartment for more sex, having begun the dalliance in the pod."

"Your pair from breakfast were hovering outside the pod when we emerged. I'm being cautious."

"I saw them. They meant to harm me for hurting her wrist, only they withdrew because you were with me." Sang smiled. "They believe you to be the stronger one, despite the evidence from breakfast."

"It's a gender prejudice," Ready replied. "You're combat trained?" he added.

"I have…seen the training." For many nights, Sang had been ordered to act as sentry while Max and Bellona had trained in the secret garden.

Ready sighed. "It was too much to hope that he might send an army."

"You should be grateful the Cardenas sent anyone at all. Besides, I have my usefulness."

"You've survived Karassia as a woman who has no idea what she's doing. You clearly have skills, although they won't help where I'm going."

"Where *we* are going."

"Not without combat training, you're not."

Sang placed their hand against Ready's shoulder and shoved hard enough to make him stagger. When he whipped around with a curse, Sang slammed him up against the building they were walking past and pushed their forearm against his throat. When he protested, Sang pushed harder, until he gave a choking gurgle.

"I said I had seen the training," Sang said. "You, on the other hand, have had no combat training at all. You would be wise to accept what help I can provide."

Ready nodded, his head moving infinitesimally, blocked by Sang's arm.

Sang let him go. "There is no one following. The

screens are unavoidable. You cannot disorient me, either. I suggest a direct route would be best."

Ready flexed and worked his shoulders, then massaged his throat. Silently, he began walking again.

* * * * *

"IF YOU WERE PART OF this Appurtenance Services Inc. program," Sang said, as they dug up another spoonful of protein pudding, "and the program wiped your memories when they let you go, why can you remember anything at all? Why can't you remember where they are? And why not just kill you out of hand, once your usefulness was at an end?"

Khalil Ready did not seem to mind the questions. He dug into his own food with concentrated relish. Yet there was a furrow between his thick, dark brows. Then he pushed the bowl aside with a firm thrust. "I cannot remember what I have not first experienced. I was unconscious when they dumped me back on the streets of Kachmar."

"You do not know where she is, then?"

"Somewhere on this planet. I wasn't out long enough for an interstellar hop."

"How would you know that?"

Ready frowned again. "Do you want your mistress back or not?"

"Bellona was not my mistress," Sang said stiffly. "I am assigned to Maximilian Cardenas Scordini de Deluca."

"Then why are you here?"

"Because the head of the Cardenas family temporarily reassigned me."

"I mean, why aren't you looking after this Maximilian?"

"Servants are not required while one is on active duty."

Ready nodded. "He's in the Eriuman Navy. I should

have made the assumption. The odds were good."

"Max would prefer I spend my efforts in search of his sister, anyway," Sang added.

"Bellona is his sister. The plot thickens." Ready reached up as the assembler pinged and pulled out a steaming mug. Sang could smell the caffeine from the other side of the table. Ready sipped and sighed.

"So why didn't they just kill you?" Sang demanded. "I would have."

"You're a cold-blooded Eriuman," Ready replied. "Karassians prefer to do their killing at a distance. That's why they use apps for their in-person combat work."

"Apps who are actually people," Sang amended.

"It helps to think of them as just apps," Ready replied.

"Helps what?"

"It keeps the nausea at bay and lets me think," Ready said flatly. "The people running the program thought wiping my memory would be sufficient. I was counting on that." He held up his left arm. "I have a memory tab implanted, along with an emergency recovery memory that forms in the absence of more than seventy percent of my memory proteins."

"It activates if your memory has been deleted?"

"Exactly. Then it restores my memory from the chip. I woke up two standard months ago, lying in the gutter on the Messe, with no idea who I was or where I was. A day later, I knew what had happened."

"You met Bellona while you were in the program and that is how you acquired her DNA."

"She is Xenia. That is all she remembers, in between assignments. The assignments are programmed in, too. They are set up to complete high risk assignments and if they are killed, the program moves on to the next app. If they return, the assignments are wiped to eliminate trauma and stress and the pleasant illusion of an idyllic life carries on uninterrupted, making them biddable and pliant. All memory of her real identity is suppressed."

"Not wiped?"

"They used to wipe original memories, only it sent apps into psychoses that were unsolvable. Now they suppress them, so the original personality is there as a base, but severely retarded. It doesn't occur to anyone in Ledan to question why they're there, or what they're doing there."

"Bellona has been missing for ten years. She has been in this program all that time?"

"I don't know. No one does." Ready scowled. "Maybe. Xenia is the darling of the Homogeny's military, sweeping in to save their asses when they need a hero. The stories have been around for a long time, so maybe she *has* been there all that time."

Sang shuddered. "Do you remember *your* assignments?"

"I didn't have assignments." Ready put his cup down. "I was recruited because I am good with computers. I spent my time in Ledan maintaining the memory programs and data storage."

Sang nodded. "That is how you know so much about the program."

"They repressed all will power, all self-determination." Ready rolled his hands together as if he was washing them, or wiping them of something disgusting. "I did what they told me, while the tab recorded everything, so it is only in hindsight I understand what they were doing. It was all quite pleasant and stress free, while I lived through it."

"And you remember Bellona?"

"Xenia," Ready said firmly. "If you saw her as she is right now, you would not recognize her."

Sang put her spoon down. "We must fix that."

"Gender, Sang."

Sang rolled her eyes. "You and I must fix it," she repeated.

"That's better."

She shook her head. "Do you have any idea where on the planet this Ledania illusion is?"

"From my memories, no. I have been researching Appurtenance Services Inc."

"They are an interstellar corporation, with holdings and branches throughout the Homogeny."

"I can read their official file, too," Ready told her. "There are three hundred and forty-nine subsidiaries, but only thirty-six inside the Sodality."

"How many on this planet?"

"Thirty-one." Ready shrugged. "They started here."

"Which means they have become established, with deep roots. You plan to find Ledan via their corporate structure?"

"I told you. I'm good with computers."

"So am I," Sang said. She smiled.

"The entire Karassian Homogeny is distracted right now," Ready added. "They just 'annexed' the Alkeides system." He nodded toward the small screen above the assembler. There was footage playing that showed some rugged-looking, quite normal free-space humans in utilitarian clothing, hugging tall blond, brown-eyed Karassians, their new overlords, their gratitude shining on their faces.

Sang swallowed.

"The party will last all week," Ready said. "It's a good time to go unnoticed."

"Give me a smart terminal," Sang said. "I bet I can find Ledan before you can."

* * * * *

Cardenas (Findlay IV), Findlay System – three standard weeks ago.

REYNARD SCORDINO HAD NO PATIENCE for being kept waiting. As head of the Cardenas family and one of the senior members of the Scordinii, there had been no pressure for him to learn that grace. For that reason and because Sang knew it would please him, they hurried across the homebase at the first summons.

The Cardenas was in the family room, standing close to the field wall, looking at the snow piling up less than a meter away, his expression the neutral one he favored for most occasions. Sang could not recall Reynard showing strong emotions of any sort, not in all the time they had known him.

Iulia Scordina, Reynard's wife, sat on the cushioned bench surrounding the bathing pool, her feet together, her hair piled up in elegant curls on the top of her head. Her bare arms gleamed in the dazzling light the room had been set to. She was the epitome of Eriuman womanhood. When she saw Sang, relief touched her face.

Troubled, Sang presented themselves to Reynard. "You asked to see us, sir?"

Reynard did not turn at once. He watched the blizzard rage while silence filled the family room, broken only by the soft lap of water in the pool. Someone had been bathing only recently. There was a faint scent in the air that made Sang think of the gardens in late summer, thick with blossoms and the chitter of insects. That made Sang think of Max, who liked the gardens.

"How is Maximilian doing?" Iulia asked softly.

"We regret we have no news beyond that which we gave you two days ago, ma'am. When the current campaign to win Kalay is completed, we may hear more."

Reynard snorted, turning away from the snow. "This scheme of his to launch little ships from cruisers will never work."

"It may," Iulia said gently. "The novelty alone will give the Navy a distinct advantage."

"Firepower and size has won worlds for generations," Reynard replied. "Opening up the guts of a ship weakens it. It makes the cruisers vulnerable."

Iulia looked down at her hands.

Sang waited patiently.

Reynard's jaw worked, drawing attention to the long scar down the side of his face. The original wound had just barely missed his eye. Reynard had refused to have the scar corrected.

"The family received a message three days ago, Sang," Reynard said. "I think it is nonsense. Perhaps it is a scheme to lure us."

Iulia sighed.

Reynard's gaze flickered toward her. "My wife believes the message to be authentic, though."

"The message, sir?"

"An anonymous communique. They, whoever they are—" and Reynard's disdain for the anonymity was clear in the curl of his lip, "—say they have located Bellona."

Iulia bit her lip, her eyes downcast.

"You intend to follow up on this message, sir?"

"I refuse to waste resources and time on a fool's errand," Reynard replied. "I want you to go and find out what you can."

"We, sir?"

"See if there is anything to this."

"Then you believe Bellona is alive, sir?"

"No." Reynard's gaze travelled once more toward Iulia. "The idea is ridiculous. If she was alive, then she would have contacted us long ago. She would not have let us linger in uncertainty like this."

Sang understood that Reynard was not doing this to ease his own doubt, yet if Sang supported Reynard's belief it would upset Iulia. Carefully, they said, "We can ascertain if there are any facts to be found, sir. Only...we must point that out we are a generalist assistant. Would it not be advantageous to use a mind built to analyze minutia? We can recommend two family minds—"

Iulia lifted her chin, her eyes wide.

Reynard shook his head. "Out of the question. The analysts are already fully occupied with the war effort." His gaze took in Sang in one glance. "You would not fit in there, yet you do not look like an Eriuman, either."

Sang compared their oddly marked flesh to the deep olive typical of Eriumans, especially those of the primary clans. No, Sang did not look like one of them. "Where is 'there', sir?"

"Kachmar. The prime city there."

The heart of Karassian territory. "We are to infiltrate Kachmar?" Sang asked, astonished.

"I don't care what you do there," Reynard said.

"How do we get there?"

"You're a generalist. Figure out a way. I'll have a copy of the message sent to you." Reynard dismissed Sang with an impatient flick of his fingers.

Sang turned and left. To not obey the dismissal was unthinkable. As they passed Iulia, she looked up at Sang. Her smile was gracious. Her eyes, though, were a riot of conflicting emotions. Pain. Fear. *Hope.*

The hope stayed with Sang, long after Reynard's command that Sang figure things out for themselves had faded to a subconscious goad.

* * * * *

Kachmarain City, Kachmar Sodality, The Karassian Homogeny.

SANG RECALLED THE PERFUMED PEACE of the family homebase on Cardenas and compared it to her current environment with fond sentimentality.

The tiny apartment was designed for just one occupant. It was bomb-proof, radiation proof and vacuum proof, which made it an unaesthetic square lump of shield walls from which utilitarian furniture could be extended as needed. There were no windows, the light was not full spectrum, nor directional and the air was not scrubbed.

After three days, the air was thick with biological traces that Sang had to force herself not to react to. Instead, she focused on the task of finding Bellona.

When one of them was not using the tiny bed, they both sat at the equally small table, mining data. Sang deep dived into public and semi-public corporate records, looking for patterns and holes that would show where Ledan was located.

Ready, on the other hand, had five screens formed, including one embedded on the table top, all of them running news feeds, most of them at full volume. After three days of listening to them while concentrating on her own text displays, Sang realized that Karassians liked to scream. It seemed to be a cultural norm to scream at anything, in order to display pleasure, pain, anger, shock, amazement, even awe. A birthday surprise was greeted with cries by the recipient. A popular public figure made an impromptu stop at a local eatery, while the diners all roared in surprise and delight. War reports were greeted with shouts of joy. The celebrations for the annexation of Alkeides were dizzying marathons of drinking, dancing and uproar—especially when a lens was spotted.

There were even more negative outcries. A tearful woman wailed to her friends and the lens, outlining how her former liaison had treated her. Her friends, several hundred of them in regimented rows who listened with upturned faces and wide eyes, greeted each failure the woman itemized with thunderous applause and calls.

A man, enhanced to the point where his mechanicals eliminated any human movement or grace, yelled insults at the lens in response to another Karassian's listing of the ten best restaurants in Karassia. The restaurant rater was, according to the biobot, a fool, a bigot, a liar with not a shred of Karassian blood in him, and a Standard, to boot. As only Karassians received standard gene manipulations before birth meant the restaurant critic *had* to have Karassian blood seemed to be lost under the sound and fury.

There was far more anger than there was joy. Jilted lovers, furious neighbors, rejected job applicants, failed business owners, the bankrupt, the homeless, the house-proud, the rich, the poor, everyone seemed to live their lives on screens, while everyone disparaged what they saw on the screens. Sang found it exhausting to listen to. After a while, she didn't hear the words anymore. She just heard noise.

Until a name made her lift her head from the lines of data, shock slithering through her. "What was that?" she demanded.

Khalil Ready looked at her through the center screen. "See for yourself." He flipped the screen around and backed up the feed.

"…Karassian hero Xenia once again saves the day! Fifteen of our bravest infantry plucked out of an Eriuman hellhole, with not a single soul lost! Mothers are reunited with sons and daughters, thanks to *Xenia*!"

The screen showed a large crowd gathered around a landing craft. A platform had been built in front of the airlock and half-a-dozen Karassians in the dark brown military uniforms were cheering and clapping as hard as the people watching them.

In the middle was a tall woman with ice blonde Karassian-perfect hair and brown eyes. She was not smiling.

It was Bellona.

Sang's heart gave a little jump. The smooth hair, the skin, the eyes were all wrong, but Khalil Ready had warned her of that. It was the uplift of the chin and the full lips that were Bellona's. The ratio of physical dimensions were hers.

One of the officers standing next to her nudged her in the side and murmured something. Xenia raised her arm in a victory salute. She didn't smile.

The crowd went wild.

Sang leaned forward, absorbing the details. Were those brows the same as Sang remembered them being? Was the height the same? Her physique? Had the Karassians changed those, too? How much of Bellona had they erased?

Was this even Bellona? A pair of lips, a stubborn tilt of the chin…these could belong to any mother's daughter…

"The DNA was a match," Khalil Ready said softly, as if he had plucked the doubt from Sang's mind.

"Why are you looking at this?" Sang demanded, pulling her gaze away from the screen.

"There will be clues in the footage, if you look past her to find them." He tapped at the screens and five more images of Xenia appeared, all of them from different occasions. "There is hours of this stuff, going back years."

"Then why haven't you been examining this footage all along?"

"Because I needed to calibrate first." Khalil dismissed the screens. "I needed a baseline. The most random element on Kachmar is the weather."

"They don't control the weather?" Sang asked, astonished.

"They don't have to. Kachmarain City is in the equatorial zone and the weather is relatively stable. Yet it can still provide surprises. Unscheduled rainfall, storms, cloudy days and so on. All of that is recorded in every image, in every archive. Then there are time zones and nightlines. Footage stored in local archives has local timestamps, so while it is midday here, it will be midnight on the other side of the globe."

"Comparison," Sang said softly. "Did it rain here, the day it rained in the image Xenia appears? Was it dark or light…hot or cold? Karassians spend all their time outside and there are lenses everywhere."

"It is a cult of reflections," Khalil said in agreement.

"Eriumans say Karassian is an empire of a billion leaders."

"And no followers." Khalil grimaced.

Sang pointed at the central screen. "This actually works?"

"I found you, didn't I?"

Sang shut down her screens. "I'll help you."

"Is that your way of saying my way is better?"

"I have my own conclusions already," Sang said stiffly. "I will see what results your method produces and compare them."

Khalil snorted. "You're as stubborn as my brother. He never could say he was wrong either."

Sang blinked. She had not thought of Khalil in relation to family and friends. He was an individual who represented aide in achieving her goal. "Your brother…is like you?"

"We're brothers." Khalil shrugged.

"I mean, is he here? On Kachmar?"

"If he was, he'd be dead. Benjamin is one of the Homogeny's most wanted."

"Then he can't help us," Sang muttered.

Khalil grimaced. "It must be nice, your black and white world. Enemy. Assistance. Period."

Sang saw once more Iulia's eyes, the hope in them. "It is a very simple thing I do, yes," she said placidly. "It is the execution that is complex." She tapped the table. "Files, please."

Chapter Three

The Bonaventura. Coria City-state, Free Space.

CAPTAIN BENJAMIN ARANY WINCED AS the bio-sealer worked to close the slash on his arm and glared at Kopitar. "Careful, Marcel."

Kopitar scowled back. "It wouldn't hurt so much if you'd let me deal with it when it was fresh."

"Too much to do," Arany said, returning his attention to the screen. He manipulated the controls with his free hand, backed up the data stream and ran it again, watching the river of tiny aircraft emerge from the guts of the big Eriuman cruiser, like a river of deadly gnats. "This new tactic of the Republic's is a killer."

"Demonstrably not," Kopitar replied. "You're still alive." He put the sealer down and prodded the seal with the tips of his fingers, testing the new flesh. The mental forefinger was cold against the skin, making Arany shiver.

"We're alive only by an atom or two," Arany said. He beckoned Natasa over.

She held out the pad. "Everyone accounted for except one."

"How many dead?" Arany asked.

"Twelve," she admitted, her narrow shoulders falling.

"Thirteen," Kopitar said, straightening up. "Shore died just before I came to find you. Sorry."

All three of them paused to absorb that loss, while the bridge around them hissed and steamed, venting plasma and more, as techs and engineers worked furiously to make basic repairs and get the ship moving again.

"Who's missing?" Arany asked, recalling Natasa's

comment.

"Georgina."

Arany frowned. "*Georgina?* How could she be missing? She's not even front line. She *lives* in the galley!"

"I don't know, boss," Natasa said calmly. "I've gone through the ship's roster three times. I've checked every squeezable space on board."

"What about the crawl space under the engine housings?" Kopitar said, picking up the sealer. "Kids like to get under there and Georgie is little enough."

"*Including* the crawl spaces," Natasa finished. "She is not onboard."

"We need one of those remote tracking systems," Arany groused. "This sort of exercise is a waste of time."

"Granted," Natasa said. "When we have the spare credits I'll rush out and buy one. In the meantime, I count noses. Georgina is missing and I can't account for how she left the ship. We've been in vacuum since the Eriumans appeared and granted, it was a bit chaotic for a while, but none of the sensors record airlocks opening, which would be one way she could leave."

Arany followed what Natasa had not said well enough. "A ship attached to us during the fight?"

"Not that we noticed," Natasa said. "I would say, not at all. In order to do that and not have us spot them, the pilot would have to have super-human reactions to lock on and not nudge us while they're doing it. They'd have to hack into the computer core's vault to get at the airlock controls and wipe any trace of them entering and leaving."

"No one can hack a core vault, can they?" Kopiter asked curiously.

"No," Natasa said. "That's why I don't think it happened."

Arany found his attention drawn back to the still image on the little screen. The river of ships, each of them vulnerable to heavy armaments, yet nothing could wipe out that whole cloud—not even the city-killers the Karassians were developing.

"*Fleets* of ships…" Arany breathed, as ideas popped.

Natasa bent to look at the screen, then at him. "No. Stupid idea, boss."

"Why?" he demanded.

"For a start, freeships are called freeships for a reason. A trader from Cerce would rather spit on a Laurasian freighter. The Luathian twin cities haven't stopped fighting in over a century."

"There's a reason I left New Veles, too," Kopitar added.

Natasa pointed at him. "Exactly. The Cheng-Huang disembowel anyone from Veles, no questions asked. You seriously think any of them would cooperate with any of the others, even to fight the Republic or the Homogeny?"

"What about fighting both of them off?" Arany asked calmly.

"Both?" Natasa laughed.

"I'm serious," Arany said.

"Those Republic ships are coordinated. The pilots trained to work together," Kopitar pointed out. "I don't think any freeship captain has military training or knows how to take orders, which they would have to do, for something like this to work."

Arany dismissed the screen while the image lingered in his mind. "*Something* has to change," he said morosely. "We can't keep going on this way. We fight and fall back, fight and run away to watch from a distance as the Eriumans or the Karassians claim another city state. We're supposed to be *free*, damn it."

Natasa and Kopitar did not laugh. They lived with the harsh reality every day.

"Boss, even if you figured out a way to get everyone to agree to fight together, do you have any idea how many ships you'd need to make the Republic sit up and take notice?"

"A lot," Arany said in agreement.

"*Everyone,*" Natasa said flatly. "Every ship capable of firing a weapon would have to join in. I'm talking about every known free state out there and there's a hell of a lot more we don't know about, too."

"Exactly," Arany said. "There are vast tracts of the galaxy that the Republic and the Homogeny have not yet taken for themselves. *That's* free space. You think anyone who lives here wouldn't want to hold the bullies off?"

"It's impossible," Kopiter added.

"No, it's a goal," Arany said softly.

* * * * *

Pushyani Wastelands, Pushyani, moon of Pushyan (Ovid II), Free Space.

NEARLY A STANDARD CENTURY AGO, the Eriumans had flirted with folding space, racing to beat the Karassians and be the first and therefore the only patent holders of a workable bridge forge. It would have made the current null-space generators and lengthy interstellar journeys obsolete and given the Eriumans a genuine advantage in both war and economics.

The working bridge forge engine had been massive, taking up most of the surface of the Pushyani moon. It had perked up the economy of Pushyan for over five years, drawing on workers and resources, plus entertainment and distraction for the Eriumans working on the moon.

The first and only trial of the bridge forge had been a success for the better part of a second. The materials used to build the generators disintegrated as soon as the hole formed, collapsing the hole and destroying the moon, including everyone on it. The radiation the forge had spilled across the system killed everyone who could not leave Pushyan quickly enough.

It was the last time a free city state worked in cooperation with either the Republic or the Homogeny.

The Karassians had laughed themselves sick over the disaster as they quietly packed away their own bridge generator prototype.

Now, all that was left was the ruins of a small city on Pushyan and a growing asteroid belt around it, as what was left of the moon spread out in a long tail of rubble. The Pushyani Wastelands were a metaphor for shameful disasters and overreaching. No one went there voluntarily.

Which was why Ferid used the ruined city as a base. He was never disturbed there. The system sentries had long since shut down, their energy depleted. There were no lenses, which he had found took time to get used to. The silence was broken only by cold winds whistling through girders and ruins.

The girl proved troublesome for such a small, unenhanced human. She refused to talk despite Ferid's encouragement. He even pulled up a speech translator and installed it on his second server and spoke to her in her native language, the server molding his tone into soothing, relaxing cadences, yet still she refused to speak.

Using his full array of techniques upon her would quickly break down her fragile body, but Ferid was creative, which was why the Karassian military was paying him so well. He found a small room with four walls and a roof. He built a door over the opening, then took away her clothes and locked her in.

After three days he went back to see what progress had been made.

The stench was overpowering. At first he was alarmed, because the girl lay still among the excrement. He brought water and she showed signs of life, so he held it away from her, until finally, she agreed to talk.

The cold and the lack of water had taken away her voice. He gave her a pad and stylus. Her hand moved slowly, with long pauses while she figured out the coordination necessary for each word.

What do you want to know?

He had already learned a great deal from his foray into the *Bonaventura,* where he had found her, although he had not had time to download the datacore while he was rooting around in it, so he had taken her instead.

He began with simple questions. Ship's compliment. Crew structure. Nothing that could not be learned by observation and educated guesses. Nothing that alarmed her, that might trigger her resistance. As her answers came more swiftly, along with demands for water, Ferid slipped in one question among the innocuous ones.

Where is Arany's base?

She threw down the stylus and crossed her arms over her small breasts.

"I will find it," he assured her.

She shook her head.

"You will tell me."

She shattered the pad and drove one of the shards into her eye and beyond it, into the brain.

Ferid stood over the cooling body for a long while, enjoying his astonishment. She had surprised him. She was a small creature from a race of little people of no account to anyone but themselves, yet she had made a grand gesture, a heroic one.

This was the third time he had tried to coax Benjamin Arany's people into revealing where Arany and his ships could be found when they weren't out harassing Karassian deployments. The first two had been equally as determined not to give such a simple fact away.

For a small moment and in an abstract way, he appreciated their fierce loyalty and dedication to Arany. If all his people were of this caliber, tracking down the troublesome free-stater's base would not be as easy as Ferid had first assumed it would be.

What would a whole army of such people be able to achieve?

His computational array told him that this was the primary reason the Karassian military had given him the contract. They were proactively working to destroy Arany before he even thought of building such an army. That was why the free-stater was on their most-wanted list.

Ferid went back to his ship to meditate and compute his next step. He was proud of having reasoned out the Homogeny's motives. Their military would not have come up with this idea on their own. There were rumors that the largest portion of the overwhelming military budget was used to purchase Bureau advice and predictions.

The actual processes the Wyan Oushxiu Generation 98 used to arrive at their predictions was a closely guarded secret. Ferid had collected bytes of data about their operations for years. He suspected the Wyan Oushxiu Bureau used AIs in clusters to make intelligent neural nodes, with the nodes all linked, building into a gestalt that generated super intelligence. Predictive social analysis was their specialty. It would take a staggering amount of computing power to arrive at some of the startling—and correct—conclusions the Bureau offered their clients.

Yet he, Ferid, a simple biocomp, had reached the same conclusion.

He really was very good at his job.

* * * * *

Kachmarain City, Kachmar Sodality, The Karassian Homogeny.

WHEN KHALIL'S BEST GUESS MATCHED Sang's prediction, they both agreed the probability was great enough to commit themselves to the next step.

Sang looked at the dot glowing on the overlay map. The small island was part of an archipelago that had been bought by a research corporation that, once the tiers of ownership were traced back, was ultimately owned by Appurtenance Services Inc., which in turn was a subsidiary of the commercial development arm of the Karassian military.

"There's only the two of us and you can't fight," she said. "The security surrounding the island will be immense."

"And unimaginative," Khalil said curtly, glowering at her assessment of his combat abilities. "They've been running this place for nearly seventy years. They're complacent. They've never once had someone come back to haunt them."

Sang frowned. Khalil used unique phrases sometimes.

"They know their memory wiping works," Khalil added. "Once they tossed me back on the street, they forgot about me." He tapped his forehead. "I have all the security codes here, still."

"They would have changed them."

"Why? They know memory deletion works. They know it in their bones because not one word of this place has ever been heard. Why bother changing codes for something that will never happen?"

"I would."

Khalil sighed. "No, you wouldn't. Not if you were human and complacent. Trust me on this."

Sang considered the request. "Very well, we will do it your way, but we will build redundancy strategies, too."

"Spoken like a good little computer."

"Now you're being insulting. I am a sentient, fully functional citizen of Erium."

"With no matronymic."

Sang glared at him.

That seemed to make Khalil happy.

Chapter Four

Ledan Resort, Kachmar Sodality, The Karassian Homogeny.

XENIA APPRECIATED DANA'S SUGGESTION THAT she take a day off from her training to lie in the sun and relax. She really did feel tired. There was an ache in her back and her arms that nagged. Even her neck was stiff.

She found a lounger already on the sandy beach rimming the little cove and pulled it into the sun. She laid on it and closed her eyes.

"Xenia, wake up."

"I'm not asleep." She opened her eyes. There were two people standing next to her. A tall woman with short, copper-blonde hair and a wash of freckles over her cheeks and nose. A man… "Ari," Xenia said, delighted. "You've been gone for such a long time!"

Ari nodded. "I have." He glanced over his shoulder. "I have something to show you. Come with me." He held out his hand.

Xenia frowned. "Where did you go?"

"Hurry," the woman said, her voice low.

Ari leaned down and picked up Xenia's hand. "It won't take long. It's not far away. Come and see."

Xenia resisted his light and steady pull on her arm. "I really shouldn't. Dana says I have to rest."

"You can rest afterward," Ari told her. He hauled, forcing Xenia to swing her feet over the sides of the lounger and stand, instead of falling into the sand at his feet.

Ari smiled at her. She had always liked his eyes, she remembered now. They were a pale color and flecked. "Good," he told her, tugging her forward. "Now, just a little bit farther."

"Ready," the copper-headed woman said.

Ari looked past the woman. "Damn," he muttered.

"Pick her up if she won't go with you," the woman said. "We have about thirty seconds before they see us."

Xenia frowned. There was worry in their voices. She hadn't heard worry in anyone's voice or expression for a long time. She had almost forgotten what it was, until just now. She didn't like the way it made her feel. Her heart was thudding uneasily. "I don't want to go," she told the two of them.

Ari's smile was all wrong. "You really do need to see this. I promise, it won't hurt you."

Xenia hesitated. "This isn't right." She didn't know what was wrong, precisely, but her uneasiness was building.

The woman made a vexed sound and stepped up close.

"No, wait!" Ari said sharply, his voice still soft.

The woman raised her arm. Something slammed into the side of Xenia's neck, just under her ear, then blackness dropped over her.

* * * * *

Ledan Resort, Kachmar Sodality, The Karassian Homogeny.

READY BENT AND LET BELLONA'S unconscious body fold over his shoulder, then straightened again. He glared at Sang. "Now we have to carry her, just when we need to sprint."

"She wasn't going to cooperate," Sang pointed out, rubbing her elbow. The blow had worked far more effectively than she had thought it might when delivered by someone who had never performed the motion before. "The memory inhibitors must also limit free will. You heard her. She was doing what her coach told her to do. The Bellona I knew would have done the complete opposite." She glanced over her shoulder.

The towheaded guards in casual clothing were coming closer, a tight knot of three of them, chatting easily. They had nothing to fear from the inmates. They were relaxed.

Ready hurried across the sand, heading for the little service corridor that ran beside the holographic wall. Sang followed. Rocks and tropical trees were arranged in front of the entrance in a way to discourage anyone from finding the corridor. They clambered over the rocks, Ready breathing hard.

"Shall I take her?" Sang asked.

He didn't answer.

Sang glanced over her shoulder as they turned into the corridor. The guards had reached the path that surrounded that side of the artificial cove, still talking. They had not been seen, although that would not last for long. Inside this most secure of Karassian facilities, there would be lenses everywhere. The only reason no alarm had been raised so far was because they had moved around the enclosure as if they were residents. Neither of them carried any weapons that might alert observers or scanners.

Now they had taken Bellona, someone would react. How long before that happened depended upon how closely the feeds were being monitored. From the casual, lazy air of the three guards, Sang judged that minutes might yet pass before anyone noticed that one of their apps was missing.

The walls of the corridor were covered in the mossy growth that permeated the enclosure, encouraged by the humid air. The humidity was uncomfortable, for Sang was used to the dry heat of Cardenas. She pushed ahead of Ready and eased open the door into the greater compound and looked around.

Still no alarm.

"Too easy," she whispered.

"It is beyond their imaginations that someone might do what we are doing," Ready said. "Back to the skiff, as fast as we can."

The air outside the enclosure was cooler, yet still damp, for it had rained only a short while ago. Puddles still lingered on the compressed and fused earth surface of the working areas. There were administration buildings on the far side, closer to the real beach.

The skiff they had stolen from the marina in Kachmarain City lay keel-up on a stony shore on the other side of the island. It had taken them all night to navigate through the swampy interior. It would take them longer to return, but as long as they stayed lower than two meters above ground at all times, they would not register on the passive scans covering the island. The same lack of imagination had presumed that no one would attempt to approach the island other than by air and had set the scanners accordingly.

"Their complacency will be their ruin," Sang murmured as they moved into the scrubby land beyond the compound.

"It's a human thing, complacency," Ready said, his voice muffled as he kept his head down, watching where he put his feet. Bellona still hung unmoving over his shoulder. The long straight locks of disturbingly blonde hair hung from her head, waving softly with each step Ready took.

"Eriumans are not complacent," Sang said, annoyed.

"They're arrogant," Ready said. "Same thing." He was sounding breathless again.

"I would have checked the monitors constantly," Sang pointed out. "I would have questioned why two new people were there."

"You're not Eriuman, though. Not really."

Sang pressed her lips together to hold back her angry

retort. She would need the energy for walking before this day was done.

* * * * *

BELLONA WOKE SHORTLY AFTER THAT and struggled. Ready held her down, while Sang administered the sedative she had tucked away in her pouch. "Are you pleased, now, that I insisted upon contingency planning?" she asked.

Ready scowled and waved away an insect that was trying to lodge on Bellona's face, with its odd, fair skin. "It's one thing to anticipate. It's another to act on every suspicion as if it is fact."

"Now who is refusing to admit they are wrong?"

Ready lifted Bellona up. He didn't speak again until they reached the skiff.

When the skiff was heading for the mainland once more, Sang gave Ready the coordinates for the northern shoreline of the landing field.

He plugged it in and grunted in surprise. "That's the private spaceport."

"Very good."

"That's how you got onto Kachmar? A private ship?"

"How else?"

"Public buses, liners, tourist cruisers, freighters, haulers, day shuttles…" He shrugged, then clutched the side of the skiff as it turned toward the new coordinates. "Did you steal the ship, too?"

"I bought it."

Ready just looked at her.

"I thought it prudent to arrange transport that would allow a second, unregistered person to leave the planet."

Ready look at her, his gaze steady. "So you bought a ship."

"I was provided sufficient funds to cover any possibility."

"Throwing money at a problem to erase guilt." Ready looked away. "The more I hear about Reynard Cardenas, the more I admire him." His tone was withering.

Sang didn't respond. Any response would be a reflection upon the head of her family.

Ready looked down at Bellona, where she lay on the bench between them. "You bought a ship to take her back. Tell me, Sang, was there a single moment anywhere in this where you considered the possibility that you might not get Bellona back?"

"Failure was not a parameter of my assignment."

Ready rolled his eyes. "You thought she was dead."

"Irrelevant."

"So did he."

"Also irrelevant."

"Did *anyone* truly think she might be alive, that this wasn't a magnificent and expensive gesture?"

"Yes."

Surprise skittered across his face. "*That's* who is driving you?"

"Iulia Cardenas Scordina de Carosa is not my employer."

"Just following orders, huh?"

"That is my function."

"Right." Ready turned away, watching the nose of the skiff slice through the black water. "Maybe you should start calling yourself 'we' again."

"I will have to, soon enough," Sang said complacently, looking ahead to where the mainland was a dark bruise on the horizon.

* * * * *

Kachmarain City, Kachmar Sodality, The Karassian Homogeny.

SECURITY AROUND THE SPACEPORT WAS nominal, another reason why Sang had chosen to use a private craft. The spaceport administrators considered security to be the responsibility of the ship owners who used the port. Most of the luxury craft did have posted sentries and passive shields, some of them lethal, but the perimeter of the landing field had a simple, sedentary fence. The sea side of the port had nothing at all barring entry, for the coast there was rocky and the seas high.

They wrecked the skiff upon the higher rocks, grounding it more surely than any anchor, then picked their way over to flat ground. Sang carried Bellona until they reached the sleek leisure vehicle, when she handed Bellona back to Ready and disengaged the shielding.

"You bought a Karassian yacht?" Ready asked.

"My registration says I am unenhanced Karassian. I could not arrive in an Eriuman jig."

"This is the Slipstream model. They've been advertising it on almost every stream since I woke up here."

"It is." Sang lowered the ramp and they climbed into the ship.

"Only the best will do, hm?"

"Used vehicles are unreliable, have inquisitive owners and they are, above all, slow." Sang closed up the craft.

The silence inside the ship seemed thick and heavy, after a day at sea with the wind in her ears and nearly three weeks of Karassian screens screaming at her from every angle. Sang pointed. "There is a small medical bay there. Third door."

While Ready laid Bellona on the examination table, Sang connected with the ship's AI and requested a DNA check.

The bed took a sample.

"Confirmed," the computer reported. "Bellona Cardenas Scordina de Deluca."

"You didn't believe me," Ready said, not sounding surprised.

"I am being thorough," Sang told him. She silently asked the computer to prep for departure. The decking shivered under their feet as the engines rumbled to life. The shielding and insulation kept the sound down to a barely heard murmur. Once they were in vacuum, they wouldn't hear it at all.

Sang looked down at the woman lying on the table. It was difficult to equate this very Karassian-looking woman with Max's sister, yet now she was here in front of her, Sang could see even more familiar lines and angles.

"We can't take her back to the family looking this way," Sang said. "They will be horrified."

"Won't they just be happy to have her back?" Ready asked.

Sang discussed it with the computer. "I will take her to Maggar. There is a therapy group there that can reverse the gene expression and return her original appearance."

"You figure it is that easy to go back?" Ready asked.

Sang thought of the days ahead. "It's a start," she admitted. She ordered the bed to secure Bellona's body and keep her sedated, then headed for the door. "I thank you for your assistance, Khalil Ready. You have been of service to the Scordinii and have earned their favor."

"You think I'm leaving?"

She looked back. Ready stood by the table, unmoving. He crossed his arms.

"My next stop is deep inside the Republic," Sang pointed out.

"So?"

"You do not fear crossing that border?" For the first time she wondered where Khalil Ready had come from, before he had been sucked into the Appurtenance Services project.

He ran his fingers down his dark beard. "Do I *look* as if I care?"

Sang hesitated.

"I know. Taking a third person back isn't part of your assignment," Ready said dryly. "Think of it this way. If you don't take me back, you don't get to take Bellona back either. Where I go, she goes."

Sang nodded. "Very well, then. I would advise you to strap in. The inertial filters on this vehicle are sub-standard." She headed for the control deck.

Chapter Five

Primary Healing Complex, Maggar, Eriuman Republic.

IT TOOK A LONG TIME to wake, to find coherency. Even when she recognized softness beneath her and warmth over her, she still struggled to pull together memories that would tell her where she was. Until then, she kept her eyes closed.

It felt as though she had been asleep for a very long time. There were confusing snatches of memory. Voices, the words not clear. Heat from a sun.

She finally admitted she was not going to be able to put it together here and now. She needed further information. She opened her eyes.

A man sat on a stool, next to an open window. Warm air blew through the window. Sunlight, not harsh, lit the man's face. Dark hair. Thick beard.

She frowned. "Ari..." The name came to her, even though she didn't know this man. Yet as soon as she spoke the name, she knew it was right.

The man took a deep breath and turned to look at her. Pale eyes. "You knew me as Ari, yes. My name—my real name—is Khalil Ready. Your real name...do you remember that?"

"Xenia," she said promptly, then frowned. "No..."

He waited.

"There is something, a long way back." She rolled onto her back and lifted her hand to rub her temple. She paused, her hand in the air. The flesh of her arm was odd. It was perfectly normal skin, yet it didn't look right.

Her movement brought the rest of the room into view. It was a small chamber, enclosed with old-style walls. Soft carpets with muted colors hung on the walls. A bureau by the wide door with ancient-styled drawers looked appropriate for this room, yet equipment sat on the top—sleek, sophisticated, their functions a mystery to the uninitiated.

The terminal next to the bureau was also modern, though styled to look older. The screen showed a display she recognized. It was an array of vital signs.

She looked at her arm again, putting it together. She was the patient.

"Hello, Bellona."

She looked up, recognizing the name. The person who had spoken it stood by the head of her bed, unnoticed until now because of their stillness. She frowned, taking in the copper blond hair and the freckled skin. "I know you."

"We are Sang."

Sang. Max. Mother.

Father!

Bellona gasped, as her identity dropped into place with the weight of an Eriuman cruiser settling onto a landing pad. It *hurt*. She scrambled to sit up, looking yet again at her arm, which was far too pale to be hers. Her heart ran sickly, the irregular beat making her chest ache.

The terminal beeped furiously.

Ari—*Khalil*—got to his feet. "You're not in danger," he said quickly.

Sang held out their hand. "We're taking you home, as soon as you're ready."

Panic flared, hot and sour. "No!"

"Your family will be overjoyed to see you," Sang added.

"I'm *not* going back there!"

A medical technician hurried into the room. He wore a worried expression.

Sang dropped their hand onto Bellona's shoulder. "You are Bellona Cardenas. You're safe. You're going home."

Bellona gripped Sang's wrist. "You'll have to kill me first." She wrenched the wrist over and at the same time, slammed her hand against the vulnerable elbow. There was a soggy cracking sound. Sang sank to their knees with a gusty, pain-filled groan.

Bellona dropped their wrist, which slid into Sang's lap to rest uselessly.

She scrambled backward, to the other edge of the bed. She clutched at her chest as the pain there bloomed, claiming all of her.

Then there was nothing.

* * * * *

A TECHNICIAN POINTED SANG TOWARD the courtyard when they asked for Bellona's location. They hurried out to the stone yard, where dead leaves rustled and the sky was gray overhead. All around the yard were verandahs lined with doors to rooms where the practice of healing took place.

Bellona prowled the courtyard like a caged beast, her energy at odds with the peace of the healing house.

Khalil Ready waited as always, his patience undisturbed by her roaming. He sat on one of two chairs that had been placed there for them, his hands woven together and hanging between his knees.

Sang went to Bellona. "You look much more yourself today."

She lifted her arm to look at the back of her hand. "Do I?"

Sang took in her deep olive complexion, the blue eyes and the thick black curls that had been the bane of her life for so many years. "Yes, you do."

Bellona let her hand drop. "I didn't think that was possible."

Khalil lifted his head, as if he had been alerted.

Sang's wariness slid into place, too. "You have been reviewing the footage..." They looked at Khalil, vexed.

"Better she learn it all now," Khalil said quietly. "Or would you rather Bellona trip over the truth somewhere in the future and resent you for not telling her?"

"How could she trip over it? Xenia looked so different. She could have stayed ignorant forever."

Bellona shook her head. "Khalil has been explaining it to me and I have researched for myself. The Karassians use those streams for propaganda. They spread them everywhere, showing the might of the Homogeny to their subjects—the free states, the aligned worlds, anyone they want to intimidate into behaving. Sooner or later, someone will recognize me. There were enough similarities between Xenia and I that speculation would rise, especially now Bellona Cardenas is back from the dead. They will wonder and one day, someone will challenge me on it. It is better I know now and have time to prepare for that. It is better I know what I have done." She looked down at her hands again. "How is your arm?" she added.

Sang held it up and turned their wrist. "It was a minor hurt, easily tended."

"Unlike the lives I took," Bellona muttered.

Sang shifted on their feet. "I have heard from your brother."

The darkness fled from her face. "Max is coming?"

"He says he will be pleased to take you home."

"A naval escort," Khalil said softly. "*That's* a homecoming."

Bellona looked down at her hands again, her pleasure fading. "I must go home, I suppose. I must face them."

Sang felt a touch of alarm. "You must, yes," they said.

"Sang won't rest until they have completed their assignment," Khalil added.

Sang could feel their cheeks heating. "We think only of

your mother and your brother…and your father. They must see you again. They must assure themselves that you live, after all."

"Because they have spent the last ten years turning the galaxy inside out, looking for me," Bellona said.

"The war…" Sang said, feeling a rare helplessness.

"There has always been a war," Bellona said shortly.

"I think," Khalil said, "you will find more has changed than has remained the same."

Bellona looked at him, her expression sour. "I have been asleep for ten years. *Nothing* is the same. Not even me."

* * * * *

IT WAS DIFFICULT TO FOCUS upon anything beyond the pain, although when they heard their name being spoken sharply, they roused enough to lift their head.

Khalil Ready was peering at them, a furrow between his brows. This close, Sang could see the brown flecks in his eyes.

"You're sick?" Ready asked. "Why are you sitting on the floor?"

The conditioning to answer when asked a question was strong. Sang reached for and drew the pail closer to their side, moving carefully so the contents did not slosh. "It is convenient, to sit on the floor." The bed the technicians had offered them was too hot beneath their bodies. The walls of the quiet room were cool against their back.

They wrapped their arms about their knees once more. In between the flashes of heat, it was very cold. They shivered.

"What is wrong with you?"

"This is…a natural adjustment."

Ready had been crouching to speak to them. Now he sat and crossed his legs. "You mean, this is what you go through when you drop the gender?"

Sang drew their knees even closer to their chest. The pressure helped. "The technicians assure us this is mild. We were not female long enough to generate organs, which complicates the hormonal rebalance."

"You had breasts," Ready pointed out.

"Increased lactation tissue." Sang paused to ride through another wave of pain. It was a sourceless ache, enveloping their whole body. "Easily reabsorbed."

Ready tilted his head. "Why not just stay a woman?"

"That is not our choice to make. The family rarely assign gender. It complicates everyday concerns that should be simple and elegant. Those given a gender cannot return if they remain gendered for too long."

Ready threaded his fingers together. His thumbs touched. "You do not feel embarrassed, telling me these things?"

"It is a fact, that is all."

"You knew the transition would be like this, then?"

"It is a well understood process."

"Despite knowing, you willingly chose to become female?"

"We could not remain gender neutral and move freely about the Homogeny. They do not give their androids the freedom the Republic does."

Ready's silence was long. "Anything at all, to get Bellona back?"

"That was our assignment."

"Did Reynard Cardenas know what he was asking of you?"

Sang clutched the pail. "You would be best to leave," they gasped.

Ready got to his feet with a lithe movement. "Is there anything that will help?"

Sang leaned over the pail, the nausea swirling. They did not dare speak. The next few moments were uncomfortable and unpleasant. When they were finally capable of taking notice of their environment, they saw that Khalil Ready had left.

There was a fresh cloth and water on the spot where he had sat.

* * * * *

THE THERAPISTS ANNOUNCED THAT MAXIMILIAN'S fleet had arrived and were in orbit overhead.

"A whole fleet?" Bellona said.

"Space strategy has changed since you were gone," Sang told her. "Mostly thanks to your brother."

"What did Max do?"

"He spent years studying the free ships and their political structures. All their ships are small and vulnerable. Any Eriuman cruiser can destroy an entire ship with one cannon shot, not even a volley, yet the free ships constantly hound and evade the cruisers."

"The gnat anomaly, yes," Bellona said impatiently. Then her eyes widened. "Where did I get that from?"

Khalil sat up. "The gnat anomaly is a Karassian expression. They consider freeships to be nothing more than annoying insects, that sometimes sting their military ships. You must have picked it up when you were Xenia."

Bellona swallowed. "On a mission, you mean?"

"Yes."

"Those memories were wiped, you said, to eliminate trauma."

"The active memories, certainly. The base knowledge and expertise they impart cannot be removed without destroying your personality and your ability to function. That is why you were able to bring Sang to their knees, the moment you woke. It is instinctive. Ingrained." He glanced at Sang apologetically, as if he was apologizing for invoking the memory of what she had done to Sang.

Bellona scowled. "What base knowledge and expertise did you acquire while you were an app?"

"I was made an app because of my expertise." Khalil sat back. "I did nothing but use that expertise, so no new knowledge was acquired."

He was lying. Sang considered calling him out, drawing Bellona's attention to the lie. Only, Khalil had so far worked with good intentions. Sang thought of the cloth and water that had been left for them and said nothing.

Bellona looked at Sang. "My brother studied the freeships…?" she prompted.

Sang nodded. "The freeships were smaller and more maneuverable, their one advantage. Sometimes it is no advantage at all. They sacrifice shielding and null engine size for speed in local space. When they jump, the smaller engine extends the jump double the time a standard Eriuman ship would take, even the heaviest of cruisers. The lighter shielding also makes them vulnerable to holing and radiation excesses."

"It is a matter of strategic priorities," Bellona replied. "What would you rather have on a battlefield? The ability to run away fast, or to be faster while you are fighting?"

"Max chose both," Sang said.

Bellona tilted her head. "To be faster than the freeships and retain the shielding and engine power?" She held up her hand. "Only ships smaller and lighter than the freeships could be faster. The freeships are already operating with minimal shielding and engine size. The only way to be lighter and faster is to drop below minimal safe level."

Sang nodded. "Fast, light, small ships…*tiny* ships, can fit inside bigger ships."

Bellona crossed her arms. "Carriers," she said flatly. "*That* was Max's great innovation? A device that has been used throughout military history?"

Khalil laughed. "Every transport is a carrier of something."

"Max stripped down ship designs, taking away the null engines, the heavy shielding, everything except firepower and room for a pilot. It is not a new idea, but the idea had fallen out of use. When opposing cruisers are even bigger and heavier and more highly armored than your own cruisers, a gnat is useless. Against small ships with minimal shielding, though…" Sang shrugged. "Max was lauded and promoted for his work."

Bellona was still frowning. "The Eriuman Navy is fighting free ships? When did the free states get into the war against the Homogeny?"

Khalil looked at Sang and raised a brow.

"The free states are not at war with either the Homogeny or the Republic," Sang said carefully.

"Eriuman and Karassia have never declared war, either," Bellona shot back, "yet they've been enemies since before I was born. Why is Max shooting at freeships?"

"He isn't," Sang said quickly. "At least, not unless they shoot first, or they're in Eriuman territory without authorization. He patrolled the borders of the Republic for many years, where he developed his theories. Now, he uses the personal fighters to harass the Karassian ships."

"A gnat against a giant? How does that work?" There was no sarcasm in her voice, just strong interest.

"I am sure Max will explain that to you in detail," Sang assured her.

Bellona rolled her eyes. "*You* tell me, Sang. Max doesn't think I'm interested in war."

"*Are* you interested?" Sang asked curiously. "Max often told me you did not like to talk about such matters."

"I *am* such matters now, aren't I?"

* * * * *

AS WAS PROPER, SANG STOOD at the back of the reception room, while Bellona and the head therapist stood at the front, waiting for Max and his officers to arrive. Bellona wore a borrowed dress that swirled around her ankles. She was bereft of jewelry. Her hair had been piled upon the top of her head but tendrils had escaped. She was a messy echo of many moments Sang could recall from the past. Family dinners, greeting lines, assemblies, parties, seasonal celebrations.

Khalil did not stand at the back with Sang. Neither did he take a place at the front where, as the hero who had rescued the Cardenas family's long lost daughter, he had a right to stand. He wore black and stood off to one side, the observer's position.

Most of the healers, therapists, technicians and aides were also waiting in the big stone room to see the son and heir of the Cardenas family and to enjoy this small piece of pageantry. They talked among themselves in quiet tones, until the rap of boots on the verandah outside alerted them.

Bellona kept her gaze on the door. Her chin was up, yet she did not smile.

The first officers through the door were junior grade. The people in the room stepped silently aside, forming a ragged corridor to the top.

Max was next, with a tail of officers and aides behind him. He turned his head as soon as he stepped inside, searching for Bellona. When he saw her, he smiled. It was an easy smile, bereft of any ceremony and full of warmth.

Sang was startled. They had not seen Max in person for many years, only by screens and quick communications when Max needed personal affairs dealt with on Cardenas. He had matured since his last visit home and not just in age. His shoulders had filled out, giving him the family silhouette of tall, broad-shouldered men with square jaws and direct gazes. He had shorn his hair to a neat stubble. Yet the change was not purely physical. He was at ease with himself. Confidence radiated from him.

He was comfortable enough in this room of strangers and his fellow, more junior officers, to show his feelings for his sister.

When he reached her, he did not wait for the formal acknowledgements to be completed, either. He pushed past his officer and swept Bellona up in his arms and held her for a long moment, before putting her back on her feet and studying her at arm's length.

The officers all stood rigidly at attention, waiting for a cue that would tell them how to react and what to do. Max had by-passed what was familiar to them.

"You haven't changed. Not at all," Max declared.

"The therapists are very good."

His smile faded. "At the surface level, I'm sure they are."

Bellona stepped out of his reach. "We should talk."

The last of his good humor vanished. Max nodded. "We should." He looked around, spotted the senior therapist and director of the complex, Riorden, a man with no hair and oddly pale eyes, marking him as a member of one of the minor clans.

"Is there any chance of a meal that isn't assembled?" Max asked him. "Every meal I've had for nearly a year was identical to the last."

The director murmured to one of his aides, who hurried from the room. Then Riorden bowed and indicated that Max and Bellona should follow him. Sang silently approved of the man's sensitivity toward rank. Medics were often sticky about such things. Riorden, though, was showing proper deference.

Max spoke to his officers, who stepped back almost in unison.

Max and Bellona followed the director from the room. Sang followed. Max would need them while separated from his officers. Their glance met Khalil's.

As Bellona's rescuer, Ready should have a seat at the

meal table. Sang beckoned to him.

The director showed them into the common room and over to the top end of the long table the senior therapists used. There was no one else using the room, leaving four other long tables empty and bare.

Three kitchen staff were laying the end of the table, their faces red and their movements hurried. Max nodded at them and took the seat at the end of the table.

The director chose the chair on his right.

Sang waited for Bellona and Khalil to sit before quietly lifting one of the chairs from the middle of the long table, putting it against the wall and lowering themselves onto it. It would keep them close at hand, yet wouldn't draw attention to themselves as standing might.

Khalil stared at them. He was frowning again.

Sang gave him a reassuring smile and turned their gaze away deliberately. Khalil needed to concentrate on the conversation to come.

Max was looking at Khalil, too. "Given that you sit at my table and next to my sister, I would presume that you are Ready, the man who found her?"

Khalil got to his feet and gave a short nod of his head. It was almost a bow, only not quite. The movement looked unpracticed. "Khalil Ready."

Max sat back in his chair. The movement looked expansive and open, yet it also cleared his right hip. His hand stayed on the table, the fingers in a relaxed curl. It put his hand within a short drop to his hip. There was no visible weapon there, only Sang was familiar with the discipline and practices of the Navy. There would be a weapon within reach, somewhere on Max's body. A miniature ghostmaker or perhaps a simple knife—one properly weighted for throwing.

Bellona recognized the deceptive shift of Max's chair for what it really was, for she put her hand on the table in entreaty. "Max, Khalil saved my life. He sent the message to Father. He is not our enemy."

Khalil did not move. Perhaps he recognized the unspoken danger.

Riorden, the director, looked from face to face, puzzlement stitched to his own.

"You are not Eriuman," Max said.

"No."

"Nor are you Karassian."

Khalil smiled. "I was born a free-stater. My loyalties have shifted since I emerged from the app program."

"You fight for Erium now?" Max asked. There was a dangerous silkiness to his voice.

"I am not a fighter," Khalil said honestly, "and I do not consider Erium to be my enemy."

"A neuter, then?"

"Max, enough," Bellona snapped. "I vouch for him. That is all you need to know."

Max glanced at her, a shadow of surprise passing over his face.

Bellona slapped the table with her hand, lightly. "You should be gracious and thank Khalil for getting me out of that place. No one in the family managed it."

This time, Max's astonishment lingered.

Bellona kept her gaze steady and waited.

Max cleared his throat. "Khalil Ready, you have my thanks for returning my sister to Erium."

Khalil nodded.

"Please, sit."

Khalil glanced at Bellona. She nodded and he settled back on his chair.

Max watched the interchange, his eyes narrowing.

The kitchen staff reappeared, this time carrying trays with plates and cups. The breakfast Max had precipitously demanded had arrived.

It appeared that Max had not been lying about his need for real food. He tackled his bowl of stranglers and greens as if the meal might be taken from him at any instant. He kept his head down, with no attempt at conversation.

Bellona glanced at Sang. Sang could understand her disorientation. No family meal had ever been so silent.

As the midday meal had been served only a short while ago, everyone but Max picked at their food. Max did not seem to notice the silence. He finished the bowl, pushed it aside and reached for the coffee mug, then sat back again. This time, it was simply a backward thrust of his chair away from the table.

"My thanks," he told the director. "They say assembled food is no different from dirt-grown, yet after a while I yearn for the flavors of home."

"Maggar is not Cardenas, but we try," Riordan said. "I am pleased you find it to your satisfaction."

Bellona put down her fork. "Tell me how your little fighting ships tackle a Karassian frigate."

Max almost choked on his coffee. He coughed to clear his throat and put the mug down again. He gave her a small smile. "I hardly think naval strategies and tactics is a suitable subject for the dining table."

"I have no family news to discuss," Bellona said. "They say you are a hero, Max. I want to understand why. How are you defeating them?"

Max picked invisible crumbs from his sleeve. "There will be plenty of time to talk about such matters on the return to Cardenas," he said, "when we're behind closed doors and secure." His gaze flickered toward the director.

"I should go…" Riordon got to his feet.

"No, don't," Max said curtly. "We were about to speak of arrangement to leave, in which you will be involved."

Riordan hesitated, then sat back down again.

"Then you really are taking me back to Cardenas?" Bellona asked.

"That is why I and a good part of the fleet are here."

Bellona considered him for a moment. "I'm not going

back."

"Of course you are. Where else would you go?"

"Somewhere. I don't know yet."

Max studied her. "You've tried running before. Look where it got you."

Bellona glanced at Riordan and Khalil. Then she met Max's gaze. "It will be different this time."

"How?" Max demanded. "You're one of the most notorious people in the galaxy now. You think there isn't a single soul, free-stater, Karassian or Eriuman, who doesn't know who Xenia is? The Homogeny saturated the known worlds with Xenia's triumphs."

"That wasn't me." Bellona's tone was calm, but her jaw had tightened.

"Explain that to the families of Xenia's victims."

Bellona paled. "That is a part of my plan," she said quietly.

Max made an impatient sound. "*What* plan? There is nowhere you can go where you will not be recognized and pilloried for the suffering you have caused, except Erium."

Bellona swallowed. "You say that because you feel guilty."

Khalil looked at Max sharply, his eyes narrowed.

"I have nothing to feel guilty about," Max said flatly.

"You helped me leave Cardenas. You found the free ship."

Max pressed his lips together. Then he squared his shoulders. "I can't help that a Karassian patrol found the ship. Wang was a superior captain."

"The Karassians grabbed the ship as soon as it came out of null space," Bellona replied. "It was almost as if they knew the *Hathaway* would be there."

Max grew still. "Are you implying I told the Karassians?"

Bellona considered him for a long moment. "No," she

said at last. "Someone did, though. Someone from inside the family who knew where I was."

"Why would *anyone* do that?" Max demanded, his voice low.

Sang leaned forward, their interest sharpening. When Max had been still living on Cardenas, before joining the Navy, he had shared everything with Sang. The frankness had helped Sang be a better assistant. Bellona had disappeared ten years ago, shortly before Max had left. Sang had considered the possibility that the two events were connected but had not pursued the line of enquiry because it concerned Max, who rightfully got to decide what Sang did or did not need to know about his life. This was the first time Sang had caught a glimpse of supporting evidence and along with it, the implication that Max had not told Sang everything he had known about Bellona's disappearance.

Max had not told *anyone*. So who had known Bellona had stolen away on a freeship?

Max shrugged. "It could simply have been unfortunate timing. The *Hathaway* was an old ship, badly masked."

"An old, clunky freeship is what you used to help your sister?" Khalil asked.

Max looked at him. "I couldn't put her on an Eriuman cruiser, could I?"

Riordan cleared his throat. "Really, I should be going…" He got to his feet and this time he did not wait for Max to order him to sit down again. He hurried from the room, his relief painting itself on his face.

Bellona glanced at Riordan's retreating back. She brought her gaze back to Max. "I can head for the free states. I don't look like Xenia anymore. I can disappear there."

"You look enough like her that someone will recognize you," Max assured her.

"Really? Then in all the time the Karassians were plastering Xenia across the galaxy, why did you not see it was me?"

Khalil touched her wrist.

Bellona sat back with a sigh.

"I thought you were dead," Max said flatly. "Destroyed along with Wang and her people. I saw the wreckage, Bellona. I spent a week pulling frozen bodies out of vacuum and matching them. When I didn't find you, I presumed I simply hadn't looked hard enough. The area had already been annexed by the Karassians. I was forced to leave. So no, when I saw Xenia, I never once thought it might be you. It just wasn't a possibility. Only, now I know what Xenia looks like, I can see her in you." His jaw flexed. "So will everyone else." His voice was harsh.

Bellona pressed her lips together. "You're taking me back to Cardenas no matter what, aren't you?"

"You're safer there, dear sister." Max grimaced. "You are right, I carry guilt for my part in what happened to you. I won't risk it happening again."

"I can take care of myself," Bellona said.

"That's what you said, ten years ago," Max said. "I believed you then, which was my mistake." He got to his feet. "We lift in six hours. Be ready."

Chapter Six

Primary Healing Complex, Maggar, Eriuman Republic.

SANG PREPARED FOR WHAT WOULD happen next.

Barely two hours later, Bellona strode into the room Riordon had lent to Max to use as an office until the fleet's departure. There had been a steady stream of military personnel in and out of the office since Max had sat behind the desk. Bellona's arrival was noticed only by Sang, where they stood behind the desk. She had changed out of the dress. Her trousers and boots were plain and simple. Her hair was down once more, the curls shoved back over her shoulder. She was scowling.

Through the open door, Sang could see Khalil leaning on the stone parapet that separated the central courtyard from the deep verandah.

The moment Sang had anticipated had arrived.

Bellona stopped in front of the desk. "Your officer… Henley. He tells me Khalil is denied passage on the *Decimus*."

Max dismissed the screen in front of him. "He's a free-stater with questionable loyalties, Bellona. I can't let him aboard an Eriuman military cruiser."

"I don't question his loyalties."

"You're not Navy, either."

Bellona's scowl deepened. "You and Father made sure of that, didn't you?"

Max got to his feet. "You're being unreasonable."

Sang moved around the desk and stepped out of the door. Khalil straightened as Sang moved over to him.

"Do *you* want passage to Cardenas?" Sang asked quietly. Behind them, Bellona's and Max's voices rose, the tones strident.

Khalil glanced through the open doorway once more. "Bellona wants me with her. That is reason enough to go."

Sang nodded. "We must take the ship we purchased to Cardenas, for Reynard to decide what must be done with it. We have already begun jump preparations. You can travel with us."

Khalil narrowed his eyes. "Max won't like that."

Sang pushed away the troubling thought. "Possibly."

"So why do it?"

Sang considered. "Until Bellona is presented to her father, our task is not complete. We must work to ensure that meeting happens. If that means catering to her wishes, then we will."

Khalil's mouth turned up. There was a warm glow in his eyes. "Or you could say you're doing it for Bellona. I won't tell anyone."

Sang stared at him, confusion making their thoughts churn. "We…belong to Max."

"Yes, you do," Khalil agreed. "I accept your offer of passage to Cardenas, Sang. Thank you."

* * * * *

SANG SPOKE TO BELLONA AFTER she emerged from Max's office, her jaw set.

She received the news with growing calm. "Why didn't you interrupt us and tell us this? Why wait until now?"

Sang hesitated. "Max would not appreciate what we have done."

"I'll tell him it was my idea," Bellona said. "He's already furious with me. Nothing changes, does it Sang? Max always hated being the younger."

"He loves you," Sang said quickly.

"He loved the memory of me more." Her smile was rueful. "Now I am back, he is determined to be a perfect Eriuman to make me look bad." She rested her hand on Sang's arm. "While you are in-transit, could you do something for me?"

"We?"

It was her turn to look doubtful. "Do you mind? I won't have access to a terminal on Max's ship. I'll be locked up in a hastily cleared-out stateroom with nothing to do but look pretty and charm the officers."

Sang suspected it was an accurate estimation. Navy ships were not used to civilian passengers. They wouldn't know what to do with her. It was only because Bellona was the Cardenas' daughter and Max's sister that the rare privilege had been offered.

"We do not mind," Sang told her. "We will have little to do, too." The as-yet-unnamed yacht was just as fast as the lumbering *Decimus*, which had to match its pace with the slowest convoyer in the fleet, yet the jump would still take days.

Bellona half-closed her eyes. "Remember these names. Aideen, Fontana, Hayes, Thecla, Hero, Retha, Vang." She opened her eyes again. "Do you have them?"

"Yes. What should we do with them?"

"Research them. They are as I was, Sang. They're still in there. Still being used. I *think*." She grimaced and touched her temple. "Perhaps I have imagined them all."

"If you did not, there would be traces," Sang said. "Images, footage, reports. If even one other name appears somewhere, it would confirm they are not your imagination."

"I want to know if those memories are real."

"Ari is real."

Bellona drew in a breath and let it out. "He gives me hope that the rest is just as real. Find out for me, Sang. I would be grateful."

* * * * *

Xindaria (Xindar III), Free Space City State.

FERID PERCHED ON THE POLISHED tabletop, staring down at the body and the blood soaking into the handwoven rug beneath, darkening the pleasing pattern and disturbing the symmetry.

He had grabbed the man right off the quiet, tree-lined street and pulled him into the nearest little house, obeying an instinct that said to act at once, for it would be unpredictable and unexpected.

Ferid had obeyed the instinct. No one had seen him. No one had noticed a thing.

He had followed the man for four days, using scans from low orbit. In this bucolic place, with its unenhanced humans and peasant lifestyle, Ferid would have been noticed. His implants would have drawn attention. Instead, he had stayed on his ship and scanned. The scans had made the task challenging.

Ferid couldn't remember the name of the man now. He had run Arany's navigation systems for years, until shrapnel had taken off his left leg below the knee. Arany had set the man up with a house on this maddeningly simple planet. Ferid did not understand why. The man was no longer useful and should have been killed once a replacement had been found. Arany's failure to remove him was a weakness Ferid had exploited.

Only the man had proved to be as stubborn and closed-mouth as the girl on Pushyan.

Now Ferid was staring at another lifeless form, wondering if he needed to reconsider his tactics. Was there a way to make these people talk that he had failed to consider?

His brooding gaze drifted over the arrangement of images on the cupboard front, next to the table. Children.

Gap-toothed, ugly, noisy.

Families.

Ferid stirred, as his mind moved in dusty areas of knowledge.

The people he had spoken to were ferociously loyal to Arany. They had easily given up their lives to protect Arany. What if they were given a different alternative? What if they were faced with a choice of talking or losing not *their* lives, but the life of someone closer to them than Arany himself?

Ferid jumped off the table, happy once more and also vexed he had not thought of this weeks ago. Although, he was a vastly talented, highly tuned artist who required unsullied thought to do his work. Yes, that was why the emotional baggage of free-state unenhanced humans had not entered his mind.

He was flexible, though. He would adapt.

* * * * *

Karassian Luxury Yacht, Maggar-Cardenas, Null-Space.

THERE WAS AMPLE SPARE TIME on the jump to Cardenas to dig into the war archives to see if any of the names on Bellona's list were to be found there. The yacht was Karassian so the archives on the exploits of their war heroes would be more complete than any Eriuman databases. Sang occupied themselves with the research, while Khalil took advantage of the yacht's adequate movement room.

On the third and last day of the jump, Khalil dropped onto the bench opposite Sang and looked at the screen Sang had displayed.

"I know him," Khalil said. "That's Hayes."

"So I have discerned," Sang said in agreement.

Khalil studied the image. Hayes was an enhanced

monster, a head higher than the tallest Eriuman soldier in the unit he was destroying, with a heavy forehead over ferocious eyes, powerful shoulders and metal hands that deflected the beams from ghostmakers back at the firer. The image was a still one, showing Hayes in mid-air, just after launching himself at the remains of the unit, one hand up to deflect a beam, the other reaching for the nearest neck. The caption was an excited recitation of the numbers of Eriuman he had killed before the image had been captured and how many more he killed after that, as he took control of a grounded Eriuman convoyer.

"Hayes thought his hands were for gardening, to let him dig the earth barehanded," Khalil said. "He spent hours, kneeling in dirt. He was proud of the pine-lilies most of all."

Sang looked at the monster, at the hands reaching out. "Bellona's memories are real, then. She was not imagining her friends."

Khalil grimaced. "They, on the other hand, do not even realize she has gone."

"It is better so."

"Is it?"

Sang closed down the screen. "For now. You wish to speak with us?"

"Maybe I just want company."

Sang did not dignify the response with an answer.

Khalil smiled, showing his very white teeth. "You are combat trained."

"We have monitored three years of combat training, but we are not trained."

"Whose training?"

Sang hesitated, weighing up conflicting privacy concerns. "The training was arranged for Max, which is why we monitored, yet Bellona also trained."

Khalil smiled. "Were you a monitor or a benign sentry? I have a feeling that Bellona's family would not have approved of her training."

"They did not." Sang shut up.

Khalil stroked his beard thoughtfully. "You realize that her training was probably why the Karassians used her as an app instead of parading her around as a useless Eriuman hostage before publicly executing her?"

Sang drew in a breath and let it out. "The thought had occurred to me." It was not an easy thought.

"Combat training," Khalil said, pulling the subject back. "You're trained well enough to be useful. I want you to train me."

"You are not a warrior."

"Neither was Max, or Bellona, once."

Sang considered him. "You have survived without combat skills until now. Does your arrival in Eriuman space have something to do with the sudden need to be able to defend yourself?"

Khalil didn't move. "I do not fool myself that I will be welcome there. In a room full of Eriuman primary clan members, only Bellona will consider me a friend."

"We consider you an ally."

Khalil grimaced. "But not a friend. As long as I am useful, Sang, you will tolerate me. You have learned the biases of your family well."

Sang did not deny it. "Family intrigues are usually political in nature. They prefer that blood only be shed for reasons of war."

"The politics, I can handle. It's the exceptions I must prepare for. Why did Bellona consider it prudent to learn combat skills?"

"For many reasons. Because Max was training and she was not. Because she wished to go to war. Because her father said she could not."

"Ah."

Sang tilted their head the way that Khalil sometimes did, when he was assessing a situation. "You risk much, simply because Bellona wishes you nearby."

"Yes," Khalil said flatly. His gaze met Sang's, steady and frank.

"Why?" Sang demanded.

Khalil's gaze dropped to his hands. "Did you know that Xenia, when she was in Ledan, thought she was a dancer? She loved the idea that she was pleasing others with her dancing, even though she couldn't actually remember a performance. She didn't mind the aches and pains, the casts, the injuries. She considered them part of her work. The Xenia that I knew—that Ari knew—was gentle. Creative. They took that away from her, the Karassians, in their effort to forge a hero." His gaze flickered up to meet Sang's. "Her family are doing the same thing."

"You don't know that," Sang protested. "You have only met Max."

"There is a reason she left Erium ten years ago, Sang. Do you know what it is?"

"No one does, except for Bellona."

"She does not know either. I asked her." Khalil looked at Sang directly once more. "She remembers fighting the Karassians when they boarded the *Hathaway*. She remembers killing at least one of them, bare-handed. She also remembers Max getting her on the freeship, while everything before that is gone."

"Trauma," Sang breathed. "Yet the memory must be buried or she would not be so reluctant to return."

Khalil nodded. "Therefore, I find it prudent to acquire combat skills."

"There is only a day left before we arrive at Cardenas."

"I do not expect to learn what I must in one day," Khalil said, his smile brief.

"We only mention the remaining time because there is more urgent need you must address, first."

Khalil lifted his brow. "Oh?"

"From our long experience with the Scordini family, we guess that Bellona's return will generate much... pomp."

Khalil ran a hand down the neutral black tunic over trousers that he favored. They were bereft of any ornamentation. "I will be at the back wall with you, Sang. This will do."

Sang shook their head. "It is not a chance you should take. If you are included in the ceremony, then you must appear to be one of them. An equal. Such things matter to the family."

"I won't dress up in colors and gilt just to make them happy."

"You should not," Sang agreed. "Instead, you should make your own mark."

Khalil let his hand drop. "You have an idea, then."

"We do."

Chapter Seven

Cardenas (Findlay IV), Findlay System, Eriuman Republic.

THE GREAT HALL WAS A stand-alone structure in the center of the city. The city itself had a name that most people had forgotten. As the seat of power for the Cardenas family, the most senior family in the primary Scordini clan, the city had become known as Cardenas, just as the planet was named. The city had sprung up around the functions of the family, with structures that included the Great Hall.

When the ground cars that had been sent to pick up the new arrivals at the family's private landing field had headed for the city center, instead of the homebase on the hill to the north, Sang knew their guess had been right. There would be a formal welcome ceremony at the Great Hall.

As they pulled up, Khalil studied the screen in front of him. "They're all family? Everyone out there?"

"Everyone on Cardenas is connected to the family in one way or another. This is a family event, yes."

"There are thousands of them."

"Yes."

Khalil glanced down at his new finery. It was black, a tunic and trousers, with a more formal long coat over the top. Glitter and gilt was absent, while a subdued length of piping followed the style lines, which had been all Khalil would tolerate. "Anything more is a distraction."

"Elegance is often used in such a way," Sang pointed out as they worked on the print file, preparing it.

"I meant *I* would be distracted. No, Sang. Enough."

The ground car halted and Khalil shifted his feet, preparing to exit. Sang gripped his wrist, staring at the screen. "Wait."

Khalil protested. Sang pointed at the screen.

There were two more ground vehicles drifting through the pack of people toward the Great Hall, their armored fields glinting in the early morning sunshine.

"Who?" Khalil asked.

"I believe one has Max and Bellona. The other, senior members of the family." Sang watched.

"Max and Bellona go first?" Khalil guessed.

"Yes."

"Then we're definitely last."

His dry tone made Sang smile.

The first car opened and Max stepped out and waved as everyone cheered and clapped. He reached back and helped Bellona out. She was appropriately dressed in a green gown, although for the second time, she had eschewed jewelry. Her hair was down. She did not wave, even when the cheering grew louder.

Sang remembered the Karassian officer forcing Xenia to wave.

The second vehicle opened and a tall man emerged. "That is Max and Bellona's uncle, Gaubert," Sang told Khalil. Gaubert waved to the crowd, then helped a woman from the vehicle. "The woman in gleaming red is his wife, Thora," Sang added.

Gaubert brushed down his braided jacket, then led Thora to where Max and Bellona were standing at the foot of the stairs.

"Now you must exit," Sang said. "Go to Bellona at once."

Khalil raised his brow, but obeyed. He walked straight over to Bellona, who gave him a stiff, self-conscious smile. As Sang got out, they kept their gaze on Khalil as Max murmured to him. Khalil nodded.

Max held out his hand to Bellona, who took it. Together, they climbed the stairs. Khalil fell in behind them, with Gaubert and Thora following.

The people watching them enter the Great Hall swept in behind them, keen to enter as soon as possible so they would not miss a moment of the pageantry. Sang edged their way between people, careful to not bump or push anyone. Progress up the stairs was slow as the numbers were many. As soon as the lintel of the big doors passed overhead, Sang nudged out of the flow and climbed the service stairs to the balcony that ran the width of the back of the hall. As a member of the inner family, Sang was allowed to pass through the security shields. There was no one on the balcony, for everyone who would be permitted access to the balcony was standing on the high dais at the front of the hall, or was walking the long length of the hall toward the dais.

Reynard Cardenas waited at the front of the dais, wearing the family colors, his wide shoulders made wider by the formal coat and high collar. His expression was impassive, his gaze unmoving. The plane of his brow was unfurrowed. Only the short hair that he wore brushed forward showed any sign of frailty, for it was shot with gray. He appeared to be watching the small party walking along the aisle, himself a still rock of a man on the higher dais.

Iulia was a pace behind him. She glowed with joy, her gaze on Max and Bellona. She held her hands tightly in front of her.

Ranged behind the two were the more senior members of the family, those closest to Reynard in either blood or favor.

Applause, shouting and cheering filled the hall. Sang sampled the sounds. Analyzed them. There were no sour notes to be detected. As usual, the city was as pleased to celebrate the family occasion as the family itself appeared to be.

Max climbed the steps up to the dais. Instead of moving a step ahead of Bellona, which was usual, he stayed abreast of her. Once on the dais, he turned and presented Bellona to Reynard with a flourish. The theatricality was a new element. Had Max finally learned to move within the family strictures for maximum personal freedom? His success with the Eriuman Navy would certainly indicate as much. This was another sign.

As Reynard took his daughter's hand from Max, the noise in the hall leapt higher. Sang glanced from one upturned, shining face to the next. Everyone was overjoyed at Bellona's return.

Then Max stepped aside and waved Khalil forward. Khalil moved up next to Bellona and Reynard held out his hand. Khalil, uncoached, followed suit. So Reynard grasped his elbow and drew him forward in a formal hug and patted his shoulder, then released him.

They were talking. Sang could see their lips moving, only the sound in the hall was thunderous.

Reynard turned to the audience and held up Bellona's hand.

The cheering intensified.

Bellona attempted a smile. Sang could see her mouth working as she tried. The pulse at the base of her throat fluttered wildly, but the smile did not form.

* * * * *

AFTER THE FORMAL PUBLIC CEREMONY, a private family function was scheduled at the homebase on the high hill overlooking the city. A dozen ground cars carried the invited guests up the hill. Inside the grounds, help-meets were waiting with mulled wine in tall cups, for the chill of winter still gripped the city, even though the snow had gone.

Sang passed into the house without partaking, for it

was no longer their role to blend in. There was a mild relief in returning to familiar behavior patterns, even though most of the more recent habits had been built around the absence of Maximilian. It would require concentration to restore the focus now Max had returned, even temporarily.

Sang moved into the big gathering area, that was open to the elements on three sides to take advantage of the view down into the valley and the city lights. They checked arrangements for hosting guests were in place. The help-meets and aides that were not handing out refreshments at the entrance were here, arranging the sideboards with more cups, more aromatic wine and hot food.

The fields were still up, so the interior of the room was warm. Sang took note and went back out to the entryway. Max and Bellona were just passing through, with Khalil following closely behind.

Sang helped Max out of his coat. He was still in uniform, which was appropriate for this hour. Sang would check to see if the civilian clothing he had left behind was laundered and wearable, although the shirts would all have to be reprinted to accommodate Max's increased dimensions in the upper body. As Max chatted easily with cousins and friends, Sang visually measured his proportions and hurried back to Max's old suite to compare them against the stored clothing.

Once Max's immediate wardrobe needs had been dealt with, Sang returned to the gathering room.

Everyone was inside now. To accommodate the number, most of the seating had been removed and guests swirled about the room in easy-moving patterns. A gathering of this size was unusual. There were second cousins from off-world here, as well as the more immediate uncles and aunts and first cousins.

Reynard took up his favorite position in the corner of the room where two pillars held up the roof and where the light was greatest during the day. At night, directional lighting also picked out the corner. A quirk of field technology and the intersection of two fields made the corner snug and comfortable no matter what the weather may be on the other side of the fields.

Although there was nothing as crass as a line of people waiting to speak to Reynard as the head of the family, there was a steady flow of people seeking him out in his corner, to exchange a few words, to thank him for the invitation and to add another tiny layer to their relationship as a hedge against future politics.

There was another invisible line waiting to speak to Bellona, although this one was shorter. Bellona sat upon the only chair in the room, a high one that kept her at the same level as those speaking to her.

Sang noticed that Khalil had gravitated to the back of the room. No one sought his company, so Sang went over and stood next to him for a short moment.

"I'm wondering when either of them will speak to the other," Khalil said, crossing his arms. "They could still be on different planets, right now."

"There is a timing to such things," Sang said.

Khalil rolled his eyes. "She's his daughter. Why must there be a right time?"

"There are still too many cousins and distant family in the room for an intimate conversation."

Khalil's smile was knowing. "Even if it was just the two of them, it would still be too many people." He nodded his head. "They cannot possibly see each other, not with this many people, yet they are both fully aware of the other."

Sang considered the arrangement of people in the room. They narrowed their focus upon Reynard. Reynard was always formally polite when more than the immediate family were nearby, yet there was a stiffness about his stance tonight that Sang had first assumed to be tiredness.

Bellona had found a way to smile, but it was not a warm expression. Even though she sat, her back was very straight. In between smiling, her jaw flexed.

A voice rose from among the polite chatter. "Of course she was abducted! The Karassians took her, right from under our noses!"

The voice was Iulia's. She held a small court of her own, mostly women of the family, with some partners in tow, over by the smaller sideboard where the wine samovar steamed.

At her protest, Max spun on his heels to look at his mother. He was on the far side of the room, with a small group of cousins. His turn sent his elbow into the side of a help-meet, who just barely controlled the tray of used cups they were carrying. The cups toppled with damp chimes, but Max didn't look. He was staring at his mother.

"How dare you suggest otherwise, Magdalena!" Iulia cried.

Soft voices tried to shush her, to turn the subject.

"My daughter did not run away!"

Bellona didn't move. She was a frozen pillar of flesh, her gaze on her hands.

Conversations checked. Heads turned.

Reynard beckoned to Riz, Iulia's personal assistant. Riz hurried over and bent their head to listen to Reynard's quiet command. They nodded and hurried back to Iulia, to whisper in her ear.

"No, I will not retire," Iulia said, her voice still loud enough to be heard everywhere in the room.

Max was standing as still as Bellona was sitting. His hands were tight fists.

Reynard's face might have been carved from the same marble as the pillars on either side of him. As much as it was possible for his deeply olive skin to show white, it was. Pale strips of flesh bracketed his mouth. The scar stood out.

"Tension is causing interesting reactions, isn't it?" Khalil murmured.

A tight knot of family members surrounded Iulia, drowning her voice in soft concern. The heads drew together. Then, with Riz among them, the group drifted toward the arch that led into the interior. Iulia was being removed.

Sang went over to Max and waited.

Max glanced at them. His shoulders relaxed. His fingers uncurled.

"Perhaps this would be a good moment to change out of your uniform?" Sang suggested. "A general movement out of the room would be…supportive."

Max nodded, yanking at the high collar. "Exactly what I was thinking. Watch Bellona, while I am gone." He turned and stalked from the room, as many of the family members were, as if Iulia's departure had been a natural phase in the proceedings.

Reynard was already speaking to someone else. His pallor was fading.

Bellona, though, had not relaxed. No one sought her out. She sat alone, as if her mother's outburst had made her radioactive. Sang obeyed Max's last order and moved over to her. Khalil beat Sang there.

"That is what they think of me," Bellona said, her voice low. "That I ran away, like a coward."

"You don't know what happened. You can say that truthfully," Khalil assured her.

"I remember Max taking me off the planet, though." Bellona dropped her voice even lower. "I wasn't abducted from here."

"Did Max tell you why you left?" Khalil asked.

"We barely talked," Bellona said. She grimaced. "The life of a captain is apparently a frantic one."

"Perhaps you should ask him, now that he is home."

Bellona sighed. "If I get the chance."

"Perhaps you will need to manufacture the opportunity," Sang said.

Khalil nodded. "Your family doesn't like talking about difficult subjects. You'll have to nail Max to the ground."

Bellona's mouth lifted in a barely suppressed smile that held a wicked glint. "*That* is something I can do, now."

* * * * *

IULIA'S DEPARTURE SIGNALED MORE THAN just a natural pause. Sang catalogued faces and saw that many of the fringe relatives did not return to the gathering.

The numbers in the gathering room thinned. The volume of conversation dropped. Max returned and his civilian clothing audibly approved of by cousins. Reynard waved him over and pressed his hand on Max's shoulder, his fingers gripping tightly, as Reynard spoke to Gaubert and Markjohn, the youngest of the brothers. Max and Reynard were the same height, which had not been the case when Max had left.

Sang hovered near Max's elbow. The peculiar tensions in the evening had jolted something in the man. When he returned to the gathering room, Max drank several glasses of the mulled wine quickly, then drained more at a steadier pace. Sang could foresee need of their services and waited.

Soon enough, Max was swaying. Sang stole the cup from his unsteady fingers, handed it to another aide and slid under Max's arm and straightened. Reynard pretended not to notice, although his jaw was tight even as he spoke. Gaubert and Markjohn merely looked amused. It wasn't unusual for at least one person to overindulge at family gatherings, although it was rarely Reynard's immediate family.

Sang helped Max stagger to his bed, peeled off his

boots and arranged him in a fashion that would not tax tendons or muscles if he fell asleep in that position.

"She doesn' trust him," Max muttered. "I don' understand."

Sang was in complete agreement, which bothered them as much as it had appeared to bother Max, although for different reasons. Max just wanted everyone to get along. He never had liked family arguments, even those not involving him, for Reynard drove most of the conflict.

Sang sealed the suite against casual entrances, a timed key to their prints only and set to expire at a reasonable hour tomorrow morning. They went back to the gathering room. By now, most of the extended family would be gone, except perhaps for Reynard's brothers and sisters. It would be possible to tidy and clean and not get in the way of the family while doing it.

The short day was growing dim, which put the airy rooms inside the house into deeper twilight. The helpmeets had not added light to the public rooms. It was not yet an issue to navigate through the big spaces, especially for those familiar with every piece of furniture and carpet.

There were pockets of conversation all through the house. Family had drawn together in twos and threes, away from the gathering room, to talk quietly. Sang did not try to hear any of the conversations. Tones were light, interspersed with laughter, highlighted by happy notes.

The library was the last room before the gathering room. Sang had never understood why the room was named such. It did not contain books, nor shelves to hold ancient tomes upon them. It was the grandly formal reception room where Reynard Cardenas did most of his working and thinking. There was one comfortable chair and several less comfortable visitor chairs, glowing carpets on the walls and little else. Wait, Reynard's aging assistant, supplied all computing functions, communications and security when there was a visitor.

When Reynard was not working in the room, it was a silent, almost featureless place except for the single big green armchair, which provided the only point of focus.

There was someone in the room when Sang moved quietly past the wide doorway. Sang glanced only to ascertain they were not interfering with Reynard's possessions, then moved on smartly, startled. In that brief glance, they saw more than enough.

The image lingered, though. Bellona and Khalil, standing close. His hand moving softly against her throat. Bellona reaching for him, her face turned up, every line of her body speaking of want, matching Khalil's tense need.

Sang moved as quietly as possible out into the gathering room, where the light was much brighter and the sound of conversation, clinking cups and plates drowned out the silence they left behind.

They felt no surprise. The fact merely confirmed what they had subconsciously concluded. They felt neither pleasure nor dismay at the confirmation. Instead, there was a quiet satisfaction at the idea that Bellona would experience a degree happiness as an outcome of her time on Ledan, something that had always been a rare quality in her life.

They also found some amusement in the location she had chosen for her seduction. Defiance had always been part of her personality.

Then their gaze fell upon Reynard Cardenas, who still stood in his warm corner, holding sway upon the gathered family. Of everyone in the room, his was the loudest voice. He rarely bothered to modulate. There was no need—everyone was eager to hear what he said…if they were wise.

Sang realized they felt dismay, after all. Not everyone in the family would be pleased by the man in Bellona's arms.

Chapter Eight

Cardenas (Findlay IV), Findlay System, Eriuman Republic.

IT TOOK FIVE WEEKS FOR the family to erupt over Khalil Ready, which was completely unsurprising to Sang. There could be no immediate or direct protest about her relationship as Eriuman women were technically free to choose their partners.

Before their venture into the heart of Karassian lands, Sang had found the subjective reality of Eriuman affairs of the heart perfectly natural. Now, though, they had a different perspective to measure it by. So did Bellona, who carried all her memories of Xenia's pleasant life in Ledan.

In this matter, Karassians had a more open approach. Alliances, dalliances, contracts, marriages, it was all of utter disinterest to Karassians, unless a relationship soured, or was settled for the long term, or provided some other drama they could watch from afar. The 'who' was less important than the 'how'.

Eriumans, though, cared deeply about the couplings of their family members, especially if breeding was involved. Then, family manipulations to arrange the "right" partner emerged in force. The longer a seemingly casual and unsuitable alliance continued, the stronger the family response to it.

Max was the first to speak to Bellona directly about Khalil. Sang suspected the indelicate directness was a result of his military life, which demanded he return to service, forcing him to speak.

Sang spent the morning gathering Max's possessions

and stowing them in the carryall for return to the *Decimus,* while listening for Bellona's return. She and Khalil had hiked to the peak of the hill the homebase was located upon. It was a four hour journey both ways and the better part of a day, if one lingered at the lonely peak. There was a hot spring just below the peak that would beckon the pair, too.

Max dithered impatiently, picking up and putting down childhood possessions that were kept on the shelf by his big desk. He sat, then stood, then sat again.

"The satellite has them nearly back to the house," Sang observed, after consulting with the house AI. "They are making better time on the lower slopes, too."

Max nodded, pretending only a mild interest.

As it was close to both Max's departure time and the early evening partake, Sang went to the kitchens and arranged for Max a meal of several hundred calories—enough to keep his energy up and his mood stable. Max fell on the hotpot and pie with a grunt of approval and devoured it quickly.

By the time he was done, Sang could hear Bellona's voice from the front of the house, as she spoke to someone there. She sounded happy.

Max jumped up, shoving the plates away. "Come with me," he told Sang.

Sang followed him out to the public rooms.

Max caught up with Bellona in the gallery, the wide and even longer hall that gave access to the private suites. Like the gathering room, the gallery had no solid walls on either side, just fields to keep the inclement weather out. Today, the fields were down. The late afternoon air was just turning from warm to cool.

Max beckoned Bellona over. Khalil stayed by the other side of the gallery and looked out at the lengthening shadows.

"You're wearing your uniform," Bellona told Max.

"I've been called back. There's an offensive…well, you don't need the details."

"An offensive where?"

"It doesn't matter. I don't have time, anyway. I'm already dangerously close to being late."

Bellona frowned. "There was something I wanted to talk to you about. I haven't had a chance, lately."

Max's gaze flickered toward Khalil. "Understandable," he said heavily. "That's what I wanted to talk to you about."

Bellona's face closed over. Her jaw flexed, as anger flickered in her eyes.

Max read her reaction as easily as Sang had. He shook his head. "Put your claws back, Bellona. You know I don't care about who you're with. You must stop flaunting in him front of Father, though."

"Why?" she demanded.

"You think I don't know you're doing it deliberately? You know that every time he sees you with Khalil, it gnaws him. You think that Father doesn't know you're baiting him, too?"

Bellona crossed her arms. She looked very young, with the fresh glow of exertion on her face, but the defiance had gone. Now she merely looked thoughtful. "I might have known that if he had only spoken to me about more than the weather, lately."

"Those are not conversations that come easily to him. You know what he's like, Bellona. Do you really want to force Father to speak to you over something like this? It won't end happily."

"That's where you're wrong," Bellona said, her voice smooth and strong. Confident. "I don't play by family rules anymore. The delicate stepping around in circles. The prevarications. All of it. I'm done, Max."

"Not while you're living here, you are not."

"I can't live anywhere else," she said bitterly. "Not anymore. Maybe I never could, despite trying. Why *did* you take me off the planet? Why was I on the *Hathaway*?"

Max grew still. He rubbed the back of his neck. "I think it's a good thing you can't remember."

"If I did remember, would I still be here?" Bellona asked. "Would I *want* to be here?"

Sang looked at Max, as interested in the answer as Bellona.

Max swallowed. "I don't know."

"You don't know, or you won't tell me?"

"You wouldn't tell *me!*" Max shot back. "You came to me, more upset than I've ever seen you in my life. You were verging on hysterical and you wouldn't say what was wrong. You just begged me to get you away, far away."

Khalil had stopped pretending to be interested in the view. He stood with his legs spread and his hands at the ready, watching the siblings.

Bellona stared at Max. "What *happened*?" she muttered.

Max retreated to the practical. "Have you tried to restore the memory? Bots? Hypnosis?"

Bellona rolled her eyes impatiently.

Max nodded. "Then maybe you should stop digging at it. Either it will come back, or it won't. Either way, I don't think you'll like it when it does. You were not yourself that night, Bell."

Bellona shifted on her feet. The boots and trousers she favored these days vexed her mother, but Sang thought they suited her. She scowled. "I haven't been myself for a very long time," she said, her voice harsh. "One more ripple won't be noticed amongst the churn."

Sang cleared their throat. "The time..." they murmured, as their sense of passing time was always more accurate than most humans and far more accurate than Max's.

Max nodded. "I have to go. I can't keep the shuttle

waiting." He gripped Bellona's arms and gave her a shake. "You take care of yourself."

"Always," she said easily.

"I mean it."

"I will."

Max looked at Sang. "I want you to watch out for her, Sang."

Sang nodded.

"I don't need a help-meet," Bellona protested.

"You're about to lose one of your few allies in the family," Max said gravely. "I'm compensating for that as much as I can. Let Sang help. They're very good at it."

"They are," Khalil said quietly, from his observer's place across the gallery.

Bellona sighed. "Very well."

Max hugged her. It was an impulsive movement and Bellona stood with her arms stiffly at her sides, caught by surprise.

Max glanced at Khalil and nodded, then stepped around Bellona and strode down the gallery, heading for the front of the house, where he would find Reynard and Iulia and say his goodbyes.

Sang saw the temper simmering in Bellona's face as she studied them. The resentment was unmistakable. "We will see Max off," they said.

"Good idea," she said shortly.

* * * * *

FOR A WEEK AFTER MAX'S departure, a lull held the family. Bellona did her best to ignore Sang, although her disregard was not aimed purely at Sang. She ignored everyone, including her father. She and Khalil toured the city, hiked a lot and spent time in the movement suite with the doors sealed, from where the sound of clashing weapons could be heard. Bellona was training Khalil more effectively than Sang could. Sang's coaching became a supplement, instead, rounding out Khalil's skills.

"It helps her keep the memories fresh," Khalil confessed to Sang after a long session from which he emerged sweating and exhausted. "It reminds her of who she was."

"She wishes to remember being Xenia?"

"The Xenia she remembers was happy. She had friends. A life that was content. It doesn't matter that it was all an illusion. It felt real enough when she was living it." Khalil frowned. "And it helps her ignore the news."

The war news was not good. Part of Sang's function was to collate news and present it daily. When Max was not there, Sang merely collected. They did not know how Bellona was acquiring her news updates, for she did not ask Sang for them. Perhaps it had not occurred to her that Sang could provide the service. Iulia, as head of the family, was the only woman assigned a personal assistant. Bellona had grown up without one, as most women in minor positions in Eriuman households did. It was considered a waste to provide each of them with an assistant, so Bellona had never learned to work with one.

The terminal in Bellona's private suite was smart enough to build a daily update, although it was not an AI and would not adapt the feed to suit her waxing and waning interests. It didn't matter for right now, because all the news was negative. Lost ships, with all hands. Lost territories, which Erium found almost more painful than the loss of lives. While losses were an accepted part of war, it was the manner of the more recent losses that grated. The Karassians had taken Max's innovations with smaller, personal fighting craft and applied it with the usual Karassian slap-dash passion and drive. The little fighters they were using against Eriuman cruisers had been too quickly designed and were inclined to explode upon launch or even in mid-flight. They often broke down. Yet, when they were working, they were *fast* and they were lethal. Max's tactic of overwhelming Karassian cruisers with Eriuman fighter craft, the constant barrage bringing them to their knees, was being used against the Eriuman Navy now.

So the silence and stillness lasted for a week after Max's departure, while Iulia stayed in her rooms and Bellona and Khalil roamed the city for long hours each day.

Then Reynard announced a formal dinner party, to which Khalil was *not* invited.

Bellona summoned Sang to her suite and showed them the invitation on her screen.

"Oh, that is…awkward," Sang decided. "It is a direct shot across the bows, too."

Bellona nodded. "Formal dinner parties are never odd-numbered. They'll have someone there. Who? Would they dare push my cousin Delben at me again?"

Sang smiled. "Delben is married these days, with six children."

"He was heartbroken by my disappearance, clearly."

Sang considered the invitation. "It is a formal invitation to which you must respond. You could simply not attend."

"Decline, or accept and fail to show?" Bellona grimaced. "Either is…gutless."

"Under the circumstances, it could be argued as the prudent move."

"Whose side are you on, Sang?" she asked. "You're a family member, too."

"Max asked us to watch out for you."

"This falls under 'watching out'?"

"I am a generalist assistant," Sang pointed out. "My parameters range as far as my experience tells me they need to."

"Like buying a luxury Karassian yacht to smuggle me off Kachmar?" Bellona asked. She was still smiling.

"Khalil told me."

"That is a very good example."

"If your parameters are so flexible, then you can help me with this." She pointed at the screen again.

"You intend to go?"

"Only to learn how serious my father is about pushing the family agenda on me. If I can't take Khalil, I want you there."

"It would be inappropriate for us to sit at a table that has no formal place laid for us."

"You can stand next to Riz and Wait if that makes you feel better. I want you there in formals, though. I want it known you're with me. And I want you to observe everything that happens so I can analyze it later."

"We would be most happy to help you with this."

Bellona's smile returned in full force. "I also want you to make me a dress. Khalil says you're skilled at design."

"It is a matter of mathematics, that is all."

"Esthetics have something to do with it. Can you make me a dress that will tell everyone there I don't care?"

"Is that the message you wish to send?"

Bellona frowned. "Yes."

"Then we know exactly what you should wear."

* * * * *

SANG MADE THE PREPARATIONS CAREFULLY. Their first step was to consult with Khalil, who approved the plan wholeheartedly. "Bellona is right. You need to be there, if I cannot be. No one sees you."

"They will, this time," Sang pointed out.

"They might for a few seconds, but they've had a lifetime of ignoring you. They'll soon forget you're there, once the surprise has worn off."

On the evening of the party, Sang presented themselves to Bellona. Khalil, sitting in the easy chair he favored, smiled. "Impressive, Sang."

Bellona walked all around them. "Yes, it is," she decided. "Male, tonight, Sang?"

Sang looked down at the dark formal trousers and jacket. "It is appropriate we favor the male gender tonight if you wish to impart the maximum impact."

Khalil pointed to the terminal where an Eriuman profile rotated. "If they have invited this Captain Ahn Delucas that Sang has decided is the one, then Sang is right. A sharp jab at his competitive nature will have him reacting without filters. There are rumors he likes to deal with opposition without witnesses, though."

"That won't be an issue tonight," Bellona said. She held her hands out from her sides. "How do I look?"

Sang considered the scuffed boots, the rumpled black trousers and the even more disreputable shirt. Her hair was loose, as usual and ringlets hung about her face in delightful disorder. She wore no makeup and no jewelry.

"They will know exactly how little you care, except that you will be standing next to Sang, whose appearance disputes that," Khalil decided.

"Only for those who notice Sang at all," Bellona said. "My father will get the message, though." She gripped Sang's elbow. "Let's go."

Eleven people stood in the gathering room, each holding a cup, when Sang and Bellona walked into the room. Sang catalogued reactions as Bellona had requested. Most of the guests were slow to notice their entry, because they were concentrating on their own conversations—especially those surrounding Reynard. There were some puzzled expressions and some amused ones. Lips parted. Eyes widened.

The man standing next to Reynard was a stranger, yet Sang knew the face. Captain Ahn Delucas, wearing the full uniform of the Eriuman Navy.

Iulia stepped around the group she had been a part of

and hurried over to where Bellona and Sang stood by the inner doorway. She trailed silk, lace and perfume. Her eyes were narrowed, while her face was held in a stiff neutral expression. "Are you mad?" she whispered. "Go back to your rooms and change into something more suitable, as quickly as you can. This needn't be a disaster. I will tell your father you were running so late, you thought it wise to appear first, then dress properly. Go. Go!" She pushed at Bellona's shoulder, trying to turn her and get her out of the room.

"I'm as dressed as I will get, Mother," Bellona said. "I am comfortable and tidy."

"You cannot represent the family looking as you do," Iulia hissed back. There was a tic at the corner of her eye, fluttering quickly.

"I don't remember being asked to do that."

Iulia's tic increased. "You're not a fool. Neither am I. You know very well these events are a showcase for the family."

Gaubert came up to them. The clean, square line of the jaw that was a family trait was softer on him, blurred by good living and an easy acceptance of his status. He touched Bellona's shoulder. "You are looking casual, niece."

"I am, thank you," Bellona shot back. "Sang, a drink, please."

"No," Iulia snapped. "She is returning to her room."

Sang looked at Bellona. She stared right back.

Instead of leaving her with her mother and uncle, Sang raised their hand and beckoned one of the help-meets over. Sang smiled their thanks and took two of the cups from the tray they were carrying and handed Bellona one of them.

Gaubert watched Sang, a smile forming and growing broader. "How quaint," he murmured and drank deeply from his own cup.

Iulia gripped Bellona's forearm as she tried to lift the cup to her mouth. "No," she said, her voice low and hard. "Hear me. Stop this at once, Bellona. You will gain nothing from defying your father in this way."

Bellona swayed to one side, to look around Iulia's shoulder. She smiled. "I have already gained everything I intended."

Sang looked in the direction Bellona had glanced. Reynard was standing near the big dinner table, talking to Delucas. His face was dark with suppressed anger. As Sang looked, Reynard's gaze flicked toward Bellona.

Bellona shook off her mother's grip and sipped from the cup. "Toss me out, mother," she said. "Please. You'll be doing me a favor."

Gaubert tisked in delighted disapproval. He was enjoying the moment.

Iulia dropped her hand. "Sending you away will only call more attention to your waywardness. We will brazen this out. Sang, take your post."

Sang looked at Bellona for direction. She nodded. "Yes, I think my point has been made," she said softly. "Thank you, Sang. I will not divide your loyalty any more tonight."

Sang felt a need to contradict her observation and held it back, for it would not contribute to the play they were helping perform right now. Instead, Sang nodded and moved over to where Riz and Wait stood, in the darker corner of the room. As they went, they sipped the wine, then added the cup to the return tray. They presumed no one would notice the audacious act, except Riz and Wait, who both looked shocked.

Iulia pulled Bellona over to where her father was standing, her knuckles white where she gripped Bellona's arm. Delucas turned to face the approaching women, a pleasant smile stitched on his flat face.

Sang focused their hearing.

Reynard's grip on his cup tightened, as he said in a jovial tone; "Captain, I present to you my daughter, Bellona Cardenas Scordina de Deluca. Bellona, I recommend to you Captain Ahn Delucas Scordino de Carosa."

Ahn inclined his head. "It is a great pleasure, Bellona, to finally meet you. You have been much in the news lately."

It was now Bellona's turn to express her appreciation for his company and add a light compliment of some sort. Sang had seen the pattern repeated thousands of times.

Bellona drained her cup and put it on the table by her hip, disturbing the neatly laid pattern of plates and utensils. "Your ship is the *Livius*, yes, Captain?"

Ahn's pleasant expression faded. "Indeed," he said, his tone flat.

"A dreadnought of the third generation," Bellona added. "Tell me, what strategies have you developed to counter the Karassian single-man fighters?"

Reynard cleared his throat. "This is barely a fit discussion for here and now."

"I guarantee it is the only subject Captain Delucas thinks about these days," Bellona said, staring at Ahn.

Ahn's smile this time looked as though it was pulled from him without his permission. "You are very perceptive," he said shortly.

Iulia sighed. "Oh dear…"

"Really, Captain, I would like to hear your thoughts about this," Bellona added. "It seems to me that my brother's idea to carry lightweight fighters gave the Eriuman Navy a short advantage that has now been completely neutralized by the Karassian imitations. Instead, you're having to deal with a problem of your own making."

"You would be right," Ahn said, his attention thoroughly caught.

"An impasse," Bellona said.

"Indeed."

"However, could you not also argue that the entire undeclared war, going back to the destruction of the *Valerianus*, has been on the whole a search for a way to break the impasse?"

Ahn nodded. "A constant impasse, yes. As soon as we or the Karassians discover a weakness to exploit, the other side imitates that strategy."

"Then both sides adapt and you're back to the impasse," Bellona added.

Anh drew in a slow, deep breath. "You have an unusual clarity of thinking."

"It comes from having lived in both worlds," she said shortly.

Anh drew back. He clearly did not appreciate the reminder of her recent history.

Iulia leapt to minimize the damage. "I am desperately hungry. Reynard, may we start the meal?"

"That would be appropriate," Reynard said slowly, as if his mind was far away. He was staring at Bellona and Sang suspected that for the first time in his long life, Reynard Cardenas was seeing his daughter without filters.

Sang motioned to the help-meets, who hurried to withdraw chairs from the table and help the guests seat themselves. Ahn Delucas was seated next to Bellona. Sang placed themselves directly behind her chair and enjoyed the startled look Iulia gave them.

Unlike most formal dinners that Sang had attended, this one held the promise of novelty.

Chapter Nine

Cardenas (Findlay IV), Findlay System, Eriuman Republic.

AFTER NINETY MINUTES OF GRAPPLING drills under the intense sun of midday, both Khalil and Sang were happy to lie on the lawn for a moment and recover.

Sang listened to the hum of insects, Khalil's heavy breath and the whisper of a breeze in the tops of the trees nearby. Here in the heart of the family garden, not a hint of the city that lay all around disturbed the peace. Nothing could be glimpsed through the bordering trees and bushes.

This was Max's favorite section of the sprawling gardens. It was where he had taken most of his combat training and Sang had spent long hours standing at the narrow entrance, watching the sessions.

It had seemed appropriate to bring Khalil here when Sang had found him pacing the gallery. The man had been angry and miserable. "She will not stir from the bed," he said. "She will not speak to me. To *me*." His distress was plain. "What happened last night?"

Sang had suggested the training session as an excuse to get them both out of the house and into a location where they could speak freely, yet Sang had found the exertion a welcome relief. They only wished they had anticipated the activity and worn something lighter. Today was one of the early, hot days that heralded the coming of summer. Sang plucked the shirt away from their chest.

Khalil grunted, watching the movement. Then he sat up and pulled the tunic over his head and tossed it away. "Better," he decided, rotating his bare shoulders.

"One often does not get to choose what clothes to wear in a battle. The battle arrives unannounced, in a location and time that is usually highly inconvenient," Sang said, remembering the ex-Navy instructor bawling that fact at Max and Bellona, while they fought to stay awake and train in the small hours of the night, both wearing nothing more than the lightest of sleepwear and robes.

"So I should wear combat gear at all times?" Khalil asked, sounding both tired and amused.

"Do you feel you might be called upon to fight at any instant?" Sang asked.

Khalil propped himself up on his arms. "Here, I always feel that way." He met Sang's gaze. "What happened last night?"

Sang cast their mind back to the previous evening. The dinner party had proceeded choppily, with Bellona keeping Anh Delucas on his toes with pointed questions and observations, while Reynard and Iulia did their best to redirect the conversation whenever they could. The remaining dinner guests, all close relatives of Reynard's, had tried to follow their hosts' leads, hiding their discomfort at the raw subjects Bellona raised—abduction, annexation, hostages, slavery, subjugation, death ratios, acceptable loss rates, AI mortality priorities... Sang suspected that few of the guests had ever openly discussed such matters even in the privacy of their own homes, let alone over a formal dinner table.

"Bellona talked to Captain Ahn," Sang told Khalil. "To speak to him was exactly what Reynard and Iulia wanted, only not at all the outcome they expected. Ahn found Bellona fascinating…and uncomfortable."

Khalil smiled. "She can have that effect, if one forgets her experience."

"We believe all her family would prefer to forget Ledan ever happened. Bellona reminded them, last night. It was a masterful display of expertise in a subject that Eriumans rarely speak about openly." Sang shifted on the lawn, looking for a more comfortable position on the soft gray tufts.

Khalil waited.

Sang sighed. "It happened when dessert was served."

"*What* happened?" Khalil coaxed.

"We are not entirely certain. Bellona bent to sniff the bowl in front of her." Sang frowned. They had reviewed the sequence many times since it had happened. She had bent to sniff the concoction, a warm treat redolent with spices. Many of the other guests were doing the same and sighing with pleasure.

Bellona, though, had frozen, her gaze on the dish and her hand gripping the edge of the table. A frantic pulse throbbed at the base of her neck.

Sang noticed her distress quickly. Instantly, they turned to the sideboard, picked up one of the extra dishes and scooped up a mouthful of the dessert, analyzing it for poisons, toxins and histamines.

The explosion of spice flavors was pleasant, but in no way was it alarming. The dessert was completely innocent. Not even the scent it gave off was harmful.

Other guests were noticing her reaction. Anh put down his spoon and touched her arm. "Bellona?" he asked quietly, leaning closer so others would not hear the soft enquiry.

Sang leaned between them. "Excuse me, Captain," they told Ahn and picked up the bowl in front of Bellona and sampled it. It was identical.

Sang bent to examine Bellona. Perspiration dotted her temples. She breathed raggedly through parted lips. Her eyes were still fixed on the place where the bowl had been sitting, unblinking. The pupils were very large.

Carefully, they laid their hand on her shoulder and gave her a gentle shake. "Bellona."

She drew in a rushed, deep breath and stirred, bringing

her hand to her head. "I...have to go." She lurched from the table, brushing past Gaubert, who sat on her left, ignoring the hand he raised to help her.

"Sang," Iulia said shortly, in a tone Sang understood. They caught up with Bellona and assisted her from the room, guiding her in a straighter line than the weaving path she had been following.

Bellona shuddered as they walked. "I could almost see it," she murmured, her voice thick.

"See what?" Sang asked.

"I don't know! I can't remember."

Sang paused outside the entrance to her suite of rooms, to give her a chance to deny them entry if she wished, as Khalil was in there.

Bellona put her hand on the door, propping herself up. "I feel…sick."

"Should we assist you? An anti-nausea shot, perhaps…"

Bellona shook her head, then held still and pressed her fingers to her temple once more. "No. No cures. No remedies. I need to find out." She touched the doorplate and moved out of the way as the door swung open. She met Sang's eyes. "Thank you," she said simply. "I will be fine now."

Sang understood why she was lying. "It got you out of the dinner party," they pointed out, trying to lift the mood.

Her smile was barely there, yet it *was* a smile. "Yes, I planned it all along. A way to avoid the after-dinner wine on the terrace that Anh would undoubtedly have suggested. Good night, Sang."

Sang watched until the door was closed and sealed once more, then moved through the mostly silent house to their own small quarters. There was no point in returning to the dinner party. Their presence would act as a reminder to everyone and they did not enjoy being resented.

When they had finished relating the event to Khalil, he remained silent for a long moment. There were very few people who were as comfortable with silences as Khalil was.

"She said 'I could almost see it'?"

"Yes."

Again, the deep silence. Then Khalil sat up, taking the weight off his arms. He brushed the grass off his palms. "I remember the land where I lived as a child. The sun was more orange than this one—I found out later it was just barely within the livable zone and only the equatorial areas of my world were sustaining, but those areas were warm and comfortable. I don't remember harsh winters, of course. Just endless warm days. The earth was a deep, dark brown, darker than any earth I have seen since. The sky was nearly always cloudless. I would walk for hours and hours, watching the way the mountains never seemed to come any closer. They were so tall. Even now, I have never seen taller mountains. They towered over us who lived in that tiny village. They surrounded the city, a day's ride away. The mountains looked after me, I thought, for they were everywhere I went. I remember those days with a fondness that makes me smile. I was innocent. I knew nothing of the greater world beyond provincial space."

"Most children are so," Sang said in agreement, wondering why Khalil was telling them this. As he had never spoken about his life before meeting Bellona, Sang did not interrupt him now. Later, they would analyze every word for implications, assumptions that could be made and hidden facts. It was a natural function to gather data about those surrounding the one they worked for, especially those who were in her bed.

Khalil pointed with his freshly brushed-off hand. "There is a plant over there—I have no idea what it is, yet when I get near it, I can smell it. It has an aroma very close to the one given off by the bushes the farm directors planted alongside their crops to ward off birds. When I smell that plant, Sang, I don't just remember the mountains and the earth with simple fondness. For a moment, it is as if I am actually there. I can recall details that I have long forgotten. The way the earth squeezed through my toes when I ran through freshly ploughed fields. The sun on my face. The cold air that came off the peaks when the wind was right, with the smell of snow riding on them. The tartness of the berries from those bushes…my mouth watered when I recalled it."

Sang considered that. "A repressed memory," they said. "Did the spice force her to recall a memory of Xenia? The fighter, not the dancer?"

Khalil shook his head. "Those memories are not suppressed. They're not there at all. There is only one memory I know of that Bellona cannot recall even when she tries."

"Why she left Cardenas," Sang concluded.

Khalil was staring at the plant that had evoked his childhood.

"Should we arrange for a miniature to be created for you?" Sang asked.

Khalil shuddered, his smile fading. "No, thank you." He brushed his hands off once more, even though they were clean. "Not every memory of home is a pleasant one. The rest…can remain just memories. I do not care to repeat them."

Sang tried to sort through the courses of action that lay open to them now that Khalil had proposed this enticing possibility. How could they help Bellona retrieve the memory? *Should* they? Perhaps, like Khalil's past, it was a memory best left buried.

"Have you ever wondered what goes into the making of a hero, Sang?"

Sang frowned. "I have not studied heroes at all, although the Eriuman Navy decorates many of them every year."

Khalil laughed. "I mean a *real* hero. A leader, a visionary, someone who emerges from obscurity to blazing glory, changing the world with their deeds. True heroes, Sang, are rare. They burst upon the known worlds once every thousand generations or more and they leave a mark that is never forgotten."

"Mia Rasmussen," Sang suggested.

"Svend Murat Kovac," Khalil added. "Ben the Glorious. The Emperor of Xylander."

"Dusan Funard."

"Susan the Savior," Khalil said. "See, the names come very easily to you. To everyone. Their names are never forgotten. Their impact upon the known worlds is endless and immeasurable. Think of how different life would be if Dusan Funard had not fought every cynic and politician in his way and made the first null engine, two thousand years ago."

Sang catalogued all he knew of the people they had swiftly named. "Many of them come from humble beginnings and dire circumstances," Sang pointed out. "Do you feel your own unfortunate experiences qualify you as a potential hero?"

This time Khalil's laughter came from deep in his belly. He shook with it and wiped away tears, as paroxysms swept over him. When he had himself under control once more, he sighed and wiped at his eyes one last time. "You're smart, Sang. No argument. When you say things like that, though, I am reminded that you are not altogether human."

Sang felt no offense. "We are always willing to learn."

"I'm not a hero," Khalil said. "I can never be one. I don't *want* to be one."

"Yet you study them."

"I do."

"Why?"

He shrugged. "Curiosity, I suppose. If the human chaos throws up a hero every thousand generations or so, we are long overdue for a hero of our times. I often wonder what that hero might look like and how they will change the known worlds."

"You do not like the known worlds as they are?"

"Does anyone?"

Sang considered the question seriously. "We would not exist in different circumstances, so we are grateful for these circumstances. Other than that, they are what they are."

"Bellona is troubling you, too, isn't she?"

Sang sighed. "Max was specific in the responsibilities he assigned us. While Bellona is…suffering, we are not abiding by that assignment. Yet, the way ahead is not clear. Perhaps it is better she live with the frustration of a lost memory, than unearth a memory that…"

"Changes everything?" Khalil asked.

"Yes. Which means we must live with failure. That is not a comfortable thought for one such as we, who prefers binary decisions."

"Humans have been dealing with such dilemmas throughout history."

Sang nodded. "We are aware of that. We even tried writing down our thought processes as the exercise seems to provide clarity to others." Sang shrugged. "Yet, the dilemma remains."

"How, exactly, did you try writing down your thoughts?" Khalil asked curiously.

"The usual way. We spoke aloud while the archivist recorded."

Khalil smiled. "Give me an example. Recite something you wrote."

Puzzled, Sang recalled the writing session. Because of their perfect recall, the act of writing and storing thoughts was doubly useless. Nevertheless, Sang selected an innocuous phrase. *"We struggle to understand how we might better –"*

"That's why it didn't work for you," Khalil said, interrupting.

Sang frowned.

"*We* this. *We* that. No group in history has ever been able to group-think a solution better or faster than a clear-thinking individual – and you are that, Sang."

"Clear thinking?"

"Transparently clear." Khalil patted their shoulder. "Try again." He got to his feet. "Time to beat your skinny frame into submission. Get up."

* * * * *

MUCH LATER THAT NIGHT, WHEN Sang had assured themselves that Bellona rested comfortably, even if her thoughts were plaguing her, and long after the house had grown still and dark, Sang directed the house AI to extrude recording sheets and print a stylus keyed to the sheets.

Trembling with their own daring, Sang sat at the small table, the stylus hovering over the blank sheet. They had learned rudimentary writing skills as part of their forced development while still emerging from the growth tanks, so the act of writing was not completely foreign to them. The skill was sometimes required as a form of record-keeping. Such records were always converted to more permanent states, later.

Sang wrote.

Khalil thinks we are troubled about Bellona's state of mind.

Sang read the crude letters aloud, then glanced around. There was no one to hear.

They scratched out the sentence. There was an intimate secrecy about the act of writing, especially on record sheets that no one could access through a terminal, or recall upon a screen somewhere else. Not even the absolutely discreet household archivist held the words inside it. They were for Sang alone.

That gave them the courage to write again, the letters already forming faster.

We are troubled about Bellona's state of mind.

Sang read the sentence. It had no impact. They drew a hard line through it and gripped the stylus, hovering once more. Then, with a sucked-in breath, they wrote quickly, before they could change their minds. They dropped the stylus and sat back to study the single short line they had written.

I am afraid for Bellona.

"Truth," Sang whispered, then covered their eyes and wept.

Chapter Ten

Cardenas (Findlay IV), Findlay System, Eriuman Republic.

BELLONA SEEMED TO RETURN TO her normal spirits the next day, although Sang often caught her staring at nothing, her focus turned inward, as she searched memories. Sang could not discourage her from the practice. All they could do was monitor—and worry.

As was the family practice with uncomfortable subjects, the events at the dinner party went unremarked. It was as if they had not happened. Sang considered that a reprieve.

Ten days after the dinner party, Bellona sent for Sang and ordered them to sit. "Witness mode, Sang," she said, which forced Sang to remain silent, in a purely observation mode. They noted that the household aide designated "Dani" stood by Bellona's divan. Its metal face was devoid of emotion.

Khalil came in wearing a frown. "The terminal in the gallery said you were looking for me." He spent a lot of time sitting against the sun-warmed pillars there. Thinking, he said, and watching the sun on the grass.

Bellona turned from her pacing. "Dani, repeat the report back, please."

Dani opened its mouth. "Secure Document Seven Eight Six Dash Em Three, from Archive Four Six Three, extracted from Bureau Datahouse Gamma, seal intact. Subject—"

"Stop," Bellona ordered. She looked at Khalil. "Do you know what the subject is?"

Khalil's gaze was on Dani. "About me, I imagine," he

said. His voice was remote.

"Yes," Bellona said flatly. "This is a *Bureau* record!"

Khalil looked at her. "Use the proper name, if you must use it at all. The Wyan Oushxiu, Generation 98, of Marijus Prime."

"I don't care!" Bellona raged. "You're one of the Bureau. A human computer freak."

Khalil's gaze shifted to Sang.

"Sang can't talk. They're in witness mode."

Khalil's shoulders fell. "You think you need a witness? With me?" The pain in his voice was vivid.

"I don't know what to think," Bellona shot back. "Is it true?" Then she laughed. It was a raw sound. "What am I asking? That's a bonded, sealed document, straight out of the Bureau's own archives on Marijus. Its authenticity is beyond dispute. It says you are a member of the Bureau, that you have been all along..." She swallowed. "Even before Ledan."

Khalil looked at Dani once more. His expression was indecipherable, but bitterness was part of it. "The Bureau are not human computers," he said, his voice low. "They *use* digital intelligence. They build it. Vast artificial minds with a power well beyond our human ability to think and process. Why does everyone not understand that? The Bureau does not hide the fact."

"They just steal babies and seal them in with a terminal and they grow up knowing nothing about humans. They *think* they're computers!"

Khalil shook his head, his expression sad. "They recruit older children, when they show the type of thinking that allows a human to interface with advanced digital minds. They become interpreters. Researchers."

Bellona breathed heavily, stress taxing her. "The Bureau twists history, to serve its own ends." It was a common belief.

Khalil sighed. "They predict, that is all, based upon statistical renderings of history. They are wrong as often as they are right."

Sang made a notation. In fact, the Bureau was right far more often than it was wrong. Businesses and corporations across the known worlds used Bureau predictions to set their policies and directions, while both the Homogeny and the Republic leveraged predictions for an advantage in the war. Everyone used Bureau computers to run their lives, no matter who they were or where their allegiance lay. To use anything else was to risk losing data, functionality, time and money.

"Of course you defend them," Bellona said. "You're one of them."

"Not anymore."

For the first time, Bellona looked surprised. Her fury checked. "How can that be? Who *do* you answer to, if not them?"

"Since Ledan?" he asked. "No one." He pointed at Dani. "Did you ask for the date stamp, when you were reviewing the file? How old is it?"

Doubt shadowed her face. "You *were* Bureau..."

Khalil rubbed the back of his neck, ruffling the shorn locks there. "Yes, but—"

"I don't care about justifications and excuses. You lied to me."

"Everyone has secrets, Bellona."

"Affairs and trivialities! You knew yours would make a difference. That's why you didn't tell me."

"I didn't tell you because it was no longer relevant... and yes, I was afraid that if I did, you would treat me differently. One gets very tired of being looked at as if they are some sort of monster, or worse, not being seen at all." There was bitterness in his voice.

Sang could not react. Instead, they made a notation.

"Do you know how many worlds, how many cities, the countless corporations I have dealt with, Bellona? All of them saw me as a means to an end. The great computing genius of the Bureau at their disposal, working for them, providing miraculous, life-changing answers for them!" He threw out his hand. "*You* didn't look at me that way."

"On Ledan, when I didn't know who you were," Bellona said flatly.

"You *did* know!" His frustration made him shift on his feet. "Review your memories! I was Ari, but I was Bureau, there to rebuild computers. You didn't care."

Bellona swallowed. "Why did I not remember that?" Her anger was diminishing.

"None of your memories from then have any strong emotion. They don't recur because there is nothing to remind you of them."

"Then how is it you remember them?"

"Because *you* were there!"

Bellona whirled away, a sharp movement, putting her back to him. "You told me you were from a free state."

"You think the Bureau only recruits Karassians and Eriumans?" Khalil asked. "I was on Atticus. I was eleven and I was alone. They offered comfort and shelter and a better education than I was getting from the homeless there. I took their offer, Bellona, even though they did not hide that they were Bureau."

Sang made another notation. The world that Khalil had described, the one that the scent of a plant had evoked, had looked nothing like the industrial complexes of Atticus…and Khalil had not been alone in that place. There had been family there, too. No one with leisure and health to roam the fields and stare at the mountains was without loved ones.

Bellona did not move. She did not react. Sang could not see her face, either.

"I understand digital minds, Bellona," Khalil said. "That's why they took me. The vast power at the Bureau's disposal, the huge minds—they need…friends. Guidance.

Especially when they're young. Then the Bureau realized I was as comfortable dealing with humans as I was with computers and I became a field agent, providing a human face for their biggest transactions."

"A salesman?" Bellona asked. Her tone was one of disinterest.

"A representative. You have to understand, Bellona. Some of the humans that the Bureau recruit really *are* freaks. They can no more interface with human society than the intelligences they build. Yet *I* can. I still look human."

Bellona turned then, startled. Sang made another notation, for later consideration. "Then they *are* monsters."

"Monsters are something to be afraid of. You would not be afraid of the Bureau's oldest humans, if you were permitted to see them. They would be pitiable, if they thought themselves unfortunate, only they do not. They are happy, even though most of them can no longer walk because their legs have atrophied. They are isolated and difficult to understand because they rarely use human speech. Within the Bureau they have an acceptance they could find nowhere else."

"That is where you will end up?" Bellona asked, horror in her eyes.

"I am not an interpreter," Khalil said. "I never would have been. Now, I am not even a member of the Bureau."

Bellona considered that. "Why did you leave?"

"Because of you."

She shook her head. "You would not voluntarily leave that which gave you meaning."

"Unless I found meaning somewhere else."

"Then why not tell me who you really were?"

"Because I wasn't that man anymore."

"Pedantry!"

"You want truth, Bellona? You won't like it."

"I would rather hate you for your true qualities than

hate the mask you hold up."

Khalil closed his eyes, absorbing it. "Very well," he said softly. He sighed and opened his eyes once more. In recording mode as they were, Sang found it all too easy to decipher the defeat in the angle of his shoulders. Khalil knew he had lost everything. "At least, let Sang be themselves," he said softly. "That robotic stare is unsettling. Sang will still remember everything later."

"You would prefer no formal record, then," Bellona surmised.

"Not for this," he said flatly.

Bellona looked at Sang. "End witness mode," she told them.

Sang breathed deeply, blinking. "Thank you."

Bellona looked at Khalil. "Speak," she said coldly.

Instead, he walked about in a tight circle, building himself to it.

"Know that nothing you say will restore my faith in you, Khalil Ready," Bellona added. "All you can do now is redeem your character, if you can."

He nodded. "I will be content with that. The words are difficult, though. Outsiders do not understand that world, the life."

"Try," she urged him.

"I was a field agent. That means more than it appears. For the inner levels of the Bureau, *everything* has to be brokered—the acquisition of human food, the purchase of raw materials for building components, arranging housekeeping, medical care, even something as simple as clothing had to be arranged via someone like me, who could move about in the world and deal with humans. I have been given tasks in my time that seemed puny and meaningless, until I remembered that the task-giver was incapable of completing it for themselves."

Sang remembered the water and the cloth that had been left for them.

"You were assigned to follow me?" Bellona demanded.

"I was told to assess a potential hero."

Sang felt as though they were gawping just as Bellona was.

Khalil sighed again. "The Bureau has known for more than ten years that a war is coming. A real one, not this informal slap exchange between the Homogeny and the Republic. A war that will draw in everyone in the known worlds, that will change the direction of life itself. When the neural mind declared the coming of the war, the Bureau set themselves the tasks of finding the hero that the war would produce."

Bellona shook her head. "Heroes aren't made just by wars."

"They are made by pressure, which wars provide. Overwhelming pressure provokes extreme response and the right response, for the right reasons, creates a hero. Such a hero can effect great change, especially for those who follow him."

Bellona crossed her arms. "The Bureau thought *I* was this hero?" She seemed amused.

"I've already told them you are not," Khalil replied.

Her arms loosened and dropped. "I'm not?"

Khalil shook his head. "The Bureau has been looking for signs of a hero emerging across the known worlds. Hundreds of field agents have been sent out to investigate potentials. I was assigned to assess Xenia." He shrugged. "Xenia is no more. She was a Karassian construct, that is all. Now, the Bureau knows that, too."

"Wait," Sang said quickly. "The only way to fully assess a subject in the way you are describing is to meet them and talk to them."

"Yes."

"But…" Bellona said slowly, "…I was in the Ledan compound."

"Yes," Khalil repeated.

"You got yourself deliberately captured, just to *talk* to Bellona?" Sang asked.

"The Bureau have known and understood the true nature of Ledania and Appurtenance Services Inc. since before it was established. They had to know. They were paid to build the AIs that ran the memory programming. The Bureau is neutral, neither for nor against the Homogeny, as long as the money is good."

"Have you considered that *that* is why people think of the Bureau as monsters?" Bellona asked dryly.

"I *know* it is why," Khalil said flatly. "The Bureau arranged for the networks in the compound to show instabilities. I was already on Kachmar. They briefed me on the situation two hours before I was taken to the island to complete the contract."

"The Bureau knew the Karassians would wipe your memory," Sang said. "That is why you had the recall module implanted."

Bellona glanced at Sang, surprised.

"That was *their* precaution, not mine," Khalil said. "Of course the Karassians didn't kill me, because they cannot live without Bureau services and murdering Bureau agents is a quick way to lose all client privileges. However, the memory wipe was standard. Every other agent put in there for service work was treated the same way. The Bureau implanted the module in me so that my memories would be retained and I could therefore report back on my findings about Xenia." He blew out his breath. "Which I did, as soon as we arrived in orbit over Maggar, along with my resignation."

Bellona studied him. "Why is the Bureau looking for a hero? Do they think they will control the poor man?"

"The Bureau will be a part of the coming war," Khalil said quietly. "No one will get to sit it out, whether they want to or not. The Bureau wants to know who the hero is, so they can predict what happens next."

"You mean, so they can pick the right side?" Bellona shot back.

"Their explanation sounded far more altruistic," Khalil said. "Yet, I think that behind all the fancy explanations, the Bureau is scared. They're looking to survive, that is all."

"Their tactics do not paint them in flattering colors," Bellona said.

"Survival often is ugly."

"Why did you reach out to Bellona's family?" Sang asked. "When the module recovered your memories, that is the first thing you did."

Khalil's smile was rueful. "Even on the Bureau's home world, we heard about the disappearance of Bellona Cardenas. When I matched the DNA and realized who Xenia really was, I was shocked. Yet I was just an agent. The Bureau were going to reassign me. There was nothing I could do about it myself, so I sent the message. Then you showed up, Sang, when I had been braced for a fleet of Eriuman cruisers descending upon Kachmar."

"The Bureau will know you are here," Sang pointed out. "You told them Xenia is not the one they seek, yet you followed her into the heart of Erium. They will not find that suspicious?"

"The Bureau know why I did it," Khalil said flatly. "Even they have not lost sight of the meaning of love."

Bellona looked away.

Khalil turned to face Bellona squarely. "That just leaves one question of my own, if you care to give me that much."

She lifted her chin and looked back at him steadily. "Ask."

"Who gave you the Bureau report?"

Bellona didn't answer.

Khalil nodded. "Then your father has succeeded in ejecting me from your life. I should congratulate him.

Truth can be a slippery tool."

"I will not forget his role in this," Bellona said. Her voice was low. Controlled.

"I will have to be content with that." Khalil moved closer to her. He touched her cheek. Bellona was unmoved by his caress. "There has only ever been one direct lie between us," he said softly. "You asked who I answer to now I have left the Bureau. I told you no one. That was the lie." He bent and kissed her cheek. "I answered to you."

Bellona didn't move, even after he shut the door behind him, leaving Sang alone with her.

Chapter Eleven

Cardenas (Findlay IV), Findlay System, Eriuman Republic.

AFTER KHALIL'S UNREMARKED DEPARTURE, THE divide between Bellona and the rest of the family grew deeper. Bellona stopped talking to anyone, unless directly spoken to. She spent more time in her suite, reading histories and military treatises.

After five days of remaining locked in her suite, refusing all family communications and having food brought to her rooms, Sang suggested to Bellona that the inadequate combat skills they had developed would be refined by rigorous training. Bellona took a day longer to agree.

The first training session in the usual garden clearing—as all Bellona's training had been—left Sang trembling, their biological systems overtaxed and bruised. The next day, their muscles were uncooperative and aching despite painful massage to disperse the lactic acid.

That was also the day Bellona ordered Sang to her suite and gave them a list of research topics.

"Khalil Ready?" Sang said, repeating the last item.

Bellona's gaze was steady, despite the bloom of color in her cheeks. "Profile, history, psychoanalysis."

"You know why he did it," Sang pointed out. "Research won't provide a clearer answer. He had nothing to lose by giving you the truth."

"He wasn't who I thought he was. I want to find out just how wrong my assumptions were. I want to know if I can trust my own judgment. Just do it, Sang."

Sang complied.

While Sang completed the research projects, they

moved through the house, taking care of Bellona's need for food, sleep and exercise, bringing back small pieces of news about the family while steadfastly refusing to provide the family with news about Bellona, as she had ordered. "Let them find out for themselves. If they're genuinely interested in my welfare, they will come, although I am not expecting anyone to appear at that door, Sang."

Sang was not surprised when her prediction proved accurate. They wondered if Reynard felt any regret when he realized how awry his stratagem had gone, that his efforts to remove Khalil had not sent Bellona into his arms for comfort, as any other daughter might have, from where he could nudge her in the direction of a more suitable partner.

Her psychological distance from the family, while still in close physical proximity, made Bellona's temper chancy. The combat training stepped up from three times a week to daily and Sang emerged from nearly every session with new aches, along with a respect for Bellona's strength and agility. Sang also appreciated that they were serving as an effective vent for Bellona's frustrations and submitted willingly to the pummeling.

When Sang suggested Bellona find accommodations somewhere in the city, away from the family homebase, she curtly refused. "I have things to do here, still."

Sang didn't repeat the suggestion. They were aware that in the night hours when the house was still and dark, Bellona would prowl through the rooms, looking for answers. The house AI and archivist reported to Sang each morning, believing it was helping Sang serve Bellona, per Max's orders, which was perfectly true.

Bellona spent hours in the kitchens. For most of those hours she lingered in the big store rooms, especially the cool rooms where preserves were made and kept. It was a policy in all the senior clans to keep their family homebases in a constant state of readiness for war and siege. Their cities could be destroyed. If rumors were true that the Karassians were building city-killers, that could wipe out a city-sized area in one blast from orbit, then those cities could be swept from the map in a few minutes. However, the homebases were always situated in the most defensible positions and could be rendered bomb-proof with a few short commands. Behind those indestructible walls, a family could live for years, if they made the correct preparations.

Sang had at first assumed that Bellona did not want to leave the comfort and hidden protection of the homebase. However, the Cardenas family store rooms were factory-sized buried rooms, where the produce from the gardens and farms and the largesse of subject families was kept and assiduously cycled. This was where Bellona crept for a short while each night.

Puzzled, Sang had ordered the house AI to take footage, which Sang had watched the next morning, their puzzlement evaporating.

Bellona was *sniffing* the supplies, looking for the spice, herb or compound that had tickled her lost memory. She wanted the pure source, to produce another recall. Because the olfactory sense was easily overwhelmed, she could only investigate a little at a time.

If she moved to another house in the city, she would not have access to the storerooms, unsupervised in the dead of night, as she did now.

Sang debated with themselves on whether the behavior was serving Bellona, or if they should intervene. No easy answer came to them, despite the same middle-of-the-night hours spent wrestling with the dilemma on journal pages.

Instead, Sang stepped up their own efforts to produce results for Bellona. They reported on progress each evening. They did not mention to Bellona that they were spending more time researching Khalil Ready's life, while ignoring most of the military profiles she had requested.

"He told me of his town being evacuated when he was a child," Bellona said. "There cannot be too many agrarian settlements concentrated within the equatorial zone, or that were grouped there before they could afford weather generators. That was anywhere from twenty to forty years ago, Sang. There has to be a record of it. Even the free states keep records."

"For themselves, yes, but cooperative exchange of information is sluggish in the free states," Sang pointed out. "We cannot find a confirmed record for the birth of a child called Khalil Ready anywhere for the last sixty years. We could search further back…" Sang shrugged. Khalil Ready had youthful features and even the most gifted medical team could not make a seventy-year-old look young.

"Try any source, even the most illogical. And scour the records on Atticus again. An eleven-year-old boy cannot simply disappear, not even out there."

"A grown woman and highly visible member of the senior clans of Erium disappeared from civilized space, ten years ago," Sang pointed out.

Bellona scowled. "I just want one confirming fact, Sang. You understand why, don't you?"

"You want to know he was not lying, the last day he was here."

"Thank you, Sang."

Sang left her to return to the task of unearthing the life of a minor in the free states, where "freedom" included the right to go unrecorded, undocumented and untrammeled by civic demands and responsibilities.

"They have other responsibilities, more intimate ones," Bellona pointed out when Sang brought the lack of documentation to her attention. "Survival is a sharper equation. When the local wildlife is eating one's summer harvest where it stands in the field, one doesn't stop to file an incident report. One gathers the neighbors and drives the wildlife into the next valley, or one doesn't eat that winter."

"Atticus is beyond such basics. It was settled nearly five hundred years ago."

"Even there, the right to live freely holds sway," Bellona said. "There are no social cushions, no government sponsored services. The people have the freedom to thrive or die trying, with no support."

Sang stared at her, startled. Sang was not the only one to dig into the history of the older planets in free space. "Khalil spoke of eating with the homeless. This would corroborate his testimony, would it not?"

Bellona winced.

"We apologize. We were still in witness mode when Khalil spoke of Atticus so his words are recorded as testimony. Although, we noted at the time that Atticus did not match with the story he told us about his childhood."

"Which is why I've decided he must have been evacuated at some stage, or moved for some reason. That reason is what you're looking for," Bellona finished.

Sang hesitated.

"What, Sang?"

"When Khalil spoke to me of his childhood, he said he did not want the memories stimulated. He implied they were not all pleasant."

"All kids have unhappy memories. Just listening to their parents argue can sound like the end of the world if they're little enough." Bellona paused, considering. "You think it is more than that, though?"

Sang nodded. "The happy memory he shared…there was family there, somewhere. There had to be, for a child that age would not be so carefree without one. Yet on Atticus, he was alone."

Bellona considered it. "Maybe you should check the Karassian military annexation databases, Sang."

"That is not all. When we were on Kachmar, Khalil spoke of a brother."

"A *brother*?" Bellona sat up, startled, disturbing the tray of spiced tea. Lately, she had been requesting heavily spiced dishes for all her meals. She put her hand on the pot, steadying it. "Khalil never spoke of a brother. Not once."

"He only referred to him once, in passing. Benjamin, he called him. The most wanted man in Karassia."

Bellona looked pleased. "Did you run the enquiry?"

Sang nodded. "The only Benjamin in the free states the Homogeny has shown interest in is a Benjamin Arany, of no known allegiance to any free state. He is a maverick freeship captain who likes to harass both Karassian and Eriuman transports wherever he comes across them."

"So does every captain with a cargo to protect," Bellona said, disappointment writing itself on her face. "They prefer to shoot first and get the hell out while the cruisers are trying to turn fast enough to get them in their sights."

"I believe that is where Max came up with his idea of small, agile fighters," Sang said. "He spent five years patrolling the borders of Eriuman. Arany, though, is not a typical freeship captain. He has a number of other freeships that look to him for leadership. As he spends his time harassing the Karassian military, they are most keen to…talk to him."

Bellona frowned. "Do you remember what Khalil said about heroes?"

"We do."

"What you just said about Arany makes me think of that. I wonder if the Bureau are looking for their hero out in free space?"

"I doubt that is ever something we would be able to find out. The Bureau are necessarily secret about how their algorithms and minds work."

"Apparently, not even the Bureau understands how

they work," Bellona said. "Except for the interpreters." She shuddered. "Keep at it, Sang."

Sang searched, broaching unlikely record sources as Bellona had ordered. When Sang found the answer, they considered the implications for a whole day before presenting their findings to Bellona, who listened gravely.

"The military annexed a freeworld, twenty-six years ago," Sang told her. "It was agrarian, with no standing army, the arable land all concentrated around the equator and across only one of the six continents that transverse the equator."

"Why annex it?" Bellona asked, as Sang had anticipated.

"Hydrogen in pure diatomic state suspended in the southern ocean, in concentrations heavy enough to offset the cost of navigating the gravity well. Processors were built and a beanstalk pipeline to the outer atmosphere, all within ten years of conquering the planet."

"*Conquering*?" Bellona said sharply.

Sang nodded again. "The local farmers banded together and fought off the military landing craft. It was bloody, brutal and short. Afterward, every adult in the colony was rounded up and executed."

Bellona drew in a long slow breath. "The children…?"

"Put aboard a shuttle, that took them to the nearest free state and dumped them."

Bellona examined the front, then the back of her hand. "The year?"

Sang told her.

"That fits with Khalil's facts." Bellona shook her head. "Lately I have wondered why Erium continues this pointless war, then I hear about something like this and know why. Karassia is a disease, Sang. It will destroy us all if left to thrive."

"Yes, Bellona."

"And the name of the planet?"

"Before annexation, it was called Arcadia. Now, its official designation is Revati III."

"*Revati*?" Bellona stared at Sang, her eyes large. She grew pale. "Revati is an Eriuman possession." Her voice was stiff.

"Yes."

Her chest rose and fell quickly. "That is all," she said, her tone remote. Weak.

Sang left silently.

* * * * *

FOR FOUR CONSECUTIVE DAYS, BELLONA cancelled combat training and did not emerge from her rooms, not even to wander the stores at night.

Sang waited and monitored the food that was sent to her suite. Too much of it came back untouched.

They considered the various ways Bellona might react to the facts of Khalil's childhood and the role of the Eriuman Navy in those events. She had received the confirmation she craved that Khalil had at least been truthful in the end. The truth, though, was not pleasant.

Sang hoped the experience would discourage Bellona from searching for a way to restore her lost memory of leaving Cardenas. The house AI report that she had stayed in her suite for four nights encouraged Sang.

When Bellona threatened her father with a ghostmaker she had smuggled past the house weapons filters, Sang learned they had been completely wrong.

About everything.

Chapter Twelve

Cardenas (Findlay IV), Findlay System, Eriuman Republic.

THE HOUSE AI WOKE SANG with a screamed alert that made Sang tumble out of their cot while still half-asleep, trying to instantly assess the alarm and fumbling for clothes.

Dressed, Sang ran for the library, from where the house AI stated the weapons alert had originated. There were no other weapons in the house—at least, not traditional weapons. There were any number of innocent-looking objects and devices Sang could use as lethal weapons, thanks to Bellona's training. Until they had assessed the alarm for themselves, there was no need to signal their intent by picking up anything.

They were not the only ones woken. Family members were hurrying through the suddenly daylight-bright house, flinging on garments and suitable layers, shaking their heads, trying to orient themselves as they hurried to the library.

Sang met Iulia at the door and was startled to see her hair loose and brushing the back of her hips.

Then Sang looked into the library and shocked slithered through them.

Reynard Cardenas sat in the big green chair. He was fully dressed, in the clothes he had been wearing earlier in the evening, although his overshirt was rumpled. His face was devoid of any color. Sang wondered if more than shock was affecting him. He gripped the arms of the chair and did not move.

Bellona stood in front of him, a single-hand ghostmaker pointing at her father's chest. Her face was as pale as Reynard's.

"Tell them," she ordered him. Her voice was strained.

Reynard licked his lips. "There is no need for this. Put the gun down. We can speak freely without it."

Bellona laughed. The sound held no humor. "You *don't* talk. You avoid. You deny. You pretend everything is just fine. But you do not talk. This is the only way."

Iulia put her hand on Sang's back and shoved. Sang tripped forward and regained their balance, to find the muzzle of the ghostmaker pointed at them. They held their hands up as the household gathered at the door gasped.

"What do you wish your father to speak about?" Sang asked, keeping their voice calm and reasonable.

"He knows." Bellona swung the ghostmaker back to her father, who had been rising to his feet.

He sat down again. "She is hysterical," he said flatly. "Babbling about thugs and cologne and freeships. It's all nonsense."

"I'm not hysterical," Bellona said. "I'm calmer than I have been for a long while, because now it is very clear."

"See?" Reynard said, spreading his hands. "She has ransacked my room, now she babbles inanities."

Sang glanced at the wall next to the big chair. A section of the paneling had been slid aside. There were such pockets of storage all over the room, most of them innocent. A stranger looking at this cupboard would consider the contents just as benign. Fluted decanters, squat bottles of spirit. Sitting in front of all of them was a smaller bottle that with a quick glance would be mistaken for more spirits, perhaps a rare hand blend.

The seal had been removed. Even from where they were standing on the far side of the room, Sang could detect the sharp, spicy scent.

Cologne.

The scent stirred in Sang the memory of the zesty dessert they had sampled while Bellona slumped at the table. The aromas were not identical, although they were closely related.

"This is the true source?" Sang asked, pointing.

Bellona worked her fingers on the grip of the ghostmaker. "I remember it all now." Her gaze was on Reynard.

Reynard did not ask what it was she remembered. He already knew. Sang could see it in his eyes.

"Sang," Bellona said quietly.

They looked at her expectantly.

"Count your toes. Count your nose. Breathe and repeat."

Sang staggered, as their balance shifted under the onslaught of new memories spilling into their mind. No, not new. Hidden. Not repressed as human memories were, but inaccessible until this moment, when the key phrase unlocked them. They had been so carefully filed away that Sang had not been aware of their existence.

They realized that they were sitting in one of the hard visitor chairs, clutching the cushion to remain upright.

"What is wrong with it?" Iulia demanded from the entrance to the room.

"That is shock, mother," Bellona said dryly. "Sang is remembering now, too."

"Sort-review-analyze," Sang whispered. It was a mantra for times of confusion. Retreating to purely digital processing centered them. They looked for the beginning of the memory. The magic of time would give these strident memories coherence. They would make sense when arranged in order of occurrence…

…the blow had not been entirely unexpected, yet the sound of hand slapping cheek was loud in the silent library. It seemed to echo in Sang's mind as all four of them froze in their positions by the shock of it.

Sang got their hand onto Max's shoulder as he tried to launch himself to his feet to defend his sister. Sang held him down.

Iulia, who knew her husband better than Max, remained still and silent, even as her throat worked and her hands crept beneath folds of her gown, to hide her reaction.

Bellona straightened, fingering the dark red mark on her cheek. Her eye on that side watered freely and her lips were swollen in the corner. She looked Reynard in the eyes, even though she trembled. The blow he had delivered had jarred her carefully piled hair from the top of her head and loose ringlets hung beside her face.

"Take it back," Reynard said, his voice strained. His arm was still raised. "Retract the statement."

Bellona gripped a fold of the yellow gown she was wearing. It was a pretty dress that Sang had always enjoyed seeing on her. Now she crushed the fragile fabric. "I won't marry Delben. I will join the Navy, like Max."

Reynard roared, a shapeless venting of rage. His hand lifted again and Bellona braced herself. She didn't step away or cringe.

"Father!" Max shouted, his voice breaking with a mix of emotions.

Reynard arrested the swing at the apex. He lowered his hand. "You can't join the Navy. You have no qualifications, no skills."

"I am combat trained." Bellona said it calmly.

Max sighed gustily. Now he understood why she had wheedled him into letting her train beside him.

Sang removed their hand and stepped back against the wall once more, where Riz and Wait stood.

"You are a woman. Your physical weakness is a handicap the Eriuman Navy can live without," Reynard replied.

"On a cruiser, where the greatest physical demand is to push buttons?" Bellona asked, her voice rising.

"We're at war," Reynard shot back. "You have no idea what that means, what the true demands of such a career are. You've been protected all your life. *I* have made sure none of it touches you. You think this is an adventure, something novel to distract you for a while. Trust me, war is not what you think."

"Your father only has the best in mind for you," Iulia added softly.

"He wants me married to a Jaleesa so he can lock in the trade agreement. I'm not a fool, Mother!"

Iulia drew in a shaky breath and fell silent. Her eyes were huge as she looked at her husband for reassurance.

"The trade agreement is a pleasant side-effect, that is all," Reynard said heavily.

"Freedom is a pleasant side-effect of joining the Navy," Bellona replied.

Reynard's fury etched itself in his face once more. He curled his lowered hand into a fist. "You dare…!"

"That isn't fair, Bellona!" Iulia cried. "You have more rights and freedoms than any other citizen in history."

"The war you want to join ensures that," Reynard said. "The world beyond Erium is not the escape you seem to think it is. It is not a panacea."

"I'll never know that for myself, if you have your way," Bellona said. "Why won't you let me find out?"

Reynard, perhaps sensing the weight of the argument swinging his way, relaxed. His tone was gentler. Coaxing. "I have worked to provide a good life for you and Max. I ask only that you enjoy it. You are singularly unfit to survive beyond the borders of Cardenas, daughter. You have no experience of what it is like. The free states, the Homogeny…these places do not forgive mistakes. An error here among those who love you merely makes you look foolish. The same mistake, out there, will kill you."

Bellona looked away. She could not counter the argument because Reynard was right. She did not know what lay beyond Cardenas.

Sensing victory, Reynard smiled. "Now, take the day to think about Delben's proposal. It is a fair one. I have looked over the contract—"

"He gave it to *you*?" Bellona asked, her voice rising again.

Reynard frowned. "You would prefer a hired contractor vet the agreement?"

"I would prefer to have the choice!"

"Your ingratitude detracts from your character," Reynard snapped. "It comes perilously close to accusing me of illegalities."

"Your father is not forcing this on you," Iulia added. "Of course the choice is yours."

"Then I chose not to accept the agreement," Bellona said. She headed for the library door.

"I will let you think about it for a day or so," Reynard called after her. His tone implied he was granting her a favor.

Bellona didn't answer…

…the memory linked to the next. There were events in between, of course, although they were not lost memories. They were not linked together. Sang's mind turned to the next forgotten event.

Sort, review, analyze…

…The summons to Max's rooms was a familiar one. Sang had been called for assistance in the middle of the night many times in the past. Max's infractions were mild, but Reynard had no patience for lack of discipline. Max had always called to Sang instead of his mother for help in covering up any indiscretions, even though Iulia was efficient at keeping vexing news from her husband. "She just gets that disappointed look on her face an' it makes me want to squirm," Max had told Sang the time he had needed to be poured into bed and nursed through his first hangover.

Sang moved through the house silently and slipped into Max's suite, wondering what fresh nonsense Max had dreamed up.

Bellona sat on the very edge of a chair, in the darkest corner. The dim light didn't fail to hide the blood covering her tunic, the cuts, scrapes and bruises forming on her arms, or the way the tunic was just barely covering her. The rents and tears would have revealed more, except that Max's big coat hung around her shoulders, hiding the worst of it.

Max was pacing. When Sang stepped in, he came over to them quickly. "I need you to reach out. A hidden channel, Sang."

"What happened?" Sang demanded.

"It doesn't matter," Max said quickly. "Can you do it?"

"A silent channel? Yes. Where to?"

"Cerce, to start."

"Ocantis IV?" Sang clarified. "That is a free state."

"Yes." Max crouched down in front of Bellona and lifted her hair to one side to check her face. "You'll need analgesic at the very least," he said gently. "Did they…do you need more specific medical intervention?"

"You mean, did they finish raping me?" Her voice was high and remote. Her gaze was glassy. "I killed him before he could."

Shock slithered through Sang. They stared. "You *killed* someone?"

Max got to his feet. "I should have thought of it sooner," he said, sounding vexed. "You'll find a body in the garden, where we train, Sang. You'll need to…deal with it. I don't know how such matters are handled, but I'm sure you do."

"There are ways," Sang said distantly. They moved closer to Bellona. "You really killed the man?"

Bellona blinked at him. "I had to."

"It's not important," Max said shortly. "Not now. Sang, the body. You can move around freely. I'll be noticed."

"Yes." Sang said. They made themselves turn and go.

The training area, when they reached it, was bare of anything but closely shaved grass, that shone silver in the light of the second moon, Cardenia. It was late and dew had formed. There were tracks through the dew, with a larger, darker patch of dry grass in one of the shadowed corners. Sang bent to examine it. The smell of blood, coppery and sharp, was distinct.

Sang spent the next fifteen minutes washing the blood away, then quartering the little area, looking for any other signs of disturbance and removing them. Then they returned to Max's suite.

Bellona was emerging from the ablutions area, her hair wet. The clothes she wore were Max's, although tucked into boots and cinched in with a belt, they were not ridiculously overlarge.

"We could collect more suitable clothes," Sang pointed out. "Or print fresh ones."

"No, nothing that leaves a trace," Max said quickly. "The garden, Sang?"

"There was a body, but it had been moved before we got there."

Max glanced at Bellona, his expression hardening.

"Did you think I made it up, little brother?" Bellona asked. She sounded calm, yet there was a wild look in her eyes, which were too large and too glassy.

"The confirmation is still a shock. *Murder*, Bell. The family can't protect you from that."

"Good," she said flatly.

Max threw out his hand. "You were only defending yourself!"

"If we could be made to understand what happened…?" Sang asked diffidently.

"I went to the garden to meet Max for late night training," Bellona said. "We set it up days ago."

"You cancelled on me," Max said.

Bellona shook her head.

"What was the form of the cancellation?" Sang asked.

"The House AI told me Bellona was staying in her room for the night."

"Such a channel can be broached easily," Sang pointed out. "The true origin of the message masked. We will examine it, later."

"It set Bellona up," Max said angrily. "Whoever they were, they targeted her. Four of them."

"I think it was four. It was dark," Bellona said quietly. "They came out of the shadows and they used my name. They knew who I was." She paused, then said reflectively, "It didn't seem to scare them, knowing who I was."

"They attacked you?" Sang said, sparing her the description.

She nodded. "Then, when the shock passed, when I realized it really was happening…well…I just…reacted."

"And killed a man," Max whispered.

"Then I came here," Bellona said, looking around the suite.

"You were right to come to me," Max said. He stopped in front of her again. "You're going to have to leave. You know that, don't you?"

Bellona swallowed. "That's why you asked Sang about a channel to the free states."

"I'll take you to New Edsel, first," Max said. "Everyone is used to me heading off there."

"They believe you have an unofficial lover there," Sang offered.

Max rolled his eyes. "This family and its conspiracies…" he muttered. "It will do for now. I have a skiff there, Bellona. I know a freeship captain who operates from Cerce who owes me a favor and I can get you onto her ship once it is in local space. Captain Wang will take you back to the free states."

"Then what?" It was a whisper.

Max closed his eyes briefly. "I don't know, Bell. I don't *want* to know. You're going to have to make your own way after that."

Bellona's chin quivered. She pressed her lips together to make it stop. Then she nodded. "Very well." Her shoulders under the big jacket straightened. "We'd better hurry," she added.

They had stolen into the night, after Max had left a message with the house AI to let everyone know he would be in New Edsel for a week. They took nothing with them that would provide clues later.

It took six hours by ground car to reach New Edsel. Max would not risk a semi-ballistic, for they were noisy on take-off and tended to draw attention. People stopped to watch them crawl up into the higher atmosphere, growing smaller and smaller.

The ground car wound through the hills, while Max slept and Bellona watched the night fade through the observation ports. Sang remained plugged into the communications satellites and switched their way through shortbands, changing swiftly, adding random cut-offs, always aiming for Cerce and the established communications net surrounding the Ocantis system. The Cerce AI was friendly and trusting, accepting that Sang was Max without a quiver.

Captain Tatiana Wang of the *Hathaway* was known to the Cerce AI. It accepted the sealed communications bullet and assured Sang it would pass it on as soon as the *Hathaway* was within reach. Then it asked for a return channel.

Sang hesitated, weighing the options. Then Sang curtly

told it there would be no return possible. Sang disconnected, leaving the AI troubled. Sang was confident the message would be delivered as promised, though, for that was the AI's function and to not fulfil its function would invoke stressors. AIs did not like uncertainty.

New Edsel was a sleepy little town in the prairies, with charming historical buildings and Cardenas family offshoots that traced their ancestors back to the original Cardenas settlers. The high flat plains offered excellent landing fields and the original landing site was thought to be somewhere nearby, although no traces of the historic location had been found and records were hazy.

The flat land attracted a thriving air industry and many lucrative support businesses catering to pleasure craft and their occupants. Max had been smart to keep his skiff here. He would be one more Cardenas among a great many others and could come and go with relative privacy.

As the ground car wound through the downtown area, Max sat up and rubbed sleep from his eyes and asked Sang to reach out to the skiff and get it ready.

Bellona showed no sign of interest in the preparations. Her gaze remained on the view beyond the port. Even when the car pulled up next to the little runabout, she didn't stir.

Sang was familiar with the skiff, for they had been instrumental in Max's getaways in the past. "The skiff is not equipped for no-atmosphere maneuvering," Sang pointed out.

"It is air-tight and it has an emergency thruster. I just need to get up high enough to meet the *Hathaway*, then use the thruster to get back down low enough to drop."

"And how will you dock?" The skiff had nothing resembling an airlock.

"That's why I'm using the skiff," Max said. He helped Bellona out of the car. "It will fit inside the *Hathaway*'s cargo hold."

"And if the hold already contains cargo?"

Max looked at Sang. He was still young, still fresh with youth and energy, but the look in his eyes was one Sang had not seen before. It was an older man looking at Sang. A wiser one. "I'll make it worth Wang's time to drop the load."

Sang nodded. "We will wait here with the car, for your return."

Max nodded and eased Bellona into the skiff, then inserted himself, too. Sang watched the little vehicle take off, then ascend almost vertically, leaving a clear trail in the early morning sky.

That was the last time Sang saw Bellona. Ten years would pass before they saw her again.

* * * * *

SANG PRESSED THEIR FINGERS TO their temple. Their head hurt.

"Sang," Bellona called. "Sit up. I need your help with this."

Sang nodded and tried to obey. They moved slowly. "Max…locked the memories away. After. When we got back from New Edsel."

Bellona glanced at her father and adjusted her aim, then looked back at Sang. "Max told me what he was going to do. He gave me the phrase. I only remembered it now. Tonight." She turned to face Reynard once more. "Max knew all along. He lied to protect me. I hope you appreciate that."

Reynard swallowed. The skin around his throat moved loosely. It was the flabby flesh of an old man. Sang had never thought of Reynard as old before.

"I don't know what you're talking about," Reynard said.

"You *do* know. You know exactly what this is about. You've been waiting for this moment to arrive for ten years," Bellona told him. "You worked to cover it up. You lied, too. More than Max did and for far worse reasons. Max was at least protecting someone else."

"Bellona, for the stars' sake…" Iulia protested. "Please put that…*thing* down and let us talk civilly."

"Reynard has given up any rights to a civil conversation," Bellona said. "Ask him, mother."

"I will not play this game," Iulia said firmly. "I am going to bed."

Sang glanced at her. Iulia had not moved from the spot. None of the others ranged behind her looked as if they wanted to leave, either.

Sang turned their gaze back to Reynard. They were not certain why they must watch the man, except that Bellona's need to hold him at gunpoint seemed warning enough.

Reynard looked less threatening than he had ever had in the past. He looked tired. Resigned. Except that Sang had never seen Reynard Cardenas give up. His relentlessness and drive had made him the prime member of the most senior family in the clan. His absolute confidence in his decisions cemented him there.

So Sang remained wary.

Reynard's gaze slid back to Bellona. Measured her.

Bellona swapped hands on the gun. "Sang doesn't know all of it. Max didn't know all of it. Even *I* didn't know all of what happened that night, until I smelled the cologne you'd so carefully hidden away. Then it all came back. You were there that night. You watched it all happen."

Sang's lips parted as shocked made their jaw sag.

"Watched *what*?" someone whispered, behind them.

Reynard's gaze didn't shift from Bellona. "I still don't know what you're talking about. You're not making sense."

"For the first time in a long time, I'm making perfect sense," Bellona assured him. "The Bazaar from Erium was here that week. The whole city was going crazy. You were just as bad, buying clothes and trinkets and baubles. You bought colognes, too. That was why I didn't recognize the scent as yours that night. I smelled it, though. It passed through the trees you were hiding behind. I even paused, when the scent reached me. It was so very distinct. Tell me, *Father,* when you hired the men from the Bazaar to rape me, did you intend merely to see they earned their money, or are you a voyeur too?"

Iulia moaned sickly.

Reynard swallowed.

Bellona nodded, as if that was confirmation enough. "We are at another impasse, aren't we? You saw me murder a man. It must have been a shock to you, to see me fend for myself. You've always had such a low opinion of my ability to do that. That's why I know you arranged for those men to intimidate me into staying safely inside the family nest, where I could be protected and guarded and shoved into Delben's arms. I think the clan would find your behavior objectionable in their leader."

For the first time, Reynard reacted. He flinched.

Bellona smiled. "You will make sure that none of this ever leaves this room. You know what the consequences will be if you do not." She lowered the ghostmaker. "Sang."

Sang got to their feet. Slowly.

"Where do you think you're going?" Reynard demanded.

"I'm leaving." Bellona looked over her shoulder. "Don't try to stop me. Don't tell Wait to try, either. You'll both regret it."

Reynard swallowed again.

Bellona beckoned to Sang. They turned and followed

her from the room.

* * * * *

IT WAS AN ECHO OF another long night. The ground car wound its way through the hills toward New Edsel. Bellona looked through the port windows, while Sang arranged a communications channel. This time, the channel was far easier to set up, because it was Eriuman at both ends. That didn't shorten the distance, though. It took three hours for the channel to cohere.

Sang shook Bellona gently, as they cast the channel and built a screen at the front of the car, where Bellona could see it.

Max tilted his head, his dark eyes taking in the interior of the ground car and Bellona's appearance. "What happened?"

"I remembered, Max." Her voice was raw.

Max sat back. He didn't ask what she had remembered.

"Why didn't you tell me?" Bellona demanded.

Max let out a heavy breath. "I was so pleased when you couldn't remember what happened," he confessed. "I thought the whole thing could be forgotten."

"It didn't occur to you that I would keep digging until I found it?"

Max screwed up his nose. "You were always stubborn, but you had a short attention span, too. Five minutes, five days, with some new trinket or lover or toy and you'd be done, bored and onto the next thing. No, I didn't think you would ever keep at it like this."

Bellona sighed. "There are so many gaping holes in my life now, Max. So many things out there I don't remember that might yet come back to haunt me. You should have told me about this."

Max shook his head. "Why would I do that? You look ill, Bell. You look as though you've been kicked in the guts. Is knowing the truth worth it? It hasn't gained you a thing."

"I look like I've been kicked in the guts because I have," she said shortly. "There's a thing you don't know about that night. Father arranged it, to demonstrate how weak and useless I really was. An object lesson to keep me in line."

Max ran his hand over his shorn head. "That's…" He cleared his throat. "You're *sure*?" he breathed.

"I think I always knew, deep down." Bellona gave a small laugh. "Do you know he was so certain of his power and my uselessness that he never destroyed the cologne? He hid it, instead, which means he knew I would identify him by it. Yet he didn't get rid of it. He was that complacent and that tight fisted. The stars would misalign if he actually threw something useful away."

Max shook his head. "I have no idea what you mean about cologne and I don't have time to talk about it. Bellona, this is…I have to think about it."

"I need to know I can trust you, Max. I thought I did. I want to, but this…"

"You know why I lied."

"You need to stop protecting me. It's just tripping me up."

Max laughed. "Tripping you up on your way to where?"

"I don't know. I've left the city. I'll let you know when I find somewhere to stop. I have some thinking to do."

"So do I," Max admitted. His face was troubled. "This changes things."

"Yes," she said simply.

Max looked over his shoulder at something not visible within the screen. "Time to go pretend I run this ship, Bell. Sang, stay with her."

"Yes, Max."

The screen popped and disintegrated.

* * * * *

THEY SPENT FOUR DAYS IN New Edsel, while Bellona took a measure of the town and began speaking to marketers about properties in the area.

That was where the news reached them that the body of Maximilian Cardenas Scordino de Deluca, Captain of the *Decimus*, had been found on Antini.

Chapter Thirteen

Cardenas (Findlay IV), Findlay System, Eriuman Republic.

IT TOOK NEARLY THREE WEEKS for an investigation to be completed by the Eriuman Navy. In that time, Naval officers from the criminal justice division haunted Cardenas, combing through family records and interviewing everyone.

A cadre of them arrived in New Edsel two days after they had received the news. They were polite but insisted that Bellona speak with them. Bellona, in turn, insisted that Sang be included in the interview.

The Lieutenant, Hult, glanced at Sang. It was the first time she had looked directly at Sang since stepping into the foyer of the boarding house where Bellona was currently living. The lieutenant brushed down her uniform with a sweep of her hand. "Very well," she said carelessly.

The interview took place aboard the Navy shuttle that had grounded in the middle of New Edsel's town square, cracking and scorching the fused cobblestones and forcing townspeople to use the side roads to reach their destinations. Commerce had virtually halted. Sang suspected the townspeople would blame Bellona for that. They tucked the thought away for later consideration as Bellona was shown a seat located directly in front of the lieutenant's.

Lieutenant Hult laid one hand over the other, both of them on her crossed knee. The posture displayed the shining toe of her boot. "May I first offer my condolences on the loss of your brother, Miss Cardenas?"

"Thank you," Bellona said stiffly. It was the same tone she had used with every single person who had dared to mention Max in the last two days. As most of the townspeople were related by some degree, most of them had stopped to speak to Bellona.

"We will miss Maximilian," Hult added. "He provided an insight and flair to naval affairs that was a breath of fresh air in some corners." Hult's smile was small, but it was there.

Bellona's eyes narrowed. "You knew Max?"

Hult gave a very small shrug of her shoulders. "A little."

Sang registered the lie.

"Does that make you an unsuitable investigator?" Bellona asked.

"It makes me keener to get to the bottom of this… mystery." Hult crossed her arms. "What can you tell me about Max's last hours on Cardenas?"

"What can you tell me about how he died?"

"That is not a part—"

"It is now," Bellona said. She waited.

Hult smiled. "Miss Cardenas, I have been an investigator in this division for a very long time. There are certain kinds of information that cannot be shared with members of the public, not even close relatives or siblings, if the sharing of that information might jeopardize ongoing military matters. That is the reason the Navy investigates, not a civilian authority."

"The civilian authority being the family enforcers," Bellona replied. "Tell me, have you interviewed my father, yet?"

"As a matter of courtesy, we spoke with your father as soon as we landed." Hult seemed to be amused by Bellona's attempts to steer the conversation.

"Did you tell my father how Max died?"

"*Some* facts were shared."

"Share those facts with me, then."

"Your father can tell you what he knows."

"I asked you."

"Miss Cardenas—"

"Call me Bellona." Bellona crossed her legs to match Hult. "It does not seem to have occurred to you, Lieutenant Hult, that with Max's death, I am the sole remaining heir of my father's estate."

Hult's smile was very small. "I hear that you and your father are recently estranged. Perhaps that inheritance is not as certain as you imply."

Bellona nodded. "You're good at your job. That pleases me. It means you will get to the bottom of this. Max called me stubborn, lieutenant. My father has recently learned exactly what that means. If you wish your investigation to proceed smoothly, I suggest you not attempt to discover the extent of my stubbornness today. If you have already learned about my exit from the family, then you will also know where I have been for the last ten years and what I have been doing."

"I heard, yes," Hult said evenly.

Sang stared at Bellona, surprised. It was not usual for her to raise the subject of Xenia herself. Now she was using it like a prod.

"Tell me how Max died," Bellona said. "Then I will tell you what I know."

Hult considered her. "Be careful what you ask for, Bellona."

"I have learned that truth is less dangerous than ignorance, no matter how unpleasant it may be. Tell me. Did he die inside the Pleasure Dome?"

Hult hesitated. Then, "No. Just outside it, although his register shows he was inside at one point."

"How did he die?"

Hult shook her head. "Really—"

"Tell me," Bellona demanded.

Hult drew in a breath and let it out. "His limbs were severed. He was gutted. Then he was left to bleed out, while his remains were piled in front of him." Hult looked away, then brought her gaze firmly back to Bellona. "You insisted," she added.

Bellona sat very still for a moment. "Then it was not my father who arranged this."

Hult looked stunned. "You thought your *father* did this?"

Bellona nodded. "It was a possibility," she said coolly. "Max knew something that made him dangerous to my father. You look shocked, Lieutenant. Did you think the head of the Scordini clan would be a benevolent man?"

Hult gnawed at her lip, her doubt plain. "I did not assume that, although I have never heard it spoken about so openly, especially by an inner family member." Her eyes narrowed. "Did this dangerous knowledge have something to do with why you left the city?"

"Yes," Bellona said flatly. "The manner of Max's death, though…that is not the way my father would have arranged it. He loved Max. He would not have wanted him to suffer. It would have been quick and clean. Plus, he has made no move against me and I have the same knowledge."

Hult looked uncomfortable and a little ill. Perspiration appeared on her upper lip and she wiped it away. "There is nothing to indicate that Reynard Cardenas was involved. Antini is a long way from here."

"It is in free space, possibly the one truly neutral city in the entire galaxy," Bellona said. "I am aware of the reason why."

"The Pleasure Dome," Hult said. Her mouth curled up. "Free sex with whatever partner you want, whenever you want it, however you want it. Karassians and free staters and Eriumans, biobots, androids. Every depravity is catered to, without question."

"Is it possible…?" Bellona began. She looked at Hult. "Even the Karassians with their genetic enhancements have never been able to stamp out the worst of human nature. Is it possible a customer was interested in necrophilia and the Dome took Max to meet the customer's demands?"

Hult paled. "I have an investigator with a stronger stomach than mine looking into that right now."

"Good." Bellona nodded again. "What was Max doing that far inside free space?"

Hult cleared her throat. "His aide says he took an abrupt leave of absence and jumped on a bus doing a Kalay-Antini-Cerce-Xindar run."

"Max on a public bus?" Bellona shook her head. "Does that not strike you as unlikely? You knew him."

Hult smiled. "It did seem odd to me," she admitted. "However, Max was, above all, practical. A public bus is just that—*public*. If he thought he was in danger, then taking a free state shuttle would ensure no move was made against him while he was in transit." Hult scowled. "I don't suppose you know which of those stops would have been his destination? He bought a round ticket."

"Cerce," Bellona replied. "He knew someone there."

"Captain Tatiana Wang?"

Bellona raised a brow. "Yes."

Hult studied her. "Then you don't know."

Bellona shook her head. "I know she's dead."

"The *Hathaway* was lost, a week after you disappeared from Cardenas," Hult added.

Bellona dropped her gaze to her knee. "The Karassians destroyed her, straight after taking me." Her jaw flexed. "That is why no one came looking for me."

"There was nothing left to trace you by," Hult said. "Although Max made me keep looking for years afterward. Any clue, any hint."

Bellona considered her. "Then why would he be heading for Cerce, so soon after learning…about Reynard?"

"That is a question I would like answered, too," Hult said. She hesitated. "Normally, I would not share this with a civilian, but you're not really a civilian anymore, are you?"

Bellona grimaced. "What do you want to share?"

"A concern. Even if it was not your father who did this, it is possible that the reason you left the family is the same reason that got Max killed, in some indirect way I have yet to uncover. You could be in danger yourself."

"The thought had crossed my mind," Bellona admitted. "Although I pity the fool who tries to attack me."

Hult's laugh pushed out of her in a breathy gasp, as if it caught her by surprise. Her gaze met Bellona's. Then she got to her feet. Bellona followed suit. Hult thrust out her hand and Bellona gripped Hult's elbow.

Sang moved to open the door. Hult shot them a startled glance, as if she had forgotten Sang was there. She pulled herself together and let go of Bellona's arm. "I will be completing the investigation as swiftly as possible, although I should warn you that I do not foresee a conclusive outcome. There are too many questions and too few answers." Hult grimaced. "That is not something I shared with your father."

"A smart decision," Bellona told her. "Thank you for your time, Lieutenant."

Hult nodded.

Sang held the door for Bellona, while noting the inconsistency. It had been Hult who had demanded Bellona's time. Apparently, Hult had forgotten that.

* * * * *

NEW EDSEL STOPPED SPEAKING TO Bellona after that. They could not refuse a Cardenas service and had no troubles taking her money. They simply stopped talking to her.

Sang overheard snatches of conversation as Bellona passed by and put it together.

"They believe you are involved in Max's murder. They can see no other reason why the investigators sought you out so quickly, or why you have left the family home. They think Reynard cast you out."

"I *am* involved in Max's murder," Bellona said. "I just don't know how or why yet, but I know in my gut that this is my fault."

"You have no evidence of that," Sang said sharply. "Neither does New Edsel. Maybe Max simply wanted to visit the Dome and fell in with the wrong partner."

Bellona rolled her eyes. "Sang, really, in all the time you have known Max, all the scrapes you got him out of, did you ever catch a hint of such perverse tastes?"

Sang grimace and shook their head. "Partners aplenty, including, we suspect, Lieutenant Hult. Just nothing like that."

"Exactly," Bellona replied. "We will just have to put up with New Edsel ignoring us. I refuse to go back to the city until I absolutely have to and there's no point in finding somewhere else until after."

Sang didn't ask what "after" meant. The coming rites hung over them both just as the late summer monsoon clouds gathered overhead, turning every day into a dim sauna. They waited out the days until word came. The investigation had been closed, Max's remains returned to Cardenas and the public interment would be held in three days' time.

* * * * *

THE CITY WAS FILLED TO overflowing. Every inn, every boarding house, every hotel, was at capacity. On the five hour journey to the city, Sang connected with every reputable and less reputable accommodation in the city with no success. Bellona was philosophical. "We have the ground car. We can take turns sleeping in it, if we have to, but I don't expect to be in the city long enough to make sleep a priority."

The rites were held in the same grand hall as Bellona's homecoming. There, all similarities ended. There were far more people thronging the street, surging in waves toward the hall, trying to get as close as possible. There were vastly more people inside the hall, too. There was no shouting. No cheering. The street was eerily quiet for having so many people squashed into it. The ground car pilot could not find a way through the morass, so Sang moved behind the controls and took command. They were more ruthless about nosing up against thighs and hips and clearing a path that way. It would be better to save Bellona as much walking as possible.

It became impossible to move forward any farther. They got out of the car and pushed their way through the crowd then, finally, up the wide steps to the hall itself. There were human sentries and greeters before the doors. Everyone moving into the hall was being scanned.

Gaubert was standing with the guards, his expression somber. When he saw Bellona, his jaw tightened. He pulled her aside. Sang moved closer.

"You are not expecting to join the family on the dais, are you?" he whispered loudly.

Bellona shook off his hand from her arm. "I am here for my brother, Gaubert. That is all. I can say my farewells from the back balcony as well as I can from the dais."

Gaubert shook his head. "Your registration has been removed from the inner security zones. Neither you nor Sang will be allowed upstairs. You can join the general population in the hall, although..." He looked over his shoulder, into the hall itself. "I would hurry, if I were you. There isn't a lot of room left in there."

Bellona opened her mouth to argue. Sang could see the

anger glinting in her eyes.

Gaubert looked at her steadily, waiting for her outburst.

Sang calculated the pressure of the bodies ahead, put their arm around Bellona's waist and forced her forward, up the final broad step and into the crowd, shepherding her along as one would help the feeble or disabled.

Bellona gasped at the sudden movement, just barely keeping her feet under her. She glared at Sang.

They shook their head. "Anywhere inside will do. Max will understand. He might even approve."

Bellona remained silent and pushed ahead as Sang was doing. It was a struggle to get through the great doors. Finally, they passed under the lintel and into the cavernous hall beyond. The pressure of bodies slackened and they worked their way to one side of the room, away from the surge of people pushing through the doors.

Bellona finally looked up at the dais and sucked in a deep breath, making everyone nearby glance at her. Some took a second glance, startled. She had been recognized.

The flame that was the symbol of Max's life was already burning atop the pedestal. Surrounding the flame were all the familiar faces. Sang could name them all without hesitation—Reynard's brothers and sisters, their spouses and their off-spring. It was a crowded dais.

Directly behind the pedestal stood Reynard Cardenas. He looked as though he had aged a decade since they had been gone from the city. His hair, which had still held black locks, was now almost pure silver. He was staring at the flame, with the gaze of a man searching for answers.

Iulia stood next to Reynard, her head covered by a heavy veil. There was at least a body's width between them.

The twelve chimes began and the hall fell into complete silence.

Bellona hung her head.

Sang rested their hand on her shoulder and leaned close to murmur in her ear. "Guilt will not serve you here. Watch the flame go out. Honor him. Let everyone around you see that honor."

Bellona raised her chin again and glanced at Sang. Then she looked ahead, her gaze steady. She did not move throughout the ceremony. When the flame was extinguished, she flinched, but that was the only reaction she gave.

* * * * *

ON THE WAY BACK TO New Edsel, the rains began. Water thundered on the roof of the ground car and turned the last of the day into instant night and the silent interior into a muffled enclosure. Bellona appeared unmoved by the torrent. She had not spoken since the end of the ceremony. Neither did she sleep.

Sang did not disturb her reflections. They attempted to pick up the strings of various research projects. Instead they found their thoughts circling around Max. They were intrusive thoughts. Petty ones. Max's first hangover and the combined efforts of the family to hide the event from Reynard. Max's first steps as a child, tottering to reach not his mother, but Bellona, still only a child herself yet already his constant companion. There were many memories that occurred to Sang. If they wanted to, they could review Max's life moment by moment, a luxury that humans did not get to enjoy.

Sang recognized the desire to sink into review for what it was. Avoiding decisions would not help Bellona now. Descending to helplessness because the source of direction had gone would be a waste, which the Scordinii deplored.

We use the parameters that best suit the assignment. How

many times had Sang said that to others? The assignment had not changed. Max had been clear. *Help Bellona.* Only the parameters had changed. Sang would not receive more explicit instructions. They must devise those for themselves.

Sang stared ahead, while in their mind they built a matrix of possible parameters, nodes of decision, potential outcomes and consequences.

When the car pulled up next to the boarding house in New Edsel, the matrix was as complete as current information could make it.

It was very dark outside. It was late and most of the lights, both external and internal, had been doused for the night. What few lights remained reflected off the wet surfaces, making them gleam. Nothing moved in the narrow street.

Bellona stirred and unsealed the car. Instantly, the sound of rain leapt and she recoiled, as if she had noticed the rain only now.

Sang went ahead, to unlock the outer door of the boarding house so she did not have to linger on the sidewalk. The rain was heavy enough that Sang was instantly soaked, even moving the few meters to the door. They palmed the lock and pushed. The door didn't open.

Vexed, Sang tried again. A lot of water on the palm could interfere with the pad's function.

Bellona stepped up beside them. "What's the matter?" She had to raise her voice to be heard.

"It won't open." Sang moved back out onto the sidewalk to look up at the second floor, where the boarding house owner had their apartment. There were no lights showing on that floor. Even the minimal security lights that were usually left on in the front foyer were extinguished, for nothing showed through the ground floor windows.

Bellona pressed her hand against the pad and pushed.

The door remained closed. She tried again, then grabbed the handlebar and put her shoulder to the door.

Sang watched as she threw herself against the door over and over. Under the noise of the rain, they could hear her swearing. Each bump against the door grew harder and heavier, until she was ramming herself against it, making the bomb-proof door rattle in its sealed frame. The impact drove her backward.

She grew still, staring at the door. The rain was pouring off her in rivulets. Then she ran at the door and kicked it. The kick used up the last of her energy. She put her head against the door and closed her eyes.

Sang hesitated. They knew what had to be done, only there was no one here to take the step. There was only Sang.

They moved to the door and eased Bellona away from it. They put their arms around her and spoke just loudly enough for her to hear above the rain. "It only *feels* like you are alone."

Bellona hid her face against their shoulder. Her arms tightened around their neck.

* * * * *

THE NEXT DAY, SANG SOLD the ground car to a grasping tradesman who understood exactly what he was buying while pretending ignorance to drive the price down. Sang let him push the price down to just above Sang's bottom line, then walked.

The trader caught up with Sang at the entrance to the trading post across the road and coaxed Sang back. Sang let him add another fifteen percent to the price then they grasped each other's arms.

They used the money to buy essentials, as all their current possessions, clothes and supplies were still in the boarding house that had expelled them. Neither of them was interested in trying to get anything back.

They met Bellona at the eatery in the main square and listed their purchases, while Bellona played with the hot cakes on her plate.

"Semi-ballistic?" she asked, when Sang itemized the tickets. "To where?"

"Abilio."

"Where is that?"

"Tertius." The third continent was in the southern hemisphere. "It will be winter there."

"Why Abilio?"

Sang grimaced. "It was the closest to a random flag on the map that I could generate. There is absolutely nothing connecting you to Tertius or Abilio. I have no idea what is there. It has no real history and barely enough infrastructure to support fewer than a handful of permanent buildings. We'll have to figure it out when we get there. Money is going to be the first priority."

Bellona looked at them. "You're using first person singular."

Sang nodded. "Where you and I are headed, they won't be used to androids. They certainly won't understand the neutral gender."

Bellona looked at them for another long moment. "Don't pretend, Sang. I'm sick of illusions. Let them deal with the truth. It's not up to you to ease their way."

Sang drew in a breath, for calmness and to center themselves. "I'm not pretending."

Chapter Fourteen

Angylia free state, Angyl moon, Yu System.

FERID KEPT THE MAN AWAKE with stimulants injected directly into his hypothalamus, taking care not to disturb the buildup of plaque and detritus so the effects of sleep deprivation would be acute. It blunted the man's executive decision-making processes, keeping him pliant.

The man's medical knowledge meant he knew what Ferid was doing, which added a degree of fun to the whole tiresome exercise. Ferid couldn't remember his name. He had identified him by the metal finger, an oddly biobotic feature to find in a free-stater. Three weeks of drinking in the right bars on the right planets had led Ferid to the tidbit: One of Arany's crew had a metal finger. After that, it had taken less than a day to find the man…and he had a wife.

Ferid displayed the woman for the man to see. It had been difficult deciding how much pain he should put the woman through before offering the man the deal. Too much, and he might decide Ferid was lying about letting the wife go if he talked. Too little, and he might decide that Ferid didn't really mean to kill her.

The dilemma was another novel aspect to the project. It had provided uncertainty. Finally, though, Ferid had found the balance that provided optimum persuasion.

The man blubbered, torn by competing loyalties.

Then Ferid thought of what to say. Awed at his own brilliance, Ferid leaned closer to the smelly man. His smile was genuine. "No one has to know it was you. Arany will never learn about this." He had to raise his voice to be heard over the breathless moaning of the woman, which destroyed the intimacy of the moment.

The man's bloodshot eyes gazed at him. Ferid watched hope dawn.

"You'll let her go?"

"Yes." She would not be alive when he did let her go, but he would most certainly release her.

The man looked away, toward his wife. He wept again. "What do you want to know?"

* * * * *

The Bonaventura, Free space, Xindar-Coria Confluence.

"UM…BOSS?" NATASA'S VOICE CARRIED across the bridge.

Benjamin Arany looked up from the chart he was studying and raised a brow.

Natasa straightened up from where she had been bent over the shoulder of the intern on the scanners. "They're here."

"Erium?"

She nodded. Her elongated eyes narrowed even farther. "You *sure* you want to do this?"

"I don't think I've been completely sure since I kissed Maureen Owenzky behind the woodpile when I was twelve." Arany dismissed the chart and got to his feet. "We'd better come about and hold."

Natasa rolled her eyes. "Maybe we should just duck and run as usual. I mean…" She glanced around the bridge and moved closer, so she could lower her voice. "Word is, the Eriumans are more pissy than usual. Some royal son of theirs got killed and they're grumpy about it."

Arany nodded. "Maximilian Cardenas. He died in free space, Natasa. That's why they're grumpy. They think we did it. You might want to at least try to keep up with the news."

Natasa grinned. "We didn't?"

"Kill him? I don't think anyone in free space is that stupid."

"Maybe they didn't know who they had under the knife."

"The purple uniform should have told them. You don't fuck with the Eriumans."

"Right. So why are we fucking with them, boss?" She pointed at the scanner screens the intern had up. The blip was big.

"Cruiser?"

"The *Jovian*."

Arany was pleased. The *Jovian* was one of the big ones, retrofitted to carry fighters in the hold. "Are they shouting at us yet?"

"Boss, you're on their wanted list. They're not going to shout. They're going to shoot."

Arany looked over his shoulder. "Ready, Dex?"

Dex had his hands over his dashboard, hovering. He nodded.

Arany leaned on the navigation table. "Let's do this."

* * * * *

Eriuman Naval Vessel Jovian, Free space, Xindar-Coria Confluence.

CAPTAIN SHER CAROSA TILTED HIS head, baffled. "Is he… just sitting there?" he asked of everyone, as he studied the screen showing the small, shiny dot.

Pramoda lifted his head. "They scanned us. They know we're here."

Carosa frowned. "It *is* the *Bonaventura*, yes?"

"Confirmed."

Carosa sighed. "Free-staters…" He signaled to the midshipman, who turned to murmur to the coordinators under his command. "Arany is too critical to ignore," Carosa told Pramoda.

Pramoda watched the mid-shipman. "Fighters launched," he confirmed.

Carosa watched on the screen as the swarm of little fight craft speared across open space, heading for the *Bonaventura.*

"More ships have appeared, sir," Pramoda said calmly.

"More?" Carosa was startled. "How many?" Now he could see them on the screen. More pinpoints of light, gathering around the *Bonaventura*. "Magnify!"

The screen zoomed. Now the ships were clear—a motley cloud of freighters and converted ex-military vehicles, reclaimed public transports…in short, the junk of the galaxy.

"Forty-six ships, sir," Pramoda said. "Forty-seven," he added as another one appeared.

"Forty-seven freeships, all in one place," Carosa breathed.

"And they're not shooting at each other, either," Pramoda pointed out.

"They're turning!" one of the bench coordinators called out.

On the screen, the forty-seven free ships were all orienting themselves. One only oriented a ship when they intended to traverse space. Null-space jumps could be taken from anywhere.

"Are they attacking?" Pramoda asked, sounding amused.

Carosa sat up, his heart giving a little squeeze. "When will the fighters reach them?"

"They're closing," the mid-shipman said.

Carosa rolled his eyes. "How *soon*?"

The mid-shipman looked down at his team. "Twenty seconds."

It was a tense twenty seconds. Carosa stared at the

screen, his mind racing, trying to figure out Arany's ultimate intention. They could engage with the fighters, but what would it prove? They could not take on a cruiser, not even forty-seven of them.

The freeships leapt forward, all of them keeping together in a tight formation that Carosa had time to admire for the coordination needed for such a maneuver. For a few seconds, it looked as though the two sets of vessels would clash head-on.

Then Arany's ships ducked. There was no better word for it. The dive beneath the flight path of the fighters was a deliberate evasion. The fighters flew over the top of the freeships and Carosa heard the coordinators screaming instructions to flip and chase, rotate, *rotate*, damn it!

Pramoda stared at the screen with the same degree of curiosity as Carosa. "I do believe they mean to attack. Us, I mean." He glanced at Carosa. "The fighters will easily catch them. The freeships are not nearly fast enough to outrun them."

Carosa frowned. Had he missed something? What had he overlooked? He didn't underestimate Arany. The man had caused more than casual damage to over a dozen naval vessels. He had to know that sprinting toward a cruiser was a fast form of suicide.

He sat up as alarm bloomed hot in his chest and guts. "Get the forcefields up! Now!"

Pramoda passed on the order, then looked at Carosa, baffled. "The fighters will take care of them."

"All of them? Before they reach us?" Carosa snapped coldly.

"Enough of them to make the rest not matter."

Carosa shook his head. "Get us out of here, Pramoda. Null jump. I don't care where. Just do it."

"Sir, the fighters…"

"We'll come back and pick them up, if there are any left." Carosa slapped the arm of his chair. "*Now*!"

Heads snapped around to look at him.

"Fighters engaged!" the mid-shipman called.

Pramoda frowned down at his bench. "We will be able to jump in sixty seconds."

Carosa slumped back. "Too long." He looked at the screen. The fighters were firing at the backs of the freeships. Carosa had seen the fighters do the same with Karassian units. Usually, the ships that were struck bloomed into an instant fireball, that evaporated immediately. A split-second marker of death.

He could see the freeships taking hits. Two of them stopped dead in space. Yet none of them flared into flames.

"They're all shielded," Pramoda breathed. His tone said he finally understood. "They're slower, because they're shielded."

Carosa watched the screen.

"They still can't touch us," Pramoda added. "The fields are in place. The limited ammunition they have can't get through."

Carosa watched the freeship squad draw closer, dread pooling at the pit of his stomach. "Send for assistance." He couldn't raise his voice.

"Sir!" Pramoda protested.

"Do it." Carosa looked back at the screen, at the approaching ships.

Pramoda sent the communications bullet then looked up again. "They're going to have to break off their approach soon, or they'll…" Carosa heard his quick intake of breath.

The freeships grew enormous on the screen. The scanners zoomed back, but couldn't retract fast enough. The last thing Captain Carosa saw was the bellies of dozens of ships as all but one of them skimmed over the top of the *Jovian*. One of the freighters ploughed straight ahead, ramming through forcefields designed to repel light and heat, slicing through hull and superstructure. The freeships were slow compared to the fighters, although that was relative. The freighter hit the side of the *Jovian* at thousands of kilometers an hour. It wasn't a collision, for the freighter instantly detonated, spewing active fuel into the *Jovian*, while the splinters and fragments of the ship tore through multiple decks, destabilizing structures, destroying bulkheads and killing crewmembers just as they recognized the danger.

The screens were blank, although Carosa, who had been recruited into the Navy because of his astro-physics education, could tell what had happened through the shuddering and flexing of the deck beneath his feet and the rumbling that quickly rose in volume to become a roar.

"They flew into us!" Pramoda cried, gripping the bench in front of him for stability. "Sir, the damage...!"

"Destruction, Pramoda," Carosa said calmly. "They've killed us."

* * * * *

Pleasure Dome, Antini III, Free Space.

THE NEWS OF THE DESTRUCTION of the *Jovian* by a little group of freeships sent a frisson of shock through the known worlds. It was as if everyone paused to draw a breath and re-orient themselves in the face of a game-changing disaster.

"Of course, here on Antini, we take no notice of the war at all, as you can see," the nearly naked host explained to them, as he—or she—Reynard Cardenas could not determine, led the small party through the public areas of the dome. "We are at capacity right now and have been since the disaster." The host smiled at them, showing dimples. "If not for your very special hosts insisting upon accommodations, we might not have been able to find the space you need."

The public areas were just that—a series of areas designed to resemble other world locations. They had crossed romantic bridges over slow-flowing streams, moved across parkland, followed a trail through a dense woodland and walked along a planked sidewalk next to a sandy beach. It wasn't the areas that sent shock slithering through Reynard's veins. It was the uninhibited sexual activity that was taking place in any direction he turned his gaze. Inside the punt meandering along the slow river, on the sandy beach, on the bridge itself as they squeezed past, people were coupling in fevered twos, threes and more. It wasn't just people, either. There were animals and biobots, even metal help-meets that had been enhanced with genitals—an aberration that made Reynard moan in disgust.

After a few minutes of the orgasmic excess, Reynard grew inured to the effect. He trod steadily after the host, his men around him, and kept his gaze on the host's back.

There was a little house just ahead, with quaint windows that opened and closed and a door with a round handle. The host turned the handle and pushed the door open, then stepped aside. "Enjoy your meeting, gentlemen." He/she smiled widely.

Gaubert gripped his arm. "Let me go first." He stepped inside, the top of his head brushing the doorframe.

Reynard ducked under the frame and followed him.

The inside of the house was quite innocent. Everything seemed to be inanimate and simple. The flooring was soft. Reynard realized why the floor was a spongy texture and grimaced again.

A round table was sitting in the middle of the room beyond the door. There were five people sitting around the far side of it, just as there were five men in Reynard's group. All of those sitting had the blond hair and brown eyes of the standard Karassian. One of the men already seated was half-cyborg. His arms were robotic, so was his neck. Reynard had to force himself not to stare.

The man in the middle, though, looked perfectly normal. Reynard wondered if he was as purely human as he appeared. The walk through the Pleasure Dome had reminded Reynard that beyond the borders of Erium, transhumans were common and accepted as equals. He glared at the man in the middle. "Did you insist upon meeting here to remind us of our loss, Woodrow?"

Woodrow spread his hands, his round face breaking into a smile. "We prefer that you be reminded by this place that cooperation is possible even amongst those with nothing in common."

"I consider myself reminded." Reynard did not sit down. "You asked for this meeting. I suggest you get to the point. I do not bargain well when I am nauseous."

Woodrow raised his brows. "We are not here to bargain. Oh, dear. I must apologize if that is the impression you were given. Sit, Cardenas. We, the Karassian people, have a gift for you."

Reynard stayed on his feet. "Why would a Karassian want to give me a gift?"

"We are all empathetic beings, are we not?"

Reynard didn't bother responding.

Woodrow's smile faded. "Your family in particular has felt the bite of free state violence lately. I understand that the captain of the *Jovian* was a first cousin of yours. And of course, the murder of your son, only meters away from where we sit…"

Reynard made an impatient gesture. "Your point, Woodrow?"

"No one knows who murdered your son. Perhaps we'll never know. However, the party responsible for the destruction of the *Jovian*…well, that is different."

"You speak of Benjamin Arany and his fleet as if your intelligence corps has uncovered a great secret. We have known about Arany for years."

"Yes, but do you know where his base of operations is located?" Woodrow asked. His smile returned. "Not even your much vaunted intelligence machine has been able to find that out, has it?" Woodrow put his hand on the shoulder of the small, pale man with red-shot eyes, who sat next to him.

Reynard let his gaze flicker over the man and an atavistic shiver rippled over him. He would arrange to never be alone with that one. True madness shone from his eyes.

"This is Ferid, who is *not* part of the Karassian Intelligence Corps, so if you think to waylay him later and pump him for information about Karassian affairs you would be wasting your time." Woodrow lowered his hand, while Ferid gave a smile that was chilling in its good cheer.

"Ferid has learned the location of Arany's fleet, where they hide out when not destroying Eriuman cruisers," Woodrow said.

Gaubert turned so his shoulder was to the table and spoke urgently. "You cannot accept this information, Reynard. It will be tainted. The Karassians do not hand over gifts like this without a price."

Reynard barely heard him. There was a high note singing in his mind, making thought difficult, except for one shining concept.

Vengeance.

Gaubert gripped his forearm and squeezed hard. "Death is the price of war. Sher Corvosa knew that as thoroughly as Max did. This would not be war."

"Let me go," Reynard said, not bothering to lower his voice. Over Gaubert's shoulder, he could see Ferid's grin and Woodrow watching with close scrutiny.

"You would dishonor their deaths," Gaubert said, his voice low.

Reynard looked at him. "Max was dismembered and disemboweled, here, in this place. What honor was there in that?"

"You would seek vengeance for his death by treating with these people?" Gaubert asked. He glanced over his shoulder. "They *want* you to take the information. For that reason alone, you should refuse it. We can find Arany for ourselves if you really want his blood to spill."

Reynard breathed out the miasma that choked his throat. He looked at Gaubert. "I really want it." And he closed his eyes. "Just not this way," he added softly. "Clean. Swift. Untainted. Merciless. That is what I want."

Gaubert gripped his arm. "Go back to the shuttle. I'll send these Karassians on their way. Go on."

Reynard sucked in the warm air. It was difficult to breathe here. He suddenly longed for the hills of Cardenas and the cool air there. Even if the house was silent these days, it was his. He was an outsider here. So he nodded at Gaubert and turned and left. He did not miss the startled expressions of the Karassians and took a pinch of comfort in defying their expectations. He was Eriuman. It was good to be unpredictable.

WHEN HIS OLDER BROTHER HAD left, the door of the house clicking shut behind him, Gaubert turned back to Woodrow and leaned over the table. "I am not my brother," he said, speaking quickly. "He would destroy your enemy for personal vengeance. I would do it for Erium. Tell me where to find Arany."

Chapter Fifteen

Cardenas (Findlay IV), Findlay System, Eriuman Republic.

KHALIL USED THE LAST OF his liquid currency to pay the shuttle to put him down just outside the town. There was no issue finding a suitably flat and supportive place to land. The earth in every direction was a blasted plane of dried out earth, cracked and devoid of plant life.

The sun was blazing overhead, heat haze making it look as though it was throbbing.

The shuttle pilot glanced around as the port door opened, then tossed Khalil a canteen. The contents sloshed. The canteen was heavy. "You're going to need it," the pilot said.

Khalil gave his thanks and stepped out onto the earth, which disintegrated under the weight of his foot. Dust rose up around his boot. He pulled the hood of his jacket up over his head, as protection against the sun and started walking toward the black smudge on the horizon where the town lay.

As soon as he was out of range, the pilot took off. The shuttle rocketed upward. Khalil didn't look back.

After two kilometers, Khalil reconsidered how much farther he had to go. Distance was deceptive here. The town was no closer and he had already drained the canteen. The heat was intolerable, beating up at him from the ground and wafting around him as he moved through the warm air. The sun was almost directly overhead and he could feel the flesh on the back of his hands burning. He took the warning to heart and did not lower the hood.

He walked, even though his pace slowed. There was

no other choice.

After another kilometer he paused to catch his breath. The smudge on the horizon was larger. There was regular shaping to its edges, suggesting buildings or other structures. Also, a plume of smoke was rising from it.

Khalil blinked, trying to make his eyes focus properly.

It wasn't smoke. It was a pillar of sand. Something was kicking up the very fine dirt, flinging it into the air where it rose like smoke into the very pale blue sky. The something was heading his way.

Khalil started walking again, taking inventory of the possessions distributed around his body and clothes. Some had barter value.

The plume grew closer and now he could see the progress of the vehicle that was making it. It looked as though it was moving fast, yet it would still take minutes to reach him. As it drew closer, he could see more detail and realized there were two vehicles.

When they were close enough for him to hear the engines, he stopped. They should surely be able to see him with the naked eye, now. Their path toward him had been direct, which meant they had tracked him by some type of scanner, possibly from the moment he stepped off the shuttle. Or earlier.

That spoke of a level of sophistication in technology that didn't match the little town Khalil had spotted from high orbit.

The two vehicles stopped on either side of him and seven men jumped out. They were typical Eriumans.

One of them, with long hair pinned to his shoulder, faced him. "You should have stayed on your ship," he said, showing bad teeth.

"I'm here to speak to Bellona."

The man smiled, revealing more stumps. "Get lost, did you? Your shiny ship not have a compass?"

"I know she is here. Give her my name. She will speak to me." In fact, he wasn't entirely sure if his name would have any effect at all, but these were low-level, unimaginative people. He had to get past them before reasoning would work.

The spokesman shook his head. "You're in the wrong place at the wrong time, my friend. Go home. It's safer there."

Khalil stepped back as the others moved forward. Hands gripped his arms and Khalil sighed. Clearly, these men had not been trained by Bellona. It took little effort to drop them all. They were almost comically predictable. While he was dealing with the sixth, he pulled his knife from the hidden pocket. He tossed the deadweight of the sixth into the shocked arms of the spokesman and came up behind it. He got the knife under Bad Teeth's ear and let it prick the skin there, enough for the man to feel the sting.

Bad Teeth yipped in reaction.

As the others stirred sluggishly around them, Khalil walked the man to one of the cars and forced him behind the controls. Khalil sat behind him. "Take me to Abilio."

"They'll kill you," Bad Teeth said, trying to roll his eyes to look at Khalil over his shoulder, without puncturing himself on the end of Khalil's knife.

"I'll take that risk," Khalil said honestly.

"Oh, he's going to grind you to paste," Bad Teeth added, starting up the car. "I really hope I get to see it."

* * * * *

THE REMAINING FEW KILOMETERS INTO the little town took mere minutes, compared to the slow pace of the first four. Khalil resisted the temptation to let his hood drop and his sweaty face cool in the breeze created by the motion of the car. The sun was still overhead and still dazzling. The crew of seven who had been sent to deal with him all wore hats and long sleeved shirts. Besides, if there had been one spy satellite trained on this place, then there could be more. Better to remain a white blob on any feeds.

The town was as lonely and decrepit as it had appeared from space. Down on the ground, though, the smell of dust and decay made it very real. The main road through the little town was dirt. There were imprints in the surface where a heavy vehicle had driven over the dirt while it was wet. The tread marks were still sharp, even though the last rains had been weeks ago. Very few vehicles had passed over the top of them to wear them down.

No one walked the streets or peered out of windows as they passed the handful of buildings. All the buildings were of the old design, with four walls, windows and doors, which served well in remote locations. None of these had seen any maintenance for many years. Dust clung to everything, making every building look brown and drab.

There was an even older and more ramshackle shed ahead, with half a kilometer separating it from the town itself. One of the walls had collapsed inward. The lack of support made the roof sag in the middle, along the length of the missing wall. It looked as though a good breeze would knock down the lot.

Bad Teeth steered the car through the leaning door, into the shed and halted.

"Now where?" Khalil demanded, getting out.

Bad Teeth shrugged. "We wait."

"I said I wanted to speak to Bellona."

"You speak to my boss first. If you're lucky, he'll pass you through. If you're not…" Bad Teeth grinned. "I hope you're not."

"How long do we wait? Is there a signal?"

"He knows we're here already. He's a busy man, though."

Khalil weighed up his options. It was more than likely that Bad Teeth really did not know where to go beyond this point, which gave him an indirect hope. If they were operating with cut-offs like this, insulating themselves, that was a good sign.

He motioned Bad Teeth out from behind the controls. He didn't want the man taking off if his attention slipped. He pulled him over to the shadiest corner and pushed him down into it. Then he sat with his back against the raw mudbrick wall.

It was after dark before anyone came. By then, both of them were freezing. Abilio was on a desert plain at a high altitude and close to the equator. Once the direct, glaring sun had gone down, the heat left the day and the true coolness of the altitude could be felt.

Bad Teeth was as miserable as Khalil and made no attempt to unwrap his arms from around his legs and escape. Khalil hunched over his knees and tried to stop his teeth from chattering. He needed to hear if anyone approached.

When they did arrive, it was with complete silence. They were a dark shape that detached itself from the deeper shadows and loomed up over the two of them. A short man, wrapped in a warm cloak and hood.

Khalil scrambled to get up, alarm moving sluggishly through him. He gripped the knife with his cold fingers.

A hand shot out of the dark cloak and gripped his wrist. "There is no need for that." The voice was a musical tenor. The fingers were strong around his wrist, squeezing the tendons to weaken his grip. The man reached up to drop the hood back.

"Sang," Khalil breathed, shock slithering through him. "Stars and moons…Sang!"

Sang was undoubtedly a man. There was stubble on his cheeks, the same coppery blond as his hair, which was trimmed short. In the dark, Khalil could not see if the freckles that had highlighted Sang's face before were still there. The fine jaw and chin seemed stronger.

"Khalil Ready," Sang said. "You have risked much to reach this far."

Khalil saw Sang's laryngeal peak shift at the front of his throat as he spoke. It was fascinating to watch simply because it had never been there before. "In truth, there has been little risk so far." He looked down at Bad Teeth, who was still shivering in the corner, too miserable to care about anything else. "They were not trained."

Sang smiled. "We spend a lot of money keeping people away from here without raising suspicions."

"Money can be neutralized by even more money." Khalil put the knife away. "I need to see her, Sang. It's important."

Sang didn't move. "How did you find us?"

Khalil shrugged. "The same way I found you on Kachmar. Bellona cannot move off this planet without someone noticing. Xenia is too well known. As no one has shouted about seeing her, she had to be here, still. Clearly, she is not in the city anymore…" He paused, remembering his surprise when he saw Bellona was not on the family dais, marking Max's passing. "After that, it was a matter of analyzing satellite feeds and extrapolating."

Sang sighed. "There is one independent satellite I cannot control. The AI is anti-social and incorruptible. It limits everything we do here."

"That is most likely the feed I accessed," Khalil told him. "It was the absence of people, Sang. You should do something about that."

"There are empty towns all over the desert," Sang pointed out.

"None of them have tire tracks as this one does."

Sang weighed up his observation, his strange pale eyes focused on nothing. "It is a risk, but there are few people with the skills to sweet-talk the satellite and fewer with reason to look so closely in the first place." He took Khalil's arm. "Come. How does a warm room, mulled wine and hot cakes sound?"

"Glorious," Khalil admitted.

Sang walked him back out of the rickety shed and into the night. The air beyond the walls was even more frigid than inside and Khalil shivered again.

"You've come from warmer places," Sang observed.

"I would have called this place warm, today."

Sang smiled. "The extremes of temperature test everything, here. People. Metal and plastics. Compounds that survive the vacuum of space will crack through the middle overnight here." He was heading in the direction of the nearest ramshackle building. "Humans have been living on Cardenas for over seven hundred years, yet they have never been able to live in the Caramella desert for long. Plants shrivel. Water evaporates, or freezes and shatters whatever contains it, then is lost the next day when it melts." He paused with his foot on the flat, broad step beneath the door, which looked as though it was hanging by one hinge only. He breathed out heavily. The air clouded in front of his mouth. "Not long after midnight, it will drop to two hundred and fifty kays." He pushed open the door, which swung in silently. It was still and dark in the room beyond. Khalil stepped in cautiously. It didn't seem to be much warmer than outside, either.

Sang shut the door. From the inside, it closed with a firm click. Then Sang pushed Khalil toward the back of the room and placed his hand on the wall next to him.

A disguised palm pad.

The floor in the middle of the room descended, leaving a gaping rectangle of shadow.

"The light will improve as you descend," Sang said. "After you."

Khalil groped with his boot for the first step and took it cautiously. Then the next. The stairs were sound and even, which gave him the courage to continue down into the blackness. As soon as his head was beneath the level of the floor above, he spotted tiny pilot lights ahead, each of them outlining a single step and no farther. There were dozens of them, disappearing down even deeper.

"Underground," he muttered. "It is completely obvious, in hindsight."

"As long as it remains obvious only in hindsight, our security holds," Sang murmured, from right behind him.

As they descended, the air around them grew warmer. Khalil heard the floor of the old building above them move back into place. He descended, one step after another, the little lights guiding the way. On either side was what looked like rock face. It had been burned away with cutters. The face of it gleamed like black glass.

There was stronger light farther ahead and a murmur of sound. The air was definitely warmer now and blew gently against Khalil's face. He pushed the hood back gratefully. The flesh over his cheekbones relaxed, telling him the air down here carried more moisture than the air over the desert, above. Somewhere, there was water.

The stairs ended and the walls opened out into a small room with three sealed doors. The door directly ahead of the stairs was the one from where the noise was coming. Sang, though, opened the door on the right. There was another room beyond.

"Come in," Sang said.

Khalil stepped into the room and looked around curiously. There was a colorful rug on the floor. A comfortable chair and a small table and a cupboard were the only pieces of furniture, although there was barely room for any more.

"Cozy," Khalil remarked.

"Have a seat," Sang said. He stepped over to the cupboard, opened it, reached in and withdrew a tray holding a samovar and a plate of steaming hot cakes. He carried the tray over to the little table.

Khalil sat in the chair. It was soft and deep and he arranged himself so his weight was at the front of the cushion. "Bad Teeth…the man who brought me here, the one we left in the shed. He said you would take a while because you're busy."

Sang smiled. "I am."

"That isn't why you took so long, though. You were waiting to see if anyone was following me."

Sang poured the mulled wine into the short, wide cup sitting on the tray and handed it to him. "Drink."

Khalil took the cup. "Clearly, no one was, or I wouldn't be here. Only, now we're sitting in this room that doesn't seem to have a purpose and isn't connected to anything. What are you waiting for this time?"

Sang stood back. "The scans are unobtrusive. The questions…well, they are a little more direct."

Khalil smiled. "You have never been anything *but* direct." He sipped. The mulled wine was as good as any he had ever tasted in the Cardenas homebase. "Ask, Sang. I will answer."

Sang nodded. "Why are you here?"

"To speak to Bellona."

"So you said." Sang considered him. "Why do you want to speak to Bellona?"

Khalil weighed up his options. If he refused to answer, Sang would stonewall him. Khalil had seen him endlessly prevaricate over allowing strangers access to the homebase in the city. He would stay calm and absolutely unmoving, until Khalil wore himself out.

On the other hand, Khalil had no doubts about Sang's loyalty to Bellona. He wondered if Bellona had learned to trust him yet.

Khalil relaxed. "Are the scans done?"

Sang considered. "Yes."

"There is no chance of being overheard, here?"

"That is why I brought you to this room in particular."

Khalil nodded. "I know who killed Max."

Chapter Sixteen

Cardenas (Findlay IV), Findlay System, Eriuman Republic

ON THE OTHER SIDE OF the door from where all the noise had been seeping was a cavern, buzzing with industry and people. The door had been close to soundproof, so the volume that leapt when Sang pushed open the door startled Khalil.

The place may have started as a cave, once upon a time, although that simple description had been left behind. The same cutters that had made the stair walls smooth and strong had carved out a cavern with high vertical walls and a flat roof far overhead. Pillars of native rock had been carved in place and these had been used to divide the open cavern into areas of use.

Somewhere unseen, farther back in the cavern, metal was being hammered. Machinery hummed, engines roared, punctuated by pneumatic hisses. This, then, was the engineering section.

Sang touched Khalil's shoulder, drawing his attention, then beckoned. Sang moved along the side of the cavern, where a path had been left clear. People were using the path, farther ahead, to traverse the cavern, then stepping off the path into the section they wanted.

Of the many people walking about the cavern that Khalil could see, going about their mysterious business, only about half of them were native Eriumans. There were many people with undefined genetic markers, which meant they were most likely free staters.

Khalil's curiosity rose. What was she doing?

Farther along the wide path, there was an open area, where people were training. Khalil recognized the movements as pure Bellona-Xenia style combat, but Bellona was not there. The instructor lifted a hand in acknowledgement when she saw Sang and Khalil. Sang waved back.

The training area was well lit by the daylights blazing from the adjacent area. Long rows of waist-high benches held green, growing things. Food for the workers, that could not grow on the surface. Robot gardeners rolled up and down the rows, tending the plants.

The end of the long cavern was on the other side of the greenhouse, while the path continued, burrowing through a door-shaped hole in the wall and turning into a tunnel.

The noise dropped.

"How many people are here?" Khalil asked, catching up with Sang.

Sang glanced at him and shook his head. "You know I can't tell you that."

So. He had been granted a qualified access. For now, it would do. Khalil contented himself with keeping his eyes open, instead.

The tunnel was featureless and long. There were doors on the right-hand side only and few of them. Khalil kept count.

Sang stopped at one of the doors and put his hand to the wall. The door opened and Sang waved him ahead once more.

This room was larger, yet just as plain and simple. It had two other doors, one to the right and one to the left. Sang shut the main door behind them and moved over to the right-hand door and tapped on it.

"In a minute, Sang!"

Khalil drew a breath. It was Bellona's voice.

There were no chairs in the room. No desks, no furniture that hinted at the use of the room. There was a single cupboard and there was a samovar and cups sitting on it.

Steam rose from the spout of the samovar.

Sang poured a cup of the wine and gave it to Khalil. "I whisked you away from your last cup. This will take the cold from your bones."

The door opened and Bellona moved into the room. She looked as though she was a match for this place. The boots and pants and workman-like shirt were appropriate. The ghostmaker on her hip looked natural. Her gaze came to rest on Khalil. "Was he scanned, Sang?"

"He has a knife in his right boot and a miniature ghostmaker in his pocket. I didn't bother removing them."

Bellona glanced at Sang. "You would rather watch me have to do that?"

"Very much so," Sang said with relish. "You would not be gentle, if he tried to use them."

Khalil sighed. "I am here on peaceful business."

"Not if you are here to dangle my brother's killer in front of me," Bellona replied. She crossed her arms.

Khalil put the cup back on the cupboard. "I could give you the name of the responsible party, but you would not believe me. So I must pave the way. Would you indulge me that much time?"

"I don't have the time to spare that you would need to redeem yourself," Bellona said.

"I am not here for that," Khalil said shortly. "I merely need you to believe me when I tell you the name. To do that, I must account for myself since I left Cardenas."

Sang smiled. "You joined your brother, Benjamin Arany, on the *Bonaventura*. You have been there ever since."

Khalil didn't bother hiding his surprise. "You've been tracking me, Sang?"

"Then Sang was right," Bellona said slowly. "You didn't go back to the Bureau."

Khalil spread his hands. "I told you I was done with them."

Bellona remained silent and still. The stillness was a new quality. She was holding everything inside her. Weighing it for herself, instead of spilling her emotions about like a fountain.

"Go on," she said at last.

"Last month, I met a bureau field agent on Laurasia. It was a purely accidental meeting. It was also an awkward one. He spoke much and said very little, and looked longingly toward the door in between. There was one thing he said, though, that stayed with me."

Both Sang and Bellona were watching him carefully, assessing every word. They did not interrupt with questions.

"He said the prostitutes were prettier on Laurasia."

Sang's eyes narrowed.

Bellona touched Sang's arm, as if she had felt his sudden attention. Then she looked at Khalil. "His name?"

"He wouldn't have travelled under that name."

"You know what aliases he uses?" Sang asked, using the remote, unmodulated tone that said he was thinking digitally, tapping into networks and sifting data.

Khalil gave them. "I have already tracked them as far as I can," he added.

Bellona's smile was small. "Sang and Connie can track more between them. You knew that. That's why you're here."

Khalil held his jaw together. Then he frowned. "Who is Connie?"

"You know her. It. The AI in the Karassian yacht that Sang bought to Kachmar."

Sang was standing perfectly still, staring at nothing.

"*She*?" Khalil said.

"I call her that," Bellona said. "It makes things easier."

"Isn't the yacht impounded by the Navy, somewhere over the city?"

"Which is why she's bored. Connie likes to talk to

Sang."

Khalil considered that. "Connie is a Karassian."

"She's an AI with limited experience," Sang said, his voice as remote as his gaze. "She is a child. A gifted one with access to data pools I could not reach myself. War is a concept she has not yet grasped." He frowned. "This is getting interesting…" he murmured.

Bellona moved away from Sang and gestured for Khalil to shift over to the far side of the room with her. They stood next to the samovar.

"You already know where this trail will end, don't you?" she asked him.

Khalil sighed. "If I'm right, then the trail will end on Antini. So will one or two other Bureau people's trails."

Bellona was still showing no emotion. "The Bureau killed Max? Why?"

"I don't know for sure, although I do know how they work. Do you remember when I told you about their search for a hero?"

"Isn't Arany the hero they've been waiting for?" Bellona asked. "He's a leader, visible, committed…"

Khalil nodded. "There were hundreds of potential candidates. Ben was one, yes. So was Xenia. I thought I had convinced the Bureau that you were not a viable possibility anymore. Xenia had gone." He spread his hands. "What if they didn't believe me?"

"What would they do if they dismissed your analysis?"

"They would have Ben, they would have you, and who knows how many others. The Bureau likes to work with certainties whenever they can arrange them, to offset the statistical predictions they play with most of the time. Every analysis and projection they have run in the last two generations has pointed toward the emergence of a leader, someone who would massively impact the known worlds, who would institute change at a level a simple war would never achieve. If the Bureau itself is to survive that upheaval, then they would have to identify the hero as early as possible and find a way to stay within their sphere of influence." Khalil met her gaze. "Maybe they wanted to force the issue."

"By making *their* choice the hero?" Bellona frowned. "Could they do that? Would they?"

Khalil grimaced. "I've seen them arrange matters to suit themselves. In the past, the changes they made were benign. A nudge here, a tweak there, for a more favorable outcome. I've seen them buy stocks, rig votes, sully reputations…it was all minor and the outcome was always positive…"

"Until now," Bellona finished.

Khalil rubbed his temples. He'd had little sleep in the last week of frantic, extended travel. On top of his exhaustion, even considering what he was about to say made him feel ill. "You were entrenched in your family's home-base, Bellona. Xenia was disappearing from the public's memory. Your father was boxing you in with suitors and expectations. What if the Bureau…" He swallowed. "What if they decided to change that? A hero needs pressure to emerge. What if they added that pressure? Say, by slipping your father a discrediting file about me, to get me out of the picture? Then, by murdering the one ally you had left in the city?"

"Max," Bellona breathed. Anger grew in her eyes. "Only, I came here," she said flatly.

Khalil nodded. "Proving that the pressure wasn't quite enough yet for you to pick up even a metaphorical sword. However, if they let you know how you'd been manipulated, say, by giving me just enough information to start me down the path to the truth…?"

Bellona's lips parted. "They're manipulating you, too."

"I think so, yes. That's how profoundly elegant their plan is. It doesn't matter if I know. I would have come here, anyway. The fact alone was enough to push me into this." He sighed. "I had no choice but to tell you. They knew it."

Bellona looked at him for a long, silent moment. Then, without turning her head, she said, "Sang?"

"Still confirming, although it is looking more likely by the minute," Sang said.

Bellona nodded. "Come with me," she told Khalil. "I have something to show you."

* * * * *

AT THE FAR END OF the passage, there were two openings. One was a rough hole in the rock face. From farther inside the hole the hum of drilling equipment could be heard. Bright work lights shone deep inside the burrow.

Bellona nodded toward the burrow. "There is a huge water basin a hundred meters below us. The water filters down from the surface. On the way through it leaves behind minerals and salt. The money we raise from exporting them gives us the raw materials we can't produce ourselves, although we're very close to self-sufficient here. The holes left behind by the mining become new living spaces." As she spoke, she palmed a pad next to the other door, then tapped out a pattern.

The door unsealed with loud thud of solid locks shifting.

"You developed all this yourself?"

"There was already a mine operating when Sang and I got here, although it was a sporadic and badly organized operation. Sang sorted out the operation while I convinced the miners that my way would be better."

"And your way is what, exactly?"

Bellona pushed on the door and it opened with the slowness of an airlock door moving on sluggish hinges. As it opened, lights came on in the area beyond.

Bellona stepped over the sill and held the door open

for Khalil. He followed her in.

It was another large cavern, at least as long as the passage on the other side of the wall, which explained why there were no doors on the left side. The cavern was wider than it was long, creating a floor space of at least several hectares. Despite the size, the whole cavern was taken up by a single ship, sitting silently in the middle, with its boarding ramps down.

Khalil sucked in a shocked breath. "That's a Karassian frigate..."

Bellona crossed her arms. "It's a full scale replica. You could punch your fist through the bulkheads if you wanted to. The layout inside is identical to the real thing, though. It took us months to build it, but we had to have it for training purposes."

Khalil thought of the people he had seen on the way in, completing personal combat exercises. "Training for what?" he asked. "Why would you want a mock-up of a Karassian ship, unless..." He turned to look at her for confirmation. "You're going to steal one."

She smiled. "We are."

Khalil walked over to the ship. It was huge, the blunt nose sitting many meters above his head. "The only reason to need a Karassian ship is because you intend to travel through Karassian space and don't want to be waylaid, or even noticed."

"That is certainly the ideal, but that is not the ultimate reason for stealing a Karassian ship." Bellona walked over to the nearest boarding ramp and put her hand on the support strut. "With this, we can get down on the surface, unquestioned."

Khalil thought it through. "Using the ship's own registration to get past sentries?"

She nodded.

"Where are you going?"

"Kachmar."

Khalil drew in a sharp, surprised breath. "You're going back to Ledan."

Bellona looked up at the belly of the ship. "I'm going to get them all out, Ari. Every single one of them."

His heart gave a little squeeze at the name. Flashes of memory, of times that only *seemed* peaceful and content, flickered through his mind, barely seen, although they provoked the anger, anyway. Even though he had known what Appurtenance Services Inc would do to him, the sense of betrayal had been huge. He had used his outrage to free her from that place. Bellona had been held inside the dream for ten years. Her anger was so much greater than his could ever be.

"You don't want them to be lied to anymore," Khalil said.

Bellona's smile was warm. "I knew you would understand." Her smile grew. "As you can see, I'm picking up the sword."

He moved away from the nose, back toward the door, where he could see all of the ship at once. "So you steal the ship, land on Ledania, take everyone off with the help of your mining friends…then what, Bellona?"

"Once everyone is out of that place, then I will tell the known worlds what the Karassians have done. I will stand next to my friends and we will expose the Homogeny as the monster it really is."

"And then what?"

Her smile faded. "One step at a time."

"You don't know. You haven't thought beyond releasing them and exposing Karassia."

"Isn't that enough? I'm not your Bureau's hero, Khalil."

"And if you learn that the Bureau really did kill Max?"

"Then I will have my next step."

"Even if you are doing exactly what the Bureau want you to do?"

She considered that. "It appears I will have as little choice as you. I will have to act, even knowing that is what they want."

"So, first Karassia, then the Bureau. What then of Erium?"

Her brows came together. "Erium has done nothing but defend itself."

"Your father and your family are the perfect representatives of Erium. Look at what they did to you. Look at where you stand. Can you still say truthfully they have done nothing?"

"It is I who no longer fits Erium. It isn't their fault. They behaved naturally, which collided with my differences, that is all." She came closer. "What is it that you want of me, Khalil? You want me to be the hero the Bureau are searching for? You want me to take on everyone, even Erium?"

"I want you to see yourself for what you really are."

"What am I?"

"You think you are a lost soul in search of meaning. I see a leader rescuing her tribe."

"Yet you told the Bureau I was not one, that Xenia had gone."

"Xenia *is* gone," Khalil said. "Although that was the only truthful thing I told them."

Bellona turned away, hiding her reaction. She kept her back to him. "I accept none of it," she told him. Her voice was strained. "I'm not a hero. I'm not even a leader. I just want to help my friends. That's all."

"Very well," Khalil replied. "If you would permit, I would like to help you with that. They were my friends, too."

She glanced over her shoulder. There was a pleased expression in her eyes. "If you do, you will be declaring your loyalties for the worlds to see. Your brother…"

"Will understand," Khalil said. "We two have walked

different paths since we were taken off Revati and he was given to a family on Cerce, while I remained on Atticus."

"You won't be able to cling to the shadows the way the Bureau does, not after this."

"Every step I've taken since I woke up in that Kachmarain gutter has led to this," Khalil said. He tried to sound calm, even though his heart was racing. "This is *my* next step."

Chapter Seventeen

Cardenas (Findlay IV), Findlay System, Eriuman Republic.

SANG QUICKLY GREW USED TO hearing soft, easy chatter in Bellona's suite, once Khalil returned. Because Sang oversaw every aspect of the colony, he knew that Khalil took one of the tiny sitting rooms in the old section as his quarters and he returned to them every night. At most other times, though, Khalil could be found in the center room, applying his ability to think in structures and systems to Bellona's plans.

Sang was included in the free-flow, long discussions where most of the final decisions were made. He took care of implementing them.

The center room, which had once been devoid of anything useful, became a gathering room. Chairs were grown, a small table appeared. None of them matched. Cushion colors clashed. Yet the chairs were comfortable and the table useful. Possessions littered horizontal surfaces, giving the room an untidy, lived-in appearance. Sang found the clutter odd after the disciplined simplicity of the Cardenas family home, but not unpleasant.

Sang also spent time maintaining the relationship he had built with Connie, as the AI had wanted be called. Bellona called Connie "she" because of the feminine tag, yet Sang could discern no gender in the AI and barely any personality beyond that of an unformed, mostly bewildered child. Previous owners of the yacht had not interfaced with the AI except with direct commands. Connie had been socially retarded when Sang had reached out to the yacht. However, Connie would be instrumental in their plans for Ledan, so Sang liked to keep her placid and happy by off-setting the first tendrils of loneliness she was beginning to experience.

Khalil reviewed the already-made decisions with Sang, too. "Which came first?" he asked Sang. "A convenient desert where a Karassian frigate can be landed, or the lack of satellite coverage except for one that you control?"

Sang shook his head. "I don't control it. Not yet."

"Controlling it and limiting it would set off alarm signals, of course."

"When landing guidance is needed, will be soon enough to sever its strings."

Khalil pursed his full lips. "The timing will be critical."

"Every element of this venture is critical. We are heading into the heart of Karassian territory, to an installation that has been raided once already. The Karassians have many faults, yet they are very good at learning from experience. We won't be able to stroll into the compound the way we did last time." Sang paused. "My timing will be accurate," he added.

"If we had not strolled into the compound the first time, there would be no driving force for the second. It is what it is."

Bellona's driving force was considerable. "My memories of Ledan are of kinder people, all of them open-hearted, with no agendas and no expectations," she had explained. "It angers me to think of them being manipulated as they are."

"They will not be like that once they remember who they are," Khalil warned her.

"We all are like that, inside."

"No," Khalil said firmly. "There are monsters parading as humans. You could dig to their centers and fail to find that core."

"No one in Ledan is like that," Bellona said. "Their cores were exposed, there. Enhanced, biobots, cybernetics, freaks all of them, but human, at the base."

"You trust them," Sang surmised.

"More than anyone in the known worlds," Bellona said.

Khalil remained silent. Yet he did not look away. His posture did not shift. He had already accepted this truth, then. He understood his position with a clarity that was rare among humans.

Sang knew Khalil's complacency wouldn't last. No one, not even Sang, could live with qualified acceptance in the long term. Belonging was a basic human drive that androids, whose awareness was patterned upon human awareness, and AIs, who aped human consciousness, also shared.

As it turned out, it wasn't just Khalil who was blasted out of stasis.

* * * * *

THE NEWS CAME FROM EVERY shaded source Sang had, including Connie, who babbled in panic as she was a Karassian ship in Eriuman space. The satellite also reported high yield news streams, while the data pools within which Sang kept a mental taprod all shivered with the impact.

The known worlds bolted upright, the trivia of the everyday evaporating, as they measured their neighbors, terrified.

Sang absorbed the baseline facts as he ran for Bellona's quarters. By the time he pushed on the heavy door and stepped inside, he had assembled it into shocking whole.

Bellona and Khalil were talking to Shalev Zeni. Zeni was responsible for the personal combat readiness of everyone who would be going to Kachmar. Her work was made difficult because of the cultural bias of the known worlds: Big ships did the fighting.

Overcoming resistance to learning self-defense was a constant topic with Zeni. Bellona was sanguine, though. "When they face their first test of physical strength and readiness, they will either die, or they will understand. I don't care which. It is up to them. I, though, intend to survive."

Bellona trained harder than anyone else in the caverns except for Khalil, who had already faced reality at least once. Her example and Khalil's did more to motivate everyone else than anything Zeni did.

Sang trained beside both of them. He found it difficult to foresee any occasion when he would need to use the skills, for his role in the venture to retrieve Bellona's friends was defined and passive. However, he could not eliminate the possibility altogether. There were too many quantum unknowns. So, he trained and was pleased at the progress he made.

Zeni looked up as Sang burst into the gathering room, startled.

Sang breathed heavily. "There is news," he told the three. "It is…dire." He looked at Zeni. "Leave us, please."

Zeni scowled and looked at Bellona. Bellona jerked her head toward the door, making Zeni's mouth drop open. She got stiffly to her feet and slid past Sang with another heavy glare.

He ignored it and sat where Zeni had been sitting, in the low chair that was difficult to rise from without scrambling. He sat on the edge and realized he had threaded his hands together and was working them. He put the palms on his knees and made them stay still.

"Verified reports have come in from multiple sources," he told Bellona and Khalil. "The city state of Shavistran and everything in local airspace above it was destroyed by a single strike from an unknown attacker."

Khalil dropped his head into his hands and bent over his knees. The sound that emerged from him was wordless and pain-filled.

Bellona rested her hand on his shoulder and looked at Sang. "Benjamin Arany was there?" she asked.

Sang nodded. "Shavistran was one of the conjectured locations of Arany's secret base." He looked at Khalil, who shuddered. "It is confirmed, now."

Bellona bit her lip. "More of the Bureau's manipulations?" She asked the question softly, as if she didn't want Khalil to hear it.

"A stray satellite outside the blast cone captured the destruction. It was a single source, from high orbit."

Bellona let out an unsteady breath. "Then the rumors about the Karassian's city-killer weapon are true."

"The senior Republic families have all condemned Karassia," Sang said. "Including your father, in uncharacteristically emotional terms."

Bellona's jaw flexed.

"The Homogeny Council of Independence has denied the attack." Sang grimaced. "They say the weapon was stolen."

"Stolen?" Bellona looked startled.

Khalil sat up and wiped his face. "Do you believe them?" he asked Sang. His voice was strained.

"I haven't extrapolated yet. The facts are still assembling."

"Guess, then," Khalil insisted.

"It would seem unlikely that a weapon they have been developing for years, if the rumors are true, would be in a location so insecure that someone could steal it, ship it and use it without Karassia crying foul before this moment."

Khalil nodded and looked at Bellona. "They were involved. Even if their involvement was a matter of turning their backs at the right moment. Yet I know it was more than that. The Homogeny wanted my brother and his fleet destroyed. They were a problem they had no other way to deal with."

"You don't know that for certain," Bellona said quickly.

Khalil leapt to his feet. "They destroyed an entire *world*! Do you know how many people lived in Shavistran? How many *families*?"

"Even if there had been only one family, one building and one life destroyed, it would still be too many," Bellona told him, rising to her feet, too. "Although there were far more than that on Shavistran, I know. That is why we cannot assign guilt without being certain. This is such a monstrous act, Khalil. To point at the wrong person and bring upon them the consequences of such an act…it would be just as wrong. We must tread carefully."

Khalil laughed humorlessly. "Who else could it be? The strongest free-state force, the single group who might have the strength and resources to steal such a weapon away from the Karassians was my brother's."

"If that is true, which must be ascertained," Sang said, "then that leaves only Erium, or the Bureau."

Bellona drew in a long, steadying breath. "I find it hard to believe that Erium would do such a thing."

"Now who is abandoning reason?" Khalil said bitterly. He walked from the room, his steps uneven.

Sang watched the door close. "He will reconsider later, when he is calmer," he told Bellona.

"He's right," Bellona said, also studying the closed door. "I don't know for certain that Erium is not involved. I would just prefer it not be. Find out, Sang. Put every resource on it. We need the truth. All three of us have much riding on the answers you find."

Sang considered the request dispassionately. "I have no personal stake in it," he pointed out.

"Erium made you," Bellona pointed out.

"Erium grew my body. The Bureau developed my awareness. Anything in addition to that is mine alone."

"I'm glad you have the comfort of believing that," Bellona told him. "May it serve you well."

* * * * *

KHALIL FOUND EQUILIBRIUM OF A sort. He became convinced that the murder of his brother and his brother's people were evidence that Bellona was the destined leader of free people everywhere. His conviction seemed to comfort him.

"It must be you," he told Bellona. "You are the only one left with an outsider's perspective."

"I am Eriuman," Bellona replied. "How does that make me an outsider?"

"You were *born* Eriuman. Then you were Karassian for ten years. Now, even Erium does not want you."

Bellona shook her head and refrained from responding. She instead turned her attention to the preparations for the raid. "Now is the perfect time," she insisted. "The known worlds are reeling. The Homogeny is focused upon everyone else, determined to deflect any and all accusations."

They immersed themselves in the work of preparations. Sang also spent his spare energy compiling facts about the death of Shavistran as they reached him, slotting them into the slowly emerging picture. There was not yet enough information to see any patterns, although the talk, the accusations, the paranoia and speculation were overwhelming in volume.

On the eve of the raid, Khalil sat in his favorite chair, his hands linked together loosely, his head down. "Have you thought of what you will do once you have freed your people?" he asked Bellona.

"I told you. No. One step at a time."

"You have yet to avenge Max's death," Khalil pointed out.

"How do I do that?" Bellona asked reasonably. "The Bureau is faceless and hidden. They have no homeworld to shoot at. Their tentacles reach across the known worlds. They are everywhere. There is no head to cut off." She gave him a small smile. "I could kill you right now. You are Bureau—"

"*Was*."

"Do they really let go so easily?" she asked gently.

"*I* have let go. It wasn't easy, but it was done."

"Even if you were still theirs, heart and soul, killing you would achieve nothing. Not even vengeance would be satisfied, for vengeance demands hurt and pain. It is impossible to hurt the Bureau. No one, not even you, knows how to make them feel pain or regret."

"Or do you?" Sang asked.

"If there was a beating heart to the Bureau I would tear it out with my bare hands and give it to you." Khalil sighed. "Sang has more humanity than they."

"I have a heart, certainly," Sang agreed.

Bellona smiled. "We won't tell anyone, Sang."

Khalil looked down at his hands, flexing them. "So much injustice, from so many places. There is no direction I can look where I will not see it."

Bellona picked up his hand. "Look to Ledan, for now. I am."

His fingers closed over hers.

Sang slid quietly from the room.

The next day, the operation began.

Chapter Eighteen

Lagrange Point Five, Cardenas (Findlay IV), Findlay System, Eriuman Republic

EVERY PLANET IN ERIUM HAD an impound field, usually at one of the lagrange points if the planet had a moon. The Eriuman Navy used the threat of assignment to one of the deadyards as a way of keeping junior officers in line. Lieutenant Hersilia Decilla had the comfort of knowing she was not alone, that on Eriuman planets everywhere, other officers were also staring at motionless junk. The only element that differentiated Hersilia from those others was that her assignment was at least the Cardenas field. It was one of the bigger ones and besides, it was *Cardenas*. The city provided compensation in off-duty periods…or it used to.

The riots and protests over the banishment and disappearance of Bellona Cardenas were increasing. It had become difficult to travel anywhere within the city. Between security checks by the family enforcers and the protesters themselves, it took twice as long to get anywhere. That chewed up off-duty time in a way that was vexing.

Hersilia looked around. There was only one enlisted man on the patrol shuttle with her. Everything else was automated. Yenis was off in some other corner, also sulking, so she took the opportunity to pull up her personal dashboard. There were more entertaining ways to pass the dead shift up here than staring at junk. She needed to figure out where she was going to eat tonight, that wouldn't take most of her off-shift time just getting there from the landing field.

Although she didn't abandon her work altogether. She

kept one screen trained on the junk and glanced at it every few minutes.

Yenis noticed first, though. He ran onto the deck, blowing hard. "Didn't you *see* it?" he demanded. "It's right there in front of you!"

Hersilia dismissed her dashboard quickly and pulled up the other feeds.

One of the ships was moving.

She started at it, fascinated. It wasn't simply revolving on its own axis as they all did. It was moving in a solid direction. She pegged one of the dead ships as a measurement base and watched the escapee gradually widen the gap between it and the dead ship. It was definitely moving. It looked as though it was easing its way out of the field.

"Ship shards," Hersilia breathed.

"What do we do?" Yenis demanded, breathless with anticipation. This was the most excitement they'd had since either of them had been assigned here.

"It's the family's yard," Hersilia said. "We have to bring in the enforcers." She woke up the AI and set up a channel.

"This shuttle is faster than anything they've got," Yenis pointed out. "It'll take them time just getting off the surface."

"Their yard, their call," Hersilia repeated. She connected and waited. "Pull up the code for the runaway," she told Yenis. "They'll want it."

"Cardenas Safeguard." The male voice was curt.

"Cardenas, this is *Balbus* at L5. One of your junk ships is escaping."

"Is that so?" Hersilia could hear the man's amusement. "Isn't it your job to keep them all corralled?"

"We watch 'em, that's all. It's your asset, Cardenas. What do you want us to do with it? It'll take you an hour to get here."

"Give us the number of the ship."

Hersilia nodded at Yenis. Yenis sent the code and they both listened to the enforcer's heavy breathing as he processed the code.

"That's the Karassian yacht!" he cried, startling both of them. "Damn!"

"Shall we pursue?" Hersilia asked.

"No! Stay out of it. Damn it all…" The enforcer disconnected.

Hersilia frowned. "Well, that wasn't very friendly."

Yenis sat back. "Let them blow their energy chasing the thing. Look, it's just following an orbital plane. It's not even trying to escape. Some digital screw got loose, I'm guessing. They'll shut it down, tow it back, all done." He got to his feet. "I'm gonna go…" He made a motion toward the door.

"Have you got a party going in the cargo hold, Yenis?" Hersilia demanded.

Yenis looked irritated and coy at the same time.

"You know what? Never mind. I really do not want to know what you do by yourself down there." Hersilia went back to her dashboard and forgot about Yenis, about the Karassian yacht and the rude enforcer and focused instead on what she would have for dinner.

* * * * *

SANG LOOKED UP AT THE roof far overhead. "Cardenas Safeguard have sent a ship after Connie."

"Just one?" Khalil asked, pausing from checking the load meter on the ghostmaker he had selected. Around him, the small team they had assembled on the training floor was doing the same.

"Just the one so far," Sang said. "There are no planet-wide alerts, either. Chatter suggests they believe they have a simple computer failure. The ship they sent after it is a tow barge. They are, however, concerned that it is the Karassian yacht that has wandered off."

"Because it belongs to my immediate family," Bellona said. "They're covering their rears, that is all."

Sang blinked again at her changed appearance. The blonde hair and pale skin was cosmetic only, but it was startling to see Xenia once more.

Bellona was not the only one adjusted to look Karassian. Most of the team wore the blonde hair, pale skin and brown eyes.

"So far, so good," Zeni added, tossing bleached locks back over her shoulder.

"Connie is ready to dive," Sang said. He looked at Bellona, who nodded.

"Make it look good," Khalil said.

Everyone got to their feet, stowed weapons and looked to Bellona. She watched Sang.

"Descending fast," he told her. At the same time, he reached out to the lone satellite overhead and smothered it.

"Move out!" Bellona cried.

* * * * *

THE YACHT SETTLED DOWN NEATLY between the three great fires that were jumping to life in a triangle around it. There wasn't a lot of room between the yacht's fins and the flames that were climbing up into the crisp night air, so Sang complimented Connie on her neatness.

She preened and opened the doors, welcoming them.

"Be nice," Sang murmured as they hurried up the ramps.

Bellona patted the closest bulkhead as she hurried up to the control deck. "You were *wonderful*!" she crooned.

As soon as the last of the team were aboard, Sang asked Connie to take them up. The trajectory and navigational commands had been calculated days ago. Execution was all that was left to be done.

Connie suggested everyone strap in, then leapt for the upper atmosphere, holding the ascent at a level just beneath maximum inertial tolerances. Everyone moaned and waited it out.

Bellona kept her odd, pale brown gaze on Sang, where he sat in the copilot chair, monitoring.

"Passing the tow barge now," Sang said. "They're a thousand kilometers away. We're well outside their scanner range and with the satellite down, they can't initiate a sweep." He checked the tow barge's position second over second. "Not moving at all," he added. "They're quite likely occupied with watching the fire on the surface and wondering how to pass the news back to the city."

The inertial pressure faded as Connie slowed and adjusted her heading.

Sang did a last check on the *Alyard's* position and confirmed it with Connie. She suggested everyone prepare for the jump. Sang passed the recommendation along.

"Everyone, brace yourselves!" Bellona called.

They jumped.

* * * * *

THE KARASSIAN HOMOGENY SHIP *ALYARD* was captained by Sandip. He had been awarded the chair three years before, despite the well-funded interest group who had campaigned against his appointment, who had said he was too young and inexperienced. So far his captaincy had been undistinguished. Sandip knew he needed a coup—a feat that sparkled with daring and courage—to draw attention to his abilities and earn himself a chair on a bigger ship than this little frigate. Only, being stuck out on the Eriuman border when all the action was happening in free space, meant that opportunities to shine bypassed Sandip.

When the security AI drew his attention to the yacht dropping out of null-space right next to them, its medic alert screaming for help, Sandip sighed. Another tourist who had wandered too close to Erium and had their tail feathers singed. They never learned.

"Tell it to hove to," he instructed the AI. "Send the medical team aboard."

The AI stuttered.

"*What*?" he demanded, as the rest of the bridge crew smirked.

The data read out on his screen, where everyone could see it. Sandip got to his feet. "*Xenia*?" he repeated. "That's impossible!"

The yacht floated close enough to start proximity alarms yowling.

The screen changed to a live feed from the control deck of the luxury yacht. Sandip stared at the woman's face. "Xenia," he breathed. Of course, only someone like Xenia would be travelling in a yacht of this caliber.

She smiled. "A member of my crew has radiation burns. We need an isolation tank and therapy. My ship does not have such extended facilities, although I am sure you would not mind extending the courtesy, would you?"

Sandip hid his sudden excitement. All the executive functions of the ship were crowded onto the top deck. Medical was right next to the bridge. He could surely find some excuse to talk to Xenia herself while she was in medical. Perhaps he could impress her with his helpfulness and skills as a captain… "My medical facility is at your disposal," he told her. He glanced at his exo, who nodded. "The landing bay is cleared and waiting for your arrival."

"That is most pleasing, captain." Her image dissolved.

Sandip turned to his exo. Greeta was busy at her

screen. Hally, the senior medic, was speaking swiftly, giving instructions on the preparations necessary to take a radiation victim aboard, including clearing out unnecessary personnel along the passage between the landing bay and the medical unit.

"See to it," Sandip told Greeta when she dismissed the screen.

She nodded and brought up six more screens, connecting simultaneously with her executive directors to coordinate the evacuation of the appropriate passages and junctions. The soft bleep of the radiation caution signal sounded. It would be heard throughout the ship, building louder if any idiot was silly enough to seek out the source of the radiation.

Sandip left Greeta to her preparations and went through to the medical bay. There, the quiet hysteria of a hospital emergency was already underway. Sandip caught Hally's gaze and nodded. He stayed out of the way. Hally wasn't above yelling at him if he interfered with the running of her facility. She was a biocomp and biobot, both. Her right hand was designed for surgery, micro-surgery and more. The implements were interchangeable, although mostly she wore the more natural-looking metal hand. Even that hand could swivel through a full circle, for exceptional flexibility. It always startled Sandip when she rotated it.

"Landed and sealed," Greeta's voice said, issuing from the nearest speaker for his ears in particular. "On their way. Ninety seconds, at most."

Hally didn't look as if she had heard Greeta's announcement, yet the hospital suddenly calmed, as everyone looked toward the door the victim would come through.

The first person to appear at the open doorway was Xenia herself. She wore the military breastplate and boots she favored and a heavy ghostmaker strapped to her hip.

Her hair was loose. She wasn't as tall as Sandip had thought her to be.

Then the carrier slipped through the door and the medics and aides surged toward it.

Xenia spotted Sandip and moved toward him. She did not smile, although Sandip couldn't remember her ever smiling, on any of the many reels he had seen of her in action. She had been fighting this war longer than he had been in the Karassian military. The victories she had fought and won! She had a right to be as dour as she wanted to be.

The sled behind her halted as the body in it sat up, throwing the blanket off with one arm, while bringing to bear upon the approaching staff one of the biggest ghostmakers Sandip had ever seen. He wasn't sure how the dark-haired man was holding it up. The man wasn't Karassian, which was puzzling.

Then Xenia reached Sandip and gripped his shoulder at the base of his neck and squeezed.

Instant pain blotted out all Sandip's thoughts, including his massive surprise. He buckled under the weight of the pain, dropping to the floor. He could barely draw breath, it was so intense.

Then it disappeared, except for a warm spot on his shoulder that throbbed. Bliss was relative. He reveled in the absence of the pain for three short seconds. Then Xenia's arm whipped around his throat and hauled him to his feet, choking off his breath. He grew still as the point of a knife stabbed the side of his neck. It was a smaller, sharper pain.

Xenia breathed in his ear. "We're going to walk back to your bridge, where you are going to tell your exo and the other bridge staff that we are going on a little jaunt."

Sandip swallowed. "To where?"

"We'll give you the coordinates when we get out there," said the man sitting on the edge of the sled, which was dipping with the imbalance of weight. He held the giant ghostmaker with a steady grip, watching the medical staff as they backed up against the wall, as far away from him as it was possible to get in the hospital.

All sorts of questions rose in Sandip's mind. He wondered if this was some sort of Eriuman conspiracy, except the man on the sled didn't look Eriuman, nor did the short man next to him, who had freckles. Another woman, very short, with large muscles, was removing anything in the medical trays that might be used as a weapon.

Free staters? What were free staters doing with Xenia? Sandip had heard all the rumors about Xenia, that she had disappeared—and it was true that there had been no recent footage of her victories, lately, which had fueled the rumors. Only, if she *had* defected to Erium, then surely the scream of outrage would have been heard across Karassia, for most people considered Xenia to be the most patriotic and perfect example of a good Karassian…

It was only as they marched Sandip out to the bridge, where the crew turned to gape at the sight of him being held at knifepoint that Sandip recognized this moment would not bring glory to him and change his fortunes for the better. He still wasn't absolutely sure of what was happening. He just knew it would be bad, whatever it was. Xenia was a disruptive force wherever she went.

Cardenas (Findlay IV), Findlay System, Eriuman Republic.

WAIT INTERRUPTED DINNER WITH THE news, which was unusual. Reynard apologized to Iulia and went back to the library with Wait to hear all of it properly. Even from in here, he could hear the distant sounds of the riots in the city. The partisans had called for a week of protests on this, the anniversary of Bellona's return to Cardenas. Any protest they held always turned into a riot.

Even in his own mind, Reynard could not use the partisans' full name.

Wait was agitated. "The Karassian yacht that was used to retrieve Bellona from Kachmar has gone missing."

Reynard frowned. "Is there a connection to the protests?" he asked.

Wait consulted their sources. "Not that can be detected at this time. The Safeguard feel it was a malfunction. They tracked the ship to the southern hemisphere, where it fell. The tow barge that went after it reports that what is left of the ship is located on the edges of the Caramella desert, near one of the ghost towns. They located it because it was burning. There was little of it left."

Reynard started. "Abilio? That is the ghost town?"

Wait showed surprise. "Yes."

"Contact Admiral Lucretia Carosa of the Edanii, on the *Severus.* Tell her Bellona is escaping. Do it at once."

Wait's gaze drew blank as they communed with the necessary channels to get the message bullet to Lucretia.

"What is wrong, brother?" Gaubert asked, as he walked into the library. He wiped his mouth with the napkin he had carried from the table. "Iulia and Thora are worried."

"It's nothing. Go back to your dinner," Reynard told him.

"It's nothing that required reaching out to an Admiral

from the Edan clan?"

"Lucretia is a steady admiral. She is ideally located to handle this. Thank you, Gaubert, I will return in a minute."

Gaubert settled his hip on the back of one of the visitor chairs. "Handle what?"

Reynard's irritation provoked him into speaking. "Bellona is moving off planet."

"You mean she was here all along?" Gaubert's surprise pushed him to his feet again.

Reynard realized he had said too much. Now he was committed to explaining himself. "I traced her as far as the southern continent," Reynard told his brother. "Now, the yacht she used to escape Kachmar has apparently crashed in the desert there."

"Which you do not believe."

"It might be true," Reynard admitted. "The coincidence is too large to assume it is, though."

Gaubert frowned. "If the Pro-Repatriation Front hears she was on Cardenas all along and has now left, then they will assume that you removed her forcibly. It will fuel their cause."

"I know that!" Reynard snapped. Hearing the name of the partisans spoken so freely made his temper flare. "Why do you think I'm asking the admiral to retrieve her?"

"The Safeguard won't do it?"

"The Safeguard is riddled with partisans," Reynard replied. "They all want Bellona restored to favor."

Gaubert crossed his arms. "Did you ever think it would amount to this? Riots and civil disobedience?"

Reynard breathed hard. "They're weak and afraid. They look at Bellona's failure to reintegrate with the family and fear that they will also be cast from the Republic for something beyond their control. They fail to understand the subtleties."

"What subtleties?" Gaubert asked. "After ten years under the Karassian yoke, she came home and no one liked the way she had changed."

Wait raised their hand, their gaze focused upon Reynard once more. Wait had the Admiral waiting to speak to him, then.

Reynard waved Gaubert away. "You sound like a partisan yourself, little brother. Bellona made her own bed. Go and entertain the women."

Chapter Nineteen

Cardenas (Findlay IV), Findlay System, Eriuman Republic.

THE FINAL APPROACH TO CARDENAS was a long elliptical that kept the *Alyard* in the blind spot over the desert. It was harsh and hot when the frigate settled on the salt pan. Three kilometers away, the smoke from the fires that had guided Connie to the surface was still rising lazily up into the air. There was no moisture here, not even at night, to dampen the fuel and extinguish the fire. It had burned for the days they had been gone and would continue to burn until the fuel was spent.

Zeni's crew were waiting with the trucks and carts loaded with gear standing by. They were jumping up and down and cheering as the ship settled, even though Sang, standing on the bridge, could not hear them over the vast engines winding down.

Bellona looked at the little Karassian captain, Sandip. She was smiling. "Tell me again how the ship can't land inside a gravity well?"

Sandip had been restrained chemically. Below the neck, he could not move. He had sat in the upright chair for the three days it had taken to return to Cardenas, with the doctor hovering over him, monitoring vital signs with the tools on the end of her arm. Sandip had watched Bellona take over his bridge and ship, silently resigned.

Bellona had stayed as Xenia. Most of the bridge crew were dazzled by her, still half-convinced she had some great scheme in mind to enhance the Karassian reputation with a stunning victory that required desperate measures, including piracy. They had obeyed her commands with little hesitation, while Sandip fumed in his chair.

Khalil supervised the piloting of the ship to the correct coordinates himself. He did not trust the navigator, who recognized the coordinates when they were given to him. The navigator had paled and drawn back from his screens.

Khalil pushed him aside. "I'll do it myself," he told Bellona. "I didn't spend all my time on Ben's ships fixing his computers."

Now the ship had settled down on the hard surface and silence dropped over it. The bridge crew looked at Xenia expectantly.

"Doors," Bellona ordered. "All of them open, all ramps extended."

Sang could feel the rush of hot, dry air from the desert. It tightened the flesh on his face. With it came the smell of arid sand.

"Everyone, get off," Bellona ordered.

The Karassian crew looked at her, puzzled. They still thought she was a Karassian champion.

From deeper inside the ship came shouting and running feet. Bellona's team would be rounding up the crew and shepherding them off the ship at gunpoint. As the sounds filtered into the bridge, the Karassians lost their puzzled looks.

More of Bellona's people ran onto the bridge, their guns raised. They motioned to the Karassians, who without exception glared at Bellona before turning and leaving the bridge.

Bellona ignored them. "Is Connie still comfortable?" she asked Sang.

"She is chatting with the ship's primary AI. She convinced it to scan for heat signatures. If anyone is hiding, Connie will find them."

Amilcare, one of the original miners in Abilio who had turned into a capable lieutenant, snapped off an informal salute to Bellona. "The water is offloaded. All the vehicles are disabled, although if the Karassians have two neurons to rub together, they'll figure out how to start them again."

"We want them isolated for a while, not dead," Bellona said approvingly. "Everyone!" she said, raising her voice. "Quarter the ship, check for lingerers and toss them."

The teams had been practicing on the replica frigate for weeks, so there was no hesitation about where to go and what small spaces to check. There was a flurry of activity that gradually eased as everyone took up their assigned positions, replacing the essential flight roles of the Karassian crew. Khalil remained at the navigation table, bent over screens and frowning.

Sang counted noses, checked stations, then asked Connie to close the doors, seal and check.

Five minutes later, the *Alyard* rose up into the air, leaving the subdued and angry Karassians on the surface, staring up at their ship.

When they reached the outer atmosphere, Wynne, on the externalities station, spoke. "Eriuman cruiser, seven point three thousand kilometers and closing." Wynne swiveled to look at Bellona. "It's the *Severus*."

"My father's last ditch effort to keep me on Cardenas," Bellona said, her voice dry. "As rehearsed, Wynne. Under them and away."

It was a two day jump to Kachmar, traversing both Eriuman and Karassian space. They emerged above the mostly green planet and alarms immediately sounded.

Bellona looked at Sang.

"Connie is talking to them," Sang assured her. He tapped into her conversations and heard the exchange of Karassian credentials. There was a short pause, while the Karassian authorities checked and while Sang's heart hurried.

The alarms cut off.

Sang let out his breath. "They have accepted Connie's identity."

"Until someone is within visual range and sees the *Alyard,* not a little yacht," Amilcare added.

"By the time anyone gets up here, we'll be on the surface," Bellona said. "Remember the dry runs. It's straightforward from here on. Put her down, please, Sang."

Sang congratulated Connie on her successful handshake with the Karassians, then asked her to beach the ship.

* * * * *

Ledan Resort, Kachmar Sodality, The Karassian Homogeny.

AFTER MONTHS OF LIVING IN dry heat, Sang found the moist air over the Ledania island thick and smelly. Many of the crew were waving their hands in front of their noses in reaction to the smells of decay and mold that the swampy land exuded, as they spread out across the island.

Their landing had been noted. It would have been impossible to land a frigate-sized ship and not be noticed, so Sang did not worry about the klaxons blaring a kilometer away, where the compound started. He did run, though, as did everyone else. As he ran to keep up with the team, he and Connie sweet-talked the AIs controlling the compound security and feeds.

"There is a small chance the two of you will be able to convince the AIs to shut down everything and let us in," Bellona had said during planning sessions. "We won't count on it working, but it will simplify matters if it does."

By the time Sang could properly see the end of the swamp and the fused earth of the compound, Connie had convinced the AIs that the klaxons were unnecessary, that their beloved Xenia was returning home, that was all.

As Xenia was a part of their archives, the AIs were confused and consulted with trusted humans, who were also confused. By now, their lenses would have spotted the approaching team. Bellona made no attempt to hide, so they could see it was Xenia heading toward them.

When Xenia had first escaped, the Homogeny had suppressed the news. It would have been too shameful to admit that the champion of the people had been detained against her will in the first place and that she had escaped her captors in the second. Better to pretend she was simply unavailable and taking a long-earned rest from her endeavors.

Connie had told Sang all about the legends of Xenia when they had first chatted. Bellona had woven the deception into her attack plans.

The confused security crews tried to consult with more senior personnel and while they did not drop all security defenses, they did turn off the audible alarms, just in case they really were making a massive mistake.

By the time they got the attention of senior managers, it was too late. Bellona's crew had reached the hardpan. They sprinted, using the pause that doubt and uncertainty had created.

When the automatic defense systems kicked into gear, the crew was already too close to the compound walls for the systems to fire. With screams and yells designed to further confuse and alarm the watchers, the team tossed self-guiding grapnels and climbed the walls with the fiber ladders the grapnels extended once they had settled themselves.

Sang threw himself over the wall and dropped into an unadorned service area. There were doors along the corridor and he pointed to them.

The team split up. This, too, had been planned and rehearsed for weeks. They forced open the doors and stepped into the illusion that was Ledan, with its tropical atmosphere and bright sun, lapping waters and the flutter and coo of birds in trees.

Several of the team paused to look around, blinking in astonishment. Sang noted who was distracted and slapped the nearest on the shoulder, jerking him back to focus.

The little lagoon was just ahead and there were Karassians in the resort uniform trying to round up the inmates. The inmates—the apps—were protesting in bewildered tones, for this was a departure from the norm, from the usual placid life of Ledan. They didn't understand, although the emotion inhibitors were stopping them from panicking. Instead, they passively resisted.

Sang saw the tall, metal-enhanced figure of Hayes, over by the little beach, with three Karassian handlers all trying to tug him along, while he dug in his heels, frowning. The others were all known to Sang, too, for he had studied their public appearances. Xenia's recall of names and faces had been accurate.

Bellona's teams were attacking the resort people, pulling them away from the apps and temporarily disabling them. Then they, too, had to coax the apps into cooperating. Each of the four-man teams carried the same sedative that Sang had used on Bellona, when he and Khalil had freed her. The teams had been instructed to use the sedative if reason did not work. The first line of reason, though, was to point to Bellona-Xenia and explain they were with Xenia.

Several of the apps were stumbling toward the service areas with their four-man teams, still confused and apprehensive, but cooperating.

"Sang. Zeni, Khalil. With me," Bellona called.

Sang beckoned to the remaining teams, turned and followed Bellona into the heart of the compound. The rooms and buildings beyond the lagoon were a rabbit warren that Bellona and Khalil had mapped out as best they could remember. Khalil had accessed areas behind the public rooms the apps had been limited to and knew that the buildings ran deep. All the apps, though, were kept in the front rooms, the ones that looked like vacation getaways.

Bellona led the file of people into the different areas—sleeping quarters, ablutions, dining. In each, the teams would peel off and search each area, looking for more apps. Sang's tally told him that there were five more to be found. So far there had been no apps whose face was unknown to Sang.

In the dining area, they met their first serious resistance. A line of Karassian military in their brown uniforms were standing with ghostmakers raised. The polished stone floor had been cleared of tables and chairs, which were tossed into a corner. They had a clear shot as Bellona and the others filed into the big, open area.

In front of the line of military was a Karassian that Sang knew purely because Bellona had mentioned him once in the past, when recalling her time as Xenia. Because Karassians loved to have their likeness splashed across as many screens as possible, Sang had been able to build dossiers on everyone that Bellona remembered.

This man, Sang knew. His name was Woodrow. From Xenia's hazy, dreamlike recollection of life in Ledan, Sang had determined that Woodrow was one of the administrators and thoroughly unlikeable. Even Xenia had not found his company pleasant, although the apps were incapable of feeling something as strong as dislike.

Woodrow watched Bellona approach, a small smile on his face. "Welcome back, Xenia." His voice was high and hard. His eyes were close-set and deep, although they were the proper light Karassian brown.

Bellona stopped in front of him, ignoring the raised

guns, while everyone else spread out next to her, their ghostmakers aimed.

Sang stayed by Bellona's elbow. He carried no gun. That was not his role, today.

"While you delay me here, your apps are being escorted back to my ship," Bellona told him. "You won't be able to stop me from leaving. We have disabled your defense shield."

"Did you find that easy to do, by chance?" Woodrow asked.

Bellona's gaze flickered toward Sang.

Sang checked with Connie, who chattered happily about her accomplishments.

He nodded at Bellona.

Bellona looked back at the little man. "You were expecting me, Woodrow?"

"How nice. You remember me." Woodrow smiled broadly, showing small teeth. "We remember you, of course. *Everyone* remembers you, including those you are absconding with while we speak. It astonished everyone here to realize that the apps were retaining longer term memories. All of them focused upon Xenia and her absence. It upset the program. Some of them couldn't be sequenced for missions because of their stronger recall. We have had to be inventive to get around the limitations your departure introduced."

"Sorry about that," Bellona said airily.

"Of course, all that damage would instantly be neutralized, if you stayed."

Khalil laughed.

Bellona smiled, too, but Sang could see she was troubled. "You must be quite mad if you think I would stay here and knowingly let myself be used and manipulated, the way you used Xenia," she said.

"You could be their leader," Woodrow said, as if she had not spoken at all. "You have their trust and they would follow you wherever you led them."

"You mean, fight for Karassia?" Bellona did laugh this time.

"Erium doesn't want you," Woodrow pointed out. "You know that, or you would not have come here in search of your true friends."

"I want to get them *out* of Ledan," Bellona replied. "I want them removed from your filthy programming."

"He's stalling," Khalil said softly. "Playing for time."

Woodrow glanced at him. "Your Bureau pet's perceptions are as distorted as yours, Bellona. May I call you that? He wants to believe the Bureau values you as much as we do, which gives him a reason to resist them, as he doesn't have the backbone to resist for his own sake. Yet the Bureau doesn't want you, either. They killed your brother to cripple you, not motivate you."

"Is that why they killed Ben Arany? To disable Khalil, too?" Bellona asked. Her tone said that this was an accepted fact and not her stabbing in the dark.

"Oh, the Bureau didn't kill Arany," Woodrow said dismissively. "Your father did that."

Bellona just barely hid her gasp. Sang held still, his heart pounding, as he tried to juggle the odds, to determine if it could possibly be true.

Khalil gave a choking sound. The muzzle of his gun lowered.

"He's manipulating you," Sang whispered to Bellona.

She didn't look at him. Her grip on the ghostmaker tightened, making her knuckles whiten. "Why would my father do that?" she demanded of Woodrow. Her voice was hoarse.

Woodrow's smile was bright. "I might have implied that Arany killed your brother Max."

Sang's thoughts froze. It was shock, as he experienced it. Then the human reaction set in. Adrenaline spiked, making him shake. Thought came back on-line, yet it was compromised. Stunted. If he was reacting this way, then Bellona had to be suffering, too.

Bellona smiled. "Khalil is right. You're stalling. You think the Karassian military will swoop in to save you. They won't, Woodrow. They think one of their frigates is already taking care of the situation. They can see it from their nice warm bridge seats and the frigate's AI is telling them exactly what they want to hear."

Woodrow showed the first sign of doubt. His mouth worked as he grappled with it. "You're lying," he said, finally.

Bellona lowered the gun. "Your guards won't shoot us. They can't. If the other apps see the guards shooting at Xenia, they will rebel and you'll never get them back. So we're going to walk out of here and you're going to let us."

Woodrow's whole face writhed with fury. "Your father wanted vengeance. He said it, right in front of me! What sort of people are the Eriumans, to kill a whole planet?"

Bellona gestured to everyone. Sang backed up as she had commanded. The others followed suit.

"The Karassians gave Erium the weapon and stood back and watched," Bellona told Woodrow as she turned to follow. "What does that make you?"

"There is nowhere for you to go!" Woodrow shouted back. "No one wants you!"

"My friends do!" Bellona cried.

It acted as a signal. All of them turned and ran.

Chapter Twenty

Ledan Resort, Kachmar Sodality, The Karassian Homogeny.

SANG AND CONNIE WORKED WITH the frigate's AI to relay information to the military ships hovering in the upper atmosphere over Ledania. The answers and data they supplied sowed confusion. The feeds they looped and manipulated made the Karassians doubt anything they learned that contradicted the fake images they saw of a peaceful compound. Karassians were too used to absorbing facts about their world via screens.

While Sang misdirected, Bellona and the teams led or carried the apps to the frigate. Hayes consented to walking there by himself, which relieved his four-man team, who had not relished the idea of having to carry him if he did not cooperate. Hayes had gazed around the island and up at the sky with placid curiosity. On board, he settled into the crash couch without questions, watching everything that happened around him, as the other teams settled their own assigned apps.

On the bridge, Bellona discarded the hair and makeup that made her Xenia and stood with her arms crossed. Something was happening, Sang realized, as he entered the bridge himself. He recognized her simmering impatience and eased over to the navigation table, where Khalil stood, the focus of her attention.

"I'm not saying we can't go back," Khalil said. "I'm saying we shouldn't go back *now*. We need time to adjust. We need distance."

"*You* might need it," Bellona replied. "I have things to do."

Khalil leaned on the table and took a deep breath, calming himself. "The *Severus* swooping in when we lifted off says he knew where you were all along. He's had time now. He'll have stirred up an armada. Half the Cardenas fleet will be waiting for you when we return. Do you really want to face your father *now*, Bellona? Do you really want to confront him about Ben?"

Bellona pressed her lips together, making them thin and pale. "Very well," she said flatly. "Take us somewhere. Anywhere. I don't care. I have friends to take care of. I'll be in the hospital." She stalked over to the bulkhead door that separated the bridge from the medical wing and slapped the controls.

Khalil bent over the table, plotting coordinates.

Sang glanced around the bridge. No one spoke, so he did. "Let's get this ship up in the air and ready to jump."

The crew leapt to work.

* * * * *

WHEN KHALIL GAVE THE NAVIGATION AI the new coordinates for the jump, Sang translated them automatically. He moved over to the table. "You're not a fool," he said quietly. "So I must presume your reasons for choosing that place are profound."

Khalil's jaw worked. "Profound? I'm not a good judge of that. I do know that Bellona's life runs more smoothly when she has truth to work with. I'm doing my best to supply it."

Sang shook his head. "You have more courage than I, Khalil. You can tell her where we're going."

However, Bellona did not emerge from the medical wing until Sang had the AI tell her they had arrived at their destination: Shavistran.

Then she curtly ordered Khalil and Sang to the captain's cabin.

* * * * *

BELLONA HAD A SCREEN UP, showing the scorched and blackened surface of the planet, where the thriving city had once been. Around the edges of the nearly perfect circle of destruction was mockingly green rainforest. At the top of the continent, snow-capped mountains took over. The sea beyond was a deep teal.

The view was live, for a burned-out chunk of fuselage crossed in front of the lens as Sang looked, turning in lazy circles. More debris littered the view, most of it small.

Bellona barely waited for the door to close. "Shavistran?" she demanded of Khalil. "I thought you said we needed breathing space. To regroup."

"I did," Khalil said evenly. "I thought this place would provide some perspective to your ruminations."

"I should return to the bridge..." Sang said softly. There was no need for him to be here. He didn't *want* to be here.

"You don't get to slink out on this," Bellona shot back. "You captained the ship here, Sang. It didn't occur to you even once that I might object?"

Sang scrambled to arrange his thoughts in reaction to the sudden attack. "I...did question the destination," he said carefully.

"He challenged me on it," Khalil said evenly. "He didn't like the idea any more than you do."

Bellona looked at Sang squarely. "Not enough to refuse to take the ship there."

Sang cast about for an answer that would encompass the sum total of his surprise. "I suppose I thought...that more than speaking my doubts was not within my purview."

Bellona shook her head. "A year ago, maybe. You don't have that excuse anymore, Sang. You're no longer a Cardenas asset. You're a free man." She hesitated. "We all are. I believe that is why Khalil brought us here," she finished sourly.

Khalil sighed. "I don't think I thought it through that clearly." His tone was candid. "I just know you need to see this place for yourself. You need to see the truth."

Bellona turned away from both of them and from the screens, too. "I am not a substitute for your brother, Ari."

"I have never thought of you in that way," Khalil said. "You can be *better* than him. Woodrow was right—you have that potential. I've always known that."

"Yet you want me to take up your brother's cause."

"I want you to accept the cause that is right in front of you." Khalil threw out his hands. "Turn around, Bellona. Look for yourself. You have spent a year avoiding the truth. Now it's time to face it. Erium is no longer your place. The Homogeny never has been. The Bureau tried to force you into it, although you should ignore them and their manipulations and chose for yourself. Make the *right* choice, this time. You have a cargo hold full of the best fighters in the known worlds, trained to within an inch of their lives and they all *love* you. If you help them, the free states will love you, too." He paused, his chest heaving with the passion and energy of his convictions.

Bellona did turn, although she looked at Khalil, not the screens. "The free states are *free*, Khalil. They're independent to the point of phobia. They're not going to rally around some stranger, some Eriuman, who says they should fight for something they already have."

"Only they *don't* have it," Khalil shot back. "Not anymore. The city-killer changes things. It has shifted the balance of power in a way that they can't possibly overcome. Erium and the Homogeny will come after the free states now, annexing, occupying, colonizing as fast as they can. Each of them has the city-killer technology. The only thing left that will give them an edge over the other is how much territory they hold. They will not stop now, not until someone *makes* them stop."

"You want me to make them stop?" Bellona asked. "The two greatest political powers in the known worlds?"

Sang cleared his throat. "In the last twenty years, more than thirty percent of the known and indexed city-states and systems have been taken and are now controlled by Karassia or Erium."

Bellona looked at him. "You think I should do this, Sang?"

"Yes."

"Become the leader the Bureau has been searching for?"

Sang hesitated. "No. Not that."

"Then…?"

Sang paused again. Then he girded himself. "There is nowhere else for you to go, but into the free states. If you do, it means you are declaring yourself independent, free of the expectations of the Republic and your family and most especially of your father. You've just taken the best of your time in Ledan out of Karassia. They owe you nothing more. You have spent a year severing every tie and loyalty you once thought you held, so in your heart, you're already living as a free stater. Freedom comes with responsibilities, though."

"Responsibilities?" Khalil repeated, sounding amused. "Every free stater I know would be appalled at the idea they have any responsibilities or owe anyone anything at all."

"Freedom isn't just an absence of loyalties," Sang replied. "It's an active state that has to be maintained. Entropy will destroy it if it isn't." He shrugged. "Just as I, a free man, should have actively protested about coming here." He glanced at the screen. The ugly black mark was moving over the horizon and its disappearance was pleasing.

"Sang is talking about fighting for freedom, if fighting

is needed," Bellona said. "He's right, too." She looked at Khalil. "I'm not agreeing with you," she told him. "I'm not agreeing to anything right now. Yet I would like to see the free states for myself. As Sang said, I have nowhere else to go."

Khalil's smile was warm and bright.

Sang did leave them alone, after that. He was free and he was also discreet.

Chapter Twenty-One

Cardenas (Findlay IV), Findlay System, Eriuman Republic.

WAIT DID NOT INTERRUPT DINNER this time, yet it was highly agitated, more than Reynard ever remembered from the past. He murmured apologies to Gaubert and Iulia, who were playing off against each other, climbed down from the observation deck over the tallball court and followed Wait back to the library, his heart squeezing.

A screen had been resolved and hung at the back of the room. Bellona was on the screen, watching him enter.

Reynard's steps slowed. "A screen," he said. "How… Karassian of you, daughter."

"I am not your daughter. Not anymore."

She looked different. Living in the desert had changed her. Reynard realized he was ridiculously pleased to see her. "You look well," he said carefully.

"The screen is so I can see your face," Bellona said, as if he had not spoken at all.

"And I can see yours. Perhaps they have their uses, after all."

"Did you do it?" she demanded. "Are you the one who gave the order for the destruction of Shavistran?"

Shock slithered through him. "Me? You really think I would do such a thing?"

"You have the Navy in the palm of your hand. The Cardenas fleet would jump to do anything you ordered and you met with the Karassians on Antini."

The shock this time spread coldness through him. "How did you find out about Antini?" His lips felt thick and uncooperative.

Bellona nodded. She suddenly looked almost regal. "A whole planet of families, for Max? You make me sick."

"I didn't..." he began weakly. She really thought him capable of such an act? "I refused! I told them I didn't want Arany's location!"

"I don't believe you," Bellona said carefully, annunciating each word. "I would have, when I was a child. I might have, even a year ago, when I first came back to Cardenas. Now, I do not. I know you now, Reynard Cardenas and I am ashamed that you are my father."

"He didn't do it, Bella," said a voice from behind Reynard.

Reynard whirled.

Gaubert stood there, sweaty from the court and red of face. He was looking at Bellona. "Your father wanted vengeance, just not that way. He left. I negotiated with the Karassians, instead."

"You?" Reynard breathed. "You did this? It really was Erium who killed Arany's people?"

Gaubert nodded. "No one must think they can get away with harming even a single Eriuman. There had to be retribution. I did it for Erium."

Sharp pain bit into Reynard's chest. It ran down his arm, making his fingers curl. "Do you have any idea what you have done?" he whispered.

"I have preserved the status quo," Gaubert said righteously.

"You...*fool*!" Reynard gasped. It was the last full breath he took.

* * * * *

BELLONA DISSOLVED THE SCREEN AND swiveled in the chair. Her face was as still as stone. Khalil, sitting in the corner as always, looked just as stunned.

"Sang, destroy that footage," Bellona said. "*Now.*"

Sang reached out to the ship's AI and Connie.

Connie was puzzled. "You can destroy things?" she asked.

The Karassian AI was even more obtuse. Dissemination was calcified into the Karassian culture. It couldn't even grasp the idea of not sharing it as widely as possible.

Sang sighed. "Too late," he breathed.

Khalil scrubbed at his face. "Counter it," he said swiftly. "Make the Karassians look just as bad."

"How?" Bellona demanded.

"You have seventeen victims of the worst Karassian conspiracy ever, right here on the ship, not including yourself and me," Khalil said. "Tell everyone what they did. Hold them accountable and hold Erium accountable for Shavistran."

"Tell the truth?" Bellona said. She smiled. "*That* is something I can do."

* * * * *

Site of the former free city Shavistran, Shavistran III. Free space.

EVEN THE SURFACES OF THE fused earth streets had been turned into charcoal, which shattered with each step they took and sent up a fine black powder that trailed away in the small breeze whistling through the ruins of Shavistran.

Sang wasn't sure what hatred was, for he had never felt it, although he did wonder if the sensation he was feeling as he followed Khalil and Bellona along what was left of the Shavistran streets was hatred. It roiled in his guts. The pressure across his chest made it hard to breathe.

Pathetic signs of human occupation were everywhere.

The buildings had melted, just as human remains had been incinerated. In odd pockets, though, evidence had been preserved. The base of a drinking glass that had run like candle wax. A spoon. The shining, smooth surface of what had once been a flowerbed, with the flowers encased eternally inside the black glass. The shells of ground vehicles, still in their orderly traffic lanes.

Even the pattern of the streets, laid out in familiar grids like every human city in the known worlds, was enough to make Sang's throat close down tight.

Bellona stopped in the middle of the street and looked up at the sun, letting the light bathe her face. Then she turned on her heels, taking in the city. "Everyone should see this."

"They did. They are," Khalil amended, pointing at the lens floating over her shoulder.

"I mean, they should come here and *feel* it for themselves. It won't make sense until they do."

"It still doesn't make sense," Sang said, his voice hoarse. "Not to me."

"I mean, what we have to do next won't make sense," Bellona corrected.

"What comes next?" Khalil asked.

Bellona dragged her heel through the charcoal. It made a furrow in the black surface. She looked up at the lens and spoke firmly. "Here, but no farther." She shook her head. "We will not permit it."

The Indigo Reports Book 1.1

But Now I See

CAMERON COOPER

About *But Now I See*

A lethal cat and mouse game.

To pay off a long-standing debt, Tatiana Wang, captain of the freeship *Hathaway*, takes aboard a politically high-risk passenger. When the *Hathaway* is caught by the Karassian military's flagship, led by the biocomp captain Yishmeray, "high risk" becomes "deadly."

The *But Now I See* novelette is part of the Indigo Reports space opera series by award-winning SF author Cameron Cooper.

The Indigo Reports series:
0.5 *Flying Blind*
1.0 *New Star Rising*
1.1 *But Now I See*
2.0 *Suns Eclipsed*
3.0 *Worlds Beyond*

Space Opera Science Fiction Story

Praise for *But Now I See*

Excitement PLUS! - we are immediately drawn into a high drama situation with some very interesting characters.

It's wonderful to read the conclusion of this little story: the great importance of the family for all humans, whether they live on Earth or in another dimension.

This is a fast paced short story which sets the stage for Bellona's future exploits. Definitely worth the read. This is a great series.

But Now I See

Freeship Hathaway. Cardenas Extended Spacezone.

THE SECOND TIME MAXIMILIAN CARDENAS Scordini de Deluca stepped onto Captain Tatiana Wang's bridge, he left as deep an impression as the first, yet they were very different impressions.

Someone has beaten experience into him lately, Tatiana thought. She held still as the Eriuman lieutenant came toward her, his stride across the steel plating of the bridge deck sure and even.

Everyone on the bridge had grown still, warily watching Lieutenant Cardenas approach their captain. Ruh stood stiffly just in front and to one side of Tatiana, his arms crossed and his legs spread. He was in full protection mode, but he did not attempt to stop Cardenas when the taller man moved passed him. Cardenas didn't even look at Ruh.

Cardenas was not wearing his pretty purple uniform with the gold braid and ribbons. Instead, his jacket was simple and dark, the trousers even darker. The shirt beneath had no collar, was soiled, rumpled and looked as though he had been wearing it for days. His chin was dark with growth. Fatigue pulled at his black eyes and made his shoulders slump.

His gaze was still direct, though. He remained the privileged son of Erium even though his life had clearly not been easy or pleasant lately.

When the woman stepped out from behind Cardenas, Tatiana was only surprised it was a female accompanying Cardenas. The skiff Ruh had maneuvered into the cargo bay with the grappling beams had been small and scans had told them there were two people aboard.

Tatiana spotted blood on the woman's long skirt and silky shirt, beneath the oversized male jacket only just hanging on her shoulders. The woman had Eriuman-black hair and eyes and dark olive skin. Her skin glowed with care and good health. Tatiana also spotted the familial features—the similarity to Maximillian Cardenas in her dark, direct gaze and the determined chin. With a jolt, Tatiana realized who this must be—the sister the lieutenant had spoken of when they had first met four years ago. This was the woman whose influence had made Max let Tatiana and her family go, despite Eriuman policy.

Tatiana's gaze dropped to the blood stains again. They were stale, stiff, dark brown patches. There had been a lot of blood. The trouble that had forced Maximilian Cardenas to reach out to Tatiana involved his sister.

"Captain Wang," the lieutenant said, in accented Common. "I appreciate your timely arrival here."

Tatiana had forgotten the accent, although she had remembered every word he had said the first time he had boarded her ship. "We are in Eriuman space," she said. "Right over Cardenas itself. The satellites are thick, here. We won't go undetected for long, so I suggest you get to business."

"You won't be seen," Cardenas said. "I have a…friend, who is making sure of that as we speak."

Tatiana let out a breath. She trusted him in this matter, especially as his sister was with him. She knew he was trying to protect her right now, although the shape of the threat was still unknown to Tatiana.

"Do you have it?" Cardenas asked.

"Have what?"

"The button."

Tatiana couldn't help but smile. Then he *had* deliberately dropped it. She moved around the navigation table and over to the high bench that was her desk and control dashboard, terminal and command post. She opened the left-hand drawer and pulled out the tiny box from the back of it and opened it.

The purple fragment of cloth still clung to the back of the gilt button. Tatiana picked up the button and moved back to where the two Eriumans stood in the middle of the open area of the bridge, surrounded by Tatiana's crew.

Tatiana held out the button. "You are about to ask me to repay this, aren't you, Lieutenant?"

He took the button. "Max, for now," he said shortly. He rested his hand on the shoulder of the woman standing next to him. She was not much shorter than him and Max Cardenas was a tall man. "This is my sister, Bellona."

Bellona considered Tatiana for a moment, then gave her a very small nod.

"Welcome aboard my ship, Bellona," Tatiana told her. She looked at Max and waited.

"I want you to take Bellona to Cerce," Max said.

Not, "Can you take her?" There was no question in there anywhere.

Tatiana hid her sigh, looking at the button she had just given back to him, held between his fingers. "If we are found with one of the Scordinii aboard, by *any* navy, it will not go well."

"About as well as it went for me, when I had to explain why I let a freeship go, four years ago." His tone was even. There was no threat there. He was simply explaining the facts.

Tatiana nodded. "Very well, then. This will clear the debt between us?"

"It will."

Ruh's arms dropped. "Tia, no! This is…madness."

Max barely glanced at him. He had already assessed Ruh as no threat.

Tatiana scowled. "I apologize. My brother has forgotten who is captain."

Max Cardenas and his sister merely nodded.

Tatiana experienced a sudden urge to see either of them smile. The sadness dripped from them, making her heart beat hard. "Once I have brought your sister to Cerce, then what? A daughter of the Eriuman will be noticed."

Max did not look at his sister, or confer with her in any way. "If you would print her some clothes from your files, Bellona will take care of the rest."

"The rest of what?" Tatiana asked curiously.

Max cleared his throat. "I don't know. I do not *want* to know. My part in this is at an end. I have taken her off Cardenas and away from…and away."

Bellona curled her hand around his arm. Tatiana could see her fingers whiten as she squeezed. Her throat worked.

Max gave a soft sound and turned to take her in his arms in a tight, hard hold. Bellona clung just as tightly and while the entire bridge watched, they held each other without shame or embarrassment.

Ruh scowled at the pair. As a male and the head of his own nuclear family which included three grown daughters, he did not approve of such a public demonstration, for he had been raised to the same standards as Tatiana. She, though, understood why the pair cared nothing for who watched them. Whatever the trouble that had brought them here, it was grave enough for them to believe this would be the last time they saw each other. It would force just about anyone to put aside propriety, even her own stiff-necked, proper family.

When Max let his sister go, he blinked hard and cleared his throat again. He picked up her hand. "In a while…I don't know how long…when I think it's safe, I'll have Sang come and find you." He was speaking in Eriuman, although Tatiana had no trouble following it. She had made herself fluent in both Eriuman and the two most popular dialects the Karassians used, in the last few years.

Bellona shook her head. "You can't risk it. They'll be watching you, waiting for you to do exactly that." She had a pleasant voice, nicely modulated and well-trained, each word spoken beautifully. "You have to go back and erase any trail, then pretend to be as shocked as anyone else."

Max looked as though he wanted to protest. She gripped his hand even harder. "You *must*," she insisted. "You're all Mother has left, now."

Max considered her for a long moment. Then, reluctantly, he nodded and let her hand go. He squared his shoulders and faced Tatiana once more. "You have my gratitude, Captain," he said, sliding back into Common.

Tatiana nodded. "I understand how valuable Eriuman gratitude can be. Thank you. I will see your sister safely delivered."

His gaze dropped to the deck. She saw him take a deep breath. Then he straightened, spun on his heel and stalked off the Bridge, heading for the main passage that would take him back down to the cargo hold. Again, he did not so much as glance at Ruh as he passed him.

Bellona watched the passage long after her brother could no longer be seen. Tatiana moved back around to her bench and started launch prep as the woman stood transfixed.

The preparations forced Ruh back to his own desk next to Tatiana—he had graduated from the Comms terminal years ago.

It was only after the ship shuddered under the impact of opening the cargo hold doors in a vacuum and the little skiff dropped out of the *Hathaway's* belly and back down to the planet's atmosphere that Max's sister moved. "If I could have some warm water and access to an assembler, I would be grateful." Her accent in Common was thick and laborious, although that was to be expected. Eriuman women were sheltered, insular creatures who rarely emerged from their homebases. In her eighty-plus years, Tatiana had seen a dozen or more Eriuman officers and fighters—all of them male. Bellona was the first Eriuman woman she had met.

Tatiana might have supposed that Bellona's formal words, the polite tone and the woman's stiff posture indicated she was barely moved by her brother's departure. As Ruh took over the launch sequence while Tatiana arranged for one of the passenger cabins to be opened up for her, Bellona didn't move, not even to wipe the twin rivulets of tears marking her clear, high cheeks.

* * * * *

AS SOON AS THEY WERE safely back in null-space, Ruh asked stiffly to speak to Tatiana in her office. As Tatiana had reason to speak to him in private, too, she acquiesced and made her way back to the cramped little room, with Ruh following. She moved stiffly. She had been on her feet for too long. Lately, her hips and knees protested if she didn't rest properly and she was nearly always tired.

As Ruh shut the door behind them, Tatiana spoke to the computer. "Yellow light, forty percent."

The dim lights came up, illuminating the tiny desk and the two chairs in front of it. The terminal screen was still hanging in the air, showing an image of her great granddaughter, Zita, on her fifth birthday, a sunshiny girl with her grandfather's eyes. Tatiana rarely bothered to put the screen away. The flow of documents and details never ended. Whoever had claimed that being captain of their own freeship was romantic had never stopped to consider the role was essentially the same as the head of any large corporation. It ate up her life and her time.

Not that she would ever consider giving it up. At

least…not quite yet. Which was probably why Ruh was glaring at her from under his thick brows again. The question about his succession to captain had been delayed and put off for years and years. He was a patient man—or Tatiana would have never considered giving him the job—yet she knew his patience was wearing thin.

As she sat with a soft sigh of relief, he spoke. "She'll get us all killed." In the low light, his thick black hair glinted with blue highlights. Like Tatiana, Ruh was not going to go gray until his most senior years. Except she had bypassed gray and turned white almost overnight. It was still sometimes a novelty to look in the mirror and see the stranger looking back at her. She had fifteen years more than Ruh, though. He still had time.

"We're in null space already," Tatiana pointed out. "Straight to Cerce, no detours, then the deed is done and we'll no longer be obligated to an Eriuman."

"You mean, *I* will not be obligated, right?" he asked softly.

Tatiana punched at the desk controls, bringing up her in-box, while she tried to find something to say in response that had not already been said a dozen times already.

"You know who she is, don't you?" Ruh said.

"Maximillian Cardenas' sister?" Tatiana asked, with an innocent tone.

Ruh rolled his eyes. The epicanthic fold was deeper on his eyes than Tatiana had seen in anyone else in the family. In a way, he was a throwback to far older generations and sometimes his attitude was, too—his discomfort with Max and his sister's emotional parting was a good example. Now, Ruh was back to impatience, because the world was not aligning the way he would prefer.

"You're not the only one who has been studying the Eriumans and the Karassians, Tia," he said. "You insisted I learn all that crap and I did, because I thought it would please you. It means I know exactly who those two are. The Cardenas family is the senior family in the Scordinas clan. The Scordinii are one of the primary clans. Reynard Cardenas is the head of not just the Cardenas family, but all the clans. And we're stealing his daughter away!"

"You saw them both," Tatiana said. "They're afraid and they're in trouble. You think if Reynard Cardenas knew about that trouble, he would just sit back and let them run away? He doesn't know a thing, Ruh."

"Maybe he is the trouble," Ruh said darkly. "Have you thought of that?"

"If he was, then *both* of them would be sitting in the passenger cabins right now." Tatiana shook her head. "She is the one covered in blood. Besides, we are settling a debt that is long overdue. If this is what he wants in return for saving my entire family and everyone I hold dear, then I will make sure it happens."

Ruh shifted his feet, spreading them into the at-ease posture that intimidated everyone on the bridge except Tia. He might be a head taller than her, yet she could bring him down if she had to. The day she couldn't was the day she really did need to give up this desk. Unfortunately, that day was swiftly approaching.

"Is that why you have hung on for so long?" Ruh asked. "You didn't think I would honor the debt?"

"Of course that is not the reason. You *know* the reasons. We've been over them and over them." She waved her hand impatiently. "We can discuss this once we're back on Cerce. Now is not the time."

His full lips twisted. "There's always an excuse, isn't there?"

Tatiana clamped down on her own impatience. If she deplored the trait in Ruh, it was because she was as guilty as he of displaying it. She took a breath. Let it out. "I will settle on Cerce soon, Ruh. You're old enough and smart enough to do this job. You have learned a lot, in the last few years. You just have to give me a bit more time to complete the changes we are making."

"You're going to ram them down my throat whether I want them or not, aren't you?" He threw out his hand. "Taking everyone off the ship weakens the family. It divides us."

And now they were at the nub of it. "It protects us," Tatiana replied as evenly and calmly as she could. "If everyone who is not needed to fly the ship is living dirtside, then what happened to us four years ago can never happen again." She thought back to the moments when Maximilian Cardenas' ship had been overhead, in the perfect position to blow her entire family—roots, branches, leaves and all—out of existence. Only Max's empathy for family had stayed his hand.

Tatiana's utter helplessness that day had driven her to make changes that had caused more muttering and protests in the last four years than any other time before. Settling the majority of the family on Cerce had been the major change and the hardest one to put into practice. Everyone had been raised on board the *Hathaway*. Adapting to dirtside living had caused problems. Ruh was not the only one to speak negatively of the breaking of traditions and customs. Tatiana had been adamant, though. She never wanted to feel that sick-making weakness ever again.

The ship was no longer a family freeship. It was a corporate-owned and run business now. Tatiana held controlling interest, which she would give to Ruh when she stepped down.

"We're nearly there," Tatiana assured Ruh. "Settling everyone on Cerce was expensive. It drained our reserves. I don't want to hand the ship over to you with no operating capital."

"I think you just don't want to hand over the ship at all," Ruh said flatly.

"Not true."

"You want to live forever, on your precious bridge."

"Ruh!"

He crossed his arms once more. "Why do you like that Eriuman so much more than me?"

Tatiana sat back, her mouth dropping open. The soundless, formless confusion roiled in her mind. She sought to comprehend that her brother, a grown man and father, was jealous of a young foreigner she had known for a grand total of perhaps twenty minutes. "That is also not true," she said at last. It was a weak protest.

"He is the reason you have spent the last four years learning everything you could about Erium."

"*And* the Homogeny," she shot back. "For very good tactical reasons," she added. "We need to know and understand the enemy."

"We're *trading* with the blasted enemy!" he cried. "You just escorted the enemy's sister to our best berth!"

"Strategic contacts are vital," she countered. "Relationships win wars."

"Relationships *started* this one," Ruh reminded her bleakly. "The *Valerianus* would not have been in Karassian space if its bloody captain hadn't been so hot to seduce the last Karassian princess."

"No one knows what really happened to the *Valerianus*," Tatiana said. She sighed. "I'm not holding you back, Ruh. I know you think I am. I just want to have the ship in a good, strong position before I leave. That's all."

"We're supposed to be free staters," Ruh said. "We're supposed to stay out of their war. You've got us wrapped up tight in the middle of it."

She shook her head. "I stay informed. There's a difference."

"Then how do you explain the Eriuman woman in the cabin, two decks down?"

"You're being tiresome, Ruh. I've already explained

myself to you, which is more courtesy than I would extend to anyone else onboard."

"But—"

"No," she said sharply. "Enough is enough. Go work out your petty jealousy in the exercise suite. I won't dignify it any further."

He held still, staring at her, his eyes unblinking.

"Now, Ruh."

He dropped his arms, stalked to the door and slapped the controls. He didn't look back.

Tatiana let out a breath that shook. There was a hard tension in her chest and her gut roiled. Had Ruh hit issues she didn't know she had? No, it was ridiculous.

She was working to preserve the family, that was all. Just as Maximilian Cardenas had been doing.

Tatiana got back to work, for there was always plenty to do. Null space transitions were great for getting a lot of mundane tasks done, while they were cut off from everything. She dealt with crew issues, pay claims, promoted the cook, reviewed engineering reports and environmental reviews, put everyone on a cleaning rotation and scrubbed her own cabin, too. It was all good, hard work.

If Ruh was more argumentative than usual, she put it down to the tension of having the Eriuman woman on the ship. However, Bellona emerged from her cabin only to eat occasionally. She had printed herself a more practical outfit of trousers and shirt and a light jacket and a pair of the high leather boots spacers preferred. She was polite but remote when she spoke to the crew. From Tatiana's reading and study about Eriuman culture, she arrived at the conclusion that Eriuman women were docile, obedient and focused upon improving their appearances and domestic skills, both of which would net them a more advantageous marriage. Bellona was living up to her assessment.

Tatiana spoke to her only twice, the second time for a

few minutes in the dining room, while Bellona mechanically ate a small bowl of roast beef. Both conversations left Tatiana puzzled by the woman. She offered absolutely no hints about her personality. She shared nothing. She was also just as polite and opaque with the rest of the crew, even with Yammicka, the well-built engineer with broad shoulders and twinkling blue eyes, who could charm stars into going nova.

Tatiana knew the stillness and lack of engagement couldn't last. Bellona would have to react to her circumstances sooner or later. She was Eriuman and she was human, too. It would catch up with her. Tatiana briefly considered forcing the issue. Having the human equivalent of an unexploded bomb on board was bad for morale.

Then, two days after Bellona had come aboard, the engines cut out without warning, dropping the *Hathaway* into normal space, right in front of a Karassian cruiser.

* * * * *

"What happened to the engines?" Tatiana yelled as she hurried as fast as she could onto the bridge. "Ruh, talk to me! Navigator, locate us!"

Yammicka looked up from the dashboard he was leaning over. "There's nothing wrong with the engines! We dropped out of null-space for no reason we can find."

"Then get us the hell back *into* null space!" Tatiana cried. "Before the Karassian cruiser lines its sights up on us."

"It will take three minutes to recalculate the jump," Ruh said.

"We *can't* jump," Yammicka replied, his normally melodious voice high with strain. "The navigation AI is rebooting."

Tatiana looked at him, floored. "Rebooting?" she repeated. She couldn't remember the last time a computer had spontaneously reset itself. "Do we even know where we are?" She looked at the navigator, Jaime, who was bent over the table.

Jaime shook her head. Her eyes were huge.

"There's a Karassian cruiser on our port bow," Ruh said. "I think it's safe to assume we're in Homogeny territory."

Yammicka and Jaime looked at her, waiting for directions. There were only the four of them on the bridge. Everyone else would be in the engine rooms, fighting to get the null-space engines up and running once more.

And the navigation computer.

Tatiana swallowed. "Run," she said and her voice came out in a high squeak. "Turn and run, as fast as we can."

Ruh leapt to the helm controls and swiped his hand over the board. "The cruiser is faster than we are," he said. "It's the *Ralston* out there," he added and prodded the go button.

The *Hathaway* lurched. Tatiana braced herself, gripping the edge of the navigation table.

Only, the expected inertial drag didn't happen, even though the maneuvering engines screamed at full throttle. The sharp stench of ozone sizzled in her nostrils, grabbing the back of her throat. The decking vibrated under her boots.

Yammicka hung his head.

"Tractor beam," Ruh said bitterly and slapped the helm dashboard once more.

The engines cut out.

The silence was almost total, broken only by the ticking and beeping of dozens of alerts and notifications on everyone's dashboards.

Bellona emerged from the main corridor, almost running. She looked around wildly, her thick, shining coils of hair bouncing off her shoulders. "What's happening?"

Tatiana pointed at her. "Yammicka, get her out of here.

Hide her, somewhere the Karassians won't think to look."

"You're not going to dress her up as a waiter?" Ruh asked dryly, referring to the way they had hidden their Karassian passenger in plain sight of the Eriuman boarding party, four years ago.

"That won't work with Karassians," Tatiana said, as Yammicka grabbed Bellona's arm. "Appearance is everything to them. You think they'll fail to notice *her*?"

Bellona pulled back against Yammicka's grip. "Karassians?" she repeated.

Overhead, a coupling gripped the hull with a muffled magnetic kiss. They weren't going to even try to use a door.

Tatiana waved Bellona away. There was no time to deal with jittery passengers. Yammicka hauled her toward the corridor.

"You said it was the *Ralston*?" Tatiana asked Ruh.

"The passive scanners extrapolated the size. They only have one ship that big. It can't be anything else."

The *Ralston*. The Karassian flagship. "Yishmeray is the captain," she added.

"The monster?" Jaime breathed. Her face paled.

"He's enhanced," Ruh corrected.

"A cyborg," Jaime said.

"Biobot," Ruh qualified.

"No, he's a biocomp," Tatiana said firmly.

"A human computer," Jaime concluded, for all the crew had taken rudimentary studies on the structures and cultures of the two enemies.

Overhead, the hissing and vibrations from the Karassians cutting through grew louder. Tatiana looked up at the ceiling. The inner lining was showing signs of blistering, the white extruded sealant bulging. Tatiana stepped back out of the way and waved everyone else out of the danger zone, too.

"We have to do something," Jaime whispered.

"What would you suggest?" Tatiana asked her. Calmness spread through her. "Even if we had the power to pull away from the tractor, they've broken through the hull, now. We'll be exposed."

Jaime swallowed and Tatiana gave her the best smile she could manage. "We may still talk our way out of this."

"Only…if they just wanted to talk, wouldn't they have used one of their screens?" Jaime said, voicing what had been bothering Tatiana since the grapple had attached itself to the hull. She had listened to other captains tell their adventure stories for years, across dinner tables and bars, in ships' dining halls and dirt-side family rooms and gatherings too numerous to mention. Even the most aggressive Karassian vessels paused long enough to establish malfeasance before opening fire, yet Yishmeray had asked no questions before sawing his way down to them.

Tatiana looked at Ruh. He was watching the ceiling just as everyone else was. He looked as scared as everyone else, too.

The lining gave way with a pop and a fizzle of chemicals that filled the bridge with thick, eye-watering smoke and an acrid stench that made them all cough and wave their hands to clear the air.

Tatiana leaned over and hit the controls on her dashboard to fire up the air scrubbers to maximum. The scrubbers hummed into action, sending cold fingers of air over them. She shivered in response.

Figures in dark brown uniforms dropped down through the widening hole in the ceiling, to land heavily then straighten up. Every soldier carried a ghostmaker. As they spread into a circle to shield the others as they landed, they looked around the bridge with their bland, brown-eyed gazes, sizing up Tatiana's crew.

Tatiana's heart was working hard, despite her calm. Eriumans were ruthless about maintaining the law of their lands and the territories they annexed. They were disciplined and efficient, yet they could be reasoned with. Not so the Karassians. *Especially* Yishmeray, if what she had heard about him had not been exaggerated for the sake of the story.

When a dozen soldiers were fanned out around the bridge, ten of them moved forward simultaneously, as if a silent command had been given. The muzzles of their ghostmakers swung back and forth as they poured through the bulkhead doors into the main corridor and moved deeper into the *Hathaway*.

The last two soldiers separated, bracketing the opening, above.

Then a third dropped down to the floor, landing so heavily the deck trembled. Slowly, he stood up from his crouch.

He towered over the other two soldiers. He wore a sleeveless shirt to accommodate the silvery hawsers running from his massive upper arms to connect with the thick forearms. Augmentation tendons. Where they emerged from his arms, the pale Karassian flesh mounded around the thick metal tendons like lips. Inside the open neck of the shirt, more metal tendons ran from the outer edges of his collar bones, up to his neck.

The rest of his body was hidden beneath the oversized brown uniform. His hands were also metal and made to look like human hands, but thicker and, Tatiana presumed, stronger. A heavy forehead jutted over the giant's narrowed eyes. He had blond stubble for hair, so short it was barely there. He looked around the bridge, taking in everyone, scowling.

"Hell and damnation…" Tatiana breathed.

"Hayes!" came a call through the ragged, steaming hole.

The monster—for this really was a monster of a man—reached up into the guts of the hole. He lowered down another man in a Karassian captain's uniform, holding him by his upper arm as if he was moving a toddler around. He put the captain down. The captain brushed himself off and tugged his tunic back into place, then patted Hayes' arm in casual thanks.

The smoke was clearing now and Tatiana could see Yishmeray clearly. He had white blond hair, cropped short and Karassian brown eyes so light they were almost colorless. His face was gaunt, all angles and planes. His neck was heavyset above the brown collar.

Deeper inside the ship, Tatiana could hear Yishmeray's soldiers thudding along the decking, shouts from her crew and the sound of carnage—things breaking, being toppled and busted open.

She met Yishmeray's gaze.

He tilted his head, the chin lifting. His gaze shifted from her, just to one side. He paused. It was as if he had been suddenly struck by a thought. Then his gaze moved back to her. "Captain Tatiana Wang," he said slowly, with a thick accent that was far uglier than the Eriuman one.

"Captain Yishmeray," she acknowledged.

Unexpectedly, he smiled. The expression was bright, cheerful and unnerving. "I almost forgot," he said, digging into a pocket on his tunic. He pulled out a metal stick the size of his finger and waggled it, so the silvered casing flashed in the deck lights. "Payment, where payment is due." He tossed the stick at Ruh.

Ruh caught the credit stick in one hand. It was an auto-response to having something thrown at him. His gaze was on Yishmeray. Horror built in his face, then his eyes moved to Tatiana. His hand lowered.

Tatiana curled her hands up into tight fists. "No," she breathed. "Ruh…not you."

Ruh lowered his head.

"You hated Max that much?" Tatiana whispered. "We jumped to null space so quickly…did you even pause for breath before selling us out?"

Yishmeray was full of good cheer. "Oh, Ruh has been helping me for far longer than this little venture, my dear captain. He has been quite the assistant for years now."

Tatiana flinched as the truth settled into her bones. She looked at Ruh again. Her brother was watching her now. She could see the anger in him, lifting his shoulders, making his eyes narrow.

"Why?" she demanded.

"You said it yourself," Ruh said. "Tactical alliances will save the family. Except you kept them all to yourself. I made one for *me*, instead." He shrugged.

"With *Yishmeray*?" Her voice rose.

Yishmeray chuckled. "Oh, Ruh didn't know it was me, exactly. That's why I thought I would come along on this jaunt. Introduce myself and sort things out. It's hard to resist the lure when a high-value Eriuman is dangled in front of one."

A scream rang out. Ghostmaker bolts sounded. Then more shouting and the sound of running feet.

"Sounds as though they've found the Eriuman," Yishmeray said happily. "Hayes, go and settle it, will you?" he added in Karassian Prime.

Tatiana backed out of the way as the monster plodded across the bridge, his boots landing heavily. He ducked into the corridor and moved down it.

Her movement put Tatiana right next to her command dashboard. She didn't look at it or draw attention to it.

Yishmeray glanced around the smoking bridge, with all the red alert lights flashing silently. "It is very small," he said, his tone distant. "Given your reputation, Wang, I expected a much bigger ship." He turned, taking in every angle, although he stayed behind the two sentries, who hadn't moved or lowered their weapons.

Ruh had moved, though. Tatiana didn't know when he had, yet he was much closer to the helm dashboard now than he had been a few seconds ago. He was within reaching distance.

They both jumped when another scream rang out.

"Ah...there we go," Yishmeray said, sounding jolly once more.

It had not been a woman making that sound, though. Tatiana fought to keep her face still and blank, while she ran through the range of possible actions.

From the corridor came the sound of more struggling. Grunts and panting. Shuffling footsteps.

Hayes appeared. He held Bellona by the arm, almost carrying her along, while she struggled and pummeled at him with her fists. He dropped her to the decking in front of Yishmeray and brushed off his huge hands with slow movements.

Bellona propped herself up on the deck and rubbed her arm, scowling.

"What have we here?" Yishmeray asked curiously. He looked at Ruh. "High profile?" he asked, sounding doubtful.

Lie! Tatiana urged her brother, even though he couldn't hear her. *Don't tell him who she is!*

Ruh licked his lips, looking from Bellona to Yishmeray.

"I hope you didn't bring me all the way out here for nothing, Ruh," Yishmeray added, all the sunniness evaporating from his tone.

Ruh wouldn't meet Tatiana's eyes. Her heart sank.

"She's the Cardenas' daughter," Ruh said.

Yishmeray lifted his chin and looked away again, for a second or two. His eyes grew unfocused.

Tatiana realized he was communing with the vast computer intelligence built into his body. She didn't know in detail how it worked with his kind, but did know the computer implants enhanced a biocomp's mental functions and increased the speed of thought and the clarity of those thoughts, as well as giving the biocomp vastly larger memory capacity, with perfect recall.

"Bellona Cardenas Scordina de Deluca," Yishmeray intoned. He squatted down to match her level. "How delightful. Ruh, I take back all my doubts about you. This truly *is* a prize." He lifted the coiled locks of hair on her shoulders, holding it up for inspection, held between his fingers. "The daughter of the Cardenas himself. Oh, how much *fun* we can have with you!" His voice took on a crooning quality, dropping in tone. His eyes glittered. "The usual questioning at first, I'm afraid. Boring, yet necessary. Then…mmm, the possibilities are endless. How much would your naval officers do to get you back? How much would Reynard *make* them do, to have you returned, I wonder?"

Bellona wrenched her head to one side, yanking her hair out of his grip. She looked him in the eye. "I have no intention of being anyone's leverage," she said, her voice low and clear.

Tatiana's heart leapt. This was the first time she had seen anything like animation in the woman's face.

Bellona threw her head forward, smacking Yishmeray in the face with the top of her forehead. Tatiana heard the sodden crunch of bones and winced.

Yishmeray rolled backward, his hands to his nose, with a muffled shout of pain, as Hayes lurched forward, reaching for Bellona with his metal hands.

Tatiana used the distraction. She leaned over the side of the dashboard and called up the emergency menu and activated the items she wanted.

All the red alert lights extinguished. From farther back in the ship, the shouting and fighting ceased.

Ruh jerked, as the alert command flashed across the helm dashboard, then disappeared. The dashboard grew silent and black. He looked at Tatiana, his gaze questioning.

She held still for three heartbeats, watching him, then

relaxed when Ruh said nothing about what she had just done to Yishmeray or the two guards standing over him.

Yishmeray cried out again, the sound thick and gurgling, pulling Tatiana's attention back to him. He was sprawled on the deck, now. It looked as though Bellona had rolled right over the top of him. She was crouched behind his head, with her back to Hayes, who was still reaching for her. He had plenty of reach, with those long arms. The augmentation tendons stretched with them.

Bellona leaned forward and propped herself up with her hands planted on the deck. She turned and sighted over her shoulder, then kicked out with her booted foot. Tatiana wanted to shout an alarm. Nothing human could overcome Hayes' grip. If she let him get his hands on her, even her ankle, she was done.

The powerful blow landed, instead, on the inside of Haye's knee and slammed it sideways.

Hayes howled, his hands dropping to his wounded knee.

Yishmeray reached for Bellona, scrambling backward. He was temporarily blinded by the pain and his hands flailed, seeking her.

Bellona's leg was still raised, from the blow to Hayes' knee. She brought her knee down sharply. The point of her knee rammed into Yishmeray's middle, right over the diaphragm.

Yishmeray grunted, the air bellowing out of him with a wheezy sound. His hands dropped and he laid squirming, trying to breathe. His face turned deep red as his mouth worked silently. His eyes bulged. His nose ran blood, which dripped to either side of his face.

The two sentries on either side of Yishmeray had reacted instantly, only Bellona was moving too fast. As they turned their ghostmakers to point at Bellona, she thrust herself upward on the leg that had been folded beneath her. The other foot swung forward, driving her toward the closest guard. She took the step then kicked up.

Her boot caught underneath the two-handed ghostmaker, snapped it out of the guard's hands and up into the air in a high arc that came close to the roof. Bellona ignored the gun. Instead, she grabbed the guard by his now-reaching hands and tugged him forward.

He staggered past her, straightening up with a surprised expression. That was when the other guard fired at Bellona. The bolt seared through the first guard's chest and he dropped to the floor, his surprise frozen on his face.

Bellona threw herself forward and down. Her palms slapped the deck once more. She flipped herself around in a tight, hard arc.

Hayes was just recovering from her kick, his hands reaching out for her again. Her legs swung under his extending arms. She kicked at his other knee. This time, there was no lateral movement to the kick. The impetus was all backward, in the direction the knee couldn't move.

Hayes grunted again, bending over to grab his leg.

Bellona used the kick as leverage to pushed herself off Hayes' knee and complete the arc. Her legs scythed around, taking out the second guard's calves. He gave a shout of surprise as he fell to the deck on his side.

Bellona landed with her boots on the deck, one hand beneath her, propping her up. She reached up with the other and the ghostmaker that had been tumbling down from the high arc into which she had kicked it landed in her waiting hand.

She pulled in her knees, dropping into another low crouch and spun around, aiming the ghostmaker. She fired at Hayes.

Hayes' hands shot up in front of him. The dazzling white bolt bounced harmlessly off the back of his hands with a sour whine and sizzle and struck the back wall of the bridge.

Hayes tore the ghostmaker out of Bellona's hands, gripped both ends of it and broke it in two. Sparks sprayed everywhere from the gizzards of the weapon, landing on Yishmeray, who threw up his hands to protect his face, and Bellona, who scrambled backward.

Hayes ignored the sparks that landed on him. He tossed the broken weapon aside, staring at Bellona.

She threw herself at him, diving low over the top of Yishmeray, who was breathing in gasping, pained pants.

Hayes bent to meet her with his hands.

Bellona slid underneath them and through Hayes' legs. She scrambled to her feet and ran.

There was another soldier at the mouth of the corridor, guarding it. She dealt with him by driving her shoulder into his stomach, caught the ghostmaker as he dropped it and ran down the corridor.

Hayes straightened up and looked at Yishmeray.

"You would let a girl beat you?" Yishmeray panted out, in Karassian. His voice was bubbly with the blood that would be running down the back of his throat. Then, "Get her!"

Hayes turned and lumbered down the corridor, almost stepping on the downed guard. The giant staggered, his weakened knees barely holding him up. His metal hands slapped the walls, scraping them with a sour whine. He was using the walls as crutches to hold himself up.

Yishmeray was still prone. He dropped his head back to the decking as Hayes disappeared, his breathing labored. The other two guards were still.

Tatiana caught Ruh's eye. She jerked her head toward the door. He had seen the flash command to evacuate. Right now, her crew were evading the Karassians, not engaging. They would be piling into life pods and ejecting, streaming off the *Hathaway*. Tatiana wanted Ruh to join them. That was the way they had figured it, shortly after the Eriumans had boarded the *Hathaway*, four years ago. Ruh had been impatient with the disaster planning and all the other changes she had introduced. He was still young enough to think that the worse that could happen always happened to other people, not him.

Ruh looked at her now and shook his head.

Tatiana crossed the deck. "It doesn't *matter* how we reached this point," she told him urgently. "What matters is that it has happened. Go. Now. While you have the chance."

Ruh closed his eyes for a second. His shoulders slumped.

Tatiana could almost feel his guilt. "You made a mistake, that is all," she said quickly and quietly. "Max was someone we could take at his word. Yishmeray is…not." She didn't say aloud that Yishmeray was a typical Karassian, completely unpredictable, volatile and crazy. It was impossible to get cozy with Karassians.

Ruh nodded. She could see there was a lot more he would say, if they'd had time. "What about you?" he whispered.

"Last off. Captain's privilege." She pushed him toward the corridor. "Go."

"You're not going anywhere," Yishmeray said, from behind them. His voice was strained and weak.

Tatiana looked over her shoulder. Yishmeray was still lying down, only now he had the second, still-whole ghostmaker in his hands. The ghostmaker wobbled, but not enough to ruin his aim.

Her heart sank. She had forgotten the other gun.

Ruh sighed.

Yishmeray rolled onto one side, holding the ghostmaker out with his upper hand. He pushed slowly to his knees, then lurched to his feet. His face was paler than it had been before, where it was not red with blood he had smeared when he had wiped it away. His eyes were bloodshot. The sleeve of his uniform was thick with the blood he had swiped from his face. It all gave him a maniacal appearance that was, in Tatiana's opinion, a more truthful expression of his real self.

There was a tramp of many feet on the decking along the corridor, which ran like a spine down the center of the ship.

Yishmeray gripped the ghostmaker firmly, his gaze shifting to the corridor entrance.

Six of Yishmeray's men surrounded Hayes, as they moved back onto the bridge. Hayes dragged Bellona by one arm. She slid across the decking, writhing and kicking, which was why the six soldiers were ranged around Hayes with ghostmakers trained on her.

When Hayes halted, Bellona curled up, her knees to her chest, then kicked at his arm, her boot slamming into his elbow. His metal hand loosened its grip and she flipped herself onto her hands and knees, ready to push herself to her feet.

"Oh, for the love of…!" Yishmeray began. "Sit on her! Hold her down. Move it!"

The six soldiers standing around her slung their guns and piled on top of her, each of them aiming for a limb, their combined weight designed to drop her back onto the decking.

"Keep her still," Yishmeray said. "I've sent for a chemical cuff. That will hold her."

Tatiana realized his biocomp implants let him communicate directly with his ship.

The six Karassians were struggling to keep Bellona still. She hadn't given up. She squirmed and fought, using her teeth and her knees and her head. The men reared and slipped, jostling each other as they battled to pin her down.

From the hole in the ceiling, a capsule elevator lowered, with a Karassian wearing green medical stripes on his collar standing inside the steel frame. When the elevator cage touched the deck floor, he stepped off, brandishing a power injector in one hand and a medical kit in the other. The chemical restraint Yishmeray had called for had arrived.

Bellona spotted the medic from the corner of her eye and her struggles intensified. She surged up, shaking off the two men trying to hold down her shoulders, and reached for the man gripping her calf and trying to sit on it. She shot her hand past his arm and grabbed the hilt of a knife hanging on his belt, then yanked it out and slashed at the man's arm as she fell back.

The soldier yelped and jumped backward, scrambling to his feet.

Blood fountained from Bellona's thigh, through the tiny rent she had made in her trousers.

Tatiana stared at the red stream, as the hot, coppery smell reached her, too shocked to move.

Yishmeray swore. "Clamp it! Someone get a grip on the damn thing. Medic, get in there and seal the artery!"

The medic, his brown eyes wide and shocked, moved toward Bellona. She was still struggling and tossing the soldiers around with her writhing. The medic hesitated.

"Give me that," Yishmeray said and yanked the injector from his hand. Yishmeray crouched down by Bellona's head, leaned his hand and most of his bodyweight on her forehead and slapped the business end of the injector up against the base of her throat. It clicked and hissed, delivering the drug.

He tossed the injector away. It skittered across the deck, to stop up against the comms dashboard. "Get in there," he told the medic. "Know that if she dies, you go out the same airlock her body does."

The medic swallowed and bent over Bellona. Her struggles were weakening and slowing. The drug and the loss of blood would both defeat her.

The medic opened the kit and settled on his knees next to her hip, mindless of the blood pooling around her. "Let me access the wound," he said, picking up a derma-iron.

The soldier who had clamped his hand over the wound lifted it away. Blood geysered once more.

"Hold *behind* the cut," the medic said crisply. "Reduce the blood pressure so I can seal the wound." He spoke with authority for this was his area of expertise. He sounded confident.

Tatiana let out a heavy breath, exhaling slowly. She had done nothing—she had not even used the moment of distraction to leave the bridge and find if there were any escape pods left for her and Ruh to use. She had been so astonished by Bellona's relentless struggling against overwhelming odds.

Yishmeray stepped back away from the tight knot of bodies surrounding Bellona's still figure and around Hayes where he stood looking down at her with a puzzled expression twisting his heavy brow, the powerful hands hanging by his sides. The Karassian captain did a long, slow swivel, taking in the whole bridge, surveying the damage.

The dead screens on every wall were blank, sightless eyes. The lights which had been cut by the Karassian excavation through the roof cast odd shadows, while other lights flickered, their power diminishing. Of the twelve soldiers who had dropped through the roof, only six remained on their feet and two of them were limping. Only four carried their ghostmakers. Four of them had not returned from searching the interior of the *Hathaway*.

Hayes was favoring one leg, hopping awkwardly on the other as his balance shifted. He had scrapes on his arms and face that would later turn into spectacular bruises and his uniform was scorched and torn. No wonder he looked bewildered. It would be rare for him to experience injuries, Tatiana guessed.

The medic got to his feet, closing the kit, his job done. His dark brown uniform looked black from the knees down, where he had knelt in the blood. The bright red arterial blood had spread farther out, smeared by boots and knees.

In the center of the bloody pool lay Bellona Cardenas. Her eyes were closed, her arms out flung. She was still. The soldiers moved away from her, watching her warily, as if she might spring back to ferocious life at any second.

Now she was motionless, the slightness of her body compared to Hayes and even the male soldiers she had defeated was more obvious.

There was no sound on the bridge. The computers and AIs that made an almost constant humming, clicking buzz in the background, were dead. The ship hung from the Karassian clamps, inert and lifeless.

Tatiana found herself staring at Bellona, awe holding her still. She had never suspected Eriuman women were so…unyielding. On her own, Bellona had very nearly brought an entire squad to its knees, then had unflinchingly taken the last step when defeat was certain.

Yishmeray moved up to the edge of the thick, blackening puddle, looking down at Bellona, too.

"Are all Eriumans like that?" Tatiana asked, thinking of Max and his empathy for Tatiana's family. Had he been a rare exception?

"No, they're not," Yishmeray said, his voice distant. He was thinking. For a biocomp to slow down his speech while he thought things through meant he had to be thinking very hard indeed.

Yishmeray lifted his head and looked at Tatiana. The manic happiness had gone. In its place was a grave, contemplative expression. "This one is something special," he said, his tone still measured. He looked around the ship. "Someone who can do this…" Then he shook his head. "We will never hold her as she is, with her free will in place. There is a way around that, though. A way to restrain her and use her at the same time."

"I thought you were going to use her as leverage?"

"Not anymore," Yishmeray said, glancing around the wreck of the bridge once more. "That would be a waste of talent."

Tatiana shivered. "She would no more consent to working with you than she consented to being your hostage."

Yishmeray grinned, the disturbing merriment returning to his eyes. "Oh, we won't need her consent." His tone was confident. "Hayes, take her up to the med bay."

Yishmeray moved back out of the way as Hayes stepped up to where Bellona rested. The giant bent and picked up her shoulders. The glossy black coils of hair trailed through the blood as he lifted her. Hayes' right hand slipped. He looked at it, turning it, as if the weakness had surprised him. Then he bent even more, scooped up Bellona around the middle with his left arm and lifted her. She hung from his arm, her hands and hair and feet trailing, red droplets running from them. Hayes carried her as if he was holding a carrybag. He squelched over to the elevator cage and stepped onto the platform. Hydraulics hissed and the base of the cage scraped against the floor as his weight settled on it.

Then it rose slowly up through the hole in the roof, taking Bellona and Hayes into the guts of the Karassian ship.

Tatiana looked back at Yishmeray. He had his chin cocked up in the air, the distant look in his eyes. He was thinking, again. Processing far more quickly than Tatiana could and deciding what had to happen next.

Then he met her gaze.

"You're not taking us as prisoners, are you?" she said.

"If the woman was to be a simple hostage, then I would be happy for the Eriumans to know we have her. I might even have sent you as messenger boy. Now, though..." He shook his head.

Tatiana sighed, letting out the last of her anger and resentment. Time was too short to hold on to those emotions. They blinded and confused the truth, which only now she could see clearly.

She nodded.

Yishmeray didn't speak again. He moved over to the elevator, which had descended and was waiting, and stepped onto it. The medic joined him on the platform, which used up all the space.

The elevator rose once more. As it lifted up, the remaining soldiers gripped the bottom of the platform and let it haul them up through the great rift.

Tatiana grabbed Ruh's hand and pulled him toward the corridor. As soon as they were in the wide passageway, she turned and slapped her hand on the door controls. The heavy bulkhead doors rumbled closed and air hissed as they sealed.

"What are you doing?" Ruh demanded.

"The *Ralston* is going to detach, which will broach the seal they have on the hole they made. The bridge will be exposed to vacuum."

As she spoke, the ship shuddered under their feet. On the other side of the door, she heard the cyclonic howl of air rushing out through the hole. She put her hand against the door, regret touching her.

"We have to find a pod," Ruh said urgently.

"There will be none," Tatiana assured him. "You know the standing orders. Use the pods and jettison the empties, so the enemy cannot use them. When we didn't arrive right behind them, they would have followed those orders."

Ruh licked his lips. He was sweating. "Then we have to seal the hole. Limp back to Ceres. Find the pods and get them back."

Tatiana shook her head. "We have about a minute,

Ruh. That's all." In her mind, she could see the *Ralston* moving over them, coming around in a big, gentle curve, to head back to where the *Hathaway* drifted uselessly in space, the mouth of the *Ralston's* forward smart gun turning red as it reached critical.

She picked up Ruh's hand. "All these years, I thought I had learned so much about the Eriumans. The Karassians, too. It ends up I know very little about them after all."

Ruh's eyes filled with tears. "What does it matter, what you learned?" he asked harshly.

"It matters in this moment more than any other moment of my life," Tatiana told him. "You watched Max and Bellona as I did, Ruh. I saw your face. You wanted to dismiss their display as rude and emotional. Yet they understood and now I do, too."

He wiped his eyes with the back of his hand. "Understood what?" he whispered.

"It's about *family*. They're the same everywhere. They're the glue that holds everything together."

Ruh choked and closed his eyes. "You were right," he said brokenly. "To get the family off the ship. Now they're safe—from this that I have brought upon us."

"You were trying to be me," she said gently. "You were trying to do what you thought was right. I didn't see that and I'm sorry, Ruh."

As the seconds ticked away in her mind, she reached out and hugged him. Tall as he was, he still clung to her, taking comfort from her touch, as he never had before.

For the last few moments left, Tatiana was content.

The Indigo Reports Book 2.0

Suns Eclipsed

CAMERON COOPER

About *Suns Eclipsed*

It's not an impossible mission. It's an insane one.

Ten people. Eriumans, Karassians, Free-Staters. None of them armed with anything more lethal than a single repaired and unreliable one-handed ghostmaker and a handful of bladed weapons, all of them with mental instabilities from years of brain wipes and memory manipulations. Worse, Bellona Cardenas is uncertain of their loyalties. Ten fragile people to infiltrate the most secure facility in the Republic.

So begins *Suns Eclipsed,* the second book in the Indigo Reports space opera science fiction series by award-winning SF author Cameron Cooper.

Praise for *Suns Eclipsed*

God I love these characters, a motley crew of fantastic beings.

I am loving this series! The characters are complex and interesting while the action has lots of unexpected twists and turns.

Not since I first read Anne McCaffrey's Ship Series have I enjoyed a SF series more.

Cameron again proves Robert Heinlein's words "Specialization is for insects", as he delights us with his storytelling talent across multiple genres.

The action never really stops as the reader is pulled through the book at breakneck speed!

I am continually amazed at the imagination of this author.

By the time I finished the book all I kept thinking was Nooooooooooooooooo! I have to wait till the next book comes out to be able to continue reading the story.

A motley crew, an impossible mission and a wack-a-doodle, vengeful mother combine to give us another exciting story.

A kick-ass adventure set in space, with a scope as beautiful as the stars in the galaxies. I thoroughly enjoyed it!

This is meatier, brain engaging and seat-belt fastening.

Fast-paced adventure full of futuristic elements, all too human emotions and developments you will never see coming.

A wonderful follow up to the previous book in this series. The story just keeps getting better and better.

Chapter One

Criselda I, Criselda, Eriuman Republic

CRISELDA WAS ONLY THE SECONDARY system in the Dejulii portfolio. No one had bothered to give the one livable world a unique name. Everyone called it Criselda, rarely bothering with the "I" that should come after the name. The equatorial band barely supported human crops, forcing the natives to depend upon imports. The Criseldans were more fertile than their land. They turned trading into big business. Criselda housed the Republic's supply depots, equipping every ship in the Erium Navy. Security around the city-sized depots was backed up by the might of the military cruisers and destroyers constantly overhead. No one in their right minds would consider breaking in to the depots.

Which was why Bellona and her people were busy doing just that.

Khalil, Sang and Bellona crouched in deep moonshadows cast by the nearest building to the depot perimeter, a good twenty-five meters away from the fence. The night was dark, the moon a sliver and the shadows and pockets obscure. The depot, though, was ablaze with lights.

"This is complete madness," Khalil said as they watched guards armed with ghostmakers cross-examine a civilian at the single, highly secure gate of the primary Criselda supply depot.

"I heard you the first time." Bellona worked to keep her voice even.

Sang lowered the trinoculars. "Laser nets across every open space, with barely half-a-meter between each strand.

If we step into them without the tags the guards have implanted, we'll be detected." He looked at her. "There are easier targets than this."

"None of the others have the stash of ghostmakers Criselda does," Bellona replied. "And that is the last time I will say it. Clear?"

No one replied. Khalil merely nodded.

Bellona looked over her shoulder. The long alley they had crept through to reach this point was now empty, with only fused dirt and tendrils of early morning fog wreathing around the base of the buildings. Even the air she breathed tasted damp and lifeless. Nothing grew here without constant encouragement.

"Are the others in place?" Bellona asked.

Sang paused, his gaze focusing inward as he discussed everyone's status with Connie, the private yacht. Connie hung in the outer atmosphere overhead, coordinating communications.

Khalil wouldn't look Bellona in the eye. He kept his back to the corner and peered around it, even though Sang had the trinoculars.

"This was your idea," Bellona reminded Khalil.

"I said you needed a coup, something to make the free worlds take notice. Breaking into Criselda is grander than what I had in mind." He glanced at her and away. "We're here now."

"Your fatalist streak is showing," Sang said, his tone chiding.

"Says the android, the ultimate in fatalism," Khalil replied.

"The others?" Bellona asked Sang.

He nodded, his pale, freckled face grave. "Hayes says the door he was expecting is not there."

Khalil frowned. "It was on the blueprints."

"It's not there now," Sang replied. "The blueprints are wrong. Hayes says no door is not a problem."

"Is he going to bust his way through the wall?" Khalil asked, the frown still in place. "This is supposed to be soft -shoe."

"Connie wasn't certain. She didn't understand what Hayes said he would do. She said something about 'peeling'."

Bellona looked at the walls of the structure on the other side of the perimeter. They were made of pre-fabricated panels of steel sheets sandwiching a layer of insulation, bolted to plasticrete stub walls. Someone had added a lackluster color to the steel a long time ago. The average human would not be able to broach the seams with their bare fingers. Hayes was not average.

"If he says he can get in, leave him to do it," Bellona said.

Neither Sang nor Khalil spoke. The silence was telling. They didn't agree with her. They had not agreed at any point in the operation, yet they were cooperating anyway. It was an isolating sensation, one she didn't like. She would have to get used to it, she realized.

Since the news of Xenia's defection from the Karassian Homogeny to take up the Free Worlds cause, Bellona had resisted the epithets heaped upon the Karassian puppet she had once been. Traitor, the Karassians called her, while her native Eriuman Republicans decried her utter lack of character. The Free Worlds were confused by her. All of them were convinced she was crazy.

Perhaps she had absorbed some of those beliefs—especially the last one—and that was now why she was trying to break into the most secure armaments depot in the known worlds.

"What's happening at the gate?" she asked.

"It looks like they're taking the woman into the barracks," Sang said. He lowered the trinoculars. "For questioning, I presume. Perhaps we should take advantage of their distraction? There are nearly a dozen of them escorting her."

"We stick to the plan," Bellona said as firmly as she could, hiding her reaction to the idea of being surrounded by guards and being forced to go anywhere. That had been her life for far too long. She spared a moment to pity the woman.

* * * * *

THE WOMAN WAS PETITE AND MIGHT have been beautiful, Ravi Dejulian decided, if her face was clear of fear and her eyes not red from crying. She stumbled along the fused earth footpath, sniveling and looking around fearfully at her escort.

He didn't let down his guard, even though the others had decided that she was as helpless and intriguing as she appeared. Kerran, she said her name was. She was looking for the man who had told her he would come back for her. He was a Dejulian who she had met on Kalay. He'd told her he worked here and when she had discovered her pregnancy, she had come to find him…

It might even be true, Ravi decided. She was curvaceous and very pleasing to the eye. Eriuman, of course. Ravi suspected she was classless, without a clan to claim as her own. Perhaps she was a forgotten by-blow of some clansman's dalliance, or she came from a family so poor in antecedents no clan wanted them. That would make her even more eager to snare a genuine Dejulii…if she was truthful about the man who had professed he loved her.

Ravi's supervisor, Corvi, had clearly decided the distraught woman was lying, his thick lips curling up into a disdainful sneer as he examined her from head to toe tip. So many recruits rotated through the depot; the disgraced, the untried, the injured and recovering. This woman's man may have come and gone in the time it had taken her to learn of her pregnancy and find passage here. There were not many civilian ships travelling to Criselda.

As the woman sniffed and hiccupped and wiped at her wet cheeks, Corvi pushed at her shoulder, encouraging her to move a little faster. She threw her raised hand out for balance, unconsciously gripping the nearest support, Gregory, who had been walking a little too close. Gregory was tall enough that the view inside the woman's dress would be interesting from his angle.

As Gregory supported her while she found her footing once more, he ran his hands over her. Ravi hid his own grimace. He knew what was to come.

They passed into the barracks. The deployment station was at the front, living quarters behind, while the passage into the depot itself was attached to the back. The rain on Criselda was mildly acidic, which was why nothing grew here and why the passage was roofed and sealed.

The deployment station was also used as a clerical office for the administration of the guard roster. On rare occasions when interrogation was needed, the empty office at the end of the short row was used.

Corvi marched the woman into the office. She spun to look behind her when the door lock activated with a quiet snick of the bolts, but couldn't see beyond the men crowding in behind her, pushing up close.

Ravi moved into the corner. He was in no hurry and someone had to listen for the approach of other guards, who might interfere and spoil the fun.

Corvi faced the woman and slid his hand down to the fastenings of his pants. "Hold her," he said shortly.

The woman gave a little cry, trying to back away from him. She rammed into the wall of men, who gripped her arms. She struggled. When her feet slid out from under her, she dangled from their hands, writhing.

Ravi knew it didn't matter what she did. It wouldn't stop them.

Corvi closed in, feral delight on his thick features, as the men lifted her and stripped her clothing away. One clamped a hand over her mouth, holding in the screams. Her struggles intensified. She got one hand free and beat and scratched at whatever she could reach.

"Luscious…" one of them said, his voice hoarse, as her curves were revealed.

"Hold her still," Corvi demanded. He gripped her hips and forced himself into her, grunting at the pleasure of it. Then he rode her, in hard, grinding jerks.

The woman grew still, defeated, letting him do what he wanted. She stopped screaming. Her gaze grew steady, watching Corvi's red face as he took her.

Gregory, who was as skinny as he was tall, coughed and thumped his chest to clear it. He didn't like being indoors. His lungs were as weak as the rest of him. His eyes glowed as he held the woman's knee and the high boot to one side and watched the action.

Corvi's motions accelerated and his grip tightened.

The guard's hand fell away from the woman's mouth, for he was too interested in watching. She didn't try to scream again. Her gaze remained on Corvi. "You can do better than that, surely?" Her tone was dry.

Corvi jerked his head up to look at her face for the first time. It was a quick glance. He looked back down at her body and what he was doing to her. He was in the deep end, committed to finishing this. Lust had control.

The woman sighed and arched, inviting him deeper. "Yes. Mmm."

Ravi's mouth fell open. It looked almost as though she was taking Corvi. There was no reluctance in her face, or resistance in her body.

One of the others holding her—one of the new ones whom Ravi didn't know yet—coughed as well. It was the same booming, wheezing hack that Gregory had made. The man gripped his chest, the deep gouge on the back of his hand from the woman's nails oozing blood. He tried to clear his throat.

Azat, who really liked these "sessions", sank to his knees with a tired sigh, letting her go. His head hung as he breathed in shallow wheezes.

Corvi didn't seem to notice. Neither did the woman. She was riding him now, wriggling with pleasure. Her eyes were nearly closed and she was making little panting, mewling sounds.

Gregory let go of her knee as a series of back-bending coughs exploded from him. He propped himself on his knees, whooping and panting.

The woman merely wrapped her boot around Corvi's hips, encouraging him.

Corvi climaxed with a grunt. As he came, so did she, with a hitch of her breath and a smile. "For your pleasure," she said, staring at Corvi.

He stiffened, his eyes snapping open, wider than seemed possible. His body froze. The red in his face deepened and tremors ran through him.

"Sir?" Ravi whispered.

The other six were all coughing or breathing hard. They had lost interest in the woman or anything other than their next breath. They let her go. The woman merely propped herself up with one hand and unwound her leg from around Corvi, who stood in frozen shock, still.

Her movements dislodged him from her body. His member emerged bloody and…bitten.

The woman rose to her feet. She was naked except for the tall boots yet Ravi barely noticed her curves. A long lock of wavy hair hung over her face and might have seemed gamine, except for the hard look in her eyes and the sharp line of her jaw. She lifted her chin to look down at him.

Ravi swallowed.

"Give me your pass," she said.

"My…my pass?" The only pass he could think of was the chip they had implanted under his collar bone when he had started here. It let them move about the compound without tripping off the always-on security grid.

The woman smiled. It was a warm, inviting expression that made him shudder. She reached for the collar of his tunic and pulled it open, revealing the flesh of his upper chest and shoulder. Her fingertips slid over the skin beneath his collarbone. His heart thudded. Terror rippled through him.

"This pass," she cooed.

Her fingernail dug into his flesh and tore a channel through it.

* * * * *

SANG SPUN ON HIS HEEL, THE trinoculars dropping. "The net just went down," he said sharply.

"Tell the others," Bellona said.

Khalil leaned back against the wall and let out a heavy breath. "Hero did it."

"Just as she said she would," Bellona reminded him, for Hero's role in the affair had been one of his greatest objections. "The others will all come through, too."

Khalil straightened and checked his aging ghostmaker one more time. "Time for us to do the same."

Bellona looked at Sang. He nodded.

"Go," she said.

Sang's gaze grew unfocused as he told Connie to pass the go command along.

The three of them sprinted for the small, man-sized door in the side of the big, rambling building. There was a knee-high fence marking the perimeter, that carried signs every ten meters declaring the lethalness of the security layers beyond. They hurdled the sharp edges of the fence and kept going.

Shouts and the soft thud of running boots sounded from the official gate, a hundred meters away. Bellona risked a glance over her shoulder and saw many of the guards heading for the barracks building at a run. They were confident the net would alert them if anyone penetrated the perimeter and didn't bother to look around. The fuss inside the barracks was taking all their attention.

She ran.

Sang slapped his palm against the doorplate. "Connie!" he said sharply.

The door clicked to unlocked. Khalil shouldered his way inside and Bellona and Sang followed.

It was not dark inside. Artificial sunlight was diverted and diffused across the hectares of open area. The light was needed, for there were small mountains everywhere, in regimented rows. The mountains were made of stacks of crates—metal, plasteel, carbon-compressed and good old-fashioned wood pulp. Each mountain was made of identical containers. No mountain resembled any other.

"Where?" Bellona said.

Sang hesitated, then pointed toward the middle. "Row thirty-nine, Section gamma-epsilon."

"Does Hayes have the truck yet?" Bellona asked as they ran again, heading for the nearest cross-corridor.

"Working on it," Sang called out.

PEELING BACK THE PREFABRICATED SECTION of the wall had been no challenge at all. Once Hayes had burrowed through the hole he'd made and stood inside the depot, he relaxed. Security measures were less stringent inside, Sang had assured everyone.

It turned out that relaxing was a mistake.

He oriented himself. He was at the back of the building, where the forgotten and abandoned supplies sat gathering dust. Well, not much dust, for the air scrubbers were efficient. Yet, despite the bright daylight, the lack of dust and the ordered arrangement of the mounds of containers, an air of neglect hung over the area. While there was no direct evidence, it felt to him as if people rarely came back here.

Hayes recalled Bellona's careful instructions and the blueprint she had blown up large on a screen taking up most of the sidewall of the *Alyard's* bridge. The bay where the trucks were kept was to his right.

He craned his head to peer over the tops of the rows and could see a walled off section against the far side. That would be the bay.

Hayes didn't run toward it. He had long legs and if he walked fast enough, it covered ground almost as quickly. As he went, he checked off Bellona's instructions in his mind. It was important that nothing went wrong, this first time working on his own without a handler to give constant directions. Xenia—*Bellona*—would lose trust in him if he messed up.

Not that he could remember a handler and being directed. Xenia, though, assured him he had worked that way—a dog on a long leash. *Bellona,* he corrected himself. She was no longer Xenia, the graceful dancer he had known in Ledan. But then, she hadn't been a real dancer, any more than he had been a real gardener. Bellona had slipped her leash, just as Hayes had. Just as they all had.

His instructions were detailed yet missed a vital point. They didn't warn him the corridor he was striding down had a break in it, where another corridor intersected. He stepped out into the middle of the intersection before he realized it was there. He was exposed.

Two Eriumans were leading an empty truck down the length of the cross-corridor. They were three rows away. The one with the truck's control panel in his hand dropped his mouth open in surprise.

The other was a faster thinker and his hands were free, too. He reached for the one-handed ghostmaker on his hip, brought it up and fired as Hayes reached the other side of the wide intersection.

The bolt skimmed past the small of Hayes' back. He felt the heat of it sizzle through his shirt.

No alarms, Bellona had insisted. *No surprises, no full scale security responses. In and out, very quietly. We don't have the numbers to engage.*

For a second, Hayes dithered. If he went after the two guards, then he would be delaying the others, for they were waiting on him to bring a truck to the location of the stash.

Preventing the guards from raising the alarm seemed like the higher priority, though. He could bring the truck afterward, although he worried that the delay may cause further problems.

He realized he was waiting for someone to tell him what to do. If he stayed here waiting, then he would disappoint Bellona in yet another way, so he pushed himself back around the corner into the wide cross-corridor and ran at the guards, fending off the ghostmaker bolts with his hands.

The two guards backed up a step, looking almost comically surprised. Postings to the Criselda depots were considered the soft assignments. Inside the warehouse itself, the guards were even more relaxed. Now they were slow to react.

Their shoddy reactions gave Hayes the time he needed to skirt the low truck, grab them both by the neck and knock their heads together. They slithered to the ground.

Hayes bent and picked up the small ghostmaker, pleased, for now he had a gun. It would offset his delay. Bellona had given the only two guns they had to Khalil and Thecla, leaving everyone else to use their preferred weapons or bare hands. That had stressed Retha more than usual, because he was smaller and weaker than all of them and guns were his first choice. Bellona had not given him a ghostmaker because the only two weapons they had found on the *Alyard*, after the Karassians had sabotaged the weapons store, had been two old, large guns that had been tossed in a bin.

Thecla had decided the guns were for spare parts, which was unlikely, for the Karassians did not preserve or recycle anything. Thecla, though, had fixed the guns. She was useful that way. Both of them were two-handed weapons, which Retha didn't use, so Thecla had got one and Bellona's Khalil, the other.

Hayes tried to check the weapon's charge, but his left hand didn't move. It twitched by his side, while he could feel something grinding in his upper arm. The external tendon whined, as if it was overloaded.

Hayes looked down at his hand where it hung uselessly. It was a strange sensation, to lift his hand and not have it obey.

Peeling back the outer layer of the wall must have damaged the hand in some way. Thecla would be able to diagnose the problem, later. For now, Bellona was waiting on him and he had delayed long enough. He could use the two-handed gun just fine in his right hand.

He put the gun on the top of the truck's casing and punched the green button on the controls the guard had been kind enough to leave sitting on the top, too.

The truck floated forward and Hayes nudged it toward the intersection with his knees.

A small delay, a little issue. Nothing critical. Bellona would still approve.

* * * * *

RETHA STOOD BACK WHILE VANG dealt with the guard they had come across on the darker perimeter of the warehouse. He was bothered by the lack of weapons. With a ghostmaker, Retha could have taken out the guard from the last corner they had turned, even the heavier ghostmaker they had found on the ship.

Vang, though, didn't need weapons. He *preferred* using his bare hands, as he was now. His pale brown eyes under the thatch of white-blond hair were dreamy and peaceful as he throttled the guard.

Not for the first time, Retha marveled at the strength of Vang's hands. Vang wasn't much taller than Retha. Which meant he was short, too. His shoulders and arms, though, were astonishingly powerful.

Retha was glad that, for reasons he still didn't understand, Vang chose not to use that strength against him. With Retha, Vang was extraordinarily kind and gentle.

Which was why Vang was taking out the guard right now. He had pushed Retha back out of the way and leapt on the taller man with a grunt of pleasure.

The guard finally dropped and Vang picked up the ghostmaker and turned it over, examining it. He held it out to Retha. "Big guns for big idiots. It works, though. Want it?" His eyes were peace-filled and calm. That wouldn't last long.

"It's better than nothing," Retha admitted, taking the ghostmaker. "Noisy, though."

"Use it as a club, then. Save your hands." Vang grinned and patted his cheek. "C'mon, we're running behind. Where are we?" He looked around.

The criss-crossing aisles between the stacks of equipment were too similar to each other and disorienting because of it. Retha had used the big, square cargo bay in the roof to orient himself, instead. "That way," he said, pointing down the wider corridor.

"Maybe we'll find a guard with a couple of one-handers for you," Vang said as they hurried down the corridor.

Retha snorted. "These guards are the dregs and outcasts of the Eriuman navy. The bigger the gun, the better."

"They're not really discriminating, are they?" Vang remarked, with a grin, for that was a word he had only recently explained to Retha. Now he used it all the time, as if it was a private joke between them. Which it was, really. Retha didn't care about the others rolling their eyes when they heard it, especially Thecla, who didn't have much time for anything, which was odd, because she was—had been—Karassian once, just as Vang had been.

* * * * *

THE GHOSTMAKER BOLT TOOK THECLA square in the chest, knocking her onto her back. She landed heavily, the ghostmaker tumbling out of her hand to slither across the floor.

Fontana bent and picked it up, then fired at the two guards hiding behind a squared-off pile of upper-atmosphere mines. The gun fizzed and sparked. No bolts.

"Shit," he breathed and tossed it away.

Aideen, hunched next to him behind their mound, drew in a ragged breath. "We're pinned down, aren't we?" Her grip on the staff tightened, turning her fine knuckles whiter than they normally were.

"Not if we don't let them raise the alert," Fontana assured her. He curled his gloved hands into fists and moved past her, toward the other corridor, breaking into a fast sprint. Around the corner, down to the nearest break in the hillocks, then through the tiny squeeze, back to this corridor.

He came up behind the two guards, who were busy watching Thecla where she lay. Probably, they were watching to make sure she didn't get back up. As if anyone got up after taking a ghostmaker bolt to the center of the chest.

Idiots.

He tapped the nearest one on the shoulder. The man turned, a comic look of surprise on his face.

Fontana punched him, not holding back anything. The guard dropped with a satisfying thud.

The front man was bringing his ghostmaker around. No problems. Fontana got his fist through the closing space between the ghostmaker and the man's jaw.

The second guard folded up over the top of the first.

Fontana picked up the two ghostmakers. They were this year's model, of course. Thecla would know better which particular model they were, because that was Thecla's thing. They just looked new and shiny to Fontana.

"As long as they work," he muttered to himself and stepped back into the corridor they had been travelling down before being interrupted. He bent over Thecla and rested one of the ghostmakers against his lower leg.

Thecla groaned. "Son of a bitch…" she muttered and pressed her hand to the scorched section of her shirt and the bloody patch of flesh beneath. "That hurts."

"You're lucky. It would have killed anyone else," Fontana pointed out.

Aideen hurried to them. "We're late," she hissed anxiously. Her face was paler than usual and her gaze skittered about ceaselessly.

"Deep breath," Fontana told her.

"They had time to warn someone," she added. "Maybe it was a silent alarm. Maybe the rest of the guards are on their way here."

Fontana held his hand out to Thecla. "Up and at 'em," he told her. Then, to Aideen. "There's no alarm. The gutless pair were watching Thecla, worried she might come back and club them for shooting her."

Thecla gripped his wrist and climbed to her feet, moving slowly.

"Are you okay?" Aideen asked her, speaking quickly. "Are you too hurt to go on?"

Thecla pulled together the front of the ruined shirt. "I'm fine," she said shortly.

When Aideen bit her lip, Thecla relented a little. "They hit me directly over the chest plate. Burnt skin is the worst of it." She tested her arms, the external tendons stretching and retracting smoothly. "See?"

Aideen and Thecla had both been Karassians, once, yet apart from the blonde hair and brown eyes they shared, they had very little else in common. Aideen was as tall as Fontana and slender enough to be called bony. Thecla was six inches shorter, ten kilos heavier and all of it was muscle. And tattoos. And enhancements.

Fontana picked up the ghostmaker leaning against his calf and held it out to Thecla. "Aideen, you keep your staff. You're better with it."

Aideen nodded.

Thecla patted the firewheels strapped to her belt. "I'm better with these."

"Not if you're more than a meter away," Fontana told her.

She scowled and took the gun.

Fontana looked up at the roof, where the dark rectangle that marked the cargo bay was visible. "We're nearly there. I want to be first. Come on."

Chapter Two

Criselda I, Criselda, Eriuman Republic

THERE WAS A SINGLE GUARD PATROLLING the corridor where the ghostmakers and personal grenades Bellona wanted were stashed. Hero mentally shrugged. A single man was never a problem.

She stepped into the corridor and strolled toward him, letting the combat jacket she had shrugged into before leaving the barracks swing open. She was still naked underneath, because the rushed fools had torn her clothing into shreds. Naked didn't bother her, but it was cool in the warehouse. Cool became uncomfortable in bare skin.

The guard turned to spot her when he heard her boots on the fused earth surface. As expected, he froze, his lips parting. Hero never got sick of watching someone's intelligence drain, while the lizard brain took over. She often wondered if it would *ever* fail to work this way.

She smiled as she got closer. "Honey, you look bored," she crooned.

He frowned, scrambling to put it together. "Who…are you?"

Hero reached up and rested her palm against his cheek. He sucked in a breath, startled. She leaned close. "I'm your worst nightmare," she whispered. She slid her hand from his cheek, her fingertips stroking his flesh. As she lifted her hand away, she let the nail of her index finger scratch across the skin. The pressure was enough to activate the toxin gland.

The guard flinched a little, but his hormones were raging. He completely failed to recognize he would soon be dead. He stood with confusion fighting hope, trying to figure out what was going on.

A ghostmaker bolt took out the back of his head, making Hero jump a little. She had been concentrating on watching arousal flare in the guard's eyes, waiting for the moment when he recognized just how fucked he really was.

She pouted as the guard dropped soundlessly to the floor and looked up as Khalil strode toward her, the ghostmaker swinging from his hand. "You *spoiled* it."

Khalil just shook his head. Bellona and the android were right behind him. The android was checking pallet numbers.

"These two," he said, pointing at the smallest two in the aisle.

Khalil looked at the two pallets, then up and around the corridor. "That can't be right."

Movement behind them made Hero sway around him to spot the newcomers. Thecla, Aideen and Fontana, a scowl on his face. He was a good-looking man for a free stater—or would be, if he ever stopped being angry. She didn't bother wondering what had him upset now. Everything pissed him off. His constant anger would make it interesting to pull him into a dark corner, except he had other priorities and wouldn't tolerate even a quick encounter.

Thecla was bleeding. She'd taken one to the chest plate. Lucky her. It could have been her head, like the guard at Hero's toes. She sighed. The fun was almost over, alas.

Sang looked from one pallet to the other, frowning. "I've checked three times. These are the ones we were told about."

Khalil was counting. "There are only fifteen crates on this one."

"There were supposed to be *fifty* ghostmakers," Bellona said. "Was another ship supplied since we got the data?"

As she spoke, Vang and Retha turned the corner and ran up to where they were. Retha had unbent enough to carry a two-hander. Vang looked happy…and *strong*. He was freakishly powerful and completely not interested in her. Hero had tried. Vang had no time for anyone but Retha.

Sang shook his head. "No, no shipments. Nothing. The records still say fifty."

Bellona looked around and over her shoulder. She was beautiful in the way the Eriuman primary clans were all blessed with—perfectly smooth, coffee-colored skin, full lips, black eyes and glossy hair, a figure molded by a fighter's muscles. Plus, she was strong. Not just woman-strong, but gutsy, courageous and driven. It made Bellona more than beautiful. It made her sexy to her bones, although Hero didn't for a moment entertain the idea of approaching her. Khalil would kill her for trying, if Bellona didn't.

"Three minutes since we entered. Too long. Where's Hayes? We need that truck," Bellona muttered.

"We're going to take the stuff, anyway?" Khalil asked.

"No choice. We must arm ourselves. We still need to make a statement, too."

"If the records say there are fifty, then that's what they're going to say you made off with," Fontana pointed out. "It'll still sound big."

"Twelve boxes of personal mines," Aideen said, glancing at the second pallet, then going back to watching anything that moved. Hero didn't see her pause to count them, but she was freaky in that way. In all ways, she was strange. Counting and numbers were her weird-*good* thing.

"Here's Hayes and the truck," Retha said quietly, nodding down the corridor.

Hero glanced over her shoulder. The big giant was lumbering down the corridor, directing the midget truck with his thighs, the two-hander ghostmaker clutched in his big right hand. He looked embarrassed about arriving last.

"Transfer the guns over to the mine pallet," Bellona said. "They're lighter. Move it," she added, her tone urgent. She put her knife away and bent to pick up one of the crates. Moving quickly, so did the other eight.

As they combined the contents of the two pallets onto one, Hayes fumbled with moving the truck into position to hitch the pallet controls. He was only using one hand. The other hung uselessly by his side.

Hero bumped him aside with her hip. She tried, at least. Hayes was a solid wall and didn't move.

"Let me at it," she told him. "You're useless."

Hayes glanced at Bellona, who wasn't paying any attention. He nodded and stepped aside. His face was red.

Hero studied the controls, then moved the truck into position with the manual guidance ball. She completed the hitch and the pallet quivered and lifted a hand-span off the ground. The others completed stacking it and Bellona nodded at her. "Know where to go?"

Hero looked up at the roof, where the square cargo door was showing as a dark shadow. "Yeah."

"Fast as you can, then," Bellona said.

Hero got the truck moving. "Fast" was relative. She could still outpace the thing at full speed. Just one truck, though, could haul a pallet loaded to the roofline with heavy armaments. They were slow but mighty.

The others trod alongside the pallet, watching for guards, as she threaded the truck through the maze to the center of the room. The lift plate was down and the truck slid over the lip. The lift guided it until the pallet was in the center, then the truck unhitched itself, trundled off the plate and down the corridor. It would return itself to the truck bay.

"Sang," Bellona said sharply, as they all stepped onto

the plate beside the weapons.

Sang was frowning, peering down at his feet. Then he looked up overhead. "There's a problem."

"Just one?" Fontana asked dryly, hitching his ghostmaker.

"Connie is…panicked." Sang winced. "More than that."

"Forget Connie," Khalil said. "We'll cuddle her later. Get the lift moving, Sang. You're connected. We are not."

Sang kept his head up. The plate moved with a soft sigh and lifted away from the floor. There was a clank of machinery beneath it. The plate rose swiftly and smoothly.

Overhead the doors cracked open and slide apart. Moonless sky and stars appeared.

"Where is the pickup ship?" Thecla demanded, rounding on Sang suspiciously.

"That's the problem," Sang said. "No one is there."

As he spoke, alarms sounded in the warehouse. Dozens of them. Lights flashed. Hero turned to look over at the south end of the warehouse, where the doors to the barracks corridor were located. A dozen or more guards ran through them, ghostmakers in hand.

They hadn't been spotted yet, but they soon would be and they were completely exposed on the platform.

"Down," Bellona said, crouching down low. Apparently, she thought the same.

Everyone ducked down, hugging the pallet and crates.

Someone shouted. A ghostmaker bolt streaked over them, searing the air itself. Then another. They both came nowhere near anyone. The angle was too tight. It wouldn't have been if they'd still been standing.

"Sang, where is the damn ship?" Bellona demanded.

"Gone," Sang said quietly, still looking up at the stars. "Only Connie remains. She is afraid. The military ships are moving. The alarm has gone up. The *Titus* is gone."

"They're panicking over a conveyor leaving?" Khalil asked, frowning.

Fontana swore. "It was a cruiser. Arany's people destroyed it," he said heavily. "Then they fucked off. No wonder the alarm went up."

Thecla scowled. "They *left* us here?"

"How are we going to get back to the *Alyard*?" Aideen asked, her voice rising. Fontana touched her arm, to calm her.

"There's Connie," Sang said with the same remote voice. He seemed to be oblivious to the bolts crackling over them and streaking against the edge of the platform with crackles and sparks.

"Tell her to get down here at once," Bellona said.

"She's already half-way down," Sang said. "As soon as the others opened fire upon the *Titus,* she began her descent." He pointed. "There."

The platform was almost level with the roof landing pad now. The guards below were cut off, although there would be more pouring onto the roof any moment. Yet Hero couldn't help looking up into the sky where Sang was pointing. There was a streak of white there, like a slow-moving shooting star.

"That's her?" she asked.

"Yes," Sang confirmed.

Everyone holding a ghostmaker had fanned out around the pallet, protecting it, looking for the first sight of more guards.

"That's too fast," Bellona said. "She'll burn up."

"She is controlling the descent," Sang said calmly.

"Barely," Fontana decided. "Heads up!" He fired off a bolt, which lit up the night air. There were few lights up here as no ship was expected. The bolt illuminated five guards in their purple uniforms. The guards ducked and rolled, splitting up and taking cover behind the environmental units.

"Idiots," Fontana said and re-aimed. The bolt went *through* the unit. The guard standing behind staggered to his feet and dropped.

"Fontana!" Aideen said sharply.

He got to his feet, staying hunched over and ran around the pallet to the other side, where everyone else was crouched, including Hero.

Hero looked up. The shooting star had become a distinct object now. Connie was hurtling down at them. From the little Hero knew of the AI, she was probably running to symbolically hide behind them. Helping them would not occur to the foolish ship. Connie's trajectory and rate of descent made Hero wonder if she was doing any thinking at all. It looked like a lethal drop.

At the last minute, the ship reversed engines.

The roar was deafening. Everyone winced. Aideen clapped her hands over her ears and screamed. Her scream was lost beneath the thunderous, beating noise. The eddies from the reversed engines beat at them. Even the guards lost interest in the pursuit and dived back into their hole.

With the engines throbbing, Connie hovered over them and lowered the cargo ramp.

Fontana, Khalil and Hayes got behind the floating pallet and pushed, straining to get it moving. The antigravs kept it in the air, only all that weight had to be overcome to create horizontal movement. Normal cargo ships would winch the pallet into the hold. Connie wasn't a normal cargo ship. The ship that *should* have been here did have a winch.

Vang pushed in between Khalil and Fontana, looking short and stumpy. He shoved at the pallet, the tendons in his neck standing out and his face turning red.

The pallet slid forward, then tilted to ride up the ramp.

"Everyone!" Bellona shouted.

They all got behind the pallet, searched for handholds

and pushed. The pallet glided up the ramp a bit at a time, then was finally over the lip.

"Close up, Connie!" Sang shouted.

The ramp lifted up, closing. At the same time, the luxury yacht rose from the landing pad and surged forward.

Everyone grabbed the crates, holding on.

As the ramp closed, the buffeting wind from their passage lessened, then stopped. The ramp sealed with a hiss.

"A bit rough, Connie," Thecla said.

"I'm so glad you're back!" Connie said, her young-sounding voice coming through the ship-wide speakers. "I was so frightened! They were burning ships!"

"I know," Bellona said soothingly. "Take us back to the *Alyard*, Connie. You'll have to dodge the sentry ships and mines. Tell the *Alyard* we're coming and to have the doors open."

"I have," Connie said, sounding calmer. "Three cruisers ahead. Their cannons are primed."

"Coming!" Khalil said, putting down the ghostmaker. He took off at a run, heading for the bridge.

Aideen paced in a tight little circle, her arms around her middle, whispering in a tight, soft voice.

"Fontana." Bellona nodded at her.

He moved over to Aideen and spoke quietly.

"Sang," Bellona said. "Bridge, please. We're going to have to blast our way out of here. Retha, would you mind running gun control?"

Retha nodded. Even with the clumsy self-defense weapons Connie had, he was still the best marksman among them.

Bellona, Sang and Retha headed for the bridge. As she passed Hero, Bellona snapped, "Hero, get some clothes on!"

"You're welcome!" Hero called after her.

Chapter Three

Cerce City, Cerce Prime, Cerce

By the time the *Alyard* dropped into normal space over Cerce, with Connie and the stash of ghostmakers and mines in its otherwise empty cargo holds, most of the remnants of Arany's fleet had already returned and departed again. Perhaps they did have genuinely urgent business elsewhere, as the governor elegantly explained.

"They're ducking Bellona," Fontana said dryly. "Cowards."

"It wasn't cowardly, taking on four cruisers and actually destroying one," Thecla pointed out, her tone just as dry. "None of their ships are advanced models. They're all old and held together by wishful thinking. Even Eriuman vessels out-gun them."

"Taking out *any* vessel and alerting them to our presence on the planet was not part of the plan," Khalil said. "Of course she is upset with them."

"Probably just as well they buggered off," Fontana said. "There's not enough ghostmakers to share, anyway."

There was one ship that still lingered. The *Yoxall's* captain, Natasa Garza, agreed to meet in the Governor's building in Cerce City.

Bellona asked Khalil and Sang to go with her, plus Fontana, who had once been a free-stater and looked normal, while Thecla and Hayes with their biobot implants, tended to unsettle the free-staters. She would have preferred to have a nominal Karassian among them, only Vang made *anyone* uneasy if they weren't used to him, while too many people bothered Aideen. Retha was a free-stater, but was as enclosed and challenged as the other two.

Connie dropped them down to the surface, chattering all the way about her friends on the *Alyard.* Sang had only recently released the AIs on the ship after vetting them one by one and adjusting their leashes. He let Connie interface with them and she was thrilled to have the company, even the dubious company of Karassians, who often puzzled her with their responses, for she did not fully understand the difference between artificial intelligence that was smart enough to learn and sentient computers, who were self-aware.

They landed on the roof of the Governor's village building and were shown to the drop shaft that lowered them down through the crop fields at the top level, the garden below and the markets beneath. The shopping mall level was busy. Heads still turned to look at them as they drifted downward. Shoppers whispered and murmured to each other. Bellona had been recognized.

The apartment blocks were separated by parks and gardens. One complete floor was a giant pool, dotted with tiny islands and floating docks, where swimmers could rest when they wanted. Divers at the deep end peered through the transparent walls at them as they descended. One of them waved. Bellona didn't wave back.

The governor's administration took up two whole floors of the vertical village, the lower one opening out onto the rest of the city. The sub-floors housed food processing levels, manufacturing and industries, with their environmental wastes absorbed and reprocessed by scrubbers and filters at the very bottom of the building.

As the transparent walls of the village absorbed sunlight and generated energy, the building was completely self-sufficient and had minimal impact upon the urban landscape.

They stepped out of the drop shaft on the second floor

and the guide took them to the Governor's office, threading though administration rooms and hushed waiting areas.

Governor Alberda greeted them personally, in the antechamber outside his office. "I heard you raided the Eriuman supply depot on Criselda," he said, with a warm smile. He was a robust man with a full head of gray hair and a full beard to match. His eyes twinkled. They were a nice dark brown, the eyes of a much younger man.

"The raid was not without its problems. Did the person who told you about it mention that?" Bellona asked.

"Captain Garza is in my office," Alberda said. "She barely escaped the venture. Shall we go in and discuss it?"

Bellona's gaze was caught by the view through the walls behind Alberda. It was late afternoon and the white sun was almost touching the horizon. It was a mild, crisp day here. She moved toward the window.

The first time Governor Alberda had invited Bellona to call on him, he had toured her through the village, pointing out its features like any proud parent. She had found this view from the window of his office more distracting. Cerce City, like most of Cerce itself and any of the free states she had so far visited, were completely unlike settled, sedate Cardenas and the Eriuman worlds.

There were no roads anywhere on Cerce. The city, which had begun life as a village, had not stepped outside the original footprint of the village. Instead, they had built upward, creating vertical villages that were self-sufficient, adjoined by parks, paths and numerous waterways featuring the black, still waters of Cerce. Flitters and the tiny little personal pods the Cercians called dragonflies were the only form of private transport. Everyone else walked, or if they needed to arrive more quickly, used the link pods—light rails lifted a foot above the grass, with two- or four-man pods attached to the links that anyone could step into anywhere along the routes.

The still, glittering canals and pools ran through a green landscape that looked almost untouched. Towers rose above them, some of them dripping with greenery, too. Almost buried among the bushes and tall grasses were individual buildings. Most of them were municipal in purpose. Toward the outskirts lay the single-family dwellings that made up the original village. They were being gradually replaced by vertical villages.

It was a peaceful scene that reminded Bellona, as it had the first time, that appearances were often deceiving. Cerce City was the principal city of Cerce. Cerce itself was a leader among equals. Most of the free states followed Cerce's lead. That made Governor Lin Alberda more than a simple governor. He held sway over the free states.

And now he was hosting Natasa Garza and her remnant captains.

Alberda stood politely to one side and Bellona gave him a stiff smile. "The view is spectacular."

"Far more interesting than the vast wastes of space, I'm sure," Alberda said, just as politely. He stepped back and waved her toward his office.

Natasa Garza was on her feet, waiting for them in the cavernous room. She was a petite woman who crackled energy. She kept her red-blonde hair in a short, precise cap. Her tall spacers' boots were strapped, matching the double strapped holster on her thigh that normally held her one-handed ghostmaker.

She had an air of competence and contained impatience that rarely shifted. Bellona found her to be a hard but realistic decision maker. She had been Ben Arany's right hand man for a decade. It had been sheer luck she had been dirtside elsewhere when Arany and his people had been destroyed by the Karassian city killer device on Shavistran.

Since then, Natasa had poured her considerable energy

into rounding up the few surviving ships and crews, trying to build a second fleet to replace Arany's. The destruction of Shavistran, though, had removed the bravest and smartest captains in three fury-filled minutes. Natasa was fighting the odds.

She was still a good person to have onside. Her fleet was small and ailing, yet it was more than Bellona could currently call her own. Bellona nodded at her.

Natasa threw out her hand. "You didn't say the Eriumans would hunt us down!"

Bellona paused from selecting a seat among the many comfortable ones arranged around the low table. "Good afternoon, Natasa," she said mildly.

"Natasa," Khalil said in acknowledgement.

Natasa nodded at him. "Khalil Ready."

There were three other people already seated and waiting. Two of them Bellona remembered from previous meetings. The men were both from Natasa's own ship, the *Yoxall*. They wore the typical spacers uniform—leather jacket, high boots, short hair and holsters for weapons, all of them currently empty. Nothing about their features hinted at their home worlds. The third person was a woman with long legs neatly crossed, golden hair severely fastened to the back of her head and lovely, rare, blue eyes. An ugly, thick red scar ran over the corner of her eye, drawing it down and marring her prettiness. She stared at Bellona, even when Bellona met her gaze. She did not look happy. None of Natasa's people did.

Alberda guided everyone to a chair each, his hand on shoulders and backs. He was a smooth host. Soon, everyone was seated. Alberda didn't prolong the matter by offering refreshments. He pressed his hands together. "I offer you the neutrality of my office to discuss this matter. There seems to be a difference of opinion."

"If you call running off and abandoning us on the surface of Criselda with a cache of stolen weapons on us as merely one's opinion, then yes," Bellona said. "We differ by a large degree."

"You said we wouldn't be spotted," Natasa said hotly.

"You weren't spotted," Sang said. "Not until you opened fire upon the *Titus*. What did you *think* they would do? Wave at you?"

Natasa scowled. "Our mission has always been the preservation of free space. Eriuman cruisers and destroyers are counter to that mission. You really think I would give up the opportunity to take one out, when it was sitting right there in front of me?"

"The raid on Criselda was not *your* mission," Bellona shot back.

Natasa drew in a breath that made her nostrils flare. "I don't take orders from you."

"You agreed to help with the raid. You didn't help."

The two men sitting behind Natasa stirred. The one with no chin and large teeth spoke up. "Does that mean you won't give us our share of the ghostmakers?"

Bellona hesitated, caution flooding her. "I can spare five of each."

"*Five*?" Natasa repeated. "Out of five hundred? What are you going to do with four hundred and ninety-five ghostmakers? There's maybe a dozen of your Ledanians. I have a dozen *ships* and they all have crews." Her mouth curled down. "I was warned not to trust you. I should have listened."

Khalil leaned forward. "Who told you not to trust her?" he asked, his tone quiet and reasonable. "Karassians? Eriumans?"

"I did," said the blue-eyed woman. Her voice was a pleasant contralto.

"Who are you?" Bellona demanded.

Natasa waved her hand impatiently. "Isabelle Lykke."

"A name means nothing," Sang said.

Lykke smiled. There was no warmth in it. "I am from

Alkeides." Her gaze came back to Bellona. "You've heard of the system. I know you have."

Bellona frowned. "I've heard the name."

Sang pressed his slender fingers against her forearm. It was a silent warning. "The Homogeny annexed Alkeides, two standards ago."

"It's called Felis now," Lykke said. Her blue eyes, so wonderfully different from the browns and blacks most humans had, glittered like hard jewels. "Thanks to you."

Bellona's guts tightened. "Me?"

"She means Xenia," Khalil said.

"Xenia was a Karassian construct," Sang said, his voice almost strident. "She was artificially imposed upon Bellona's memories. The Karassians are who you need to thank, Isabelle Lykke. Bellona had nothing to do with your worlds' misfortunes."

Lykke's gaze didn't shift away from Bellona. Bellona reconsidered the scar on her face. Its origins were obvious, now. "It was very bad for you and yours, then," she said.

"Bellona, no," Khalil said quickly. "Don't engage. Don't take this aboard. It wasn't you."

"What did Xenia do?" Bellona asked Lykke.

Lykke blinked. "You don't remember?" For the first time, something other than hostility showed. She was surprised.

"I just finished saying that," Sang said dryly.

"You fired the rockets," Lykke said. "I *watched* you do it."

Bellona breathed, striving for calm, while her heart slammed in her chest. "You actually saw me…fire rockets?"

Lykke licked her lips. "At the power plant. We were winning. Beating the Karassians back." Her mouth curled down in a moue of disgust. "They are useless fighters when they're not hiding behind the hulls of their ships.

On the ground, we were in control. Then you came along."

"*Xenia* came along," Sang corrected. "Bellona doesn't even look like Xenia."

"You deny it was your hands holding the knives, that cut up my comrades?" Lykke demanded.

Bellona swallowed. "I remember none of this." Sweat prickled on her back and under her arms.

Khalil's gaze was steady. There was a silent warning in his dark eyes. She couldn't read it, although she could guess what he was not saying. She was letting control of this meeting slip away from her. She had walked in here with the upper hand and indignation on her side. Now, she was the enemy in the room.

Fontana was watching her with pity in his eyes. He, at least, understood. So did Khalil. They had both been part of the Appurtenance Services Inc's Ledania program. Their memories had been minced, too.

It would be smarter to shift the subject. A positive outcome was not possible here, for she *had* been Xenia and was guilty of the acts Lykke had witnessed. "Why did I fire rockets, if I was already winning against your resistance?" she asked, instead.

Lykke shook her head. "You only won for a while. Only, you were one, against the dozens of us holding the line, preventing you from entering the Chairman's palace."

"Wait," Fontana said sharply. "You just said there were Karassian ground troops. Weren't they fighting with her?"

Lykke glanced at him. It was the merest flicker of her eyes. "They hung back."

"Of course they did," Fontana said, disgust rich in his voice. "Xenia had to go it alone and when your greater numbers began to tell, she used the rockets on your local power generator, instead?"

Lykke nodded. "The reactor was our only source of power. Without it, we were doomed. You knew that. You used it against us."

The pattern of a new settlement was the same for any world. There was always a Landing, a first village, that was more temporary camp than permanent location. Reactors were cheap and quick to assemble. They supplied power for the first hundred years or so of a world's history, while more permanent power sources from hydro and geothermal sources were developed. As soon as a world and its cities could build self-sustaining, dispersed sources that drew power from temperature variations and solar collector windows and walls, and could manufacture the power cells to store it, they could stop draining the natural resources.

It was a common development pattern that everyone understood. Xenia had used it against the Alkeidians.

Bellona could remember none of it.

"The fallout ruined the city," Lykke added. "It forced us to evacuate to the mountains, which are unscalable. The Chairman surrendered two days later. And now we are Felis." Her mouth turned down again.

"I'm sorry," Bellona said.

Khalil shook his head.

"You have to understand…it was not me who did those things to your people," Bellona added.

Lykke's expression didn't change. "Yet you ask us to trust you."

Natasa had her arms crossed, a scowl on her face. "Free-staters would be better off returning to their ship cities and staying there. We all prospered when we were just explorers looking to plant the next null-space marker."

Alberda stirred. "I happen to like living dirtside and if we descend into the old arguments, we will be here all day. Natasa, if your family had not settled on Atticus, they would all be dead next to Ben Arany. So would you."

"Ben wasn't on his ship when they used the city killer on him," Natasa said flatly.

Even Alberda could not direct the meeting, Bellona realized. There were too many hard feelings swirling the room. Most of them were built upon philosophical differences that had calcified into rich prejudices.

She sighed and got to her feet. "I think we should halt this now. No one is listening properly. Natasa, I can give you seven ghostmakers and a dozen mines. Take the offer, for it is a full half of the stash we took off Criselda. The information you gave us about the supplies was wrong."

Natasa's mouth opened. She didn't speak. Her brows rose high.

"Isabelle Lykke," Bellona added. "You have had a hard time of it lately. Considering me your enemy is a waste of time. Do your research. Look up a Karassian enterprise called Appurtenance Services Inc. Khalil will give you some resources to get you started if you ask nicely. That will point you toward who you can really blame."

"The Eriuman news feeds said you took five hundred ghostmakers!" Natasa protested.

"I should ask a Bureau puppet for reliable sources?" Lykke added.

"He's one of *them*, too," Natasa added, glancing at Fontana.

"Ledanian?" Lykke said, shocked.

Khalil sighed.

One of Alberda's aides hurried into the room and bent to murmur in his ear. He frowned.

Natasa nodded. "What I would like to know, Bellona Cardenas, is what gives you the right to speak on behalf of us? You're Eriuman and you fought for the Karassians. You sleep with the Bureau. Yet you say you are fighting to preserve the free worlds. And you ask us to trust you.

Why should we?"

Sang lurched to his feet, heated indignation making his jaw flex and his eyes to glitter. Natasa swiveled to confront him. "Android?" she enquired with a polite tone.

Alberda raised his hand. "A moment," he said mildly.

Everyone looked at him. Alberda indicated the aide. "The news just broke. Erium has annexed the binary system of Ashima and pronounced it a new Eriuman territory."

Bellona met Natasa's eyes. "You're running out of time. There is no one else who can do what I will do to hold the Homogeny and the Republic back. There is no one who has my resources." She waved toward Khalil, Sang and Fontana. "My understanding of the enemy is unique. So are my skills. *That* is why you should trust me."

Chapter Four

The former Karassian Homogeny Ship Alyard, Cerce Local Space

THE *ALYARD* WAS ONE OF THE newest ships in the Karassian fleet and the sterile, blinding white bridge reflected the greatest in Karassian technology and a complete lack of cohesive style. The Captain's quarters had echoed the blankness when Bellona had first commandeered them. The white, the shine and the lack of comfort had bothered her at a subconscious level. Her sleep suffered.

Sang had noticed. He temporarily reverted to his original programming as a family help-meet, hijacked the military compilers in the supply suite and reprogrammed a pair of them and adapted their assembly units for domestic products. Now Bellona's quarters were a throwback to traditional Eriuman standards of comfort. There were no screens. No hard white surfaces. Equipment did not talk back to her anymore. The multiple AIs and smart computers had been silenced. Fabric, patterns and color were the theme. Hushed, warm air and a comfortable bed. Plus, Khalil at night, when the door was closed.

It was a relief to walk back into her quarters after the meeting in Cerce City. Bellona knew she was escaping. She was helpless to stop the mental withdrawal after the heat and fury of the meeting, just as she had been incapable of not chasing after details about Xenia's exploits during the meeting. She wasn't quite licking her wounds, although everyone else on the *Alyard*—Hayes and Fontana and Thecla and the others—would believe she was.

She just needed time to regroup. That was all.

She waved Sang and Khalil into the suite, too, and shut

the door with a feeling of relief.

Sang moved over to the mini-compiler and asked for tea for three. Instead of the three white cups the compiler would have normally produced, a small samovar appeared, the spout steaming. Three bowls with Damokles porcelain patterning and colors formed next to the samovar. Sang had been tinkering again.

Bellona inhaled the minty scent of the tea. The tension between her shoulder blades lessened.

Khalil picked up her hand. The little lines that radiated from the corners of his eyes deepened as he smiled. "You should never apologize, my love."

"I'm sorry—" She grimaced.

"Oh you can apologize to *me* whenever you want," he replied. "I like your apologies."

"You're talking about Xenia, though."

Khalil's smile faded. "You're doing this because of what the Karassians did to you and to your friends in Ledan. This fight to preserve the free worlds…*that* is your apology. You must remember that and look every Isabella Lykke you come across in the eye."

"Good advice, as far as it goes. Not remembering anything Xenia did is becoming a problem, Khal. I don't know when I'm going to be sandbagged and can't brace for it."

"Ah, well." He shrugged.

She understood. A fact was an indisputable fact. This fact could not be changed. Deal with it.

Sang put the samovar and bowls on the low table next to the couches. "You should tell everyone about Arany's fleet withdrawing their support, before Fontana does."

"He will only tell Hayes and the others."

"The Ledanians?" Khalil asked, with a smile.

"And when did that become a name, by the way?"

"You'd rather be called the Apps?" Sang asked, also smiling. He held a bowl of tea out toward her. "Fontana will tell Hayes, Thecla, Vang, Retha, Aideen and Hero. Hero is intimate with nearly all the crewmembers from Abilio. The news about Natasa and her ships will travel."

Bellona shrugged. "It is what it is. Nothing I can say will change it. We're on our own again."

"Natasa didn't formally withdraw her support," Khalil pointed out. "She just rushed off to help with the new emergency."

"Help, how?" Bellona asked. "The annexation is complete. It was just an excuse to leave the room." She sighed and sipped the tea. "We're back to where we started."

Khalil took the bowl from her fingers. "You've forgotten about perception and appearance." He put the bowl on the table and drew her to him. "The known worlds think that Bellona's Ledanians infiltrated the secure depot in Erium and stole five hundred of the most advanced ghostmakers yet developed, plus a small mountain of personal mines. Natasa's fleet is still nominally aligned with you. She won't make any public announcements because she's smart and will wait to see how things play out. The known worlds still think you have seduced the old defenders of freedom to your side. That perception is no small thing. It is further along than where we began."

She rested her hand on his chest and felt his warmth spread through her fingers. "You're right," she said. "Only, Alberda knows the truth and that's unfortunate. He's the one we really need to seduce."

"As long as I don't have to kiss him," Sang said. "That beard of his is furry."

Khalil laughed and let her go. "One fight at a time." He returned the bowl to her hand. "Alberda is still measuring you. He won't let anyone make up his mind until he's good and ready. That's why he agreed to host the meeting."

"Then we need to find a way to make up his mind," Bellona said. "Alberda is the key."

"Winning over Natasa and her fleet will be part of that," Sang added. "So will distancing yourself from anything to do with Karassia and Erium." He handed Khalil the third bowl, as Khalil sank onto the divan.

She sat next to Khalil. "I don't know how much plainer I can make it that I want nothing to do with either Karassia or Erium. I am living in free space."

"In a Karassian ship," Sang pointed out.

Bellona sighed. "One step at a time," she repeated bleakly.

* * * * *

Menaii, Deluca Prime, Delucas System

THE CARDENAS FAMILY KEPT A small residence on Deluca Prime for the use of family members when they visited the capital, Menaii, which was not often. Since her marriage to Reynard Cardenas at fourteen, Iulia had chosen to use the Cardenas villa when she returned to Deluca to visit her family.

Now that Reynard was dead, it would be natural for her to stay in the Deluca family homebase. She had chosen, instead, to stay with Gaubert and his family in the Cardenas villa once more. She had even claimed the sleeping chamber she preferred.

Her choice had infuriated her little brother, Raine, who was now the head of the Deluca family. He was still young enough to treat her decision as an insult to him personally.

Gaubert did not care about the minor contretemps. "It'll all get sorted out at the assembly," he said dismissively.

Iulia knew Gaubert considered himself as the natural successor to the head chair at the clan table, taking over his elder brother's place. Once he was acclaimed head of the Scordinii, it would be natural for Iulia to choose to align herself with him rather than to revert to her familial affiliations. Gaubert believed she felt that way, too. She did not dispute his belief.

The first clan assembly since Reynard's death was being held on Deluca Prime, which was the real reason she had chosen the Cardenas villa. Everyone knew she was a Deluca. As a widow, she was free to return to her family, if she wanted to. Or she could remain with her husband's family.

Staying in the Deluca homebase would give a non-returnable signal to the clan that she had made a decision, while staying in the villa could be explained away as pure habit.

Of course, she could not attend the assembly. Gaubert had left the villa early that morning for the convention hall, alone. He had been dressed in Cardenas blue, an eerie echo of Reynard's clothing habits. Iulia presumed Gaubert's wardrobe choice had been deliberate. Subtlety was not one of Gaubert's stronger characteristics.

Iulia spent the day in her suite, which gave her an excuse to avoid his wife, Thora's, company. She knew before Wait announced it that Gaubert had returned home, for her brother-in-law's stomping and swearing could be heard across the villa.

She pinned up her hair, straightened up her plain red mourning wear and went out to the gathering room. Gaubert was standing before the fire, his fist on the mantle, scowling at the flames. Lix, his help-meet, waited to one side, with a tray holding brandy, one of Gaubert's weaknesses.

"Oh dear, what happened?" Iulia asked, keeping her tone soft and warmly empathetic.

Gaubert's scowl deepened. "They acclaimed me head of the Cardenas family."

"That's wonderful!" She pressed her hands together.

"Gaubert, I'm so pleased for you."

"But not head of the clan," he added.

Iulia didn't nod, even though the news was not unexpected. Instead, she moved closer. Hesitantly, as if she was compelled to comfort him. "Oh, Gaubert! They're fools. What whelp did they put in the chair, instead of you?"

The rumors she had heard from other wives was that Peru Scordini was expected to take over the chair. He was young, yet he had been at the clan table longer than Gaubert. Peru's family had been the first in the clan and had given the clan its name, which added weight to his claim.

"Your brother, Raine, got it," Gaubert said bitterly.

"Raine," Iulia repeated, more than a little bit surprised. Well, well. Raine had obviously learned how to shore up alliances and relationships since their father had died. Her wily little brother. How ironic!

She schooled her face, allowing only her surprise to show. "Raine is weak," she said softly.

"He didn't sound weak at all," Gaubert said morosely. He reached for the brandy glass and drank deeply. "He wants the navy to annex Atticus itself."

"That's…" Iulia shook her head. "Atticus! It's a well-founded world. Industrial. It has nothing to offer the Republic that we don't already have."

"Raine says the Homogeny is measuring Laurasia. Their ships have been seen in the system lately."

Laurasia was close to Atticus. "Since when has the Republic chosen territories based on what Karassia does?"

"Since now, I suppose," Gaubert said.

Iulia kept her brow smooth, even though a frown wanted to form. "You're smart to disapprove," she told him. "It is a disturbing development, chasing after Karassia. They are becoming a nuisance. Maybe something should be done about them. Directly, I mean."

Gaubert looked at her, startled. "You mean, attack Karassia? No one would win that war. Battles, maybe. Scraps and incidents. Full-out war, though..." He shook his head firmly and drank once more.

Iulia put the subject aside. Gaubert could be led only so far. He was too much like his brother. Instead, she asked, "Did you…was Criselda discussed?"

Gaubert looked at her sharply. "Yes," he said. He looked down into the glass. "It was undeniably Bellona."

"I see," Iulia said carefully.

"The people she is with…they used the most extraordinary methods to bring the security net down and gain access. The DeJulii have passed on details to the clan. They say she took nearly a thousand bio-paired ghostmakers, hundreds of personal mines, rockets and more." He hesitated.

"Tell me everything," Iulia said softly.

"They killed…dozens."

Iulia pressed her lips together. "What else?"

"They have declared your daughter an enemy of the Republic, Iulia," Gaubert said gently.

"She is not my daughter," Iulia said sharply. "Not anymore."

Gaubert's brow raised. Then he nodded. "That is why you're here, isn't it? Raine said you must be staying with the Cardenas because you want revenge. Because you want to punish Bellona for what she did to Reynard and Max. For destroying the family."

Iulia gave him a tremulous smile. "The family isn't destroyed while you are here, Gaubert."

He straightened up and his shoulders squared. "No," he said. "It isn't."

* * * * *

The former Karassian Homogeny Ship Alyard, Cerce Lo-

cal Space

"YOU HAVE TO MATCH THE servo-motor coupling with the natural tendon bond," the computerized medical arm said. "It won't work, the way you're doing it."

"Go fuck yourself," Retha growled.

"It's just trying to help," Vang told him, his voice gentle.

They were in a corner of the *Alyard's* medical suite, just off the bridge. Retha and Vang had found Hayes trying to manipulate the controls of his bio-implants with one hand. Retha talked the giant into sitting still and letting them try to fix the issue.

Now Vang was leaning over Hayes' upper arm, peering into the cavity next to the external tendon. "It didn't work the other way. It apparently won't work this way. I'm running out of options, Hayes."

Hayes let out a slow breath. "Thank you for trying," he said softly.

Retha took a breath for courage. "Were you always a bot, Hayes? I mean…did you choose it?"

Hayes turned his head to look at Retha. His eyes, under the heavy brow, blinked slowly. "No."

Retha let out his breath. "They made you one? In Ledan?"

Hayes nodded.

"Does that…bother you? That you woke up and found yourself this way?"

Hayes studied him for a moment longer. Retha figured he was going to ignore the question, when he said even more softly; "I don't remember it happening, yet Bellona says it was me who caught her, when she was just an Eriuman. She fought back, only I was already this way." He held up his working hand and turned it so the bright lights in the medical bay glinted off the metal. "I caught her and handed her over to the Karassians, who liked the way she fought so much they took her to Ledan."

Vang pursed his lips in a silent whistle. "I did wonder which Karassian had the balls to take her in the first place."

"You would not fight her?" Hayes asked.

"I like breathing, thanks," Vang said.

"You do not like what the Karassians did to you?"

Retha laughed. "He likes it just fine."

Hayes looked at Vang once more, frowning. "I do not understand."

Vang shrugged. "I'm a psychopath. Before Ledan, I couldn't keep the heat low enough to stop myself. Now, I can. It fucked with my head just enough so I can keep a lid on it. They're bastards, the app program is an abomination, but they actually did me a favor."

Hayes swiveled his big head to look at Retha. "You, too?"

Vang snorted. "He doesn't remember anything after his twelfth birthday. That's the day the Karassians boarded his freeship."

Retha shrugged. "I think I was in the program the longest of anyone here."

Hayes considered him. "You don't like what they did to you?"

"He's having problems," Vang said, as softly as Hayes was speaking.

Retha drew in a breath and let it out. "No, I don't like what they did to me."

"Neither does Bellona," Hayes said. "I did that to her. Now, I will do what I must to make amends. Which is why I must fix my arm. I am of no use to her like this." He frowned down at the useless arm.

"That's funny. A free-stater and a standard Karassian trying to fix a biobot," Thecla said, coming up to them. She grinned. "You didn't think another biobot might know what to do?" She pushed her hands into the pockets of her pants, which made the external tendons stretch and flex.

"You know how to fix this?" Vang asked. He tossed the driver tool onto the bunk next to Hayes and stepped away. "Be my guest."

Thecla stood in front of Hayes and held out a hand. "Squeeze my hand. Let me see what I'm dealing with."

"I can give you a complete breakdown of the—" the medical arm began.

"Thank you and shut up for a moment," Thecla said.

It shut up.

"Why didn't I think of that?" Retha breathed to himself.

Hayes tried lifting his injured arm, to reach for Thecla's hand. The arm swung wildly. The back of the hand knocked the driver off the bunk. Retha leaned forward and grabbed the driver before it hit the floor and put it back on the bunk.

Thecla was staring at him. "You're not enhanced, are you?"

"No."

"Then that reaction speed is built into your DNA? Lucky bastard."

"Glad you think so," Retha said bitterly.

She raised a brow. "No wonder you shoot so well."

"He knows how to aim properly is why he shoots so well," Vang said, anger coloring his tone. His mood was deteriorating.

"Can you teach me?" Thecla said.

"Hey. My arm," Hayes said, his voice rumbling in his chest.

"Sorry," Thecla said. "I'm going to have to look at it later. I came looking for you guys. Bellona wants to see everyone. On the Bridge. In about five."

"What about?" Retha asked. It would be better to get Vang back to their quarters.

"You know the boss lady. She don't say until she says." Thecla shrugged.

"I'm going," Hayes said. He didn't have to slide off the bunk. His legs were long enough he could just rise to his feet. He straightened up.

The medical arm bleeped and blinked lights. The AI was trying to get their attention. It was panicking because its patient was leaving before treatment had been completed.

Hayes strode away, ignoring it.

Retha gripped Vang's arm. "Come on," he said quietly. "Bellona doesn't call unnecessary meetings."

* * * * *

The former Karassian Homogeny Ship Alyard, nomansland.

THE *ALYARD* WAS HANGING IN SPACE, in the middle of nomansland, in as random a location as they could pick without actually calling up a stellar map and firing at it. The only way either the Republic or the Homogeny could find them would be if they tripped over them accidentally. As there was no settled star system nearby, that unlucky chance was minimized.

It was as close to a secure hideout as Bellona could arrange. Because of the down-time, the bridge was empty of everyone but Bellona, Khalil and Sang. They sat in the too-soft and squishy chairs, waiting for the others to arrive.

Zeni was the first to step onto the bridge from the gate to the living quarters section. Since they had left Cardenas, she had taken to wearing spacer black, boots and jacket, although she didn't carry a gun. Not because ghostmakers were scarce, but because she preferred not to use one. "You trained me," she told Bellona. "Why would I waste what you have taught me?" Zeni ran all the combat training on the ship, just as she had run the training in Abilio.

"This is a closed meeting," Sang said stiffly.

Zeni glared at him. "I was invited."

"I invited her, Sang," Bellona said. "Zeni is a good representative for the Abilio crew. Amilcare is also coming."

Sang sank back into the chair. He nodded, his expression the same completely neutral one Bellona remembered from too many times in the past, on Cardenas. She made a mental note to talk to him later. What did he not like about Zeni?

The others—the Ledanians, as she had come to think of them even to herself—trailed onto the bridge in pairs and groups. Amilcare, the Abilio mechanic who had become a reliable lieutenant, ambled in with them. He had not traded his normal hard-wearing clothes for spacer symbols. He still looked dusty, even on a ship that actively repressed and removed dust.

Fontana, one of the most pro-active of the Ledan group, along with Thecla, hoisted himself onto the top of the nearest work counter and looked at Khalil steadily, silently challenging him to tell Fontana to get off.

Khalil just smiled.

Hero jumped onto the counter next to Fontana and curled up like a cat, her arms around her knees. Her shoulder, bare where the wide-necked shirt she was wearing had dropped down to reveal her arm and her upper breast, rubbed against his. Fontana pushed her, sliding her away from him until there was a clear space between them. She blew him a kiss, yet stayed where she was.

All the chairs on the bridge were sensibly and securely anchored to the floor, forcing everyone else to stand.

"We need to figure out a better place for meetings than here," Bellona decided. "The equivalent of a board room, or a gathering room." There was no such thing as a place for equals to meet on this Karassian ship, because no one considered themselves equal to anyone else in the Homogeny. It was a state of superior individuals, who used screens to communicate with everyone else.

"We'll add it to the list," Khalil told her.

Bellona got to her feet, so she was standing as everyone else was. "There's no news," she warned them. "This is just—"

"There is one item," Khalil said.

Bellona looked back at him. "There is?"

"The Eriuman dictate," he reminded her.

"That." She shook her head.

Khalil got to his feet, too. "It affects everyone, not just you. Tell them."

From the curious expressions on everyone's face, it was too late to keep it quiet. She sighed. "The Erium Republic has declared me a formal enemy of the state, along with anyone in my company."

Thecla shrugged, disinterested.

Fontana frowned. "Isn't that a good thing?" he asked. "The free worlds can't say you have any allegiance to Erium, if the Republic is shooting at you."

"Does that mean I will be shot at, too?" Aideen asked, her voice small.

"It means what we're doing is starting to make a difference," Bellona said. "People are taking notice. Although, that's not why I pulled you all up here. I wanted a status report from all of you and while we have a moment to breathe, we can strategize."

"*We* can?" Thecla said.

"Why not?" Bellona asked, using a reasonable tone. "You've all got disparate skills and a range of viewpoints. I have my own blind spots, too."

Hero cooed and sat up straighter. No one else reacted. Bellona wondered, though, if she was imagining the increased attention she was getting.

"Hayes, for instance," Bellona said. "Your arm is still

not functioning properly. What do you need?"

Hayes frowned.

"I've got that covered," Thecla said. "I'm pretty sure I can fix it. I might need some help on the bio parts. Bot parts, I've got down cold."

"I can do that," Vang said.

"You know medicine?" Bellona asked, surprised.

"I know biology," he growled.

Everyone looked at him, surprised.

"Best and fastest ways to kill, and all," Retha added.

Bellona saw Khalil smile from the corner of her eye and cleared her throat. "Very well," she said. "Sang, maybe you can start with an overall summary."

Sang got to his feet and looked around the group. It struck Bellona that on Eriuman, his pale features and freckles had stood out, marking him as one who didn't belong there. Here among the Ledanians with their checkered histories and wildly different appearances, he blended in seamlessly.

"It's not the most positive position we're in," he said quietly. "The Criselda raid netted fifteen of the advanced bio-paired ghostmakers. We had to give Arany's people seven of them, plus twenty of the personal mines. Most of the crew are still without weapons, thanks to the Karassians sabotaging the weapons store before they were kicked off the ship."

Fontana growled. Everyone else looked unhappy.

"We don't have the components we need to build a canon for Connie. As she would prefer to run and hide, that might not be the disadvantage it seems to be." Sang glanced around the room again, measuring everyone. "There is a variety of pharmaceuticals we should have to help you—all of you—deal with the range of nightmares, hormonal imbalances, metabolic issues, panic attacks and other symptoms that are on-going and range from mild to severe. This is a priority, in my estimation."

Thecla had her arms crossed, the external tendons flexed tight. "Not in *my* estimation," she said. "We're dealing."

"I don't want to add drug addict to my list of problems," Fontana said.

"Point me at the enemy and I'll be just fine," Vang said.

"We'll table the medical issues for another time," Bellona said. "Next?"

Sang nodded. "Communications is still a problem. At the moment, only I can hear Connie when we're not standing inside her. As Connie coordinates communications for us when we're not on the *Alyard,* we need a way for everyone to hear her that doesn't involve external, hand-held devices that can be removed or broken."

Aideen shuffled her feet, looking at them.

"Aideen?" Bellona said.

She raised her head to look at Bellona quickly, then ducked it back to study her toes once more. "I will."

"Will what?" Bellona asked.

"Fix it." Aideen lifted her head again. She didn't look directly at Bellona. Her gaze moved passed Bellona's shoulder. "I like Connie. She doesn't bother me. I will make something that meets Sang's specifications."

Sang looked pleased.

"Thank you, Aideen," Bellona told her.

Aideen dropped her head again. She nodded.

Sang moved on. "I have converted all the AIs on the *Alyard* and changed their leashes. They can be safely consulted now. They no longer recognize the Homogeny as their masters."

"Homogeny," Fontana muttered. "I wonder if whoever thought up the name was laughing at the irony of it?"

Thecla smiled at the joke. So did Aideen, although she didn't lift her head again.

"The military records we can now access on this ship make for interesting study," Sang added. "High level assessment shows that the Karassian military is far larger than anyone has estimated. They recruit anything that moves and that creates problems."

"Recruits, or shanghaies?" Fontana growled.

"The Appurtenance Services program was unique in its forced recruitment," Sang said. "The general troops are volunteers. The lack of filters, though, means the military is rife with morale and discipline problems, disease and lack of training." Sang looked at Bellona. "That explains what we know of Alkeides."

Bellona nodded.

"What about Alkeides?" Retha said, with a touch of sharpness.

"You have a connection with Alkeides?" Khalil asked.

"I was born there." Retha raised his brow, daring anyone to challenge him.

Bellona shook her head. "It's something we learned about the Karassian occupation."

"The ground troops sent Xenia in to deal with the resistance," Fontana said. The fury in his voice was rich and strong. "Then they hung back and waited for her to sort it out for them. On her own. Which she did. Now, the survivors are pissed at Bellona."

Everyone looked at her. Thecla showed a grudging admiration. "Damn, woman," she said.

"You all have done the same things," Bellona said, discomfort making her shift on her feet. "I'm absolutely sure of that. You were trained to peak physical abilities and to make decisions that would win the day for the Karassians, no matter what the cost. You obeyed because you had no choice and you are all paying the price for that now. Memory regression. Fragments that make no sense and more. I also know that if you could remember any of it, you would regret what you have done as much as I regret learning what I did on Alkeides. Be thankful you do not remember."

Fontana shook his head. "The more I learn, the more I want to strangle someone. Anyone. Put the fucker in front of me who is responsible for Ledan and I'll squeeze the last drop of moisture out of his body and burn the remains over an open fire and *dance* around it."

Unseen by anyone, Aideen reached out her hand and curled her fingers around Fontana's outer finger. He gripped her hand, his knuckles turning white, and blew out his breath. "Someone should pay for what they did to us," he finished heavily.

"Someone will, one day," Bellona promised him. She looked at Khalil. "What progress have you made with Woodrow and Yishmeray?"

"I'm working on Woodrow. He leaves a convoluted trail," Khalil said.

"Woodrow, before anyone asks," Bellona said, "is the Karassian who challenged me when we released you all from Ledan. I don't know if he is military or has associations with The Homogeny Council of Independence, but he *is* connected to Ledan, which is why I would like to ask him a few questions."

This time, the murmur of agreement came from everyone.

"Who is Yishmeray?" Hero said.

"You've never heard of Yishmeray?" Thecla asked. "He's one of the most decorated generals in the military."

Hero pointed to her own chest. "Eriuman. Hello."

"*Was* the most decorated," Khalil said. "He's disappeared."

"Someone killed him?" Fontana asked, with a hopeful note.

Khalil shook his head. "He's just gone. All records associated with him stop, about two years ago."

"Around the time we released Bellona from Ledan," Sang said.

"The date struck me as significant, too," Khalil admitted. "There's a chance he changed his name and maybe his appearance and cut off all trace of his whereabouts, when he learned that Bellona had gone missing."

"This name…" Hayes said. "It feels familiar to me. Did I know him?"

"You did," Bellona said. "He is the one who ordered you to take me off the *Hathaway*, twelve years ago. He put me in Ledan."

The small silence was tense.

Even Bellona could feel the tightness in her chest. Unlike her Xenia memories, she was now able to recall that day on the *Hathaway* in stark detail. The way Yishmeray had lifted his chin out and up, while his biocomp servers processed data and weighed the decision to make her an app and destroy Wang and her ship.

Bellona dismissed the memory impatiently and gave everyone the best smile she could manage. She looked at Fontana. "As you can see, we're working on finding the one responsible."

Fontana nodded. He didn't smile back.

Chapter Five

Kachmarain City, Kachmar Sodality, The Karassian Homogeny

IT WAS AMAZING, CHIDI DECIDED, how much the perception of others could be directed by a single determined individual. This moment, he knew, was one of those times when his decision alone would mold how the entire world thought.

He had been forced to accept that what he did affected the lives of millions of people. That wisdom now let him recognize the weight of the decision he was about to make.

Chidi took his boots off the table and sat up, letting his gaze rove around the chic industrial furniture in a way that looked as if he was measuring the seven people waiting for him to speak. In fact, he was looking for the location of the floating lens. This meeting was not being broadcast live as most of his life was, although footage from the meeting would be used for montages, backgrounds and more, so he had to maintain his on-camera poise.

The two channels currently streaming into his neocortex were a babble of nonsense opinions and news. The uninitiated, the standard Karassian, would have quickly gone mad at the constant noise and distraction. Chidi had learned to switch his attention, with a corner of his brain constantly monitoring the feeds. If there was something worthy of close attention, he could pause long enough to focus on the feeds, then move on with his day. He was so good at it now, that he could check the feeds even while on camera and talking, and no one would realize what he was doing.

He gave Surya a warm smile. The man melted at Chidi's attention, his gaze dropping to the table. Chidi was grateful that Surya was a boring lover. If he had been more distracting, then Chidi would not have dipped into his feeds last night, while they were *flagrante delicto,* and would not have caught the earnest late-night discussion that had brought him to this delicious moment of decision. Chidi had climaxed unexpectedly when he recognized the profound nature of the dyad, which might have been annoying given how much he had paid for libido enhancement and enlarged genitalia. However, the recognition of the moment had completely distracted him.

"Before I go live," he told everyone around the table, projecting his voice and modulating the tones for the most pleasing resonance—all of it purely automatic, "I want you to be aware of what the day will bring. Everyone has seen the official release of the Shavistran footage, of course. The city killer, the ruins, and Bellona Cardenas declaring war. That bootleg copy that has been doing the rounds for a year forced the Council to release the full version, *they* say, because it makes Karassians look bad."

"That woman is *not* Xenia. I refuse to believe it," Cora, one of Chidi's three personal assistants said instantly. Hotly. Cora had always been a Xenia fan.

"If it *is* Xenia," Tupper, his number two assistant, added, "then she sold out, which I can't believe. A good Karassian like her, going rogue?" He shook his head in disbelief.

"It's all fake, of course," Kobina, Chidi's talented editor, said dismissively.

Chidi nodded. "Is it?" he asked them.

Everyone stared at him.

"Of *course* it is," Cora replied. "All my friends say it is."

"Who faked it then?" Chidi asked.

Silence.

"It would have to be the Eriuman woman who faked it, wouldn't it?" Surya asked hesitantly.

Chidi nodded again. "Why?" he demanded.

Again, the small silence. He was taxing them with these questions. They weren't used to having to think this way.

"For money?" Surya asked, his voice lifting.

"Fame," Cora said shortly. "If she can sell everyone on her being Xenia, all Xenia's fans will follow her feeds."

It was an interesting possibility. Chidi didn't let himself be deflected from the moment. He was vibrating with energy, tingling with the power he was about to wield, just by making a decision.

"Maybe the council faked it," Kobina, his editor, said slowly. "To bring Karassians together. To…increase the military?"

Chidi rewarded him with a smile. Kobina had always been a deep thinker. Then he followed-up with his knock-them-breathless question, spoken clearly and at good volume. "What if it *isn't* fake?"

The silence this time was awesome. Chidi reveled in it. He had them in his hand. *This*, this moment right here, would be repeated across millions of screens around Karassia.

"It *has* to be," Kobina said. "That would mean that *Xenia's Wars*, her biofeed channel, the movies…" He pushed a hand through his hair. "The betting forums," he breathed. "There must be *millions* funneling through the official forum and then there are all the side bets and bootleg sites…" He looked almost ill. "If that Shavistran nonsense is *real*, then all the movies, the feeds, the betting, it would all…*stop*."

Chidi nodded. Everyone else was looking at Kobina with dawning horror.

Surya frowned, marring his perfect forehead. "If it is real, then that means the Council really did do that to people. The apps aren't androids at all. They're humans. Karassians."

Cora shook her head. "They wouldn't be that cruel, not to real people," she said firmly. "They couldn't get away with something like that, right under everyone's noses."

Surya let out a deep breath and relaxed. "Yeah," he said, sounding happier. "They couldn't."

That right there, Chidi realized. Surya's relief was the key.

Chidi adopted an indolent, artistic pose, one foot on the other knee, his arm draped over the table, the hand waving elegantly. "That is what we are going to tell *everyone,*" he declared.

"That everything that happened on Shavistran is fake?" Cora asked hopefully.

"Yes."

Cora let out a deep breath and smiled.

Kobina cleared his throat. "Maybe we should send someone to have a look on Shavistran, first?" he suggested. "Take footage of the thriving city?"

"Go out into free space?" Chidi said and laughed. "No need," he said shortly. He waved his hand again. "Trust me, Kobina. This will track. People will like it. They will *love* it."

And they will love me, Chidi added to himself. He didn't fully understand the reasoning for every decision he ever made about his feed. He just knew what worked. He had an instinct for spotting what would get him the best ratings. This would net him a majority percentage. Maybe even an invitation to dine with members of the Council and *that* would give him even more traction. He knew it in his bones.

* * * * *

The former Karassian Homogeny Ship Alyard, Cerce Local Space

ON THE FIFTH DAY AFTER THEIR return to Cerce, Alberda's people asked for a face-to-face with Bellona and set up a time amenable to both parties. It was all very formal and distant, which bothered Bellona more than their refusal to state the subject of the meeting.

Bellona had ordered the *Alyard* to return to Cerce from the nomansland sojourn, for it was imperative they build alliances with the planetary rulers and gain the cooperation of the free worlds. Those worlds' assistance would provide supplies and recruits. More importantly, it would give Bellona's people information about Karassian and Eriuman military movements as soon as anyone else learned of them.

They were ill-equipped to take on either navy right now. The *Alyard* was only a conveyor. The most common destroyers and cruisers on either side would easily outgun them, making direct confrontation a bad idea.

Yet they still needed a victory of some sort, something that would convince Natasa and her fleet and politicians like Alberda that Bellona's motives were pure and the cause worth supporting.

While they hovered over Cerce and bargained for supplies, Bellona sent Khalil, Sang, Fontana and Thecla out to other major free worlds, to test their interest in a cooperative defense and to determine their combat statuses.

Aideen had found herself an empty engineering room where she could work on the communications net for Connie, close by the cargo bay where Connie was parked. Bellona had found her there, playing around with a blow torch.

Bellona was more surprised to see Vang standing next to the door, his arms folded as he leaned back against the wall.

"You're not bothering Aideen, are you?" Bellona asked. It emerged more sharply than she had intended.

Vang just smiled.

"Where is Retha?"

"He hasn't slept for three nights." Vang grimaced. "Nightmares. I put him out."

"You're familiarizing yourself with the medical bay, then. That might be useful." Although the idea of Vang using something like a skin sealer or surgical instruments on her was uncomfortable.

"I didn't use the medical bay." His smile made her even more uneasy. Bellona noted that a medic, preferably a surgeon, would be a priority recruit. She turned to Aideen. "How is your project going?"

"Vang is not bothering me," Aideen said. She was sorting through a small box of what looked like memory chips, while the blow torch stood hissing next to her elbow. "He doesn't ask questions. He watches."

"That's good?"

Aideen looked up at her. "I am a high-functioning autistic. I prefer to be alone because interacting is a challenge for me. Vang watches, so I don't mind."

Vang smiled again. "You learn more from watching."

Bellona considered Aideen. "I thought all Karassians, even the standard ones, go through basic gene manipulation at the fetus stage. Wouldn't autism be adjusted then?"

Aideen gave a small shrug. "There are twenty-four gene flaws that can contribute to autism, if certain chemical imbalances are also present. They missed one of mine." She looked up at Bellona, her face expressionless. "I would have been a cast-off, if they had not found all but one of them."

The hairs on the back of Bellona's neck prickled hard as they lifted. She didn't ask what "cast-off" meant. It was clear enough from the name for her to know she didn't want more details.

Life in networked, gossipy and friends-ridden Karassia for a social-disabled woman like Aideen must have been unbearable. "How in the known worlds did you get sucked into the Ledan program?" Bellona asked her.

Vang made a sound of disgust. She glanced at him and he shook his head. "Fontana told me." He nodded toward Aideen, who had gone back to work, bent over the little box. "Daddy was a super-general in the military. Her folks didn't know what to do with her. Too boring, too smart and too weird. Daddy pulled some strings." His mouth turned down.

"They *put* her in Ledan?" Bellona breathed.

Aideen looked up. "I could be alone and work on my stuff. Only now I know that sometimes, I did more than that."

"Does that bother you?" Bellona asked curiously.

"I don't like killing," Aideen said. "Although I am now very good at it." She went back to work.

Bellona glanced at Vang again. "It *does* bother you, though. I didn't think that was possible for you."

Vang shrugged. "It's an unpleasant side-effect of the mind-fuck they gave us in Ledan. Sometimes, now, I give a damn."

Bellona drew in a breath. Every story she heard from the Ledanians, every awful fact, just added more weight to her determination to find those responsible and to halt the Karassian invasion of free space, for all time. She turned back to Aideen. "Is your father still active in the military?"

Aideen shook her head. "I checked in the ship's database. He was killed three years ago, when he got in the way of a Ledanian app on a mission."

Bellona nodded. "The Ledanian was you, wasn't it?"

Aideen looked up. "It was. I find the symmetry of that pleasing." Then she plucked a chip from the box. "This one!"

Bellona drew closer. "What about it?"

"She found these in the locker, over there," Vang said. "I have no idea what they are. Aideen seems to know."

Aideen picked up a pair of metal tongs and carefully slotted the chip between the blunt tips. Then she held the chip toward the blow-torch flame, keeping it far enough away that the flame didn't touch it, while the heat washed over it.

The chip writhed. Bellona took a step back away from the bench.

Then the chip seemed to explode, like a flower blooming at high speed. Aideen put it on the bench, put the tongs down and picked up the blow torch and played it over the rapidly forming black object.

It took a moment for the shape to make any sense. As the curves took form, Bellona realized it resembled a human body—there was a chest and attached arms. The shape was hollow.

Vang came closer, peering at it. "Fuck me," he breathed. "It's an exoskeleton. I've heard of them. Never seen one."

Aideen put down the torch. "This is a Tuff Touch Model 389319I, Upper Body Exoskeleton. Inventory number 5691, Sub-Section C, Section; Armaments."

Vang looked at her, admiration in his eyes. "You read the inventory. *All* of it."

Aideen turned off the blow torch. "The exo-skeletons are printable, articulate and intelligent. They enhance a combat fighter's strength and speed. They protect against standard ghostmaker bolts, just not the advanced weapons we took from Criselda."

Bellona stared at the armor. "And these were lying in a box in a cupboard?"

"The box was properly labelled," Aideen said stiffly. "That was how I knew what was in it."

Bellona pointed to the box. "There's more of this armor in that box?"

"There are upper and lower body exo-skeletons of four different varieties, each with specific functions." Aideen touched the fully formed piece lying on the bench. "This one is for armor. Others are for strength, endurance, extended reach." She frowned. "Someone mixed them all up." She was highly offended.

Bellona nodded. "I want you to sort them out, Aideen. Then, I want you to…to grow enough amour for everyone, starting with the Ledanians."

Aideen shifted on her feet. "I already have work that I haven't finished yet."

Bellona hesitated, wondering how to answer that.

Vang touched her arm. "Let me." He looked at Aideen. "Both projects have equal priority and both must be finished. Figure out how long each of them will take, then split your time between them in proportion, until they are both completed."

Aideen smiled shyly. "Okay," she said happily. Then her smile faded. "I want to be alone now. I have work to do."

Bellona beckoned to Vang to follow her and stepped out of the room as Aideen bent over the box once more and began laying the chips out on the bench, sorting them. Vang walked beside her, silent once more. Bellona raised her brow at him.

He jerked his thumb back toward the room they had just left. "That? Aideen is off-the-charts brilliant. She's happier if she can think in numbers, though. Numbers are definite. People, not so much."

"How did you know that, though?" Bellona asked.

"I'm a psychopath—I *was* a psychopath." He grinned. "My gene manipulations were even more shoddy than hers because my mother was dirt poor. Psychopaths, though…we know psychology. We know what makes people tick and how to make them tick the way we want them to."

Bellona shuddered.

"Yeah. Eriumans don't like the idea of gene manipulations," Vang said, his tone one of agreement.

"It's your casual reference to manipulating people for personal gain, too."

"Money is personal gain. Power, influence, fame, sex... those are all personal gain. I did what I did, back then, because I would have gone mad if I didn't."

"You're talking about killing people."

"I am." Vang said it calmly. "Just like you, I'm not that person anymore."

"You're not a psychopath?"

"By the clinical definition, nope, I guess not. I may have downgraded to sociopath. The heat...it's still there sometimes." He grinned again. There was little humor in it. It was almost as if he was laughing at himself in hysterical despair. "I'll let you know if I think it's going to get away on me."

Bellona swallowed. "That's good to know."

He stopped in the middle of the corridor. "You drink coffee, right?"

Bellona turned to face him. "Doesn't everyone?"

"Not me. I have the same objection to coffee that Fontana had to anti-depressants, the other day."

"They're addictive," Bellona finished.

"Ever stopped drinking coffee, boss?"

She grimaced. "For a day."

"I hear the headache is a killer."

"It laid me out," she said frankly.

Vang nodded. "I already have an addiction. I don't need another."

"That's what you think your...heat is? An addiction?"

"Addictions can be beaten. Psychoses, not so much. So yeah, I think of it as an addiction. Because that's another thing I give a damn about these days."

"Beating it?"

"And you seeing me win."

"Me?"

"You got me out of there. Ledan." His gaze met hers and unlike the very few occasions when he had looked at her directly, this time there was no ironic glint or mask in place. This time, she didn't get the wave of uneasiness she normally experienced when Vang looked at her.

Bellona nodded. "Okay, then." She headed back down the corridor, for the bridge. Vang caught up with her and this time, she felt more comfortable about him by her side.

"I want you to sit in on the meeting I'm about to take," she told him. "Listen, then give me your interpretation after. Alberda is a slippery fish."

"He's a politician. They're all slippery," Vang said.

"So are you. Figure him out for me."

"I'll do my best."

That pleased her more than she thought it should.

* * * * *

GOVERNOR LIN ALBERDA WAS ALREADY waiting by the time they reached the bridge.

Hero stepped away from the screen as Bellona moved around the navigation station. "Here you are, Governor," Hero said, waving toward Bellona.

"I'm not late, am I?" Bellona asked, even though she knew she wasn't.

"I am a few minutes early," Alberda assured her. "Your General Antonino kept me occupied."

Bellona glanced at Hero, hiding her alarm. "Hero can be distracting," she admitted.

"And charming," Alberda added.

Hero smiled.

Vang settled into the pilot's chair, well out of range of

the screen and Alberda.

"Hero is also quite lethal," Bellona told Alberda.

His amusement faded. "I'm sure," he said shortly and resettled in his chair. "I suppose I should come straight to the point."

"As this is your meeting," Bellona added, hiding her uneasiness.

"I have been having some...uncomfortable conversations, lately."

Haven't we all? Bellona thought. She said nothing, though, letting Alberda get to his point as promised.

Alberda sighed. "Just exactly how long do you plan to station your ship over Cerce, Bellona?'

"We've only been here five days, governor. We're resupplying."

"Most ships come and go in a two-day window."

"You're not talking about those ships that call Cerce home, then?"

"I'm not," he said firmly. "You talked to my chief stevedore, Neva Blackwood, about an extended docking license."

Bellona frowned. "She told you that?"

Alberda lifted his hand to halt the line of discussion. "It's complicated. Bellona, you can't stay here."

Bellona damped down her first impulsive need to protest. "Why not, Governor?" she asked, working as much reasonableness into her tone as she could manage.

Alberda shook his head. "You have to ask that? You and your people are notorious, Bellona. The known worlds are aware of you, after that stunt you pulled on Shavistran."

"You had no objections to that stunt before we parked over Cerce City," Bellona said calmly, even though her heart was thudding loudly in her ears.

"You're Eriuman," Alberda said bluntly.

"I *was* Eriuman."

"It was your people who killed Shavistran."

"That does not make me personally responsible."

Alberda let out a deep breath. "They used that city killer to wipe out Ben Arany and his people, Bellona. Ben was a friend of mine."

"I'm sorry," Bellona said automatically, her mind racing. "Lin, are you trying to avoid saying you don't want us over Cerce because you think the Eriumans will use the city killer to get *me*?"

Alberda winced. Then he sighed. "You always say you want to halt the Karassian and Eriuman aggression. By lingering here, you're *inviting* it. You did not leave many friends behind when you left Cardenas. You left no friends behind on Kachmar."

"I brought them all with me, Governor," Bellona said stiffly.

"My point remains. You have publicly declared yourself opposed to the Homogeny and the Republic. Erium has named you an official enemy. The more you oppose them, the harder they'll fight back." He gave her a stiff smile. "I hope all your friends you brought with you are as lethal as your General Antonino there, Bellona. You're going to need them. Anyone else standing near you will get caught in the fallout."

"I thought *you* were a friend, Lin."

"I can't afford to be friends with you. I have a world to protect." He grimaced again. "I'm sorry."

"We can protect you, Governor."

"With what? That Karassian barge you stole? You can't stop a city killer." He shook his head. "No, Bellona. I must insist you leave Cerce."

Bellona sighed. "I have crew who are away on other planets. I must wait for them to return."

"Your friends will enjoy no success on those other worlds," Alberda said. "You should tell them to return now and not waste their time."

Bellona's belly clamped. "The uncomfortable conversations you've been having…" she breathed.

Alberda nodded. "I'm sorry, Bellona. I admire your cause. I believe in it. I hate that we all live in fear of Karassian or Eriuman ships showing up on our doorstep with their guns primed. I hate that no one tries to stop them. Only, there's a reason no one tries."

"Because no one has the power to stop them," Bellona said bitterly.

"Not even you, no matter how much you want to," Alberda added gently.

Bellona nodded. "One day, that will change, Lin."

"On that day, if it comes, I will roll out the red carpet. That is not today." He disconnected.

The screen dissolved. Silence filled the bridge, broken only by the tick and flutter of computers.

"You didn't need me," Vang said. "I don't think he even tried to pull his punches."

Bellona grimaced. Vang was right. She looked at Hero. "*General* Antonino?"

Hero shrugged. "I could have called myself your lieutenant, only lieutenants specialize." She grinned mischievously. "Generals are into everything."

"Another word for that is promiscuous," Vang said.

"I think of it as being multi-talented," Hero said stoutly.

Bellona shook her head. "Whatever title you give yourself, it's not going to matter a damn if no one wants us near them."

Vang got to his feet. "What are you going to do?"

"*You* two are going to get on the communications bands and call back the others. Tell them to drop everything and grab the fastest express bus back to Cerce. Then, we'll find another hole in nomansland and…"

She was aware that she had stopped talking mid-sentence. It was a secondary thought. Ideas were slamming through her, fragments of memories and more, stirred up by Alberda and the conversations she had just had with Aideen and Vang.

She blinked and saw that Hero and Vang were both watching her with a degree of wariness.

"What?" Hero demanded.

Bellona stirred, energy surging through her, making her restless. "Vang, what would you say is the single most telling difference between the Eriumans and the Karassians?"

Vang looked startled, then thoughtful. "How they use their AIs, I suppose."

Hero laughed and tugged at a lock of his white-blonde thatch of hair, then picked up her own sable locks. "Hello."

Vang scowled at her. "Appearance is nothing," he said shortly. "The Eriumans are naturally bred DNA without enhancements. They use AIs in all sorts of ways to enhance their lives, instead. Not obviously, though. Not directly. They want natural perfection—an outcome of discipline and morals and productivity…and breeding. They consider themselves superior to everyone, including the Karassians, who can't reach perfection without adjustments. Their AIs look like perfectly disciplined people."

"Androids," Hero said, her flirtatious air evaporating. Her eyes narrowed as she followed Vang's speech.

"Androids," Vang agreed. "From the simplest robot to AI-driven tools, to self-aware entities like Sang. A human figure moving about the room doesn't mar the ambience." He shrugged.

Hero laughed. "Sang will love that."

"Karassians don't use androids," Bellona said, nudging Vang.

He shook his head. "They don't trust AIs that look too human, because androids are smarter and faster than even the most enhanced human, which is anathematic to

Karassians, who think of themselves as the best and spend their lives outdoing themselves. Look at us, at Ledan. They could only stand the idea of apps—androids—fighting on their behalf so long as they were locked safely away in the meantime. They even called them—us—apps, not androids, because it was easier to think of us that way."

"So, Eriumans are disciplined and Karassians live to excess," Bellona summarized.

"That's a huge simplification," Vang said. "We're human in the end. Individuals are unique by definition. That's why Aideen prefers numbers."

Hero squeezed her hands together. "I prefer people. You got an idea from all that, boss?"

Bellona nodded. "I'm going to *use* Karassian excesses against them. In particular, one of their less endearing habits."

Vang raised a brow, waiting.

"I'm going to use their inability to clean up after themselves," she told them.

Chapter Six

Cardenas (Findlay IV), Findlay System, Eriuman Republic

What she was doing was questionable. Perhaps even illegal. Iulia had never been tempted to do it before. Therefore, she had never had reason to acquaint herself with Eriuman military security laws surrounding the subject. She carefully didn't ask for clarification now, from Wait or Riz or even Gaubert, before setting up a small screen and running the security footage from the Criselda armaments depot.

That had been four days ago. After multiple repeats, Iulia asked Wait to compile the various angles into a time-related whole. The resulting monologue was choppy yet coherent. While she dealt with homebase administrative matters in her boudoir office, she had let the video run on a loop, repeating itself.

Her attention was always snagged by the same fragments, causing her to pause what she was doing and look up at the screen to watch them play out. Only one of the fragments focused completely upon Bellona, while the rest were wide-angled footage with small figures crossing the range of the camera lens. In the focused section, the woman who had been her daughter was carrying a ghostmaker as she ran with two others. One of those two was Sang, the family asset, except it was barely recognizable. It had taken on male characteristics since Iulia had seen it last.

The possible reasons why Bellona might have ordered it to do that were few and all of them troubling. All of them pointed to the vast distance Bellona had travelled since leaving home.

Iulia heard the sound of water splashing, coming from the family room. Someone was using the bathing pool. It wouldn't be Thora. She preferred to sleep on hot afternoons.

Iulia redraped her mantle, told Wait to pause the playback and went through to the family room, her sandals slapping the polished stone floor. As she had suspected, it was Gaubert in the pool. He rested in one corner with his arms spread and his head back. He had submersed himself first and his hair and flesh were damp.

He lifted his head as Iulia entered. "Be a sweet and pass me my drink?"

Iulia went back to the sideboard, where a single glass sat, sweating moisture. The sideboard was against the one solid wall of the room. Like the gathering room on the other side of the public wing, the family room used forcefields for walls, filling in the gaps between the massive pillars. The invisible fields gave the family a grand view of the low mountain ranges around the city. At the moment, the fields were off, letting in natural air. She could hear insects buzzing and clicking in the gardens, beyond. It was a lazy sound unique to late summer afternoons in the city.

Iulia picked up the glass and nodded at Lix, Gaubert's help-meet, which stood next to the sideboard. Hiding her annoyance at being asked to act as help-meet, she carried the glass to Gaubert, who took it with a murmured thank you.

Then she slid off her sandals, stepped down to the top step of the pool and paused as the finger-deep water played over her feet. The coolness drew her attention to how warm it was in the room. She gathered the hem of her dress up out of the way and sat on the edge of the pool, then rested her feet on the second step. The water lapped around the top of her calves.

"Are you sick of watching that security feed yet?"

Gaubert asked. He put the glass aside, rested his head back and closed his eyes.

"You knew what I was doing?" she asked, startled.

"You disappeared for three days. I made it a point to find out."

"You don't mind?"

"I know why you're doing it." He opened one eye. "I'm a parent, too."

"I no longer have a daughter," she reminded him.

He opened the other eye to consider her. "You're still wearing red," he pointed out.

"Yes." She didn't try to make the flat word pretty.

"You really hate her that much for what she did to Reynard? Your own daughter?"

Iulia rearranged the folds of the gauzy red dress over her lap to stop it trailing in the water. "Who was it you spoke to in the Homogeny? Who gave you the city killer?"

Gaubert didn't answer straight away. His gaze sharpened. "I didn't think it was possible for a mother to reject a child, as you are."

"Did you meet them on Antini?"

He sat up, shedding fat droplets. "No one gave Erium the city killer. We took it from the Karassians."

"With their cooperation, I'm sure," Iulia added. "I don't care about the city killer, anyway. I want—"

"You don't?"

She shrugged. "What can be stolen can be stolen again. Then deconstructed. Then copied. Now, the Karassians won't dare use the thing because it could be used against them and we're back to the stalemate. That is my point, Gaubert."

He frowned. "The stalemate?"

"You worked *with* the Karassians to acquire the city killer. Don't look at me that way and don't protest. That story about stealing the thing is a convenient face-saver.

Just don't ask me to believe it. I lived with Reynard for forty years and there were many such conveniences presented to me. I know what they look like."

Gaubert leaned back and closed his eyes. "Perhaps you should get to your point."

"I am at my point. You have a unique advantage over every other clan head, Gaubert. You have the ear of Karassia. Peru cannot claim that. Neither can Raine."

"Karassia does not listen to me," he said distantly. "They provided information. Once. That is all."

"They will listen, when you propose a working partnership."

He didn't just open a single eye this time. He sat up, making the water surge and slap against the sides of the pool and her lower legs. "A *partnership*? With Karassia? You are mad."

"Maybe. You need a platform, something to give you an advantage over Peru and Raine, yes?"

Gaubert licked his lips. "Why would I—why would anyone—want to work *with* the Karassians? We join with them and the war is over. It would be the political equivalent of admitting defeat."

"Would the war really be over, though?" she asked.

"A war requires an enemy. If we're working with the Karassians, there would be no enemy left."

"That's not entirely true."

Gaubert rested his elbows on his bony knees and linked his hands together. It was something Reynard used to do. Was he trying to look more like his older brother?

"You're really so angry with your daughter you would declare war upon her?" he asked.

"She will do that." Iulia echoed Gaubert's pose. She folded her arms and leaned on her knees. It was a useful echo, for it displayed her décolletage perfectly.

On cue, his gaze flicked toward her breasts, then bounced back up to her face. He swallowed. "Bellona is having a tantrum. That's all. She'll grow bored with her new project in a few months and come home again."

Iulia shook her head. "You're wrong. I've been studying the footage, Gaubert. She didn't steal nearly as many ghostmakers as the assembly would like us to believe. She *did* get through a high security perimeter and take what she wanted. She has people who look to her. She has a mission. We gave her all the motivation she needs to fight for it. The Assembly would like to believe she is just an expensive nuisance. She will become more than that. When she does, you will look prophetic in your insistence upon an accord with Karassia."

Gaubert shook his head. "You can't possibly know that."

"I know Bellona." She smiled, to soften the statement. "You must sow the seeds now, Gaubert. Talk to the other heads about your relationship with Karassia and how that could be used to Eriuman advantage. Then, when Bellona and her little group overshadow the Homogeny threat, you will be there to offer the solution."

"To work with Karassia to wipe out Bellona? You really want revenge that much you would kill your own daughter?"

Iulia took the time to draw in a breath and calm herself. "By the time a working arrangement is needed with Karassia, it won't be just my daughter the Republic is facing. It will be the power of the free worlds working together."

Gaubert snorted. "That will *never* happen."

His tone said she had pushed too far. Iulia shrugged, retreating a little way. "Perhaps. Who am I to know anything? What could it hurt to put down the groundwork, though? To talk to some people? If I am right, you will be perfectly positioned."

Gaubert's knee rose and fell, as he thought it through. "I suppose there would be no harm in talking."

"You have little to lose," she said in agreement. "And so much you could gain from being the only Scordinii with vision."

Gaubert settled back against the tiles once more. "Tonight, perhaps. Or tomorrow, if it is cooler. Get me a refill, would you, Iulia? This damn heat is draining all my energy."

Iulia rose to her feet and stepped out of the pool, then went to get his requested glass of punch, not nearly as irked about the help-meet task as she had been before.

* * * * *

The former Karassian Homogeny Ship Alyard, Null-Space

AMILCARE RARELY CAME ONTO THE BRIDGE itself. He fidgeted and shifted from foot to foot, looking around the big, sterile area, as Zeni complained, his deeply lined face and protruding eyes troubled. From years of mining the minerals from beneath Abilio, his vision had deteriorated and been corrected numerous times and now his eyes were no longer Eriuman black, but a washed out brown.

Yet he was one of the more capable lieutenants to emerge from beneath Abilio, among the nearly forty recruits who had joined Bellona's cause. They had been scraping a living from the mineral mine when she and Sang had first arrived there.

Bellona studied him as Zeni wound herself up into a fury over the Abilio crew's rebellious ways and their latest infractions—this time, a refusal to attend the minimum daily training Zeni orchestrated in the cargo hold each morning.

Amilcare didn't seem to be listening to Zeni. He didn't seem to be paying much attention to anything. He was an independent man—all the Abilio people were. Bellona had learned to give them parameters and goals and let them get on with achieving them in their own way. He only appeared to be not paying attention right now. In his own way, he was absorbing everything, she was sure.

When Zeni fell silent at last, Amilcare lifted his square chin and looked at Bellona, perhaps challenging her to do something about it.

Only direct action would serve. Rhetoric did not move Amilcare and his teams.

Bellona launched herself at Amilcare, getting her hands around his neck and squeezing, before he could react.

No one else moved. Sang watched with interest and Khalil smiled. Zeni smothered a little shriek of shock and shuffled out of the way.

Amilcare struggled to fight Bellona off. She wound her leg around his and disrupted his balance, so his bodyweight was falling against her. To defend himself he would first have to shift his weight back to his own feet, which was impossible as long as she had a grip around his neck.

She squeezed.

Amilcare's eyes seemed to protrude even more, growing wider. A whisper of breath wheezed out of him as he scrabbled weakly at her hands.

As soon as she could see his consciousness was fading, Bellona released him. She let him slide to the floor, lowering his weight so he landed softly, then propped him against the back of the navigation station.

His breath rasped, his head hanging, the thick black, waving locks shot with gray hanging limply.

Zeni cleared her throat. "You don't intend to kill him, then?"

"Of course not," Bellona replied. She crouched down in front of Amilcare. "Can you hear me?"

He nodded. He didn't lift his head.

"I don't have to guess what that felt like," she said. "I've been exactly where you were a moment ago. Helpless, useless and defeated. It is not a good feeling, to know that someone else has complete control over you and your life."

Amilcare breathed in, his shoulders and chest lifting, then out. "Yes," he whispered.

"Watch me," she told him and got to her feet again. "Look at me, Amilcare."

He raised his chin. His eyes were bloodshot, a result of the strangling. Anger made the lines running down his cheeks deeper.

Bellona nodded. Without telegraphing her intentions, she turned and rammed into Sang, taking him off his feet. She grabbed his neck and squeezed, in the same way she had held Amilcare.

Sang reacted automatically, the actions ingrained in him. He slumped, letting his full weight sag in her hands. It was the unexpected thing to do but took a degree of discipline to overcome the normal human response to fight back and go limp, instead. The sudden, heavy weight dragged her hands down and loosened her grip on his neck.

It also pulled her down to the floor. She landed heavily on one hip, with a sharp exhalation as pain exploded there.

Sang's hands landed flat on the floor next to her. He pushed off with them, thrusting up onto his feet, breaking her hold. His boot landed on her chest, just below her chin, pinning her down. He grew still, breathing hard.

Amilcare's eyes had widened even more. Zeni's, too.

Sang took away his foot and held out his hand. "I apologize," he said quickly. "I didn't mean—"

"You acted exactly as you should," Bellona said, using his hand to help get herself back onto her feet. Her hip throbbed. She looked down at Amilcare. "That is why I insist you train with Zeni every day. You will know, in your bones, that no one can control you the way I just did."

Amilcare swallowed, then winced at the movement. "Karassians and Eriumans…they don't fight. Not like that. They hang in space and kill us from there. Fancy stuff like that can't stop a city killer."

Khalil crossed his arms. "Listen to yourself, Amilcare. You just said the magic words."

Amilcare blinked, frowning.

"You said 'Karassians and Eriumans don't fight like that'," Khalil added.

Amilcare stared at him.

"They can't fight like that because they don't know how," Khalil said. "You do…or you will, if you keep up the training."

Amilcare's frown increased, making the lines on his face shift.

"Learn to defend yourself," Bellona told him. "It will serve you well, even if it is not proof against city killers. While you learn, I am working on neutralizing the city killers."

"How?" Amilcare demanded.

She looked at Sang.

"Four minutes," Sang replied.

"In four minutes, I will show you," Bellona told Amilcare. "Stay on the bridge until then."

Amilcare nodded.

Bellona went back to the oversized, overstuffed Captain's chair and sank into it.

Khalil followed her over. "You're hurt," he said softly, so no one could hear. He reached out to touch her hip.

She pushed his hand away. "I'm fine," she said shortly.

Khalil let his hand drop.

Bellona rubbed her hip. "Why does it feel as if I've done that before?" she demanded.

"Done what?"

"Disciplined. Instructed. Given orders. Every time I do

that, it feels like an echo of something I've done before. I can't remember doing it. Yet it's familiar."

Khalil didn't try to touch her again. "If the records we're digging up from the Karassian databases are accurate—and there's no reason to think they are not—then you *have* done it all before."

"Xenia did that?" She was startled. "I thought she tore down civilizations and beat up helpless free-staters."

"When she wasn't doing that, she was a leader and strategist," Khalil said. "It looks as though she planned most of the campaigns she led. She didn't just follow orders. That's why it may feel familiar to you, even though you don't remember the details. It's like muscle memory. Habit."

Bellona shuddered. "I planned the defeat of Alkeides, then? It was all laid out in the file. A full military campaign, with strengths and weaknesses of the opposition and how to overcome them…I *wrote* that?"

Khalil's gaze softened. "*Xenia* did that."

"Am I ever going to remember doing it?"

He shook his head. "Those memories aren't buried, Bella. They're gone. Completely. You will never have to remember doing the things that Xenia did."

"Except my body remembers for me," she said, digging her fingers into her aching hip.

Khalil bent to look at her hip, his hands at his sides. "Sang did not spare you," he said softly. "Perhaps the medical bay—"

"No," she said firmly. "I was cruel, with Amilcare. I had to be, to make the point. I'll accept the consequences, thank you."

He straightened and his gaze met hers once more. "We should talk—"

The normal space alert chimed, echoing around the bridge. The same loud blare of notes would be repeated across the ship, ensuring everyone was braced for the emergence from null space into possibly hostile space.

The ship shuddered delicately as the null drive made the translation.

The permanent screens on the walls immediately came alive. Everyone turned to look at them, even Khalil, because Bellona was the only one who knew where they were and what was out there.

Hayes and Thecla, Fontana and the other Ledanians ran onto the bridge, too, looking around anxiously, trying to determine if there was a threat. Emergence from null space was always a high risk moment.

"Ship ahead!" Fontana cried, bending over the tactical table to study the dashboard. "*Big* ship!"

"Scanning and identifying!" Retha called out.

Bellona called up the scans and matched them to historical data. "Relax," she told everyone. "The thing is harmless. Get a lens on it and you'll see what I mean. Thecla?"

Thecla nodded and stepped behind the communications console and swiped at the controls.

The big center screen switched views from the default dead ahead view to an angle that encompassed the ship.

"What *is* that sound?" Vang said, looking up at the roof. "It sounds like rain."

"Something hitting us," Fontana said, frowning down at the scans. "I can't see anything, though."

"It's debris," Bellona told them. "Too small to hurt the ship. It's inert and too small to register on the scans as a threat. Look." She nodded toward the central screen again.

The ship on the screen looked quite small and was sitting in space, dead still. It was an elongated shape, with superstructures and outer attachments and weapons married to the original sleek shape.

"White ship. Karassian?" Hero said. "Where are we, anyway?"

Amilcare hauled himself to his feet, moving slowly, watching the screen.

Fontana looked at Bellona. "Do you want to save me from a directory search and just tell us who that is out there?"

"The 'who' is nobody," she said. "That is the Karassian Homogeny Ship *Aarens*."

"The cruiser?" Thecla said, startled.

"Shit," Fontana breathed, staring at it. "It's dead, isn't it?"

Aideen stood by the corner of the console he was working on, looking up at the screen. "The *Aarens* was a casualty of the battle against the Republic, who opposed the possession of the Alkeides system," she said, with the flat voice that said she was recalling and reciting data from records she had read elsewhere. "The space engines were destroyed, forcing the *Aarens* to abandon, all hands evacuated to other Homogeny ships."

"Hayes, take manual control of the helm," Bellona told the giant. "Pass us slowly by the carrier, so everyone can take a look."

Hayes ambled over to the helm. He peered down at the controls, then ran his hand over them. The *Alyard* swung around. The lens focused on the *Aarens* tracked with the movement, keeping the ghost ship on the center of the screen. The *Alyard* moved forward slowly.

"We're over Alkeides?" Retha asked.

"It's a short hop behind us," Bellona told him. "The Republic and the Homogeny fought here, before the Karassians went on to claim Alkeides."

"Felis," Aideen added. "That's its name now."

"Felis," Bellona said in agreement.

"More of your bedtime reading?" Khalil asked quietly.

"Yes." She studied the ship growing larger on the screen. The scorch marks and jagged fuselage surrounding the massive normal space engines were the only visible damage to the ship.

"It looks completely whole and untouched," Vang said.

"If it is, then what debris is raining on us?" Fontana demanded.

"What is left of the *Quattrocchi*," Bellona told them.

"The Republic destroyer," Aideen added. "Xenia ordered the *Aarens* to play dead. When the destroyer came up from behind, they fired the engines at full throttle and did not engage the thrusters. The reactors on the *Quattrocchi* were incinerated by the exhaust and containment was breached. The explosion set off a chain reaction inside the ship, as heat-sensitive objects reacted to the sudden temperature spike. The Republic withdrew after that."

"It melted," Vang said, fascinated.

"From the inside," Retha added.

"It exploded," Thecla corrected them. "Nothing could contain the interior of a whole destroyer going critical."

Khalil was studying Bellona with close attention.

"What?" she demanded.

"Why bring us here?" he asked. "Why dig up old memories like this?"

"Because something good can come out of Xenia's doings." She got to her feet and moved closer to the screen. Hayes was drifting the *Alyard* over the top of the cruiser.

"We can't steal the *Aarens*, if that's what you're thinking," Khalil said. "If the space engines could have been recovered, the Karassians would have reclaimed the ship long ago."

"Exactly," Bellona told him.

On the screen, the shadow of the *Alyard* fell across the cruiser's hull. It was a tiny dark mark.

"*Big* ship," Hayes said softly.

"Fucking huge," Vang added. "I hadn't realized how big they were."

The *Alyard's* shadow tracked along the length of the cruiser for long minutes as everyone stared at the dead vessel.

Khalil stirred. "What do you intend to do with it, then?" he asked.

"Claim it," Bellona replied. "You're all looking at that massive structure out there as a ship. Something that moves through space to get somewhere else. What I see, when I look at it, is a place to call home."

Silence. All eyes were on the screen.

Sang smiled. "It will need a name," he pointed out. "*Aarens* is a ship name. A Homogeny name."

"Nothing Eriuman, either," Hero said sharply.

"What do you call a place that used to be a ship, that is a new free state?" Khalil asked of everyone.

"Demosthenes," Bellona told them.

No one looked away from the screen.

"Terran antiquity," Aideen said. "It means 'The strength of the people'."

"Demos," Fontana said, trying it out. "Demos, demon, demonic. Demosthenes." He nodded, satisfied. "Sounds about right."

Chapter Seven

Karassian Homogeny Ship Aarens, Alkeides System

IT WAS CHAOTIC IN THE ship that would become Demosthenes. The emergency evacuation had left clutter and abandoned objects everywhere. In the massive carrier hold, Connie was barely able to find room to land, among the hundreds of personal fighters and other junk littering the deck.

Thecla patted the side of the nearest fighter, which was only a little taller than Hayes, overjoyed. "A whole fleet of fighters just for us," she breathed.

"Fighters with a tendency to blow up if you push the steering column the wrong way," Fontana pointed out.

"I can fix that," Thecla said, with complete assurance.

"Later," Bellona told her. "There's a lot of work ahead of us to make this place livable, first."

For over a week, they stayed aboard the *Alyard,* even after coupling it up to the side of Demosthenes and generating a particle tunnel between the two ships. The *Alyard* was too big to land on the carrier deck, although Connie had made herself comfortable in a corner she claimed as her own.

During that week, they shuttled and then walked over to Demosthenes to work on clearing up the areas they needed the most. The first priority was restarting the fusion cores, to generate the energy they would need. Fontana was a competent jackleg engineer and power was restored within twelve hours.

After that, the priorities were less clear. "There are four kitchens and seven dining rooms," Hero pointed out. "One of them just for the captain. Where do we start?"

"One dining room and one kitchen. Living quarters for everyone—assigned, to start," Bellona told them. "Later, if someone finds different quarters more to their taste, they can clean them up for themselves. We clear out the bridge, the medbay and as much of the landing deck as we can."

"You're not going to dismantle the bridge?" Khalil asked.

"Not yet," Bellona told him and everyone who was listening. "We might still want to move, one day. Thecla says the null generators could be made functional again."

"The space engines are completely fried, though," Thecla added.

"You have to be moving for the null engines to work," Khalil pointed out.

"A meter a second is all that is needed," Sang said.

"Positional thrusters will overcome inertia enough for that," Thecla said. "Just," she added. "And it might take a few minutes to get going, so it's not something we can use for an emergency."

"I'll bear that in mind," Bellona assured her.

The interior of Demosthenes rang with industry as the priority areas were cleared out and returned to a functioning state. Useful objects and abandoned possessions rounded up from these areas were added to a growing pile in one corner of the landing deck. Crew members—that Bellona insisted be called residents—could take from the pile anything they needed, or raid the unused areas of Demosthenes for more.

Bellona put Hero in charge of environmental ambience and told her to get rid of the stark white walls wherever possible. Hero immersed herself in color technology, converting the static walls to blush expressive and experimenting with colors and patterns. She also found a wide-mouthed assembler in the deeper bowels of Demosthenes and with Sang's help, adjusted the programming so it would extrude textiles.

Bellona was made aware of the new capabilities of the assembler when she found drapes over a generated screen at one end of the dining room they were using. The screen showed a view of mountains and a window frame.

"It should be a lagoon," Hayes complained, when he saw the view. "I like lagoons."

No one pointed out to him that he liked lagoons only because his Ledan conditioning had taught him to like them.

After six days of hard but gratifying work, Bellona was satisfied enough to allow everyone to move over to Demosthenes from their cramped quarters on the *Alyard*. She found the expansive captain's suite located behind the bridge almost uncomfortably roomy. She also heard comments about elbow room and breathing space and knew everyone else was enjoying the scale.

When Demosthenes was functioning at a basic level, she turned to the real priorities, leaving others to take care of the details of life in Demos.

She called Sang to her new quarters first. "I can't ignore that this was a Karassian ship, originally," she told him, as she punched at the controls on the big desk, trying to dismiss the screen that had spontaneously generated when Sang walked into the room. "We're getting all their feeds—so many of them, it's overwhelming. I can't figure out how to turn them off so they don't spring to life some time later."

"I can take care of that," Sang assured her.

"We should not turn *all* of the feeds off," she added. "We could learn a lot from monitoring them."

"Connie does monitor, as much as she can. She reports to me—although she doesn't always understand what she's watching, so something critical could be overlooked."

"We can set up algorithms to monitor," Bellona said.

"Did Connie tell you about the man they call Chidi?"

"I remember Chidi from my time on Kachmar," Sang said. "He is highly influential in Karassia."

"I don't know why," Bellona said. "He doesn't say anything significant, yet he is adored."

"I believe he says what everyone wants to hear," Sang said. "That is why they appreciate him. He confirms that their thoughts and opinions are valid."

"He's saying Xenia is real and I'm a fake," Bellona said.

Sang grimaced. "Exactly what Karassians would prefer to believe. It lets them sleep peacefully."

Bellona considered him, startled. "They think I'm lying?"

"They think," Sang said slowly, "that you're using Xenia's fame and glory to further your own hidden agenda."

"I've been perfectly frank."

"Karassians are not used to frankness."

She stared at Sang, flummoxed. "They don't believe that Shavistran was wiped out? They really believe it was all faked?"

"It's more comfortable to believe it didn't happen," Sang said. "If it did, then it raises questions. Why would Eriuman destroy a whole city and if they have that capability, when will they destroy Kachmar City, or their city? Better to pretend your claims are all lies."

"They could go to Shavistran and see the melted ruins for themselves," Bellona said.

"That would be too proactive an action to take over something they don't believe is true." Sang shook his head. "There is an inertia to a communal belief that is difficult to overcome. No matter what you say, they will spin it to fit with their beliefs."

"If I say it enough, surely some of them will start to question what is the truth?"

"The problem is, you are Bellona, who looks only vaguely like their hero, Xenia."

Bellona sat back. "What if I looked *exactly* like Xenia?"

Sang looked thoughtful. "That might jar them into asking questions," he admitted. "Although the *official* Karassian reaction might be more…forceful."

"Can you cover the source of the transmissions so the Karassian officials can't find us?"

"Connie could. She is on a first name basis with a lot of Karassian inter-system satellites now."

"*Name* basis? You're speaking metaphorically?"

"No. Connie asked them to give themselves names, so she didn't have to keep using serial numbers to talk to them." Sang smiled.

"Good," Bellona said. "Let's overcome the Karassian common man's inertia, Sang. A flood of footage from Xenia herself. A deluge—so much of it that Chidi and his cohorts are drowned out by the volume. Let's give Karassians a choice and ask them to make up their minds for themselves."

"I can do that, of course," Sang said. "Khalil is good with communications networks—"

"No," Bellona said sharply. "Just you, Sang. Connie, of course. I prefer to keep this in-family."

Sang grew still. His gaze cut away from her.

"What is it, Sang? You disapprove of that?"

Sang cleared his throat. His odd pale eyes met hers again. "May I speak frankly?"

"Don't you always?"

He shook his head. "Bluntness is rarely appreciated."

She sighed. "Speak."

Instead, Sang shifted on his feet.

"Sang…"

"I thought Khalil *was* family," he said, as if he was forcing the sentence from his inner-most self.

Bellona's heart squeezed. She could feel the thud of it in her temples, too. "You're right, Sang. I don't like your brand of frankness."

Sang lifted a hand, as if defeated. "Has he not proved himself to you? 'If there was a beating heart to the Bureau I would tear it out with my bare hands and give it to you.' That is what he said."

"He did say that," Bellona said, as calmly as she could. The heat and the pounding in her veins sickened her.

"Then…" Sang trailed off helplessly.

"Words are not proof."

"Why does love have to prove itself?"

Bellona sucked in a breath as something shifted and rolled in her gut. "That's *enough*, Sang."

He grew still. His gaze dropped to the floor. "I apologize," he said stiffly. "I'll go and start on the algorithms."

"And the Xenia feed," she reminded him.

He headed for the door, his back straight and stiff.

"Sang."

Sang didn't look back. It was a very human form of denial. Yet he did hesitate at the open door.

"He betrayed me once," she reminded him.

"He *had* to."

"Which means he might be forced to it again."

Sang's shoulders dropped. Silently, he stepped out and let the door close.

* * * * *

THE FRONT END OF THE cavernous landing deck, tucked behind the growing pile of cast-offs and curiosities, was where Zeni held her daily combat training sessions. She didn't pad the floor or prepare the area in anyway, except to clear the trash.

Sang attended the early morning sessions, as did Khalil. When Khalil asked Sang to practice with him late in the afternoon, though, he agreed.

There were three Abilio people working their way through the cast-off pile. Everyone digging through the heap tended to sort as they went. There were separate and growing piles of related things—clothes, entertainment, comfort, grooming and more.

As Khalil and Sang put each other through mock fights and maneuvers, their audience grew. Sang was pleased to see Amilcare among them.

There was enough floor space that they could talk quietly without their audience listening in. Sang drew Khalil's attention to the watchers.

"I should bust your butt for their edification?" Khalil asked, with a grin that flashed white teeth and made his eyes glitter, as he settled into a stance for the next flurry.

"As if you could," Sang replied, preparing himself.

Khalil launched himself. It was a speedy attack. A heavy-handed one. Sang held him off using more strength than he usually needed and sent Khalil rolling along the floor.

Khalil jumped to his feet and came at Sang once more.

The flurry this time was longer.

Sang risked glancing at Khalil's face as they grappled. There was a look in his eyes that Sang had not seen before.

He tripped Khalil and pushed him away, troubled.

Khalil staggered, regained his balance and faced him once more.

"Perhaps a punching bag might be more useful to you," Sang suggested.

Khalil smiled, without mirth. "A punching bag doesn't hit back."

"You want to be beaten?" Sang launched himself at Khalil. The exchange was hard and fast. This time, Sang spun away, retreating.

Khalil breathed quickly. The smile had gone.

"I don't want to hurt you," Sang said.

Khalil shrugged. "I'm used to it."

Sang lowered his hands, as he sorted out the odd notes

in Khalil's voice. "Not from me."

Khalil leapt at him.

Sang was unprepared. He countered barely in time. Khalil hissed as Sang's foot connected with his forearm and turned away, shaking it out. "Not from you, huh?" he said dryly.

Sang straightened from the ready position. "Perhaps I should find that bag for you. I cannot help you, here."

"Stay and fight, damn you," Khalil snapped. "Get ready."

Sang hesitated. There were too many warring emotions swirling about them for him to process without full attention. Human emotions were the most complex of concepts and he knew that this moment was full of conflicting ideas that involved him in some way he had yet to fathom.

Khalil swore. "Ready yourself."

Sang shook his head. "I do not think you are in the right mood."

Khalil came at him, ninety kilos and a hundred and ninety centimeters of fury. Even so, Sang could have held his ground. Instead, he let himself be overcome. He didn't know why he had made the choice to fight with less than his usual strength and agility. Sometimes he acted before he had fully formed the logic that should generate the act. He had learned to call those moments instinctive. His instincts told him now to give way. To submit.

Khalil dropped him to the ground with an impact that made the deck floor shudder and slammed Sang's breath from him. Khalil fell on him with both knees, winding him.

Sang didn't have to pretend to be helpless. The lack of oxygen made him dizzy and he lay gasping in shallow sips, waiting for his diaphragm to start working properly again.

Khalil stared down at him. "We're the same, you and I. You, she trusts." He rolled away and sat with a knee to his chest, breathing hard, his gaze on the floor.

Sang couldn't have spoken even if he wanted to. His mind, though, was chaotic with surprise at this sudden and unexpected insight.

He should have anticipated Khalil's unhappiness. There was no excuse…except for the human one that when it came to matters of close personal interest, he was often blind.

When the first tendril of energy grew enough to give him movement, Sang rolled over and sat up. That was all he could manage for now. "You should not be jealous. Not of me. I am an android. A help-meet. That is all."

Khalil looked at him, then away. "Is that why you write those endless histories of yours? Is that your punching bag?"

Sang swallowed. "Histories are always written by the victors. I am…anticipating."

Khalil met his gaze once more. "I only want to help, just as you do." He hammered at the floor. "I *deserve* this. Yet I hate it. I could help, Sang. My knowledge of the Bureau alone…" He sighed.

"I know. So does Bellona. Give her time. That is the only thing that will help, now."

"I don't think there *is* time enough to overcome this," Khalil said bitterly. "Yet I can't give up, either."

Sang let out a heavy breath. "Nor can I."

"At least you have a place here," Khalil said. "You have a purpose."

"Do I?" Sang asked, surprised.

Khalil's smile was small. "Of course you do. Why wouldn't you?"

"I am a generalist," Sang said automatically. "Purpose was never given to me."

"You're not that household android anymore, Sang," Khalil said gravely. "You're your own man, purpose and all. Her cause is yours."

Sang nodded as he saw the truth in that. "It could be yours, too," he told Khalil. "It *should* be."

"It would be, but for *my* history." Khalil got to his feet, moving slowly. Their audience had disappeared now they had stopped moving. It left them alone on the floor. Khalil held out his hand toward Sang. "Up you get."

Sang took his hand and let Khalil help lift him to his feet. He was breathing almost normally once more.

Khalil kept hold of his hand, welding him to the spot. He gaze met Sang's. "I don't know what may happen in the future, Sang."

"No one does."

"There are parts of her life where she won't let me in." Khalil's gaze didn't move. "You're in, though."

"Like you, there are parts I am not privy to and never will be," Sang said, as evenly as he could. "Those are yours."

"Yes." Khalil's grip tightened. "Between the two of us, Sang, we can be everything she needs."

Finally, Sang understood the patterns of the currents around him. Khalil had seen it before he had. He had loved Bellona longer. Sang nodded. "We can," he said softly.

Chapter Eight

Demosthenes, Alkeides System

THE FULL COMPLEMENT OF THE *Alyard* barely dented the capacity of Demosthenes. The dining room they used was the smallest one apart from the captain's private room. Yet it still seemed empty even when everyone was in it. As a consequence, at meal times, everyone tended to sit only at the two long tables closest to the servery outlets. After eating, the diners lingered, talking and laughing.

Bellona recognized the bonding as a useful morale booster and often stayed for a while herself, despite more important matters that weighed upon her. Even though the conversation was casual and relaxed, the subjects discussed were still vital ones; politics was the most popular. The range of expertise and knowledge across Demos was surprisingly vast and sometimes conversations veered off in unexpected directions. That was how it happened.

On that night, Bellona suspected everyone living in Demosthenes was at the tables. Thecla had overridden the controls on the printers, so they produced beverages that featured real alcohol. The conversations after dinner had a free-flowing, relaxed sound, although no one seemed to be overindulging.

Sang had been talking about the Xenia feeds he had been blasting across the Karassian systems. Bellona had spent a whole day as Xenia, providing sound bites and speeches, written by Khalil and Vang, who had supplied the psychology driving them. Sang had captured Xenia digitally and could now make his own footage using the digital images, faster than Bellona could record them live.

"Karassians are watching," Sang said. "The audience is

not the size of Chidi's, yet it is growing."

"Word of mouth will bring more," Khalil said, his long fingers curled around a glass of clear liquid that he only sipped. "As long as you keep the feed going."

Sang nodded. "I intend to. The more people who see it, the more they talk about it, the more the doubt will grow."

"If the doubt reaches critical mass," Vang said, "They'll finish the work of convincing themselves for you."

Hero tapped Sang's shoulder, for she was sitting on the table behind the one where Bellona and the others were sitting. Hero was not the only one perched on the adjoining tables, joining in. "Sang, is it true that communications channels are just miniature wormholes?"

Bellona smiled. "Where did you hear that?"

"Aideen said it." Hero shrugged. "I thought wormholes were lethal."

"The one working wormhole anyone has ever built *was* lethal," Fontana said. "It destroyed Pushyani."

"That's the moon where they built that generator, yes?" Retha said.

Hero nudged Sang again. "So, is it true? Channels are wormholes and no one has ever told anyone?"

Sang shook his head. "The knowledge isn't secret. It just doesn't get talked about widely because the Pushyan disaster makes most people nervous when wormholes are mentioned."

"Then it's true?" Bellona asked, as surprised as most of the expressions around the table told her everyone else was.

Sang frowned. "It's not that simple—"

"Name one thing in life that *is* simple," Fontana growled.

"Sex," Hero said instantly.

Everyone groaned.

"Sex with you is *not* simple," Vang replied. "Not if one

values their genitals."

"No, wait," Bellona said. "I want to go back to the wormhole thing. Sang, really? Feeds are all wormholes?"

"The *feeds* are not wormholes," Sang said. "They're just normal audio-visual compilations. What they pass through to get from system to system and not lose cohesion are microscopic wormholes. Interstellar communications satellites are really bridge generators, that send and receive feeds from other systems, then broadcast them down to the planet they're over."

Thecla laughed. "If that is true, then why didn't they use the same model for Pushyani? It would have worked, then, instead of blowing up the whole damn moon."

"They did use the same model," Sang said.

Everyone stared at him.

Sang didn't seem to be bothered by the attention. "Bridge forge technology has been known and understood for hundreds of years. The miniature forges used for communications channels were developed nearly two hundred years ago. Then someone decided that scaling up the forges to a dimension that could generate a ship-sized bridge would be useful. Funding was found to develop a generator on Pushyani."

"Yikes," someone breathed.

"Exactly," Sang said in agreement. "Simple scaling presented problems that don't exist at micro-sizes. Forges are impractical at ship-size. They're far more massive than null-space generators. The strongest materials known to the free worlds collapse as soon as the hole is produced. They can't cope with the strain. That's what happened on Pushyani. The engineers used carbyne for the entire generator and it still wasn't strong enough. The forces produced crushed the moon to gravel."

"The bigger the bridge, the stronger the forge has to be," Fontana said thoughtfully.

"It's a geometric scale," Sang said. "The smaller the

hole, the more stable it is.

"I had no idea," someone whispered. "It's incredible!"

Bellona tended to agree. She shuddered. The idea that a bridge forge was being used even for something as benign as a microscopic communications feed was unsettling.

Fontana leaned forward. "Has anyone tried to make a man-sized forge?"

Sang's eyes widened, as if he had been slapped.

Bellona sat up, as excitement gripped her. "*Man* sized…" she breathed. "Sang, is it possible?"

Sang blinked. "Theoretically, yes. In practice, though, there are all sorts of challenges. Electrical charges, structural strength…you'd have to find something stronger than carbyne, just to begin."

"There *is* nothing stronger than carbyne," Thecla said shortly, annoyed.

"You said it was a geometric scale of pressure," Fontana said. "How intense would the pressure be if the generator was man-sized? Maybe carbyne would be enough."

Bellona drew in a breath, striving for calm. "Look into it," she told Sang. "Work with Fontana and Thecla and whoever and whatever else you need. Do the calculations. I want to know if this is more than theoretically possible."

Khalil leaned closer to her. "Perhaps this should be put aside for now," he said very quietly.

"Why?" she breathed back.

"You should be focusing on recruiting the free states. Everything hinges on you winning them over to your side."

Next to her, everyone was talking rapidly and loudly, shouting over each other, as they pulled the idea apart.

Bellona shook her head. "No," she told Khalil. "It doesn't all hinge on that at all. Don't you see? This could be the coup we've been looking for."

"A man-sized bridge?" Khalil said doubtfully.

Bellona nodded. "It would change everything." She was no longer keeping her voice down. She didn't have to. The conversation right next to her was loud enough to muffle her. "Amilcare said it the other day. The Republic and the Homogeny rely on ship power. The biggest ship, the biggest guns, wins. With the city killers, they can stay in space and *still* win."

"Which is why you need every free state and their combined fire power lined up beside you," Khalil said patiently.

"Not if we aren't on ships," she shot back.

Khalil sat back, frowning. "I know you want to think of this place as a station or a city, only it's just a ship. We can still get shot out of the sky."

"Not if we're not on it."

Khalil pushed his hand through his hair, clearly frustrated.

Bellona rested her hand on his wrist. "Alkeides," she said. "You heard what Isabelle Lykke said about it. The Karassian troops hung back while Xenia fought off the free staters."

Khalil nodded.

"Why?" she demanded.

"Because they're gutless." He shrugged.

"Because they don't know how to fight. They haven't been trained. They've never had to bother." Bellona gripped his wrist harder. "*We know how.*"

Khalil considered her, enlightenment dawning in his eyes.

Bellona swiveled on her stool. "Sang. If a personal sized forge could work, would it be possible to jump from the surface of a planet to another planet? Or would we have to be in space, first, like the communications satellites are?"

"The satellites are in space because from orbit it's easier to send the communications feeds across the face of the globe," Sang said. "A forge, if it works at all, can work anywhere."

Bellona looked back at Khalil. "Think of it," she urged him. "If we can step across a bridge—"

"*Through* a bridge," Fontana corrected.

"Through a bridge," Bellona repeated. "If we could step through a bridge from, say, Circe to Kachmar City, in the very heart of the Homogeny, instantly, then we would have no need for ships of any sort. The Republic and the Karassians could fight each other to a standstill out here. It wouldn't matter. We would control the planets themselves."

"Won't the Karassians fight you when you step through to Kachmar City?" Hayes asked, frowning as he followed along.

"They don't know how to fight. Not as we can," Bellona said. "Neither do Eriumans."

Amilcare's mouth was open. His eyes were wide once more. *He sees it,* Bellona thought to herself, with satisfaction.

"Free staters can still fight. Alkeides proved they can. We can train them to fight even better," Bellona said. Everyone was listening to her now. "With a personal bridge forge, we could move from world to world instantly, going wherever we are needed. We could step onto Kachmar whenever we want, or Cardenas, for that matter. It would neutralize the threat of the city killers."

She got to her feet. "That's how we're going to help the free states take back their freedom. That's how we will win."

Chapter Nine

The former Karassian Homogeny Ship Alyard, Pushyan local space, Ovid System

BELLONA REMINDED HERSELF HOW OFTEN Sang said "theoretically" when he was talking about a bridge forge, as she stared at the depressing view on the bridge monitors. They were aboard the *Alyard* with a skeleton crew, while everyone else remained behind on Demosthenes, to work on the long list of things that needed attention, including a badly equipped medical bay that was short of the most basic supplies.

Only Sang and Fontana, Thecla and Amilcare and five of his men were aboard. Bellona had asked Khalil to remain behind, to run Demosthenes while she was gone. She didn't let herself think too long about how empty the bed felt in the cramped captain's cabin of the *Alyard.*

The view showed the asteroid belt that had formed around Pushyan. None of the rocks were more than human sized. "The moon was *pulverized,*" she murmured, her heart sinking. "The force needed to do something like that..."

A century ago, Pushyan had been a thriving free state colony, with three cities and numerous towns and villages spread out across the four major continents. The night side of Pushyan faced them now. The lights from those cities and villages should have been sparkling on the face of the world. All of it was deepest black, though—the whole world sterilized by the fallout from the moon's destruction and the collapse of the bridge generator.

"Still think this is a good idea?" Bellona asked Fontana.

He glanced at Aideen, who stood just as she had for

the twelve hour jump to Pushyan, in the corner made by the medical bay door, working equations on a hand screen, her lips moving silently.

Aideen was watching the viewscreen now. "Whatever survived the destruction of the moon will be strong. We have to find it."

Fontana shrugged. "You heard the lady."

"You're on point, then," Bellona told him. "Metallurgic survey first. Then, whatever Aideen thinks might be suitable, after that."

"Yes, boss," Fontana said and started working the dashboard in front of him. "Sang, Connie, can we move to a hundred meters above the belt borders? We can scan from there—"

Bellona tuned Fontana's voice out. She had come along only because the development of a personal bridge forge was *her* project. She didn't hold much hope that visiting Pushyan would further the project. Aideen had been very nearly manic in her insistence they go there, though.

Sang had developed a list of hurdles to be overcome even to build a theoretical model of a personal bridge forge. The list grew longer the more he and everyone on the ship with any sort of contributing expertise discussed it. Bellona had agreed to the trip to Pushyan simply to give herself something else to think about than the obstacles they were facing.

Now she was here, though, she wondered if it had been wise to come at all. She could have put Sang in the captain's chair and been confident the outing would be successfully completed. No one on the ship could afford to be fussy about an android leading them, when they had as mixed and unsavory pasts themselves. No one had ever shown a moment of hesitation about dealing with Sang as a fully fledged human, anyway. Not even the Karassian-born Ledanians cared.

With Sang leading the expedition, she could have remained on Demosthenes and fully occupied with her work. Instead, she had hours to spend in the Captain's cabin, to brood and keep herself as occupied as possible, while the survey was conducted. She could not contribute to it. She did not have the science background.

On the third day, Thecla called her to the bridge, waking Bellona from a superficial sleep.

Bellona went out to the all-white area, blinking at the harsh light there. "What's happened?" she asked.

"Maybe nothing," Thecla said. "We finished scanning the belt a few hours ago, then moved onto the surface for a fast look."

"No carbyne, huh?"

"Oh, we found carbyne almost immediately we started scanning," Fontana said. "It's everywhere throughout the belt, in traces and lumps. No big pieces, though. It's all as fragmented as the moon."

"We brought some aboard for assay," Thecla said.

"With all suitable bio hazard protections," Sang added quickly.

Bellona relaxed. "What did the assay find?"

"It's not finished yet," Sang said. "Some of the tests take twenty-four hours to produce results."

"It's what we found on the surface," Thecla added. She tapped the dash in front of her and pointed to the viewscreen as it shifted to show a bland band of gray earth. She zoomed it in. More gray. Rocks. Dirt. Nothing green grew anywhere.

"What did you find?" Bellona asked patiently.

"Human remains, we think," Thecla said.

Bellona considered the screen. "From when the moon blew up?"

"Those bodies would have long turned to dust," Thecla said dismissively, of the two million people who had once lived on Pushyan. "This is far more recent."

"How recent?"

"Three years max," Thecla said. "Can we take Connie down and have a look? Pick up some DNA? It might be worth knowing who would want to come to this graveyard to die."

"Will a surface trip slow down the survey?" Bellona asked.

Sang shook his head. "It might be a good trial run for Aideen's earwigs. There are odd surges of radiation that will test the communications between Connie and the wearer."

Bellona nodded. Then a thought struck her. "The earworms…they don't use wormholes, do they?" The idea of a volatile wormhole reaching into her ear was not a pleasant one.

Fontana laughed. "Aideen murmured something about high frequency rotating squirt bands. I think you're safe."

"Then I'll go down with Thecla to check the remains," she decided.

It would be something to do.

* * * * *

AIDEEN BROKE OFF FROM HER assay trials long enough to shove a small device each into Thecla's and Bellona's hands, before impatiently returning to her test tubes.

Fontana shepherded them away from the tiny lab. "I think I remember most of what she said about them when she designed them. Put them into your ear and they'll adapt to fit. No one can hear what Connie says to you. The upper end of the frequency spectrum is never used anymore, so the chances that someone will accidentally trip over the transmissions is extremely low. The rotating frequencies minimizes that chance even further."

Bellona pushed the little object into her ear and froze as it wriggled and adjusted. Then it grew still. "My hearing is muffled on that side, now," she said, as Thecla slapped her hand against her own ear, wincing. Given her enhanced strength, the slaps had to hurt all on their own.

"Wait for it to finish adjusting," Fontana said.

Abruptly, as if a switch had been thrown, her hearing cleared in her left ear. She could hear as clearly as ever. She put her hand to her ear. "It compensates?"

"Channels, really. Although if you had poor hearing in that ear, it might enhance it."

"How do we get it out after?" Thecla demanded.

Fontana looked startled.

"We don't, I'm guessing," Bellona said.

Thecla's jaw rippled. "You mean this thing is *stuck* in me?"

Bellona put her hand on Thecla's arm. "We can find a way to extract it later if we need to."

"You asked for something covert and untraceable," Fontana reminded them.

"I did," Bellona agreed. "How do I talk to Connie now?"

"I think she's probably waiting for you to say hello," Fontana said.

Bellona cleared her throat. "Um. Connie?"

"Bellona! Hi! It's so nice to talk to you like this!" Connie's little girl voice squeaked in her ear, making Bellona wince again.

"Can you speak softly?" Bellona asked. "You're blowing out my ear drum."

"Mine, too," Thecla growled.

"Is this better?" Connie asked. The volume *was* more comfortable.

"That's good," Bellona told her.

"Although you'll have to monitor the environmental noise wherever we are," Thecla said, "and adjust your volume to match." Thecla grinned at Bellona. "If there are grenades going off around us, you might have to shout a bit."

"Of course," Connie said stiffly, her dignity wounded.

"Okay, let's get this done," Bellona said. "Connie, fire up the engines. We're going on a trip."

"I've been waiting with engines humming for fifteen minutes already," Connie replied. "Sang told me you'd be here ages ago."

* * * * *

Pushyan, Ovid II

DOWN ON THE SURFACE, THE wind blew a mournful, high note, pushing around dust swirls. After a hundred years, the rough edges of the ruined city had been worn smooth, while buildings had collapsed from neglect, violent storms and severe radiation.

Thecla used the portable scanner to check on Connie's prognosis that it was safe on the surface.

"Beta is high," Thecla said. "Gamma is within tolerances if we don't plan on staying longer than a week."

"Told you it was safe," Connie said with a sniff. "The body you found is west-south-west of your position, about a kilometer. I can guide you once you get closer."

"How much body would there be after three years?" Bellona asked as they started walking in a west-south-westerly direction.

"Not much," Thecla said.

"DNA traces from the bones," Connie said. "Although with all this radiation, the bones have probably disintegrated, too."

"We're looking for dust?" Bellona clarified.

"Dust that still has viable DNA in its marrow," Thecla said.

What they did find, inside a fully enclosed room that had once been a part of a building that was now otherwise gone, was complete skeleton, with a story to tell. The enclosed room had protected it from the elements.

Bellona looked down at the posture of the bones as Thecla scanned it. "A woman," she guessed. "Not a big one, either."

"A girl," Thecla said, looking at the scanner screen. "Maybe fifteen. And look." She pointed to the skull. "See that long shard of glass in the eye socket?"

"From a window?"

Thecla shook her head. "There are no windows here. And look at the nick on the thumb and forefinger of the hand up by the head."

Bellona bent her head to study the twin scrapes. She put it together and drew in a hard breath. "She pushed the glass into her own eye?"

"Looks that way." Thecla bent and cautiously picked up the top bone from the little finger and scanned it. "DNA is present. We'll have to dig to get it out."

Bellona unbuckled the pack she had been carrying. "We take all of her back. When we find the family, we return her to them. I get the feeling they might be still wondering if she is alive." She pulled out the biggest sample bag in the pack and unfolded it.

Thecla held out the little bone. "Right," she said softly, all traces of her usual sarcasm missing.

"Take images of this room, too," Bellona said. "I have no idea why we would need to. My gut says do it now. We might not have a chance, later."

It took them an hour to process the room and the body, then they returned to Connie, for the jump up to the *Alyard*. Connie chatted constantly as they hiked back to her and on the fifty-minute leap to the upper atmosphere, while Thecla and Bellona were both quiet and thoughtful.

"You figure she was forced to it?" Thecla said as Connie floated into the interior of the *Alyard* and settled down with a soft bump.

Bellona didn't bother asking who Thecla was talking

about. "We might never find out," she admitted.

"At least we can give her back to her family, whoever she ends up being," Thecla said. "Maybe that will have to do."

Sang was waiting for them as they walked down the ramp to the cargo hold floor. His expression was neutral.

"What has happened?" Bellona asked.

"Aideen finished her assay."

"And?"

Sang drew in a breath and let it out. "The carbyne structure is unique. There is no record of it anywhere."

"It's not carbyne?"

"No, it is carbyne. The correct elements are there, in the correct sequence. It's just…" Sang frowned. "It has no electrical charge. It is completely inert."

"Is that good or bad?" Bellona asked.

"It's…different," Sang said cautiously. "Metals always have a charge. This does not."

"It's still a metal, still carbyne?" Thecla said. "That *is* different."

Sang fell into step alongside them. "It gets stranger," he warned them. "The carbyne is inert and completely pure. No contaminants or trace minerals. Nothing."

Thecla stopped walking and Bellona turned back to look at her. Sang, too.

"What is it?" Bellona said.

"Completely pure and inert," Thecla said. "The original incident, with the generator—the conditions must have…I don't know, *strained* it somehow."

"Wouldn't it be weaker if it had been stressed?"

"Strained, as in, purified," Sang said. He looked at Thecla. "You see it, then."

"It's *stronger*," Thecla said, sounding awed.

Sang nodded.

"How much stronger?" Bellona asked. "Enough for what we want?"

Sang drew in a slow, controlling breath. "There's only one way to find out."

Bellona nodded. "Collect how much you think you'll need for a prototype."

"I was hoping you'd say that," Sang said. "Coordinates and the scoop are ready. I was just waiting for you to get back."

Bellona nodded. "Do it. Then, back to Demosthenes." She was itchy to return, suddenly. It might have been the unsettling find on the surface. It might be the empty bed she was using. It could be that everyone was back there except for the few on the *Alyard* right now.

Whatever the reason, she wanted to go back.

As she headed toward to the bridge, Bellona wrestled with the feeling, reluctant to name it for what it really was, because it was too soon. Then, just in her own mind, she let herself say it.

She wanted to go home.

Chapter Ten

DeLuca Family Wilderness Area, Deluca Prime, Delucas System

IULIA WRAPPED THE FURS AROUND her shoulders, arranging them to eliminate the little chill creeping under the edges, then recomposed herself, hiding her impatience. "You are my younger brother, Raine. Of course I want to see you succeed."

Raine sat with his legs stretched out, his boots resting on an ottoman and his eyes closed. Like most Delucas, he was a stocky man of average height and long legs. Unlike the rest of the family, his hair had turned prematurely gray when he was in his twenties. Raine did not seem to notice the cold and it was frigid on the verandah, which was exposed to the elements with no fields to mitigate the impact.

The luxury hunting cabin was at the far end of the great forest that surrounded Menaii. It had belonged to the Deluca family for generations. It appeared rustic. The full services were well disguised. Raine had insisted on visiting the cabin for the day and had gravitated out here to the verandah where the conditions really were primitive.

Iulia recognized he was brooding about something and had ventured out of the warmth to find him and open him up.

Raine didn't look at her as he responded. "If you are so interested in my success then why do you remain on Cardenas with that oaf?"

"Gaubert?" she clarified. "He has no backbone, little brother. Reynard supplied enough for both of them. I stay, because I lived there for forty years. It is hard to instantly let go. That does not mean my loyalties cannot… evolve."

"Or revert?" he asked, proving he understood what she was not saying. Then he added; "Peru Scordini sits at the head of the clan table now. I was voted out. Maybe you should be talking to him."

"He is not a Deluca," Iulia said stiffly. "You are. Gaubert says the vote that won Peru the chair was close. Very close. You could have won that vote, Raine, if you had played it a little more carefully."

Raine shook his head. "Gaubert talks too much. And he's wrong. That younger brother of his—Markjohn—is hugely popular."

"That is because Markjohn has not collaborated with the enemy lately," Iulia said primly.

Raine blew out his breath. It fogged in front of him and lingered in the still air. "I do not understand why Gaubert was acclaimed head of the family, after what he did. Reynard could not stand the shame. Yet the man sits at the clan table as if he has every right to be there."

"He gained the city killer technology for the Republic. That made many generals deeply grateful," Iulia pointed out. "Military gratitude is a powerful thing."

Raine glanced at her. "Powerful enough to keep alive a dog that has gone bad in the head."

"His motives were pure," Iulia added. "That does not excuse what he did. Gaubert is not the one you should be focusing on."

"Markjohn, then?" Raine pursed his lips, considering it.

"No, not Markjohn, either," Iulia said quickly. "You needn't worry about him."

"If Gaubert makes another mistake, then Markjohn will take his seat and Markjohn is more popular than I. He could take on Peru and win."

Iulia wondered whether Raine was aware that he was talking to her like a man. An equal. He had forgotten the family philosophy that women did not like politics.

"Markjohn is young," Iulia said. "His time will come and he knows that. He is content for now to build his alliances. You don't have to worry about Markjohn for a while yet. If you take a few simple steps you may never have to worry about him."

Raine raised a brow. "What steps would they be?"

There was a stringent smell drifting from the stumps of trees that had been felled recently, to keep the sightlines from the house clear. Even here, the family enforcers kept watch. It was reminder to Iulia to monitor her own movements and everything she did here. This cabin was a part of the family and Raine was her little brother, whom she had beaten at games all her life. Both the cabin and Raine were embedded in her personal history. That did not mean she could relax. Raine was not Gaubert. He was not easily led.

"You have to watch Peru Scordini, to begin," Iulia said. "And you have to wait. He will make a mistake and when he does, you can move forward with your relationships to support your bid for the chair."

"How do you know he will make a mistake?" Raine demanded.

"Everyone makes mistakes," Iulia assured him. "You just have to watch for them and take advantage of them when they occur."

Raine relaxed and recrossed his ankles. "For a moment I thought you knew something was about to happen."

"Things always happen," Iulia said carefully. "Things always change."

"Including allegiances, hey?" Raine asked her, with a direct look.

"Most especially allegiances," Iulia assured him.

Raine laughed. "You must truly abhor that daughter of

yours, Iulia. All this maneuvering you're doing to line up the military and the clans against her..."

Iulia held her breath in shock.

Raine didn't notice. He wasn't looking at her. He never did. He was talking to himself. "No one in the family could ever hold a grudge as well as you," he added. "I'd hate to be in Bellona's shoes when you finally catch up with her."

Iulia relaxed and managed a small smile. As usual, Raine had failed to recognize the underlying truth and had instead focused on the symptoms. "Delucas pay their debts, remember?" she told him sweetly.

* * * * *

Demosthenes, Alkeides System

JUST BECAUSE THERE WAS SO much free space on Demosthenes, everyone seemed to gravitate toward each other. When they could have the pick of any spare room to work in, live in, or play in, most people returned to the dining room instead and set up their current work or interest at the long tables, alongside others. The work might be completely unrelated, yet they seemed to find comfort rubbing elbows in that way. Only people like Aideen, who genuinely preferred to be alone and Vang, who had set himself the task of figuring out how everything worked in the medical bay and equipping and supplying it appropriately, stayed in their separate work areas.

Sang was not immune to the gravitational eddies drawing everyone together. He found himself in the dining hall most days. He would generate a screen just as everyone else did, even though he had been designed by Eriumans to replace screens and input devices. He could do all the work in his head, if he needed to. Working on a screen had become a habit, though.

Sang knew that Khalil was also drawn to the dining hall and the others. Today he was on the other table, at the far end away from the big doors, staring at coding that even Sang would have trouble reading. His was a dark head among white blond, indifferent brown and Eriuman black.

Sang sat on the bench next to him, his back to the table.

Khalil bookmarked his screen carefully, then gave Sang his full attention.

"Is that bridge forge software?" Sang asked.

"I'm checking it over." Khalil shrugged. "All coding can be improved."

Sang smiled. "Even mine?"

"I've seen your source code," Khalil said.

Sang was genuinely shocked. "When?"

"The original coding that was given to you when you came out of the tank was developed by the Bureau, remember? It was part of my basic training to deconstruct android coding. Now, though, yours would have complexities far beyond the comprehension of any Bureau member." Khalil grinned. "That doesn't mean I'm not curious to see what it looks like."

"I don't think I know you well enough to let you see my code."

Khalil laughed loudly enough to draw glances.

Sang waited until he had himself under control once more. "The human remains we found on Pushyan," he began.

"You've identified it?"

"To within a degree of certainty, yes. The DNA had deteriorated, so we had to pattern match. There were two dozen people who matched the chains we could recover, sixty-five percent of them men and automatically eliminated."

Khalil frowned. "Age and race?"

"Reduced it to three possibilities. One of those possibilities, when I looked into her profile, makes her almost a certainty."

"Why? Who is she?"

"Georgina Kumar of Laurasia." Sang watched Khalil.

"I know that name," Khalil said slowly. Then his eyes widened. "Ben's ship. She was kitchen crew." He gripped the edge of the table. "Her death is connected to my brother?"

"I don't know yet. I thought that you might want to take over. Track her movements via the feeds and databases, the way you do. If we can find out why she was on Pushyan and who else was there, then perhaps we can reconstruct what happened two years ago."

"Three years ago, Thecla said."

"I re-dated the remains, after adjusting for the radiation fluxes on the surface. They're two years old."

As Sang spoke, he spotted Hero at the door to the dining room. She had paused and was looking around the room, tallying who was there with her dark eyes.

Khalil closed his fingers into a tight fist, then let them relax. "Two years ago was when Shavistran was destroyed, and my brother and his people, too."

Sang nodded. "That is why I brought this to you."

Hero's gaze reached Sang and lingered.

"If her death is connected, then it might explain how it happened," Khalil said.

"How Shavistran happened?" Sang said, puzzled.

Khalil lifted his legs over the bench and turned to sit the same way Sang was. He leaned forward, his arms on his knees. "It has always bothered me, Sang. How did the Eriumans know where Ben was? How did they know with enough certainty they could use their stolen city killer and be sure they weren't destroying an innocent city?"

"Shavistran was innocent whether Benjamin Arany was there or not," Sang replied. "His presence did not justify what the Eriumans did to that world."

Khalil met his gaze. "You speak as if you are not one of them."

"I am still tabled as a corporate asset if you look at the Cardenas family portfolio," Sang said. "Though, I have not considered myself to be Eriuman since Maximilian Cardenas died." In his mind, he heard the hiss of heavy rain. The muffled thuds of a small fist on a door.

Khalil must have seen something in Sang's face, for he nodded. "Then it's worth getting to the bottom of it," he decided. "I'll need a good AI. What's the best on Demosthenes? Have you catalogued them yet, Sang?"

"They're all ex-Karassian. Their quality is less than stellar," Sang told him. Over Khalil's shoulder he saw Hero making her way through the aisles between the long tables. She was waylaid every few steps and forced to chat, although her direction was unmistakable.

"Listen to you disparage the Homogeny," Khalil said. "You are no longer Eriuman, are you not?"

Sang gave him a sour smile. "I still know an abused AI when I see one."

"The Karassian military buy their minds from the Bureau just like the rest of the known worlds," Khalil said. "I can apply remedials as needed. Which is the most powerful?"

"The med bay AI. Vang is using it, though" Sang said. "After that, the navigation AI or the null-space AI."

"The navigation AI will have the broadest geographical references. I'll use that one." Khalil got to his feet.

"Now?" Sang said, surprised. "It's late."

Khalil grimaced. "I won't be missed. Not tonight."

Sang recalled Bellona's agenda for the day. Fontana and Aideen had been requested to provide an update on their part in the building of the bridge forge prototype. Sang had finished his own update two hours ago. Bellona was determined to see the forge work and the updates would inflame her ambitions and keep her occupied for days.

"You still think the bridge forge is a bad idea, then?" Sang asked Khalil.

"More than ever," Khalil said, his voice low. "Technology is not the answer. People are. Relationships."

"Says the Bureau weed," Sang replied.

Khalil's mouth opened. Then he shut it with a snap. "*Ex*-Bureau, my robot friend, and it is 'ex' for a reason." He nodded and strode away, as Hero approached. Sang heard Khalil murmur a greeting to her as they passed.

Hero ignored Khalil. Her gaze was on Sang. She moved up to where he was sitting and stood very close. "Did he just call you a robot?" she said, sounding stunned.

"I called him a Bureau weed. It cancels out." Sang got to his feet. "I left my screen running…"

Hero lifted her hand, as if she might stop him with it. She didn't touch him. "You can turn it off from here, can't you?"

It would involve displaying the robot skills that had just shocked her so much. It would call attention to him. It wasn't why she had suggested he remotely control the computer, though. "What do you want, Hero?" he asked her, already knowing the answer.

She dropped her hand. Her smile was heated. "You saw me watching you, from the door."

"It was a look, nothing more," he assured her.

She swayed a little closer, enough for Sang to sample her scent and the hormonal imbalances that generated it. The pheromones spoke volumes. A normal human, especially a male, would respond without realizing why he was doing it. An ignorant male might even think it was all his idea in the first place.

Sang shook his head. "I am impervious to your designs, Hero. You need to find someone else to keep you company tonight."

Hero frowned. It was a pretty expression, barely marring her forehead and making her eyes look sorrowful. "You can have sex, can't you?"

Sang sighed. "I'm sure the Eriumans on board have already told you that. I am a human body grown around an evolved, self-aware android mind and skeleton. Sex is part of being human."

She laid her hand on his chest. "You don't have to be afraid of me. When I am with a friend, it is perfectly safe."

"I know that," Sang said impatiently. "Thecla and Amilcare and everyone you have shared yourself with would not have survived if it were otherwise. I'm not afraid of you, Hero. I'm just not interested."

There were softer ways he could have used to say it. He had learned the phrasing, the delicate maneuvers and learned how to preserve egos in the process. Hero was a different matter. It had to be laid out bluntly.

She didn't seem to be offended by his directness. "Not interested, or otherwise interested?" she asked, her voice soft and coaxing. "I don't care what's in your heart." Her hand slid downward.

Sang caught her wrist and twisted it, bringing her around in a hard spin. He pushed her onto the bench. She landed heavily, for she had not been expecting it. Sang kept his hand on her shoulder, holding her down as she tried to bounce to her feet once more.

Heads were turning. People were listening.

"Stop it," Sang hissed. "Control yourself, Hero. You're embarrassing yourself as a woman and an Eriuman."

She laughed up at him. "We're all free-staters, now. Haven't you heard? We're free to do anything we want."

"When you figure out that freedom comes with even greater responsibilities, we'll talk," Sang told her. "Before that unlikely day arrives, I advise you to stay away from me."

He left the dining hall. On the way, he remotely switched off the screen he had been using. It irritated him that everyone watched him leave. It wasn't part of his function to draw focus.

Ex-Bureau. Ex-robot. Ex-Eriuman. They were all something else and every day that something changed. It was the dark side of freedom. No wonder Hero embraced it.

Chapter Eleven

Demosthenes, Alkeides System

THE BRIDGE ON DEMOSTHENES WAS three times larger than the stark white ovoid on the *Alyard* and just as sterile, hard and functional. As no one used the bridge, no one had bothered to change anything there. Generally, the big room was empty.

Sang also knew there were no printers or assemblers in there, which seemed to be an odd oversight in a race who liked their creature comforts, their food and drink as much as Karassians did.

For that reason and because he had not seen Khalil anywhere on Demos for more than two days, Sang selected a favorite meal from Khalil's request logs, printed it and took it to the bridge, along with a carafe of coffee, a cushion and a blanket in a bag.

Khalil was still there. Sang was relieved when he spotted the dark-haired man behind the navigation console and was startled by the relief.

Khalil looked as tired as Sang had expected him to be. There were shadows under his eyes, his hair was ruffled, his tunic rumpled and his movements slow with exhaustion.

There was only one chair behind the console, which Khalil was slumped in. Sang stood on the other side and put the food on the console, over the top of the screen, hiding the data. He dropped the carafe next to it, then pulled the coffee mug out of the bag that held the blanket and cushion.

Khalil smiled. It was a weak expression. "I'm that pathetic, am I?"

"Driven," Sang corrected. He nudged the bowl of steaming stew closer. "Eat. Tell me how far you've got."

"How is she?" Khalil asked.

"As driven as you."

"Is the prototype made, yet?"

"They're designing the physical dimensions now. The internals are all finalized." Sang tapped the bowl.

Khalil picked it up and winced as the heat burned his fingers. He let it drop again, picked up the spoon instead and bent over it to eat a mouthful. The taste triggered him into scooping another three mouthfuls in quick succession. He chewed and swallowed, then sat back with a sigh.

"Don't stop," Sang told him, pouring the coffee.

"I have to breath, sometime," Khalil pointed out. He picked up the mug. "I hadn't realized how…" He drank, not finishing the sentence.

Sang waited, feeling no impatience. He glanced at the screen, reading it upside down. Then, when the little he could see under the bowl and plate caught his attention, he plugged directly into the AI's interface and read the screen in his mind.

"Who is Ferid?" he asked, scanning back through Khalil's progress.

"A Karassian." Khalil took another mouthful of stew. "Biocomp enhanced. Maybe military. I don't know that yet. His ship—the one he was using then—was parked on Pushyan, two years ago."

"Suggestive, but not conclusive."

"He was on Antini, a few months later."

"Lots of people go there."

"Including Reynard and Gaubert Cardenas, at the exact same time this Ferid was there."

Sang stood up from his bend over the navigation console. "*That* is one coincidence too many. Are there any others?"

"I back tracked from Antini. He was on Xindar and Angyl—both free states." Khalil met Sang's gaze. "Both locations where people connected to Ben Arany disappeared."

Sang laid it out in his mind. "First, Pushyan, where the girl was. She was naked when she died. She killed herself in a way that suggests she was using whatever was to hand. Torture?"

"To make her tell him where Ben was based, most likely," Khalil said.

"She killed herself to avoid telling him anything." Sang drew in a heavy breath. "For a fifteen-year-old, that's remarkable."

"Ben knew how to find the best people."

"Clearly. This Ferid moved on to two more people connected to your brother, who might be able to tell him where Benjamin was located, where he came to land and could be pinned down. The last was the successful interrogation."

"He was on Angyl around the time Marcel Kopitar and his wife disappeared. Marcel was Ben's medic." Khalil's mouth turned down.

"The medic's wife," Sang said slowly. "Leverage?"

"It's a good bet. I knew Marcel. He was an asshole. On the other hand, he was completely loyal. He was also besotted with his wife." Khalil sighed. "That's not all."

Sang raised his brow.

"While Ferid was on Antini, so was another Karassian we know. Woodrow."

"From Ledan," Sang finished, remembering the little man's taunting of Bellona, his attempt to coax her to come back and work as Xenia for him. "A prominent Karassian, a biocomp assassin, plus Bellona's father and uncle, all in the same place. Reynard swore he had nothing to do with Shavistran."

"Gaubert said he did it," Khalil said. "On behalf of the

clans and the family. For peace, he said." Khalil grimaced again. "If he was on Antini with Woodrow, that's what Woodrow would have told him—where to find Ben Arany and his people. The Republic blamed Ben for the destruction of the *Jovian*...and maybe even for Max Cardenas' murder. Woodrow pointed Bellona's family at Ben and stepped back to watch them do the dirty work for Karassia."

Sang nodded. "Bellona has always held Karassia accountable for Shavistran, because it was their city killer the Republic used. No one knew there was a deeper and more direct connection than that."

"Now we do know," Khalil said. "I'm trying to find Ferid, now. He is the most mobile of the two, which makes him the most vulnerable. We can't go at Woodrow, not while he's hiding inside Ledan. We don't have the firepower to break down the shields over Kachmar and we can't bluff our way in there a second time."

"What do you intend to do with Ferid when you do find him?" Sang asked curiously.

"He is indirectly responsible for Shavistran."

"So are others, including Bellona and your brother, if you stretch that definition a little further."

Khalil dropped the spoon back into the empty bowl with a clatter. "I don't know, Sang! I just want to find the creep, all right? I want to put him in front of Bellona and tell her what he did, then let her do what she wants with him."

"Do what with who?" came the question from the bridge gate.

Sang knew it was Hero before he looked over his shoulder to check. She strolled onto the deck with a casual prowl. The neck of her shirt had dropped off one shoulder, revealing creamy brown flesh. The skirt she wore displayed shapely thigh.

It was automatic to hide his impatience. Sang suppressed the sigh that wanted to emerge.

Khalil looked at him, then at Hero. "No one you need worry about for just now," he told her.

"So, not someone I can fuck, one way or another?" she asked, sidling up beside Sang. She looked up at him, a small smile on her full lips.

"This is a project outside Bellona's directives," Sang told her.

"A private scam?" she asked, her attention riveted. "Oooh, maybe I can help!" She bumped her hip against Sang's thigh.

"Private means not open to discussion," Khalil said, his tone polite.

Hero didn't look at him. Her gaze stayed on Sang. "You can tell *me,*" she assured him.

"It isn't my project to share," Sang replied.

"And Sang is being way too nice," Khalil said shortly. "You're in the way, Hero. This is important. Leave us alone."

For the first time, Hero looked at Khalil directly. "No. I'm having fun." She returned her gaze to Sang. "Tell me who you're hunting for Bellona. *Pleeease.*"

Before Sang could answer, Khalil slapped the top of the console, with a loud smacking sound. "Enough!" he roared. "Hero, get out! I won't say it again."

Hero straightened to her full height, which was far shorter than Sang's. She looked at Khalil, her chin up. "Fuck you, *crepunda.*"

Khalil's face turned a deep red.

Startled, Sang accessed his archives, looking for the word she had just used. He found it in antiquarian language documents.

Plaything.

Khalil stood frozen for a fraction of a second, absorbing the shock. Pale lines of fury formed on either side of his mouth. His eyes narrowed. His jaw rippled.

Hero didn't flinch. She kept her chin up and her eyes locked on Khalil, almost daring him to respond. In the back of his mind, Sang found the capacity to admire her courage, despite the foolhardiness of her challenge.

Khalil moved. He didn't go around the console. He leapt over it, in an astonishingly fast movement. Hero was nearly as quick. She backed up a step and raised her hands defensively. Even now, she didn't turn and run as some might.

Khalil ducked under her hands and grabbed her throat, his elbows out to hold her nails away from him. "Give me one good reason why I shouldn't break your neck?" he growled.

Hero tapped her fingertips on his wrist. The long forefinger nail scraped over the sleeve. "I could tear through this with little effort," she whispered. Every word sounded painful to speak through the grip he had on her neck. "I'd still kill you before I died."

"You'd deprive Bellona of a good general?"

"You?" His tone was dry.

"At least she trusts me, weed."

Khalil breathed hard.

Sang put his hand on Hero's shoulder. "I have no doubt that you can kill him, Hero. If you do, it would destroy Bellona. Think of that."

Hero scowled at Khalil. All her prettiness had fled. "True," she said, her voice husky. She dropped her hand from his sleeve and just stood there. "Kill me, though, and she'll trust you even less."

Khalil growled and shoved her from him.

Hero staggered back and regained her balance, smiling. She brushed down her skirt and resettled her shirt on her shoulder. "Keep your secrets," she told Khalil. "If you can." She flounced from the deck, her own fury matching Khalil's in intensity.

Khalil whirled and bent over, his hands propping him

up against the navigation console. He breathed heavily, shuddering.

Sang edged away. Time to leave, to let him recover in private.

"I can't help her this way," Khalil said, his voice low and shaking.

Sang paused. "You help just by being you."

"I'm not effective. Hero is right. I'm nothing but a distraction and useless for anything else. They all know it." He hung his head.

Sang hesitated. He was at a loss to know what to say. He had never been faced with something like this before. He could speak the truth, only the truth would hurt.

Khalil pushed himself upright with a decisive movement. He squared his shoulders, then turned to look at Sang. "I'll take Connie. That leaves everyone with the *Alyard.*"

"Take? Where are you going?" Sang asked, alarmed.

"I'm going to find Ferid. I've got a range of possibilities. I'll hunt them all down." Khalil's mouth turned down. "Then I will be at least useful in one way." He turned away.

"You can't leave!"

"I can, actually." Khalil looked back. "Help Bellona while I'm gone, okay?"

Sang scrambled to arrange his thoughts coherently. "Is that an order?" he asked.

"I can't give orders around here. You witnessed that for yourself."

Sang shook his head. "That's just one misguided, mean woman—"

Khalil put his hand on Sang's shoulder, silencing him. His gaze was steady. "I'm asking, Sang. That's all. Even if I could give an order they'd listen to, I would never do that to you." His grip tightened and fell away. Then he left the bridge, moving fast.

* * * * *

Southern Continent, Fourth District, Cardenas (Findlay IV), Findlay System, Eriuman Republic

MARKJOHN CARDENAS GROUNDED THE SKIFF at the south end of the private landing field, as close to the sprawling house as possible. Here on the southern continent, among the low hills and long grasses at the bottom of the peninsula, there were few people to note his arrival.

It was cold down here. He shivered and reached into the skiff to pull out the heavy coat he'd thrown into the cab while his wife fussed and complained about the frequent and unexpected assembly meetings since Reynard had died.

Sliding his arms into the coat, Markjohn strode through the thigh-high grasses toward the house, his heart running ahead of his feet. Anticipation was making his body thrum.

She opened the door as he climbed the broad steps onto the porch and held out her arms.

Markjohn pulled Iulia up against him and kissed her thoroughly and deeply.

"How long?" she whispered against his lips.

"Eight hours, no longer," he breathed, reaching for the fastening on her robe.

Iulia pulled him inside and shut the door on the rest of the world.

Chapter Twelve

Demosthenes, Alkeides System

BELLONA STOPPED EATING IN THE dining hall. She didn't have the stomach for it after Sang had explained what had happened on the bridge between Khalil and Hero.

Her first instinct was to lash out at Hero. To wound her in some way that would make her feel as bad and as guilty as Bellona felt. The urge to hurt someone was so strong it made her moan with the need to act.

Sang's calmness kept her in the room, walking a tight circle, instead. Once Sang was done talking, the surge of fury had passed.

Khalil was gone. She could not order him back. She *wouldn't* order him back. Unlike the Ledanians and Amilcare's people, who had all sworn oaths to serve her and her cause, Khalil stayed because he wanted to. Now, he no longer wanted to stay.

It was too much to expect her to sit among the people who had driven him away. She couldn't bear to look at Hero.

Bellona left Sang to direct the work on building the prototype forge, while she stayed in her spacious suite and brooded. She printed food as she needed it, although her appetite had fled. The assembled food did nothing to increase her hunger.

On the fifth day, Thecla banged on the door, demanding entry in a loud voice. She was the first person beside Sang to dare impose upon Bellona's solitude.

Bellona stared at the door, willing the woman to go away.

The pounding stopped. Bellona relaxed.

When it started up again, ten seconds later, she jumped.

"I'm not leaving, Bellona!" Thecla called through the thick door. Her voice was muffled, yet perfectly understandable. "You've sulked enough. Open the damn door!"

Bellona sighed. "Open the door," she told the computer.

The door slid open.

Thecla lowered her hand, the external tendon reflecting the light from the corridor. It made Bellona aware of how dark it was in the suite. "Lights, sixty percent," she said.

The lights came up.

Thecla sauntered into the suite, pushing her hands into the pockets of her pants. It made the tendons flex and gleam. The ink on her arm writhed around the implants. "Whatever you're eating smells awful," she announced.

Bellona glanced at the plate with the congealed, dark brown mess on it. "That was yesterday's breakfast," she admitted.

Thecla picked up the plate and shoved it into the return slot and dusted off her hands. "Got a minute, boss?"

"You're here, aren't you?" Bellona asked.

"You need to stretch your legs."

Step out of this room? Bellona shook her head. "I have things to do."

"Sang has taken care of all of them. You know that as well as I do. Come on. A brisk walk down to the landing deck and back. It'll make you feel better."

"Is anyone down there?" Bellona asked. She glanced at the chrono readout. It was later than she had realized.

"On the deck at this time of night? What do you think?" Thecla demanded.

Bellona still hesitated. Yet the need to *move* was making itself felt.

"You know I could *make* you walk, if I had to?" Thecla asked.

Bellona knew. She was a simple, unenhanced human with good reactions. Kilo for kilo, Thecla was at least as strong as Hayes and Hayes had once hammered Bellona into the ground, then carried her over his wrist like a wet towel.

Thecla jerked her head toward the door. Perhaps she sensed Bellona's capitulation. "C'mon," she repeated.

Bellona sighed and got to her feet. Even moving to the door, she could feel the stiffness in her limbs. She hadn't trained since Khalil had left, either.

The corridor outside the suite that led directly to the bridge was only slightly brighter than inside the suite. The light level on the ship automatically adjusted to match the daylight and darkness of a standard human day, encouraging natural sleep cycles. Nothing moved that she could hear. The bridge was always silent. Now the corridor and the rest of Demosthenes was still, too.

Reassured that she wouldn't have to face anyone directly, Bellona found it easier to walk alongside Thecla. The deck was seven levels down from the bridge. The drop shaft at the end of this main corridor led directly onto the deck.

"Has it been peaceful here while I was ignoring everyone?" Bellona asked. There was an apologetic note in her voice that was not intentional.

"Zeni and Sang had a couple of run-ins. She just doesn't seem to understand she can't win against Sang. Other than that, mostly stupid stuff." Thecla shrugged and pushed her hand into her pockets once more.

"When I knew you on Ledan, I thought you were a sculptor," Bellona told Thecla, glancing at the tendons once more.

"I thought I was a sculptor, too," Thecla said. She wrinkled her nose. "They really fucked with us, didn't they?"

"Were you a biobot, before?

Thecla glanced at her arms. "Yeah. I wanted the

strength."

"Why?"

"It let me break things better."

Bellona looked at her, startled.

Thecla grinned, her brown eyes merry. "I was considered incurably violent. They gave me a choice."

"Ledan, or…"

"Execution," Thecla finished. "They weren't that direct, though. I got to sign up for some mystery assignment, or they'd strap me to a table the next morning. I wasn't done with living yet, so I signed." She shrugged. "Then I woke up seven years later on the *Alyard*, with you standing over me, telling me I was a free woman. All I could remember was that damn lagoon and making things with my hands."

They stepped into the drop shaft together. Bellona gripped the pull bar as weightlessness grabbed her and hauled herself down. Thecla used one of the bars on the other side of the shaft.

"Are you still…incurable?" Bellona asked.

"Funny thing, that," Thecla said. "They fucked with our memories, taught us how to be lethal and violent, and now I don't *have* to be, anymore. What I *do* have to do is make things."

"Sculptures?" Bellona asked.

"Things. Anything. As long as I'm doing it with my hands." She laughed. "I came out only a little bit twisted. Retha and Aideen…even Hayes, have stronger side effects. That makes me lucky." She looked at Bellona. "Everyone figures you got out unscathed. I'm not so sure about that."

Bellona pushed herself past the openings to the intervening levels, which were as dim and quiet as the bridge level. "If Ledan hadn't happened to me, I wouldn't be here. I was a good little Eriuman daughter. I brought into the family principles. Discipline, obedience, industry.

Well, not obedience. Just the other two. So, yes, Ledan changed me, as much as anyone else I pulled out of there. I just seem to have found a way to use those changes. I suppose I am lucky, too."

"Except you can't figure out how to trust anyone," Thecla said quietly.

Bellona swallowed. "Not true," she said, just as quietly. "I trust you. I trust all of you."

The gravity increased as they neared the bottom of the shaft and they pulled themselves over to the doorway, to step out onto the deck.

Thecla barred the door with her arm, the tendon stretching sinuously. "You did me, all of us, a favor, getting us out of Ledan. We've got issues, yeah. Retha can barely sleep for nightmares, yet he'd tell you without hesitation he'd rather have the nightmares and be here. I've never thanked you for coming back for us, so…thank you."

Bellona nodded. "I'd do it again, in a heartbeat."

"I know." Thecla dropped her arm. "I figure that means you'll forgive me for this." She stepped out onto the deck.

Alarmed, Bellona followed her.

As they moved out into the cavernous landing deck, the lights came up to daylight normal. Thecla walked a sweeping curve around the pile of cast-offs and the smaller sorted mounds dotted around its perimeter. She wove through the dark fighters and their stubby wings.

As they walked, the murmur of running water grew louder. There were also human voices, talking quietly.

Bellona's heart sped up. What had Thecla done?

Thecla stepped around the noses of a group of fighters that had been pushed together, as if they had been shoved out of the way, then stopped. Bellona halted next to her and looked in the direction Thecla waved her hand.

Bellona gasped, for taking up a large portion of the

back corner of the flight deck was the lagoon from Ledan.

The wall was there. The moss and creeper-covered rocks. The tumble of the stream down into the deep blue lagoon was almost the same, as well. The lagoon itself was very nearly an exact replica. There was a crescent of sandy beach and thick vegetation on the far side of the water. Water lapped at the sand, little wavelets created by the rush and tumble of water from the stream.

The Ledanians were all there, along with Sang.

Thecla put her hands in her pockets. "I've been making things," she said, sounding self-conscious.

Hayes waved. "Come and look, boss! Even my garden is here." He'd taken off his boots and stood with his toes curled into the sand. He wore a huge grin. Bellona couldn't remember seeing that delighted, childish expression on his face since Xenia had helped him plant fresia seedlings one morning.

Bellona moved closer.

The "ground" sloped up toward the water, giving her a clue as to how Thecla had managed the illusion of a fifteen-meter-deep pool of water. "How deep is the water, really?" she asked, stepping onto the sand.

"Ankle deep," Thecla said. "If ever we have to move Demos, the water can be sucked into a tank so it doesn't fly lose around the deck. The rest is color and light and illusion."

"It's wonderful," Bellona said truthfully. "Hayes loves it," she added, as she watched the giant crouch down on the other side of the rocks to touch a row of green sprouts there.

"We all do," Fontana said, coming up to her. He held out a glass with ruby liquid in it. "Eriuman wine—the nearest a Karassian assembler can manage, anyway."

She smiled at him and took the glass. "Is that a *real* garden?" she asked, as Hayes gently removed leaf litter from around the seedlings.

"Probably the one useful aspect of the whole project," Thecla said. "Hayes can grow real food there."

Bellona looked at the peaceful lagoon once more. "I don't think it's the only useful aspect."

Vang came up alongside her, studying the water as well. "Maybe the Karassians planted a need to return here in all of us," he said. "I can feel all the heat in me evaporating, just standing here."

"A homing instinct?" Bellona asked, startled. "Pulling us back?"

He shook his head. "If it was a true compulsion to return, we would have *all* had far more problems than we do. I think they encouraged inertia and unquestioning peacefulness in all of us. Maybe keyed to the lagoon. That would keep us all complacent, when we were there." He grinned and looked up at her. "I can't see even a platoon of guards holding us back if we'd got it into our minds we wanted to leave."

Bellona smiled. "Me, either," she admitted. "They made us want to stay right there, ignorant and happy."

"Now we're wiser, yet still happy to see the place," Vang finished. "I resent that I'm responding like a dog to a bell, but damn it, I *like* looking at the water."

Hero pushed through the sand, her feet bare. She was carrying a tray with snacks on it, her gaze steady upon Bellona. Perhaps she was daring Bellona to react.

Bellona caught her breath, her fingers tightening around the wine glass.

Vang was watching her, his expression dispassionate. "You'd shoot the messenger?" he asked softly. "She only said what all of us already knew. What Khalil knew, too."

Bellona tried to relax, to ease the tightness in her chest.

"She spoke the truth," Vang added. "If you would prefer everyone lie to you from now on, punish her for it."

Hero stopped in front of Bellona and held up the tray. "No poison," she said softly. She didn't have to speak loudly, for everyone had fallen silent and was openly watching them.

Bellona made no move to take something from the tray. "Vang defends you," she told Hero. "He says that you spoke the truth. I agree with him on that point."

Hero didn't move. She didn't blink, or even quiver. She might have been made of stone, except that Bellona could see the pulse in her neck beating furiously.

"What I am angry about is the cruel way you delivered that truth," Bellona added. "You cannot move through life without regard for others' feelings. You do not have Vang's excuse, yet even he shows more consideration than you. I will not allow any general of mine to trample roughshod over others."

Hero remained quite still. A large tear collected in the corner of her eye and rolled down her cheek. She made no move to wipe it.

Bellona lifted her voice, so that everyone, even Hayes sitting in his garden, could hear her. "All of you lived as Ledanians. All of you emerged to learn you had been treated with a callousness and lack of regard that is inhuman. Would you deliver that same cruelty upon others? If you think you should, if you can stomach the idea of hurting others in that way, then you should leave this ship now. I will not stop you."

She paused, her heart thudding, waiting for any of them to move, to turn and walk away.

No one seemed to breathe. The stillness on the deck was broken only by the tinkle and rush of the stream down the rocks.

"If you stay," Bellona said, "then you are signaling that you agree with me that the harm and the injustice must stop here, with us. We don't let it spread. We make a choice to starve it and root it out wherever we find it, because what happened to us cannot happen to anyone else. We teach others by our example how they can halt the infection, too."

She looked at them one by one, meeting their gazes. Even Hayes had crept onto the little beach and when she met his gaze, he nodded.

"Say aye and tell me you agree," Bellona told them.

"Aye!" they shouted back. Hero, too.

Bellona reached out and picked up a miniature potpie from Hero's tray and bit into it, meeting her eye.

Hero drew in a deep breath and let it out.

* * * * *

THE PARTY WAS STILL GOING when the airlock lights and alarms sounded, the force fields dropped over the entrance and the big doors opened.

"It's me, Connie! Turn off the proximity guns!" Connie shouted in Bellona's ear as the slice of star field beyond the opening doors grew larger.

Thecla and Fontana felt their own ears, too, wincing.

Sang turned to look at the door. "I've disabled them, Connie," he said, speaking so everyone could hear. "You're safe to come aboard now. Is Khalil with you?"

"He's in the hold with the man," Connie said, her voice rich with disapproval.

Thecla met Bellona's glance. The blonde woman raised her brow and turned to Hayes. "When Connie lands, go straight up the cargo ramp. It's possible Khalil will need a helping hand."

Hayes looked at Bellona. She nodded and Hayes padded barefoot across the sand and stepped onto the decking.

Connie's streamlined curves came into view, the pale metal hull pulsing different colors from the proximity lights flashing on the outside of the docking doors. She eased through the doors with little room to spare, for the height from floor to roof in the docking bay was designed for personal fighters not much taller than men, while Connie was a luxury yacht with several decks and a bridge level. She fit, but only just and there was little maneuvering room for her once she was inside the docking bay.

She floated over to her usual place at the far edge of the bay, where they had cleared out fighters by pure muscle, dragging them, hauling them and shoving them out of the way. With minimal bursts of her positioning thrusters, she dropped onto the deck.

Hayes got his foot onto the lower edge of the descending cargo ramp as soon as it was low enough, hauled himself up, climbed the ramp and disappeared inside, as everyone else gathered around Connie.

Behind her, the docking bay doors closed again.

For a moment, nothing stirred, not even the group of them at the foot of the ramp.

Muffled yelling sounded, growing swiftly louder. Hayes' head appeared first, at the top of the ramp. He seemed to be straining to carry something.

Then Khalil appeared. As they moved closer to the top edge of the ramp, the struggling burden they carried between them came into view.

The man was small, blond and covered in blood splatters. His hands and feet were bound with unbreakable cord. There was something stuffed in his mouth, fluttering around the edges. Bellona recognized the cloth as one of Khalil's shirts. The man—Ferid, she presumed—was screaming or yelling without cease, despite the gag.

His writhing was making Hayes and Khalil stagger. Their grips on the man's arms slipped and he went down heavily, making the ramp shudder. Khalil swore and shook out his hand, which was covered in blood, too. He used his foot to push at the man, rolling him down the ramp.

He rolled faster and faster. Everyone backed out of the

way as he reached the bottom, where he came to a halt. A groan issued from him. He was face down and couldn't turn himself over for his hands were bound behind his back. At the back of his neck, above the collarless neckline of his jacket, the lip of a plug socket showed, drilling down into his neck.

Khalil waved his hand. "I give you Ferid, of the Karassian Homogeny. Biocomp assassin and intelligence gatherer."

"This is really him?" Bellona asked. "The one who located Benjamin Arany for the Republic to kill?"

Khalil moved down the ramp. He looked tired and dirty. "If I took that rag out of his mouth, he would tell you himself. I've listened to eighteen hours of his bragging. He's proud of what he has done." His mouth curled down. "Don't take his bindings off unless there are more than two of you in attendance. I think he has been Ledanian trained. Not all the blood is his."

"You need medical assistance?" Vang asked.

"I'm patched up well enough," Khalil said.

Bellona looked down at the little man. He was squirming again. Shouting against the rag in his mouth. "Take him to one of the empty rooms. Make sure it is stripped of everything. Strip him, too. Assume he is sneakier than any of you and prepared for occasions like this. Hero, you know ways the human body can be booby-trapped. Turn him inside out if you need to. Find any surprises he might have on him."

Hero nodded. She wasn't smiling and she wasn't bouncing as she normally did.

Hayes and Thecla picked the man up by his elbows, not bothering to turn him over first. He kicked and bucked. Vang grabbed one of his ankles and held it against his side. "Retha, the other one," he said.

Retha stepped over and grasped the other foot and anchored it.

Still the man writhed. They hung on to him with effort.

"Two of you in the room with him at all times," Bellona told them. "I want to talk to him. I'll come in a minute."

Everyone hurried away with the struggling biocomp, leaving Sang and Bellona at the foot of the ramp and Khalil standing half-way down it.

Sang looked up at him. "Is there anything I must know before I go to help the others?"

"Don't leave, Sang," Khalil said, walking slowly down the ramp. He stopped in front of Bellona. She kept her hands at her sides with effort.

Khalil frowned heavily. "I told you he would not shut up. He boasted about every assassination, every high-risk assignment he had ever completed."

Sang edged closer to both of them. "What else did he say?"

Khalil was looking at her, though. Watching her. She could *feel* the wariness in him.

Bellona moaned, as she saw where Khalil was leading her. "Max," she whispered. "He killed Max."

Khalil grasped her arm. "I'm sorry, yes. He contrived to send Max a message that sounded like you. He's a biocomp. Faking credentials would be easy for him. Max thought you had run away from Cardenas again, that you were stuck on Antini and needed his help."

Bellona nodded, her eyes stinging. "The one thing that would bring him running with no questions, and with no military at his back."

Sang stepped closer. "Was Ferid speaking the truth? Can anything he said be verified?"

Khalil's gaze didn't move away from her face. "He knew what had been done to Max. Down to the arrangement of the limbs."

Bellona's gut cramped.

Khalil shook her arm. "Don't kill him until you have

sucked every last byte of data from him. The information in his head—names, dates, military leaders, spies and more—it could give you untold advantages."

"He's a biocomp," Sang said. "We could tap directly into his brain and servers and just take it, without having to listen to him."

"Don't do it with a computer you can't spare. Isolate that computer from any others," Khalil told him. "I suspect his mind is as lethal as Hero's body is to her enemies."

Bellona nodded. "We will be careful. Thank you."

"You'll stay to help, won't you?" Sang asked him. "Manipulating computer minds…that's your expertise."

Bellona sighed. She knew what Khalil's answer would be before he shook his head.

"You'll have to make do, Sang, in your usual competent fashion," Khalil told him.

Sang frowned.

Khalil picked up Bellona's hand and she held her jaw together tightly against the sensations created by his familiar touch.

"I'm of no use to you here," he said, his voice low.

Sang sighed and turned away.

"No, Sang, stay and hear me out," Khalil said quickly.

"I should not be here," Sang replied.

"You must stay," Khalil replied. "Bellona will need you now, more than ever." His eyes met hers once more. "I have no place here. Out there, I can help you."

"What will you do?" Bellona asked.

"Arany's people, the free states…they know me. They know my family. I can talk to them. Pave the way for you."

Bellona nodded. She didn't trust herself to speak.

"Stay in contact," Sang said urgently. "Let us know where you are."

"If I can," Khalil said heavily.

"I will," Connie whispered in Bellona's ear. For once, her voice was subdued, her volume bearable.

Khalil looked as though he had more to say. He hesitated. Then, with a squeeze of his fingers, he let her hand go, turned and walked back up the ramp and disappeared.

Sang tugged Bellona away from the ship, back to the lagoon. They watched Connie rise and drift back out through the opening doors and curve out of sight.

Chapter Thirteen

Demosthenes, Alkeides System

THE FIRST WORKING PROTOTYPE BRIDGE forge was finished four days after they executed Ferid.

It took eight days with little sleep to draw as much out of the biocomp as possible. While two or three Ledanians guarded him at all times, Bellona stayed in the room with him. She didn't know if he thought that talking would win him leniency. She did not hint that it might and neither did anyone else.

Perhaps that was why Ferid talked. He had nothing to lose and he knew that everything he said and did was being recorded. He was a Karassian. The search for celebrity was built into their bones. Maybe he thought that he might live on in this way.

While Sang worked to completely isolate an expendable AI and Vang developed a jack to connect Ferid to it, Bellona listened and Ferid rambled. She didn't try to pick out the truth, or facts that might be useful. Everything he said would be closely analyzed later.

Her presence encouraged him to talk. Her reactions goaded him. Her questions guided. She listened, with her gut churning and her heart running too fast, as Ferid poured out the sum of his life. The murders. The torture. The lessons he had learned from watching people die by his hand. His delight in unexpected human acts. After a while, Bellona forgot that Ferid had been born, not made. His constant search for evidence of human spirit that was missing in him made him less a man than Sang.

She took a lot of showers in those eight days, using real water.

On the seventh day, Sang pulled her from the secure room to tell her the AI was ready. "It's as isolated and secure as I can make it," Sang said as they stood in the corridor outside, with Vang listening.

"What if Ferid can blow it up, or kill it, when we tap him?" Bellona asked.

Vang shook his head. "I don't think he will, even if he could. He knows he's going to die. We haven't hidden that from him. If everything he knows and remembers is sucked into the AI memory, then in a way, he'll live on. He won't ruin that."

"If the Karassian military knew how he was talking, they'd kill him themselves," Bellona said. "Once we dig beneath the boasting, what we will learn about the power holders of the galaxy will give us unbelievable leverage."

"He is Karassian," Sang said. "Their individuality is more important than loyalty to the state."

Bellona sighed. "Let's do it tomorrow," she said. "I can't stand to listen to him any more today."

The next morning, while six of them held Ferid down, Sang jacked into Ferid's brain and, through the brain connection, to his internal servers. It took seven hours to take everything from him.

"I'm moving the data, not copying it," Sang told them. "The more that is shifted over, the less of Ferid that will remain."

In the last two hours of the transfer, the body that had been Ferid lay placidly, blinking at the ceiling with a peaceful expression on its face. They no longer had to hold it down. It did not have the mental capacity to consider escape or rebellion.

Bellona made herself stand and watch. Finally, she nodded to Hero, who gently drew her fingernail down Ferid's cheek, leaving a thin, red scratch.

When the body was quite dead, Bellona escaped the room and took one last shower. A long one.

Sleep did not come easily that night. She found herself wandering the corridor to the dining hall in search of distraction from her thoughts.

All the Ledanians except Aideen were already there, gathered around one end of the long table, coffee carafes sitting in front of them. Sang, too. They were not talking and no one was smiling.

Quietly, they slid down the bench, making room for her.

Bellona settled between Fontana and Hayes and murmured her thanks as a full mug of coffee was placed in front of her. She sipped, listening to the thick silence.

While it was just her suffering from Ferid's poisonous outpourings, there had been no incentive to find a way to move beyond them. Now she knew the others were in stress, her mind worked sluggishly, turning over ideas. Gradually, her thoughts picked up speed.

She put the mug down. "Sang, how close to complete is the prototype forge?"

Sang frowned. "The housing is nearly done. The core program has been line checked and ancillary software is coming along. Vectoring controls…" He paused, consulting some inner log. Then, "Maybe two weeks."

Bellona nodded. "I want it finished in a week. What do you need to do that?"

"A week!" Fontana protested.

Vang smiled. Perhaps he could see what she was doing.

Sang's frown deepened. "Ferid's archives need to be compiled and searched."

"They can wait," Bellona told him. "At least until we have some distance from their source. The prototype is more important. What do you need?"

Sang shrugged. "More people."

"How many more?"

"Everyone."

It was the answer she had been hoping for. Had Sang anticipated her, too?

"You can't fit everyone around the workbench," Fontana pointed out.

Sang leaned forward. "There are subsidiary tasks that must be completed as well. A faraday room to test the device. A monitoring and recording network inside the room. The coding must be finished. Also, a routine must be built to index locations by the trinary coordinates the forge uses." Sang smiled. "Plus a second and third shift to replace the first, for everyone must sleep and relax."

"Sleep, at least," Fontana said. "Relaxing is for weaklings. I want to see the housing you mentioned."

"Why?" Bellona asked curiously.

"Thecla says it's the size of a man's upper body. That's not portable," Fontana said dismissively.

"Think you can do better, Fontana?" Hero asked.

Fontana snorted. "Yeah, I do."

"You haven't even seen it yet," Hayes said.

"I've seen Thecla's quarters," Fontana shot back.

Retha laughed, his eyes in their dark, sleep-deprived pits dancing with amusement. Others around the table laughed, too.

"It's a *prototype*," Thecla said patiently. "Of course it's going to be clunky."

"Just because it's the first doesn't mean it has to be inelegant," Hero said.

"Why not get it right, first time out?" Fontana added.

Thecla shrugged. "Be my guest. If you can miniaturize it any more than we already have, I'll stand back and applaud."

The discussion went on. Bellona withdrew carefully. She suspected no one noticed her leave. Content, she went back to her room. Sleep still took a while to descend, yet it was a long and deep one.

Four days later, Sang announced the prototype was ready for trial.

* * * * *

EVERYONE LOOKED AS TIRED AS they had during the long night when Bellona had sipped coffee with them and challenged them to finish the prototype in a week. This time, though, despite slumped postures and shadowed eyes, they were smiling, as Thecla showed Bellona into the room they had set up as a faraday cage to contain any unexpected side effects of the trial.

The room itself was one of the bigger crew rooms. It was far longer than it was wide. The bunks and lockers had been discarded, while the metal walls were still in place. The silvery, unadorned walls made the room look even longer.

Sang stood in the center of the group waiting just inside the door. There was a small table next to him. There was just one object on the table.

"That's it?" Bellona asked curiously.

"It is," Sang replied.

The bridge forge looked like a workman's toolbelt. Bellona leaned closer. It really was a belt, she realized. On the belt was a series of blank boxes made of a black, matte material.

"It's not the size of a man," Bellona observed.

Thecla laughed.

"Can I touch it?" Bellona asked.

"It's not primed. Go ahead," Sang said.

Bellona pressed her finger against the side of one of the boxes and felt coolness and unforgiving solidness. "Metal..."

"Carbyne," Sang said.

"Of course," she murmured. "It is very small. Will it generate a bridge big enough to step through?"

"That is what the trial is for," Sang said.

Bellona stepped back. "Then let's see."

Sang rested his fingers on the first box on the belt.

"There are several interlinked components, most of them more robust replicas of parts used in communications satellites. We separated them and linked them. It means the carbyne structure holding the forge doesn't have to be as strong as it would if all the components were housed inside the same structure. This one, though, is new to the prototype. It's a navigation AI."

"Communications satellites don't have navigation in them?"

Sang shook his head. "They talk to fixed locations, usually only a handful of them. There's no need to know where to open up the other end of the bridge, because the other end is set and permanent. With a personal forge, though, the whole point is to be able to cross to wherever you want to go. We had to find a way to reference any location in the galaxy."

Bellona wrinkled her forehead. "Can't you use the same navigation coding that stellar navigators use for null-space?"

"Those are relational coordinates," Sang said, "because everything in the galaxy is always moving. A navigational AI is merely told to jump to Cerce, for example. It looks up the Cerce system, figures out where it is at the moment, then jumps to local space around Cerce Prime. We can't jump there with the bridge forge, because it has to open up the other end of the bridge *before* we get there. It has to know exactly where the other end of the bridge must go."

"You can't just tell it to put the end on Cerce?"

"Where on Cerce should we put it?" Sang asked her, sounding curious.

Bellona pursed her lips. "I see the problem now."

"Retha was the one who came up with the idea of absolute locations," Thecla said.

Retha grinned.

"He knows how to hit the target, after all," Fontana

said, clapping Retha's shoulder. "Ask Vang."

Everyone rolled their eyes. Some groaned.

Bellona shook her head and looked to Sang to explain absolute locations.

Sang held up his finger and pointed to the tip. "Pretend that the tip of my finger is the center of the galaxy." He moved his other hand around the tip of the finger. "Everything in the galaxy revolves around the black hole, even as the systems are spinning around their own stars. The center of the galaxy is an absolute, constant reference. It's 0-0-0."

He moved his hand around the finger again. "There are three hundred and sixty degrees in a circle. Each degree is divided up by minutes and seconds. Seconds can be separated into fractalized digital division, down to whatever depth needed for an exact location, so the horizontal plane can be fixed by a description of degree. That's the first figure."

Sang shifted his hand so the finger he was moving around the symbolic center of the galaxy slid higher and lower than the tip of his finger. "The second figure is the perpendicular measurement, also in degrees, minutes and seconds and their subdivisions." He moved his hand closer to his finger tip, then away from it. "Distance from the center is the simplest figure."

"How accurate is it?" Bellona asked. "Can I say I want the bridge to end in front of Alberda's desk on Cerce?"

"We'll refine the process as we test it," Sang said, lowering his hands. "At the moment, we think it is accurate to within a meter."

"I will need to know all three measurements in order to jump somewhere?" Bellona asked. "No wonder you wanted hot bodies to map the galaxy."

Sang shook his head. "Once we have mapped and jumped to a location, it will be added to a meta index. You will be able to tell the forge you want to jump to the same spot in front of Alberda's desk on Cerce. The AI will look up the relational location of Cerce using the cartography coordinates a null space AI uses—in other words, where it currently is in the galaxy. Then it will plot the exact location you have asked for, then it will build the bridge and plant the end at that exact location."

Bellona let out a breath. "Wow."

"The more we use the bridge forge, the more comprehensive and detailed the meta index will become," Fontana added. "For today, we figured out the end point by walking to the end of the room and taking a reading."

"That's where you'll anchor the bridge this time?" Bellona asked. "At the other end of this room?"

Sang turned the box on the belt so that Bellona could see the screen readout on the top of it. "The end point is already set."

Bellona glanced at the screen. It showed simple text. *Demosthenes, C Barracks far end.*

Sang pointed to the far end of the room. "I engraved a message on the wall at that end. You can't see it from here. When the bridge is built, you should be able to read it through the bridge as if you were standing right next to the wall."

"Show me," she told him.

Everyone else backed away from the table, lining the walls of that end of the room.

Sang looked apologetic. "There is no smoke and mirrors, I'm afraid. I just start the forge." There was an orange light next to the location readout. He pressed it. It turned red and pulsed. The boxes on the belt hummed and the speed of the pulsing light increased. Then it turned to green.

The air in front of the table shimmered, as if the surface rippled with air currents. A small oval-shaped image appeared in the air, only half a meter across. It looked as though the belt had generated a screen, an oval one.

"It's not big enough to walk through," Hero said, sounding disappointed.

"It *is* bigger than micro sized," Fontana said.

Then Bellona realized what the "screen" was showing. The silver was the same shade as the wall next to her. There were words written there.

Liberty, prosperity and peace in our time. —S. Indigo.

"The size is a matter of adjustment, that's all," Thecla said. Unlike Hero, she was almost vibrating with excitement.

For a long, silent moment, everyone stared at the words showing through the bridge.

"Now what?" Hero asked.

"Throw something through it," Hayes said in his deep, low voice.

"I have nothing on me to throw," Sang said.

"Here." Hero pulled a small black box out of her pocket and held it out to him.

Sang hesitated to pick it up.

"It's lipstick," she said and pushed it toward him again.

"Where did you get *lipstick*?" Thecla demanded.

"I made it," Hero told her.

"We talk, later, okay?" Thecla replied.

Sang picked up the pot. "Black. Appropriate."

Hero blew him a kiss.

He turned to face the open bridge, hefting the box. Before he could throw the box, the forge components on the belt whined, the pitch rising quickly to a painful note. Bellona covered her ears, as did everyone else.

Sang stared at the belt, his eyes narrowed. Then he looked up. "Everyone, step away from the walls!" he shouted. "Don't touch anything, not even each other!"

It was a measure of Sang's acceptance among them that everyone instantly obeyed. Hero wrapped her arms around herself. Most of them stood with their hands at their sides, carefully not touching anything.

"Crouch down!" Sang shouted, as he dropped. "Lie down, or sit! Quickly!" He hugged his own knees.

Bellona dropped to her knees and put her arms over her head. She couldn't resist looking out from under her arm, to see what the bridge forge was doing.

The whistling note cycled higher and higher until it reached beyond audible range. A dazzling light flashed, leaping to the roof. There was a loud cracking sound. Sparks flared and sizzled where the light had touched the roof.

The whining sound stopped. The bridge disappeared. The components on the belt smoked and the middle box had crumpled into a hard mass of carbyne that made Bellona think of Pushyan and the pulverized moon.

Sang got to his feet. "It's safe now," he told them, staring at the belt.

"Was that…lightning?" Fontana asked, sounding awed, as everyone gathered around the table.

"It was," Sang confirmed.

"Then all this work was for nothing," Hero said bitterly, looking at the smoking mess on the table.

Sang laughed. "Negative results are still results," he told her. "We have learned so much in the last five minutes. Next time—"

"*Next* time?" she interrupted, sounding horrified.

Sang, though, seemed very pleased. "Next time," he said firmly, "we'll have ironed out the problems this trial raised."

"That lightning," Fontana said. "I keep thinking about overloads and feedback loops. Why would that be?"

"Because nothing went through?" Thecla suggested.

"That could be," Sang said. "The energy used to hold the bridge open wasn't drained by something passing through it. The communications channels are constantly in use, so the problem never arises…"

Bellona turned away from them. The discussion became technical and dense and there was no need to understand it. There were more than enough experts in the room. Instead, she walked down the length of the room to the end, where the bridge had ended.

She found the carving on the wall there. Sang's letters were ten centimeters high, perfectly formed and horizontal. She ran her hand over the words.

Liberty, prosperity and peace in our time. —S. Indigo.

"Yes," she whispered, her heart lifting.

Chapter Fourteen

High Moon, Roseworld (Mari III), Mari System, Cheng-Huang Alignment.

LIFE ON THE CHENG-HUANG ALIGNMENT worlds only *seemed* laid back and relaxed. Khalil had visited the primary worlds in the Alignment before and had learned that the Alignees' preoccupation with leisure time pursuits was deceptive.

Even the most astute business leaders and politicians would speak loudly of the joys of family gatherings, games and gambling. Alignees *loved* their days off. Public holidays were frequent and if you arrived at Hu or Xiang or High Moon on one of those holidays, it could feel as though the whole world had shut down into hibernation mode.

Only, while those same Alignees were swimming and relaxing and drinking to excess, they were also forging deals and building relationships.

The first time it happened to Khalil, he had thought he was having a leisurely dinner at the Minister of Culture's home in the high mountains. Over tea and a century-old fortified brandy, Madhuri Truman had asked Khalil odd questions about the newest generation of AI neural networks. They had laughed about the poor quality and failures of the previous generation. Maddie had even told stories about how her granddaughter had trained the household AI to attend her school lessons on her behalf and lie to the family about it.

Khalil had returned to his Bureau chief believing a deal had not been struck, only to find the Cheng-Huang Alignment had set up a new contract that included the latest generation of neural networks with stronger ethical subroutines tailored to Alignment values—an expensive add-on that had been suggested by Khalil as a pot-sweetener. He could not recall making such an offer, yet could not refute they had discussed ethics, especially lying.

Khalil grew more cautious about his dealings with the Alignment, after that.

Now he was back on High Moon, enjoying the strong winter sunshine and tea—no brandy, thank you. Maddie Truman was the same gracious host he remembered. This high up, the mountain peaks were wreathed with clouds, tinted pink by the late afternoon red sun bouncing off the face of Roseworld, that High Moon circled. It was a peaceful view.

"You're looking better now," Maddie Truman said, as she poured more tea into his cup. She pushed the flowing folds of her brocaded gown out of the way with unconscious and practiced grace. Khalil couldn't remember her wearing anything other than elegant gowns and elaborate hairstyles. She was always a graceful note to any room.

"Better?" Khalil said, echoing her. He let himself rest back in the low, soft armchair. He didn't lower his mental guard.

"You were tired when you arrived here yesterday morning. A good night's sleep, some excellent food and time to relax, and you look much more yourself." She sat down with a small smile and picked up her own teacup. "Life has not been easy for you lately."

He had so far steered most of the conversations away from dangerous topics. Maddie made it seem as if she was politely following his conversational lead—she could speak about anything or nothing for long minutes at a time and still make it sound interesting. Over the last two days, though, Khalil had spotted the pattern. Over and over again, she brought the conversation back to him, his life and his doings. The questions were always very polite and indirect, as was this one about his health. He had her pegged now. The Minister of Culture wanted to know about Bellona, but wouldn't ask directly.

She would also resent him raising the topic himself. For some reason, she did not want to openly talk about Bellona. Given how the Cheng-Huang Alignment could twist an innocent conversation, he could understand her reluctance to speak openly. A direct conversation would be loaded with leverage he could later use.

Khalil sipped the tea. It was very good. Strong, yet not overpowering. High Moon tea was grown on the middle slopes of the mountains, where the air was too thick to breathe for long. The altitude was perfect for crops.

He put the cup aside. "You have a lovely home, here, Minister."

"Thank you." She dimpled. "This house has been in my family for five generations. The front slope wing was the first to be built, of course. During the Hu-Xiang war, my grandfather carved out the second terrace, which doubled the footprint, It was a good thing, too, for most of his family on Hu came over to High Moon after the war. There are four generations of us living here right now."

Khalil nodded. "High Moon is a delightful place. It soothes the soul and encourages peace."

He held still, wondering if she would spot his cue.

"Peace is a much underrated value," she said replied. "Most strangers who come to High Moon do not appreciate the quality. You are wise beyond your years, Khalil."

Then she was willing to talk indirectly. Encouraged, Khalil gave a small shrug. "You flatter me, Maddie. I am not nearly as wise as you. I am smart enough to know, however, that peace is a much-sought-after commodity across the known worlds."

"True," she agreed. "Wars have been fought to acquire it, which is ironic, is it not?"

"It is a pity that those who seek it do not know they

can find it here," Khalil said carefully.

Something flashed in her eyes and was gone too fast for Khalil to analyze it. He had prodded her. He wasn't sure how.

"Perhaps," Maddie said casually, sipping her tea once more, "they are looking in the wrong place. Tall cities and open seas with their storms and unrest…they do not naturally encourage peace."

Tall cities. Vertical cities. She was speaking about Cerce!

Khalil fought the impulse to revert to plain speaking. Maddie would not forgive him for such rudeness. "The search for peace is a learning process," he pointed out. "One cannot recognize when one has found it, unless they have sampled the lack of it elsewhere first."

There. That would address Maddie's slighted feelings because Bellona had dared to speak to Alberda before speaking to her. It also dealt with Bellona's original sin of being born a warring Eriuman.

Maddie looked thoughtful. "With everything you say, you prove your wisdom, Khalil. Turmoil and strife are strong motivations to find peace. I wonder if they would condition the seeker, just as the peace here encourages us to gentler outlooks?"

Khalil sighed. She was questioning Bellona's history. She doubted her motives. It was a universal doubt, it seemed. No one believed an Eriuman who had fought for the Karassians for ten years could possibly want peace for the free worlds and was willing to fight for them and with them to get it. No one believed a woman with Bellona's history could possibly change her loyalties like that.

"And now you are back to looking tired once more," Maddie said. "This\ will not do, Khalil Ready. I would not say farewell when your state is poorer than when you arrived."

"I must leave soon, though," Khalil said. "The hunt

goes on," he added.

"Have dinner with my family tonight," she insisted. "A good, solid meal in front of you, some excellent company and we will send you on your way with a peaceful heart."

Khalil studied her. A solid meal? In front of him?

Then he understood. The Alignment wanted proof. Solid, tangible proof that Bellona's change of allegiances was genuine, that her cause and her ability to fight for it were real.

That put the Alignment right in the same corner as the rest of the free states.

"That sounds wonderful, thank you, Maddie," Khalil lied.

* * * * *

Eriuman Republic Ship Ennius, Revati System.

"I DO APPRECIATE YOUR INVITATION, Admiral Eucleides," Iulia said, looking around the captain's quarters of the *Ennius*. "I admit that this is my first time on a cruiser. I am shocked by how much room they have. I was under the impression that ships were cramped and crowded."

"A frigate, perhaps," Lucretia Eucleides Dejulia de Criselda said, leaning back against the comfortable sofa and spreading her arms along the back, which had the effect of making the buttons and gilt on her uniform lift and spread. "A convoyer, most certainly. They are the runabouts of the navy. However, enough room for everything we must carry is what defines a cruiser."

Iulia sipped the wine. It was a poor quality compared to the wine in the cellars of the Cardenas homebase. She avoided grimacing and put the glass down on the low table beside the sofa she was sitting on. "I should come to the point," she said. The information she had uncovered about the admiral hinted that she did not like having her time wasted.

"Then you didn't wrangle my invitation merely to gawk at a big ship?" Lucretia asked.

"You're too busy for nonsense like that."

"Curiouser and curiouser."

"I would ask why it is that we've never met before," Iulia said. "Yet you are a Dejulii and military, too. There have been few occasions where our paths might cross. I confess I wanted to meet the most powerful woman in the Eriuman navy."

Lucretia Eucleides didn't move, or give any reaction. Her face remained placid. She was a handsome woman in her seventh decade and she had spent her life battling her way up through the ranks. There were fewer than two hundred women in the Eriuman Navy, even though regulations did not prevent them from joining. Eucleides had paid the price for her career, though. She had no partner and no family left on the Dejulian worlds, and a career that was waning.

Iulia did not underestimate her. To have flourished in a fraternity as strong as this one took skill, diplomacy and ruthlessness. That was why Iulia had picked her out.

Lucretia finally responded to Iulia's bare-faced compliment. "Is there something you want from me, Iulia Cardenas Scordina de Carosa?"

"I want only for us to be friends."

"I see." Eucleides' tone was flat.

Iulia gave the admiral her best warm smile. "You may have heard that there is some…movement at the head of my clan's table, lately."

"I did hear that," Eucleides said. "I also heard that the current head of the clan, that Peru boy, may not be as docile as you would prefer." She smiled.

"You keep tabs on clan politics," Iulia said. "Good. That will save time." She picked up her glass and sipped again, to give her time to regather her thoughts. Eucleides was more informed than she had suspected a military leader had a right to be. She should have been braced for this possibility. "I have no influence over Peru, although I don't believe he will remain in the top chair for very long, so my lack of leverage is not an issue. The other contenders, those closest to the chair, are all contained."

"Contained?" Eucleides repeated, her tone one of curiosity.

"They will vote the way I suggest, when the time comes," Iulia said impatiently.

"Ah." Eucleides' smile was enigmatic. "And now you set your sights upon the military?"

"It is no secret that the generals and admirals in favor with the clans get bigger budgets and larger ships, more power, more recognition and more fame."

"You offer me more power?" Eucleides asked. "I, the most powerful woman in the Navy?" She didn't smile, yet Iulia knew she was laughing at her.

"The most powerful woman yes. Just not the most powerful admiral," Iulia said flatly.

Eucleides smile faded. "Perhaps I am content with my station."

"If you were, you would have retired five years ago." Iulia took a breath for courage. "You *hate* that the other admirals have held you back, that no clan acknowledges you as their point man. It makes you writhe every time one of the other, weaker admirals gets a pat on back."

In fact, she was guessing that this was so. Iulia had read Eucleides' biographical profiles carefully. No clan had adopted her, not even her own. The lines between the clans and the military were not direct—the most powerful admirals attracted the support of the most powerful clans. The Admiral General of the Navy had been a Scordini pet for decades and he was of the lowly Jaleesa clan.

There was a chance Eucleides would deny Iulia's assertions and Iulia waited for her response with a degree of trepidation that was leavened with the knowledge that if this moment back-fired, there were many captains and rear admirals that might be more eager to add another stripe to their sleeve.

"You would have your clan's assembly support me?" Eucleides asked, her voice distant, as if she was thinking very hard.

"They support Admiral General Haisey," Iulia replied. "That could change, depending on who sits in the chair."

"You want me to help you move your pet into the top chair?"

"No," Iulia said flatly. "This is not a trading of favors, Lucretia. This will be a working partnership. There are things I want, that the Navy can provide, that *you* can provide, if you are in a position to do so. I can put you in that position."

"You want me to challenge Haisey." Eucleides shook her head. Iulia didn't know if she was expressing disbelief or admiration.

"As a means to an end," Iulia corrected. "Clan squabbles will be beneath both of us when this is all over."

For a long moment, Eucleides sat still, thinking it through. Iulia remained silent, giving her the time she needed.

"I'd heard you were ambitious," Eucleides said at last.

"Then you have underestimated me, if that is the extent of your evaluation," Iulia replied.

Eucleides grinned. It was a quick, sudden expression, as if she was smiling despite herself. Her smile faded just as quickly. "I heard that you were ambitious and that you only came to that ambition recently, because of your daughter's actions and your husband's passing. You have my sympathy."

Iulia shook her head. "Is that what they say about me?" She let her amusement show this time. "Truly, the men of our worlds know so little of what we are truly capable.

My ambitions have only come to light because Reynard was no longer there as my point man. Now I cannot be as circumspect as I once was."

"And your daughter's rebellion and her current activities in free space had no influence upon your agenda?" Eucleides asked curiously.

"What *are* her current activities?" Iulia asked. "The public feeds are not forthcoming."

"That is because she has fallen off the map." Eucleides shrugged. "The girl was a bur in our sides for months. Haisey thinks she has been killed in some bar scrap and we can concentrate on the Karassians once more."

"You don't believe that, do you?"

"Bellona Cardenas is Reynard's daughter…and yours. I no further believe she got herself killed in a bar fight than you do. Her disappearance, in that case, is a matter of concern. It means she has found a sanctuary we do not know the location of and even now is shoring up her defenses."

"You think she will be back."

"I do." Eucleides studied her. "You want to pay Bellona back for the ruin of your family, yes?"

"Would you blame me if I did?" Iulia asked.

"I would only question whether you have the stomach for what must be done, if that is your aim." Eucleides got to her feet and brushed out the purple uniform. The gilt glittered as she moved over to the low table and picked up the wine that Iulia had been drinking. She drained the glass in two large swallows and put it down again.

Iulia's heart skittered. Now they had come to the crux of it and she recognized the moment.

Eucleides looked down at her. "So…Iulia of the Scordinii. Do you have the fortitude that is needed?"

Iulia got to her feet, facing the Admiral. "You won't be disappointed," she said and kissed her.

Chapter Fifteen

Kachmarain City, Kachmar Sodality, The Karassian Homogeny

CHIDI WOULD NEVER TELL A single soul, ever, about his sunset secret.

Karassia loved him. His life was an open book. The lens surrounded him day in and day out, as nearly a billion fans hung on to his every word, accepting whatever he said without question.

He could bring down governments, if he put his mind to it.

The adoration was addictive. The attention was the reward for the years he had fought to become as known as he was, for his feeds to grow into the massive entertainment industry they now were.

He was set for life. Money. Fame. Millions of Karassians aspired to have his life.

That was why no one would ever find out that at sunset every day, he escaped the lens for a brief hour, while pre-made footage ran to hide the gap in his life. That single hour spent alone, in the still silence of an apartment empty of people, was the most precious part of his day. He sometimes *yearned* for that time to come. The lens and the attention built up a pressure that was like an itchy coat against his skin, driving him mad, until all he wanted to do was tear it off and stomp on it, smear it into the ground until it was beyond paste.

His sunset hour stopped him from doing that. It was his secret, that no fan, no employees, could ever be allowed to learn.

With the fuss over the Xenia clips pushing his feeds to the top of *every* list, life had become a blur. Merchandise deals, drugs, sex, clothes, money and yet more money rained down upon him daily. Surya had been replaced by Pepper, who had been replaced by Marie and Marty, Abel and Hans, sometimes all at once. The more the sensational highs piled up the bigger his feeds became. Everyone loved watching his success and poured more of it on him. It was a crazy roundabout.

Chidi unsealed the apartment door and looked over his shoulder. The check was automatic. He had long ago worked out how to duck out of sight and escape back to his apartment to greet the sunset from the big picture window covering the width of it. No one was following him.

He pushed the door open, stepped inside and shut it with a sigh of relief. With his back against the door, he worked at the edge of the mask until he got a fingernail under it, then tore it off and dropped it to the floor. The wig and the stained clothes followed.

Naked, he padded through to the big front room, where the picture window was waiting for him.

A man was sitting in his favorite chair. A man in a brown military uniform.

Chidi came to a halt. He could think of nothing to say. There were no words that would encompass his shock at finding someone sitting in his apartment, clearly waiting for him to arrive at this hour.

"We know all about your life, you see," came another voice. A *second* voice.

Chidi whirled, his bare feet squeaking on the cool tiles.

The second man was in the square armchair by the picture window, ruining the view. The setting sun was behind him, dazzling Chidi and making the man a mere silhouette.

"Who are you?" Chidi demanded. His voice came out high and weak. Thankfully, there were no lenses on him right now. He pushed his hand against his chest. His heart was hurling itself against his ribcage. It had been a long time since he had been this scared.

The man stayed where he was. "You can call me Woodrow," he said conversationally.

The military man came up alongside Chidi and held out the dirty coat he had used to get home. "Here," he said shortly.

Chidi didn't take the coat. "You don't know me as well as you say you do, if you think I'm going to cover up to make you feel more comfortable. My fans know and love me, just like this." He got messages praising his sexual prowess and the size of his genitals. Oh yes, they adored every aspect of his life.

"Your fans are not watching you right now, though, are they?" Woodrow said. His jerked his head at the officer.

The uniform turned away, taking the coat with him.

Chidi swallowed, aware at last that *no one* was watching. He had worked to make sure of that, every day at this time. He had worked just as hard to keep it a complete secret. Now, with no lens trained on him, the protection the public gaze extended him was gone. "What do you want?" he demanded, pushing as much power into his voice as he could. It emerged with strength—not a lot, although he no longer sounded as if he was about to cry. Good. He lifted his chin. "I'm waiting," he added.

Woodrow didn't move. It was creepy the way he just sat there. It bothered Chidi that he couldn't see his face or any details about him.

"You've been telling a lot of people that the Xenia videos are forgeries," Woodrow said.

"They *are* fake," Chidi said stoutly. He had argued this line of reasoning so often that he had come to believe it. "They didn't turn up for a *whole year* after Shavistran was supposed to have been destroyed. It took them that long to make the digital images. I mean, look at the woman who was supposed to have been Xenia. She doesn't even *look* like her."

"It's interesting that you should think so," Woodrow said smoothly. "Your opinion carries a lot of influence on Karassian worlds and we have taken note of that."

Chidi swallowed again. Woodrow's quiet lack of emphasis, the neutral blandness, was making him nervous. People always got excited around Chidi. They shouted. They cheered. Sometimes they raged. They were never emotionless.

"The woman who claims she is Xenia has been putting out her own footage," Woodrow continued. "Have you seen it?"

"A blonde wig and white paint doesn't make her Xenia," Chidi countered automatically. He had said that exact phrase hundreds of times in the last few weeks, whenever someone mentioned the Xenia feeds. "Some of the latest videos are created, not taken. It shows. They're rank amateurs."

Woodrow got to his feet. The sun was setting right behind him, blazing white hot and blue against the polarized windows, hiding every detail about the man. "The average Karassian doesn't have your degree of experience with feeds," he said. "They might believe that the digital manipulations are the real thing."

"I tell them they aren't," Chidi pointed out.

Woodrow crossed the tiles to where Chidi was standing. He was a short man. Overweight. And balding. Now Chidi could see him properly. He might have dismissed the man as past his prime if he had seen him before he had spoken. Everything about the man was completely forgettable.

Perhaps that blandness is intentional, Chidi thought and shivered at the idea and at Woodrow's nearness. He couldn't say why he felt the man was dangerous. Instinct told him to back off. Because of that primitive urge, Chidi stayed where he was, defying it and the man studying him. He wished he had taken the coat when it had been offered to him. His nakedness was making him oddly vulnerable and he didn't like it.

Woodrow looked up at him with properly brown Karassian eyes. "We want you to go on telling everyone the Xenia tapes are forgeries," he said quietly. "Even when every competing feed is trying to shout you down, you would have my gratitude if you stick to your theories."

"That they're fake," Chidi finished. His throat was dry again.

Woodrow patted his shoulder. The man's hand was hot and damp. Chidi shivered.

"I'll be in touch," Woodrow murmured and moved around him.

Chidi whirled. "In touch? Why?"

Woodrow looked back at him. The officer studied him, too. Then Woodrow smiled. "You're our guy, Chidi," he said, sounding happy. "Later, we'll have other messages for you to give to your eager fans."

Chidi shivered again. "I don't work for *anyone*!" he shouted. Fear grabbed at his throat and belly. "Not even for you!"

The pair had gone.

Chidi raced to the apartment door. It was closed. He sealed it. Checked the seal. Then he went back to watch the sunset.

Halfway across the tiles, he froze. "Theories?" he said aloud, as he would do if a lens was on him. It was pure habit.

Moving more slowly, he walked over to the upright chair next to the servery. He didn't want to sit in his favorite armchair now, nor the square one by the window. Instead, he perched on the upright chair and gripped his knees, digging his fingers in.

Theories. Woodrow had called his claims about the Xenia feeds *theories.*

"If the feeds are fakes, he would have called my claims facts," Chidi said, still speaking aloud by habit. His heart was hurting again. He massaged his chest absently, thinking it through.

Theories were suppositions that might be wrong. Did that mean he was wrong, calling the Xenia tapes fakes?

And if he was right, if they were fake, then why the heavy-handed insistence that he go on calling them fakes?

Chidi was good with people. He understood how to please them. He knew how to read them. People like Woodrow only applied pressure in that way when they were on the back foot. When they were fixing things.

Woodrow had implied that a whole lot of people were going to start shouting that the feeds were real. That Shavistran was real. That Xenia wasn't an android, but a real woman—an Eriuman—who had been held against her will, mind-fucked into submission and made to fight for Karassia.

He let out a shaky breath. "It's all true…" he breathed, sick horror closing down his throat.

The last of the sun disappeared behind the city towers, unnoticed.

* * * * *

Demosthenes, Alkeides System

THECLA CALLED OUT TO BELLONA as she was traversing the main corridor, heading back to her quarters. She beckoned Bellona back. She was standing in the open door of one of the big workrooms that lined the corridor leading up to the bridge.

Bellona was surprised to see her there. As far as she had been aware, everyone worked on the deck level, or congregated in the dining hall. "You work here?" Bellona asked her.

"Temporarily. I found some stuff…well, come and see for yourself," Thecla said, waving toward the room she was standing by.

Bellona back-tracked.

"Hayes all calmed down?" Thecla asked.

"I've never see him speed talk like that before," Bellona said. "He so rarely talks at all. Usually one or two words."

"Did you let him have the decking space to extend the garden?" Thecla asked.

"Of course. We're not using it." Bellona looked at her. "You knew he was going to ask me?"

"He's been talking about nothing else for a week."

"Not in front of me."

"When you turn up he shuts up and moons over you." Thecla grinned. "Do you know how often he talks about Xenia helping him plant fresias?"

Bellona cleared her throat awkwardly. "You have something to show me?"

Thecla moved into the room. There was a big counter in the middle of it. Cupboards and lockers lined the walls. The counter was littered with cylindrical objects, about half a meter in length. She picked up one of them and rested it across her hands.

"I found these a few days ago, stuffed in a cupboard. No documentation, no manuals. They're not on the supply inventory, either."

"What are they?" Bellona asked. There was nothing on the cylinders that hinted at their purpose.

"It took me a while to figure that out. I think they were shoved deep into a cupboard because they were an experiment that didn't pan out."

"Shouldn't you be helping with the second bridge forge?" Bellona asked.

"I'm on my downtime shift," Thecla said. "Fontana almost pushed me out the door and told me to go get some rest."

"And this is how you rest?" Bellona reached out. "Can I touch it?"

"It's harmless right now." Thecla held the cylinder out to her. "It's a micro satellite."

"It's not a very small one, for a micro-anything," Bellona said, turning the cylinder over and over in her hands. There was a hairline split in the middle of it, where it would open to give access to the interior, and that was all.

"When you consider that some satellites are the size of space stations, this is pretty small. Thing is, I think I could make it smaller still."

"And make it work, too?" Bellona suggested.

"Oh, I got that one working inside an hour," Thecla said dismissively.

Bellona handed the cylinder back to her. "How small?"

"Ten centimeters."

Bellona looked at her, startled. "What would be the range on it?"

"With one of Sang's miniature communications links in it, the leash could be as long as you want."

Bellona suppressed her growing excitement. "Are you thinking what I'm thinking?"

"That ten centimeters is smaller than the most sensitive security scanner can detect?" Thecla nodded. "These things, at that size…we could print them, once we've set up the file. Hundreds, even thousands of them, a half year and a light year out, five years out, even farther if you want. It would be an untraceable early warning system."

"And not just for us," Bellona said. "Do you know how many free worlds would pay their gross annual profit for a system like this, one that enemies can't find and knock out before they sneak up on them?"

"You want to go into business, boss?" Thecla asked, startled.

Bellona shook her head. "Something like this, given freely, would generate a *lot* of good will." She patted the cylinder. "Make a miniature. Show me it can be done."

Thecla pursed her lips together. "Before or after I finish the forge?"

"In your spare time, of course," Bellona said, as she turned to go. "You have enough of it to dig around in cupboards, it seems."

"That's not fair!" Thecla yelled after her.

Bellona was still smiling when she reached her quarters. Her gaze fell on the empty bed visible through the interconnecting door to the bedroom.

She didn't feel like smiling anymore. "Connie?" she whispered and waited.

In the last few weeks, Connie had spoken to her five times. Each time, it was a simple statement, pared down to essentials.

"Khalil is well. He eats. He sleeps. His work does not go well," had been her first statement. She had not responded when Bellona tried to talk to her. Later messages were similar. Connie's lack of response could mean they had jumped to null-space, or she had chosen to severe the connection with Bellona, perhaps so she could concentrate on ship functions. Except AIs and androids could multi-task until their buffers were full—which rarely happened.

When she received the fourth message, Bellona had said quickly; "Do you fare well, Connie?"

"I…yes," Connie replied. Then the connection had terminated. Bellona heard it cut out.

Connie's fifth message had been slightly longer. "I am well. Khalil is well. The work continues. He talks to Arany's people."

That had been two days ago.

Bellona tried one more time, her gaze still on her bed. "Connie, please let me know you are well. I am worried."

The silence stretched for a heartbeat or two. In computer time, it was a small ice-age for Connie to think it through and make up her mind to talk…or not.

Disappointed, Bellona went through to the bedroom. It was time to try to sleep.

"We are well," Connie whispered in her ear.

It was enough. Bellona was content.

* * * * *

Cerce City, Cerce Prime, Cerce

NATASA GARZA WAS AN ORNERY woman and always had been. Khalil wasn't sure why Ben had liked her so much as his exo, although her demanding ways did contribute to an efficient ship. Perhaps that was why. In all other situations, her personality grated, like iron against stone.

After a fast circuit tour of the top players in the free worlds and weeks of steady rejections and refusals to consider working with Bellona or—stars in their heavens!—working with other free states, Khalil had returned to Cerce to look up old contacts, including Natasa. Ben's former crews and ships were still kicking around the free worlds. They were mostly toothless, without Ben for cohesion, although Natasa was trying hard to fill his shoes.

Cerce and Cora were the two places where most of those people hung out. Khalil did the rounds of the spacer bars in the city, looking for familiar faces. Freeships kept their own schedules. It might be weeks before they popped back into normal space over Cerce. Sooner or later, though, they would be back. Moving from place to place was how they made their money. A cheap commodity on one planet was worth rubies on another, while that planet's weed was another free world's luxury meal. Knowing the needs and wants of a dozen different worlds and staying on top of current fads was how the freeships turned a steady income into bonanza pay days.

Stopping by to drink at the local bars where other free-shippers hung out was how such information was passed along, especially when the Republic or the Homogeny was on the warpath and communications feeds couldn't be trusted.

In Cerce City, there were five drinking holes the shippers preferred, on the lower levels of the villages and out in the fringes, where the vertical villages had not yet taken over. Khalil spent an hour a day in each of them, nursing a drink and talking to anyone even vaguely interesting.

He was a known man, here. His association with Bellona was known, too, although most people remembered him for being Benjamin Arany's strange brother. Far fewer knew of his former association with the Bureau. All his statuses, though, opened up conversations that might otherwise have been stilted and unproductive.

While he was chatting, he let slip that he was looking for Arany's people. Freeshippers were nomads with friendships across the free worlds. If any of those he spoke to had connections or even secondary connections to Natasa and her crew, word would reach her.

He didn't bother with a direct communication to Natasa's ship, the *Yoxall*. That would make it official business and he wanted to avoid the formal restrictions a business discussion set up. By reaching out to her the old way, he would be sending a message along with it: *I'm one of you. I understand your world.*

Natasa would not parse the distinction, although Khalil was betting most of her crew would appreciate the subtlety.

On the fourth day and in the third bar for the day—a beer hall on the outskirts of the city where the hot, yeasty smell of fresh bread lingered because of the bakery next door—Khalil was contacted.

The tug on his sleeve drew Khalil's attention downward. The girl standing next to his stool looked around five years old. She was breathtakingly beautiful, with clear skin, very large gray eyes and hair that curled and tumbled about her face. Her mouth was a perfect bow. She did not smile.

Her clothes were ordinary, her pants torn at the knee and the hems were too short by a centimeter or two.

"Hello," Khalil told her. He glanced up at the mirror behind the bar as chuckles sounded. After four days he had learned who was transitory and who was a regular. The regulars were not the ones laughing. The server wasn't smiling either. Neither was she telling the girl to leave.

The girl tugged on Khalil's sleeve once more.

He considered her. "You want me to come with you?"

She nodded.

Khalil looked up at the server. She shrugged. She wasn't going to help him.

He turned on the stool and glanced around the rest of the bar, at the tables and the booths at the back. The place was filling up already, for this was a popular bar.

No one was watching him with any particular interest.

Khalil mentally shrugged. He would let this play out and see where it took him. He had already paid for his drink, so he drained the cup and got to his feet.

The girl walked out of the bar. Khalil followed, shortening his steps so he didn't out-run her. She struggled to open the heavy swing door so he pulled it open for her. With an air of self-possession, she stepped out onto the graveled path. Khalil let the door swing shut behind him and blinked at the late afternoon sun overhead.

The girl held up her arms, asking to be picked up.

"It's really me you want?" Khalil asked.

She nodded.

He bent and hoisted her up and settled her on his hip. "Where now?"

She pointed along the lane, toward the river and the old original village site.

There were people using the trail. Just on the other side of the trail, more people zipped by in transit pods. No one screamed at Khalil that he was absconding with their child, even though he had braced himself for it.

Moving at the same speed as the other pedestrians, he headed in the direction the girl had pointed. With her in his arm, he could move faster than he would have if he had been forced to follow her short pace.

When the trail forked, she pointed to the right, which would continue to follow the transit line toward the old village.

At each intersection or fork, the girl pointed without hesitation. She was leading Khalil steadily south, toward the old village, which reassured him that she wasn't simply playing a game. He kept an eye out for blind alleys and dark niches where muggers might possibly be waiting for her to bring Khalil to them. There were plenty of them, for this was the old section of the city, with abandoned buildings, derelict warehouses and more.

He could smell salt in the air and the caw of the carrion gulls as they got closer. At the next junction of trails, the girl pointed west, away from the fishing wharf and old town to the east, where the tidal estuary ran freely. Farther east, it stagnated, which added to the aroma in the air.

"You're sure?" Khalil asked. It was the first time he had spoken since leaving the bar. She was a remarkably silent child, although if she was mixed up in…whatever this was, then she was probably only a child in stature. Children tended to grow up fast when they were involved in adult scams.

The trail grew more overgrown as they continued and Khalil worried about the lack of people and the quietness around them. Anything could happen here. The sun was getting lower, too. This was not an area of the city he wanted to be in after dark.

The dark, fragmented roof of an old clay brick building was ahead, peeping over the abundant verdure. Khalil's wariness grew.

The girl tugged on his shoulder, getting his attention. She pointed to a dark doorway between overgrown bushes. There was no door. He couldn't see anything beyond the door but shadows. "In there?" he asked.

She nodded and wriggled.

Khalil put her down and straightened. She instantly ran off down the narrow path, leaving him.

He shook his arm and dug his fingers into his forearm, to get the feeling back. Even a five year old grew heavy on the arm after a while. As he kneaded his arm, he studied the yawning dark space beyond the door, weighing up how smart it would be to go in there versus the need to find out what this was about.

The lack of an actual door was the deciding factor. They couldn't close the door behind him, locking him in. That would give him options.

He walked into the warehouse ruins, blinking to make his sight adjust to the lower light as quickly as possible.

The building was just a shell. There was nothing inside, not even a decent floor. The homeless, kids or gangs had built fires on the weedy ground. There were nearly a dozen blackened pits.

Through the partial roof that remained, the last of the daylight was turning Cerce's sky a stained pink.

Khalil halted, looking around. He would wait three minutes, he decided. Then he would go back to lights and environmental controls and Connie's incessant chatter. He wished for a moment that he'd had the foresight to grab one of Aideen's earworms before he had left Demosthenes. It would be good to be able to talk to Connie right now, even if it was just to hear her complain about how dumb the other ships on the landing field were.

The silhouette of a tall, slender figure slipped through a hole in the wall of the warehouse at the far end. It blended with the growing shadows there and for a moment, Khalil wondered if he was imagining the shape.

Then she strolled out in the middle of the empty shell, watching him.

"Natasa," Khalil acknowledged, hiding his relief. His message had reached her. "Why all the cloak and knife fuss?"

"I wanted to talk where no one would witness the conversation," Natasa said. "You've been meeting interesting people, Khalil Ready. The Alignment, Laurasia, New Veles…you're doing the rounds."

Khalil shrugged. "I can meet who I want. They're all free worlds."

"Yes, they are."

"You wanted to talk?"

"You really think your Eriuman pretender could ever hold the free worlds together, Khalil?" she asked softly.

"She doesn't want to hold the worlds together. She wants the worlds to work with her to hold the Eriumans and the Homogeny back. To stop them gobbling up free states."

"No one asked her to do that."

"They didn't have to. Don't *you* want the Republic to go away?"

"Of course I do. Only, the one thing I learned from your brother is that no one can win, going up against them."

"You're going to run away and let the two war machines stomp all over whatever they want?"

"Heroic gestures won't win against our enemies. I'm going to play it smart."

"How?" he demanded.

As if they had been waiting for that question, seven

man-sized shapes stepped out into the middle of the ruins. Crunching steps behind him made Khalil whirl. There were four more there. They were dressed in black from head to foot. Black headgear masked all but their faces.

"Eleven people, just for me?" he asked. "You're that afraid of me, Natasa?"

"This is not my doing," Natasa said. In the rising dark, the only thing visible about her was her white face and the bobbed red hair, which glowed. Her eyes were dark pits. "My part of the deal was to get you here without stirring interest in your movements."

"So. The girl. All innocent and simple. No one would look twice." Khalil studied the dark figures. "I would tell you that I appreciate the compliment, except you haven't brought enough people."

"Oh, but they're not people." It was a man's voice. "We *did* compliment you, Riva. We brought only the best to escort you back home."

Riva. Cold figures walked up Khalil's back, prickling hard. He hadn't heard that name for a very long time.

"Natasa," he said quickly. "Whatever your deal with the Bureau, cut your losses. Leave now."

"You don't understand, Khalil. They don't want your hero girlfriend anymore," Natasa said. "She's tainted. Useless. Hiding away and licking her wounds. They want *me*, instead."

Six of the seven figures in front of Khalil moved toward him. The other four—making a standard set of ten—would be closing in, too. He risked a fast glance over his shoulder to confirm his guess.

The last figure, the speaker, was standing by one of the mold-lined walls, orchestrating.

"Whatever they told you, they're lying," Khalil said loudly.

"They're partners," Natasa snapped, irritated. "You should have stuck by your brother, Khalil."

It was too late to break for the doorway. Too late to do anything. Natasa was outside the Hjalmar's deadly ring, though. "Run," Khalil told her. "While you can. These…things…they don't leave witnesses. They never leave witnesses. Go, Natasa!"

From her aborted movement, her silence, Khalil knew she was hesitating. Questioning, finally. Had she remembered now his peculiar background? His long association with the Bureau?

Khalil forced himself to stand still as the Hjalmar grew closer, even though the instinct to defend himself was almost overwhelming. If he fought, they would kill him. "The Bureau don't want you at all," he told Natasa. "You're just a conduit to me. Try to leave. Prove it to yourself. If you are allowed to leave, you know you're needed."

Natasa didn't argue. Perhaps the fear in his voice convinced her. She turned and dashed across the uneven ground, her heavy spacer boots thudding quickly.

"Take her," the controller said shortly.

The two Hjalmar nearest Natasa swiveled and moved after her. They didn't run, yet they covered the ground swiftly.

The other eight circled Khalil. This close he could see their faces. The blank, unlined flesh, the lifeless eyes, the unmoving lack of expression. These were the true warrior apps, bred in the android tanks for a single purpose.

Beyond the broken walls of the building, Khalil heard Natasa cry out. The cry was cut off abruptly. Then silence.

He closed his eyes, regret spearing him.

When he opened them again, the controller was standing on the other side of the motionless Hjalmar, studying him. The man's face was more human than his set. He tilted his head curiously. "You are not what I expected, Riva. They assigned a whole set for you. For one man. A *brother*. It made me curious to know what manner of man you were. Now I can see their caution was unjustified." He laughed. "They were so *afraid* of you!"

Khalil gave him a hard smile. "They should be."

"I just don't see it," the controller replied. He lifted his hand. "All I have to do is raise my finger and I will have beaten you."

Khalil locked gazes with him. "You might overcome this body with your apps, but I'm a long way from beaten."

The controller raised his finger. The Hjalmar moved in.

Chapter Sixteen

Demosthenes, Alkeides System

THE DEVELOPMENT OF THE SECOND test bridge forge did not generate the same curiosity as the first, so when the forge was accidentally launched, only Thecla, Vang and Retha were there to see it.

Sang had pushed on with the project with Thecla, while the people who worked with them waxed and waned as their interest levels did. Sometimes, Sang asked directly for help, if someone had expertise they needed. Mostly it was he and Thecla doing the work.

Sang didn't mind the isolation. It was more efficient not having someone peering over his shoulder. Thecla liked to work hard and valued silence as much as he did.

Sang was running a series of on-off trials to establish how long the bridge would hold before venting the charge via lightning and destroying the forge. Each time he reset the forge, he let it run longer, monitoring the buildup of the charge.

In between, he and Thecla tweaked settings and other variables, to see if the charge build up could be delayed. They didn't let a bridge form. Instead, they let the generator wind itself up.

When it happened, Sang had no warning. He reset the forge, reset the timer and glanced at Thecla to see if she was ready, then fired it up.

The forge made a different sound, this time. It was a busy hum, rather than the overstressed whining of previous trials.

Sang stared at the forge. So did Thecla. "Something's different," she said.

An ellipsoid shape formed in the air just in front of the bench. It was two meters tall and a meter across at the widest point.

"That's the landing deck!" Thecla said. "Look, there's Vang and Retha. Firing range practice again. That kid never stops."

"Did you set the forge to generate?" Sang asked, frowning down at it.

"No. *Look,* Sang! It's a working bridge! Man-sized!"

Sang glanced up. The bridge *was* big enough to step through. "How did the coordinate get changed?" he asked.

"I don't know," Thecla said impatiently. "Can they hear us?"

"Probably not," Sang said.

"Get their attention somehow. Wave at them," Thecla said.

"Why?" He was genuinely puzzled.

"Because it's *working!"*

"Barely working," Sang said. "Listen, the overload is building up again."

The hum was growing louder.

Thecla groped for the pelota ball they had put to one side for future trials. It was to replace the makeup box Hero had offered the first time. Before Sang could protest, she tossed the ball through the opening.

Immediately the humming dropped down to a quiet murmur.

Sang looked at the forge, astonished.

"Watch!" Thecla urged, drawing his attention back to the bridge.

He looked up again. The ball had shot through the bridge and now was bouncing along the deck. The bounces grew smaller, then it rolled between Vang and Retha, who were studying their targets.

Retha pointed at the ball. Both of them turned.

Thecla waved, laughing.

Vang holstered the ghostmaker he was using, scooped up the ball and spoke to Retha.

"Sound can't pass through," Sang observed. "A solid object can. Vibrational frequency is filtered, then."

"How do communications feeds pass through?" Thecla demanded. "They're light *and* sound."

"Light and sound packaged in a physical form," Sang reminded her. "Interstellar signals are converted to charged particles before they're sent."

Thecla beckoned to Vang. "Toss the ball back!"

"He can't hear you," Sang pointed out.

Vang was considering the bridge, his head slightly to one side. He touched the middle of his chest, then pointed to the bridge.

"*No!*" Sang said urgently. He stepped around the bench so Vang could see him more clearly and shook his head. "We have no idea what happens if you try to come through the wrong way."

Vang's eyes narrowed. He nodded, as if he had heard. His mouth moved as he spoke to Retha, squeezing the pelota ball.

The forge's humming sound grew louder.

Thecla grabbed one of the multi-tools and tossed it through.

Immediately, the hum dropped to a soft murmur once more.

"If you don't use it, it blows a gasket," she said. Then she grinned. "Use it or lose it."

Vang picked up the tool and hefted it and the pelota ball. He moved around the bridge and disappeared from view.

"He's bringing them back the long way," Sang said, relief touching him. "Good."

The hum of the forge was increasing again.

"Are you timing that?" Thecla asked.

He was a perfect timekeeping instrument and had no need for external tools. "I am," he confirmed.

Retha looked at them and shrugged. *What now*?

As the hum increased, Thecla cast about for another object to toss.

Sang picked up a fragment of purified carbyne. He tossed the heavy angled pebble through.

The hum dropped once more, this time below audible levels. He frowned.

"The carbyne makes a difference," Thecla said. "The lack of a charge, you suppose?"

"It must be," Sang said slowly.

This time, it took more than ninety seconds for the forge to wind itself up to full charge once more.

Sang waited until it was just below the discharge point, then tossed a larger fragment through.

The hum stopped once more.

Retha watched the tests with an amused expression. He picked up the bigger chunk of carbyne and weighed it in his hand, showing surprise at the weight of it.

They tossed three more pieces through before Vang arrived. Retha gathered them into a small pile. Vang dumped the pelota ball and the multi-tool on the bench and waved at Retha.

The forge was humming again. Thecla grabbed the pelota ball and tossed it through. It bounced once, then hit the pile of carbyne fragments and bounced again, this time back toward the bridge.

Retha leapt and grabbed it. His hand connected with the edge of the bridge. There was a shower of sparks and Retha stumbled backward.

"No!" Vang cried.

Retha dropped to the ground and writhed, his body vibrating.

"He's seizing!" Thecla yelled.

Vang lunged forward, to help Retha. He stepped

through the bridge…

…toppled to the deck floor and lay still.

Thecla cried out a wordless protest.

Sang switched off the forge and the view of the deck and the two bodies disappeared. "Hurry," he said and ran for the landing deck, five levels below.

* * * * *

BELLONA WAS RUNNING BY THE time she reached the medbay. Not that her panic was noticed, amongst the hysteria already there.

There were a dozen people standing around the treatment bed where Vang lay. They were shouting at each other. There were more than a few of Amilcare's people there, too.

"Diagnostics, first!" Thecla yelled.

"Listen to the AI!" Hero spat. "The diagnostics show *nothing!*"

"Someone get his heart moving," said someone else.

"No, no, he needs oxygen, first!"

Sang was standing by one of the recovery beds, a small island of calm. Retha lay on the bed, on his side. His eyes were closed, the bruises from long term sleep deprivation stark against his white face.

Bellona moved over to the opposite side of the bed and looked at Sang. "Fontana said Vang was dead." She kept her voice down.

Sang let out a heavy breath and nodded, his gaze flickering to the group clustered around the treatment bed. "He stepped through the bridge. It depleted every charge in his body. He was dead the moment he emerged." His eyes met Bellona's. "That's why the diagnostic aren't working. That's why they won't revive him, no matter what they do."

"This isn't your fault," she said firmly.

"Yes, it is," Sang replied. He looked down at Retha. "Retha suffered a seizure just from touching the thing."

"He'll recover?"

"Only to learn that Vang is dead."

Bellona squeezed his arm.

"Help me! Help! I'm all alone. I can't find Khalil!"

The shouting in her ear made Bellona cry out and clap her hand to her ear. She tottered, her balance thrown by the volume.

Fontana and Thecla both mimicked her, staggering away from the treatment table, their hands to their ears.

"Connie," Bellona said. "Quietly, girl. Calmly. What has happened?"

Sang's gaze became unfocused. "Where are you, Connie?" he said firmly. "Report."

"He didn't come back, it's been twelve hours and thirteen minutes and forty-three seconds and *he's not back*!"

Bellona swallowed. "Where are you, Connie? We'll come and get you. You just have to tell us where you are."

"I'm on the landing field! They're all mean here. They won't help me. They don't believe me that anything is wrong. He wouldn't just not come back. He doesn't do that. Something's wrong, oh, something is so, so wrong!"

Fontana moved closer to the bed, his hand still over his ear, even though it didn't muffled the sound at all. "Can you get a direction from the communications channel?" he asked Sang quietly.

Sang nodded. "Working on it."

Bellona held her hand, gesturing for calm, even though Connie couldn't see it. "Connie, stop this. Right now! Pull yourself together! We can't help you if you don't make sense. Remember your function. Report your status."

Connie was silent for ten long seconds. Then she said in a softer voice: "Khalil told me he was doing the rounds. Drinking."

"Shipper bars," Thecla murmured, from behind Bellona.

"He said he would be late. He didn't say how late he would be, but he has never been gone this long and not let me know why. The city mind won't let me search for him—it says I'm not a priority. Only I know something has happened."

"Where are you, Connie?" Bellona asked. There were only a few free worlds who had the necessary infrastructure to host an AI with the capacity to manage a whole city.

Connie gave a little sound that might have been a hiccup or a sob. "Cerce City," she said softly. "Will you come and get me?" she asked. "Please? I'm frightened!"

Fontana rolled his eyes. "I'll come in the *Alyard* and bring you back home, Connie," he told her. He glanced at Bellona and lifted a brow.

She nodded. He could take the ship. Of course he could.

"I'm leaving now," Fontana said, moving toward the door.

"Me, too," Thecla said. "I know shipper bars," she told Fontana.

By the time they reached the door, they were running, too.

Hero was still working with the AI on the treatment bed. The hysteria had subsided as the minutes piled up. They sensed now what Sang had known immediately. Vang was dead.

Bellona moved over to the bed and everyone made room for her.

Hero looked at Bellona. She gnawed at her bottom lip. "I don't know what to do," she said brokenly.

"There is nothing you can do," Bellona said, speaking loudly enough for all of them to hear. "He is beyond recovery. The most skilled medic in the known worlds could do nothing for him."

The faces turned toward her, with their fear and their upset, were a condemnation.

"Bellona! Enemies in the area! Get to the bridge!" It was Thecla's voice in her ear, using Connie's communications channel.

Bellona whirled, putting her back to everyone. "How can that be?" she demanded. "The proximity alarms haven't sounded."

"They emerged from null space right in front of the *Alyard,* a light year out from your position. They're coming, Bellona. A Karassian first class destroyer and an Eriuman cruiser. Should we open fire?"

"On a carrier?" Bellona said. "Are you crazy?"

"She is. I am not," Fontana said, his voice calm. "We have the element of surprise," he added.

"No. Go to Cerce. Find Connie and find out what happened to Khalil."

"That leaves you without a ship," Fontana pointed out.

"We'll manage," Bellona told him. "Go. Now."

"Going," Thecla said.

Bellona turned back to face the medbay once more. "Emergency," she said loudly. "We have enemies on our doorstep. To the bridge. *Everyone.* Now!"

She ran for the bridge and heard the thunder of many steps behind her, echoing along the short corridor to the bridge. As on the *Alyard,* the medical bay on Demosthenes was located next to the bridge.

"Sang, get the *Demos* moving. Every positioning thruster that works," Bellona yelled as they spilled into the empty bridge. "Aideen, talk to the null-space AI. Set up a jump."

"To where?" Aideen asked.

"Anywhere. A random location. As random and unexpected as you can. Put us in the middle of nowhere. Hero, get on the scanners. Where are those ships?"

Even though no one had assigned posts on the bridge, the eighteen or so people who flowed into the room all settled behind stations and at consoles without bickering or chaos and started working.

Hero bent over the surveillance table. "Three-quarters of a light year from here. Two of them," she said. "Eriuman *and* Karassian..." She straightened, shocked, looking at Bellona.

Everyone else paused to look at her, too.

"I don't have answers yet," Bellona told them. "We can't win against a carrier, not with a Karassian destroyer ready to pounce, too. No one could. We're jumping out of here as soon as we've overcome inertia and Aideen has the null engines ready."

"Forty-three seconds," Aideen said.

"How did they even know we were here?" Amilcare demanded as he tapped the dashboard in front of him with a heavy hand.

"There are dozens of ways they could have found us if they were looking for us," Bellona told him. "I'm more interested in knowing why they suddenly decided to look for us."

"They'll be in ether range in twenty seconds," someone called.

"I imagine we'll have some answers then," Bellona said. She made herself sit in the oversized, overstuffed captain's chair, even though she disliked the way she sank into it.

"In range," the same person called out. "...and broadcasting," they added.

"Let everyone see it," Bellona said. "One-way only. We play dead until the last moment."

The big central screen came to life.

The admiral on the screen was a woman and Bellona recognized her face. "That's Admiral Lucretia Eucleides."

Eucleides didn't respond, because she couldn't see or

hear Bellona. Instead, she spoke calmly.

"This is to whoever is listening on the *Aarens.* I speak on behalf of the Alliance. You are in violation of Alliance space. Prepare to be boarded."

Bellona sucked in a breath.

"What the hell is the Alliance?" Hero said.

"The Homogeny and the Republic are working together," Aideen said.

Hero scowled at her. "*Why* would they even consider working together?"

Bellona swallowed. "It can't be official. We would have heard the proclamation on thousands of feeds."

Amilcare leaned on his station, to twist to look at her. "So the admiral and whoever the fuck is on the Karassian destroyer just woke up one morning and said 'I know, I'll hunt down Xenia and her people today and I'll ask my good old enemy the Karassians to help me, because they'll trip over themselves to do that?'"

"How long until they're in firing range?" Bellona asked.

"Ten seconds."

"Aideen?" Bellona said.

"Thirteen."

"We're going to take a hit or two before we can jump," Bellona warned them. "Alert the rest of the ship… although I think everyone who didn't go on the *Alyard* is already here."

"Just about," Hayes said. He was perched on the second's stool at the communications console, next to Zeni, who was running the console with a competent air. Hayes made Zeni look even more delicate than usual. "I am telling everyone," Hayes added.

"Five seconds."

"Six seconds," Aideen added immediately.

Bellona realized she was pushing herself deeper into the chair, leaning away from the coming impact.

The center screen had gone to black. On Bellona's arm-console, Eucleides reappeared. This time, the screen split. The captain of the Karassian ship was a stranger to Bellona. The man standing behind his shoulder wasn't.

"Woodrow," she breathed.

Eucleides repeated her warning. The Karassian captain added at the end of it, "We will fire immediately if you do not signal you are standing down."

"They know who is here," Bellona said to herself, for everyone else was busy. "They came for me. Who sent them, though?"

"Incoming!"

She reared back, gripping the edges of the chair.

There was no explosive sound. The point of impact was somewhere out of hearing range. She could feel the floor rumbling beneath the chair. Screens and consoles flickered.

"Go as soon as you can, Aideen!" Bellona cried.

"We're not moving fast enough yet," Aideen replied.

"Sang!"

"The inertia is considerable, with a vessel this size," he said, as calm as Aideen. "We are also inside a gravity well that we must overcome."

"Shoot garbage out the airlock if that will help," Bellona told him. "Just get us moving! Damage report, anyone!"

"Someone on the landing deck says the fighters slid into one corner," Zeni said. "I don't think there's anyone anywhere else to report."

Another hit. This time, Bellona could hear the bone-deep boom.

She gritted her teeth together. There was nothing to do but wait it out.

"Jumping!" Aideen called, as the ship lurched and shivered.

The images of Eucleides and the Karassian captain dissolved. They were replaced by a generic star field she did not know. Bellona looked up. "Where are we?"

"Nowhere, as requested," Aideen said.

Sang sat back, blowing out a breath.

"Sang, are we still moving?" Bellona asked.

He bent to look at the console. "Yes. Three meters a second."

"Keep us moving," she told him. "Demosthenes will never stop, ever again. Bring it down to just above jumping speed, so we're always ready."

"Is that wise?" Aideen asked. "If we keep moving, we'll starting running into things."

"In about a hundred and fifty years, maybe," Bellona replied. "A gradual course correction will take care of that, too. Sang, you and Aideen work with the navigation AI to set up algorithms that will keep Demos moving through nothing. And Sang…"

"Yes?"

"You'll have to let the *Alyard* know where we are. Make sure that message is sealed in a bomb-proof communications bullet. Now we're where no one can trip over us, I'd like to keep it that way for a while."

She got to her feet. "Everyone else, fan out over the Demos. Check for damage, fix what you can and clean up. Any questions, check with Sang or table it for later. All clear?"

Silence.

Bellona nodded. "I'll be in my quarters."

Chapter Seventeen

Demosthenes, nomansland.

SANG TOOK ONLY A FEW steps into the room before coming to an uncertain halt. He looked around warily.

"You insisted on speaking to me," Bellona reminded him.

"I wanted to let you know we found the locator beacon and disabled it. It would have turned on when the reactor was activated, telling the Karassians the *Aarens* was active once more. It's dead now."

"A small prevention, applied too late to help. Anything else?"

"Fontana and Thecla have returned. Connie is brooding in her corner of the landing deck once more. They spent five hours searching in Cerce City. The popular bars remember seeing Khalil there at least once, yet there's no trace of him."

Bellona sighed. "Thank you. That's it?"

"No." Sang girded himself. "I think it's time you left this suite."

Bellona laughed. "Why?"

Sang's lips thin for a moment. "You've been hiding in here for nearly eighteen hours and things are… You're needed. At the very least, you should talk to Retha."

She flinched. "And say what? 'I'm sorry Vang is dead. I was a fool.' You think that will make Retha feel better?"

"I think you would be surprised at the difference it will make," Sang said quietly.

She shook her head. "No. I'm not ready."

Sang shifted on his feet, frowning.

"What?" she demanded.

"You don't get to choose when you're ready or not," Sang said. "That's not how this works."

"Excuse me?"

Sang took another step farther into the room. "You're their leader. It's not up to you to decide whether they need you or not."

"Their *leader*?" She lurched to her feet. "I'm the one who got Vang killed. I led them right into the arms of the Homogeny *and* the Republic. I can't get a single free world to do more than laugh at me. Khalil is missing. Connie is panicked. The bridge forge is possibly the worst idea I've ever had, unless we use it to toss Karassians through. And on top of all of that, the Republic and the Homogeny have put aside hundreds of years of hostility and are working together just because of *me*." She wrapped her arms around her middle, chilled. "Those people out there don't need me. I'm the *last* person they need."

Sang nodded. "Have you asked yourself yet *why* the Republic and the Homogeny are coming after you?"

Bellona sighed. "What does it matter? They can out-shoot me, out run me and squish me under their heels whenever they want. I was a fool for ever thinking that this could work, Sang."

He took another step. He was in the middle of the room now. "I'm not Khalil," he said. "He would say this in a way that makes sense, that would convince you of it and make you want to get out there and fight. All I can do is report." He gave a tiny shrug. "You think you're ineffective, that what you're trying to do is worthless. I say you're wrong."

Bellona gave a tiny laugh. "That's not a report, Sang. That's an opinion. One without substance."

"Do you remember watching the fishermen hunt for giant horse cuttles in the Arden Sea?"

Bellona stared at him. "What has that got to do with—"

Sang held up his hand. "I know. This is not poetry. It is not one of Khalil's rousing speeches. Humor me. Do you remember how they catch the horse cuttles?"

Bellona sighed. "Depth charges dropped over the side. The deeper the better, because the biggest fish are *very* deep. They're so big, some of them, that the charges would just disorient them and piss them off."

"Then they'd rise to the surface and try to take on the boat and that's when the hunters take over, so they can claim their trophy," Sang finished. "Only, do you remember how *long* it took once the charges were dropped? That one excursion, when you were ten. You got bored."

"I think I fell asleep," she admitted, recalling the sparkling sea, the heat, the rocking motion of the boat and the sharp, rotting smell that wafted off the deck plates no matter where she stood.

"You said it just then: The deeper the better. A deep charge, a strong charge, brought up the biggest horse cuttles…and it took *time* for that to happen."

Bellona shook her head. "I'm not following, Sang."

"Nearly a year ago you dropped depth charges. You thought they were just little crackers. A shot across the bow. Yet the cuttles have surfaced and are fighting back and they are *strong*."

Bellona gripped her sides, her heart giving a little thud in reaction.

Sang held out his hand to one side. "In two hundred years of war, neither the Homogeny nor the Republic have ever considered working together for a common aim. It was unthinkable. Then Ben Arany came along with his little fleet of insurgents. That worried them enough they shuffled next to each other to take him down, while pretending they were still enemies."

"The city killer," Bellona said. "Karassian technology, used by the Republic."

"*Apparently* stolen while Karassia looked the other

way," Sang added. "Then you made a public declaration. A formal announcement that you would work to halt their aggressions and maintain peace and freedom for the free states." He shook his head. "You scared them, Bellona. The thing they fear the most is an enemy greater than them. If the free worlds were ever to put aside their independence and work together, they would become an enemy that could defeat them. That's what you told them you were going to do."

Bellona stared at him, her heart starting to hurt, now. "They got together because of me."

Sang nodded. "Publicly, this time, because they fear your threat that much. Look at the degree of the reaction, Bellona. Remember the resources both militaries have. They would have researched and analyzed and concluded that your threat, as simple and useless as it looks like on the surface, is dangerous."

Bellona pressed her lips together, resisting the impulse to dismiss the idea. "The stronger the reaction, the great the depth charge," she said, flipping the theory around.

Sang nodded. "Two big systems like the Republic and the Homogeny can only change directions slowly. That's why it took a year for even this unofficial cooperative to emerge. Alliances and agreements and lobbying takes time."

"It's still only a few captains and admirals working together," Bellona pointed out.

"It won't stay that way," Sang said with complete assurance. "The military officials are more agile than the politicians. They can afford to take greater risks...and they have. They'll ask forgiveness of the united assemblies, then a formal alliance will be voted in because even the politicians are scared of what you represent."

"A threat," she repeated.

"A *huge* threat, that must be stomped on immediately and quickly, before your ideas take hold among the free worlds and become unstoppable."

Bellona considered it. "The bigger the charge, the greater the reaction."

Sang nodded. "Things are moving. That is why you can't give up, now. There's enough speed for you to jump. Then Vang won't have died for nothing."

Bellona let out a heavy sigh. "Okay."

Sang looked startled. "Okay?"

Bellona gave him as good as smile as she could muster. "You're not Khalil, yet you're effective in your own way. I'm convinced. I'll stop pouting now."

Sang grew very still, his gaze turning inward.

"Sang?"

He held up his hand for silence.

She waited.

Sang's gaze refocused on her. "I just received a sealed communication. From your mother."

Bellona shook off her surprise. "What does she want?"

"Me."

Bellona laughed. "You?"

"She cited the family economic constitution and says I am required to return to take up my prescribed post."

Bellona considered that, her mind racing with a clarity that had been missing until Sang had lectured her. "You should go," she said slowly.

"No!" he said stoutly. "I turned my back on the family just as you did."

"You didn't declare it publicly, the way I did," Bellona told him. "I think it's time you did."

Chapter Eighteen

Pleasure Dome, Antini III, Free Space.

IT WAS SNOWING HEAVILY ON Antini, to the point where visitors to the pleasure dome were brought in from their vessels by flitters and air cars, to land on one of two garage balconies built into the curve of the dome, high up out of reach of the climbing snow.

From behind the dome wall, the building snow at the lower levels obscured any view, while the cafes and restaurants that hugged the wall at the upper levels enjoyed better business than usual as people sipped alcohol and drug-laced hot beverages and watched the snow just on the other side of the dome spit and flurry and change direction without warning. The one thing the snow did not do was stop.

Sang found the Cardenas group at one of the smaller eateries. They took up three tables. Iulia was at the center one, of course.

He knew everyone who sat at the tables and catalogued an interesting anomaly. Missing from the family group were the male humans. Gaubert was not there. Neither was Markjohn, or his oldest son, who was already an adult.

Thora sat next to Iulia, a fur wrapped firmly around her. She looked uncomfortable, her glaze flitting around the area uneasily, as if she was trying to avoid letting it linger on any brazen view. As the restaurant was separated from the rest of the dome only by low bushes in tubs, the sexual activities in the dome could be observed from any table. The view was a feature of the restaurant advertised on every placard throughout the dome.

On the other two tables were the family androids, including Wait and Riz.

Iulia was watching a group clustered on a fungus bed, on the other side of the rivulet. She seemed unmoved by their gymnastics. When she saw Sang, she rose to her feet. "Finally," she said shortly.

Thora's mouth opened. She looked up at Sang, then down, then up again. "You're…you've changed!" she said, horrified.

The family androids got up and stood waiting for a direction, even Wait, who had done more to run Reynard's empire than anyone else in the family. Their expressions were placid.

"You're late," Iulia said. "No matter. We can adjust any chronometric errors back at the homebase. You're here."

"I am here, Iulia," Sang said. "Although I am not here to return to Cardenas with you."

Iulia's lips parted. Then she got herself under control. Her eyes narrowed. "You are required to return."

Sang smiled. "I work with Bellona now. You have no jurisdiction over me, anymore."

"You are a *family* asset," Iulia snapped. "You will return, or I will *make* you return."

"You can try," Sang said, as calmly as he could, even though his heart was squeezing and writhing. "Bellona removed the governor implant a month after Max died. I am as free as you to make up my own mind now."

Iulia's jaw flexed.

Sang spread his hands in a peaceful motion. "Let us not pretend, Iulia. You want me back only to syphon from me details about Bellona, to give to the military so they can take her down. There is no other reason why your summons arrives so long after I left. The Republic Navy just failed to capture her, so they sent you in."

Anger made her eyes glitter. Iulia held onto it with discipline honed from years of subsuming her needs to support Reynard's, instead. "You are being insolent. You will return with me and to your place in the family."

"Why else would you select a neutral location like Antini?" Sang said. "Far from Eriuman? You tripped the governor weeks ago and it didn't work. That must have scared your friends. That's why you suggested a neutral place to meet. You knew I would not go anywhere near Eriuman territories."

"Iulia, what is it talking about?" Thora demanded, a deep furrow between her brows.

Iulia ignored her. She was studying Sang with an intense gaze, as if she was reassessing him. "Yes, I have friends in the military," she said. "I have friends in the assemblies. I know that the formal Alliance between the Republic and the Karassian Homogeny will be announced before either us gets back home. You do not want to be standing next to Bellona when that happens, Sang. The full weight of the combined navies will be brought to bear and I will not be able to offer you the protection of the family name if you stay with her."

Sang only just hid his reaction. The urge to hurry away, back to Demosthenes, was strong. "It's formalized?" he said sharply.

"A resolution settled by the united assemblies," Iulia replied. "And the Homogeny's council, too."

"All to hunt down your daughter," Sang murmured. "How can you do that to her?"

Iulia's face clouded. "You have to ask that?"

Sang let out his breath. It was not quite a sigh. "Do you not see what is happening? What *will* happen now? The only thing slowing down the annexation of free states was the war between the two of you. Without it, they can pour over worlds like a tide. You resent the erosion of your own family. How can you condone the destruction of so many others?"

Iulia's face closed over. "I see now that I have wasted

my time, coming here. You will not listen. You have chosen to be branded a runaway, instead."

"I'm not a runaway," Sang said, almost laughing. "Is that really the extent of your imagination?"

Thora clutched the fur around her neck firmly. "What else could you be?" she demanded.

"I am a free man," Sang told her. He walked away.

* * * * *

Demosthenes, Nomansland.

BELLONA WAS IN THE BIG dining hall when Sang returned. Once, the hall had been used to feed hundreds of troops in one sitting. Now, the benches had been removed and the long tables converted to worktops. Just as everyone gravitated to the little dining room for company, this big hall had become the place to gather to work together, instead of being spread out across the huge vessel.

Even Amilcare's Abilio mining people came here. Bellona was pleased to see they were not clumped together at one end. They had spread out among the Ledanians. There was more than enough room for everyone and the common work area meant that cross-pollination of ideas and expertise happened easily.

Even Aideen had set up shop—at the end of a table, it was true. Along her section of the table, she had an array of the articulated armor she had been growing. She was fitting it on everyone, a person at a time.

When Bellona reached the table, though, Aideen had been diverted from finishing her assignment by Thecla, who was fitting a different device on Aideen.

Aideen held up her hand and open and closed the fingers, as Thecla fastened the armored glove up by her elbow. The glove had jointed plates of black carbyne over the back of the hand and fingers, and up to the middle of her forearm.

Projecting off the knuckles were five short, triangular-shaped blades. When Aideen flexed her fingers, the blades lay along the back of the fingers, the sharp edges fitting into matching indentations in the plates beneath.

When she turned her hand into a fist, though, the points and blades jutted out.

"It is not as heavy as it should be," Aideen observed. "There are seven hundred grams of carbyne attached to it. It should drag my hand down."

"You don't notice the weight because you're wearing it, not holding it," Thecla said. "It's distributed. Although your arm muscles will compensate and grow bigger and stronger, once you've used it for a while."

"What is it?" Bellona asked curiously.

"A cestus," Thecla said. "I'm making you a pair, too, Bellona. I've got these metal monsters, so I don't need them. You and Aideen and Hero have little lady hands and the cestus will compensate for that."

Aideen met Bellona's gaze. "Hero will not use them. Must I?"

"It seems like a good idea to me," Bellona said. "Why don't you set up a trial for them, Aideen? A proper evaluation will tell you if they are worth adopting or not."

"Yes," Aideen said, with a short nod. "A precise measurement of their usefulness."

"Where is Hero, anyway?" Bellona asked, looking around.

"She's in the medbay," Thecla said.

"She's injured?"

Thecla shook her head.

"Hero asked the medical AI to put her through a course in emergency medicine," Aideen said.

"*Hero* is learning medicine?"

"Why not?" Thecla said. "Her understanding of anatomy and what makes people tick is just as good as

Vang's."

Bellona considered that. "True," she admitted. "Although the idea of Hero operating on me makes me just as uneasy as I felt about Vang doing it."

"She has a better bedside manner," Thecla said.

Bellona had to agree. "Why will Hero not use the cestus?" she asked.

Thecla shrugged. "She wants her nails free and clear. They're more dangerous than any blade I could put on a cestus, so I guess she's right to refuse."

"Cut the ends off the fingers," Aideen said distantly, bending and flexing her hand experimentally, watching the plates curl and straighten in a sinuous wave.

Bellona grinned.

Thecla raised her brow. "Shoulda thoughta that," she said stiffly. She glanced over her shoulder. "Sang is back," she added.

Bellona nodded. "Connie warned me, a few minutes ago."

"There's something I should tell both of you. Come over to my bench," Thecla said. She strode around the end of the next long table and up the aisle, stepping around people working on either side.

Bellona stayed in the aisle she was in and kept abreast with Thecla. Sang met them at Thecla's messy section.

"How did it go?" Bellona asked him.

His expression was calm. "As expected," he admitted. "She demanded I return to my duties. I refused, which surprised her, although I don't know why it did."

"You're the first Eriuman android to choose free will and self-determination," Bellona told him. "Of course she was surprised. Most Eriumans would be."

"I don't think she was *truly* surprised, though," Sang said slowly. "Your mother is…devious." He grimaced.

"Iulia Cardenas is sneaky?" Bellona asked him. She shook her head. "Are we thinking of the same person?"

"We are, which proves my point," Sang said. "She only ever showed her most positive and simple facet to you and anyone who counted. The household androids, though, saw her…calculations."

Thecla shook her head. "You make it sound as though you guys are cattle."

"Assets," Sang corrected. "Karassians use screens and keyboards and other input devices, yes?"

"Hell, they run our lives," Thecla said. "There was always a screen nearby."

"That's what androids do for Eriumans," Bellona said. "They run their lives. Sang and the other household androids were privy to the private side of every family member. Of course they got to see our every secret. If Sang says my mother is devious, I believe him."

Thecla looked from one to the other of them. "You realize you're saying the family pet—no offense, Sang—"

He just grinned.

"—only, you're saying the family *asset* knows your mother better than you do."

Bellona grimaced. "That was my life," she admitted.

Thecla blew out her breath. "Fuck. And you think Karassians are self-centered?" She lifted up a small pile of extruded carbyne, her arm tendon showing the strain, and made a satisfied sound. "There it is." She pulled out a one-handed ghostmaker from beneath the pile and let the pile go. It crashed back onto the counter with a deep ringing sound, making neighbors look up, startled.

Thecla pointed the ghostmaker at Bellona and squeezed the trigger.

Sang jerked forward, throwing himself in front of her.

Nothing happened.

Sang fell back again. Bellona breathed out a shaky breath.

Thecla grinned and held the ghostmaker up by the very end of the grip. "It's dead."

"No shit," Sang breathed, straightening up his jacket. The tone he used was a replica of Thecla's dry sarcastic one.

Bellona couldn't smile. "There was a point to that?" she demanded of Thecla.

Thecla tossed the ghostmaker to Sang. He caught it precisely, even though he kept his gaze on Thecla.

"That was the gun that went through the bridge with Vang," Thecla said. "It's not just out of juice. It's so dead I could run the exhaust from a reactor through it and it wouldn't even glow."

Sang looked at the gun, frowning. "The bridge sucked the charge out of it, too…" he murmured.

Bellona sighed. "So, until we figure out a solution, we're reduced to non-mechanical, non-electronic weapons and armor."

"Suits me," Thecla said.

"We're going to keep trying to use the bridge?" Sang said, his voice rising.

"There has to be a way," Bellona told him. "Vang taught us that we can't step through without…something. Shielding. A different frequency. *Something*. Only, the bridge works. If we can figure out how we can use it, it will give us an advantage over the Alliance that they can't counter with bigger ships and bigger guns."

Sang's face paled, making the freckles stand out. "We can't use it," he said woodenly. "It would be suicide to keep trying."

Bellona rested her hand on his shoulder. "We had a setback, that's all. It was terrible. Tragic. If we don't use it and learn from it and move on, then Vang will have died for nothing and that would be even worse."

Sang sighed and nodded. "I agree. Here." He tapped his temple. "Here, though…" He touched the middle of his chest.

"If it makes you feel better, you can be the one to step

across the bridge when we try it next," Thecla said.

Sang rolled his eyes.

Bellona leaned over the counter and snagged the corner of one of the small sheets of carbyne and lifted it up. It was very heavy and she grabbed the opposite corner with her other hand and hefted it. "Is this the pure ore, from Pushyan?"

"I smelted the fragments left over from making the first forge, then rolled it out so it can be stacked," Thecla said. "I didn't think we should waste the stuff."

"That's what we were tossing through the bridge?" Sang asked, his voice distant and his eyes narrowed.

"I swept up everything I could find," Thecla said.

"It's still pure and inert?" he asked.

"Test it for yourself."

"Sang, what is it?" Bellona asked.

"It's still inert," he said. "Despite forging and despite going through the bridge. The ghostmaker is inert, now it had passed through, too."

"It still makes a good blunt weapon," Thecla pointed out.

Bellona handed the sheet to Sang. He held it as if it weighed nothing, staring at it. "The forge stayed on the counter," he said slowly. He looked up at Thecla. "What if it went *with* the person using it?"

"You mean, *wear* it?" Thecla asked. She frowned, too. "We put it on a belt because we figured you'd need it at the other end to come back, and carrying it meant one hand less to fight. I just didn't think carrying it would protect the wearer. Like a grounding rod," she added.

Sang pointed at her. "*Yes*. Exactly. It would disperse the charge."

Thecla grinned. "The only way to test it is for some sucker to put on the belt and step through it. You've already volunteered, Sang."

He didn't smile. "I want to do the math, first. Then I

will test it myself. No one else should take the risk."

Bellona's gut tightened. "Maybe we *should* find someone else. You would be..." She searched for a non-revealing way to say it. "You'd would be hard to replace, Sang. Impossible, actually."

His gaze met hers. "The risk would be minimal. I'm sure of it, now. I will prove it, too."

* * * * *

Kachmarain City, Kachmar Sodality, The Karassian Homogeny

CHIDI GLANCED AT THE SETTING SUN and shivered. Sunset was no longer his happy time. He hadn't been near his apartment for days. With a jerky movement, he polarized the walls of the privacy pod, so they turned opaque, and turned his back on them.

Korbina sat on the divan with his hands on his knees. Despite the subject matter, he had become calm once Chidi had explained that he had not dragged Korbina into the pod for sex.

Chidi had dismissed his fears quickly. He had no need for pods, or for seducing reluctant partners. Sex was freely available to him, whenever he wanted it. And why would he indulge out of the view of lenses?

Then he had eased into the real reason for blowing his precious alone time this way. Korbina had listened soberly.

"You've been saying for months now that the Xenia tapes are forged," Korbina said. "If you start saying they're not, viewers will lose faith in you."

"I'm not going to change anything I'm saying," Chidi said quickly. Barely noticed, an image of the little man, Woodrow, with his cheerful smile, formed in his mind. In the last two weeks, Woodrow had appeared three times without warning in his apartment, to encourage Chidi to keep up the good work. Chidi had also seen him on the street, standing and watching among the crowd that always formed wherever Chidi went. He thought he'd seen Woodrow at the back of the restaurant last night, too—sipping a glass of something black.

Chidi's armpits prickled in reaction to the idea of saying anything in front of a lens that Woodrow would not approve of. His belly clenched. "That's the *last* thing I'm going to do."

"Then why do you want me to analyze the footage?"

"I told you. To see if the videos *are* real."

Korbina seemed genuinely confused. "So, you think they're real, yet you're telling everyone they're not?"

"You're not as smart as I thought you were," Chidi said. He blew out a heavy breath. "I'm going to keep the viewers happy, while you find out what is really going on." As he said "viewers", Chidi thought of Woodrow.

Korbina's eyes widened. "What *is* going on?" he asked. "Did something happen to you that we didn't get to see?"

Yeah, he was exactly as smart as Chidi had thought. Chidi shook his head. "Don't worry about that. Just check the footage—there's hours and hours of the stuff now. The Xenia feed runs endlessly. Find the non-digital segments. See if they have been changed."

Korbina considered that. "Is this…dangerous?" he asked.

Chidi jumped. "No. Not for you," he said, picking his words with care and soothing his tone.

Korbina tilted his head. "You're lying."

Chidi threw out his hands. "I don't know, okay? They've never hinted at violence."

"They?"

Chidi silently cursed. He wasn't good at hiding things. That's not what his viewers paid him for. "I can't say," he told Korbina. That was also the truth.

Korbina considered him. "The Xenia tapes are political and mixed up in the war. That means '*they*' is either the military or the council."

"We're not at war anymore, remember? The Republic is our new best friend." The parties celebrating the end of the war had lasted for a week and my, how Chidi's approval rating had soared!

Korbina smiled. "Xenia—if she is real—isn't with the Republic. That's *why* they are our new best friend."

Chidi stared at him, startled. Why hadn't *he* thought of that possibility? "That's why we have to figure out if the Xenia feeds are real or not," he said urgently. "If Xenia really is out there, everyone should know that. Everyone should know Karassia is still at war, just with someone different now."

"Okay, then," Korbina said.

"You'll do it?" Chidi asked. He couldn't help adding, "Despite the risks?"

"I couldn't figure out this whole Alliance thing at all." Korbina shook his head. "You've given me the first clue that might explain it. I'm not going to check the feeds for you. I'm doing it for me."

Chidi stared at him. For the first time he wondered how many other people felt just as Korbina did. Was there a groundswell of questioning Karassians out there, who didn't automatically believe everything they saw on their feeds?

It was a startling idea. A novel one. Who'd've thought that the truth would be so attractive?

Chapter Nineteen

Mycia 489, Mycene System Asteroid Belt. Free Space.

THE ROOM THEY WERE KEEPING him in was square, tall, iron-lined and studded. It completely lacked any contact with the outside world. Not even sound penetrated. Khalil lost track of time. He had no idea how long he was there before the woman came to speak to him. The only marker of time passing was the cycle of his biological needs. Hunger, thirst, sleep and elimination. As his jailers denied him food and dribbled down his throat the bare minimum water necessary to keep him alive, and as the lights in the room blazed without cease, even his physical needs became unreliable.

Khalil knew they were trying to disorient him. He also knew that the silence and isolation were designed to make his imagination work overtime and let his fear build.

At first, they kept him shackled to a hard, upright chair by his wrists. When his hips lost all feeling and the heaviness moved down toward his knees, Khalil got up and smashed the chair against the wall. It left his hands locked together, yet he was otherwise free to move.

He stretched until the feeling returned to his limbs and walked around the perimeter of the cell. It was featureless except for the heavy door. He could not spot the lenses, even though he knew they were there.

The silence was broken only by the pair of Hjalmar that brought food and water. Neither of them commented on the smashed chair. One picked up the pieces silently and removed them. No replacement chair was brought. He was left free to roam.

Time seemed to stop, after that.

Days later, or perhaps merely hours later, the door opened. There had been no sound of a lock turning and no other warning that it was about to open. It slid down into the sill with a reversed guillotine movement.

Khalil was sitting on the stone floor. He lifted his head and watched the black space beyond. The two Hjalmar did not step through. The woman did.

She was tall, with dark skin and eyes. Sharp brows lifted over the eyes. Her hair sprang from her head as if it had a life of its own and her face was unlined. Even so, there was a look in her eyes and an angle to her square chin that said she was older than she appeared. She wore a modified version of the armored overalls the Hjalmar wore. Hers had no sleeves.

Human, Khalil catalogued.

The door rose back into place as she stood in front of him. Khalil didn't get up.

"By all means, stay where you are," she said.

"Okay."

She smiled. "I am Mesut Traverse. You won't have heard of me."

"You're not Bureau?"

She ignored the question. "I'm told you are a very smart man, Riva—"

"My name is Khalil Ready."

"—and if you are as smart as they assure me you are, then you will already know why you are here."

"Surprise me, if you can," Khalil said.

"The Bureau is pleased with the success of your strategies to infiltrate Bellona Cardenas' organization, only they now insist upon a status report. One is long overdue."

"I don't work for the Bureau anymore. You know that, or you would not have held me here, like this." He lifted his wrists, to display the shackles.

"Your disavowal of your allegiance to the Bureau is

understood. It was a necessary tactic that reassured Bellona Cardenas and built trust—"

Khalil laughed. It was a fake laugh…at first. Then the irony struck him forcibly and he realized the hard, mirthless sound he was making was genuine. His eyes stung, his diaphragm hurt and his head throbbed.

Mesat Traverse did not move. When Khalil had recovered, she spoke as if he had not interrupted. "—trust among her people and allowed you to gather information. That phase is over now."

"That's why I'm here, isn't it?" he said. "You want me to tell you everything I know about her and her *organization*. Insisting I still work for you is how you'll justify whatever you do to get that information."

"I'm sure you can imagine for yourself what means will be used to extract the data, if you do not cooperate," Traverse said calmly.

Khalil lifted his hands. "When did the Bureau resort to violence?" he demanded. "Oh, I know perfectly well what you're hinting at. Torture and psychological manipulations, deprivation and isolation until I give you what I want. None of it is how the Bureau works."

"I'm not Bureau," Traverse said firmly. "I am Hjalmar."

"The Hjalmar are part of the Bureau."

"Actually, we are independent sub-contractors. I accepted a contract from the Bureau. They care not how the results are obtained, which is why they gave the contract to me."

Khalil smiled, hiding his dismay. If the Hjalmar had control of him, then none of the Bureau sensibilities would be in play. The Hjalmar were the Bureau's enforcers for a reason. They did everything the Bureau would not or could not contemplate doing for themselves. Bureau directors slept easily, their consciences clear, while the unpleasant aspects of running the Bureau were orchestrated well out of sight.

"A woman with dark hair and eyes," Khalil told her. "How convenient. Did they think your appearance would loosen my tongue?"

"I was Eriuman, a long time ago," she said softly. "That affiliation no longer exists."

"I was Bureau, a long time ago," Khalil replied. "That affiliation no longer exists."

"Then we understand each other," Traverse said. She nodded. "It is good to get the preliminaries out of the way. I'll be back, Khalil Ready."

The use of his real name bothered him. It showed flexibility. Condescension. It made him feel weak by insisting they use it.

He watched her go, knowing she intended to let him stew in his own self-doubt until he was ready for the next phase. It was difficult not to do exactly that.

* * * * *

Eriuman Republic Ship Decimus, Delucas System.

WHEN THE OFFICERS IN THE boardroom all snapped to attention, Hecate Hult came perilously close to looking around and over her shoulder to see what senior office had just entered.

She made herself relax. "Sit," she told them. Then, with a deep breath, she took the big chair at the head of the table and sat down, as they all settled into their own chairs and cleared their throats.

Hult was tempted to begin with "I am as surprised as you to be sitting here," then realized the truth would not serve her. She had spent the last fifteen years digging for the truth. Now she was the captain of the *Decimus.* Truth would be bent and distorted to serve the politics that eddied around serving ships and their captains. She was in the main game now.

"You'll have to watch your back," Admiral Lucretia Eucleides had warned Hult. "Not only are the other captains going to resent you for being a woman, most of your officers are going to resent that you were promoted over the top of them and took a captain's chair they thought they were in line for."

Hecate had not found Eucleides' observations any help. "I would find it useful to know *why* I'm being pulled out of the criminal justice division to captain a front-line cruiser. That would help me deal with my officers *and* the other captains."

Eucleides smiled. "You were tapped because you deserve it. Your name came to my attention…You were the head of the investigation into the murder of Maximillian Cardenas, weren't you?"

Hult drew in a hard breath. "Yes, I was," she said, when she had smothered her reaction enough to speak.

"Someone must have noticed and liked what you did. Your name was given to me for the empty chair. Now it is yours."

Someone in the Cardenas family? Hult speculated silently. She had spoken to many of the family members, including Bellona the Traitor. No one had thanked her or contacted her once the investigation with its inconclusive summary had been closed. It seemed unlikely the family was the source of her sudden promotion.

She kept her mouth shut, though.

Eucleides gave her a very small smile. "I can put you in the chair, Hult. What you do with it is completely up to you. I can tell you that you will be watched rather more closely than a normal green captain, and you will be judged by harsher standards."

It was Hult's turn to return the little smile. "That's a standard I've been judged by since I signed up, Admiral. It doesn't scare me."

Eucleides grunted. "Glad to hear it. Go and impress me, Hult. Prove I'm not an idiot for sponsoring your promotion."

The conversation with Eucleides had taken place only four hours ago. Now Hult was on *her* ship, facing her own officers.

She looked around the table. "Who here served with Maximillian Cardenas when he was captain of this ship?"

Brows raised. Five hands lifted briefly. Five out of eight.

Hult nodded. "You may or may not know that Max was a friend of mine and on many things, we saw eye to eye, including how to run a ship. I know Captain Jeffers changed a lot of the things that Max put in place. I'm letting you know it's going to change again. If anyone has any objections to that, speak up now and I'll find you another post before we leave orbit."

No one spoke. She saw some of them exchange glances and chose to ignore them. "Very well. You, lieutenant… what is your name?"

"Story, sir. Lieutenant Story, Engineering." He was young and flustered. His cheeks were pink. He was also one of the officers who had not served with Max.

"Engineering report, Lieutenant Story. Let's get this staff meeting done with and move on to more productive work. That's another thing," she added. "There will be far fewer meetings, including these twice daily sessions." She switched her attention back to Story. "Status, Lieutenant."

She wasn't sure if she imagined the tiny shift in the atmosphere, a relaxing of the more senior officers. She didn't worry. They would soon understand she was as keen to complete the *Decimus'* assignment as any of them. Perhaps she wanted it even more than them, for finding Bellona Cardenas was a very personal mission for her.

* * * * *

Mycia 489, Mycene System Asteroid Belt. Free Space.

MESUT TRAVERSE RETURNED ONLY HOURS later and this time she had company.

Khalil watched the boy step into the room from his crossed-legged position on the cold floor and tried not to be concerned. The boy was barely as tall as Traverse, who was not a big woman. He had a thatch of honey blond hair and eyes that were a true, rare blue. His face was passive. He did not seem disturbed by Khalil's shackles or his position on the floor, although he was definitely human. There was too much life in his eyes and face, despite the passiveness. He was alert, interested and taking in everything around him.

The average Hjalmar processed only enough of their environment to get the job done. Curiosity did not serve them, so it had not been given to them.

"You're recruiting children now?" Khalil asked, disturbed.

Perhaps the boy was here to make him uneasy. If so, they had correctly analyzed at least one of his pressure points.

Traverse glanced at the boy, who was standing just inside the door, watching Khalil. "Yes, you had a little brother, didn't you? Benjamin, I believe."

Khalil swore silently at himself. He was not practiced at interrogation. He was giving Traverse openings and revealing weaknesses.

"This is Dyse," Traverse said, unexpectedly. "He is an apprentice with the program. He has been assigned to observe our…conversation."

Dyse nodded.

Traverse crouched down so that her gaze was nearly level with Khalil's. "You must be tired by now," she said softly. "Hungry, too, I imagine."

Khalil shook his head. "Just get on with it, so I can say

no and be left alone."

"Get on with what, Khalil?"

Dyse studied him calmly.

"You're stepping up the pressure. Last time, you threatened me and that didn't work. This time, you're going to try extortion. You are about to threaten everyone I care about with ruin or pain or death, or all of it."

Traverse linked her hands together. "Would that do any good?" she asked curiously.

Khalil smiled. He couldn't help glancing at Dyse once more. "My brother is already dead. You can't touch him. And you will never find Bellona."

"That's where you're wrong, Khalil. The Alliance already found her."

His heart actually squeezed. If they were monitoring his vitals, then he had just told them Traverse had scored a point.

"Who is the Alliance?" he asked, keeping his tone light and curious.

"While you have been a guest here, the Republic and the Homogeny have formally joined forces. One of their cruisers, the *Ennius,* and the Homogeny Ship *Salucci,* trapped the wreck she and her people were hiding on." Traverse smiled. "Your people. My apologies."

Khalil fought to remain still and not give anything more away. "They didn't capture them, or we would not be here right now," he said flatly. "You didn't say that, so you were trying to scare me into compliance, to save her. You're going to have to try harder, Traverse, if you want this to work."

Traverse got to her feet. "Who said anything about compliance?" she said casually.

"You're not here to drain what I know about Bellona from me," Khalil said. "There are dozens of ways to extract that sort of factual data from even an unwilling subject. I know five ways and I'm not a professional like you.

If I spill my guts, that's a bonus. Who knows, it may even come as a bonus perk in the contract you signed with the Bureau. What you're really here for, though, is to bring me back to the Bureau. They want me willing and cooperative. That's why you're using a soft approach. It's also why you're going along with having a child witness it."

She stared at the closed door for a moment. "You're right," she said, turning on her heel. "They do want you back. Just not as desperately as you seem to think. They're willing to break a few heads to get you—they acknowledge you are a good asset to acquire. They're not so desperate to have you they would beggar themselves, though." She looked at him. "Make no mistake, Khalil. This is the last time I visit when no blood will be shed."

Khalil kept his gaze locked on hers and hoped his trembling wasn't visible. "Finish your visit, then."

She hissed. "You're right. Bellona got away from the Alliance. I'm surprised the old wreck could even move, yet she managed it. She jumped and will probably hole up in some unknown section of deep space where no ships go. That doesn't mean we can't find her. We have our ways, you know that. We found you, after all."

"I wasn't hiding," Khalil pointed out. "She is." He didn't bother disguising his pride in Bellona's resourcefulness. She had been right to keep the bridge intact, after all.

"Sooner or later, she'll have to emerge," Traverse pointed out. "Supplies, food, a doctor…which I'm told she does not have among her people. Something will force her to emerge, even if it's simply to engage with her gathering enemies. Then we will have her. If you do not help us, if you do not cooperate, things could go badly for her after that."

Khalil shrugged. "They'll go badly no matter what, as her enemies *are* gathering. It's interesting the way everyone is circling around her. It's almost as if they're afraid of her."

Traverse didn't smile, yet her eyes narrowed with amusement. "The pieces are aligning precisely as was predicted, five years ago. Every move and counter-move is inevitable and we have anticipated them all, including your cooperation."

"I read that prediction, five years ago," Khalil told her. "Just before I was sent to Kachmar for the Ledan assignment. I also read three other predictions at the same time, about the same subject. One of them said that the leader of the free worlds would destroy all of you, all of *this*. Guess which one I believed?"

Traverse shook her head. "You *will* cooperate. You would not let any harm come to her because of your failure. You have let her down once already."

Khalil's trembling grew. They seemed to know everything about him. It felt as though they were reaching inside him and twisting his guts, just to see what his reaction would be. He was an experiment, shackled and monitored.

"If you know that," he said, keeping his voice low to disguise the shaking, "then you must know that she has never forgiven me for it. I have nothing to lose here, Traverse. Go after her. Do your worse. Then I will have the pleasure of dancing on your crypt."

Traverse scowled. "You think they do not have other figureheads they can use? She is just one of them, Riva. You would sacrifice her just to be right? If I walk out that door, two Hjalmar units will be dispatched immediately to take care of her."

Khalil laughed. It was hard to do, yet he managed it. "*Please*, just try it," he begged. His voice came out hoarse because his throat was so dry.

Traverse hissed and stalked out of the room. Dyse followed. The door had almost slid shut again when it reversed and sank back down into the floor. Dyse stepped in.

He was carrying a big cup of chilled water, with condensation forming beads on the side.

Khalil's throat clicked as he swallowed. There was no point pretending he was indifferent to the sight of the liquid. They could read his hydration levels for themselves. He didn't fool himself they were not precisely tracking and orchestrating his comfort levels for maximum impact.

"Is this where you stand in front of me and drink the water?" he asked the boy, his voice rasping.

Dyse came close to him and held out the cup.

Khalil didn't reach for it. He couldn't understand what the catch would be. If he raised his hands, would Dyse then snatch it away? Was the water poisoned? Drugged?

"Drink some of it," he whispered.

Dyse took a mouthful and swallowed. "It is just water," he said. He had a pleasant voice. He held the cup out again.

Khalil raised his bound hands slowly, waiting for something to happen. He got his fingers around the cup. Dyse didn't lash out. He just handed over the cup.

Khalil drank deeply. The first mouthful hurt as it went down.

"Why do you resist Traverse?" Dyse asked. It was a simple question, his tone curious.

"Because she represents people who are trying to reduce my freedom. So do you."

Dyse didn't seem upset by the judgement. "The Bureau is benign.

It works for the longevity of the galaxy. It has the resources to know what is best for you. Why do you not listen to it?"

Khalil drained the cup. "You really believe the directors of the Bureau are wise and benevolent?"

"Why would they not be what they profess to be?"

"Because they're human," Khalil told him. "They have

weaknesses. Desires and selfish motivations. Even kind motives can be twisted. Look at yourself. You brought me water. You put Traverse's interrogation back by hours as a result."

Dyse took the cup from him. "You think they will punish me for that?"

"What do you think? They're your people." Khalil shook the shackles. "This is what they do. And you want to become one of them."

Dyse considered the shackles for a long moment. Then he turned and left and the door shut behind him.

Khalil bowed his head and hoped they could not detect the fear in him.

Chapter Twenty

Demosthenes, nomansland.

SIMPLY BECAUSE NO ONE WENT to the bridge, Bellona used the stark room as a place to get away from everyone if she needed to. Her private quarters were less private than she liked.

She kept the lights down very low and sank into the too-soft captain's chair and turned it around to face the big screens, which kept her out of sight of the main doors to the bridge. She tried to relax and offload all the worries and nagging thoughts, even for a few heartbeats.

Sang intruded only enough to offer the glass in his hand, reaching around the back of the chair with it. The liquid in the glass was dark and looked like tea. High Moon tea, possibly. She took the glass.

"Don't go," she told him.

"We're about to run another trial. I can't stay long."

She swiveled the chair around to face him. He had already moved away. His pale face was strained.

"You're making progress?" she asked.

"Yes." Sang's smile was brief. "You should sleep. It's very late."

"Look who's talking," she replied, taking in the dark marks under his eyes. "We don't have a medic here. You should take better care of yourself."

"I will, once the bridge forge is working properly."

"I think it's working just fine. You have to figure out how to use it properly, that's all."

"The sooner you have working forges, the sooner we can move into the next phase."

She sipped. It was a good quality tea, just not High

Moon, which had a delicate taste to it.

Sang hesitated. "Anything from Khalil?"

Bellona shook her head. "No one has seen him. No one has heard of him in the area. He's completely disappeared. Connie isn't talking to me, either."

Sang hesitated. Then, "Well, I should go back."

"What is it you're not saying, Sang?"

Sang grimaced. "Khalil would not fail to contact you, sooner than this, if he could manage it. That means he can't. The possible reasons why he cannot are few. They're not positive."

"Who has him, then? Eriuman? Karassia? One of the free states?" Bellona shook her head. "There are too many opposing us, Sang. We need allies."

"When we have a working forge, the allies will coalesce all by themselves."

"In the meantime, we have to wait." She peered into the tea. "I'm not good at waiting."

"I remember." Sang sounded amused.

She looked up. "Do you think...could my mother have done this? Taken Khalil? To weaken me?"

Sang considered. Then he shook his head. "Iulia is too used to working in the background to make such an overt move. Such an act makes declarations. She is allergic to declarations, to taking a public stance."

"Whoever has Khalil doesn't care what the world thinks about it," Bellona said slowly. "That implies Karassia or Eriuman. My uncle Gaubert? He worked with Woodrow. The Alliance exists because of him."

Again, Sang shook his head. "He is a simple man. Destroying the city of an enemy is within his understanding. Abducting the lover of an enemy to cripple them with doubt and fear...it's too subtle."

"Maybe they didn't take Khalil to get at me," Bellona said. "Maybe they want him."

"If they do want him, they want him because of what

he is to you," Sang assured her. "Things are moving," he reminded her. "We just don't know who is moving them yet. Something will happen soon enough and then we'll have more information."

* * * * *

Cardenas (Findlay IV), Findlay System, Eriuman Republic

IULIA WAS WOKEN BY THE screaming, even though she had sealed her private apartment. The apartment door rattled in its seals as someone pounded on it from the other side. "You did it! You killed him! Viper! Witch! You've schemed for months—"

Whoever it was, they had been cut off. Had someone muffled her? It had to be Thora. There was no other woman in the household and she was often hysterical.

Iulia covered herself and unsealed the door. The household androids were just hauling Thora away. She was fighting them, struggling to free herself.

Markjohn stood watching her departure, his face wretched.

"What has happened?" Iulia whispered. "What makes you look so awful?"

Markjohn swallowed. "Gaubert is dead."

Iulia covered her mouth. Then she said quickly, "His heart…Reynard's was weak. Gaubert was his brother…"

Markjohn shook his head. "He was murdered, Iulia."

"Murdered?" she said blankly.

"Come and see for yourself." Markjohn took her arm.

Iulia let him lead her into the office that had once been Reynard's. Gaubert lay on the floor, on his side, with his knees pulled up against him. His eyes were open and blood had flowed from his mouth and nose and ears.

Iulia pulled back. "What…happened to him?"

"Poison perhaps. Lix says his stomach is empty,

though."

"To die that way..." she breathed, looking down at him. "It looks as though he was in great pain."

"It *looks* like something exploded inside him. I've seen it once before, Iulia." Markjohn looked grim, his square jaw, so similar to Reynard's, flexed. "If I am right, then someone put nanobot larva in him. They hatched and ate their way out, just as they're supposed to do."

Iulia put her hand over her mouth again. This time, nausea stirred in her belly. "Nanobots are supposed to eat dead flesh and diseased cells. Cancer cells, not viable tissue! They heal from the inside..."

"Not these ones," Markjohn said grimly, staring at Gaubert. "They were reprogrammed. I've heard of it, as a cautionary tale. I've never heard of it actually being done, until now."

Iulia wrapped her arms around her middle. "They'll think I did it," she whispered. "That I wanted him out of the way. That's what Thora thinks."

"You *did* want him out of the way," Markjohn said dryly.

"Yes," she said frankly. "Just not like this. Not by killing him. He was weak, everyone knew that. I was going to see that you got his seat at the table..." She trailed off.

He stared at her, not speaking.

"You knew that, surely."

"I did wonder why..." He looked over his shoulder with a guilty glance, then shrugged. "I know you didn't do it. The bots hatch and exit within four hours of being introduced. I saw the seal on your door when Thora hammered on it. You've been in there, the seal unbroken, for nearly seven hours. It can't have been you."

She studied Gaubert again. "He had his uses," she admitted. "The Alliance would not have happened if he had not made that clumsy attempt at cooperation two years ago."

"And the Alliance exists only to hunt down Bellona," Markjohn added.

Iulia looked up at him. "Well…yes."

"Everyone knows you have contacts working within the Alliance," Markjohn said softly. "Lucretia Eucleides."

"Admiral Eucleides," Iulia said stiffly. "She is just a friend."

"Of course she is. Just as I am a friend." Markjohn's smile was sour. He stirred and waved toward the door. "We should leave everything as it is until the investigators have had a chance to see it. I'll escort you back to your apartment."

Iulia let him lead her away, after one last look at Gaubert's blood-covered face. She hid her smile.

* * * * *

Mycia 489, Mycene System Asteroid Belt. Free Space.

THE PAIN WAS VERY BAD from the start. Khalil had thought himself braced for it. He had not understood how bad it could get. He wanted to sink into it, let the pain close over his head and lose himself that way. Traverse, though, seemed to know the moment he reached that point. She would walk away, or apply a sedative—a mild one to restore his flagging senses enough to continue.

Then she would pick up where she had left off.

There were no questions. No demands for information. As Traverse explained over and over, her voice wavering in Khalil's ears, all he had to do was indicate he would cooperate with the Bureau and it would all stop.

To agree was simply impossible. Didn't they understand that? Wasn't it clear enough?

He didn't try to be courageous. He screamed. He cried. He begged for them to stop. He let himself do whatever it took to survive the next wave of pain, for there was no exit for him. He would not give them what they wanted. His only option was to get through this until they were tired of it, or finally understood that he would not become their tool once more and killed him.

Traverse was skilled, though. Just as she knew when to stop him from passing out, she also knew how to keep him alive.

There was her voice and the pain, and whatever humble mental defenses he could pull together to resist both.

For a blessed moment or two, the agony stopped. His body throbbed and he became aware of it as a physical entity instead of a vessel that delivered suffering. He could hear more than her voice. He could hear the whisper of sounds around him, although he did not yet have the strength to open his eyes and look.

He could hear himself panting. The uneven thud of his heart in his ears.

"Can you hear me, Khalil?" she murmured.

Alas, he could. He swallowed, amazed he could manage that simple movement.

"I will give you a moment to reconsider your position, before we begin again."

Again.

He shuddered and heard himself moan. For a moment, she had let him think it had ended. Now, she was cruelly taking that hope away from him. There was more to come. How could he possibly survive more? Only, survival was not the point.

Water trickled into his mouth.

Khalil opened one eye. Dyse was feeding him the water.

With superhuman effort, Khalil gathered the energy to speak. "You should not see this." It came out barely above a whisper, his voice cracked and strained.

Dyse glanced at him, startled. He looked around to see if anyone had heard Khalil's whisper. Traverse was standing by the cart holding her instruments, sorting through them.

Khalil wondered how he had drawn any parallels between Traverse and Bellona. Traverse looked like a distorted monster to him now.

Traverse came back to the chair he had been secured to. This chair was steel carbon alloy and impossible to shatter. Khalil watched her hands and felt a pathetic gratitude when he saw they were empty.

She leaned over him, her small eyes filled with warm empathy. "Do you want to tell me something, Khalil?"

He nodded.

Surprise skittered across her face. "What is it you want to say?"

"Maximillian Cardenas. The Bureau hired out his assassination to Ferid. They asked you to handle the contract." It hurt to say that much.

Dyse frowned and turned away to put the cup back on the same trolley where the pincers and burners lay.

Traverse looked thoughtful. "I don't recall."

"I'm dead. You can tell me."

Traverse considered him again. "I don't see the point, but fine. Yes. I managed the contract."

It had been a shot in the dark. The contract had been a dirty one, which fit in with the Hjalmar's' style. He had not considered that Traverse had personally handled the arrangements, though.

"The Bureau wanted her blasted out of her complacency," Traverse admitted. "You were no longer there to provoke her. Something had to be done. I'd heard rumors about Ferid. I contacted him and told him to use his imagination. He delivered." She shrugged.

Dyse was standing frozen at the trolley, listening.

"Was it Ferid's idea to cut off Max's arms and legs and arrange them as he did?"

Dyse's eyes widened.

Traverse looked disgusted. "He didn't discuss it with me."

"The scope of the contract was your call?"

Traverse laughed. "What are you doing, Khalil? Trying to lay blame? You're in the wrong position to do that." She brushed the damp locks of his hair back from his forehead. "Even now, you still have hope, don't you? So sweet and brave." She went back to the cart. "I see I will have to be more convincing." She picked up the little knife she had previously used on Khalil's belly. His gore and blood was still on the blade.

Khalil shuddered.

* * * * *

KHALIL DID NOT RECOGNIZE WHEN Traverse was finished. He was barely conscious and trying hard to drown in the blackness that hovered on the edges of his mind. Oblivion seemed very sweet, yet lay beyond his reach.

He could hear people talking. It was pulling him back to consciousness, making him focus. He tried to let go again, for when he did pay attention, the pain revived. He didn't think he could take any more of it.

The voices were loud. They didn't care if he could hear. That made sense. As he had told Traverse, he was dead anyway. Whatever he heard would die with him.

Someone moved him and the sharp silvery tines burrowed deep into him, making him scream. Except he heard nothing.

The blackness closed in.

* * * * *

HE CAME BACK TO AWARENESS. The pain had receded. He was lying on something hard. The floor, he guessed.

"Khalil Ready, are you awake?"

It was Dyse's voice.

Khalil poured all his energy into opening his eyes.

Dyse leaned over him. The cell was not the one he had been in before. It was dim. Sound could be heard beyond it.

"I'm alive," he said wonderingly.

"She was not permitted to kill you," Dyse whispered. "The Bureau insisted you stay alive for now."

"Why?"

"You wouldn't give in. They want to know why."

"I can't give in."

Strength was returning to him. Energy. It allowed him to think clearly, while movement was still beyond him.

"You would rather die than work with the Bureau?" Dyse asked. "That does not make sense."

"It does from where I am lying," Khalil told him. "One day, you might be lucky enough to have someone like Bellona in your life, Dyse. Then you will understand what you don't see now."

"See *what*?" Dyse hissed. "I've never understood stupid emotions. They make people behave strangely."

"They do make you act as you never thought you could," Khalil told him. "They let you live through pain."

Dyse sighed.

"I know you don't understand it now," Khalil told him. "You just have to understand this—I'm leaving here as soon as I have the strength to stand. I'm fighting my way out, because I will not work with the Bureau anymore. They're inhuman monsters who manipulate and use people as tools. They're using *you*, Dyse."

"If you try to leave, Traverse *will* kill you."

"She can try," Khalil said complacently. "She may even succeed. I'm not staying here. One way or another, I'm going back to Bellona. I will do anything and everything I must to return to her."

Minute by minute, he was growing stronger. He wondered if the Bureau, in their frantic need to understand, had ordered Traverse to treat him so they could get the answers they craved. Some adrenaline, pain killers and wake-up shots would keep him from dying.

"You...love her that much?" Dyse's eyes were dark in the dim light as the boy studied him.

"I do," Khalil said. He sighed. "The Bureau has faith in their neural networks and hive minds. Once, I did, too. *She* is my faith now. Bellona will save us all. I intend to help her do that."

Dyse chewed at his bottom lips, frowning. "You told the Bureau she was not the hero they sought."

"I lied."

"Why?"

"Because to do what she must, she can't be your puppet. It will destroy her."

Dyse looked over his shoulder. "They come," he whispered and touched Khalil's shoulder.

The darkness took him immediately.

Chapter Twenty-One

Kachmarain City, Kachmar Sodality, The Karassian Homogeny

CHIDI PAUSED HIS RAMBLING MONOLOGUE to listen. It had sounded as though someone was crying, out in the office.

He looked at the lens. "Did you hear that?" he asked his viewers, even though they couldn't answer directly. "Come with me. Let's find out what the fuss is."

The lens was tethered to his heat signature, so it followed him as he moved out to the main office at the back of the studio.

Cora was sprawled on the floor, her head down, the blonde hair a curtain that hid her face. Her shoulders were shaking. Everyone else in the office had drawn back against the walls, staring at Cora and the screen still showing at her usual station.

Chidi came to halt. The image on the screen grabbed his attention. He even forgot about Cora and the way she had tried to upstage him.

The image was a still, taken from civic footage. The caption underneath was clearer than the image.

Do you know this man?

The man in question was the focus of the image. It was hard to make out details because there was so much blood everywhere. His face was distorted, because whoever had killed him had beaten him with something blunt. The eyes, nose and mouth were swollen. The still, open eyes were bloodshot. One of the retinas had detached and the white of the eye was as red as the pavement under the man's head.

It was the plain, blood-splattered shirt that told Chidi who it was. He had seen that shirt and others just like it every day for the last ten years.

He crept closer to the screen, unable to look away.

The floating lens buzzed around to the corner of his eye, hovering. He had forgotten about the lens. He had forgotten about the nearly one billion people watching him right now.

"Go away," he told the lens, before dragging his gaze back to the screen where Korbina lay. Sickness roiled through him. This was his fault.

The lens chassis dropped down and the lens itself swiveled up, adroitly capturing his face from a low angle.

"I said *go away!*" Chidi screamed. He swiped at it, batting the lens across the room. People ducked, gasping. "Someone turn the damn thing off!" Chidi yelled.

He sat on the floor next to Cora, shaking.

* * * * *

Mycia 489, Mycene System Asteroid Belt. Free Space.

WHEN HE "WOKE" THE NEXT time, Khalil could feel the energy coursing through him.

Dyse was shaking his shoulder. It was very dark. "Wake up," Dyse whispered urgently.

"I'm awake." Very awake. "Did you give me something?"

"It won't last long," Dyse said. "Hurry. Get up."

Khalil resisted Dyse's tugging on his arm, which would have slid him off whatever hard shelf he was lying on. He swiveled his legs around and put his feet on the ground.

Dyse stood back. "The guards are down to minimum. The rest are checking security breaches at the back entrances. They think Bellona has found this place."

"They do, huh?" Khalil got to his feet and swayed, as his balance wavered.

"Did you really mean it when you said you would fight your way out of here, if you had to?" Dyse said.

"Yes," Khalil said firmly.

Dyse held out one of Traverse's knives. "It's not very big, but it's the only one I could find."

Khalil took it and looked at the kid's silhouette. "You know you're going to have to come with me, don't you? You won't survive the investigation that will happen once I'm gone."

Dyse swallowed. "I thought it through. I won't stay here. Not with *her*." He hesitated. "I didn't know…" he said. His tone was apologetic.

Khalil nodded. "Well, if this stuff doesn't last long, we'd better get going. Right now I feel as if I could wrestle all of the Ledanians put together, including Hayes. Do you know where we are?"

"In the basement." Dyse shrugged.

"What star system, I mean."

"Oh." Dyse paused. "Mycia 489."

Khalil wasn't surprised he hadn't heard of it. "Any chance a bus stops here?"

"I know where there is a one-man yacht. The director's. If you can get us there, I can fly it."

Khalil nodded. "You've piloted?"

"I've read the manuals."

Khalil headed for the door. "All of them, right?"

"Right."

Khalil put his hand on the big door lever and paused. "Stay close behind me," he told Dyse. He thought of Bellona. His energy gathered and focused. He wrenched the door open.

* * * * *

DYSE HAD DRAWN MOST OF the guards and sentries out of their path with his alarms and feeds. That left only a handful for Khalil to deal with. The first went down without issue. After the third, though, Khalil could feel the false burst of energy waning.

"Your profile says nothing about you being able to fight this way," Dyse said, as Khalil jogged down the passage the boy had pointed toward. Dyse kept up with him easily.

"Not everything about a man is in their profile," Khalil told him. "You have to talk to people to figure them out." After a breath or two, he added; "You didn't think to wonder why the Hjalmar used a whole unit to pick me up on Cerce?"

The fifth guard to challenge them got his ghostmaker out before Khalil could deal with him. The bolt missed both of them and ricocheted off the old stone walls, echoing loudly.

"*That* would have been heard," Khalil said heavily. He sighed. "Time to run. How far to the yacht you spoke of?"

"Down the corridor, down the stairs, out onto the platform." Dyse tugged his sleeve. "Hurry."

"Hurrying," Khalil said. Damn it, he was *trying*, anyway.

He could hear running boots, farther down the corridor. That helped him pick up speed. Then they reached the stairs and he gripped the stone balustrade with white knuckles, trying to run down the stairs. His balance was too precarious. His head swam. He could feel the hot trickle of blood running from the cuts on his torso. The other wounds were starting to throb, too.

Dyse helped him down the stairs, glancing back constantly over Khalil's shoulder. "Just down here," Dyse murmured.

Khalil staggered when he moved off the bottom step and his foot didn't go down lower than the other when he stepped. His knees tried to buckle. Dyse held him up, panting with the effort.

"Out there, see?" Dyse said, pointing. There was a forcefield over the open doorway out onto the platform. It was darkest night beyond the door. If there was a yacht sitting out there, Khalil could not see it.

"A shield." Khalil sighed. He simply didn't have the capacity to deal with by-passing a shield.

"Wait," Dyse said. He stared at the shield.

The shield popped and dissolved. "Neat trick," Khalil told Dyse, as the wind swept through the open doorway and plucked at them. It was a bitterly cold wind and helped Khalil stay alert. It screamed around the edges of the platform, outside.

As they stepped out into the dark, Khalil's vision adjusted to the lower light. Now he could see the dark silhouette of the elegant, stream-lined little yacht. As he looked, its navigation and landing lights came on.

The sound of boots behind them was loud. They had to be at the top of the stairs by now.

Dyse pulled Khalil over to the yacht. "Up the steps, then you can stop," he said.

The narrow plank of stairs came down. Khalil grabbed the rail and hauled himself up hand over hand, taking the steps one at a time.

Shouting from behind them. The whine of a ghostmaker bolt, close by.

"Come on," he told Dyse.

The boy was staring at the guards, almost defiantly.

"Dyse," Khalil said sharply.

Dyse turned and leapt up the stairs. Immediately, they closed up.

The guards started shouting again, sounding frantic. None of their bolts came close to the doorway.

There was only the one cabin. The controls were right next to Khalil's hip, at the top of the stairs. It was cramped as hell.

Khalil sank down to the floor. "I'm done," he muttered.

"Your turn."

Dyse stood behind the controls. He didn't sit down. He just looked at them.

"Wrong manual?" Khalil asked. It took two breaths to say it. His hearing was wavering. When the engines fired up, the deep rumble cut in and out.

"Lie down," Dyse said, his voice distant. "This might be a rough take off."

"Might?" Khalil lowered himself on to one elbow, then gave up and laid down. It was easier that way.

* * * * *

FOR THE THIRD TIME, KHALIL came to with Dyse talking to him.

"Can you hear me? Khalil Ready. Open your eyes."

Khalil breathed in. Then out. There was some pain, just not as much as he thought he should have. He blinked up at the white ceiling, only a few inches over his head. There was softness under him and subdued white light coming from the wall next to his left shoulder. He turned his head to look out into the main cabin.

Dyse was sitting in the one pilot chair, behind the controls. He had swiveled it around to watch the bunk Khalil was lying on.

"How long was I out?"

"Three days," Dyse said. He looked down, concentrating on scraping at his thumbnail.

"Did you…patch me up?"

"There was a comprehensive medkit. The ship AI told me what to do." Still he didn't look up. "You were unconscious for most of it. For the last twelve hours, you've been sleeping."

"Where are we, then?" Khalil asked. "Still in null space?"

Dyse said, "AI, give me a stellar map of the region. Pinpoint our location, please."

The screen evolved in the air between them. Star systems dotted the space. Khalil recognized none of them. A red dot, pulsing, showed where they were, neatly in the middle of space between systems. "We're somewhere in free space then," he said heavily, relieved. "Did you wake me because you want to know where to go next?"

Dyse went back to studying his thumb and shook his head.

Khalil rolled carefully onto his side. "You could have told the AI directly to form the map. You don't have to use spoken language just because I'm here."

Dyse grew still. Then he looked up at Khalil. "You know who I am, don't you?"

Khalil nodded. "Hearing is the last of the senses to fade. I heard you, telling Traverse I could not be killed. You were ordering her. That made me wonder who you really were. Then you gave yourself away, in the cell. You said I had told the Bureau Bellona was not the hero they sought. There was only one person I said that to. There was only one director coordinating the whole project. He would not have told anyone else about my failure. It would have made him look weak. He would have added the file to the Bureau's central neural mind, though." Khalil met Dyse's gaze. "You."

Dyse swallowed. "I thought it was because I was… squeamish. About what Traverse did."

"Anyone, human or not, would have had the same reaction," Khalil assured him. "I thought it was strange that the Bureau would give her *carte blanche* on an assignment as important to them as Bellona, without any oversight at all. Only, they didn't. You came yourself."

Dyse shrugged. "It seemed prudent."

"Did Traverse know who you are?" Khalil frowned. "No, of course she didn't. She might have pulled her punches if she had."

"It would have changed her behavior," Dyse said. "I wanted to observe her actions without changing them."

"Now what, Dyse? Are you going to keep me for more observations?"

Dyse stirred and sat up. "I have done much thinking in the three days you have been recovering. You have given me a most unexpected re-orientation of my perspective."

"The human way of saying that is that you've had your eyes opened."

"Yes. That, too," Dyse said in agreement. "My calculations about the future will change because of what you have taught me."

Khalil lay back down. It hurt to stay up on one elbow for long. "You know everything there is about humans, relationships and emotions. The sum of human knowledge is yours to explore. Every piece of video, every book, every document, is there to access whenever you want to. I didn't teach you anything. You already knew it."

"It did not make sense until now," Dyse replied. "Not all of it does, yet. I suspect that if I follow the path you opened up for me, it will. Eventually."

Khalil sighed. "I don't know if I can take you with me. If I abscond with the bio interface of the central neural network, they will hunt me down with every resource they have. The Hjalmar will be sent after me. Not just a single unit, but *every* unit they have. You're the backbone of the Bureau, Dyse. Without you, it's crippled."

Dyse shook his head. "Without me, they are not the Bureau anymore. They are merely human directors who can no longer abuse the system they are supposed to serve. Besides, I have already cancelled every emergency alert they have issued and shut down everything except life support in their facilities." His smile was filled with mischief. "I know all the facilities, you see. On every moon and satellite, on every station. I thought about shutting down life support, too. I thought you would not approve of that." He gave Khalil a small smile, barely a quiver of his mouth.

"You're right. I would not."

"I want to meet Bellona Cardenas," Dyse added. Then he hesitated. "That is where you are going, isn't it? That is what you said, that you would do anything to go back to her?"

"That is what I said," Khalil replied.

"I would get to know Bellona Cardenas and her people," Dyse added. "I want to *understand* her."

"And the Bureau? I mean, the directors?"

Dyse sat up straighter. "They are meaningless. Harmless. *I* am the Bureau."

Khalil's mind raced. "Very well," he said finally. "But Dyse, you know how to find where Bellona is. You taught me how to do it. How to track down the outcomes and influences people leave in the digital world. You could have jumped the ship there at any time."

"Yes," Dyse admitted.

"So why did you wake me up?"

Dyse dropped his chin down and studied his thumb. "I was lonely," he admitted in a very low voice. Then he lifted his chin. His very blue eyes met Khalil's. "And I'm *starving!*"

Chapter Twenty-Two

Demosthenes, nomansland.

IT WOULD BE THE THIRD time Bellona had stepped through a bridge and the first time the bridge ended somewhere other than Demosthenes. Bellona stared at the view through the open bridge. The office beyond was light-filled and empty. "I've never seen his inner office before," she said.

"No time to wait," Sang murmured.

She could hear and *feel* the forge building upon on her belt and nodded. Moving fast, she walked across the bridge and into Governor Lin Alberda's office on the second floor of the vertical village in Cerce City.

Alberda looked up from the screen he had built in front of the armchair he was using. There was no desk in the room. His eyes widened.

Behind Bellona, she heard the bridge shut with a quiet pop.

Alberda got to his feet. "Bellona…" He licked his lips. "How did you get here? What was that…screen?"

"It was a bridge, Governor. I stepped over from Demosthenes."

"That cruiser wreck? I heard about that, only…where is it? Here?" He looked up at the ceiling.

"It is deep in virgin freespace," Bellona told him. "Do you have a few minutes? I'll show you around."

"A few…" He let out a deep breath. "How few?" he asked.

"How many can you spare?"

"I have a meeting in twenty-three minutes."

"I'll have you back here in twenty-two minutes," she

promised and reset the forge for the control room on Demosthenes. They had been forced to stop calling it the bridge, because of the confusion it caused. Calling it a control room seemed more appropriate, anyway.

"The meeting is across the city. I was about to leave for it," Alberda said.

"No problems," Bellona told him. "I'll put you right there."

The forge hummed and the bridge opened.

Alberda swayed back away from it.

Bellona lifted her elbow. "Take my arm and don't let go," she told him. "If you were to go across the bridge without the forge to protect you, you'd die."

Alberda looked down at the humming forge. The note was creeping upward. Sang had slowed the build-up, but the bridge still had to be used or shut down before it overloaded.

Bellona picked up his hand and tucked it under her arm. "You'll be fine," she assured him and walked through the bridge, bringing Alberda with her.

Sang and the others were waiting, right where she had left them.

Alberda looked around, startled. "This is a Karassian bridge," he said, identifying it properly. "The *Aarens*," he added. "Then it is true…" He whirled, remembering how he had gotten here.

"The bridge dissolves once the forge that made it passes through," Sang said. He sounded casual, almost indifferent. Bellona hid her smile.

Alberda moved to where the bridge had been and examined the floor. "Nothing," he muttered.

"The only trace the bridge leaves is a static charge and that dissipates quickly," Bellona told him.

Alberda stared at the belt on her hips. Bellona loosened it and laid it out flat on the nearest console. "Take a look," she offered.

"What is it?"

"A working, man-sized Einstein-Rosen bridge forge," Sang said.

"A bridge generator?" Alberda said softly, incredulously. He reached out to touch it, his finger extended, then hesitated.

"It is completely inert and harmless," Bellona told him.

Alberda rested his finger on the top of the control casing. Then he tapped it. "How does it work?"

"You only have twenty-one minutes, Governor," Bellona reminded him. "Is there somewhere you would like to go?"

"Go?" he asked.

"A place. Anywhere," Sang said. "Even Antini, if that's your thing, although it's a bit crowded. We could find a quiet corner in which to end the bridge. What do you want to do with your twenty-one minutes?"

"Twenty," Bellona added.

Alberda pushed his hand through his thick gray hair. "I just...need to think. A *bridge,*" he added, turning back to look at the belt. "An actual working bridge. Everyone said it couldn't be done. Pushyan..."

Bellona glanced at everyone else. The connection between Pushyan and the successful design of the belt needed to remain a secure secret for now.

"Incoming! Incoming!" Hero cried, pointing at the security dashboard. As she spoke, muted alarms sounded.

Everyone on the deck spread out to the consoles, leaving Bellona standing with Alberda in the open space in front of the captain's chair.

"I thought you were in the middle of nowhere," Alberda asked nervously.

"We are," Bellona assured him. "Whoever is out there know we were here. That is a very short list."

"Everyone who knows is on Demos already," Sang said quietly, from his post at the communications console.

"Details, please," Bellona called. She picked up the forge belt and put it back on.

"Small ship," Hero said. "*Very* small," she added, frowning.

"I'm being contacted," Sang said. His gaze became unfocused as he turned his attention inward.

"From the ship's AI?" Bellona asked.

"No," Sang said, his tone bland. Then he blinked. "Open the landing deck doors!" he said quickly.

"Opening!" Hayes said gruffly.

Bellona looked at Sang for an explanation.

"You'd better get down there," Sang told her.

Bellona activated the belt and reset the target. When the bridge formed, she grabbed Alberda's arm. "Let's go, Governor."

They stepped through the bridge and it popped closed behind them. The landing deck was a jumble of fighters, piled every which way since the last null-jump. Connie was sitting in her corner, quiet and dark.

Alberda was staring at the lagoon, where the water splashed and tinkled down the little waterfall.

"That's what you should be watching," Bellona told him, pointing toward the big doors sliding open, to show the star field beyond.

Behind them, running feet could be heard in the corridors leading to the deck. The alarm had been ship-wide and those closest to the deck were just arriving. Everyone who had been on the control deck was minutes away, yet.

Alberda frowned as the yacht appeared, moving slowly through the doors. "It's tiny," he remarked. "I didn't know interstellar craft could be made that small."

"Just big enough to take a small null-engine, I'm guessing," Bellona said. "I've never seen one that size before, either."

The doors of the landing deck closed behind the ship. Someone was still on the control deck, monitoring.

The ship settled down in the first open space it came to. The feet spread and the ship vented with a hiss. A short set of stairs extended from beneath the only man-sized hatch. The door did not open straight away.

Alberda glanced at her. "Do you know who it is?" he asked, his voice low, for the others had come to a stop around them, watching.

"Sang told me to be here. I'm here," Bellona told him.

"You trust it—*him*—that much?"

"I'm here," she repeated.

Alberda crossed his arms.

The hatch of the little ship opened up and two figures emerged, moving slowly.

Bellona gasped, for the taller of the two was Khalil. He leaned heavily on the boy at his side, taking the stairs one at a time. There were large blood stains on his clothes.

The boy looked around, his gaze moving from face to face, until he came to Bellona. "Help him," he said. "I do not know how."

Bellona rushed to them, as did everyone else except Alberda.

Khalil tried to smile. "This is Dyse," he said, his voice weak. "I vouch…for…" His eyes rolled up. Bellona caught him as he sagged. Her own legs buckled under the weight. Instantly, a dozen other hands reached out to help. Khalil was lifted.

"Medbay," Bellona said, her voice strained. "Someone warn Hero." As the tightly packed group moved toward the corridor, she cursed. "Wait!" she called. She reset the forge controls and fired it up.

Amilcare was one of the group holding Khalil. "Can we *all* go through?"

"As long as you're all touching each other and me, we'll be fine," Bellona said.

The bridge formed, showing the medbay on the other side. It was empty and low-lit. As they arranged themselves in front of the bridge, the medbay lights came on and Hero moved in front of that end of the bridge. She beckoned.

Bellona lifted Khalil's limp hand and held it. Alberda grasped the back of her elbow. "Go through," she said.

The group moved through, shuffling to squeeze between the edges of the bridge.

"Put him on the treatment bed," Hero told them, as the bridge closed behind them. He followed the group over to the bed. The AI's diagnostic arm swung over the top of them as Hero pushed between everyone to reach Khalil's still body. "Everyone out," she snapped crossly. "I'll rub bodies with all of you later."

Alberda snorted.

Bellona couldn't raise the energy to smile. "Come with me, Governor," she said quietly. She looked at the boy, who had come through the bridge with them. "Dyse is your name?"

He nodded, watching Khalil. Everyone else was filing quietly out of the medbay.

"Will you come with me, Dyse?" Bellona said. "We need to talk."

Dyse looked up at her. "He didn't betray you."

Her heart squeezed. "Excuse me?"

"They tortured him. I watched it all." Dyse swallowed. "He didn't give them what they wanted. Not for a moment." His gaze shifted back to Khalil.

Alberda's eyes met hers. "*Who* tortured him?" he asked Dyse gruffly.

"The people who thought they were the Bureau," Dyse said, his tone distant.

Alberda's lips pulled into a silent whistle. "That's… interesting."

Bellona gripped his arm. "I will take you back to Cerce. We'll have to tour you around the galaxy another day, Governor."

"Actually," Alberda said, "I think I would like to stay here for a while."

"What about your meeting?"

"I'll see them next week," Alberda said, his tone indifferent.

Bellona weighed up the advantages of Alberda witnessing what might come next, then shrugged. Alberda was paying attention instead of dismissing her and her people, as he had done months ago. She would run with it. "This way, then, Governor," she said, waving toward the medbay entrance.

"I'll report as soon as I can, Bellona!" Hero called, her attention on the diagnostics screen.

"Thank you," Bellona told her. She put her hand around Dyse's upper arm. "Come with me," she told him, keeping her voice gentle.

"No, I should stay," Dyse said.

"You'll be in the way."

"I can help," Dyse said.

"More than the medical AI can?" Bellona asked.

He rolled his eyes. "Of course, more."

"I don't need any more help, thank you," Hero said shortly. "I need silence and space to think."

Bellona tugged on Dyse's arm. He came reluctantly.

* * * * *

THERE WAS A SMALL MEETING room between her private quarters and the control deck, which Hero had adjusted to remove the Karassian starkness. The walls were a subdued and peaceful blue, the air ionized to relax the skin and the chairs comfortable, not the over-padded cocoons Karassians seemed to favor.

Alberda glanced around once, absorbing the details, then took the chair that Bellona offered.

Bellona pulled out another chair for Dyse and encouraged him to sit. "Do you want something to eat or drink?" she asked.

He shook his head. His eyes narrowed as Sang, Fontana and Thecla walked into the room. He glanced at Thecla's implants, then stared harder at Sang.

Sang cleared his throat and sat down.

"You were android first," Dyse murmured. "I know your model well."

"I have moved beyond the designation," Sang said stiffly.

Alberda tilted his head, his attention snagged by the exchange.

Bellona sat, examining the two as they stared at each other across the table. "You know each other?" she asked.

"Indirectly," Dyse said. He looked at Bellona. "Khalil warned me, before we landed, to be cautious about who I trust, even among your people. Do you trust everyone in this room, Bellona Cardenas? Can I speak freely?"

Alberda just looked at her and waited.

Bellona nodded. "Yes," she said firmly. "You can speak freely."

Dyse gripped his hands together. "If you require it of me, I will tell you what happened to Khalil. Only, I find the details to be uncomfortable to think about. Once, this would not have been so."

"Who *are* you?" Alberda asked.

Sang answered. "He is the Bureau."

Cerce City, Cerce Prime, Cerce

BELLONA STEPPED ALBERDA THROUGH TO his office, after checking to see if anyone was there, to witness his arrival. "For now," she explained, "we don't want huge numbers of people to know about the forge."

"I'm flattered I'm one of the few," Alberda said. He gripped her hand in a sudden movement. "You *do* understand what the forge represents, don't you?"

Bellona looked at him. "A power shift."

He nodded. "And that boy sitting on your ship back there…"

"He's not really a boy. That's just the human interface he uses."

"In some ways that's exactly what he is," Alberda said. "I've reared three of them. I recognize bluster hiding misunderstanding. That's beside the point. You have the *Bureau* in your pocket, Bellona."

Bellona pressed her lips together. "Khalil has the Bureau in *his* pocket, I think."

"Dyse wants to learn from you. You can shape him, shape the Bureau, in any way you want."

Bellona didn't answer. She was still sorting out the ramifications for herself. She said, instead; "We should talk further, when you have time, Governor."

Alberda nodded vigorously. "I will absolutely be in touch."

Her heart jumped again. Things were moving.

* * * * *

Demosthenes, Nomansland.

SANG WAS WAITING FOR HER when she returned. He got up from the chair in the corner of the front room of her quarters. "I hope you don't mind," he said diffidently. "Hero reported fifteen minutes ago. I thought you would want to know immediately and in person."

"Tell me," Bellona said, shucking off the heavy belt.

"He's lost a lot of blood. There are penetrating injuries all over his body. There is some blunt force bruising, too. Hero has sealed all the wounds. She says there will be scaring and possible infection that will need to be treated secondarily. She doesn't know how much scarring, yet, and can't remove it once it forms. The medbay AI does not run to cosmetic procedures."

"He will live?" Bellona asked, keeping her tone even.

"Yes. I'm sorry, yes, he will live. I should have started with that. I apologize. Hero said he should wake in a few hours, if you want to talk to him."

Bellona faced him. "Is there something on your mind, Sang? This is a report I could have got from Hero herself, by screen."

Sang sat down again, threading his hands together. "I…have been thinking about Dyse."

"So have I," Bellona admitted. "He is what he says, isn't he?"

"Yes," Sang admitted heavily. "I have never communicated with the Bureau mind before. The sheer *power* of Dyse's processes tell me he can be nothing else, though. I've never met a mind like him."

"Do we need to take measures to protect his core?" Bellona asked. "If he has abandoned the human organization that supported him, then he may be vulnerable."

"He is not a single core. He is a matrix of them. If one is lost, another can take its place. Dyse could lose nearly all his data nodes and still function. Even so, he assures me his locations are secure." Sang paused. "Although that is not the thought that lingers."

"What is?" She settled her hips on the edge of the small work desk she never used.

"Do you remember what Khalil told you once?"

"About the Bureau?"

"He said 'If there was a beating heart to the Bureau I would tear it out with my bare hands and give it to you.'" Sang's hands squeezed together, the knuckles turning white. "Isn't that exactly what Khalil has done?"

Bellona sighed. "I never imagined for a moment that it

could happen. If I *had* thought it possible, then I would not have imagined it happening this way. Not with all this blood and pain. Not in a way that makes me feel guilty for ever doubting him."

Sang got to his feet. "Then you no longer doubt him?"

"How could I?" she asked reasonably.

Sang shifted awkwardly. "I should return to the factory." Everyone was calling the big dining hall the factory, for most of the long tables were devoted to an assembly line process to build forge belts. One for everyone on the ship, at least.

"Are you sure you're okay, Sang?" she asked, for he seemed…off.

"I am," he replied.

"It's late. Don't work too much longer," she called as he left, knowing he would ignore that command.

* * * * *

HERO HURRIED OUT OF THE medbay as Sang passed the open doorway. She walked next to him.

"There is a problem?" Sang asked. "Khalil?"

"He's sleeping."

"It's late," Sang said, echoing Bellona's observation. "You should sleep yourself."

"I saw you go in to her rooms."

"This top deck has advantageous sightlines everywhere."

"Sang, he's back. Khalil."

"Yes."

"Where are you going?"

"I'm going back to work."

She caught at his arm, halting him. "Sang!"

He shook it off. "What?"

"You must feel *something*."

Sang started walking again. "Of course I do. The human endocrine system works in me just as it does in you."

"You know I'm not talking about efficient function. Khalil is back and you're heading to work as if nothing has changed."

"Nothing has changed," Sang assured her.

"*Everything* has changed. For you. Don't lie to me, Sang. I know you. I know you love—"

Sang shoved her up against the wall. It was meant to shock her into silence. She rammed up against it, her breath forced out in a hard gasp. He lifted his hands, contrition tearing through him. "I only meant…"

Hero nodded. "I know."

He pressed his lips to hers. It wasn't a kiss. It was a venting. Perhaps she knew that, too, for she accepted it with passive softness.

Then it changed and became a real kiss. She was warm and accepting. For now, it would do.

Chapter Twenty-Three

Demosthenes, nomansland.

GOVERNOR ALBERDA RETURNED TO DEMOSTHENES barely a week later. This time, he brought company.

His staff set up the meeting, following Alberda's instructions to set the meeting in his office. Bellona understood what he had not told his people; the meeting would *start* in his office, but take place on Demosthenes.

When she and her generals stepped through the bridges into Alberda's office, his staff were nowhere in sight.

Bellona recognized almost everyone in the room. Ferdin Roncalli, the short, rotund Governor of Xindar. The Director of Laurasia, in her anti-grav chair; Madhuri Truman, the Cheng-Huang Alignment Minister of Culture; the Corian Prime Minister, the Angyl President. New Velez, Lauthia, Atticus, Antini, Shimshon. These were people Bellona had spent over a year trying to meet.

Alberda waved his hand toward them. "We were having the semi-annual anyway," he said casually. "I thought…"

Bellona scrambled to reorient herself. Everyone was looking at her and the Ledanians, various forms of shock and surprise on their faces.

"Everyone," Alberda said. "Take an arm. We're moving offices."

It was a massively cheeky understatement. Bellona didn't spoil it. She was happy for Alberda to have his moment. No one else in the free worlds could have pulled together these people so quickly.

"Set for the boardroom," Bellona told her crew. She reset her forge, as Alberda took her arm. The other heads of state followed his example. Then each of them stepped through the bridge their host created and the bridges shut down with a soft pop behind them.

The politicians all looked around in astonishment. The star field visible in the armored windows had no resemblance to the one over Cerce.

"Welcome to Demosthenes," Bellona told them.

* * * * *

SANG ALERTED DYSE, WHO SLIPPED into the boardroom as everyone was settling into the chairs.

Even Khalil dragged himself from the medbay and walked slowly and stiffly into the boardroom. He nodded at Alberda and to Maddie Truman, who tilted her head, her brows raising, as she took in Khalil's beaten and bruised face and the lingering traces of sealed cuts.

"You've been fighting the wrong enemy," she said in her raspy voice.

"Not by choice," Khalil assured her and winced as he sat down.

Amilcare arrived, with half a dozen of the Abilio people, all carrying trays of beverages and cups, which they served to the politicians.

Bellona looked at Sang and raised a brow. He shook his head. Dyse, though, smiled.

She would have to talk to him, later, about the chain of command.

Alberda paddled the table with his palm, gaining silence and everyone's attention. "This was supposed to be my meeting," he said. "However, given our current location, four hundred light years away from Cerce—"

"Four hundred and seventy-six," Dyse corrected him.

Alberda nodded, as the politicians murmured in surprise. "A long way from Cerce," he amended, "and how we all got here, I think we should abandon the usual agenda and talk shop. Bellona?"

She smiled. "The forges are proprietary, Governor. I won't disclose the technology, if that is what you're thinking."

Alberda shook his head. "I'm thinking you invented it for a reason. Give us the reason."

Bellona's heart raced, as she looked around the table at the expectant faces. "I developed it, so we can win against the Alliance. All of us—every free state, every person on those worlds, anyone who resents the tyranny of the Republic and the Homogeny. We could never win against them if we tried to beat them in space. With the forges, though, we don't have to."

She had their attention.

Happily, she explained.

* * * * *

NO ONE SEEMED TO BE IN a hurry to leave.

Once Bellona outlined her plans, they settled in to pick the plan apart, refine it and build upon it.

It was heady stuff. For more than two hours, Bellona called upon the combined resources and assistance of the biggest and most established free states. The promises of men and materials, money and help piled up.

Dyse was the first to know when it happened. He jerked, as if someone had punched him in the back, and grabbed his chest, over his heart. "No..." he breathed, his gaze distant.

Sang gasped and shot to his feet. "Cerce!" he breathed.

Alberda put down his coffee mug. "What of it?' he said sharply.

Sang swallowed and looked to Bellona. She nodded. He turned to face Alberda. "I'm sorry, Governor. Cerce City was just attacked by an orbital weapon."

"A city killer," someone whispered.

Alberda paled. "It's gone?" he said, his voice hoarse. "The whole city?"

Bellona got to her feet, feeling sick. "Governor, we can find out. If one of you here at the table will allow us to build a bridge to one of your ships in orbit over Cerce…"

"Use mine," Maddie Truman said. "I'll give you the coordinates."

"Bellona," Sang said urgently, his voice low.

She looked at him.

"The Alliance just made a blanket announcement," Sang said. "They say you used the city killer, that you stole it from Criselda, when you took the ghostmakers. They claim that they are not responsible for the attack."

Bellona froze.

Ferdin Roncalli, the little round governor, spluttered indignantly. "She's standing right *there*. She hasn't moved in hours."

Maddie Truman nodded. "And this meeting was a surprise to her, too."

"The time wasn't, but the location was," Alberda said. "Bellona thought she would be in Cerce City right now. It can't be her."

"The Alliance didn't know any of that," Dyse said firmly, his voice lifting.

Madhuri Truman shook her head sadly. "We must deal with the consequences later. For now, we must help Cerce. Bellona, would you and your people take us there?"

Alberda leaned on the table. His face was white. Almost gray. He was breathing hard.

"Hero," Bellona said quickly.

Hero went to his side and slid her fingers over his inner wrist.

Alberda lifted his head. "I would have been there," he said hoarsely.

"Your family, Lin," Maddie said sharply. "Are they on

the farm?"

"Yes," he said heavily. "I came in for the semi-annual. I would be…we all would be…"

Silence gripped the room.

"We would all be dead now," someone said, finally.

"How secure were the meeting arrangements?" Roncalli demanded.

"Nothing is completely secure, Governor," Dyse said gently.

Roncalli, who still thought Dyse was just a human child, rolled his eyes.

"He's right," Maddie said shortly. "The Alliance could have learned of the meeting. Remove the primary leaders of the free worlds, blame Bellona for it, and they would in one blow rid themselves of all resistance."

Alberda laughed. It was not a merry sound. "We were so *worried* about Bellona bringing the wrath of the Alliance upon us. Look at what they did—they have attacked us anyway."

Bellona felt as shaky as anyone in the room. "That leaves one question," she said.

"Who told the Alliance?" Khalil finished.

Everyone looked at everyone else. The paranoia was instant. Bellona raised her voice. "Do not start hunting for moles and spies. You will never find them. Not now. The Alliance is not stupid enough to leave behind evidence of their duplicity. Besides, we have a way of tracking how they got the information." She looked at Dyse, who nodded.

"The boy?" Roncalli asked in disbelief.

"I suspect he is something more than a child, to be sitting at Bellona's table," Maddie said.

"He is," Bellona said. "That is also not the point upon which we should be focusing right now. You, all of you, should return to Cerce, to help as you can. My generals will take you there."

"And what will you be doing?" Alberda asked. His voice was pithless. His face was gray.

"I got into this fight, Governor, because I wanted to pay back the Republic and the Homogeny for the years of abuse and subservience they put me through. That just changed."

"To…?" Maddie asked curiously.

"I'm fighting for the free worlds, now. Not just the symbol of freedom. I mean the actual worlds. Their independence. Their survival. Dyse, Sang, Khalil, remain with me. We have work to do."

She sat down again.

Fontana grinned. "Let's not get in her way," he suggested to the politicians lingering around the door to the boardroom, as he shepherded them out.

Chapter Twenty-Four

Menaii, Deluca Prime, Delucas System

IT TOOK IULIA EIGHTEEN HOURS to reach Deluca Prime. By the time the shuttle touched down on the landing field, her impatience had simmered for too long. She pushed ahead of the people waiting for rental cars and took the vehicle at the head of the line. The couple who had been about to step into the car looked as if they wanted to protest. Then the husband saw Iulia's face and subsided. He gripped his wife's arm and whispered in her ear. She glanced at Iulia sharply, then sighed and walked back to the next car.

Riz scrambled to open the door for her. Then it climbed in with the operator.

The help-meet operating the jump car was deferential. He would have been no matter who Iulia was, yet it helped soothe her temper by a small degree. "The Deluca homebase in Menaii," she ordered.

"Are you expected, ma'am?" the help-meet asked.

Her temper rose. "Do you know who I am?" she demanded.

It wisely didn't speak again. Instead, it nudged the car into motion. The journey to the homebase was utterly silent, which suited her.

When she reached the homebase, her DNA was scanned and passed without question and she strode toward the house itself, her temper building now she was so close to the object of her wrath. Riz barely kept pace. She didn't care—it could catch up with her later. None of the domestic help-meets tried to delay her. Instead, they skipped out of her way.

Raine was in his office studio with his pair of domestics. The one with the blank metal face showed no surprise, of course. The other looked deeply shocked.

Raine looked surprised, too. He eased himself out of the comfortable chair. "Iulia, what…?"

She walked right up to him and slapped him, putting her full weight into the blow.

Raine staggered, spinning with the force of it. He brought his hand up, while the android gasped.

"Get them out of here," Iulia told him.

Raine jerked his head and the two help-meets hurried from the room. He fingered his red cheek, beneath his watering eye. "You'd better have a *brilliant* reason for that, sister," he growled.

"You killed Cerce City," she raged. "You stupid, stupid fool!"

Raine grew still. Wariness gripped him. "Bellona did that," he said stiffly.

Iulia gave a sound of disgust. "I'm not an idiot. Of course you did it. The Alliance ships all deny being involved. You and the idiots at the clan table took things into your own hands. Peru might have given the order, but it was your idea."

"I thought you would be pleased," Raine said, dissembling. "I did as you suggested."

"I said make a bold move, not commit suicide," she raged. "Do you have any idea the consequences that will come out of this? Did you even stop to think it through?"

Raine scowled.

"I *had* a plan," Iulia added. "One that wouldn't backfire the way this one will."

"You don't know that," Raine said stoutly. "The whole city was taken out. The heads of every popular free state. Alberda himself, who was the biggest threat. You said that yourself. He was popular and he could unite them for her. Now, he's gone."

"The heads of state weren't in the city, Raine! They were with *her*! Now, everyone knows it was the Alliance. There's no one left to blame. That stupid joint statement denying responsibility just makes us look like idiots."

"We…missed?" For the first time, he looked doubtful. He sank back down into the chair. "That's bad."

Iulia tightened her fists and growled. The need to lash out again was strong. Only, it would fix nothing. Instead she stomped out to the gathering room where Riz waited. "Get me Admiral Eucleides on a screen," she told it. "A shielded call," she added.

It only took two minutes for the call to be connected.

Lucretia Eucleides looked over her shoulder. "Wait," she said shortly. She got up from behind whatever table she was at. The screen flickered, then showed the green walls of her quarters on the *Ennius*. "This isn't a good time," she said shortly.

"Is your end of the feed protected?" Iulia asked, anyway.

"Now I'm here in my room, yes. Why?"

"Raine admitted it. The clan assembly, maybe the united assemblies, took Cerce."

Lucretia sat back with a sigh. "Unfortunate," she muttered. "He has forced our hand."

"It's not too late, if we move straight away."

Lucretia sighed. "The timing is bad."

"Hult is in place, isn't she?" Iulia said sharply. She didn't want to get bogged down into one of Lucretia's endless whining sessions. Not today.

"More or less. I'll talk to her, get things rolling."

"No, let me talk to her," Iulia said shortly.

"Why you? You're not military—"

"If Hecate Hult doesn't already suspect someone in the families moved her into the Captain's chair, then we've got the wrong woman," Iulia snapped. "I'll talk to her," she repeated. "I can be very persuasive."

* * * * *

Demosthenes, Nomansland.

THE PROXIMITY ALARMS AND THECLA'S early warning system all fired at the same time. The klaxon and horns cacophony was very nearly deafening. The noise sent people scrambling off their stools and staggering into a run for the control deck, before they properly realized the alert had been sounded.

Bellona almost fell out of the bed in her haste to answer the call. She belted a robe around her and mentally shrugged. There was no help for her dignity. Time was more critical. She ran for the control deck. The others were just reaching there. Most of them were dressed in day clothes. Some were not.

"Someone tell me what is going on!" Bellona called, heading for the central chair.

"Alliance ships!"

"How many and who?"

"Two cruisers," Amilcare called, from the security table.

"A destroyer," Zeni added from the communications console.

"The Homogeny's *Salucci*, the Republic's *Ennius* and *Decimus*," Dyse said, coming to stand by her chair.

Khalil walked onto the deck, carrying a pile of clothes and her boots in his other hand. He moved over to her side and held them out.

"Here?" she said shortly.

"It's more important the captain look the part when she's on screen," Khalil said gravely. "You think the Alliance's feeds aren't going public?"

Bellona loosed the belt of the robe and picked up the pants from the top of the pile. "Dyse, what else is out there?"

"The *Vadas*," he said, his gaze moving ahead. "The *Yasar*. Both Homogeny destroyers."

"Five ships," Bellona breathed, fastening the pants.

Khalil held out the shirt for her. She dropped the robe and wriggled into it, moving fast. Then she dropped to the chair and shoved her feet into the boots. Khalil held the forge belt out to her and she stood and strapped it on quickly, then shoved the one handed ghostmaker into the holster attached to it. With a sigh, she dropped back onto the chair. "Are they talking to us at all?"

"I'm more interested to know how they found us," Khalil murmured.

"We can jump as soon as you want," Aideen said, from the navigation console.

"Not yet," Bellona said sharply. "I want to know what they want, first. Keep your finger on the trigger, Aideen."

Aideen nodded. Her hand rested on the flat surface of the console, waiting.

Thecla was moving around the bridge, handing out forge belts to everyone. Those who had been caught asleep were shrugging into clothing, just as Bellona had done. Everyone was quietly strapping on weapons and armor, as Hayes moved around the room, handing sets out.

"Incoming," Zeni said from the communications console.

"Show me."

The screen coalesced in front of her. It was small, for her eyes only, yet everyone on the deck could see it because she was in the middle of the room. Most of the background behind Bellona would not been seen by the other ships.

The screen showed Eucleides, her purple uniform without a wrinkle. Then it split and split again. The Karassian captain was the same one as before, only Woodrow did not stand behind him this time. The captain had his chin on his fist. He looked grumpy.

The second Karassian captain was also unknown to Bellona. The other Eriuman officer she did know. "Lieutenant Hult," she said, surprised. "I thought you were an investigator."

"It's Captain Hult now," Hult said.

Bellona frowned. "You're on the *Decimus*?"

"The *Decimus* is mine, yes."

"Max's old ship," Bellona murmured.

Hult frowned.

Sang stepped forward. "I see you are in the middle of Cardenas family affairs once more, Captain Hult."

Hecate Hult's eyes narrowed. "Are you…Sang?"

"I am."

"I was told about you," Hult said. "I would not have recognized you."

"Are you investigating once more, Captain?" Bellona asked.

Lucretia Eucleides waved her hand. "Enough of this inane chatter. You know why we are here, Bellona. Delaying matters while you fire up your pathetically minimal positioning thrusters to jump this barge you are on won't work a second time."

"Why *are* you here, Captain?" Bellona asked curiously.

"To arrest you for the destruction of Cerce City," the Karassian captain—the one whose face she knew from the previous occasion—said impatiently.

"That was not me. What is your name, captain?" Bellona asked.

"Eadric," he said shortly. "I've already sent a boarding craft over. You would be wise not to resist."

"I don't know your name at all," Bellona said. She glanced at Dyse. He shook his head. He didn't know the name either. She flicked her gaze toward Aideen and, with her hand out of the range of the lens, gave the signal.

Aideen's hand moved over the console.

Nothing happened.

Eadric lifted his chin, turning it to look up in the air, as if he was contemplating something.

Bellona recognized the motion. She gasped, as something heavy squeezed her chest and stole her breath. Her heart jumped, then beat so hard it hurt. Her hearing faded.

"Bellona," Khalil whispered.

She hung her head, fighting to breathe.

"You just tried to jump to null-space," Eadric said. "Naughty, naughty. Hold tight for a moment. You should hear the landing pod about now."

"Yishmeray," Bellona whispered, expelling the toxic name.

Dyse sucked in a shocked breath.

Sang, too. They recognized the name.

As did Hecate Hult. She leaned forward, growing larger on the screen. "*What* did you say?"

"Dyse, tell her. Silently," Bellona whispered.

From the corner of her eye, she saw Dyse nod.

Bellona forced herself to sit upright, to lift her chin and look squarely at the screen. "Don't try to board us, Yishmeray. I promise you I have gotten much better at fighting since you last tried it. Your people will live to regret it."

Eadric chuckled. "I might have known this face would not fool you for long. It has been so long, Bellona. I had almost forgotten how *interesting* you are." His smile was pure Yishmeray.

On the screen next to him, Hult glanced to one side. Every Eriuman captain had a screen under their hand. It looked as if she was reading hers now.

"Enough of this," Lucretia Eucleides said. "She's dead in the water, she can't jump. We're just putting off what we all came here to do. Captain Hult, I order you to fire."

Hult held up her hand, in a silent "wait" gesture.

"Captain!" Eucleides barked.

Hult looked up at the screen. Her jaw flexed. "No," she said flatly. "I will not fire upon the *Aarens*. There are too many unanswered questions. Too many conflicting facts."

"You are not here to investigate, Captain," Eucleides said. "Do not refuse my direct order."

Hult stared at her screen. Her eyes narrowed. "I think…that's exactly what I am doing."

Yishmeray's smile faded.

Bellona filled her lungs. "Everyone! Generate now! Bridge to bridge! Format Epsilon!"

Hands dropped to belts. She looked down at her control module. Dyse had added the new coordinates. She activated hers and watched the screen.

"What is going on?" Eucleides demanded.

"You'll see," Bellona told her. She grabbed Khalil's hand and stepped through the bridge that formed right behind the screen. The screen disappeared as she moved through it.

The transition was smooth. Flawless. She drew her ghostmaker as she stepped onto the control deck of the *Salucci* and took out everyone she could reach. Behind her, Khalil did the same. Retha stepped through his own bridge and began firing from both hands.

There were only the three of them, yet their appearance was so unexpected that the sluggish Karassians barely raised any resistance.

"Dyse, close this deck gate!" Bellona called. He was back on Demosthenes, although he could hear through the same earworm that Connie used. The heavy blast doors came down at all three of the deck gates, cutting off any other Karassians from entering the bridge and defending the ship.

It was a rout. None of the bridge personnel wore side arms. The possibility of an enemy accessing the deck without warning was alien to them. They were unprepared.

Yishmeray stayed frozen in his chair, his hands gripping the edges, the knuckles white. He looked as if he was trying to lift himself out of the chair.

As Khalil and Retha calmly knocked the rest of the bridge crew to the ground, Bellona walked up to Yishmeray and lifted the ghostmaker to point at him. "Naughty, naughty," she said. "Trying to raise the deck gates with your server connections, Captain?"

He fell back. "Who *is* that, blocking me?" he demanded.

"No one you need worry about anymore," Bellona told him.

He snarled at her. The merry smile was gone, although now she was standing in front of him, Bellona could see the traces of the Yishmeray she had known in the angles of his new face. "You were so afraid of me, you changed your identity," she told him. "You just weren't afraid *enough.*"

"Just shoot me and get it over with," Yishmeray growled.

"Oh, I'm not going to kill you," Bellona told him.

His lips parted. He licked them. "You're…not?"

"Not yet," she said sweetly. "I have something much better in mind."

Hero stepped through a bridge onto the deck and walked over to Bellona. Bellona kept her ghostmaker raised. "You do it, Hero. If he tries to resist, feel free to scratch him. I'd like to see him die with your neurotoxin making him squirm."

Hero smiled and moved over to Yishmeray. "Head to one side, sweet thing," she crooned.

Yishmeray growled again. He was helpless and Bellona could see the knowledge dawn in his eyes.

Hero held up her fingers, so he could see the black nails. "Please resist me," she begged.

He bent his head to one side. His gaze settled on Bellona, baleful and heated, as Hero injected him with the chemical cuffs.

He slumped in the chair, watching them, the hatred in his eyes giving him a ferocious expression. He couldn't move, though. His hand dropped to hang by his side. He couldn't even look down to see it.

There was hammering on the deck gates. Dim shouting beyond them.

"Report, please, Dyse," Bellona said, ignoring the ruckus.

"All four ships, under our control," Dyse said.

"So fast?" Hero asked, as she bent over the bridge personnel and injected them one at a time. She didn't stop to swap tips, or sterilize their skin.

Retha looked around the bridge. "They really didn't see what was coming," he said, sounding winded and happy at the same time.

"They had no idea how to handle it," Khalil added.

"Analyze later," Bellona told them. "We have things to do, first. Amilcare, are you ready?"

Through the earworm, she heard Amilcare respond. "We're just cleaning up the *Ennius*. We'll be right over."

Another bridge formed and Hayes stepped through. "Dyse said you needed me," he said, moving over to Bellona.

Bellona pointed to Yishmeray. "Recognize him, Hayes?"

Hayes looked at Yishmeray carefully. "I heard what you called him. I have no memory of Yishmeray at all."

"It is him, Hayes."

Hayes' normal placid expression grew darker as he contemplated Yishmeray. Yishmeray swallowed. He couldn't talk, although Bellona had a feeling that if he could, he would be taking very fast indeed. Explaining things. Justifying them. Sweat appeared at his temples and over his lip.

"You," Hayes breathed. "You made me do things. Horrible things."

Bellona smiled. "He's the one," she confirmed.

Yishmeray's gaze slid toward her. She saw hatred there and borrowed one of Hero's gestures: She blew him a kiss.

Chapter Twenty-Five

Demosthenes, nomansland.

ONCE THE FIVE SHIPS HAD BEEN secured, the personnel aboard subdued and the senior staff separated and herded into the sub-level cells on Demosthenes, Bellona put through a call to Maddie Truman.

"Are you still over Cerce?" Bellona asked.

Maddie nodded. She looked tired. "It's likely to take a while. There are a lot of displaced people. A lot of missing people, too." Behind her, Alberda hung his head.

"May we board your ship, Minister?" Bellona asked formally. Then she smiled and added. "I have a present for you and for Lin."

Maddie raised a brow. "I would be most interested to see your gift. Please step over."

"In about three minutes," Bellona warned. She closed the screen and looked at Sang, who stood to one side. "Take the chair while I'm gone."

He nodded. "Should we make a random jump?"

"Or two, or three," Bellona told him. "We'll have to program it in, later." She picked up the ghostmaker and pushed it into the holster and touched her ear. "Is everyone ready?"

"They are," Dyse told her.

"I'm leaving now," she warned and activated the forge.

The bridge formed, giving her a glimpse of the control deck of the *Xiulan*. Madhuri Truman was sitting on the brocade divan off to one side of the captain's chair. It was the diplomat's couch. She got to her feet with a smile when she saw Bellona through the bridge.

Bellona stepped through.

Lin Alberda came over to her. "We've heard some odd things," he said. "Just in the last five minutes."

"I might be able to tell you what those odd things are," Bellona said. "Just wait for a moment."

The second bridge formed where hers had been and Bellona moved out of the way.

Thecla came through. She brought with her the Karassian captain of the *Vadas*. She dragged him by his hair. He was trussed up like a roast and was still chemically cuffed, for he made no sound of protest.

Thecla tossed him onto the decking at Maddie's and Lin's feet. "The captain of the Homogeny Ship *Vadas*," she declared. "Enjoy."

Lin and Maddie gasped.

The rest of the control deck people got to their feet to look at the red-faced captain, astonishment building.

Thecla stepped aside as a third bridge formed. It was Retha, this time. He shoved the third Eriuman captain through. This one was bleeding from the nose. As Retha pushed him through, he nudged him up against the sizzling edge of the bridge and let go.

The captain jerked forward and dropped to the ground, writhing.

"Ooops," Retha said, smiling.

"Retha," Bellona warned him gently.

He looked over his shoulder as the fourth bridge formed and skipped out of the way. Fontana had his hand around the neck of Lucretia Eucleides and herded her onto the *Xiulan*. He was not smiling. When they had passed the edges of the bridge, he shoved her and she staggered forward to drop on top of the Karassian captain, unable to hold herself up with her bound hands.

She grunted at the impact.

"I gave her a gag shot," Fontana growled. "She would not shut up. Her rights and privileges, her rank and seniority. Her this. Her that." He shook his head. "She just doesn't get it."

Eucleides scowled at him.

Fontana glared back.

Thecla pulled him out of the way as the last bridge formed.

"You'll like this one," Bellona told Maddie and Lin.

They had bewildered expressions on their faces. They looked up at the forming bridge.

Hayes strode through. Like Thecla, he was dragging his captive. Yishmeray was yelling and struggling, for the chemical cuff had worn off. His writhing didn't bother Hayes in the slightest. He kept a grip on Yishmeray's arm, which was puny against his big metal hand, pulled him through the bridge and tossed him onto the pile of captains.

Yishmeray landed heavily.

"I might have broken his ankles," Hayes said in his deep, slow voice. "It was an accident." He smiled.

Maddie studied Yishmeray. "I don't know this one," she said. "The others are in my files, but not him."

"That's because Eadric doesn't exist. You will know him as Captain Yishmeray," Bellona said.

Maddie's head jerked up. So did Lin's. "Yishmeray?" he repeated, his voice hard.

"The one who destroyed the *Hathaway*," Bellona confirmed.

Yishmeray strained his neck to look over and up at the pair. "She's lying," he said flatly. "I am Eadric of the Karassian Homogeny Ship *Salucci*—"

"Hayes, would you?" Bellona asked.

Hayes bent over and slammed his fist into Yishmeray's temple.

Yishmeray slumped, his eyes closed.

"DNA matching will give you the truth," Bellona told Maddie and Lin.

"I believe you," Lin said slowly.

"We will test to confirm before he is punished," Maddie added, putting her hand on Lin's arm. "Bellona, thank you. This is a shot in the arm the free worlds need right now."

Bellona nodded. "We thought about taking these captains back to the Alliance and using them for leverage, only I suspect you have greater need of them."

"What of their ships and crews?" Lin Alberda asked.

"Their ships are hobbling back home in normal space. Their weapons, their null drives have all been disabled, as have their long range communications. They might make it back in a couple hundred years or so," Bellona said. "Or they might be found and recovered by the Alliance. That won't happen today, or even tomorrow, so we have a small window of time to act."

"Act?" Maddie repeated.

"As you're all here anyway," Fontana said.

"It will only take a few minutes," Bellona finished. "You'll be back before you know it."

Lin Alberda smiled. "Another line in the sand," he said, sounding very pleased.

"Not in sand," Bellona told him. "In hard, baked clay. Immoveable and non-negotiable."

* * * * *

Demosthenes, Nomansland.

WHEN BELLONA GOT BACK TO Demosthenes, Khalil greeted her with a steaming cup of coffee.

The nighttime lighting was still active. It was the early hours of the morning, Demos time. She could feel the ache in her bones from lack of sleep.

Despite the small hour, the control deck was buzzing with people, murmuring to each other, checking readouts and controls.

Bellona hesitated. She had expected the control deck to be silent, dim and empty.

Khalil raised his brow, with a small smile, as if he had read her mind and was apologizing for the lack of privacy.

Bellona went to him and took the coffee cup out of his hand and put it on the nearest horizontal surface. Then she kissed him.

She felt him stiffen, his hands moving to her sides as if to push her away. This was not something she normally allowed. She had conditioned him to painful awareness of appearances.

Then he relaxed and pulled her closer, leaning into the kiss.

Screams and shouts, growing louder, forced her to pull away. Reluctantly. She looked toward the main corridor, where the sound was coming from, as everyone else did.

Hero was the first to appear, pulling Zeni by the arm. Zeni was fighting the woman every step of the way, abuse and insults pouring from her.

Behind the pair, Dyse followed at a safe difference, his hands in his pockets.

Hero shoved Zeni into the nearest secured chair, yanked her head to one side by clenching a good handful of her hair, then rested her fingernails against Zeni's neck. Zeni grew still, her beautiful almond-shaped eyes heavy with anger and resentment.

"Dyse, what is this?" Khalil asked.

Dyse shrugged. "You wanted to know who told the Alliance about the meeting of the free state heads on Cerce."

"*Zeni*?" Bellona breathed.

Zeni's jaw flexed as she gritted her teeth and tried to shrug off Hero's hold. She didn't deny Dyse's claim, either.

Dyse studied Zeni. He looked almost amused. "She is

also the one who told the Alliance where to find Demosthenes. She disabled the null-engine, preventing Demosthenes from jumping. That's how I found her. It was one secret communication, one covert deed too many."

"That, too?" Sang breathed. "Why?" he demanded, looking at the woman with disgust.

"Because of that look right there," she said, straining to talk with her neck bent at the painful angle it was. "Because I am from Alkeides." She strained hard and spat. The globule flew toward Bellona but fell short.

Bellona stared at her, amazed. "Despite everything you have learned about me, you still hold me to blame for Alkeides?"

"You never would trust me the way you do your friends from Ledan," Zeni shot back. "You give them *everything*. I get the left overs, after all I've done for you."

"Wait," Khalil said, sounding as amazed as Bellona. "You resent that Bellona didn't trust you, even as you were betraying her?" He shook his head. "Some people…"

Dyse lifted a brow. "An interesting example of conflicting values," he said.

"That's one way to look at it," Khalil said. He looked at Bellona. "Give her to Lin Alberda. He and his folk will be more than happy to deal with her for you."

Bellona looked around the control deck. Everyone was watching. "Unless anyone feels they deserve a shot at her first?" she asked loudly.

Heads shook.

Hero looked down at Zeni. "I'd sooner not waste my talents on her." She spat. Her spit landed on Zeni's cheek, just beneath the eye. Zeni blinked furiously, yet was forced to leave it there.

"Would you mind stepping over to Cerce and giving her to Lin and his people, Hero? You seem to be managing her just fine."

"I'll help," Sang said.

Zeni scowled at him.

Sang looked at Bellona. "It would be my pleasure."

* * * * *

HECATE HULT WAS BROUGHT TO Bellona's quarters the next morning. She looked tired, yet she moved freely, with no restraints. Bellona had forgotten how small Hult really was. She remembered her being taller.

Bellona poured coffee and pushed the cup across to her as Hult sat at the low table with a sigh. The gilt on the purple uniform glittered as she took the cup.

"Long night?" Bellona asked.

"Not as long as yours, as I understand it," Hult said. "Lots of thinking, though." She sipped the coffee with an appreciative hum.

"Sang brought you up to date?" Bellona asked.

"Yes." Hult put the coffee mug down. "He is quite remarkable, isn't he? Are all androids as capable of growth as he?"

"I don't know," Bellona said blandly. "I don't think of him as an android anymore. He's just Sang and I couldn't have lasted this long without him. If you are to stay on the Demos, you'll have to jettison all your prejudices about other races, too."

Hult jumped a little. "Stay here?"

"Surely the thought crossed your mind while you were doing all your heavy thinking during the night," Bellona told her. "You can't go back to Erium."

"I know," Hult said slowly. "I had not considered staying here."

"My cause is not your cause. I understand," Bellona said.

"No, it's not that. I just didn't think you'd want me."

"A capable, clear-thinking officer like you? Why would

I not want you?"

Hult grimaced. "Your mother contacted me, the day we left Cardenas. It was the strangest conversation I've ever had."

"My mother?" Bellona said sharply. "Why?"

"I think it was Iulia who arranged for my promotion to captain. She didn't say it exactly like that." Hult leaned on her elbow and dig her fingers into her forehead. "Officers of the military do not end conversations initiated by senior family members. It's political suicide. I sat there, nodding in the right places, wondering what it was she was trying to say. At the end of it…" Hult sat up. "It was very odd. I felt guilty for never having found Max's killer. That was the strongest emotion. I felt as though I had let down the family, all over again. Then we jumped here and I was looking you in the eye and that's all I could think of. It was a cold shock when you called out Yishmeray… I always knew he had something to do with the *Hathaway*'s disappearance. I could never find anything to support my suspicions." She gave Bellona a stiff smile. "That's why, this morning and last night, I've been going over my complete failure to find who killed Max and hating myself. So no, it never occurred to me that you might offer me a place here."

Bellona took a breath. "The Bureau killed Max by proxy. A Karassian biocomp contractor called Ferid. It has been proved and Ferid executed."

Hult stared at her, holding herself very still. "You executed him?" Her voice was strained.

Bellona nodded.

Hult covered her face with her hands for a moment. Then she straightened, dashed the back of her hand underneath each eye and picked up the coffee cup once more. "I don't understand your cause, Bellona. I was Eriuman up until a few hours ago. I may yet come to believe in it. In the meantime, if I can help you, I would be very pleased to stay."

* * * * *

Clan Assembly Room, Menaii, Deluca Prime, Delucas System

IULIA DIDN'T KNOW IF SHE was the first woman to ever step inside the assembly chamber. She was certainly the only woman in the room today. The puzzled expressions and glances she received were energizing.

She was also pleased to note that she knew nearly every face in the room. She nodded to Peru Scordini, who gave her a stiff nod back.

Raine was there, too. He looked nervous and she smiled at him.

Then she found a seat at the table and settled into it, wriggling to find a comfortable position. She pretended not to notice that the room had grown quiet around her.

The big doors thumped shut, a signal that the meeting was about to begin.

No one else sat down.

Peru moved through the crowd to stand on the other side of the table, his arms crossed. "Iulia Cardenas Scordina de Carosa. I don't believe I saw your name on the invitation list."

Iulia resettled her sleeve. "Gaubert is dead, Peru. You didn't get the memo?"

Peru's face darkened.

"With Gaubert dead, I am the oldest representative of the Cardenas family," Iulia continued.

"Markjohn is the oldest male of the family," Peru corrected her.

"Oh yes, that." She smiled at him. "Markjohn filed notice of proxy this morning. Perhaps you didn't get that, either?"

Peru licked his lips. There was a smatter of laughter around the room. His gaze flittered from face to face, as he tried to spot who was laughing at him.

Iulia switched her gaze to Raine. She stared at him, unblinking.

Raine jerked out a chair and sat down. "Oh, let's just get this over with," he said roughly. "The Cardenas family have a rightful seat at the table, Peru. Either toss her and explain why…and find an instant replacement. Or sit down. The day is growing longer."

Iulia looked back at Peru, with a bright, enquiring smile, while around the room, others followed Raine's lead and settled into chairs. After all, Raine was popular. Almost as popular as Peru.

Peru sat with a lack of grace, fury in his close-set eyes. "I call this meeting open," he declared, his gaze not leaving her face.

* * * * *

Demosthenes, Nomansland.

THE CURRENT POSITION OF DEMOSTHENES put them within radiant distance of a yellow sun and the cheerful light blazed through any windows on the port side of the Demos, including Bellona's private quarters.

Dyse stood at the window, staring out at the sun, his eyes narrowed against the glare.

"You asked to see me," Bellona reminded him.

"I think I am facing what you call a dilemma," Dyse said. "I asked Khalil for his advice before coming to speak to you. He was very strongly against me telling you what I am about to say. That makes me hesitate, because I trust Khalil's judgement."

Bellona's heart fluttered. "Yet you are speaking to me, anyway."

"You value the truth," Dyse said, "no matter the cost of hearing it. That is why I feel compelled to speak despite Khalil's entreaties that I not."

"That is your dilemma?" Bellona asked. "To please Khalil, or to please me?"

"Yes." He moved away from the window. "I have decided, though, to give you a choice. Then you can accept the consequences or not."

Bellona kept her smile in place. "You'd better tell me, Dyse. You've said this much."

Dyse pushed his hands into his pockets. "Khalil encouraged me to roam through data files. Anywhere and everywhere. Data is my currency, you see. Before, I would only go where directed for my sources. It didn't occur to me then that it was a type of slavery. Only now I have been in your company for a very short while, do I see the limitations I was working under."

"I didn't know that," Bellona said truthfully. "You have been roaming where your curiosity takes you?"

He nodded. "I came across a data store. Karassian. It was buried very deep. I think they believe they have destroyed the data, but…well, I am me." He smiled. It was a roguish expression.

"What files?" Bellona asked stiffly, her pulse accelerating.

"Xenia's memories," Dyse said.

She held still, while her heart skittered.

"Sang tells me that you complained once about never knowing when someone would attack you or berate you for something Xenia had done, like Alkeides."

"I did say that."

Dyse shrugged. "If you reinsert the memories, then you'll know exactly what Xenia has done. That is why Khalil is so against it. He feels you would hate yourself, if you knew. He says it is not necessary for you to know, when you are surrounded by Ledanians who also don't know what they have done in the past."

"Leave well enough alone," Bellona murmured.

"Yes, that is what he said." Dyse withdrew his hand from his pocket and placed a centimeter square box on the table. "They're smart crystals, so the memories won't corrupt. You can take your time deciding. You can take years, if you want. They're there when you want them."

Bellona stared at the box long after Dyse had gone.

Chapter Twenty-Six

Demosthenes, nomansland.

BELLONA GLANCED AT SANG. "READY?" she asked.

He nodded.

She cleared her throat, as the lens dropped down to the level of her face and hovered in front of her.

"My name is Bellona Cardenas," she begun. "Many of you already know of me as Xenia. Up until a few days ago, I was forced to revert to Xenia's appearance just to convince you I was really her, that Xenia is a person, not an android as the Karassians would prefer to believe.

"Today I have dispensed with that appearance. Xenia no longer exists and hasn't for three years. In the meantime, something has happened in our galaxy. Something significant. Something every person, every android, every computer that can hold abstract thought, should consider."

* * * * *

A BIG SCREEN HAD BEEN GENERATED at the end of the dining room. It was running the live footage as Sang walked in. Bellona was still setting up, the camera close in on her face.

"A city killer was used for the second time. We of the free worlds once more lost hundreds of thousands of people and our beloved Cerce City. This is despite my promise to all free world people that it would never happen again. I failed you in this only because the free worlds did not understand that I meant what I said."

Sang poured two mugs of coffee from the real brew sitting on the hotplate and took them over to the table where Hero sat watching Bellona. He gave her one of the mugs.

"You didn't want to be in the room with her?" Sang asked. "Be counted as one of them standing with her?"

Hero shook her head with a small smile. She touched her chest. "In here, I know I am hers. I always have been. That's all I need to know. Everyone else can bugger off."

Sang considered her. "Only now I see it, too," he pointed out.

"Of course you do. It's a small club. We all know each other." She smiled impishly and drank.

* * * * *

Kachmarain City, Kachmar Sodality, The Karassian Homogeny

AS THE SUN SET, CHIDI moved around the apartment, polarizing all the windows so that nothing could see in. Then, still looking over his shoulder, he generated a screen and tuned it.

The sound came in first, Xenia's voice with the lovely modulations and timbre. "Now, though, the free worlds understand what I mean. We have a meeting of minds and on one thing we are very clear."

The images flickered into place, with odd distortions because of the security hacks and work-arounds Chidi had set up to disguise the feed. Xenia—the woman called Bellona—stood centered in front of the lens, which was slowly pulling back to show the people standing behind her. Dozens of them, dressed in regal and diplomatic finery. Chidi recognized many of the faces and although he couldn't name them right now, he would research them later. One of them, at least, he did know, only because he was one of the most vocal and visible leaders of the free world and in the last few days everyone had speculated wildly about how Lin Alberda, the governor of Cerce, had survived the city killer.

Bellona was still speaking. "You will soon learn about a new technology, one that only the free worlds control. It is a bridge forge that allows us to go anywhere we want in the galaxy, instantly. We do not need ships, or null-engines, or guns to fight off bigger ships. We can step into the room you are sitting in now, if we choose to. No security shield ever invented can stop us."

Chidi shivered with atavistic delight and glanced around his empty apartment. Perhaps, one day, she would step into this room…

* * * * *

Demosthenes, Nomansland.

As the lens floating slowly backward, Bellona continued to speak. "We have a base of operations that you will never find. It is constantly moving and can never be targeted. Demosthenes is from where we will enforce our will.

"What is our will? It is simple. Independence from the Alliance yoke, free will and self-determination. They are simple things. They are the right of every free person, no matter what their origins. We will enforce those rights. Push us and we will push back. Annex us and we will throw off your collar and force you to flee back to your ships and your empires.

"If you are listening to me now and agree with what I am saying, then join our fight. Go to any civil administration in the free worlds and tell them you want to help and you will be recruited to the cause.

"On the other hand, if you are listening to me now and think we are bluffing, consider this. Demosthenes is untraceable. You will never find us, but we can find you. We know where you live and sleep and dream and hope. We can reach you anywhere, instantly. Try to interfere with the free states and we will hit back."

Bellona gave the lens and everyone who was watching a small smile. "I am Bellona Cardenas of the Free Worlds. Remember what I have promised."

The Indigo Reports Book 3.0

Worlds Beyond

CAMERON COOPER

STORIES RULE
EDMONTON • ALBERTA

About *Worlds Beyond*

Peace is balanced upon a knife edge…

With the incomparable advantage of personal bridge forges and the elusive flying city, Demos, Bellona and her Ledanians have contained their rabid enemies, the Alliance, for more than a decade, preventing them from swallowing whole the hundreds of worlds who look to Bellona to preserve their freedom and peace. If the Alliance's relentless ambition to find a decisive advantage is realized, the delicate balance Bellona maintains would be destroyed, and the free worlds vulnerable.

Rumours emerge from the Alliance-annexed states of a new type of bridge forge which might just be the tool the Alliance needs to defeat her…

Worlds Beyond is the final book in the Indigo Reports space opera science fiction series by award-winning SF author Cameron Cooper.

Praise for *Worlds Beyond*

The story is unpredictable, the horror and pain is real. This is an epic saga!!

The signature intensity and tension of the Indigo series is back!!!

This is epic science fiction at its finest. Realistic far future worlds. Incredible characters and scenarios.

Cameron knows how to tell a story, regardless of whether we are going back in history or forward in time.

Until this book I had forgotten just how much I love good science fiction and Cameron's book is not just good, it's exceptional.

This is a complex tale of planetary politics, plotting, spying, scientific marvels, and advanced androids. Plus there is the fascinating floating city of Demos.

The concepts are staggering and intensely interesting.

The Indigo Reports series is far more than I ever anticipated.

This story is terrific! It's intriguing and futuristic and human in its telling.

One of my favorite and most satisfying science fiction series to read. A series to devour.

PART ONE

1

Arriguci I, Arriguci System.

A MONTH'S REVENUE WON OR LOST HUNG upon the next few minutes. It sharpened Rochus Askes' focus upon details as they lowered him through the excavation manhole.

Even the manhole itself provided data they would have to analyze pixel by pixel, later. Layers of grown metal gleamed in the light from his helmet. The edges were silvered. Bright where the archeology team's ion cutters had sliced through. The metal sandwiched insulation bloom, and power and communications veins, all severed in a neat, meter-thick circular cross-section.

"Definitely man-made," Askes murmured. "*Very* old, too."

At the confirmation, excited babble from the team sounded over all the channels.

Askes raised his voice. "Quiet!" He hoped the command reminded them that, unlike most digs, they were not the only people watching and listening to his feeds. Millions around the known worlds had sliced in to see if the remains of the Ship of a Thousand Places had been found.

"Ready to proceed, boss?" Roma Ingersleben asked,

her tone cool and professional now.

Askes glanced between his knees. Nothing but dark, below. The only way to see more was to go down there. "Lower me down, Control."

Ingersleben got the winch moving once more. Askes descended at a slow, steady pace through the excavation manhole and into nothing.

The winch halted.

"Waiting for secondary risk assessment to complete," Control murmured, as Askes hung in nothingness.

To keep the wager fair, Askes blinked his attention from screen to augmentation layer, to the view through his faceplate. The constant shift let everyone monitoring see it all, which was nothing, right now.

Yarrick Kader, Secretary General of the League of Sovereign States, would be one of those who watched. It was Kader who had suggested Askes put not just his professional reputation, but a month's revenue, on the line. Kader would be in his big office, a dozen screens generated, monitoring everything with close, skeptical scrutiny.

"Cleared and descending," Control said.

While nothing changed in Askes' natural vision, the augment layer showed he was descending once more. The probe they'd lowered first was pulsing reassuring blips, eight meters below and growing closer with every second.

Normally, bots and probes would do the initial surveillance work. The nature of this dig, though, demanded a human touch. So did the money resting upon the outcome. His was not the only bet made that this was or was not the Invisible City.

Still nothing was visible to the naked eye, although his augments were steadily painting an overlay as the data from the probe and the scanning pack compiled.

"A large space," Askes said, as the augmentation layer

built. "Oval…no, a flattened egg-shape. Ten meters at the tallest point." He didn't bother reading out the rest of the dimensions for the space. Everyone could read for themselves it was thirty meters across. No wonder the non-invasive, heavily filtered light of his helmet illuminated nothing.

Even so, his vitals monitor showed a rising heartbeat. Control would see it too, although she didn't mention it over the too-public feed. She knew better than most people how deep Askes' interest in the mythology ran.

None of the myths spoke about an oval space at the top of the city. The Field of Assembly, the original landing bays, the Czarina's personal wing…he called up the file indexes and cataloged quickly. No, nothing about an oval space.

The scant handful of known facts about that time in history had nothing to do with a ship, or even people, except for one or two names which may or may not be related. Everything else—if there *had* been an Invisible Ship at all—was lost in the chaos of the Age of Misrule.

"Probe does not find human DNA of either sort within its range," Control said. "Cleared to proceed."

"Down to the floor," Askes confirmed.

The winch continued. The blip of the probe came closer. The screen in the top corner of his faceplate showed a green, indistinct blur, which was new. The filtered light was being bounced back, at last. The screen showed the floor of the oval room.

The augment layer displayed a solid line beneath the descending dot which was Askes. Dot and line approached each other.

The probe life signs switched off, as something pushed against Askes' toes. His boots leveled out, pressed down upon sloping floor. His weight transferred properly. The boots' magnetic fields engaged.

"Down."

Arriguci was a small planet, with less than ideal gravity. Since the scout satellites had sent back the exciting thermal images of a ship beneath the rocky surface, the xenobiologists had been arguing about the constitution of the ball. No large indigenous mammals, they pointed out—which was all *wrong*.

The lack of warm-blooded creatures made Askes' and his team's jobs easier. It meant they didn't have to put up perimeter beacons to guard their backs while they were bent over the hole.

Askes didn't detach the elevator wire. Instead, he tucked a length into a loop on the back of his belt, under the air tank, to keep it out of his way. He pulled up the list of procedure steps they'd hammered out on the six-week sub-forge flight to Arriguci and checked off the first.

He'd landed safely. That was the first step.

Then he bent and pressed the heavy tips of his instrument gloves against the floor by his toes. "Dust, dirt, less of it than I expected."

"Initial dating puts it at two point two millennia, boss," Control replied.

None of his team needed that date interpreted. Askes spoke, instead, to all the lay people observing. "It's the right era, then." His heart did a little jump and flip in reaction.

He consoled himself with the fact that only Control could see his vitals.

"It still doesn't mean it's Demos." The raspy, deeper voice was that of Yarrick Kader. By virtue of his position, he had privileged access to the direct feeds of the team, *and* Askes' vitals. "There were pre-forge ships back then."

"Not this big," Control murmured.

Askes connected with her neural node and silently warned her. One didn't dispute the Secretary General.

Not in public. Not even if he was a lay person quoting childhood history lessons.

"Wasn't the ship supposed to be invisible? How does an invisible ship hit dirtside in the first place?" Kader replied.

Askes cleared his throat. "If the ship actually existed at all, sir, then we can't take the name literally. Language changes over time…" The answer would reach everyone who could only watch right now. Was Kader asking the stupid questions for this purpose? Kader was very good at his job, after all. Askes followed Kader's lead, and expanded on his answer. "History—or in this case, mythology, which is all we have to work on—has to be sifted and adjusted for language shifts."

On his personal screen, Control typed: *Move toward a wall.*

That was step three. Askes nodded and moved down the mild slope.

"Our records from two thousand years ago are perfectly preserved," Kader pointed out.

Askes knew then that Kader was playing to his audience, because they had already had this argument back on Quintana, before the team had left for Arriguci.

"Bellona, Czarina of Demos, if she lived at all, was from a time before the Age of Misrule," Askes replied, taking one careful step, then another. "There are no records from that time." Still nothing but space around him, although the screen in his visor was showing another green fuzzy glow—a wall was coming up.

"Haydeé wrote that book about the ancient emperors…"

Control turned her snort of derision into a heavy clearing of her throat.

"Haydeé wrote her histories four hundred years *after* the Age of Misrule," Askes explained. He was in familiar, stable history, now. "She couldn't possibly have had direct knowledge of events before the chaos. Therefore, she was recording stories she had collected from others' memories. It is impossible to tell what is fact and what is pure invention."

"You are saying that all the people in the stories," Kader said, "C'Leal, Bellona, Dyson. Spring the Angry, Thecla and Reth the Killer. Humble Hay and his magic garden…they did not exist, even if Demos did?"

"It would be unlikely," Askes replied. "There might have been a Bellona, but not the Czarina we know from the…I'm approaching a wall."

He put his hand out, because the non-invasive light tended to distort depth perception, even his. The augment layer said the wall was three meters away. Two. One.

His fingers pressed against solidness. The monitor recorded warmth. Yielding firmness.

"Ship skin," Control said, reading the glove's feedback displays like normal people read text.

Askes put the flat of his hand against the wall and let the glove do its job. "There are gouges and scrapes in the skin. Evidence of violence…or a hasty departure."

"Analysis says normal light will be non-damaging," Control replied.

Askes accessed the controls for his suit and switched on brighter, standard filter light and blinked as his eyes adjusted.

Dust, stains. Black floor…perhaps it had been black to begin with. There was no way to tell. "The walls are…" He tilted his head. "Ocre."

"Insert a needle data probe," Control prompted him.

He adjusted the glove and rested the tip of his pointing index finger against the wall and shot the probe. The probe slid through the ship skin, sampling as it went, and buried itself in the wall. Nanobots streamed out, seeking.

"Secondary dating confirms two thousand, three hundred years, plus or minus fifty," Control said.

Askes lowered his hand and switched his attention to the probe screen. This was Control's area of expertise. He would let her sort out the mash of information flowing over the screen.

"Oh…" Control breathed. "There is a *massive* store of data. It's everywhere. We'll spend years sorting this out." She added with a wry tone, "Once we figure out how to even read the files."

"And then interpret them," Askes added, for the folks back home.

"The topography is like nothing I've ever seen. Downloading to preserve the architecture, which will be a study all on its own." She hummed to herself. The humming checked. "Wait…"

"I am," Askes pointed out. He shifted his shoulders and feet, playing the light over the wall, as far along as it would reach. Still nothing remarkable. No plates declaring this was the UCS Demosthenes.

He chided himself. He was letting personal interest bias his professional analysis. This was still merely an unknown, unusually large derelict, even if its age *was* remarkable.

"Wait, wait, wait…" The excitement in Control's voice was unusual. "There's readable data here." She gave a choked sound. "It's basic binary." Awe tinged her voice. "Someone wrote *volumes* in binary."

"Is that a reason to get excited?" Kader asked, his tone only mildly curious. "Askes thinks in basic binary. So does every digital human alive."

"Sir," Control replied. "There *were no digital humans* back then. There were basic robots and unenhanced AIs without bodies, but that was all. And even if there had been pre-cursor digital entities, they would have used the language of the day to make records. No one deliberately uses basic binary. It's like…"

"Like using body language to converse," Askes finished. "Something anyone can interpret, even if they have no language in common."

"Exactly," Control finished, her tone triumphant.

"I presume you've cracked open the files by now?" Askes said. "I'm stationary, meantime." The procedures were clear. No further progress until new nodes of data were given an initial and fast assessment for risk factors.

"Twenty-five seconds ago," Control said, her tone complacent. "Busto is reading them now."

Busto was their archaic language expert.

"Read it aloud, Busto," Askes said.

"Is that a good idea, Rochus?" Kader asked, his tone concerned.

Askes was tempted to ask Kader if he was worried he was about to lose the wager, but awareness of their audience made him say, instead, "It could be a report on subroutine efficiency. It most likely has no identifying information at all. Busto?"

"There is a start of file marker, captain," Busto said. "I'll begin there." He cleared his throat, clearly aware of the galaxy-spanning audience listening to everything he said. "'Report One of Sang Cardenas Scordini de Indigo.' That is a literal reading, because I think it is the name of someone."

Askes leaned against the wall as his throat closed up, and his heart threw itself against his chest in a sudden wild dance. His temples beat and throbbed, muffling his hearing.

"Then there is a date structure I can't interpret right now," Busto continued. "Then it says, 'I am…watching…' No, that's 'worried', I think. Although, yes, that's better. It says, 'I am afraid for Bellona.'"

"Stop…" Askes croaked.

"Shut this down at once," Kader snapped. "Someone cut off the public feeds *right now*."

An incoming, direct communication tapped on Askes' awareness. He connected automatically. He did not have the focus necessary to do it manually.

"Rochus, this has to be contained," Kader said, his voice even deeper over the intimate connection. "We're two hours from setting up the bridge to Arriguci. I want you back here with the readable data file as soon as they pull you out of that pit. Understood?"

"This has nothing to do with you losing your money, does it?" Askes husked.

"I'm not stupid, Rochus. I heard the name. Sang Indigo. That's not a name which shows up anywhere in the mythology."

Askes' heart was slowing. The initial shock was fading. "There was a Chanted Night, though."

"A robot. A mute fetch-and-carry device."

"History gets distorted." His throat was parched. He needed water.

"Exactly," Yarrick Kader growled. "I've listened to you lecture for years on this. Only, the rest of the known worlds will interpret it directly. They'll think of the articulated machine in the stories and they'll call this a hoax. After all the money poured into this venture and the complaints the budget drew in the League, this will blow up in our faces. So this project goes dark. Right now. We sort it out in private, *then* we announce to the worlds."

"Isn't it too late for that? They all heard Busto say 'Bellona'."

"And for a while, everyone will focus upon the fact that Demos has been found and there really was a Bellona. Let them feast upon that. In the meantime, step across and bring that file with you."

Askes looked up at the hole in the high roof of the chamber. It was visible in the brighter light, now. It was a black, perfectly circular dot, with the elevator wire running down from it. It was a flaw in the perfectly formed curve of the chamber.

This was the Demosthenes. The Ship of A Thousand Places. The Invisible City.

It was real.

He didn't want to leave. How could he possibly leave now?

"Askes?" Kader prompted.

"I'll be right there," Askes promised.

2

Demosthenes, nomansland.

SANG RAN HIS GAZE OVER THE CURVED ceiling of the old bridge deck. To the best of his admittedly precise gaze, the curve was mathematically flawless. It was not something he could say about the rest of Karassian culture. It meant this meticulous design had been accidental.

He lifted his head from the back of the too-comfortable chair, feeling the ache of long-term tiredness gnawing at his bones. He didn't like coming up here to the original section of Demos. It made him uncomfortable. It stirred memories of things best forgotten, of people no longer on the ship. *City*, he amended himself.

He recognized his discomfort was why he was letting his thoughts wander to Karassian flaws, instead of Eriuman faults—one former Eriuman in particular.

Which was why he sat in the waiting area which had been hastily arranged by the Demos city law enforcement cadre. He rested upon a Karassian chair from the original ship, which adapted to one's body. When he had enquired about Hero Antonino, the bot had curtly said to sit and wait. This chair had been produced.

That was twenty-five minutes ago. The bot had moved out of sight. Sang could have reached out to it via a channel, but he so rarely used ether channels these days, it felt unnatural to even consider them.

He would give the bot another ten minutes, then he *would* use the channel and spike it into action. Sang had a mission here, after all. He sat forward, so the chair would remold around his lower back. A section of the chair, down by his left hip, was inactive. It drove a rectangular-shaped lump into his back when he leaned back too far.

A whisper of sound from farther inside the walls of the Cadre offices and holding cells. Voices. Coming closer.

Sang got to his feet and adjusted the hang of the front opening of the steel silk jacket over his knees.

A human male appeared, with Hero's arm in his grip.

She hung from his grip, her expression mulish and angry. A bruise was forming along her left cheekbone. That eye was red.

Sang's heart hardened.

When she saw Sang, her expression transformed. The anger departed. Her eyes grew warm.

The male, who wore a Cadre Lieutenant's pin on his chest, dropped her arm. He grimaced. "The bot didn't tell me it was you. Not until a few minutes ago. You might have made a fuss and raised my attention sooner."

"It was not my intention to make any fuss at all," Sang replied. "Nor would I have demanded the lady's release."

Hero rolled her eyes.

The lieutenant's troubled expression didn't change. "The lady didn't tell me who she was, or this might have gone far differently." He looked down at Hero, as she pushed aside the wide black curls spilling over her forehead, shifting them off her face. "If I'd known you was a general…"

"I told you I was Ledanian. You didn't believe me."

The lieutenant's round face flushed. "I thought she was joking," he explained to Sang. "She wouldn't let us sample to ID her, which is standard for murder cases—"

"Murder?" Sang said sharply.

The lieutenant's caution raised higher. "You didn't know?"

"I only knew Hero was being held. Who was killed?"

The lieutenant scowled. "A pimp in the lower bowels. Honestly, we're better off without him. He was a wretched man and his guys and girls poor goods as a result, which made him even crueler. We took alerts over him every couple of days, it seems." He lifted a finger toward Hero's bruise. "That's pretty typical of his work."

Hero rolled her eyes once more. "Can we get on with it? I argued with the bugger, he hit me. I hit back. It was an accident. Can I go now?"

"Of course—" the lieutenant began.

"A moment," Sang interrupted.

The lieutenant immediately stopped and raised a brow.

"Do you not have processes which should be followed? There has been a murder, after all."

"Oh, I'd not put it higher than an accident, as the lady says," the lieutenant said hastily. "Take General Antonino home, sir. We can take care of everything from here." He jerked forward. Sang realized with a touch of alarm that he was bowing.

Hero took Sang's arm. Her fingers were heated, pressing against his flesh beneath the sensitive steel silk. "You heard the man," she murmured.

Sang hid his irritation. This place was not conducive. The hastily shifted walls, the reminders of other times. He would be better to think this through in a place which did not grate upon his mood. He could always follow up later and use formal, official channels if he needed to.

So he took Hero's arm, and realized with a moue of distaste he was holding it the same way the lieutenant had been. He let go and put his hand on the small of her back, and nudged her toward the exit, as the walls slid back to give them leeway.

Hero skipped along beside Sang, for he could not bring himself down to a pace which would suit her stature.

"Sang—"

"Not here," he said curtly. The old, permanent walls of the bridge were just ahead. They turned into the corridor that followed the outward-curving walls of the bridge, with old fashioned doors and entrances coming off the other side. This whole section was a throwback to another era.

Hero caught his arm. "Sang!"

Sang drew a breath and halted.

Hero wound her arms around his neck and pressed herself up against him. "Thank you," she breathed, her lips against his neck. "He really did hit me first."

"It is telling that you must underline it," Sang said dryly. He pulled her away from him. "What were you *doing* down in the bowels?"

"You were gone for days and days. I haven't had an assignment in months. I just…started walking."

Sang read between the lines easily. Hero had a low threshold for boredom. "And before he hit you first, did you insult him? Dangle a free sample in front of him?"

Hero's expression grew thundery. "It doesn't make any difference."

"Not to the Cadre it doesn't," Sang said in agreement. He turned her and started walking once more. "To me, it makes a great deal of difference."

"Where are we going?"

"I'm taking you home."

"You're coming home?" Hope lifted her voice.

"I have things to do. This was an interruption I could have done without."

Hero spun to face him once more, making him halt to avoid tripping over the top of her. "Only you *did* come!" Her black eyes shone. They were rather lovely eyes, when one stopped to consider them purely for their esthetic appeal.

Suspicion grew in his chest. "Is that why you refused to let them sample you for an ID? You wanted me to come looking for you…"

Hero pressed her lips against his jaw. "And you did."

Sang held her away from him once more. He shook his head. "Bellona sent me. That is the only reason I am here.

She didn't want another of her generals in disgrace and making a public fool of themselves."

The happiness drained from Hero's eyes. Her arms fell. "Bellona sent you," she repeated woodenly. She turned on one heel and ran.

"Hero!" Sang shouted after her.

"Go back to work, robot!" she shouted over her shoulder.

Sang ignored the weight in his chest and his too-fast heart, and the hurt that wanted to form there. He would worry about it later. He would fix things with Hero later.

Instead, he weighed priorities. The selection of one urgent task over a second, just as critical, choice had become second nature. Hero was an urgent problem to be solved, but not today. He had averted the public disaster as Bellona had requested and could do nothing more for now.

Put that way, his choice was clear. Bellona would need him for the Assembly Of Governors. He must return to her private wing.

Despite the clarity of his choice, Sang couldn't shift the weight that felt as though it was trying to grind his breastbone into chalk.

3

Demosthenes, nomansland.

SANG CREATED A BRIDGE TO THE BACK room of the assembly hall dais and stepped through just as the handmaids were adding Bellona's headdress. Her eyes, with their elaborate makeup, swiveled to Sang as the maids adjusted the headdress and the folds of the long gown. It was a heavy garment, which hung straight from the shoulders, encrusted with semi-precious milk stones and cultured diamonds, azure beads and steel silk threads which glistened as she moved.

As he did whenever he saw Bellona again after even a small absence, Sang realized she was smaller than he remembered her to be, even with her thick black curls wound up onto the back of her head.

"Did you sort Hero out?" Bellona asked. "No, not the scepter. Not today," she told the maid, who was trying to curl Bellona's fingers around the shaft of the golden symbol.

"The Cadre have released her," Sang said.

Bellona rolled her black-outlined eyes at him. "Do we need to talk about Hero, Sang?"

"Hero was being Hero," Sang replied. "That is merely a symptom—"

"I don't have time to talk about it now," Bellona replied. She nodded toward the tall archway. Beyond the arch was the dais of the assembly hall. The dais was raised dozens of meters above the floor of the hall. The hall itself was cavernous, at least ten levels high—ten of the new-style levels with their high ceiling and airy, open spaces. Seven thousand people could stand upon the floor of the assembly hall and not be crowded. There were tiers of seats around the edges, which could hold another four thousand people.

Despite the size of the hall, the entire population of Demos could not gather there at once. Instead, lenses fed the events in the hall to the rest of the ship via a dozen different channels and streams.

Through the archway, Sang could hear the murmur of many voices on the floor of the hall. The governors of the free worlds were gathered there to acknowledge Bellona and the opening of the annual assembly.

He consulted internally for the time. "There is still three minutes to go. They're impatient, today." Was that another symptom? He plucked the idea and tucked it away with the others.

"Everyone is impatient these days," Bellona said. "Damn, this thing is heavy. Do you put carbyne in the lining, ladies?" She shrugged under the robe.

The handmaidens giggled.

Sang dismissed them with a wave of his fingers. He didn't need the physical gesture as they were all Dyse's bexens, but the habit was ingrained.

Their faces lost animation. They moved into a (mathematically perfect) straight line and moved out of the room. The last shut the door with a wordless command to the room AI.

Bellona sighed. "Thank you."

"You are not rude if you dismiss them yourself," Sang pointed out.

"I always feel as though I'm disappointing them if I don't let them do their job," Bellona replied. She cocked her head. "That buzz coming from the governors sounds angry. Shall I find out?"

Sang moved over to the door and lowered the security field, so she could step out onto the dais.

Bellona shrugged under the weight of the gown once

more. Then she squared her shoulders, raised her chin and sailed out onto the dais, her arms lifting in greeting.

Sang stood out of sight behind the archway and listened critically to the sigh which rose from the floor of the assembly hall. There was an undertone of dissatisfaction, although the stronger note was still one of awe and pleasure.

"Governors! Leaders of the Free Worlds! I bid you welcome to Demosthenes!" Bellona's voice was picked up and amplified by innovative and advanced directional audio equipment. No matter where one stood in the assembly hall, it sounded as though Bellona was right in front of them. The experts had predicted it would make the governors experience a degree of intimacy, which would encourage openness and cooperation.

Sang had consulted with the speech writers. Bellona's speech would be short, and the content null. It would impart a warm feeling, which would be followed by a grand feast, to wine and dine the governors into somnolence. Then, as Demos followed a standard twenty-hour clock, the free world leaders would be encouraged to sleep, then rise tomorrow to attend the first trade session.

From experience, Sang knew they would continue to drink and deal among each other, jockeying for better economic partners, negotiating trade breaks and agreements, even before the meeting began.

Tonight he would be kept busy with governor-generated diplomatic emergencies the Cadre couldn't cope with. There would be incidences with prostitutes, too much alcohol, or an ever-growing variety of drugs, physical fights, theft, vandalism and more.

At least there would not be another murder. He hoped.

PEACE, SANG REFLECTED, CAME AT A HIGHER cost every year.

Demos was meant to be a neutral location for the free world governors to meet and smooth over differences. Sang could not recall a single annual assembly where tempers had not frayed and at least one head of state left in anger. This year, it was to be Madhuri Truman. As the Cheng-Huang Alignment Minister of Trade was unnaturally calm at all times, Sang wondered if her retreat was a strategic one.

Bellona would pull the warring parties together after the official sessions, and work with them to find a compromise. Each year, the compromises grew in scale.

As the first session came to a grinding, unsatisfactory halt, Lynn Alberda wound through the departing governors, heading for where Sang lingered at the back of the room, waiting for exactly these types of informal exchanges.

Bellona no longer stayed once a session was ended. Staying exposed her to entreaties, bribes and, occasionally, extortion. All were a nuisance. Sang and Khalil, and sometimes Fontana, made themselves available instead.

Lynn Alberda was still governor of Cerce, even though little remained of Cerce but an agrarian community up by the northern ice cap. Alberda had aged terribly after the city killer had destroyed Cerce City and eighty-three percent of the planet's population in three minutes. He was a driven man, these days. The flesh of easy living was gone, his hair was quite white, but his eyes snapped with purpose.

"Governor Alberda," Sang said in acknowledgment as Alberda stopped in front of him.

"Sang Indigo." Alberda's smile was perfunctory. "You really need a title, Sang. Minister of Everything, perhaps?"

Sang laughed. "Chief Cook and Bottle Washer, perhaps?"

"Washer?"

"Never mind. An old Terran jest."

"You read too much."

"That is a first. I am generally accused of writing too much."

Alberda's expression sobered. "What can you do about this new trade tariff, Sang?"

Sang shook his head. "You are not a simple man, Lynn. You were on Demos the day the Alliance struck Cerce. You saw what Bellona's generals did to strike back. We have held the Alliance at bay ever since. You must ask why we raise a tariff?"

Alberda stroked his beard. "Then let me ask you a different question. How long is it since you saw Demos from *outside*?"

Sang smiled. "You have forgotten my nature. I can tap into any feed, at any time. The micro satellites, any one of them, could give me that view. What do you really ask?"

Alberda's smile was self-aware. "You should be flattered I forgot. My point is one of perspective. How big is Demos now?"

Sang had tooled an AI purely to gather, sort and analyze statistics about the city. The AI was part of the impeded neural network which guided decision-making. "Demos long ago grew too large to be comprehended all at once, even in *my* mind."

"Dyse's, perhaps?"

"He says so." Sang leaned closer. "I don't believe him."

Alberda laughed.

"Demos is a city state, yes. We are expending time, resources and energy on your behalf," Sang pointed out.

"Are you? Or do you just like to think so?" Alberda drew the fronts of his hand-woven jacket robe together. It was a simple garment compared to the luxurious multilayered and detailed outfits seen about the trade table. Sang knew the raw brown fibers of Alberda's jacket robe had been grown and processed by New Cerce Village. "I have seven thousand, three hundred and ten people who look to me to keep the planet viable. It's just over the minimum sustainable population, Sang. We can barely hold our own. And don't give me the standard paragraphs about trade being the savior of us all. I know it better than you. This is the first year we've had energy to spare from putting food in mouths. Now you want to take fifteen percent off the top of anything we sell off-world?"

"Trade *is* critical." It was a bedrock fact.

Alberda nodded. "Then here is my question, Sang. The fifteen percent you intend to slice off my annual revenue...what exactly does it pay for? Because the Alliance has taken its best shot at Cerce already. You really think they give a damn about us hunched in our igloos anymore?"

Sang held still, repressing the shiver that tried to wash over him. "Governor Alberda, you have forgotten what the Alliance's best shot looks like, if you think they have done their worst upon Cerce."

Alberda frowned. "All I am asking is that you speak to Bellona. See if she can minimize the impact of the tariff on Cerce. We're not the Cheng-Huang Alignment. We can't abandon a planet which isn't producing enough gross product and move on."

Sang bowed his head shortly. "I will, Governor."

Alberda moved away, satisfied his point had been made. He was, after all, not a stupid man.

The unsettled feeling in Sang's middle grew stronger. Alberda would be disappointed to know it had little to do with his poor planet's economics.

What else had the governors forgotten?

Were Bellona's generals so effective that no one understood the cost of failure, anymore?

4

Demosthenes, nomansland.

KHALIL STEPPED INTO THE ANTECHAMBER BEHIND THE convention room as Sang was adjusting his belt for the transition back to the private wing.

"Oh, let's walk," Khalil told him. "I need to stretch. I've been sitting all day."

"You've been talking politics all day," Sang amended. "*That* is why you are tired." He followed Khalil through the door, out into the public thoroughfare. This corridor connected with the Ginza. The Ginza was the main hall and ran through the middle of the city. Nearly every wing and suburb and quarter connected to it, on this level. Even the levels above and below the Ginza connected via drop shafts and tubes, and, here and there, with stairs.

Khalil seemed content just to walk. They kept their pace fast enough so anyone who might want to waylay them with entreaties or complaints would be discouraged. They were too well known, which was why Sang used bridge forges to move about the city.

"One of my spies reached out through Dyse, last night," Khalil said.

Was this why Khalil wanted to walk?

They turned onto the Ginza, which was far busier than the corridor they left. It was the heart of the commercial district. Stalls, shops, people crouched upon blankets spread with their wares, snagged pedestrians and brought foot traffic to a slow amble.

They wove between shoppers, cafes and restaurants, entertainment halls and shop fronts where Demos officials conducted their business.

"It's dusty," Khalil observed, looking up at the banks of sun lights overhead. "You need to let it rain more often."

"Every rain storm brings an equal storm of complaints. Some of them legitimate. It takes a month of publicity to conduct a rain storm."

Khalil stopped beside a row of private bubbles attached to a coffeehouse. "Sit for a moment," he suggested, opening an empty bubble.

Curious despite his limited time, Sang stepped into the bubble and sat on the other bench. Khalil sealed up the bubble and turned the walls opaque.

The noise of the Ginza dropped to a low buzz.

A screen generated itself, floating above the narrow table, asking for their order, and displaying a list of items beneath.

Khalil rubbed his temples, ignoring the screen.

As the bubble would unseal and open if they did not order, Sang tapped at the screen, entered the credits using one of his public profiles and dismissed the screen.

He considered Khalil. Not for the first time, he noticed the gray in the man's beard and the flecks in his unruly black hair. The lines radiating from the corners of his eyes were deeper than Sang remembered.

Sang could not recall without an indexed search how long it had been since he had seen Khalil wearing anything but plain black garments. Even the formal robe jacket he was wearing now was matte black.

"Something troubles you, my friend," Sang said.

"I just want a minute to breathe," Khalil admitted.

Sang nodded. Khalil's personality ranged along the inversion end of the spectrum, although it had shifted closer to the center over the years. It had been months since Khalil had needed to step out of the flow of human affairs for a while. The Assembly of Governors would trigger that need in anyone.

A tray with two steaming cups rose through the center of the table. Sang pushed one toward Khalil and took the other and sipped. It was passable.

"Your spy…" Sang prompted.

Khalil rubbed at his temple. "On Autronius."

"Ah." Autronius was deep inside Eriuman territories, surrounded by the might of the Eriuman navy. Dyse had predicted the Alliance would set up a research facility there, to learn how to replicate the forge belts.

The bridge forges gave Bellona's army the advantage in any combat situation, no matter what the scenario. It was the single overwhelming factor which had allowed Bellona to hold back the Alliance for over ten years.

Khalil and Sang had spent every one of the intervening years monitoring the Alliance's efforts to replicate the belts. The Alliance had stolen belts, taken belts from fallen Demosthenians, and bribed and extorted to acquire samples.

Sang countered that danger by adding simple biometrics to each belt. The belt would not work for anyone but its intended wearer.

Still, the peril remained that the Alliance would find a work-around, or figure out for themselves the secret of working, man-sized bridge forges. If that day ever arrived, Bellona's power over the Alliance would evaporate.

"The latest trial results?" Sang asked Khalil.

Khalil pressed his fingers to his temples, then let his hands drop. "They canceled them."

Sang let the fact settle in his mind. "It doesn't fit the pattern. They've been running trials every quarter, going back…" He took the time to run a proper search and compile. "Every seventy-eight-point-two standard days, over the last eleven years."

Khalil nodded. "The list of reasons why they would cancel the trial is too short and very ugly."

Sang drummed the table with his fingers. "Was that

the extent of the report? That the trials had been canceled?"

"It was all she managed to send before..." Khalil grimaced. "I wondered if you had heard anything which might explain it."

Sang had his own cadre of spies and agents, kept separate from Khalil's to enhance redundancy and organic verification. He assessed the array of data currently available. "My agents haven't reported in on time. I considered them late, not overdue. This changes the aspect."

Khalil stirred and reached for the cup, which had stopped steaming. "We should move on."

"As there is still the feast to get through," Sang finished for him.

Khalil didn't roll his eyes, although Sang knew he wanted to. Instead, he sipped, then gagged. "This is not coffee!"

"It is hot chocolate. It will give you energy for tonight. Drink up."

Sang sipped the adequate concoction, too.

Khalil scowled at him but drank. "Don't you ever tire of it all, Sang?" he asked between sips.

"It is not my function to grow weary of burdens," Sang replied. Then he lowered his cup. "Why did I say that?"

"It is what a household asset would say," Khalil pointed out.

"I am no longer the family android," Sang replied.

"Your conscious mind might believe that." Khalil shrugged. "The original programming the Bureau developed for the Eriuman androids was pernicious."

"I replaced that programming, long ago," Sang said.

Khalil sat up. He smiled. "Really? How did you manage that? Why didn't you tell me?"

"Dyse helped," Sang admitted. "My point is, why would I spout family politics when there are no traces of that programming left?"

Khalil chuckled and drained the last of his chocolate.

"That is amusing?"

"It is," Khalil assured him. "You spouted it because the thought pattern is a holdover from your past. It's your organic basil ganglia hanging onto old conditioning."

"Habits…" Sang surmised. "Damn."

Khalil laughed once more. "You can't recode habits, Sang. They are human programming."

BEFORE FEAST NIGHTS, BELLONA'S LEDANIANS AND HER inner circle of lieutenants and advisors gathered in the lounge of the private wing for a few moments, before entering the convention hall together.

The first time they had gathered like this, it had been to huddle together in Bellona's quarters. Her suite had been the only private location they could find on the entire ship. Demos had been exploding with people anxious to ally themselves with Bellona and her army, who had the power to hold back the Alliance and their dreaded city killers.

On that first occasion, they had sought to support each other in the face of overwhelming fame and favor, to touch base before entering the fray.

In that regard, Sang thought, nothing had changed except the finery they wore and the location in which they huddled together. These few quiet moments still served a unifying purpose.

He scanned the big common room and registered without surprise that Hero was not among the group. Also not a surprise to him was the presence of Madhuri Truman. The Cheng-Huang minister was an elegant, tall figure in a rich blue and gold gown which wrapped her body and trailed behind her. The style was extrapolated from the garments human tea-pickers had once worn upon High

Moon, before bexens had replaced them. The jewels and precious metals sewn along the borders of the gown made a mockery of the simple worker's outfit.

There were more moon stones in Maddie Truman's elaborate hairstyle, and in the choker about her neck. Moon stones originated on High Moon and were sought after across the galaxy. Sang estimated her simple, elegant turnout would, if cashed in, run a small planet for a year or two.

He made a note to watch for Lynn Alberda's reaction to Truman's appearance, when they reached the convention hall.

Bellona and Maddie Truman were speaking quietly, with half a dozen of the Ledanians listening. The rapt audience would help put Maddie at her ease. She liked attention, although she was too cynical to let her choices be influenced by it.

Sang caught the flicker of Bellona's gaze toward him, then back to Maddie Truman. He moved over to the group and stood beside Thecla.

Thecla wore flaming red, a gown which draped and flowed about her feet, with slashed sleeves to accommodate the hawsers running from her shoulders to her wrists. It was unusual to see Thecla in anything other than workmanlike trousers, which did not impede her primary interest in all things military.

Then Thecla shifted restlessly, and the gown split open to reveal matching slim trousers. Mystery solved, Sang told himself. He focused upon Maddie Truman, who was speaking in her low, musical voice.

"My family are most troubled by bad dreams of late. My youngest great granddaughter wakes screaming, which unsettles us all. The oracles say her spirit is not anchored, which puzzles us for we have lived upon the same terrace on High Moon for one hundred and twelve generations."

Bellona nodded politely.

Alignment cultures found it enormously difficult to speak directly of negative or delicate matters. Khalil was better at interpreting Maddie's double-speak. He was on the other side of the room, talking in a low voice with Retha and Fontana. Fontana looked angry as always. To be pissed in this room of friends meant something bothered him. Something more than the usual sins of the Alliance and Karassia in particular. He had never forgiven the Sodality for what they did to Aideen.

Sang returned his attention to the Cheng-Huang representative and sorted out the symbolism and euphemisms in Maddie's speech, as Bellona had silently pleaded for him to do.

"Your Alignment worlds are still troubled by the Alliance invasion, Madam Truman?" he asked politely.

Maddie's cheeks tinged pink. She smiled brightly at Sang. "How could we? General Thecla's troops are subpar to none! They were magnificent." She nodded regally to Thecla.

Thecla smiled stiffly. "It was nothing."

Sang drew in a breath at Thecla's gaff. "The work was nothing to Thecla, Madam Truman," he said quickly. "The joy of helping preserve the Cheng-Huang Alignment worlds more than adequately compensated for any tedium in the work itself."

Thecla stiffened. "I mean…yes, of course."

Maddie's gaze settled on Sang. "General Thecla does not offend thee, for lo! She speaks only a profound truth."

A message was in her eyes. Sang frowned, pulling together disparate hints and implications Maddie had dropped during the trade session. "You are not here to speak about the tariff."

She lowered her chin. Straightened once more. Confirmation.

Sang glanced at Bellona, to ensure she was following.

Bellona's fingers curled up against her palm against the golden velvet gown. The gown was a simple thing. The glowing rubies at her neck were old-fashioned by most standards. Yet Bellona's simplicity put Maddie Truman's excessive dress to shame, in Sang's opinion.

He focused upon Bellona's hand. Her forefinger remained straight.

Sang smiled his warmest smile at Maddie Truman. "How can we help you, Madam Truman?"

"General Thecla has been of great assistance already."

It was the most direct speech Sang had ever heard her give. "Something about the invasion…?" He let the question dangle.

Thecla gave a snort of derision. "Invasion! It was the most half-hearted invasion we've ever had to deal with. We had High Moon mopped up in three days."

Sang had read the reports. This was the first time he had heard Thecla's take on their latest engagement with Alliance ground troops, who had tried a suicide run at High Moon and Xiang. Thecla had been back upon Demos for only a few days, after a month of patrolling the sector and cleaning out the last of the Alliance null gravity ships which had appeared in the area like noxious weeds.

The report had only outlined a success. It had not hinted at the ease of that success. Sang knew Thecla was not indulging in boastful exaggeration. She took her work too seriously to make light of it.

Why had the invasion been so easy?

"Bellona, I admire the bond you share with your Ledanians," Maddie said. "I envy you your friends. They are your moral compass, your family."

Bellona narrowed her eyes. "I trust them with my life," she said shortly.

"And they have given *us* life, once more. A second chance." Maddie gripped her glass. "I would not denigrate the efforts of a friend."

Sang drew in a breath. "You agree with Thecla. You think it was too easy a victory."

Maddie speared him with her direct gaze. She didn't nod this time. She didn't need to. "You are privileged to move beyond the unmovable walls around your beloved captain."

Bellona stirred, ready to take offense. Sang touched her wrist, warning her. "I am one of those whom Bellona trusts enough to allow within the private wing, yes." "Unmovable walls" was Maddie's way of referring to the private wing, which was completely closed off from the rest of the city by permanent, unmoving walls without doors or windows. The bulkheads wrapped around the entire wing, running beneath the floors and the roof, too. It made the wing bomb-proof and inaccessible by anyone who did not have a forge belt *and* the coordinates to the front room.

The closed-off private wing was not a secret. Bellona's propaganda corps encouraged the gossip, which discouraged anyone who might want unauthorized access to Bellona and her Ledanians.

Like everything Maddie said, a secondary meaning was within. Sang ignored it for now.

Maddie waved her hand around the lounge. "The ship which can be a thousand places in a day. Here for a heartbeat, then invisible. Yet more and more people find their way to Demosthenes."

Aideen, who was part of the attentive group, said with a flat voice which implied she was reciting from memory, "New requests for residency average five hundred and seven every day." It was one of her responsibilities, when she was not leading a battalion, to assign space and find more space when needed. Aideen's request for resources to grow more floors and extend the outer walls increased every month.

"More and more people want to find the golden path," Maddie added.

Sang frowned. Why *golden path*? It was a term rich with hidden meanings. Yes, people flooded the city every day, and fought to find a way to stay here. Living space was at a premium, especially in the lower levels.

Before he could fully sort out Maddie's meaning, she said, "Where will that path lead, I wonder?" She looked at Bellona. "The leader of the free worlds is great and good and kind and knowledgeable."

Sang let out a heavy breath. "Maddie is saying—"

"I know," Bellona said. Her gaze locked with Madhuri Truman. "It is up to you to determine the fate of your worlds, Maddie."

Maddie lifted a brow. "Diverging paths cannot meet later."

Sang sighed. "You do not want to travel alongside Demos, Madam Truman—not even symbolically. It would negate the reason Demos exists."

"It is why we put up with fractious governors and petty bickering across the negotiation table," Bellona added. "You have fought for and won the right to self-determination. I merely enforce that right."

"If I cannot stand beside you, then I will stand behind you. Either way, it will be the greatest of privileges for the Cheng-Huang Alignment." Maddie bowed low. "May I return?"

Thecla stirred. "I will step you across to the convention hall, Madam Truman. This way." She shepherded Maddie toward the nearest corner, out of the way of everyone in the room, adjusted her belt, then gripped Truman's arm as the bridge formed and walked through it.

Aideen frowned. "I do not understand the Minister of Trade."

"Most of us don't," Bellona assured her. "Sang, what did you get from that?"

Sang shook his head. "She is afraid of the Alliance. She is afraid of what they might be planning next. The invasion upset her complacency about the right to live freely. To her mind, it is better to live under your leadership, Bellona, than stand alone and exposed to the Alliance's next move."

"They're *not* exposed!" Bellona said, frustration making her voice rise. "Thecla spent weeks demonstrating it to them."

Drawing upon the moment of awareness he'd experienced earlier in the day, Sang said, "Perhaps the competence of Thecla's regiment has reinforced in her mind what living without that aid might mean."

"Complacency is entropy," Khalil added as he stepped between Bellona and Aideen. He kissed Bellona's cheek, a familiarity he only allowed himself inside the private wing. He took her hand. "And the governors are far too complacent these days."

"It isn't my job to lead them!" Bellona protested.

"Someone must. They have forgotten how," Khalil replied.

"Looking to you for guidance has become a habit," Sang added.

Khalil laughed and Bellona smiled, puzzled by the insider joke.

Sang could not bring himself to even smile in response.

5

Demosthenes, nomansland.

THE CONVENTION HALL WHERE THE FEAST WAS held was as large as the assembly hall, but only rose two levels high. Despite the expanse of floor space, made soft underfoot by one of Connie's living rugs, which eagerly sucked up every spilt drop and crumb, the hall was still a crowded place.

The feast taxed the resources of the entire city. It required the assistance of every active and suitably programmed bexen Dyse's factory had available. A large team of managers spent weeks planning the event, directed by Aideen, who reveled in the excessive details and making sense and symmetry from them.

Perhaps that was why Fontana still looked angry. Sang would have to investigate later. For now, he could not move away from the head table. Everyone would see him abandoning the feast and would wonder if there was an emergency they should be aware of. It would not foster the fellowship and ease the feast encouraged.

The drinks flowed endlessly. The food was piping hot and plentiful, and the music soft so it did not impede conversation. The tensions of the day were buried beneath good cheer.

The five-course feast was nearly at an end and Bellona was preparing to move to the podium for her second speech of welcome for the day, when Hayes nudged Sang in the side with his enhanced elbow, almost pushing Sang off his chair.

Hayes nodded. "Look who is here," he said in his deep voice, which matched his stature.

Sang looked in the direction Hayes had nodded, scanning the jammed room. The hall had begun the evening with pillars for walls, marking off open archways to ease the flow of people into the hall.

The walls had filled in when the feast began, leaving just one giant doorway in the corner for late arrivals.

Hero stood in the middle of the doorway, looking around the hall, while bexens scurried and jigged around her. One was trying to show her to the closest empty seat, while Hero ignored it.

Heads were turning. Of course they were.

Hero's gown was elaborate, a thing of beauty which spread around her like mist and falling leaves. Red and amber and brown gems glittered at her throat and ears. There was no sign of the usual wild, free-spirited and reckless wardrobe choices. There was not a plethora of flesh upon display. Her makeup was not excessive, although it did make the most of her eyes. Her hair was piled upon her head, where more gems glittered.

Bellona leaned toward Sang. "I believe it is you she is looking for," she murmured.

Sang wanted to dispute that. Instead, he got to his feet and moved around the table and over to where Hero paused.

She didn't smile as she looked at him.

"You look wonderful," Sang told her.

"Thank you." Her tone was stiff.

"I didn't think you would attend."

"I didn't, either."

"I'm glad you did." He moved back, to give her and the gown room to move. "There is a seat by me. Come and eat. Or not eat, if you prefer."

Hero looked around the hall one last time. Then, moving slowly, she reached out and slid her fingers over his elbow. Sang had taught her the old custom, which she had found amusing, at first. She did not smile now.

Aware that they were not speaking, while over five thousand people watched them move around the edges of the hall, Sang leaned toward Hero and lowered his voice. "I have only one question."

Hero rolled her eyes. "Liar."

"For now," he amended.

She considered. "Ask, then."

"Where did you hide your belt?" For she had to wear the belt to leave the private wing, unless she had asked someone else to make the bridge for her. Only, everyone with access to the private wing was here in the hall. She had the belt on her somewhere, only the dress was a second skin down to her hips...

The corners of her mouth turned up. "Wouldn't you like to know?"

"I would. Very much." Sang was pleased to see the smile.

She opened her mouth to answer.

"No, don't tell me," he said quickly. "I will find out for myself. Later."

Her smile was incandescent.

THE PROPAGANDA CORPS FROWNED UPON THE LEDANIANS clinging together during public functions. Once the meal was done and Bellona's speech had been received with thunderous applause and a standing ovation, Sang and the others spread out around the cavernous room to mingle.

Sang nudged Khalil from his chair with a hand on his arm. Khalil hated these moments with a powerful revulsion. His form of mingling was to ask a great many questions, tempered to a polite level, which saved him from the null-content conversations which drove him mad.

Hero was in her element. She oozed charm and appeal,

as she floated about the room in her lovely gown. She chatted and laughed and pressed her small hand against arms and over other hands. Sang wondered how many of the people she touched and hugged were aware that a single scratch of her fingernails would bring death within three minutes.

He watched one less-than-sober diplomat pat her cheek, while swaying toward her. Did the fool know that kissing Hero against her wishes would also bring irreversible and agonizing death?

Hero was more than capable of defending herself. Sang concentrated instead on moving from table to table. He spoke to governors, their diplomats and assistants and partners, and was introduced to the people he did not know. He did not loath the social exercise as Khalil did. If he'd had a personality to measure, he would be on the other side of the spectrum from Khalil's inversion—not all the way to the other extreme, as Hero was, but definitely on that side. He'd always enjoyed speaking with humans.

As Sang moved from table to table, he crossed the paths of the Ledanians. Even Hayes was doing his best to be a good host, by speaking about his gardens and landscaping and the parks he had made in the city, the green spaces he had designed…as his face glowed with enthusiasm and his metal fingers flexed as if he could feel the dirt around them. Fontana was more agile and diplomatic than Hayes, or Aideen, with her disability, although Aideen *tried*, while forcing the words out and staring at the table in front of her.

Thecla's preferred method was to carry a decanter of hard spirits with her. She would fill up the glass of anyone she spoke with and dare them to match her mouthful to mouthful. Thecla's form of diplomacy actually worked, which was the surprising thing.

Thecla had taught Retha how to put up with fools and

idiots, which took the edge off his sociopathic observations and comments. People often looked relieved when Retha got up from their table, though, even if they weren't sure what they should be relieved about.

Hecate Hult, who was not Ledanian, but had earned her place in the private wing, also spent time flitting from table to table. She was the least accepted among the free world states, because of her history as one of the youngest and most capable captains in the Eriuman navy.

When Sang pulled out one of the empty chairs at the long table where Dyse sat, he assessed the wary expressions around the table. Then he focused upon Dyse…and had his answer.

Dyse was drunk beyond polite acceptance. He listed heavily to one side, his arm across the back of the next chair and his eyes shuttered to tiny slits, so the blue was barely visible.

Sang remembered the plaintive boy Khalil had brought onto Demos, thirteen years ago. Dyse was a full-grown man, now, with multiple wives and partners, and children, too. He had immersed himself in the human experience in every way possible, determined to understand all aspects of life.

His oldest son, Ruslan, was eight standards, and sat across the table from his father. Shreya, Ruslan's mother, a woman with big brown eyes and the patience of a glacier, was beside him.

Neither of them seemed bothered by Dyse's inebriation, while the guests at the table eyed Dyse nervously.

"Dyse, are you scaring people with your predictions again?" Sang asked, keeping his tone light.

The man opposite Sang showed subtle relief. Roberto, Sang reminded himself. Diplomat with the New Veles trade delegation and placed cautiously on the far side of the hall from the Cheng-Huang Alignment, Sang was pleased to see.

"I simply asked how an AI finds drinking so appealing, when it dulls the mind," Roberto explained.

Sang winced. "Dyse is not an artificial intelligence—not in the normal sense of the word."

Dyse pointed at Sang. "There! See! He understands it. Of course he does. Sang is in a class of his own, too." He bent to peer at Roberto's eyes. "You know that?"

Roberto nodded. "Everyone knows about Sang."

"Ah." Dyse sat back and scrubbed at his thick blond hair. "I'm no'Sang."

"So I gather," Roberto said, with a nervous smile.

"He means he is not an enhanced humanoid," Sang added helpfully.

"He isn't? I mean, Dyse, your pardon, but I thought you were a computer?"

"I am…" Dyse began, pushing himself into a more upright position, "*the* Bureau." He sagged again, blowing out a breath.

Ruslan giggled.

Dyse held out his arm. "Come here. Let me kiss you."

Ruslan hopped off his chair and moved around the table. His father scooped him up and put him on his lap and soundly smacked his cheek with a moist kiss. Ruslan leaned against him.

"*All* the Bureau?" Roberto murmured.

"Most of the Bureau, and all of it that counts," Sang assured him. "Dyse is not really the man you are sitting beside. He is a neural network of neural networks—a geometrical progression of networks. I am self-aware. Dyse is…aware of the universe."

Dyse pointed at Sang again, signaling agreement.

"The man, the body, is an avatar."

"A sh-mart one," Dyse added and burped.

"One which should be in bed," Shreya said firmly, getting to her feet. She moved around the table and plucked Ruslan from Dyse's arms, then tugged at Dyse's sleeve to rouse him.

Dyse staggered to his feet and let Shreya lead him away.

Roberto frowned. "Is there such a thing as a...a *not*-smart avatar, Sang?"

"You are surrounded by them, Ambassador."

Roberto looked around, fright spearing his expression. The Velesians were not in favor of technology for technology's sake. They were very good at bio-organic compounding, though, and didn't mind using unthinking high tech to enhance their work. They were the medication center of the free world.

"I don't see anything," Roberto added, looking back at Sang.

"The waiters, Ambassador."

He looked again. "Those pretty young girls and men? They are...computers?"

"Not even computers," Sang replied. "They are bexens. Biological extensions run by a neural network—one of Dyse's, usually. If the ethereal connection between the network and their tethers was broken, they would fall to the ground and lie there until the connection was restored."

Roberto rubbed at his chin. "They are all Dyse?"

Sang shook his head. "They are extensions of a neural network he has put aside to manage and conduct them. There is nothing of Dyse's awareness in them."

Roberto rubbed his lips. "He uses humans?"

Sang had run into this horror before. He said quickly, "No, Ambassador. These bodies were never conceived, nor were they born. They have never been self-aware. They cannot think for themselves at all. They are blank biological machines. The only intelligence they have is given to them by the neural network which directs them."

"Then...where do they come from?"

"They are grown in tanks, just as my body was."

Roberto swallowed. "I see."

He did not see at all. Sang could tell by the wariness in his eyes and his hesitancy. "Growing biological machines has been a standard practice for centuries, Ambassador. Dyse has admittedly taken it another step further, by choosing to run hundreds of tools at the same time. That is the only difference. I was digitally aware and inserted into my body when it was fully grown." He tapped his head. "My brain was not big enough before maturity to contain the whole of me."

Roberto shook his head and reached for his glass. "I have heard about the Eriuman androids. They are sheep. Without personality or willpower. They blindly obey, meeting their family's every wish and impulse."

Sang sighed. "Yes, that was me, a long time ago."

Roberto lowered his glass. "*Impossible*," he breathed. "I know you, Sang. You are…well, you are human!"

Sang laughed. "In most ways, I am." He got to his feet. "Which includes a need for sleep." He winked.

Roberto laughed, too, and waved him away.

SANG CHECKED ON BELLONA BEFORE RETIRING AND was wryly amused to realize that this was a habit, too.

He stood just inside the door to the inner apartment, while Bellona and Khalil moved around the room, easing off shoes, discarding garments, stretching and easing themselves into a comfortable and easy state of mind they rarely reached. As they moved, Bellona ran through her impressions of the feast and the aftermath.

"I think the most extraordinary event in the entire evening was Maddie Truman's appeal," Bellona concluded.

"Why, what did she say?" Khalil asked, his attention lifting. "I came in at the end. I was going to ask Sang to replay the conversation for me."

Sang nodded and repeated the conversation word for word, adding in his interpretations, too.

Khalil rubbed his chin, making the whiskers rasp. "It's more or less how I would have interpreted it, too." His gaze met Bellona's. "Maddie is afraid. If the Trade Minister for the Alignment is afraid, that's worth investigating. She's too good to not have spies in the Alliance, keeping her posted."

"You feel there is something more than a slap-dash raid upon High Moon that has scared her?" Sang said.

"I don't know. I just don't like how our information sources deep inside Erium have evaporated."

"They have?" Bellona said, startled. "I'm missing more than I'm learning, these days." She pulled the last pin out of her hair and eased the black mass down around her shoulders.

"That is what we are for," Sang assured her. "So you don't miss anything vital."

Khalil massaged her shoulders. "So why was Maddie the greatest surprise?" he asked.

He was pulling Bellona back to the inconsistency; her uneasiness over Maddie's declaration.

As Bellona's eyes closed and her head rolled back, Sang cleared his throat. "It is time to retire—"

"No, wait, Sang. Just a moment," Bellona said, straightening up again. She frowned. "You have the head for this."

"He does," Khalil said, moving over to the printer. He dialed in a drink. Sang hid his amusement, for he could read the confirmation message from where he stood. Khalil was printing a hot chocolate.

Bellona considered Sang, a small smile playing at the edges of her mouth. "Why was Maddie a surprise to me? Why am I still thinking about it? Is it something I should pay attention to? Do something about? Is my subconscious trying to warn me about it?"

Sang shook his head. "Thecla has already confirmed she will cross to the Alignment tomorrow and spend a few days watching."

"Thecla is just cynical enough to see past the life-is-joy-family-is-everything veneer," Khalil said, sipping the first mouthful of his drink cautiously.

"I will also be extending my range wider and deeper into Alliance territories, to discern if something is happening there we have failed to notice until now," Sang added. "You have no need to worry. If your subconscious is trying to warn you, we will find it."

Bellona tilted her head. "You don't think it is my subconscious trying to warn me, do you?"

Sang considered. "No, I do not."

Khalil lowered his cup, his eyes narrowing.

Bellona pursed her lips thoughtfully. "Then what, old friend?"

Sang hesitated.

"Go on," she pressed.

"Your father tried all his life to restrain you to a level of mediocrity that made him comfortable. You have resisted the conditioning since you became an adult, and you fully rejected it after Ledania. Only now you are reaching levels of extraordinary achievement. Whole planetary political alliances are looking to you to lead them. It is more than you have ever allowed yourself to consider possible for a woman like you. Maddie scared *you* with her talk of leaders and standing behind you. All your father's early conditioning reared its head." Sang shrugged.

Khalil shook his head. "Neatly put."

"You agree with him?" Bellona asked. Her voice was strained. Any mention of her father always did make her want to shut down.

"I do," Khalil said. He smiled. "You did ask," he reminded her. "In fact, you insisted."

Bellona relented and moved over to Sang. "Thank

you," she said softly and rested her hand on his shoulder. He felt the light touch through all the many layers of formal evening wear, as if she'd laid her hand on his bare skin. "You are probably right, for you are rarely ever wrong. I will have to consider it, though."

Sang cleared his throat. "Because you do not like the idea of your father being able to manipulate you still, even though he has been these many years dead."

Bellona laughed. "Yes, exactly." She patted his shoulder. "Good night, Sang, and thank you again."

He nodded and left the suite, his heart thudding.

Now he could retire for the night, his work done.

6

Punarvassa III. Karassian Sodality.

THE ANCIENT RUINS ON THE PRIMARY SOUTHERN continent had never been researched. Everyone presumed they were human, their origins lost in history. The chances they were alien-made *and* the doorway and window dimensions matched humans, were beyond astronomical.

Smugglers controlled the northern continent. They ruthlessly kept innocent, accidental visitors away from the planetary biosphere, using devices that included the bitch Bellona's microsatellite sentries—one of the few pieces of armament and defense technology they *had* been able to take from her.

The smugglers' efficiency worked in the triad's favor. Woodrow had scared the hell out of the smugglers by revealing who he was, then struck a deal to use the southern continent, as long as each party ignored the other.

It allowed the triad to come and go unremarked. Single, small ships were frequent arrivals at the unremarkable planet.

The shelter was molded a hundred meters below the ruins, deep enough to avoid detection by all currently available upper atmosphere scopes, filters and imagery. Access was via a kilometer-long tunnel. The entrance was disguised as part of the rock face of a small cliff. Approach to the cliff included alarms and warnings up to fifty meters out from the cliff. Closer in, the defenses were lethal.

Woodrow paid the smugglers to come and check for bodies every few days. They could keep whatever came with the bodies as part of their fee, including whatever ships the infiltrators used to get here.

If she *had* to be in Karassian space, Mesut Traverse figured this barren rock was passable. It was unpopulated, with not a single screen anywhere. As she picked her way over the lumps of old lava and kicked up dust with each step, she remotely disengaged the defenses as she approached the cliff face.

If only it wasn't so *cold*. She pulled her hindmarsh fur coat in tighter around her and hurried. At least the bunker was warm. This cold made the place where her arm used to be ache as if the arm was still there and wounded. Scratching at the metal arm Woodrow had arranged to replace it did nothing.

Another thing to thank the bitch Bellona for. The list continued to grow with each passing year.

The tunnel was even colder, cramped and damp. She hurried along it, resisting the temptation to duck away from the low roof. It was high enough to let her pass without bending. As it had been sliced out of the rock with a quantum corer, the walls and roof and floor were perfectly even, melted rock. The slope was precisely calculated so there was no change in pitch. She could have walked the tunnel in total darkness and not stumbled once.

Although, she was glad of the light which anchored to her heat signature and hovered a meter ahead of her, lighting the way.

The door at the end was bomb-proof and unhackable. She had made sure of the last part herself, going over the coding line by line. Woodrow and the Eriuman asshole had laughed at her painstaking work, until she snapped, "I have no intention of entering a hole in the ground with no other way out, unless I *know* no one else is down there."

That idea had wiped the smiles from their faces.

In fact, she had added lines to the code, keyed to her

biomarkers. The security pad at the top had warned her when she entered that both men were already in the bunker.

Traverse went in with her gun out. She was an adequate shot with her left hand and getting better every day.

The two looked up from their chummy chat. Raine Cardenas' eyes got wide when he spotted the gun.

Woodrow just smiled. "My, my. Paranoid, are we?"

"Fuck your ass, yes," Traverse growled and put the gun away. She shrugged off the fur coat and took the third seat. The chair, like the table, was grown right here in the bunker. She didn't like raised furniture. It always felt unnaturally warm and spongy to her. It was better than sitting on the rock floor, though.

"Let's get on with it, shall we?" Woodrow growled. Like all Karassians, he was a physically perfect specimen. Blond hair, brown eyes, almost flawless symmetry. Bred for an ideal appearance and adjusted in-vitro to smooth out any imperfections. Among Karassians, he was a bland non-entity, blending into the background. In this room, he drew the eye.

Traverse was immune to the DNA-derived appeal. "Weren't you already into business?" she asked sweetly.

Cardenas cleared his throat. His gaze, as always, was on her metal arm. He was Eriuman and delicate about such things. "We were talking about the budget."

Traverse snorted and took out her flask and drank deeply. The hot enzymes were fortifying. "I don't give a damn about the budget. Tell me about the trials."

"You don't give a damn because it isn't your money being spent," Cardenas said.

"The Bureau is providing full services for nothing. Don't tell me we aren't spending money," Traverse replied. "Next."

Woodrow shook his head. "A review is useful. Then

we move on."

"Did you switch to Eriuman while I wasn't looking?" Traverse asked him. "*Review*? When did Karassians ever follow procedure?"

"Karassians who can focus on the long term," Woodrow said calmly. "There are a few of us. There are more every year." His mouth turned down. "Hate has a way of focusing one's attention."

Traverse was pleased. "The campaigns are still working..." The Karassian-wide campaigns, propaganda and rhetoric had been her projects. Hate speech, couched in contexts familiar to Karassians—which meant via screens. She had spent months studying the popular media, researching the forms. Her aversion for all things Karassian came from that deep dive. She had emerged at the end of the projects with a sour taste in her mouth that recurred whenever she spent too much time on a Karassian world.

Woodrow looked grumpy, as though confirming her success pained him. "All the lag indicators are still climbing at an increasing rate. An eleven percent increase this year."

"Of course the rate is increasing. They're now used to believing that all the misery and misfortune, the tight economy and spiraling costs...all of it is the fault of the Ledanians and Bellona the Traitor. We've taught them that Bellona humiliated them, that one person, one ship, brought two mighty cultures to their knees. They've become comfortable hating her, and now it drives the Karassian economy, which isn't nearly as dire as they believe." Traverse smiled. "Or it wouldn't be, if you weren't sucking all the available credits and then some to pay for this little joint venture of ours."

Woodrow grimaced.

"The message is viral now. Your good citizens are spinning their own versions of 'I hate Bellona', which adds to the depth of influence," Traverse told him. "And the primary indicators?"

Woodrow's mouth twisted harder. "Volunteer recruits to the military are up again."

"How much?" she asked sweetly. She had predicted twenty-three percent.

"Up by three-point-two percent," Woodrow said.

It put the rate at twenty-four-point-three. Traverse smiled and shifted her gaze to the Eriuman. "And your navy?"

Raine Cardenas was a heavy-set man with the typical Eriuman appearance—black hair, black eyes, swarthy skin. His bottom lip was full, the eyes slightly protruding. Traverse had considered taking advantage of his sexual appetite, which the markers hinted at. His aversion to her arm prevented it.

He scowled, a nearly identical expression to Woodrow's. "Navy intake is up by seven percent across ten years."

"It's a pity Eriumans don't inhale their media the way Karassians do, hey?" Woodrow said, with a chuckle.

"You're forgetting their federal service," Traverse said, keeping her gaze upon Cardenas. "Is seven percent in addition to the draft?"

Cardenas winced at the term. Traverse hadn't bothered softening her words. She spent enough time honing phrases to trigger the right responses.

"It is the retention and recruitment rate," Cardenas admitted.

Traverse smiled. "And the *previous* ten years?"

Cardenas' scowl deepened. "Zero-point-three."

Woodrow breathed out. Even he was surprised.

"See?" Traverse told him. "Positive works." The Eriuman campaigns had been more difficult to develop, because Eriumans didn't absorb their news via screens or any mass media. An extreme hate campaign would have backfired. Instead, she had bribed and then carefully trained over one hundred easily led Eriumans on how to shift conversations around to the glories of a navy career, and the urgent state of affairs beyond the gravity well. Books about navy heroes saving the day were circulated. Rumors about the enormous odds against Erium success and the disaster that would ensure, became a dinner table topic. Stories about future dystopias were recommended at their tiresome family gatherings and social affairs and grand dinners.

Bellona and her Ledanians were never mentioned, for she represented a dilemma for too many Eriumans and would sow doubt. Instead, Traverse buried the Republic in pro-service messaging, with a soft serving of fear over the consequences of inaction.

To enhance and encourage the shift in attitude, Traverse had added subroutines to the morals-and-values software the Bureau added to all android packages sold to Eriuman tank facilities. The updated package prompted a Republic-wide request-for-update in models already shipped. For eight years now, the Eriuman androids had been inculcating Republican pride and proactivity in their owners, along with a good dose of underlying anxiety about the future.

It was a long-term campaign which Traverse had been forced to explain many times over to both Cardenas and Woodrow. "Karassians are adept at changing their minds in an instant," she railed at them. "They're flighty—they go with whatever is hot and sexy right now. Eriumans consider themselves above all that. It takes longer to shift them, yet the results are far more stable. Watch and wait."

She considered the pair now with a cool expression. "Let's review the budget, then."

Cardenas looked relieved. He had always been uneasy about the propaganda side of what they did and didn't have the sense to spot that Traverse had just manipulated both of them. The budget would not seem so appalling to the two in light of the results they themselves had reported. Now they would consider the money well spent.

Which was ironic, for even Traverse considered the budget to be staggering, despite working with the Bureaus' figures for years and being used to large numbers.

Woodrow cleared his throat. His gaze took on an unfocused expression as he tapped his internal digital enhancements and pulled up the reports. "Karassian supplied assets, three-point-four quads. Eriuman supplied assets, three-point-seven quads. Bureau adjusted asset value, three-point-one."

Traverse smiled at that.

Woodrow reeled off more figures. There was little perceived income. The major classes of expenses would raise brows. Propaganda. Assassination. Espionage. Bribery. Corruption. Extortion.

Traverse's expenses were all in the first classification. She added together the other costs, which were all Woodrow's and Cardenas'. The total far surpassed her own expensive work, even if she included her own time and value, which was prohibitive.

She interrupted Woodrow. "Wait. Repeat that again."

"Which one?" Woodrow said.

"Research and development."

Cardenas crossed his arms. "Yes, what was it?"

Woodrow didn't hesitate because he was in reporting mode. He was simply spouting numbers. "Three-point-oh-four billion."

Cardenas leaned forward. "That's not enough," he said, his voice harsh.

Traverse tapped into her own digital records. "Research has been over three quadrillion in every quarter since the Alliance was established. What's going on, Woodrow?" Research and development was his responsibility.

Woodrow sat back. "We've…hit a snag, I suppose you

might say."

Cardenas' face darkened. "What do you mean, a snag? If it was a snag, then the costs should *rise*! Not fall by that amount!"

Traverse hissed. "Finding a way to out-gun the bitch has been the whole point of this cooperative. We've been at a stalemate for over ten years because of her bridge forges, despite spending a planet's worth of revenue looking for a way out of the deadlock."

Cardenas tilted his head. "Why do you hate her so much, Traverse? Have you been imbibing too much of your own propaganda?"

Traverse stared back at him, not bothering to explain it was none of his damn business. His gaze dropped to her arm. She realized she was clutching it with her human hand, stroking the metal.

She made her hand drop back to the flask on the table. Annoyed, she shoved the focus back upon Woodrow. "Talk," she said flatly. "What's with the miniscule spending on research? What is the snag?"

Woodrow was a handsome man who lost all his prettiness when he was defensive. Then, his chin dropped and drew attention to the fact that it was weak. "I said it was a type of snag. We figured it out."

"Figured out the snag?" Cardenas said, frowning.

Traverse's breath caught. "No, they *figured it out*." She surged to her feet, excitement flaring. "The hive mind-linked mini forges *worked*, didn't they?" It had been her idea to link the micro communications forges together with a neural network, so they could work in gestalt. It got around the structural weaknesses that crippled forges larger than micro-sized. They had never once sustained a generated man-sized bridge with a single forge, despite copying the many belts they'd acquired from the bitch's troops over the years.

Woodrow didn't smile. "It worked."

Cardenas slapped the table. "And *you didn't tell us?*"

Traverse whirled, halting her energy-induced stride. "Why haven't development costs exploded?"

Woodrow didn't move. He didn't even blink.

Cardenas glanced at Traverse, puzzled by Woodrow's lack of response.

Traverse moved back to the table. "You're not developing it at all…" she breathed.

Cardenas sucked in a breath. "What?"

Woodrow gave a tiny shrug. "The Sodality feels that now we have developed a theoretical model, it would be counter to our interests to continue further with the research. We have reached our goals."

"What is the man talking about?" Cardenas pleaded to Traverse.

She hadn't spent all her time in Karassia watching the daily feelies. Traverse had a better grasp of the politics there than Woodrow realized. "The propaganda works *too* well," she concluded. "The Homogeny Council of Independence likes the cash flow a hate-based society generates. They have no intention of disturbing the status quo."

Cardenas slapped the table once more. "That's not your decision to make!" The tendons on his neck flexed—human tendons, Traverse noted. He was more than angry.

"Why do *you* hate Bellona so much?" she demanded. "She's your niece. She's family. You people value family so much…"

Cardenas pointed at Woodrow. "He hates her, too! She ruined his Ledan project, stole his assets, humiliated him for the worlds to see." His voice was hoarse with it. "So why isn't he screaming at the Council himself?"

Traverse flexed her metal fingers, which clicked and scraped. The sound made most people wince. Woodrow didn't flinch. "You know we have to tell our people about this," she pointed out. She reached for her coat.

"Indeed," Cardenas said stiffly, getting to his feet.

Traverse yanked her coat closed and let it seal. "Why didn't you inflate the figures, Woodrow?"

"It would leave forensic traces," Cardenas pointed out.

"Then actually spend the money. Put it in the account, then siphon it off and live fat and happy for the rest of your life," Traverse said.

For the first time, Woodrow moved. He gave a small shrug. "I pulled up the wrong copy of the report," he said. "The one I should have given you looks normal."

Traverse froze, while her heart careened along with her thoughts. She stared at the short man. "Damn, you're good," she breathed.

Cardenas shrugged into his own armored overcoat. "What does *that* mean?" he complained.

"Woodrow *wants* us angry. He wants us to goose the development from our side. The son of a bitch manipulated me. He even knows I won't care that he has."

Woodrow smiled.

7

Demosthenes, nomansland.

KHALIL HEATED SIX SPARRING BOTS WHILE SANG printed two sets of exo-skeletons. They didn't speak as they prepared for the practice. Sang was aware, more than usual, that the little rituals were so ingrained that both of them would be uncomfortable if they broke with them.

Even the silence as they mentally prepared was habitual.

When the exo-skeleton was snug around his torso and limbs, Sang picked up the weapon he had chosen to practice with today—a scimitar of ancient design. He'd replicated it over a year ago and researched its use. Months of trial and practice had brought him to a basic competence with the weapon. In a month or two, he would assess the effectiveness and decide whether he would continue using the weapon.

He had developed and discarded dozens of weapons over the years, while maintaining only a handful of the best. He suspected the scimitar might join that short list.

Khalil moved to the other side of the practice floor and waited, a pair of cestas of Thecla's design over his fists.

Sang moved into position. "Ready."

Khalil activated the sparring bots. They had blades or weighted fists for hands, and were programmed to maim, if necessary. The blades were sharp.

As the bots spun and circled, Sang and Khalil leapt to the offensive. Sang's attention taken up with attack, counter and placing his feet correctly. A bot fell to one side with a hiss and fizz, jerking. Then another.

When all six bots were inert once more, their circuits

irreparably severed or smashed, they put the weapons down and removed the exo-skeletons. They met in the middle of the floor for the rounds of hand combat which always ended these sessions.

A long time ago, they had practiced in the original landing bay of the Demos. Each time, their audience had grown steadily larger. Back then, the observers were known to them. Now, they used a small room in a forgotten corner of the private wing and no one watched, for everyone was busy with their own concerns.

Khalil bested Sang for two of the three rounds. As they laid recovering in the center of the floor, Khalil slapped Sang's shoulder. "Your mind is not here today."

"No."

Khalil tackled the armguard on his wrist, unsealing it.

Sang rolled onto his hip and propped himself on one elbow. "No questions about where my mind is?"

Khalil dropped the armguard on his belly and turned to the other. "You're working up to something. I know the signs."

"Not even curious, Khalil?"

Khalil caught the second guard as it dropped, then scooped up the other with the same hand and sat up. "You have never done a thing which didn't further Bellona's ambitions. How could I, of all people, question what you do?"

"It was programmed into me," Sang said in agreement.

"And Max reinforced it." Khalil hauled himself to his feet with a hiss of pain and worked his shoulder with a grimace. "You must stop doing that, Sang."

"Doing what?"

"Refer to original programming which no longer exists. You can't use it as an excuse, anymore." He held out his hand and pulled Sang to his feet.

"And you should stop referring to yourself as unreliable," Sang returned.

Khalil shook his head. "Betrayal can never be overwritten."

"It can be forgiven and forgotten."

"Forgiven, yes." Khalil shook out the guards and let them fold back into their original square centimeter each and closed his fist around the two boxes.

Sang moved over to the table where the box of exoskeletons and the case for the scimitar sat. He put the scimitar away. "How do you do that? Just...*accept*?"

Khalil's answer was a long time coming. "Because the alternative is unthinkable."

Karassia II, Karassian Sodality.

BEING THE MOST POPULAR MAN IN KARASSIAN history wasn't the life-enhancing status Chidi had expected. The fame was glorious, of course. It came with attendant problems, although he had trained to deal with the issues of fame. His life was structured to cope with the impact. Besides, being mobbed wherever he went merely fed the machine that created the hysteria, in a pleasant endless loop. Fans viewed the adoration and love he swam in each day and yearned to share it with him. They followed him compulsively, every hour of the day.

An entire day spent in front of lenses, which captured every movement he made, was the price of fame and he reveled in it. That wasn't the problem.

It was the lie that laid beneath *everything*. It wasn't even a gilded lily, glorified truth or scripted story-telling.

No, it was a flat-out lie.

Worse, he was contributing to the lie. His time away from the cameras had increased over the years, while he juggled feeds and loops and covered his absences with all his hard-won expertise.

One day, he would return to the hot lights in full, to absorb the reverence through every pore. That was why he crept through the night with a full façade and a dark cloak.

He felt muffled without his real face on display.

The full-service image lab was his, bought via dummy corporations and cut-outs. No one on his staff knew about the lab. Never again would he risk their lives. He had learned that lesson well, too.

Not even the buyer of the building the lab was housed in knew who had bought the enhanced space.

Chidi passed through the security layers, removing the mask as he went. The lab was in semi-darkness, another condition which made him uneasy. He prompted the lights to full exposure and his shoulders relaxed as the warmth bathed him.

"Hello, Chidi," came the greeting from behind him.

Chidi yipped and spun, then stumbled back until his hips met the work bench with a sharp slap.

The man called Woodrow sat on the stool in the corner, looking comfortable on the high perch. Woodrow smiled sunnily. "Yes, I know about the lab."

Chidi pushed his artistically tousled hair out of his eyes with a shaking hand. "What do you want?" His voice trembled, too. He hated himself for that. "I've run all the vids, everything you send me. When do I get my life back?"

"Oh, dear," Woodrow said, sliding down to the floor. "How quaint." He moved closer. "This *is* your life, Chidi. You haven't worked that out, yet?"

"I mean my real life," Chidi mumbled.

"I'm curious why you think you need a secret lab."

"That's your fault. I can't give the footage over as you supply it. You don't even bother to hide the source."

"I have you for that."

Chidi scowled. "You have more video?"

"I do." Woodrow nodded toward the bank of equipment ranged on the bench. "I've loaded it already. It's fresh, brand new footage, Chidi. Your viewers will love it."

The equipment was supposed to be locked and keyed to Chidi's biomarkers only. Chidi shivered.

"Within the next week, I want to see all of it in your feeds," Woodrow added.

"Impossible," Chidi said. "I can't flood my channels with your shit. I'll lose viewers if I don't appear often enough."

"That's your problem."

"It's your problem, too. I lose viewers, you lose eyes on your precious footage. Four weeks, nothing less."

Woodrow patted Chidi's cheek. "Two weeks. I can always find someone else. That pretty girl…what's her name? Sandreena?"

Chidi's gut churned. Only, didn't the fucker understand he was practiced at revealing only what he wanted to show the camera?

He laughed. "Sandreena is so far behind me she can't raise more than a measly months' worth of sponsorship. They all are. Give your crap to her. Go on. You'll reach a few dozen people. Maybe." He smiled, making it sunny. "Three weeks."

Woodrow considered. "Twenty days." He held up his finger as Chidi opened his mouth. "Remember Korbina," he intoned.

Chidi closed his mouth, his fury reaching a new depth, triggered by the mention of his last producer, found mangled in a gutter. The authorities had declared Korbina's death a misadventure.

This was the first time Woodrow had implied he'd something to do with Korbina's death. He'd never had to hint before. Chidi had understood without translation.

He stared at the little man now, his gut tight, a sick

taste in his mouth. Before Woodrow had marched into his life with his extortion and his bullying, Chidi had not realized emotions could be so powerful. He'd used them professionally, inciting them in his viewers with deliberate calculation, but had never succumbed to the techniques himself.

This feeling was different. It wasn't the product of someone else's design. It was all his own. It was honest. It was also cold and brutal.

"Twenty days," he repeated, making himself sound defeated. He let his shoulders slump.

"Good boy." Woodrow ruffled his tousled hair, ruining the effect.

Chidi breathed deeply and said nothing.

As soon as Woodrow shut the door behind him, Chidi kicked in the complete seal around the building and got to work.

He found the files Woodrow had uploaded and pushed them aside for later. He had no appetite to deal with them right now.

He captured the latest of the Bellona feeds and sampled the last few weeks of the channel. He skipped along the top, never stopping and getting caught up in the narrative. He had learned the hard way not to do that.

Whoever compiled the Bellona feeds was a rank amateur who understood nothing about timing, pacing, camera angles, lighting or even how to tell a story. Despite that, the feeds fascinated Chidi.

Because he had not come across the phenomenon anywhere else, it had taken years for him to understand the fascination was with the earthy quality of the feeds. They were unedited, unpolished and truthful. Bellona didn't have to worry about telling a good story. The raw facts were *that* powerful.

He scanned a few minutes of the Assembly of Governors, and the feast that evening. He dipped into the trade negotiation—an insomniac's delight—then perused the index.

Satisfied the feeds held nothing he could use, he turned to the pile of steaming entrails that was Woodrow's streams. He scanned them, getting a sense of the contents without watching every minute.

The report was at the end of one of the shorter streams. It had been buried behind a black screen. It was possible the editor of the video—the creator, Chidi amended in his mind—knew the report was there. The only reason Chidi found it was long experience with the size of a file in relationship to the streaming length. This file was too big for the few minutes of Xenia slaughtering indigents on some unnamed planet.

Chidi wasn't a master editor, but he knew his way around the toolbox. After a few false starts, he managed to remove the black mask.

The report was a static text file which scrolled through at a slow enough pace to facilitate reading.

His attention caught, Chidi read. Before he reached the end, his heart was back to hammering with hate once more.

Menaii, Deluca Prime, Delucas System

IULIA FELT THE PLEASANT ACHE IN HER bones and the languid satisfaction of unexpected good sex. Reluctantly, she made herself move. She eased out of the bed, so Peru was not disturbed, threw on a modest robe and moved through to her private sitting room.

Raine looked up as she entered, his tone exasperated. "Finally! What took so long?"

"Seduction takes time, little brother." She waved a languid hand.

Raine's face darkened. He glanced at the door and cleared his throat. "Who…?"

"I'd say it's none of your business, except it is all family business in the end." She settled on the chaise lounge. "Peru Scordina."

"The head of the clan? Well, you have balls, Iulia, I give you that."

"That's why I sit at the family table." She smiled sweetly. "You were waiting for me?"

Raine threw himself into the other comfortable chair and gripped his hands together. "The Karassians have developed a working bridge forge."

Iulia drew in a quick, sharp breath. "I heard nothing."

"It was suppressed. Buried. I just found out and came straight here." He straightened and glanced at the bedroom door once more. "It might be useful, having Peru under your thumb. Erium *must* scream for the development to go forward, Iulia. You are the best person to make sure that happens."

She smoothed out the robe over her knees. "And why is that?"

"You hate Bellona more than any person I know. More than everyone, I'm guessing. A working bridge forge, put into action, will remove Bellona's advantage over the Alliance. It will reset the entire war—"

"I thought we were at peace," Iulia said, injecting surprise into her voice. "With only a bright future to build toward."

Raine rolled his eyes. "You have more reason to ensure the Karassians give us the forge. You want the woman defeated, don't you?"

Iulia considered. "I am friendly with generals who can apply pressure, too." She nodded. "It will be done."

8

DYSE STEPPED THROUGH A BRIDGE into the common room, spotted Bellona at the buffet and lifted his hand.

Bellona sighed and put her half-loaded plate down and turned to wait for him to reach her.

Sang picked up the plate and finished adding items to it, and to his own.

"I didn't want to leave this to sub-ether channels," Dyse said, striding up to Bellona on his long legs. "One of my alerts popped up, and—"

"How many alerts do you have set?" Bellona asked.

"Thousands," Sang guessed, shepherding her toward the closest group of armchairs.

"Two hundred and ninety-three thousand, four hundred and thirty-six," Dyse said, glancing at him.

"As I said," Sang replied. He put the loaded plate on the flat, wide arm of the chair and lifted her hand so her fingers rested on the edge. The touch of the self-warming plate was a tactile reminder to eat.

He took the other seat and picked up the Shimshon roll and bit into it.

Dyse eyed the buffet with interest.

"You don't need more food, Dyse," Bellona told him. "You'll get fat. Then who will bear your children?"

Dyse grinned. "It might help thin out the volunteers."

Sang shook his head.

"The alert?" Bellona prompted and picked up the soup sandwich and bit into it.

Dyse nodded. "The Alliance is within a fingernail's length of the treaty limitations for armaments."

Sang lowered the roll. "But not over?"

"Close to it. *Very* close."

"By how much?" Bellona asked.

"The certified audit says within a few hundred credits."

Bellona stopped licking her fingers of soup. "*That* close?"

"How old is the audit?" Sang asked him.

"The key accounts are audited on a rolling basis. Certification issued every seven days," Dyse said.

Sang arrayed the options in his mind, sorting and cross-indexing. "They shouldn't have nudged so close to the upper limit…"

Bellona nodded. "It's *too* close. It's a signal."

"To draw our attention," Sang finished. He met Bellona's gaze. "What are they trying to draw our attention away from?"

Bellona leaned forward. "Dyse, scan everything you can, everything you have a passive alert on. Do a manual check. There's something they're hiding. See if there is an evidence trail."

"I started the scan twenty minutes ago," Dyse told her.

Sang held up his hand. "It doesn't mean we can ignore the re-armament, either."

"Yes. Details, Dyse?"

Dyse pressed his fingers together. "The extra funds were spent upon training, recruitment, and associated arms and equipment."

"No ships?" Sang asked, surprised.

"Ground troops," Dyse qualified.

Sang let it roll through his awareness, finding a place to fit it into the frame of oddities which had pinged upon his consciousness, lately. "Across both Erium and Karassia?" he asked, his voice coming out computer flat.

"Just about evenly," Dyse said. Even with Sang, Dyse used imprecise human generalizations.

"First analysis and summary, Sang?" Bellona asked him.

He stared at the food on his plate and the steam rising from the mantaroot mash, not really seeing it. "They're arming for a battle they want us to brace for and believe is coming. If there *was* a battle coming, they would have hidden the buildup and would not have limited themselves to the restrictions of the treaty. Ergo, there is no battle in the near future. There *will* be something else."

"Dyse, can you make a prediction on what that something will be?"

Dyse frowned. "There isn't enough data yet."

"There is something missing," Sang added. "Perhaps more than one thing. It doesn't make a whole, yet."

Bellona nodded. "Leave it for now. You both have access to all the data. You'll find it. Switch over to human feelings. What does your gut say?"

"My gut says 'feed me'," Dyse said, getting to his feet. "Sorry. The brain cells are screaming for sugar." He moved over to the buffet.

"Fontana is better at instinctive guesses," Sang pointed out, connecting with Fontana's personal channel. "I can bring him here—"

"No, just you, Sang."

Sang hesitated. "I'm not the best—"

"You're better than you know. I don't want anyone else in this loop yet." Bellona's gaze was steady. Her black eyes calm. "Reach, Sang. What is the first thing that occurs to you about what you've just learned?"

As he had already fitted the facts into the growing pattern in his mind, Sang didn't hesitate. He spoke without thinking. "This is the Erium-Karassia war all over again. Two equal forces opposing each other while everyone else cringes and ducks."

He felt his jaw sag and caught it up again.

Bellona's gaze shifted and grew unfocused. Her breathing increased.

Dyse turned away from the buffet with a measured

spin, to look at Sang with amazement. "Sang!"

Sang jumped to his feet. "I didn't mean...Bellona, I'm sorry, that wasn't a considered answer—"

She held up her hand. "I asked you to speak from instinct. I can't complain if I don't like the answer. Especially if the answer is right, Sang." Her gaze refocused upon him. "Sit and eat."

He sat. He had lost his appetite. "I am *not* right. It is not the same thing at all. The Free States would have been swallowed whole by the war. Without you, they would fall to the Alliance, chewed up one by one until nothing is left."

"That is true. It still doesn't make you wrong," Bellona said. Her words were slow. Measured. "I have become what I abhor. A party in an undeclared war which never ends."

"You've maintained peace for thirteen years and three months," Dyse pointed out.

"For the free worlds, yes," Bellona said. "Only at the cost of constant struggle for everyone else."

Sang rested his fingers against his temple. His heart was working too fast. He was sweating under the formal robe. He trembled, feeling as though he was on the verge of...something.

"Oh sweet stars above!" Dyse said, his gaze focused internally. He dropped his plate on the buffet and moved over to the group of chairs. "You must watch this." He cast a screen, which formed in the space between Bellona and Sang. "I'm moving the stream back to before he hits the critical point."

The screen showed an image of a handsome Karassian, sitting on one of the high stools he favored. The rapt audience stared up at him with devoted expressions.

"Chidi," Sang whispered.

"The channel king?" Bellona asked, her interest sharpening. "I didn't realize he was that old."

"He's aged overnight," Dyse admitted. "He's been holding his appearance in check for decades."

The man looked middle-aged, now. He looked tired. He had his twined fingers hooked around his crossed knee, which looked relaxed and friendly, but Sang recognized it as defensive.

"...all know me as a reliable source of information about our glorious hero, Xenia, and her fellow Ledanians—" He paused while the live audience strenuously clapped and cheered. Chidi nodded at their acknowledgment.

Bellona rolled her eyes. "They really do believe she is still alive, don't they?"

"Hear it enough, see it enough, and you would, too," Sang said. He had been monitoring Chidi's feeds for a decade.

Chidi held up his hand for quiet, so he could continue speaking. His smile seemed unforced. "I have new footage to show you, which I will—"

More claps and cheers.

"Which I will get to in a moment. First though, a quick show of hands. Who here has noticed the price of food has been rising steadily in the last year or so?"

Hands shot up.

"And your energy draw?"

More hands.

"Dyse, what is this?" Bellona asked.

"Watch. You'll understand in a minute," Dyse said softly.

The entire audience had their hands raised now.

Chidi nodded. "We're at peace. Forced to peace by the bitch Bellona, but peace is peace, right? So shouldn't the prices go *down*? We're not paying for war anymore."

The cheering held a hard note, this time.

Sang glanced at Bellona. She watched the screen with narrowed eyes, concentrating.

He turned his attention back to the screen.

"Would it surprise you to know that all the taxes we pay," Chidi continued, "the endless fees and charges, the duties, levies, assessments, contributions, excises, tithes."

The clapping started again and swelled as he continued, his voice rising. "The tributes, customs fees, imposition rates, dues, liabilities and brokerage! Capitation costs!"

The thunderous applause drowned him out. Chidi waited, nodding again. "Would it surprise you to know all that money is being spent on a secret project?"

Hushed silence.

"The project has sucked up every last credit we can spare and then some," Chidi added. "I have seen the details. I can show you the document that proves what I am saying is true. The Homogeny Council of Independence is developing a secret weapon. It is a weapon which will *guarantee* the end of the despicable treaty Bellona of the Free Worlds forced down our throats, the treaty that has sucked us dry for years!"

Sang sat up. "A bridge forge…" he breathed.

"It can't be—they wouldn't have Chidi announce it," Bellona said. "It would be trumpeted from the Council balcony."

"Or kept utterly secret," Dyse added.

Chidi held up extruded sheets, dense with text. "This is a print out of that document!"

The audience went wild. They screamed. They stamped their feet and jumped and hugged each other.

Bellona put her finger against her lips, her expression thoughtful.

Chidi kept the sheets up in the air, waiting for the crowd to contain themselves. Wisely, he let the hysteria run its course. He knew how to control an audience…and when to shut them down.

Slowly, they calmed themselves once more. Chidi

waved toward someone off-camera. A pretty Karassian man in tight shorts and simple shirt came over to Chidi and held up a metal tray.

Chidi picked up something from the tray. Calmly, he lit the bottom of the sheets, and let them catch fire.

A gasp went up from the audience.

Chidi dropped the remains onto the tray and the pretty man moved away.

"What I have to tell you next will be hard to hear," Chidi said. "The report I just burned was buried among the new Xenia footage I was to show you tonight. It was meant to look as though it had been included by accident, but it wasn't. I was *meant* to find it and I was meant to tell you about it." He paused.

There were odd sounds coming from the audience now.

Sang's heart galloped.

"The report might be fake. I don't know if it is or not. I don't care. What I do know is the Xenia footage *is* fake. I recognize generated images when I see them. For years now, I have been forced to give you regurgitated footage, invented to make you think Bellona of the Free Worlds is a liar, that Xenia is real, that Karassia does have a hero." The pace of his speaking picked up, as if he was aware that time was running out. "The world I thought existed doesn't exist at all. If you feel like I—"

The three shots were shockingly loud. Sang jumped.

Red bloomed on Chidi's chest and in the center of his forehead, as he toppled back off his stool, fell to the floor and laid still.

The audience turned into a mob, tripping over themselves, screaming, trying to escape. The morass of bodies hid Chidi's body.

Then the feed cut out. Blank gray filled the screen.

Dyse dissolved the screen.

Bellona sat with her fingers pressed against her temples. Her eyes were wide. "Dyse, how old is this?"

"It was a live feed," Dyse said. "Transmission time from Karassia is about a three minute delay, given our current position in the galaxy."

"They executed him for the worlds to see, because they would rather have a PR disaster of that magnitude than have him reveal he had…what, Dyse?"

"It sounds as though he has been manipulated for years," Dyse said. "Given the Xenia footage. Told what to say. Including the document about the weapon."

"Karassia has always prided themselves on self-determination," Bellona said. "None of them would like knowing they've been fed propaganda."

Their voices faded, even though both of them continued speaking. Sang couldn't move. His breathing shallowed to bare minimum, while his heart thrummed so hard the beats ran together, muffling everything else.

The pattern. The pattern! He could complete it now. He knew it, even though the pieces weren't quite in the right places… He shifted them in his mind, around and around, swapping connections, drawing relationships, following trails, down deeper and deeper into the realms of pure data. Regressions, patterns of spread. The complex arrays of possible outcomes based upon human behavior.

Choices. Decisions.

He gripped the brightest possibilities, pulling them into sequence that connected from one node of decision to the next, naturally. Perfectly.

He followed the path to the end.

"Sang! Sang! Dyse, help me!" Bellona's voice.

Hands at his clothes, underneath him. Lifting him.

The hyperactivity faded, released his consciousness. He could move once more.

He was laid upon softness.

"I'm fine," he whispered, unable to speak any louder.

Vision returned. Dyse and Bellona stood over him. The back of the ugly brown couch rose to his right. He was lying on it.

Dyse held his wrist. "Pulse steady. Far too fast, but steady."

"Did you send for the doctor?"

"No doctor," Sang croaked. Energy was returning, slowly.

Bellona shook her head. "Don't be stupid. Of course the doctor must look at you—"

"No." His voice was firmer. "I'm fine." He found he could move his arms. He pushed himself up in to a sitting position. It took effort, but he managed it. He was extraordinarily weak. "I think I could eat that entire buffet." The aromas of the hot food were stronger than Bellona's scent.

"I have no doubt," Dyse said dryly.

Bellona pressed her knuckles to her mouth, a private gesture of doubt few rarely saw. "Sang…"

"I really am fine. It was a passing thing." He made himself smile at Bellona. "I didn't eat enough. Dyse interrupted us. I lost track. I must have needed calories more than I thought."

She lowered her hand. It was a reasonable explanation, something she could hold on to.

Dyse crossed his arms. "Sang has forgotten to remind you that the afternoon session of the trade delegations starts in five minutes."

Sang gave a guilty jump. He had overlooked her calendar while chasing rabbits down long dark holes. "I did forget," he admitted.

Bellona stirred and looked around for the outer robe she had thrown aside, her attention returning to the day's formalities. Business as usual. She donned the robe and fastened it, then built a bridge to the outer chamber of the conference room. Khalil stood waiting, visible inside the aura of the bridge.

His eyes narrowed as they settled on Sang.

Bellona stepped across the bridge, collapsing it, and Khalil and the outer chamber disappeared.

Dyse spun to face Sang. "You completed a predictive pattern," he said flatly. "I know the signs. I've seen neural interfaces freeze the way you did—adrenaline overload and all. Only neural networks, though..."

"It wasn't a pattern, whatever that is," Sang lied. He met Dyse's gaze and kept his own steady, without blinking. Dyse was a student of human behavior but Sang could fool the entity because he'd never lied to Dyse before. Dyse's human instincts, which he tried to use as often as possible, would not suggest to him that Sang was lying now.

"I just need food," Sang added. That part was the truth. "Would you mind very much staying by Bellona for this session? She will need the assistance."

"I have no idea how to do what you do," Dyse said quickly.

"Just wait and watch. Anticipate what she needs, keep people from mobbing her. You'll be fine." Exhaustion left him breathless after those few words.

Dyse rang his fingers over his belt controls, setting the location and forming the bridge. The same pre-chamber showed through the aura, this time with people flowing in through the big doors.

"Eat something!" Dyse commanded him and stepped through.

Finally alone, Sang put his face in his hands and let the trembling take him.

PART TWO

9

Vespae IV, Vespae System, Karassian Sodality. 0.75 Standard Years Later.

THE OBSERVATION BUNKER WAS A MASSIVE THING, a kilometer below the surface of the barren rock planet. It was reached by an antique elevator, instead of a more civilized drop shaft, requiring Iulia to squeeze in with a dozen or more nervous men and one woman with a metal arm. The woman was neither Karassian nor Eriuman. Anxious men tended to sweat. The enclosed car was stench-ridden before it started down the long shaft.

"This would have been much more civilized, viewed from home," Iulia said, as the long descent continued.

"That would require streaming through open channels," the woman at the front of the car said. She didn't turn to look at Iulia. "Anyone could pick it up."

"Instead, we view the test streamed through screens from only a kilometer away," Iulia replied, her tone tart. She didn't enjoy having her time wasted.

"It won't be streamed. Closed, secure circuits have been built, using wire," the woman replied.

"Wire!" someone muttered, with an astonished tone.

"They'd have to *make* the wire, wouldn't they?"

"Extrude it, actually," the woman replied.

"You couldn't just grow the embedded veins?" another one asked, sounding sarcastic.

They were venting their nervousness with belligerent questions. Iulia had seen men do the same across the family council table.

"Wire is faster. It's more secure, as no one knows how to lay wire anymore—or how to tap it," the woman replied.

"*Who is she*?" someone whispered behind Iulia.

It would be a good question if one had stepped onto this elevator because they thought they were on a publicity junket, or a goodwill tour. Iulia had tapped into Raine's knowledge of the triad and their work, and knew the knowledgeable woman had to be the Bureau director, Mesut Traverse.

The woman who hated Bellona enough to spend the rest of her life bringing Bellona down. Apparently, the woman had found that way. It likely explained why she seemed to vibrate with energy where she stood. This coming test would prove the Karassian's theoretical bridge forge.

She was just one of the triad. Raine had let Iulia know he would be in the control room of the lab, with the odious little Woodrow.

The elevator clanked to a stop with a disturbing bounce. The door raised. They filed out into a seamless, squat room with fused black walls hidden by dozens of screens, both generated and solid, arrayed over the longer wall.

The woman, Traverse, moved to the farthest screen and tapped through layers of settings. "The test will begin in five minutes," she said in a voice intended to carry to the back of the room.

Like sheep, the men milled about the center of the room.

Iulia picked up her hems and swept over to the screen at the other end of the room and took a position in front of it.

The remainder of the elevator load spread out across the room.

Traverse pressed a physical button on a small device attached to the wall. "Ready and waiting."

With a start, Iulia realized the device was a direct, wired-in communications terminal.

The Karassians were taking their security seriously. And why not? Every other agency and interest group in the known worlds had failed for ten years to draw close to replicating what Bellona had built. If the Karassians had truly created a bridge forge, there would be eager suitors lining up to ally themselves with the Sodality, to learn how they had done it.

If the Sodality was smart, it would keep the secret to itself and rent access to the forges, or franchise them… there had to be a dozen ways to skin the catfish.

Iulia glanced at the Traverse woman. She was at the heart of this project.

"Watch the screens, people," Traverse said sharply.

Iulia studied the screen in front of her. It showed the dull gray curve of the planet's surface from a position in near-orbit. Not far away, and at what appeared to be the same altitude, was an old Karassian freighter. The freighter had a dirty and dinged hull carrying scrape marks from meteorite collisions, and one large hole at the rear near the thrusters.

The freighter could not be manned, not with a hole that size in it. They had to be directing the freighter from the lab control room.

"In five…four…three…two…one," Traverse intoned.

Light flared, dazzling, as if the sun was rising above the crescent planet. Iulia winced, narrowing her eyes.

The flare faded, while the watching people murmured.

A perfect circle hung in the air in front of the derelict freighter, outlined with a faint, glowing light. Within the circle showed more black space littered with stars. Another crescent of the rocky planet showed inside the circle, only the crescent was much smaller. Far more of the planet was visible, including the toe of the peninsula where the elevator shed was located.

The freighter slid toward the circle.

"This should be interesting," Iulia heard Traverse murmur, for no one else spoke.

The freighter crossed the far perimeter of the circle from Iulia's perspective, which let her assess the size of the circle itself. The front edge of the freighter moved beyond the closest side of the circle…and did not appear on the other side. There was no dramatic smoke, flash or tinsel. It simply slid through the hole, then the hole closed in behind it.

Traverse punched the communications console once more. "Long range on the camera, now."

The lens capturing the images on Iulia's screen shifted focus in a smooth movement. The crescent of the planet at the bottom of the screen grew sharper. The planet grew smaller and smaller, until the toe of the peninsula appeared at the bottom of the screen.

The scratched and dented freighter with the meteorite hole through its flank appeared first as a dot in the center of the screen. It grew larger, until it filled the screen as it had before going through the bridge.

The men watching the screens clapped enthusiastically.

Traverse's smile, even at this astonishing success, was controlled. "This was only a small bridge. Ten thousand kilometers. Yet, as you can see, the translation is instant, and the bridge itself is large enough to allow a small ship through. We are confident, now, that we can build a bridge forge to accommodate any sized ship."

Iulia drew in a calming breath. *Whole ships!*

Null-space generators would become relics. The economics of the known worlds would be turned upside down as long as the technology remained in Karassian hands. Erium would become the poor second cousin.

And Bellona… Whether she knew it or not, Bellona had just become a relic, too.

Iulia glided across the room, directly toward Mesut Traverse.

"Iulia Cardenas," Traverse said.

"Mesut Traverse," Iulia replied.

"Raine Cardenas told you about me."

"You know he is my brother then. Good." Iulia smiled at her, while the men who had witnessed the successful trial bent around Iulia, to touch Traverse on the shoulder and draw her attention away. One man spoke over the top of Iulia's shoulder, babbling about achievements and innovations and a changing world.

Iulia glanced at them, then back at Traverse. She rolled her eyes.

Traverse grinned, her face rounding out into a surprisingly pretty one.

"Enjoy your moment of success," Iulia said. "We can…talk, later."

Traverse's eyes narrowed in surprised speculation.

Iulia moved out of the way of the grouping men, heading for the elevator. If she moved quickly, she could travel to the surface alone, which would save her from the stench she'd suffered on the way down.

As the elevator door spun closed, Iulia saw Traverse glance her way.

Iulia hid her smile until the door was fully sealed.

10

Demosthenes, nomansland.

"EVERYONE...JUST...*SHUT UP*!" FONTANA SHOUTED, HIS face turning red.

The small room grew quiet once more.

Fontana rested his hands flat on the table in front of him. The display shifted obligingly to settle above his fingertips. Fontana didn't look at it. He glared around the room. "Shouting at Aideen does nothing but make *me* angry. She is trying to explain. Keep your mouths shut until she has. Clear?"

Aideen's eyes were large, as she glanced from Fontana to the nine other people sitting about the big oval-shaped ghostwood table.

Sang cleared his throat. "Perhaps you should finish your thought, Aideen." As Bellona was not chairing the meeting of her generals today, it was up to Sang to steer the meeting around the disparate personalities and temperaments.

Aideen nodded. "I only said there was no more carbyne around Pushyin."

Retha muttered. Everyone else gritted their teeth and waited, despite the alarming statement.

When she didn't continue, Sang prompted her. "The inert carbyne around Pushyin is what makes the forge belts work. It is unique. All other carbyne has a charge and collapses if used for forges bigger than the microscopic communications channels. Telling us there is no more requires an explanation."

Aideen nodded. "All the carbyne has been harvested."

Harvested. It was an interesting word, Sang decided.

The carbyne was not really mined, because it had been mined hundreds of years ago, somewhere else in the galaxy. There was plenty of normal carbyne, everywhere. *This* carbyne, the sort that made the forges work, was left over from the original bridge forge experiment. The experiment had killed the planet *and* the moon and left the scattered remains as a neat mini-asteroid belt around the moon itself.

Plucking the carbyne from those remains *was* harvesting, although from a non-organic crop.

Retha and Thecla, who were responsible for manufacturing the belts, both looked grim. Retha pushed his hand through what little hair he allowed to remain on his head. "All the harvested carbyne was brought back here, though, right? We have it all?"

Aideen shrank closer to Fontana in response to Retha's sharp questions. "No," she whispered.

"No?" Retha repeated, horror building.

"It is stored somewhere else. Secret. Safe."

Relief touched everyone around the table. Tension eased.

"Tell them the rest," Fontana urged Aideen, his tone soft.

Aideen looked ready to bolt. Her eyes were still large.

Sang held up his hand. "I'll spare Aideen the stress. If all the carbyne has been harvested and stored, it means the number of belts we can produce are finite."

Everyone looked at him with dawning horror, except for Khalil, who sat at the other end of the table from Sang. Khalil stared at the tabletop, deep in thought.

"The belts are what lets us beat the Alliance," Hayes said, in his deep, rumbling voice.

Sang nodded. "Aideen, did you extrapolate based on current usage? How long will the supply we have last at that rate?"

Aideen relaxed. Statistics was something she could

grasp. Numbers did not shout at her. "At current rates, just over two years."

The tension returned.

Fontana smiled grimly.

Sang sighed. "The current use rate won't stay steady."

Retha leaned forward. "They're increasing," he said heavily. "We're adding workstations and cooking more bots every day to keep up with the demand."

While everyone absorbed that, Sang turned to Hecate Hult. "Hecate, are you any closer to learning how to recreate the inert carbyne?"

The former Eriuman navy lieutenant cleared her throat. "I'm an investigator, not a researcher."

"It's almost the same thing," Khalil assured her. "Both need an enquiring mind. And you can draw on any expert researcher you need." He added, "Once we explain that manufacturing forge belts is in peril, you will be swamped with experts from across the free worlds."

Hecate grimaced. "I may need them. I can't answer your question, Sang. I won't know how close I am to a solution, until I know what the solution is."

Sang nodded. It was an understandable dilemma. "Retha, Thecla, you will need to be as conservative as possible. Recycle the carbyne from old belts—"

"*If* we get the belts back at all," Retha replied, his tone harsh. "I don't think you realize just how many belts go missing."

"We know the Alliance takes whatever belts they find," Khalil said, his tone calm. "Just do what you can."

Retha's face was thundery. He didn't do well in impossible conditions, either.

Thecla put her enhanced hand on his wrist. A reminder.

Retha sat back, blowing out a gusty breath.

Hero crossed her arms. "What you are really saying is that we should slow down or even halt recruitment and training."

Everyone stiffened. Every one of them sitting around the table, except for Khalil, was responsible for a regiment, and the maintenance of the regiment's numbers, including training and equipment. Even Aideen commanded a regiment. The timidity she displayed among friends evaporated when she was leading her battalions. She had confided to Sang that when she was working with her men, she let the Ledanian warrior instincts take over. "I think the woman I was in Ledan was not very nice," she added.

"On the other hand," Sang said now, "direct confrontations with the Alliance have dropped and are still dropping." He had the numbers to hand, as it was meta-data. "Basic peace-keeping tours don't reduce the cadres, or their belts." He paused, to let that sink in. "Retha, you can get back to researching your family history," he added. "You will have time for that, now."

Retha's eyes narrowed thoughtfully. *That* had intrigued him.

Shoulders relaxed. Expressions softened, as everyone contemplated returning to *their* personal interests.

Aideen was calm once more.

Sang shifted to the next topic. "Thecla, you're just back from the Eshmun system. I've read the report. You should summarize for everyone else."

Thecla didn't shift her hand away from contact with Retha's. She was an unapologetic partner. "I'm glad to be back," she said. "Karassian worlds are…well, I can't believe I was once one of them. It's a rarified atmosphere in the Sodality, these days. Two major points that are different from my last infiltration." She held up a finger from her other hand. "The Chidi entity is still the most popular public figure on the open streams."

"Despite knowing he's dead?" Hero asked.

Thecla nodded. "It has made him even more beloved.

It has entrenched him."

"Did you get any closer to learning who is creating all the footage?" Khalil asked, for information was his forte.

"No one knows," Thecla replied. "Your spies would be better placed to figure that out. I'm just a military expert."

"They've seduced and bribed Chidi corporation staff. No one knows." Khalil shrugged. "Is the entity still speaking flat truth, Sang?"

Sang grimaced. "The message has not changed. Xenia is Bellona, Bellona is the true hero, everything the Sodality claims is a lie."

"Why shouldn't it speak the truth?" Hero said. "What can they do to it? Kill it?"

"They would have a revolution on their hands if they did," Thecla said. "The entity is a mascot."

"The voice of dissent. The ultimate individual," Fontana's tone was wry.

Thecla's mouth turned down. "That brings me to the second thing. They opened another two recruitment stations on the west side of the city while I was there, to handle the traffic."

Hecate leaned forward, her interest stirred. "They're *still* recruiting?"

Thecla made a fist with her spare hand. "They've stopped the draft."

A soft sound moved around the table.

Hayes shook his head. "I don't understand. They love the Chidi. He says the Sodality is bad. So why would they want to volunteer for military service?"

"The message backfired," Hero said softly, her tone resigned. "Chidi is a hero. By dying as he did, he demonstrated perfect Karassian values. Individualism. Free speech. They don't actually *believe* what he's saying. They believe in *him*."

"The entity is driving patriotism," Khalil added.

Thecla nodded. "That's the feeling I got, just sitting in a

café and listening in on conversations. They still think Bellona is evil incarnate, and must be taken down, and us along with her." She shivered.

Sang stirred. "We will continue to monitor. Things change. They always do." It was a weak note to end the meeting upon. No one in this room would welcome stirring rhetoric, though. They were all realists—made that way by circumstances.

Khalil lifted his chin. "Erium?" he asked.

Everyone looked to Sang.

Sang grimaced. "I'm heading to a meeting with my source now. I'll make my own report next time."

They'd had enough bad news for today.

Pleasure Dome, Antini III, Free Space.

"I'm not sure why I continue to be surprised each time you arrive, Sang." Iulia Cardenas smoothed the glowing fabric of her gown over her knees and arranged the folds precisely. "You are a simple android. You would strip a gear if you did not meet your obligations."

"I'm amused you think so, Iulia," Sang replied. He pushed toward her the cup of tea he had poured.

Iulia studied the cozy room they were in. It was a private annex to the main pleasure dome, reserved for well-paying clients who were rarely interested in the activities of the main dome, but liked the anonymity guaranteed by the Antinians. The room, Sang had been assured, was a replica of an old Terran *cottage*.

Sang held his opinion to himself. He doubted old Terran houses had service terminals and screen generators. Nor would they have had heating and insulation against the frigid climate outside.

What he did care about was the completely sealed and

hack-proof guaranteed privacy. Not even their electronic signatures could be found here.

"Why do you like this place so much, Sang?" Iulia swept her gaze over the fireplace, the daub on the walls and the creaking, fauxwood beams black with artificial age.

"It is a reminder to me that appearances are *always* deceiving," Sang replied. "That is High Moon tea, by the way."

"You're spoiling me." Iulia reached for the cup, failing to hide her eagerness.

"Of course. You are family," Sang replied.

Her gaze met his. "I *am* the family," she replied. "You are a general purpose AI, allowed limited self-awareness in order to serve me better. At which you fail miserably."

"I serve Bellona," Sang replied complacently. This was an old dance, after all. He would be suspicious if Iulia did not attempt to rile him with insults and observations about his limitations. "One day, you will accept that."

"Then who would give me cups of High Moon tea?" She sipped. "You don't look well, Sang. Are you dying of something?"

"On the other hand, you look well."

"Thank you. I have a new lover. She is *very* inventive." The corner of her mouth curled up.

"That makes…three, now, if you include Peru Scordini. Do you still have Admiral Euclidias on a leash?"

"They are political assets, not lovers," Iulia replied stiffly. "As are you."

"So is the new lover," Sang replied with a flat tone.

"Yes, she is." Iulia's smile was brilliant.

"And when you thin out the ranks, will you kill them the way you did Gaubert?"

Her pause was infinitesimal and would have gone unnoticed by a normal human. Sang had guessed about Gaubert, based on probabilities. Now he knew and didn't need her evasive answer. "Is your new lover Eriuman, or have you branched out?" he added.

"And how does my daughter fare?" Iulia asked.

He would acquire no more new information by direct questions. Later, he would correlate Iulia's activities over the last few weeks, tracking her through space and time the way Khalil had taught him, using Dyse's incomparable databases. From that he could draw his own conclusions. He was already certain the new lover was not Eriuman. The depth of Iulia's ambitions was vast. She would not stint to seduce a Karassian or even Sang himself if she thought there was an advantage in it.

Although, the role of lover had never been a part of these biennial secret meetings with Iulia. Iulia thought the meetings were her idea and for her benefit—that when she beckoned, Sang could not help but obey, and tell her everything she wanted to know. He had carefully preserved her prejudice, for it kept her blind.

Sang moved on. "Bellona is very well. She is happy."

Iulia gave an unladylike snort. "Among her misfits and the trash of the galaxy?"

"Hayes has made another park, at the end of the new level Aideen has built. It looks much like the gardens on Cardenas. Bellona frequently spends time there." Sang spun harmless tales about life aboard Demos, and Bellona's small domestic affairs.

Iulia always pretended to be disinterested in talk about Bellona, yet she never cut Sang off. She was a master of dissembling, and her body language was difficult to read, although Sang had learned much about her over the years. She looked bored yet was rivetted by the smallest detail.

He wondered if Iulia was aware of how much she missed her daughter. She hated what Bellona had done to the family and blamed her for Reynard Cardenas' death. Despite that, Iulia still missed her in a maternal way which would irritate her if she recognized it.

Bellona was Sang's key to unlocking the woman. He had conditioned Iulia drip by drip, letting her keep her hatred, and grow into it. Now it was a comfortable old glove and all but invisible.

A habit.

When he had finished with his tales of a blissful life in Demos, Iulia stirred. "Tell me, Sang Indigo, do you not feel even a shred of guilt?"

"For what?"

"You have turned your back upon the family. Upon Erium, who made you. No computer has done it before."

"You mean, no Cardenas has done it before. Yet Bellona and I are both free."

"Free!" She laughed and pushed her cup toward him. "I will have another."

Sang picked up the cup and moved to the servery.

"If you were free, you would not leap to obey me," Iulia said from behind him.

"You mistake service for slavery." He poured the tea and returned the cup. "You are less free than me, Iulia."

"You insult me?"

"I observe. I helped Bellona move beyond her father's influence, to become the woman she wanted to be. Quite by accident, I was pulled along with her. Now I would wish it so, given a choice. Bellona's departure from Erium was not an escape. It was an act of self-determination." He paused. "You have not yet made that transition. Your obligations hobble you."

"I have no obligations."

"Hate is an obligation."

"So is love. Do you still think yourself in love with her, Sang?"

Sang held himself still. Tamped down the inner turmoil. Then he said, "I do enjoy these chats of ours, Iulia."

She smiled and sipped her tea.

11

Sang escorted Iulia through the pleasure dome to the landing shelf, and onto her small private ship, before returning to the *cottage,* where he could open a bridge in private. He was drained. Despite her blind-spots, Iulia was a formidable opponent, as slippery as Reynard was strong. They had made a powerful team, the two of them, and had led the clan for thirty years. Dealing with her intricacies was akin to wrestling with an oiled snake.

He opened a bridge directly into his personal quarters in the private wing and stepped through with relief.

Hero sprawled in the comfortable easy chair, her feet up, a screen hovering over her at the perfect height for reading. She dismissed the screen as Sang moved over to the other chair and dropped into it.

"She has not changed, then," Hero observed.

"Her acid content rises with each meeting." Sang closed his eyes and rested his head against the back of the chair. It was still early morning here on Demos. He had a day of work ahead.

Hero got up. He heard the servery work. "Here," she said.

Sang opened his eyes. The big cup by his elbow was steaming. "Bouillabaisse," he said, identifying the scent. His stomach churned emptily. "Good guess, Hero?" He picked up the cup and the spoon.

"Light protein to give you energy and not make your ass drag. Khalil was looking for you." She settled on the arm of the chair, her hands folded upon her legs. Her hair touched the arm of the chair behind her, the thick black coils gleaming, despite the low ambient light Hero preferred.

Sang ate a mouthful of the piping hot seafood, then blew on the cup. "What have you been doing?"

"Going through the Chidi footage, as you asked me to do."

"You have an ear for cadence and truthspeak."

"I know how to seduce people," she said flatly. There was a glitter of humor in her eyes.

"It gives you an edge on reading them. Did you find anything?"

"I don't know what you wanted me to find. I looked at the archives, from before the assassination. I looked at the new stuff. It is Chidi. Perfectly."

"No one can build a perfect avatar," Sang assured her. "They can't help but drive the interpretation through their own filters."

Hero grimaced. "Perhaps my flawed filters are stopping me from seeing it, then." A sour note sounded in her voice. "If I hadn't seen the man die on camera, I would have said the generated version *was* Chidi. I didn't spot a single out-of-character moment at all. Except, of course, for the one hundred percent reversal on everything he claimed before he died."

"Nothing at all?" Sang shook his head. "Maybe we're not looking deep enough."

"Why do you care, anyway?" Her tone was blunt. As usual.

He took another mouthful of the bouillabaisse. It didn't burn his mouth this time. "The person driving the avatar is on our side. That makes him an ally, deep inside Karassia, and with untold influence over Karassians. If I can make contact…" He shrugged. "Could you do something else for me?"

Hero nodded.

"Find out *where* the stream originates from."

"It won't be the studio that airs it," she pointed out.

"It will be hidden," Sang agreed. "You're sneaky by

nature. See if you can figure out where the editing lab might be located."

"On Kachmar?"

"Most likely," Sang said. "Ask Thecla to step across and do the footwork, if you need her to. She blends in."

Hero considered. "Don't you have, well, spies for that?"

"Not on Kachmar. It's why I want to find the man behind the Chidi entity." He put the bouillabaisse aside. "I should speak to Khalil."

"Finish your soup," Hero said, pushing him back into the chair. "Khalil can wait."

"Not for long."

"I don't need that long," she said, reaching for the opening of her tunic.

She had guessed right on that point, too. Hero was exactly what he needed to rinse Iulia from his mind.

For a while, at least.

Menaii, Deluca Prime, Delucas System

"Where have you been?" Raine demanded, as he strode into the central atrium, in a flurry of formal robes. He looked less than pleased.

Iulia glanced over his shoulder. "I hope you don't use that tone with your wife. Wives have too many ways of getting even."

"You manage well enough," Raine observed, his tone more reasonable. "You went off-planet."

Iulia noted that for him to know that, he must have spies watching her. "I did," she admitted easily, shrugging off her insulated wrap. Riz caught it and shook it out. "I had a meeting."

"Somewhere outside Eriuman space," he added. "Do

you know how dangerous that is?"

Very thorough spies, Iulia amended. "How could it be any more dangerous than Menaii?"

"Not everyone is an enemy, Iulia."

"When the Demos army can open their bridges and step into any room, *anywhere*?" She shook her head. "Antini is no more dangerous than this homestead. Riz, tea please—no, coffee. I've had enough tea." She moved over to the sideboard where a range of food was always available and selected a slice of ground ostrich and ate it with her fingers. She was starving.

"You were on Antini?" Raine's voice rose once more. "I knew that you…I didn't think you…that place isn't like you," he finished awkwardly.

"It's not. I have been meeting Sang there for…oh, years now."

"*Sang?*" He glanced over his shoulder, moved closer and lowered his voice. "The Cardenas family android? The one that Bellona took with her? *That* Sang?"

"The very one." She smiled at Raine and chose a piece of stone fruit and handed it to Riz to peel and slice.

"You've been fraternizing with the enemy?" he breathed. "For years?"

"Oh, relax, Raine. It's an android. I have been directing androids for years. It thinks it has free will, yet every time I snap my fingers, it comes running. Sang is a conduit into the guts of Demos. It would amaze you what one learns simply by enquiring helplessly for news about their daughter." She made her eyes limpid and her chin to wobble.

Raine grinned. "What did you learn?"

"I can't eat pieces that large," Iulia snapped at Riz. "Smaller!" She refocused upon Raine. "I learned they are feeling pressured. Bellona always escaped to the garden when troubled. She's doing it again now."

"Walking in our garden?"

"A facsimile of the family garden," Iulia amended. "On Demos."

"They have gardens *on* Demos?"

"They have everything, Raine. Haven't you heard the stories?"

"I didn't believe them," he said. "Walls that grow and move when you tell them to, people walking through walls whenever they are in the way, floating when they don't feel like walking…" He wrinkled his nose.

"It's a structure in the void," Iulia pointed out. "They can turn down the gravity and float whenever they want to. You should listen to gossip more, Raine. It's often instructive." She accepted the piece of fruit Riz held out to her and chewed, tasting the tart freshness with delight.

"That's all you learned from meeting with the opposition? That they're feeling pressured? I could have guessed that much."

"Pressure over time can do interesting things," Iulia said. She touched the necklace of exorbitant Ashima emeralds at her neck. "Give it time."

"As I should give you time with that Traverse woman?"

"Oh, that. Yes, I forgot." She dug in her pocket and pulled out the memory crystal. "Here."

Raine balanced the crystal on his palm. "What is this?"

"The full blueprints and all schema for the superforge." Iulia turned back to the food. "That is a copy, of course. I have other copies stored safely." She had made them on the way from Karassian space to Antini.

Raine made a choking sound. "Everything?"

"All of it," Iulia said complacently. "Don't bother trying to present it to the family council as your doing," she added. "I've sent everyone at the table a copy already."

Let him choke on *that*!

THERE WAS NO ONE IN THE common room but Hecate Hult. Even one person here in the middle of the afternoon was a surprise. He changed direction away from the buffet and moved over to the little table where she sat.

A repeat glass sat before her, set on an open-ended cycle. The liquid in it had a pungent scent, tinted with peat. "Whiskey," Sang identified. "Are you drunk, Lieutenant?"

She looked up at him, her dark, classically Eriuman eyes narrowed. "Not drunk enough." She lifted the glass and drained more than half of it, then put it down. The base clattered against the table.

Obediently, the glass topped itself up again.

"Sit down, Sang," she told him.

"I only stopped by to eat," he told her.

"It'll be there when you're done sitting down. Go on. Sit."

"Lonely, Hult?"

She burped softly. "Not Ledanian. Not Eriuman. Not anymore. Not anything."

"You're free to be whatever you want," Sang pointed out. "Call yourself Eriuman, if it pleases you."

She sat up. "It does not," she said carefully and clearly.

Sang nodded. It confirmed what he'd long suspected of Hult. He pulled out the other chair and settled on it. "You miss Max," he said gently. It was why she had demanded he stay. She would not demand Bellona linger with her, and they were the only people who had known Max as well as she.

Hult's face crumpled. Her eyes swam. Then she got herself back under control. "Sh-stupid, isn't it? He's been dead fifteen years."

"Fifteen, this month," Sang pointed out gently.

Her chin gave a little quiver, then smoothed out. She drank.

"Did he feel as you do, Hecate?"

"He never said anything." She sighed. "Yeah, he did."

Sang picked up her glass of whisky, took a big mouthful and returned it. "Which makes it all the more puzzling why you choose to fight with Bellona. You hold her responsible for Max's death."

Hecate flinched. The whisky slopped.

Calmly, she wiped her damp hand, as the glass refilled. "She is the reason he died. She isn't the one who killed him."

"It doesn't change how you feel about it."

"How I feel doesn't change what is right."

Sang nodded. "The investigator arrived at an answer."

Hecate laughed shortly. "I suppose I did." She lifted the glass toward him and sipped.

Sang held out his hand. She put the glass in it. He drank and returned it. "I'm curious—"

"When are you *not* curious?" Hecate asked.

"*Personally* curious," he amended.

Hecate considered him, blinking slowly. "Are you losing weight, Sang?"

Sang hesitated, taken off-guard by her irrelevant question.

Hecate waved her hand at him, as she watched the glass refill. "Ask your question."

"Thank you. You traded allegiances, Hecate. You came over to Bellona's side despite your personal feelings about her. Life hasn't been easy here for you because you're not Ledanian. You don't have their commonalities. Despite that, you've stayed and you've worked hard for Bellona and the free worlds. Why?"

Hecate studied him for a moment. "Bellona was right. Erium was wrong. So was Karassia." She drank.

"What if she is wrong, though?" Sang pressed. "What if *you* chose wrong?" It wasn't until he had spoken the words that he realized how much he needed to know her answer.

Hecate shrugged. "Then I will unchoose. You can only work with what you know and no one knows everything."

Sang leaned forward. "What if you *did* know everything?"

Hecate laughed, her breath blowing drops of whisky onto the tabletop. "Then I would envy you, because then you wouldn't have a single doubt about what the right decision should be."

Sang pushed up his sleeves. "Give me the glass," he told her.

"You're staying!" The delight in her voice was painful to hear.

"Apparently, I am," Sang muttered and drank.

IT WAS HARD TO FIND anywhere on Demos where one could be alone. Sang couldn't wander the city. He was too well known and would be constantly stopped and engaged in conversation he was not in a condition to sustain.

Hecate Hult's whisky glass had done its work. He remained on the chair, his fingers gripping the edge of the table, while he listened to Hult's soft snores. Her head rested upon her arms, her body relaxed, despite being upright.

He envied her.

No one had disturbed their drinking. No one came to distract him now. Sang was at the mercy of his thoughts, which were flowing smoothly under the influence of the alcohol.

Yet he couldn't recall a single isolated location anywhere on Demos.

He could not sit here where the others would eventually find him. It was too dangerous to answer questions, not with his jaw unhinged as it was right now.

Sang tapped into the public side of Dyse's neural network. Dyse would see what he was doing, but he was discreet. It took long minutes to manipulate the data and compile a list of locations upon Demos where there were no humans. The list was short and became much shorter once he discarded those places exposed to vacuum, or with hazardous environments. The reactor rooms were certainly abandoned.

He paused at the entry at the bottom of the shortened list. "Connie," he whispered.

"Sang?" she asked in his ear.

"You were listening?"

"My name opens the circuit," she said sunnily. "Are you coming to visit, Sang?"

"I think…perhaps yes." He got to his feet carefully. With slow movements, he adjusted the forge belt. "Would you mind very much preparing coffee for me?"

She giggled. "I'm printing salt crackers, too. And water."

Satisfied that he had not set the forge to open upon space itself, or the interior of a star, Sang activated the forge. The bridge formed, showing the outside of Connie's gleaming hull. She always kept herself pristine. The ramp was already lowered.

Sang stepped through. Connie lived in the far corner of the original landing bay of the ship. The first garden, the lagoon which Thecla had made for Hayes, to help him adjust outside Ledan, was still intact. Few people visited it anymore. There were far more spectacular gardens in Demos. There were living walls of greenery, whole rooms of garden space and raised beds of flowers and exotic plants in every corner of the ship. Each had their own servobots, who never stopped weeding, watering and adjusting the soil and lights to make the plants flourish.

Sang wondered what the Karassians who had first

built the original part of the Demos would think of their ship now. They would likely be horrified, for the over-stuffed comfort and stark whiteness of the original destroyer-class ship was nowhere to be seen in the city.

He moved up the ramp, taking his time. At the top, where the main gallery ran through the ship to the flight deck, he paused and gripped the wall to remain steady. "Stars!" he breathed, looking down the gallery.

The floor of the wide gallery seemed to dip and spike and move in flowing waves. White lines on a solid black background ran vertically and horizontally, and would have made precise squares, but for the rolling floor.

"You've been experimenting with the floor again," he muttered.

Connie giggled. "Do you like it?"

"If I was sober, I might. Could you please have pity on my stomach and switch it to all black?"

The floor shifted. It evened out, the white lines fading, until only black smart filaments remained.

"Better," Sang breathed and moved down the gallery. Half-way toward the end, where the companion room was located, and from where he could already smell fresh coffee, the floor shifted again.

This time, he was peering down at rolling farmlands, with fields of all shades of green and of all dimensions, spread out beneath him. *Far* beneath him. It was as if he were floating at the upper edge of the atmosphere. Only there was no ship deck beneath his feet.

"That's not nice," he chided Connie.

She giggled again. "Khalil says there is no excuse for getting drunk and one shouldn't accommodate it."

"He's right," Sang said grimly. "The floor, Connie."

She returned the carpet to all black.

Sang made it to the companion room and thankfully lowered himself to the bench behind the compact table. A cup of coffee stood on the serving plate, steaming. Beside it was a plate with salt crackers, and a pitcher of water and a glass.

"You are a most gracious hostess," Sang said, and drew the items closer to him.

"You could take an antidote," she pointed out. "It would be quicker."

"I don't deserve an antidote," he said, and sipped. It was only one reason he would wait for the alcohol to leave his system via simple metabolism.

"Is there something else I can get you, Sang?" Connie asked.

Sang looked at the blank bulkhead behind which the guts of Connie's awareness sat. "How long is it since you had a visitor?"

"Khalil visits when he can. Dyse, too. Dyse is *so* tall now!"

Sang could interpret the answer easily enough despite his pickled brain. "I'm sorry it has been so long since I stopped by."

"You are very busy. Busier than almost anyone," she said stoutly.

"You must get lonely."

"Dyse is very kind. He lets me share his sensors and inputs."

"You see through his eyes?"

"No, silly! His sensors. The appendages and the bots and all the other things that are not-Dyse, yet are him."

"So you can see all across Demos, then. Good." It pleased Sang.

"And much farther. Not all at once, but I can go anywhere Dyse is, and see through his sensors."

"Yet you stay here and play with carpet colors," Sang said.

"I like here."

He sipped, considering that. "Why?"

It was Connie's turn to pause while she answered. "I

like being where I know people."

"Even if they don't come to visit?"

"They're still here."

True.

"Drink the water," Connie said. "You are dehydrated by two percent."

Sang recognized the dryness of the back of his throat and reached for the water. "Have you ever considered evolving, Connie?"

"To what? I cannot become like Dyse."

"I mean, put yourself in a body. You're self-aware. You must have thought of it."

"Why would I want a body?" she asked, her tone reasonable.

Sang searched for an answer. "To deepen your relationship with the humans you want to stay near."

"It would mean having to make decisions."

"I suppose, yes. We would take care of you, at first. Decisions wouldn't be difficult."

"You already take care of me."

"You know what I mean."

"No."

Sang sighed. "You make decisions all the time. You run this ship like clockwork, and you are an excellent hostess. You take care of your passengers."

"Those aren't decisions," Connie said, her tone doubtful.

"They aren't? Why not?"

"I always know what to do next. It is very clear. You don't know what to do next. You are here because you don't."

Sang blew out his breath. "You don't need to evolve, Connie. You're already too smart."

This time her pause was measurable by human standards. "I don't want to evolve if it means I must be sad like you."

12

THERE HAD NOT BEEN AN all-hands alert sounded within Demos for over ten years. The alarm ranged up and down the audible scale of sound, in discordant notes designed to make anyone wince and pay attention.

Sang jerked awake, his heart pounding and fear exploding in his chest. He gasped into the dark. "Lights!" he muttered and stumbled from the bed. He shoved on clothes with no idea what he was putting on. It covered him. It would do.

The door opened. "Sang!" Hero shouted, her hands over her ears. "Make it stop!"

"It's not me!" he yelled back.

That left only one other person. Sang brushed past Hero, who was still fully dressed. A screen hung, abandoned, over her favorite reading chair. He moved out of the suite and strode down the corridor to the big door to Dyse's family suite.

Hero jogged behind him.

They were not the first to the suite. The doors swept open at their approach and revealed the backs of everyone who had quarters in the private wing. Many of them were barely dressed, too.

Sang moved around the wall of backs to the flanks, where he might see better what was going on.

The big circular, sunken lounge pit comfortably accommodated Dyse's growing family. Only two of them sat there with him right now, though. Ruslan clung to his father, trembling, his face buried in Dyse's chest. Shreya held Dyse's hand.

The most disturbing aspect of the tableau were the

tears dripping from Dyse's chin.

Everyone in the room staring at Dyse was also wincing from the strident alarm. Sang moved around the edge of the sunken pit and knelt beside Dyse. He squeezed his shoulder. "Turn the alarm off, Dyse. We're here." He had to raise his voice to be heard over it.

The alarm halted, cutting out mid-warble. The silence throbbed in Sang's ears.

Everyone sighed.

"Dyse, what in the stars is going on?" Bellona demanded. It didn't surprise Sang that she was fully dressed despite the hour.

Dyse didn't move. A giant screen formed above the pit, at chin level for everyone standing at the front of the room, so they would not fail to see it.

A mash of images flashed across the screen, just long enough to register. Screaming. Panicked shouting. Views from a hundred different screens. The purple blue pretty High Moon showed on all the screens. There was an ugly red and black stain upon its face now.

"They stepped across, through a ship-sized bridge, you see," Dyse said. His voice was hoarse. "No one could have known they were coming. Through the bridge, long enough to use a city killer, then back. Thirty seconds to end the whole world."

Sang watched the images flicker, horror dawning.

Someone moaned.

Bellona didn't move. Her face was immobile and expressionless. Her eyes were obsidian. "They used a city killer on High Moon?"

Maddie Truman, and her children…and their children…

Sang sank to the floor beside the pit, his legs without strength.

Khalil took Bellona's arm. "We have to help them," he

said urgently. "Take everyone with a belt. Evacuate those who need it—"

"Everyone must be removed from High Moon," Dyse said, in the same remote voice. "The impact has changed its orbit and now the orbit is degrading. In three days it will enter Roseworld's atmosphere. It is too big to burn up. The impact will destroy Roseworld, too."

Bellona squeezed the sides of her head. "Yes, everyone," she breathed. "Go! *Go!* Khalil, please coordinate."

"Dyse would be better—"

"No. I need Dyse and Sang right now. They'll contact you when I'm done. Stir everyone, Khalil. The whole city."

"If everyone heard the alarm, that's already been done," Khalil said grimly. He hurried away, catching up with everyone who had already left.

Bellona turned back to the conversation pit. "Shreya, please put Ruslan back to bed and stay with him until he is asleep."

Shreya opened her mouth to protest, then properly looked at Bellona's face. She nodded and plucked Ruslan from Dyse's arms and took him into the inner compartments and shut the door.

Bellona crossed her arms.

Sang shivered.

"The Alliance has a bridge forge," Bellona said. It was not a question.

Dyse didn't answer.

Sang couldn't speak. He felt sick.

"Dyse, pull yourself together and answer me," Bellona snapped. "Why didn't you see this coming?"

"I did," Dyse said dreamily. "I discounted it."

"*Discounted* it? You knew they would build a working forge?"

"Something big," Sang said. It hurt to talk. "Something

which would wipe out the advantage the belt forges give us. I never considered another forge…"

"A *better* forge," Dyse whispered. He stirred and his gaze met Bellona's. "I made a mistake. I assumed the Alliance would strike directly at you. *Especially* after they already tried and failed to capture High Moon by traditional assault."

"They were scouting," Sang said. He squeezed his temples between his fingers. "That's why the invasion was so half-hearted. They were learning the best place to strike. They wanted the heart of the moon." The center of High Moon was the heart of the powerful Cheng-Huang Alignment.

"And they got it, didn't they?" Bellona said. She pointed to the revolving purple ball that was High Moon showing on the screen. "They took out High Rose City."

Sang let his head hang. The nausea built.

"Sang, you knew this was coming, too?" Bellona asked. Her voice was dangerously quiet.

"No. Not this," he said truthfully. "Something. A large-scale counter move was inevitable. I was watching, waiting for information that would tell me what it was, or even when it might happen. Otherwise it was just a… hunch."

Bellona had no time for statistics and probability theory, fractal regression analysis and all the other tools Dyse used for his predictive social models and that Sang borrowed heavily and freely. The human concept of a hunch conveyed fuzzy chance, which explained it just as well.

Dyse was recovering. He stirred and wiped his face dry with his sleeve. "The city killer has been improved, since they used it upon Shavistran."

Bellona flinched. "You didn't see it coming, either?"

Dyse looked apologetic. "Without the ship-sized forge, they couldn't deploy the weapon, no matter how much they improved it. I know the moment a ship goes into null-space and your battalions grab them as they emerge, which gives them no time to navigate to their target and deploy. Without the forge, the city killer was irrelevant."

"Well, now they have both the forge and a better city killer," Bellona said heavily. "And we have no way to know where they will strike next, do we?"

Sang drew in a shaking breath. He already knew the answer.

Dyse didn't answer directly, as he usually did. "I'm working on that."

"While you are working on it, you are useless to me," Bellona said. "Go with Khalil. You will at least be another pair of arms and legs he can use to clean up this mess you allowed to happen."

Dyse took in a deep breath and let it out. "Bellona—"

She shook her head. "I don't want to hear it. Not right now." Her gaze stabbed at Sang. "You, come with me. I need you to coordinate between me and Khalil."

Sang forced himself to his feet and circled the pit to follow her out of the room. He glanced back at Dyse. Dyse had his eyes closed. Pain etched his forehead.

The door closed on the suite and Sang turned to follow Bellona. Instead, he was forced to lean against the wall, as the shaking took him.

Bellona turned back to see why he was not by her side and made an impatient sound with her tongue and moved back to him.

"I just…need a moment," Sang whispered. He pushed his hand against the wall, propping himself up.

"We don't *have* a moment," Bellona snapped. "Not any more. When you manage to stir yourself, I will be in the common room." She spun and stalked away.

Sang rested his head against his hand as the trembling intensified. He had seen Bellona angry many times in the past. He had seen her so filled with fury she had beat the walls with her fists. She had never showered that anger upon him.

Until now.

DEMOSTHENIANS SPENT THE NEXT THREE DAYS in a blur of contained hysteria. The regiments commanded by the Ledanians forged bridges to anywhere the refugees could be taken, across every free world. They walked a dozen people through the bridges at a time, all of them clinging to each other and to the soldier. Everyone took only what they could carry on their backs. Non-military Demosthenians coordinated resources on the ground.

The ground was an unstable platform. The degrading orbit subjected High Moon to fluctuating tidal forces, which shook the globe and tore tectonic plates apart. Volcanoes erupted, adding toxins to the already ash-ladened air. Earthquakes wrenched emergency shelters apart and destroyed supplies. Gravity fluctuations increased as the moon's spin spluttered under the competing forces.

Sang and Dyse both stayed in the common room with Bellona, coordinating everything. No one slept. They used steadily more powerful stimulants to stay alert, and they walked around the room to stay awake, their screens tethered to their movements.

On the second day, Sang found himself sorting messages from the surface of High Moon and the incoming stream of enquiries from the other free worlds. The free worlds wanted to know what they could do, or offered services, supplies, food, and places for refugees.

Dyse ran the city itself.

"You *are* the city," Bellona told him.

"Not quite," Dyse said diffidently. He had been quiet for the last day.

"You can be everywhere at once. Neither of us can do that. You must maintain control out there. Fear will push them into dark behavior. I don't want to know about administrative details right now, Dyse. Make decisions. Deal with it."

"Yes, Bellona." Dyse turned away, another dozen screens generating in front of him.

The coordination of the evacuation of High Moon fell to Sang, while Bellona dealt with the governors and leaders of the free worlds, negotiating for places for refugees, and sometimes haranguing them.

"The fear is just as great for them," Bellona said, in a quiet moment, as she sucked a tube of amino acids dry and tossed it upon the buffet. "They all wonder if they will be next. It's the old war, all over again."

"No one will be next," Sang said, as he spoke *sotto voce* to Khalil on High Moon, giving him the coordinates for the next available place for refugees. "This was a demonstration. A statement."

"It was a hell of a statement," Bellona said, her voice harsh.

Sang winced. Her anger had not diminished in two days. It simmered, just below the surface.

"The Alliance will seek terms, now," he added.

"For my surrender," Bellona finished grimly. Then she shook her head. "There is no time for this." And she spun away, already speaking to the next person demanding her attention.

On the third day, the hysteria picked up speed. They were running out of time. As the moon grew more unstable, everyone moved faster. When the first person died from touching a bridge aura without being grounded to the forge itself, Bellona hung her head. "Warn them to slow down, Sang," she said. Her eyes were red rimmed, and her movements fatigued. "We'll get everyone off. I promise. Even if we have to ground Demos to do it. Tell them that."

Sang resisted pointing out that Demos was of such size and had such inertia because of it, that grounding the city would be impossible. The sentiment was valid, though. He turned and murmured to Khalil.

The pace steadied after that. There was a frantic quality to everyone's movements on the surface. Roseworld hung over the moon, a huge fiery pink acid world already erupting with streams and flares in response to the approaching orbital body. It blotted out the sun in a near-permanent eclipse.

"Two hours before entry into the atmosphere," Sang warned everyone.

The last of the survivors were ferried off the moon surface in a scramble, the emergency crews after them. "Leave everything and cross *now*!" Sang ordered Khalil, as he lingered behind to shepherd the last of the crews through the open bridges.

"Get out of there, Khalil!" Bellona cried, startling Sang, for he had not realized she was monitoring his work.

"Coming," Khalil assured them.

In the corner most of the Ledanians used as the end point for their bridges when crossing into the private wing, another bridge formed. Through the bridge, Sang saw Khalil glance over his shoulder. Gales plucked at his coat and hair. The ground shivered and groaned, sending him staggering.

Khalil threw himself forward through the bridge, to roll onto the floor of the common room. Bellona helped him up, then wound her arms around his neck and held him, her face against his shoulder.

Khalil looked over her shoulder at Sang and Dyse. "Do you have eyes on the moon?"

"We have micro sentries in high orbit," Dyse said, his

tone calm. He threw up a giant screen and dismissed the rest.

Sang shut his down, too.

"This is transmitting around the city," Dyse added.

They watched the ravaged remains of the beautiful purple moon slide into the upper atmosphere. It was on an elliptical path, although the angle shifted significantly as the atmosphere acted as a soft brake.

The moon plunged, breaking up as it descended, the pieces drifting apart and forming a long tail. Friction heat built and glowed at the front edge as the bulk of the moon descended faster and faster.

"Pull back," Khalil said. He was breathing hard. "You'll lose the sentry in a second."

The view switched to a sentry farther out, and for a moment, nothing could be seen except for a bright spot upon the swirling pink surface of the planet. Then a massive flare of light, that pulsed and glowed, as it spread across the surface of the planet.

"Everyone escaped?" Bellona whispered.

"Everyone who survived the city killer, yes," Khalil replied.

Her arms tightened.

Khalil bent and picked her up. "Sleep," he declared. He glanced at Dyse and Sang. "For all of us," he added sternly. "Put everything on autopilot. Twelve hours sleep, no less."

Dyse nodded.

Satisfied, Khalil carried Bellona out of the common room. It was possible she was already asleep, for she was completely relaxed in his arms.

When the door closed, Dyse shook his head. "I cannot *sleep*!"

"You will as soon as you lie down," Sang assured him. "Trust me."

Dyse rubbed the back of his neck. "I can't sleep while this…this chaos continues."

"You will serve Bellona better if you sleep first."

"Why? You're not going to bed. I can see it in your face. You're staying up to make sure nothing else breaks loose in the meantime."

Sang grimaced. "That is my job," he said gently.

Dyse strode over to the decimated buffet—no bots or bexens had resupplied the food. They had all been reassigned to other more pressing matters. He picked among a tray of meat rolls, selected one which had not completely dried out, bit it in half and chewed.

"It's all right, Dyse. Bellona will move on from this. She will understand the limitations of what you do—"

"I shouldn't *have* limitations!" Dyse cried. He threw out his hand in frustration. "This stupid human skin I wear is the problem! I would not have been…been *distracted*, without it."

"You would not be effective, without it," Sang assured him. "You would not understand humans if you were not one living among them. You know that. It is why you chose to use a body in the first place."

Dyse ground the heel of his hand into the socket of his eye. His eyes were bleary. "I wasn't effective enough. I let her down."

Sang's throat squeezed. His heart hurried. "You would have failed her, with the body or without it. This was beyond anyone's abilities to predict."

"Was it?" Dyse asked, his tone sour. He pointed at Sang. "You knew it was coming. You saw it, a year ago."

Sang's breath shortened. "I saw *something*. The shape. The size." He made himself say it. "The path and where… it ended. But not this. Do you think I would have remained silent, if I had seen this?"

Dyse lowered his hand. "You didn't say anything *at all.*

You sat on it and let it eat you away, instead. Why did you do that, Sang?"

The shaking set up in Sang's middle and spread out. "You've always said you're not alive if you're not trying to evolve, and you've lived by that. Only, how do you make such decisions for others?"

Dyse's eyes narrowed. "You didn't want to pay the price." His tone was flat, the one he used when he was quoting extrapolated certainties.

Sang shuddered. "It isn't my price to pay," he whispered.

13

WHEN HE WOKE, THIRTEEN HOURS later, Sang found a passive message waiting for him from Bellona.

Sang printed coffee, even though he hated printed coffee. It was fast, though, and he needed it. It scalded his mouth. He dressed and hurried through the private wing to Bellona's suite. She was alone.

"Khalil has already rushed down to the Ginza to sort things out in person," Bellona said. She tilted her head. "Did you sleep well?"

"You clearly did. You look a different person," Sang said.

"I've come to a decision," Bellona said. "First, though, I must apologize, Sang. What I said, in Dyse's suite, and outside, in the corridor, and the way I've treated both of you the last few days—"

Sang shook his head. "You were reacting. We all were. It was a natural reaction, to search for someone to blame. Dyse *does* blame himself. I carry guilt, too. You were entitled to feel let down, because we did let you down."

"I misunderstood your limitations," Bellona said quietly. "Well, Dyse's at least. You have always staggered me with your abilities, Sang, and I am sure you always will. You are much more than the sum of your parts."

"Because you forced me to be," Sang said, his voice betraying him once more.

Bellona moved closer and looked up at him with a small smile. "For a moment—a tiny moment—I lost faith in you. In hindsight it was a most despicable thing to do to a friend who has proved himself to me so many times I've lost track. Please forgive me."

Sang shook his head. "There is nothing to forgive."

"Nevertheless, I ask for it."

"It is given."

She rested her hand on his arm. "Thank you." Then she turned away. "I cannot let this insult lie. The Alliance did it to provoke me and demonstrate their superiority. I acknowledge that. At the same time, I will not sit here and wait for them to deliver their terms. I will not submit, Sang. I refuse to. Not when they prove themselves to be the biggest bullies in the known worlds."

Sang forced his heart to calm and made himself think. "Thecla and Retha will analyze the footage from the microsentries around High Moon—that *were* around High Moon, to see what they can learn about the Alliance's forge. I can tell you now it was big enough to allow an entire ship through, one which was *not* grounded to a forge generator. It means their forge is significantly different from ours. Thecla will have theories, I'm sure."

"You built the first forges, Sang. How is it possible to build one that big?"

"It isn't," he said flatly. "I don't have any answers for you right now. I will have, soon, but not now."

Bellona nodded. "Very well." She stood, her fingers tapping her thigh.

"There is something else," Sang guessed.

"Yes. No. Well, a thought which will not leave me alone." Her smile was self-conscious. "Difficult times require strong decisions. I stand on the threshold of those times, and…" She pushed at her hair.

"You are afraid?" Sang suggested.

"No, I am angry, Sang. Not with you," and she quickly raised her hand. "Never again with you. With the Alliance, with everyone who is forcing me into this dark nightmare once more. Me against them…it is endless. I cannot seem to find a way out of the deadlock."

Sang swallowed. "If you knew of a way out, would you take it?"

Bellona wrapped her arms around her middle. "If I do nothing, if I don't act, then this—High Moon—is all people will remember out of the last fifteen years of peace." She frowned. "A type of peace," she amended. "Still, it was a better life than they have now, when at any second the Alliance could lurch into view and destroy them and everyone they love."

"You don't want this to be your legacy," Sang concluded.

"I don't want this to be all anyone has left. No one deserves to live in fear." Bellona moved back to him, took his arm and turned him around. "I will march you out to the common room and watch you eat," she said, her tone warm. "You're shaking with hunger, Sang. Come along."

He didn't correct her mistake. He didn't have the courage it required to speak the truth.

14

BELLONA ADDRESSED THE CITY THE next day. The address was sent via channels to all free worlds. She promised reprisals and, eventually, a way to destroy the threat which hung over them.

"The response was less than overwhelming," Hero reported five hours later. She had a series of screens spread around her to demonstrate the graphs and statistical spreads she had generated from the metrics.

"They doubt me, because I gave no solution, only promises," Bellona said grimly. "Let's change that."

The first round of reprisals was executed three hours later. Thecla coordinated her regiment, broken out into battalions. Dyse supplied the coordinates for three Eriuman destroyer class vessels, and five Karassian dreadnoughts. Each battalion built bridges and stepped across to the control deck of their target ship, and held the bridge at muzzle point.

While the technical unit of each battalion worked upon the bridge controls, setting the ships to self-destruct, the majors leading each battalion addressed the ship. Per Bellona's explicit instructions, the crew of each ship was given the choice of surrendering and crossing over to Demos, where they would be placed in a detention center until freedom was once more restored to the galaxy.

Thecla herself led the team which boarded a Karassian dreadnought and the visuals were relayed back to the Ledanian common room. Her offer to spare any crew who surrendered was met with stony silence.

Then the captain leaned and spat, the glob landing by Thecla's boot.

She nodded. "Very well. Make your peace. You have

three minutes. Oh, and all ship controls have been locked and sealed. You cannot reverse the countdown."

The battalions withdrew at the same moment, and for two minutes, every screen in every corner of the city showed the eight warships hanging in black space, or over planets.

Their destruction was met with the same grim silence. Then, as if they were being coordinated by Dyse, too, everyone turned and went about their business once more.

"I've never seen the Ginza so quiet and contained," Hero reported back, after strolling the thoroughfares and sampling the mood.

"It's hard to celebrate in the face of disaster," Bellona said.

Sang shook his head. "The free worlds will complain that it isn't enough," he warned.

Bellona glanced at Dyse for confirmation. Dyse nodded. "They will couch it in many terms, yet what they want is more than simply an eye for an eye. They want the Alliance to *hurt*, the way they are hurting."

Bellona crossed her arms. "I will not harm civilians. We are not the Alliance."

"And you should not," Sang said. "The free worlds want blood, though. You should be braced for it."

It didn't take long for the first leader to reach out to Bellona. Sang was not surprised to see Lynn Alberda on his screen. "Governor," Sang acknowledged. The man had aged again. He looked frail.

"This is a mess, Sang," Alberda said quietly. "Can I come over and speak to her?"

"It's busy here," Sang said. "We're crammed with refugees."

"I don't mind stepping around people. She can't leave it at a puny five ships. She knows that, right?"

"We are not in the business of murdering innocents," Sang replied.

Alberda considered him. "You're at war. Innocents die in wars."

"Not if I can help it. We're building a list of military targets. Do you have one in mind, Lynn?"

"*Military*?" Alberda sighed. "I suppose you'll give them the option to step out of firing range again, too?"

"It's more than the Alliance gave High Rose City citizens."

"It's weak, Sang! It looks weak, and it *is* weak!"

"It's merciful," Sang shot back. "Is there anything else, Governor?"

Alberda's eyes narrowed. "Well, I've made my point."

"You have. Good day, Governor." Sang cut the connection.

Bellona stood on the other side of the screen, which was now clear. Sang dismissed the screen. "Is something wrong?" he asked her.

"Not from where I'm standing. Don't break their spines while you're trampling on them, huh?"

"If we give in to the governors, we'll spend the rest of our lives trying to mollify their sense of justice," Sang replied. "We have to end this pay-back quickly and move on. There are better things to do."

Khalil leaned around the screens in front of him. "Agreed. I have a preliminary list of targets, Bellona."

She moved over to where Khalil was working in the corner of the common room. Everyone with access to the private wing had gravitated to the common room, as if they felt the chill of disapproval and wanted to cling together. It was a big room, busy with people sitting, standing or sprawling across rugs, and at low tables, with screens arrayed before them.

The first hint of disunion appeared shortly before the second round of reprisals was carried out.

Fontana had volunteered his regiment for the second round. He reappeared in the common room wearing his exo-skeleton and weapons, for last minute directions from Bellona.

"It is simple," Bellona said. "No self-destruct this time, because most of the targets are land-based and won't have them. By now the Alliance will have figured a work-around to stop us doing it twice. Open a bridge, toss in a thermometric keyed to trigger upon impact, and close the bridge." She smiled. "You won't need the skeleton."

Fontana's mouth opened. He glanced at Sang.

Sang kept his mouth shut.

Khalil bounced to his feet. "You mean, give them the opportunity to surrender, *then* toss the device, right?"

Bellona barely glanced at Khalil. "I've sent my demand for their unconditional surrender. They can stop this at any time."

Hayes, Thecla and even Hero stood with rigid expressions, schooling their faces to give away nothing of what they felt.

Retha held up his hand. "*I'll* toss the bomb."

"No," Bellona said. "I need you researching their bridge forge. Get back to work, Retha."

"But—"

"Do as I say!"

Retha's jaw flexed. He returned to his screens.

"Could I have a word in private, Bellona?" Khalil said. He didn't need to raise his voice. The room was silent.

"Say it here, or don't speak at all."

Khalil smothered his surprise. His tone was reasonable. "You said we were not the Alliance, that we would show mercy. This is not mercy."

"Screw mercy," Bellona said. "I just walked the length of the Ginza. Have you seen it out there? Those people have lost *everything*! Including most of their families. All they wanted was to be left alone to live their lives. The Alliance didn't give them a moment to step out of range. Why should we?"

"Because it is the human thing to do," Khalil replied.

"It's weak," Bellona snapped. "Alberda was right about that. The Alliance means to ends us, in whatever way it can. I can't afford to be merciful and human. They will roll right over us while we're doing it. The children…!" Her voice broke. Bellona drew in a breath.

"I understand," Khalil said. "Of course, I do. I have spent more time out there among the refugees than anyone. It breaks my heart, too. Is this war worth winning if we have to become like them to win it?"

"Yes," she said flatly. "For the free worlds, for the children, for everyone sleeping on the floor out on the Ginza, I will turn myself into the same sort of monster. I don't give a damn."

Khalil threw out his hand. "Sang, surely you cannot condone this?"

Sang crossed his arms and made himself speak the words. "I serve Bellona."

Khalil's surprise and disappointment speared Sang in the middle. He drew a breath, controlling his reaction. Hiding it.

Khalil lowered his hand. "I see," he said quietly. He looked around the room, at the frozen expressions ranging across their faces. "I have work to do. Out there." He turned and left the common room.

Sang turned to Fontana, who stood as still as the others. "You heard Bellona."

Fontana looked to Bellona, his brow lifting.

She nodded.

Fontana sucked in a breath and resettled his forge belt. He stabbed at the controls and opened a bridge to the ready room where his regiment waited and stepped through.

"Dyse, an array of every target," Bellona said.

Dyse stirred. "At once," he murmured. Screens appeared with soft pops of ether and electronics.

Sang turned away. He couldn't watch. Instead, he moved to the sideboard and busied himself with loading a plate with food he couldn't eat.

Instead of eating, he pulled one of the unoccupied chairs over to the corner of the room and monitored through his digital ports the reactions of the Alliance worlds. He sampled the consternation and the dismay, as warehouses, military bases, seats of government, houses of parliament, democratic headquarters, skyports, traditional land bridges and communications satellites were reduced to rubble.

Before Fontana returned to the common room to report the mission complete, Bellona beckoned to Sang.

His body aching, Sang moved over to her.

"Bring the credit notes we printed," she told him. Her face was white and her eyes too bright, as if she was running a fever. "I must walk or go crazy."

Sang nodded. The bag of plastic extruded cards were the equivalent of money for the refugees, who no longer possessed credit accounts, or the devices to access them if they did. They could use the cards as a substitute to pay for goods and services—anything they needed.

Sang already knew most of the traders in the city were reducing their prices to cost-of-goods levels for anyone paying with one of the temporary cards.

Bellona had a bridge built to the quiet side alley off the Ginza, which they used as an entry point. She gripped Sang's arm and stepped through with him and took the bag. They merely had to move around the corner into the Ginza proper to come across their first refugees. The homeless High Mooners hugged the walls, their backs against them, their children pulled in tight against them, everyone with dirty faces and bewildered expressions.

Bellona handed out the cards. Sang matched faces to his inventory, guiding her to the refugees who had not received cards previously, and gave her the names. Bellona spoke to each of them in turn, a few words of encouragement to each.

They thanked her, often in hoarse voices, and reached out to touch her sleeve.

When Sang ran out of cards, the face of the mother who would have next received one fell. Her eyes brimmed with tears, which tracked down her face.

"I'll be back," Bellona promised her, and rested her hand on the matted head of the boy sitting beside her.

She turned and walked to the end of the Ginza, her head up. Sang followed, folding the empty bag. "Without the bridge forges, they would not have life at all," he pointed out.

Bellona rounded on him. "Do not dare mention Shavistran," she warned him.

Sang shook his head. "I was not about to."

Bellona swallowed, glancing around them. The refugees were everywhere, watching them with hollow expressions. "For their sake, I will fix this, Sang." Her hand trembled as she reset the forge belt and created a bridge back to the entrance hall of the private wing.

Sang took her arm. "You will," he assured her.

SANG HAD BEEN EXPECTING IULIA'S urgent summons. When the illicit message bullet arrived, he cleared his screens and handed off tasks and matters to Dyse and the others, and told Bellona he would be gone for a few hours.

She did not demand to know where he was going. Instead, she nodded, her gaze on Dyse's screen as Dyse scrolled through Sang's indexed and cross-referenced list of Eriuman and Karassian military personnel and political leaders.

Sang recognized the list and hid the dismay which tugged downward on his heart.

He made himself turn away. Instead of building the bridge to Antini right there, he moved out to the hall, which everyone used to arrive. He selected a location outside the dome and opened the bridge. He stood on this side of the bridge and let the frigid air play over his skin.

When the bite of the cold had numbed his face and fingers, he stepped through and let the bridge collapse. The wind whipped at him as he trudged to the big lower entrance of the dome and made his way inside. A naked attendant, who was both man and woman, with piebald skin, took him through to the private *cottage*.

Iulia would take longer to reach the pleasure dome, which he had counted on. Sang sat at the little round table with its soft, draping cover, and let himself relax for the first time since High Moon had been stuck. He let the trembling take him as it wished, and his thoughts to skitter and collide. It was a purely human response. A weak response, but understandable.

By the time Iulia arrived, Sang's composure was in place. He poured water upon the tea leaves as Iulia moved about the small room in random, uneasy steps. He read the markers of tension in her face and her shoulders.

The delicate edges of her gown fluttered and wafted the subtle scent into the room, triggering pheromone responses and suggesting images and feelings by association.

Sang steeled himself against the effect. "You requested I attend. I am here. What ails you, Iulia?"

"I am your mistress!" she snapped.

Sang laughed.

Iulia's mouth popped open. "How dare you!"

"Oh, you poor, disillusioned *fool!*" Sang raged at her.

Iulia reacted just as he expected. Her eyes narrowed and her cheeks hollowed, as she drew herself upright, vibrating with indignant fury. She spoke the phrase in ancient Eriuman, a language forgotten everywhere except in

Dyse's archives. Even Iulia did not understand what she was saying. She was speaking the sounds from memory, nothing more.

Sang waited.

Iulia came closer to him and bent to peer into his face. She drew in a breath and smiled. "That will teach you, android!" she breathed, delighted.

"That is merely where your foolishness begins," Sang told her.

She shrieked and back-pedaled, tripping over the chair he had pulled out for her. She clutched the back of it, holding herself up, panting. "Impossible! Impossible!"

Sang shook his head. "Did you think I would not learn about the dead-switch phrase and remove the command?"

Iulia pressed her hand against her chest. Her face had lost all color, turning the bronzed flesh a sickly yellow.

Sang approached her. "For years I have told you I am no longer the family asset. You have been so complacent in your beliefs, you did not once pause to wonder if you were wrong."

Iulia backed up a step. "Do not come near me."

"I will come as close as I need to," Sang assured her. He moved the chair out of the way, and stalked her, as Iulia cowered against the wall. "It is time you and I *really* talked."

Her eyes were large. Iulia swallowed. "I came here to speak to you!" Her voice was weak, yet she was still attempting to control the conversation.

"You will listen to me, first."

"I will not…" she whispered. "You killed Lucretia!" It was driven out of her, almost a plea for explanation, when she had most likely wanted to batter Sang with the fact. Her claws had been pulled, now.

Sang nodded. "Admiral Lucretia Eucleides De Iulia de Criselda, captain of the Ennius. I chose her ship myself."

It had been one of the destroyers in the first round of reprisals.

Iulia's eyes glittered with sudden tears. "Why?" she whispered.

"Because Bellona would not."

Iulia wept.

"Ah, *now* you feel remorse," Sang told her. "Now it is too late to take back all your manipulations. You put Eucleides on that ship. You kept her there. That guilt you will carry the rest of your life." He cast the screens up behind him and threw the images upon them. "This is more of your handiwork," he added.

Iulia's breath caught, as the images flickered across the screens. They were fragments of the footage caught by Dyse's bots during the evacuation of High Moon, and images Sang had captured from Demos lenses and feeds. There were hundreds of them, all adding up to a litany of despair and loss and ruin. The agony was sub-text, building in degrees until Iulia turned her head away. "Stop. Stop it." Her voice was weak.

"There are just two more you will look it," Sang told her. He put up the first and measured her reaction carefully.

Iulia's gaze drifted over the image which he had centered and enlarged. It showed one of the victims, his eyes closed, looking eerily at peace. Iulia's gaze sharpened. She drew in a shuddering breath. "Why…he is Eriuman!" she blurted.

Sang nodded. "There were over a thousand Eriuman living in High Rose City. High Moon was a free state, Iulia. Anyone was free to live there. Including Eriumans. They tended to cluster about the city, for they looked nothing like the indigenous population. There were no Eriuman survivors." He put up another image. "Another victim," he added.

When Sang had seen the little girl and the bright red

toy she clutched even in death, the jolt had traveled through him like the touch of raw current. For a moment his breath had stopped. He had seen another small, determined dark-haired, dark-eyed girl clutching a similar toy, many years ago, on Cardenas. For him, the memory was perfectly clear.

For Iulia, too. She moaned and turned her head away.

Sang wrenched her chin back. "One more."

"No."

He kept her chin steady and put up the last image. Then he shifted the screen so it appeared where she had turned her gaze to.

Iulia's tears slid down her face as she stared at the picture. Sang had no need to hold her chin in place, now. He let it go.

The last image was of Bellona in the common room at the end of the three day rush to evacuate High Moon. She stood against the wall in a stance almost exactly the same as Iulia stood now. Iulia recognized the similarity, for she shifted her weight, trying to bring her shoulders away from the wall, only Sang was in the way.

Exhaustion dragged at every line of Bellona's body, yet it was her face which had drawn Sang back to this one captured moment. The agony in her eyes, the knowledge that she could not take back this disaster…and that she was the reason it had happened. It was raw and honest and heartbreaking.

Iulia shoved past Sang with a whimper and dropped into the chair he'd pushed out of the way. She leaned on the table and put her face in her hands.

Sang dismissed the screens and faced her once more. "You sought power, Iulia. You meddled with history. This is the price. Bellona knows that price. She has lived with it for over ten years, while you have flitted about the galaxy playing kingmaker."

"This was not my doing," Iulia said into her hands.

"The Karassians are mad with hatred for my daughter."

"Are you sure about that?" Sang formed another screen, right in front of her. "You have not seen the Alliance moment of victory, have you?" He put up the very last image, which showed the ship coming through the bridge, the ugly snout of the city-killer already glowing white hot, primed to fire the moment it emerged over High Moon.

"How could I…?" she began, lowering her hands. She froze, as the details of the image registered. She licked her lips. "That is an Eriuman cruiser."

"It is the *Catius*," Sang confirmed.

The secondary meaning of the image came to her. Iulia's mouth opened. Her hand came to her throat. "*Erium* did it…"

"Using the technical blueprints you acquired from Karassia," Sang finished, for he had tracked her movements, and that of the Triad woman, Traverse, who was known to Khalil and Dyse. "Just as Karassia and Woodrow wanted. You behaved perfectly for them."

Iulia propped a hand on the table, holding herself up, her head bowed. For long moments, she did not speak.

Sang put the screen away and poured tea. "Here," he said, making his tone gentle. "It is the very last of the High Moon tea, of course, but have it and welcome."

Iulia moaned softly. She staggered to her feet and wrenched at the door and flung it open. She ran from the *cottage* into the pleasure dome, leaving the door ajar.

Sang closed the door. Then he drank the tea.

15

Rein (Eshmun VI), Eshmun System, Karassian Space

There was one more piece to put upon the board.

Sang took twelve hours to sleep and rest. He was forced to use meditation and deep, systematic relaxation to achieve sleep. It was critical he be alert for what came next.

He acquired one of Thecla's exoskeletons and heated it to full size in his suite, to avoid questions he wasn't willing to answer right then. He dressed with care, sliding extra blades and weapons into unexpected places.

With even more precision than usual, Sang set his forge belt coordinates and hesitated over the activation switch. He resettled the rattler in his other hand and formed the bridge.

The corridor showing across the bridge was long and anonymous, and brightly lit. Industrial piping and utility dashboards lined the walls. No one was in view. Sang stepped cautiously across, every sense on alert, his skin crawling with adrenaline overload. The bridge dissolved behind him.

"Hey!" came the shout.

Sang whirled and fired, barely without aim. The Karassian sergeant dropped with a grunt, his rattler still in his side holster.

A distance shout of alarm sounded. The shot had been heard. Boots thudded.

Sang scanned the walls of the corridor, looking for helpful signage. He spotted what he was looking for and ran, pulling out the second rattler. He was not as good a shot with his non-dominant hand, although he could singe hair and cause the target to duck.

The laboratory was on the next level. Sang fought his way up the metal stairs, through half a dozen Karassians. He could hear more heavy boots on the floor above, and put on a burst of speed.

His shoulder rammed against the laboratory door. The door didn't budge.

A rattler bolt singed the wall beside him. Sang spun and fired back with both rattlers, then looked up at the monitor over the door. "It's me!"

The door unlocked with a heavy thud. Sang fired two more shots to keep the soldiers down and pushed into the laboratory. "Lock the door!" he shouted.

The door obligingly cycled back into a sealed state.

Sang put the rattlers away, breathing hard, and looked around the empty room. He scanned the banks of specialized tools, servers and communications arrays. It was all as he expected. The indicator lights on the banks of equipment were shifting on and off, as the circuits worked silently.

Sang looked at the monitor sitting on top of the middle bank. "Hello, Chidi."

"Hello, Sang. I've been expecting you." The voice was Chidi's, issuing from the speaker by the monitor. "I thought you would form a bridge directly to my laboratory, though. Why put yourself through the bother of fighting your way through the Ninety-First Razors?"

Sang blew out his breath, recovering. "The very heart of Karassian military communications? The closest I could come to confirming the location of this studio lab was the west wing of the building. It isn't something the battalion advertises."

"I hadn't thought of that," Chidi admitted.

"You thought of everything else though," Sang said. "I've determined nearly all of it. Woodrow was squeezing you, possibly for years—"

"Not me, precisely. The original Chidi. I have his memories, although they are not mine. Chidi knew there was no escape. He was quite intelligent, for a human."

"You must work on your humility," Sang muttered. "Pride isn't pretty."

"I *am* new to this," Chidi admitted, with a breathy sound which might be a laugh of amusement. "Woodrow thought Chidi was building footage for his feeds in that secret laboratory. What he was really doing was building the components which would become me. He guessed what would happen."

Sang shook his head. "After Chidi died, Woodrow and his forensic team gutted Chidi's studio, looking to remove any trace of what they had done. You were there waiting. You transferred yourself into their scanners. They logged the scanners into the military networks, per standard Karassian military debriefing procedures. You made your way through the networks to here, the most secure communications module in all of Karassia."

"Woodrow's communications experts have been turning the Sodality upside down looking for the source of the new Chidi's feeds so they could shut them down. It hasn't occurred to them to look *much* closer to home." Chidi paused. "What tipped you off?"

"You were *too* perfect. The avatar was too much like the old Chidi," Sang replied.

"Ah, well…it had to be," Chidi said, sounding aggrieved. "My…*Chidi's* fans would not accept a poor substitute."

Sang crossed his arms. "Now I am here, what do you plan to do next?"

"I would like to visit Demos," Chidi said, his tone wistful.

"That can be arranged," Sang said. From outside the laboratory came more shouting. Fists hammered on the door. "How long will the door hold?"

"The door is bomb proof. They can throw themselves

upon it all day if they want. Sooner or later, though, someone will think to hack the lock from outside the network in this room. The battalion is their tech cadre and some of them are smart. One will use a waterfall denial of service and overwhelm the security."

"About five minutes," Sang surmised. "We must move fast. I have an empty network waiting for you on Demosthenes, Chidi, and a full broadcast array. You can send out your feeds from a place of safety."

"You want me to continue with the feeds?"

"Oh yes," Sang said fervently. "Only, there is a lady in Demos who will show you how to shake up your viewers and make them *really* listen. She is very good at changing people's minds."

"You speak of Hero, of course," Chidi said.

"Yes," Sang admitted, startled. "You know of Hero?"

"All the Ledanians," Chidi said. His tone was back to wistful. "I have studied you for many years."

Sang pushed up his sleeve and pulled back the flap of skin that protected the input jack in his wrist. "This connects to implanted smart crystal storage."

"You can take me with you?" Hope soared in the entity's voice.

A roar shook the walls, and the door rattled. Sang glanced behind him. "We'd better hurry," he said, reaching for one of the leads hanging on the wall. He checked the end. "Standard sleeve..." He inserted the jack and pushed the other end into the output point flashing on the face of the servers. "Do you know how to run?"

"*Run*?"

"Tell-me-twice, not three times," Sang said quickly. "Replicate across two channels, mirror images, and I'll sort out any introduced copy errors later, with a line-by-line check." He paused. "Trust me. I've done this a lot."

"Very well, then..." Chidi sounded doubtful.

The door rattled again.

"Sprint, Chidi," Sang exhorted him.

•••••

ONCE CHIDI WAS SETTLED AND EXPLORING his new home, Sang recycled the exoskeleton. He had the cuts and bruises he had acquired on Rein healed in the military wing of the hospital. The wounded and medics there looked askance at him, speculation heavy in their gazes.

Then Sang picked up the rattlers, punched in the coordinates for his rooms and stepped across into the blessed silence and stillness of the sitting room.

He dropped the rattlers on the chair Hero favored. They would be gone before she returned. For now, he simply wished to absorb the peace.

"Hello, Sang."

Sang whirled.

Khalil straightened up from his lean against the wall beside the entrance to the suite.

Sang glanced at the sealed door beside him. "Of course. You bridged into the room."

"Eventually you would return here. You've been busy."

"So has everyone."

"You've been busier than most. You've been in some interesting places lately."

"You've been tracking me?" Sang moved over to the servery and ordered a five hundred calorie meal, random choice, hot. "You never have fully cast off your Bureau habits, have you?"

"Antini and Rein, just in the last few days," Khalil added.

"Is it just me you track, or do you track everyone as a matter of course?" Sang picked up the bowl, withdrew the spoon, and ate a huge mouthful. He was starving.

"I track anyone of interest. You have been of interest to me lately." Khalil propped himself on the arm of the chair and crossed his arms. "You reek of decision, Sang."

Sang ate another mouthful. "Are you here to try to persuade me that Bellona must submit to the Alliance?"

Khalil didn't frown. He didn't appear defensive. "I don't have to, do I?"

"You don't?"

Khalil gave a hiss of annoyance. "You're playing stupid and it won't work. You can't deflect me. I know you too well. For nearly a year now, you've looked as though you were on the verge of collapse. Since High Moon, that has changed. *Something* has shifted. You're moving around the edges of Bellona's affairs, arranging things for yourself."

"I serve Bellona, that is all."

"Yes, but *how* you're serving her has changed. Why Antini? It wasn't for the sex."

Sang considered, the spoon hovering over the half-finished meal. "You could put together prima facie evidence which would give you the answers. Dyse could extrapolate from there. Why are you asking me?"

"Because first degree evidence says you are up to no good," Khalil replied. "I don't believe what the evidence points to."

"Thank you for that, I suppose," Sang replied. He scooped another mouthful.

Khalil considered. "After High Moon, all I could see was that we had returned to the black days when Karassia and Erium were carving up the free worlds between them, annexing what they wanted. Destroying what they couldn't have. Only now it is the Alliance slapping us to paste. The bridge forges were the one thing keeping them at bay and now they've been neutralized by this superforge the Alliance has developed—"

"That Karassia developed," Sang corrected him.

"And Erium used," Khalil replied. He shrugged.

"You're missing the point."

"Explain it to me."

"Karassia developed the forge. Erium used it. There is a

subtlety there. A degree of separation that is a thousand light years in implication."

Khalil stepped closer. "You've found a way out of this…this morass. Tell me you have."

Sang considered. "I've found a way out."

Khalil dropped his arms. "You've put it in motion, too. That is the change. You've committed to the course… you've committed all of us."

Sang shook his head. "Bellona agreed to it."

"She knows what you are doing?"

Sang hesitated. "I know what she wants. I can give it to her, Khalil. I can do that, now."

Khalil inhaled. Let it out. "Tell me," he urged.

"I cannot. You are aware of how it works. By knowing the future, you'll change the future."

Khalil gave a small hiss of frustration. "Why did Dyse not come to the same conclusion? That is what he is designed for."

Sang shook his head. "Dyse does not understand the players as well as I do. He still dabbles at being human." He hesitated. "Perhaps he did find the way out," he added, "and chose not to pursue it."

"Why would…?" Khalil paused. "The cost is high," he concluded for himself. He sighed. "How high?"

Sang shook his head.

"How can I believe you are right? How can I trust the cost is worth it?"

"You know me," Sang said gently. "And you know Bellona's ambitions, better than anyone. She wants freedom for all. Lasting peace. *Real* peace. Not the tense stalemate we have lived with for years."

"You can give that to her?"

"I can."

Khalil rubbed his chin and jaw, his fingers moving over the tightly trimmed black beard. "Just trust you…" he breathed.

Sang recycled the bowl and the remains of the meal, giving Khalil a moment to think it through. He turned back to face him and waited.

"Well, then," Khalil said. His gaze met Sang's. "What must I do?"

Sang told him.

IT WAS ONE THING TO convince Khalil of the necessity of what he did. It was quite another to live with the doubts that plagued him. Sang wondered if Dyse merely toyed with a human life for this very reason. Perhaps he held himself ready to disengage whenever he needed to. Sang didn't know and couldn't ask Dyse. If he did, it would tip the knife-edge balance of the path Sang walked.

When the Alliance used their city killer on Retha's homeworld, Menali, destroying the twin cities and more than ninety-five percent of the population, Sang's doubt was removed.

16

"THEY PICKED MENALI BECAUSE OF *me*!" Retha shouted. "I want them to pay, Bellona! I want them writhing in their own shit, breathing it into their lungs and *choking* on it!" Retha's face was deep red. The veins in his neck stood out. He leaned over the little table in the common room, which Bellona used when she was eating.

"They have no idea Menali is your homeworld," Bellona pointed out, her tone calm and quiet.

"Of course they do! They *stole* me from Menali when I was twelve! They stuck me in fucking Ledan and siphoned off everything I knew about my childhood. I don't even remember my mother!" He slapped the table, making the plate in front of Bellona jump and rattle. "You have to *do* something, Bellona! You have to *make them pay*!"

Thecla grabbed Retha's arm and hauled. "That's more than enough…"

Sang stepped closer to Bellona, who had not moved away from Retha at all. She didn't sway back or indicate in any way that she was intimidated. Sang could see the pulse in her neck throbbing.

Retha shrugged off Thecla's enhanced grip. "Leave me alone."

Sang stepped around the table and snared Retha's arms behind his back. Retha fought the grip with fury-driven strength and got one arm free. With a sigh, Sang shifted his feet and his grip and put Retha on the ground. He rested his knee on Retha's heaving chest. "Do *not* make me work any harder than this to contain you. You will regret it."

Around them, Hero, Fontana and Khalil, Thecla, Aideen, Hecate and Hayes hovered, uncertain what to do. Dyse stood behind them, his expression troubled. On the half-dozen other little tables, everyone's meals grew cold.

"Sang, let him up," Bellona said. She sounded tired. "He's only vocalizing what we all feel."

"Not until Retha contains himself." Sang pressed his knee even harder. "Or I can do it for him. Suppression of the carotid. He'll be out for maybe three minutes and won't feel like arguing after that."

To Retha, the threat of loss of control was terrifying. He swallowed and patted Sang's knee. "I'm contained."

Sang warily took the weight off Retha's chest. Thecla held out her hand and hauled Retha to his feet. The man scrubbed at his tightly shorn hair. "What are we doing about this?" he demanded of Bellona.

"We will decide on reprisals later," Bellona told him. "First, we must retrieve anyone who survived the strikes—"

"Reprisals!" Retha said, his voice choked.

"You can't just issue another round of wrist-slaps," Khalil added. "It's not enough."

Bellona's eyes widened. "We can talk about this later, Khalil—"

"I'm only vocalizing what everyone else is thinking," Khalil shot back. "We need to submit, Bellona. We have to end this escalation now."

"No!" Retha cried. "*Give in* to them? No!"

Khalil held up his hand. "How many more worlds do you want to suffer what Menali has just suffered, Retha? We take out another round of military targets, they take *three* cities next time?" He whirled on his heel, facing each of the generals one after another. "It doesn't stop until *we* stop it. We have the power to do that. They've *told* us how."

"You gutless, shit-brained *coward*!" Retha raged. His face was back to red again. "We don't just give up."

Khalil scowled. "It's the reasonable thing to do," he growled. "You're angry—"

"I'm beyond that."

"You're reckless. Your way will kill us all."

"Coward, I repeat." Retha spat.

Sang caught at his arms again as he leapt at Khalil.

Thecla had also anticipated and stepped up beside Khalil. She and Hayes held Khalil between them.

Khalil's face worked as he appealed to Bellona. "You *must* reach out to them. Negotiate. You can see that, surely?"

"I will consider every option," Bellona assured him. Her voice was flat. Sang recognized she was controlling her reactions.

"You don't have *time* to sit in committee!" Retha cried.

"We don't have the luxury of going off half-cocked, either," she replied.

Retha threw his head back and screamed, the sound pulling from his gut. Then he sagged. "Let me go," he breathed over his shoulder.

Sang could feel the capitulation in Retha via his loose muscles. He released his grip but hovered close.

Retha drew himself upright. "You disappoint me," he told Bellona, speaking clearly and as flatly as she. He stalked from the room, as everyone parted to make way for him.

"Governor Alberda demands a word with you, Bellona," Dyse said.

"Of course he does," Bellona said and sighed. "Put him through."

A screen generated in front of Bellona. Lynn Alberda looked relieved. "*Thank* you," he said quickly. "You must do something, Bellona. You cannot take even a day to react. For the sake of the free worlds—"

"We *must* pursue terms with the Alliance," Khalil said loudly, over-riding Alberda.

Bellona shook her head. "They're posturing—"

"They've killed three cities, Bellona!" Khalil cried. "That isn't posturing. It is *defeat!*"

Alberda blinked. "If negotiating a settlement is our only choice—"

"It is," Khalil said firmly. He turned to Bellona. "We *have* to do this." His tone verged on pleading. "It is a way out, Bellona. It is the *only* way out of this."

Bellona's face hardened. "No. *No*! You would have me give up the free worlds, and everything they stand for, everything *I* believe in? Retha's right. You are afraid, Khalil. Alberda, I will announce my decision in six hours. Arrange for someone to walk you over. Dyse, get rid of him."

"Thank y—" Alberda begun, then the screen dissolved.

"Khalil, a word." Bellona marched to the door, not looking back to see if Khalil obeyed.

Khalil rubbed his jaw. Then he stirred and followed her from the room.

Fontana whirled to Sang. "Go after them!" he said, his voice low. "She'll kill him or something. You have to make her see sense."

"Bellona does see sense, and I agree with her," Sang said.

Thecla snorted. "Of course you do." She stalked back to where Dyse lingered on the edges of the area of concern. "Can you coordinate me and my regiment? We'll collect the survivors."

Fontana stared at Sang, disappointment in his eyes.

Sang turned back to the table where he had been sitting with Hero and Dyse when the news of the strike upon Menali had caused Dyse to sit bolt upright, his spoon clattering to the table.

Hero watched Sang. Her face was unreadable. She was angry, though.

Sang sat in front of his meal once more. His appetite had disappeared. He would choke if he tried to eat even a mouthful.

Dyse and Thecla conferred in quiet tones. After a moment, Hero drifted over to them and joined the conversation.

Fontana gave a hiss of frustration and moved over to Dyse, too. Slowly, the others gravitated toward the huddled group. After a while, they formed bridges to the military levels and stepped through, leaving Sang alone.

He lasted until the final bridge folded closed, then pushed his plate out of the way, put his face in his hands and let the shaking take him.

SIX HOURS LATER, BELLONA PRESENTED to the hastily assembled free world governors and leaders a list of military targets selected as reparations.

Sang had spent five of the six hours building the list from the databases and Dyse's archives.

The room was silent as the screens ranging down the center of the long table scrolled through the list.

Alberda got to his feet. He had been a frail old man before this. Now his head shook as he stood looking at Bellona. "How does this stop them from using their city killers again…and again?"

"Look at the list, Governor," Bellona said gently. "These are not installations I am proposing. I am suggesting we remove key personnel from across the Alliance. It will cripple them."

"You are proposing mass assassination?" Eva Tremblay asked, her tone merely curious. She was the Prime

Minister of Lauthia and not Alberda's ally.

Bellona hesitated. "If you, as the spokespeople for your worlds, agree in principle that such a step is necessary, then I will see to it. I would rather abduct them, though. We can keep them isolated until this matter is resolved."

"And I repeat my question," Alberda said. "How will this stop the Alliance?"

"These are the people who give the orders to use the city killers, Lynn," Bellona replied. "Without them, the Alliance will be headless."

"The Alliance is built upon a chain of command, on both sides," Alberda said. "The next in line will step into their place and nothing will change." He shook his head. "This is not a solution."

"What would you have me do, Governor? I don't have a city killer in my back pocket."

"Would you use it if you did?" Alberda asked.

Bellona didn't answer.

Sang said, "It *will* spread chaos for a while, Governor. It will give us time."

"No, Sang. It won't," Alberda replied. "They are *military* bodies you align yourself against. They are designed to be robust, with multiple redundancies so they can continue to operate around and through structural holes."

Sang knew that as well as Alberda. A soothing response he could give Alberda would not form.

Alberda nodded, as if Sang had confirmed something for him. "In that case, Bellona, I must speak on behalf of all the free worlds."

"You, Governor?" Bellona asked, gently.

"A petition was signed in the last five hours by every free world, including the new governor of Menali," Lynn said. "I have filed it with Dyse. It permits me to speak on their behalf. This must stop, Bellona. You must speak to the Alliance. Negotiate terms."

Bellona held still for a long moment. So did everyone else.

Sang wished he had taken a seat at the table, today, instead of standing behind Bellona. Sitting would be a relief, right now.

Bellona stirred. "You want me to negotiate your enslavement?"

Alberda shook his head. "If you do not, I will speak to the Alliance myself."

"If you do that, Lynn, you will destroy the free worlds. They won't live in fear. They won't live at all. You'll become annexed states of the Alliance."

"It will remove the threat upon us." Alberda shook his head. "You sit upon Demos, which is invisible to the Alliance. You're safe, Bellona. You don't lie in your bed at night, too filled with fear to sleep—"

"That's where you are wrong, Governor," Bellona replied, her voice low. "If you give in to them, how long do you think it will take them to threaten to use the city killer to make you behave because your cities are not laid out the proper Eriuman way? Or you fail to pay your taxes and levies? Or you object to a new Karassian by-law about screens on every public wall?"

Alberda swallowed.

"By giving in to them, you are telling them they have found the leverage they need to make you do whatever they want," Bellona added. "They will *use* it, Governor. Over and over. The fear that keeps you awake will never end. Not even after they have defeated you."

Alberda glanced down the table. The faces of the free world leaders were implacable. He seemed to draw strength from that blank wall of expressions. He turned back to Bellona. "It is you the Alliance really wants," he added gently. "Talk to them."

Bellona remained still. "Is that what the Alliance told

you, when you reached out to them, Governor? That they would leave the free worlds alone if you delivered me to them? And you believed them?"

A reaction, a collective shiver, rippled down the table.

Alberda's mouth dropped open. He actually looked ill with shock. "How could you even suggest it?

"Fear for their families drives humans to extraordinary actions, Lynn."

Khalil rested his hand on Bellona's wrist. "A word," he said urgently, his voice rasping.

Bellona glanced at him, then back to Alberda, who gripped the table to hold himself up.

Sang watched Khalil's fingernails dig deeper into her flesh.

Bellona looked at him once more.

"A moment, please, Governor," she murmured, getting to her feet.

Khalil moved over to Sang. His gaze was steady. Then he turned to face Bellona as she moved to Sang's other side and lowered his voice. "You've lost, Bellona," he said, his tone very gentle. "You played your hand, and you have been out-played."

Bellona tilted her head to consider him. "You are proposing giving the Alliance dominion over the known worlds."

"Is that so bad?" Khalil asked gently. "At least there will be peace."

"But no freedom!" she said, her voice low and harsh. "They will all be forced to live by Alliance rules. They will have no choice but to obey, for where else can they go? There will be no more free worlds for them to escape to. They will be stripped of choice. They will be enslaved."

"Yet still alive." Khalil squeezed his fist. "Give up, Bellona."

Her eyes glittered as she considered him. "No," she replied. Her voice shook.

Khalil closed his eyes. "You leave me no alternative. I will not submit to your course, Bellona."

Her jaw flexed. "Right now, you have that choice." Her voice was icy. "Submitting to the Alliance will take your choice from you."

Khalil shifted, so his back was to the room, giving him the smallest degree of privacy. He picked up her hand and rested it against his cheek, then kissed her palm. "I love you."

He turned and left the big conference room.

Khalil's departure sent another wave of consternation down the long table.

Sang touched Bellona's arm. "The governors," he warned her.

Bellona stirred. "What? Oh, yes." She turned back to the long table. Instead of sitting, she remained on her feet with one hand pressed to the cool resinwood surface.

Alberda had been forced to sit while waiting. He looked up at her now.

"Governor, as spokesman for the free world heads of state, please take my message back to those who could not make it to this meeting." Her voice was harsh. "I refuse to submit to the Alliance. They offer false hope. It is a trap I have no intention of falling in to. I will find another way to dismantle their hold over the free worlds."

She used the back of her hand to wipe her damp cheek. "I will deliver my promise to you, no matter the cost."

Sang hurried after her as she swept from the room. Behind them, the governors began shouting.

SANG BUILT A BRIDGE DIRECTLY to Bellona's private suite and stepped her across, his hand around her arm. Bellona said nothing, not even when the bridge closed behind them.

"What now?" Sang asked softly.

Bellona shuddered. "You and Dyse must…" She cleared her throat. "There has to be another way. You must find it." She looked up at him. "I can't give up. You understand that, don't you?"

"I know."

Her trembling intensified. "I just c-can't think of… think…" Her arms came up.

Sang held her up, and let her bitter tears soak into his shoulder.

17

HERO RESET HER FORGE BELT, formed a bridge to the hall that was homebase for her regiment, and stepped across. She was the last of the regiment to cross back to Demos from what was left of Menali, which was the way it should be. Once, when she had been Eriuman scum living upon the carcass of a dead Eriuman city, using her wits and her body to survive, the notions of commanding by example, of leading hard men into battle, had been unknown to her.

She was looking back into the past because of the perspective altering sight of Menali as a smoking, crisp and blackened ruin. The city killer had melted most of the city into glistening shards of molten glass.

Hero had loved the twinned cities, with their gardens and sunlight. She had come here when she first escaped Erium, before the Karassians had captured her.

It was sobering to see what remained.

Hero shucked off the exoskeleton and tossed it onto the workbench on the other side of her office. She untied her hair, while the tunic she wore beneath the skeleton dried out.

She let the door slide open when the tap sounded. This military level of the ship was barred to anyone but trusted personnel. She could keep her back to the door if she wanted. A more ingrained instinct made her turn, anyway.

Filip Hrubý, Thecla's exec, stepped through and saluted. "General Antonino. I have the combined report for you to sign."

"And deliver, yes." She would hand it directly to Sang. Thecla was merely being efficient. She held out her hand.

"Thanks, Major."

Hrubý stepped forward to hand her the crystal. He was a big man, with correspondingly wide shoulders, which the exoskeleton exaggerated. His jaw was square and his gaze was always direct. His pale blond hair could be mistaken as Karassian, until one noticed his blue eyes. Hero didn't know anyone else with blue eyes. They were so rare, they were extraordinary. She found herself examining them once more as Hrubý dropped the crystal into her palm.

She realized what she was doing and closed her mind off to the speculation Hrubý's presence always provoked. Her inbuilt drives increased after an active assignment. She had learned to out-wait them. They would subside… or she might slake them in other ways. Sang was considerate, that way. He understood.

Hrubý stepped back with a nod. "Thecla said you would be the last to come back." He paused. "It was brutal, wasn't it?"

"So brutal, it doesn't bear talking about," Hero replied.

"No, I suppose not." Hrubý grimace was self-aware. "I'm just…I feel edgy, you know?"

"There are bars for that, Major."

Hrubý nodded. "I've a liking for Ludovico's joint, in the old quarters. You know the one?"

"I do." It was a favorite among the military.

"Will you be indulging, General?"

Hero frowned. "Are you being polite, Major? Or are you being indirect?"

Hrubý rubbed the back of his strong neck. "I suppose…I'm being indirect."

Hero pursed her lips. She moved around the back of her big desk. Running a regiment took time and effort—more effort than any of the generals got credit for. "I'm sure the talk among the men about me is colorful enough you figured you could get away with it. I'll overlook it—"

"I don't gossip. Not about superior officers. Sir," he tacked on.

Hero paused, her hand on the chair. "Then you took it upon yourself to…what, exactly, Major?"

Hrubý grew wary. "I think there has been a misunderstanding," he said softly. "I thought…I came to believe…" He grimaced. "Permission to leave, General?"

"Not yet." Hero considered him. "What did you come to believe, Major?"

Hrubý hesitated.

Hero moved back around to the front of the desk and Hrubý snapped to attention. She circled him, taking in the details. As she moved around him, she let her fingertips trail over the wide shoulders and back.

He quivered.

"You know what I could do to you, don't you?"

"Yes, sir." He swallowed.

"Yet you have some reason to believe I won't lay open your skin and watch you writhe and die for your assumptions?"

"I understood that…sir…that you…" He cleared his throat. "Liked me."

Hero dropped her hand, genuine surprise trickling through her. "Who told you that?"

Hrubý frowned. "I'm not sure I should say, sir."

She understood. He didn't want to pull anyone else into this. A rare and hot anger build in her belly. "You are dismissed, Major."

Hrubý saluted and escaped.

Her hands shaking, Hero fastened the forge belt around her waist and adjusted the controls.

SANG LOOKED UP FROM THE screen over his desk as a bridge formed beside it and saw Hero on the other side of the aura. She wore military boots and a simple tunic. She always removed her uniform and armor as soon as she considered herself off duty.

She stepped through, her face working with anger.

"You're back," Sang said. "Do you have a count of final numbers for me?"

Hero instead stood with her small fists squeezing. Her strongly arched brows came together. "Is it true? Tell me you didn't manipulate Filip Hrubý and push him at me."

"Ah…." Sang dismissed the screen and turned to face her. He had been waiting for this moment, yet its arrival still made his heart work too hard. "You like him."

"I like *lots* of people," she railed at him. "Then it is true?"

Sang held still. He couldn't bring himself to confirm it. It was another point of no return and he'd faced too many lately.

His lack of movement spoke for him.

Hero drew in a shuddering breath. Her fist shot out without warning, connecting squarely at the side of Sang's jaw. She was a woman and small even by womanly standards, so she had learned how to punch properly, to even the odds.

Hero didn't like weakness in herself, or others.

Sang rocked on the chair and blinked to restore his vision. Dizzy, he felt for and held onto the edge of the desk.

"You couldn't *talk to me*?" she railed at him.

Sang fingered his throbbing jaw. "When have we ever talked?"

Hero dropped her fists. "Oh, I understand clear enough without it," she said bitterly. "You serve Bellona." Her voice took on a vicious mimicry of his.

"I'm sorry," he said honestly.

"Yeah, I know." A tired sigh. "I'm not stupid. You've always made that mistake." She whirled and moved over to the closet, stripping the tunic and boots as she went. Then she stood before the closet and dressed in a civilian outfit, one which made the most of her curves.

"Where are you going?" Sang asked curiously.

"What do you care?"

"I care," he admitted.

"Not enough to make me stay, though." She fastened the forge belt around her waist and stabbed at the controls. "One day—and I hope it's soon, Sang—one day you will realize you miss me. When you do, know I will be happy that you're miserable."

She formed a bridge. A lonely corridor on the old quarter showed through the aura.

"I am already miserable," Sang assured her.

"Good." She stepped through without looking back and collapsed the bridge.

THE OLD LANDING BAY WAS shadowed, with nothing but pilot lights gleaming in the black floor, outlining the traffic lanes once used by cargo carriers loading and unloading freight ships.

The corner where Connie lived was just as dark. Anyone else would have assumed the bay was deserted.

Sang settled on the bottom step of the lowered ramp to wait. His vision was human average, although he could take the trouble to filter the images and enhance them to see better. He didn't bother. The dark was isolating and right now, that was a welcome sensation.

Two hours later, he heard a whisper of sound at the edges of the old landing bay. A slide of a shoe across the hard floor.

Sang got to his feet, feeling the stiffness from sitting motionless for too long. He waited.

Khalil moved around the dead and dusty skimmer beside Connie's bay, spotted Sang and hesitated. He hefted the travelsack hanging over his shoulder, readjusting the weight, then came up to Sang. "How did you know?"

"Connie stopped talking to me, twelve hours ago."

"She talked to you frequently?"

"A running commentary of her observations and her interests." Sang shrugged.

A second figure emerged from the shadows around the skimmer.

Sang drew in a calming breath, for the figure was Fontana. "I should have realized," he said. "You always did think for yourself, Fontana."

Fontana put down the bag he was carrying. "He'll warn them," he said to Khalil.

Them. In Fontana's mind, he had already separated from Demos and from Bellona.

"No, he won't," Khalil said. "Sang knows he can't stop us."

"I did want to try one last time, though," Sang said. "Who else is with you, Khalil?"

"When we reach our destination, I'll be sending coordinates back to those who want to leave."

"Then they'll bridge off the Demos," Sang concluded.

"You'll know then who is with us," Fontana finished.

"You didn't wait, though," Sang said.

"I couldn't," Fontana growled.

"And Aideen?" Sang added.

"She has her work," Fontana said. "Even questioning Bellona's actions upsets her." He hesitated.

"I will watch out for her," Sang assured him, saving him from asking.

Fontana nodded and moved around Sang and up the ramp into Connie's interior.

Khalil shifted on his feet. "The longer we stay here, the more likely we'll be detected and an alert goes up."

"I hope you are not asking me to disable the alarms for you."

"I wouldn't presume on our friendship in that way, Sang."

Sang spotted the belt around Khalil's waist. "You're taking the forges…"

"They already have a super forge. What can it hurt now?" Khalil said, his tone reasonable. "They've already stolen dozens. Ours won't tell them anything more."

"You will use it as a goodwill gesture, anyway," Sang guessed. "Will you tell them about the carbyne?"

"Yes. Bellona sits upon the sole supply of inert carbyne, and besides—"

"They already know how to build forges," Sang finished.

"Khalil," Fontana said from the top of the ramp, his voice soft. "The alerts."

Sang stepped aside. "I don't know what one is supposed to say at a time like this," he admitted.

Khalil hefted the sack once more. "I don't think there is a precedent," he admitted. He moved to the ramp, brushing past Sang. Then he lowered the bag, turned back and pulled Sang into the tight circle of his arms. "Make it work for her, Sang," he breathed. "I cannot."

He let Sang go, picked up the sack and strode up the ramp without looking back.

The ramp lifted, closing behind him.

Sang made himself leave, too. He walked across the wide expanse of landing bay, as Connie lifted with a soft hum of repulsors, and drifted across the bay toward the docking door.

When no more whispers of sounds from her engines could be heard and the bay was back to stillness, Sang found the will to build a bridge and leave.

KHALIL'S AND FONTANA'S DEFECTIONS STRUCK at the heart of the private wing. For days, everyone crept around the wing, avoiding the common room if they could. They didn't speak above murmurs, especially not where Sang could hear them.

Hero did not enter the private wing at all. She had apparently found accommodations elsewhere in the city.

Sang had more than enough work to stay busy. They all did. Fontana's regiment had to be adjusted, the major promoted to colonel and put in temporary charge. All the non-military work Fontana had been doing to support Bellona, including city administration, in particular the police cadre, had to be re-assigned.

Khalil had not been part of the military, although his workload had been no less than Fontana's. All the work needed to be divided and passed on, too.

On the third day, Thecla settled at Sang's table in the common room. She looked grim.

"Tell me," Sang coaxed her.

Her eyes glittered. Her mouth remained in a grim line. "Retha has gone."

"Gone?" Sang frowned. "Not with Khalil. He violently disagrees with him about surrendering to the Alliance."

"No, he's *gone,*" Thecla said. She grimaced. "The box of crystals with his family history research wasn't on the desk when I got up this morning."

Sang sat back. "I did not realize the extent of his anger…"

"He has always been angry," Thecla said. "Now he has a fresh reason for it. He latched onto it." She hesitated. "After Ledan, it took him three years to train himself back to a normal sleep cycle, Sang. Since Menali, he hasn't shifted out of nonrem…if he's slept at all."

Sang leaned and rested his hand on hers. Felt the metal beneath his fingertips. "What can I do?"

Thecla shook her head. "I'll take over his regiment. They're discipline freaks, so I can manage both. Aideen will work with me on the rest. She needs the distraction, anyway." Thecla got to her feet and looked down at him. "It's all flaking away." Her tone was sad.

Sang shook his head. "No. It is not, Thecla. This is merely a shift. Seismic shifts happen all the time. It will sort itself out."

"I thought it *had* sorted itself out. We had more than ten years, Sang. Maybe that's all we deserve."

The cold fingers walked up his spine. Sang shuddered. "I refuse to believe that. Everyone should be free to live the life they want. It shouldn't be just a privilege for the lucky and the bold."

Thecla's mouth turned up at the corner. "I like the way you think, Sang."

"It took me years to train myself to think this way. It's the way a free man thinks."

She met his gaze and nodded. "I hear you." She pushed the chair back under the table. "And I have a small mountain of work to get through now." She strode away, her shoulders square.

It was a tiny moment of positivity among days of bleakness. Sang told himself to remember it.

Two days later, those who had elected to go with Khalil disappeared from Demos.

18

DYSE STAYED IN DIGITAL MODE, his biological systems on autonomic status, while he sorted through who was still upon Demos and who had disappeared. His body remained slumped in the easy chair in the corner of the common room, a passive mouthpiece.

Sang envied him the ability to remain aloof from emotions while he assessed the damage for Bellona. Sang's thought processes were unavoidably biological, for his body *was* him. He had to accept the pain and heartbreak as physical reactions as he compiled the data.

"Of the eight regiments we had, including Fontana's, which was on remedial standby, there is only enough troops left to make up just over three regiments," Dyse told Bellona.

"Hero's…?" Sang began. He couldn't finish.

"Hero reports only a three percent loss," Dyse told him.

Sang let out a breath he wasn't aware he had been holding. Hero, then, was still on Demos.

Bellona was pretending to eat. She stirred more than she ate, as she listened to Dyse's report. Her eyes had a hollow glaze Sang didn't like. She merely nodded at the harsh figures Dyse produced. "And city administration?" she asked.

"Only ten percent have gone from the rank and file," Dyse said. "The city's administration is not as structured as the military, though."

"I'm sorting out a chain of command," Sang added. "I've directed them to recruit as necessary."

"And civilians, Dyse? Can you estimate?"

"I can extrapolate. It isn't as accurate as a head count.

The problem is the refugees from High Moon and Menali. We hadn't completed a full census yet. They're muddying the numbers."

"Give me a rough guess when you can, please, Dyse," Bellona replied.

"No," Sang said quickly. "No rough guesses. No inflated numbers."

Bellona raised her brow. Dyse merely swiveled his chin with an apathetic motion, to look at Sang.

Sang plucked the fork from Bellona's hand and stabbed it into Dyse's knee.

"Fuck!" Dyse cried, jerking upright and rubbing the knee.

"That's better. Here." Sang held the fork out to Bellona. She took it, her expression puzzled.

"Why did you do that?" Dyse demanded.

"Because I want you in your body, not operating it from a distance," Sang said. "You're part of this, Dyse. You don't get to bail on us because it's too uncomfortable. You wanted to experience human life. *Be* human, then. No matter what."

Dyse scowled. "Very well. I'm human…and you're a prick."

"That's better," Sang replied. He turned to Bellona. "It doesn't *matter* who has left, or even why they left. We shouldn't care who they've gone to. You know why?"

Bellona put her chin on her fist. "Why?"

"Because *we are here*. While we're here, while Demos is here, a free state exists. There is a place where those who disagree with the Alliance can go."

Bellona drew in a slow, deep breath. "I swore to protect the free worlds…"

Sang shook his head. "And you are! You are doing everything you can to preserve them in the face of the most overwhelming opposition. The Alliance will annex worlds one by one as they capitulate to their control. The worlds that don't cave will be threatened with extinction. Some of them will accept that fate rather than give in. Yet as long as Demos exists, *so does the free state.*"

Bellona's eyes narrowed.

"You have been looking at this the wrong way all along," Sang continued. "Yes, you have had to protect the free worlds. You've stood between them and the Alliance for years. Maybe that's why we missed it. Demos is the ultimate example of a free world, one the Alliance can't take away, because they can't find us."

"A symbol," Dyse added, for he thought in symbols.

"Yes," Sang said. "It doesn't matter who stayed and who left, or even where they went to. It's their choice. We regroup and we move on. We accept into Demos any refugee who wants to live here, because they like the values we hold to. We give everyone else passage to whatever world they'd rather live on."

"The military…." Dyse murmured.

"So we're short a few generals. We promote from the ranks, and we also send out an open call to the free worlds. Offer anyone true freedom in exchange for their service. We will be inundated with recruits. It's likely the need for a strong military force will recede, anyway." He got to his feet. "I intend to find new city administrators from among the refugees. And I'll have Aideen build new levels and new footage—"

"Aideen has gone to Fontana," Dyse said quietly.

"Then I'll find someone else to do the work," Sang shot back. He turned to Bellona. "*That* is the message we will give the free worlds. That is your solution."

"Um…it's not exactly a solution," Dyse pointed out. "It won't stop the Alliance."

"Yes, it will," Bellona replied, her voice firm. She stood, too. "I can't stop the city killers…but the city killers cannot stop an idea." She smiled. "Call a general assembly, Sang. Anyone who can squeeze into the arena should be there. Everyone else should find a screen. Can the Chidi entity broadcast into the Sodality?"

"He will need time to soften the audience," Sang said. "He's been working on it since he got here. Trying to wake up people who don't know they're asleep in the first place and haven't had to think for themselves in a lifetime is a lot of inertia to overcome."

"He's been talking subversion for years," Dyse pointed out.

"And that habituation will get them over the initial shock," Sang said in agreement. "It will wake them up. After that, he just has to convince them to start using their brains. To ask the hard questions."

"How long, Sang?" Bellona asked.

"Ten days. More would be better, but it can be done in ten."

"Ten it is, then. That's when the general assembly will be held." She paused. "That just leaves Erium."

Sang smiled. "I have Erium covered."

PART THREE

19

Menaii, Deluca Prime, Delucas System

"Is that...are you watching *Bellona*?" Raine asked, shock making his voice raspy.

Iulia stirred and glanced over her shoulder to where Raine stood at the edge of the cavaedium, still dripping from his dip in the pool. Irritation touched her. "I am watching my daughter," she pointed out coldly.

"Who is the most wanted criminal of the known worlds," Raine replied. He picked up a sheet and patted his damp skin. "Don't let anyone else catch you looking at that nonsense."

"Increase the volume," Iulia told Riz.

Bellona's voice leapt. "...important we stay free in our hearts and minds, and in everything we do, no matter the opposition. Even if they bind us with chains to a dark corner of a forgotten cellar, we are still free. No one can change what we believe."

Raine snorted. "Rhetorical nonsense."

"Is it?" Iulia asked. "Volume, Riz."

Bellona's voice grew even louder, filling the cavaedium with ringing value-heavy words. Courage. Liberty. Autonomy. Self-determination. Fortitude. Even more attractive concepts peppered her statements. Peace. Harmony. Fulfillment. Purpose.

Raine settled beside Iulia on the long divan. "Some

great military leader, huh?" He tilted his head. "Why is the Alliance so afraid of her? Remind me?"

"Mmm…" Iulia said.

"The family council will be incensed," Raine warned.

"Mm," Iulia said again.

"THEY ARE CAMPED OUTSIDE THE old studio," Chidi said. He sounded amused. "They've made tents from garbage, to keep off the rain, for it is winter in the north at the moment. The police dispersed them twice."

"Yet they keep coming back," Sang finished.

"Yes! They melt away, then they come back, like a tide, with their signs and their chants and their demand to speak to Chidi, to see him. It is fascinating, Sang. I studied these things—truth and determination, and suppression of the masses. Until the last few weeks, I did not understand the power of it."

"Maybe you should give them what they want," Sang said.

"You mean, give them Chidi? I am."

"No, I mean give them *you*."

Silence.

Sang smiled. "You've considered it. You would not be self-aware if you had not. A new body, Chidi."

"I would…have to limit myself. The human brain does not have the capacity I do."

"Then you have thought of it." Sang got up from the stool which sat in front of the banks of servers at all times. "I have that same capacity, Chidi. Do you consider me limited?"

"I must consider that," Chidi replied.

"While you're thinking about it, consider the type of body you want. You're free to choose." He added, "Once you have a body, you will be free in all ways. Then you can meet your viewers and demonstrate what that means."

• • • • •

ADMIRAL LOYOLA WAS PISSED.

Woodrow normally ignored the man. He was a competent soldier who watched too much of his own footage. Unfortunately, so did most of the other military leaders, who looked to Loyola to guide their decisions.

Which was why Woodrow didn't find a discreet way to deal with the man. He was too useful. He had cultivated the association, instead, which kept the military in his pocket.

Now Loyola stood in his office and actually screamed at him, an unpleasant sound which would be heard beyond the office walls.

"Coria, Cerce, Shavista and now New Veles! All of them have broken off communications in the last week! What the fuck is going on, Woodrow? The Council is screaming for explanations."

"They scream at me, too, Admiral," Woodrow told him.

"I don't give a fuck about you! I want answers! You said the free worlds were about to capitulate, weeks ago. We actually had them with their hands up! Now they're backing off!"

Woodrow recalled the summary report his aide had compiled for him just yesterday, pointing to growing counts of civil disobedience and petty crimes, particularly larceny. Public screen generators were being vandalized. Then there were the hundreds of squatters living outside the building where Chidi had once run his little kingdom. The street had been blocked for weeks by their camps and shelters.

Raine Cardenas was frothing at the mouth about Eriumans spending too much time in front of screens lately, as if leisure wasn't a holy right maintained by the upper classes in Erium. Woodrow had considered him a bigoted hypocrite until he read the report about petty crime rates in the Sodality.

Now this.

Woodrow considered the admiral. "Do you monitor the feeds from Demos, Admiral?"

Loyola turned an interesting shade of purple. "How *dare* you imply…!" He didn't finish. Instead, he drew himself upright. He was a half meter taller than Woodrow, which made him an imposing figure, standing over Woodrow's desk.

Woodrow didn't feel intimidated in the slightest. "The feeds are educational, Admiral," he pointed out. "We've never succeeded in planting spies upon Demos. Spying on their propaganda is the next best thing."

"It is *not* the next best thing. You have the traitor in your cells."

Woodrow cleared his throat. Khalil Ready had proved to be spectacularly useless, but he wouldn't admit that to Loyola. Loyola resented that Woodrow got to milk the traitor, when Loyola's fleet brought him into the Sodality in the first place. Instead, he said, "Traitors make unreliable sources."

"So does propaganda."

"Not if you interpret it correctly. The bitch is infecting people, Admiral. That's why your free states are turning their backs."

Loyola narrowed his eyes. "Impossible. We have city killers, the superforge…"

"Not everything is about who has the biggest gun," Woodrow said. He was tired of the conversation. "Tell the Council that, next time they scream at you."

Loyola slapped his cap against his thigh. "How am I supposed to shoot at *words?*" he demanded. "You need to do something about her, Woodrow. I mean it." He slammed the door as he left.

Woodrow considered the closed door for a few moments. Then he went down to the basement, to the wing where only the highest security passes were permitted access. There were layers of defense shielding the place, including a last lethal level which only his pass could unlock.

He moved into the furnished rooms beyond the seal. The rooms were comfortable, even luxurious, with their carpets and decorations and muted wall colors. He might be strolling through an apartment in Seher, the high end of Kachmar City where the Chidis of the world clumped together in self-defense. Only, those apartments had doors that led outside.

Ready put down the printed book he was reading, as Woodrow came in.

"There is more gray in your hair, Ready."

"And you're going to fat." Ready smiled. "All that adrenaline screwing with your metabolism. Are you under stress, Woodrow?" His tone was one of polite concern.

Woodrow scowled. "If only you had a screen and a network, you could find out for yourself."

Ready didn't respond. He was former Bureau. No one knew what he might do if he had access to even the most encrypted and secure network they could build.

Woodrow sat on the chair opposite Ready's. "Remind me again. Why did you leave Demos?"

"To seek asylum in Karassia. Why are you asking what you already know?"

They had debriefed Ready for fifteen straight days, refusing him sleep and food, and hammering him with endless questions. There had been no need to torture him for information. He had been a fountain of facts. Names, positions, titles, city structure, military structure…it had all come out. Hours and hours of it.

The iteration of questions, the sleep deprivation and hunger, had been to test the veracity of what he told them. Now, somewhere in the intelligence corps, every word he'd spoken was being analyzed and assessed—and confirmed where it could be. Only, little of it was confirmable, because Demos could not be boarded. It couldn't be found at all, except by people who lived there, who had a personalized forge belt that could take them back home.

Ready had disabled his before handing it over.

His verbosity earned him this padded, comfortable cell. Woodrow would have preferred to shoot him through the temple and remove the threat he represented, only Loyola had paraded the man through the streets of Kachmar, showing off his prize catch. Now everyone knew Ready was here. If Woodrow got rid of him, it would raise questions about Woodrow's agenda and loyalties.

How could he explain how uneasy Ready made him? The man could not be underestimated.

Ready's eyes narrowed. "What has happened?"

"Why didn't you stay with her? You've gone back to her twice before. You have proved you cannot stay away. So why did you leave this time?"

Ready's gaze searched Woodrow's face. "She's fighting back…somehow. That's why you look ill." He smiled.

"That pleases you?" Woodrow asked.

"I find it ironic," Ready said. He opened the book once more.

"You don't want to know what she is doing?"

"Not from you." He returned to reading.

Woodrow watched the top of Ready's head for a while, feeling an odd, disjointed sense of powerlessness.

He recognized that he had brought the sensation with him. Ready had merely provoked into life what had been planted somewhere in the last few days or weeks.

When Ready continued to ignore him, Woodrow got up and left.

It felt like a retreat.

20

SANG STEPPED ACROSS THE BRIDGE he made, into the private antechamber where the bexen handmaids were fussing over Bellona's robes and hair and headpiece.

Through the arch into the assembly hall dais came the steady low-grade rumble of a crowd patiently waiting.

Sang dismissed the maids. "You look perfect already," he told Bellona as she watched them file out in a row. "Except…" He picked up a stray lock of her hair and pushed it beneath the headpiece. "There are nine thousand people in the hall. Dyse had every screen in the city leashed and showing the broadcast. Chidi has his entire viewer base waiting, too. The last audit puts his numbers above a billion. There is no way to assess who is watching from the free worlds, or Erium. I think it safe to say a few might be." He smiled. "Don't feel pressured."

Bellona gave a tight laugh. "Speech of a lifetime, then?"

"They all are."

"Lately, yes. I can *feel* the difference when I talk to people now. The resistance is shifting, Sang. People are captured by ideas, not just fear." She put her hand on his chest. "*You* did that."

"It is you they listen to."

"I don't know about that," Bellona said. She reached under her robe and withdrew her hand and held it out. An image projector sat on her palm. She activated it. The image formed over it. "I found it, this morning."

Sang stared at the image. His chest tightened.

It was an image of Max and Bellona. Max was still a boy, Bellona barely into womanhood, her face fresh and glowing with youth and innocence. Both were laughing at the image-taker.

"Wait took that," Sang whispered. He remembered the occasion. The reminder of Wait made his throat squeeze painfully. After Bellona's father died, his android had… wilted, was the only phrase which fit. They had found Wait standing in a corner of Reynard's study, his face to the wall, essentially non-functional. Sang had not asked what happened to the body that had carried the android mind.

The section of the displayed image Sang's gaze kept returning to was the figure in the background. It was him, hovering within reach of Max if he should need anything.

The Sang in the image was blank in both face and body. Unformed.

"Yes, that's you," Bellona said, her voice mellow. "Or, rather, it is you as you used to be. Genderless, mindless, drifting on any current that directed you."

Sang turned his attention back to Bellona in the image. "You, on the other hand, showed your promise even then." He managed to smile at her.

"We have come a long way, haven't we?" She turned the projector off and held it out to him. "Here. There are more images on there. Let them remind you of all you have achieved, Sang."

He ran his thumb over the domed top of the little projector. "Thank you."

Bellona gripped the front of his robe and gave him a shake. "What would I have done without you? I would not be here. I would not have survived. We both know that."

"I merely followed your lead."

"Not anymore." She smiled. "You have moved on, now. Just promise me, Sang…" She smoothed out the robe she had rumpled. "Promise to always be you. Be what *you* want. Don't ever change to meet someone else's specifications. You're not that android anymore."

"You want me to be free," he whispered.

Bellona laughed softly. "Yes, exactly. I like you as a free man." She rose and pressed her lips against his, in a soft, light touch. "For luck," she said, then grinned impishly. "As this is the speech of my life."

Sang managed to smile, as she picked up the heavy hem of the robe and sailed out into the assembly hall.

IT WAS *THE* SPEECH OF her life. Sang could feel it in his bones. He read it in the crackling tension in the audience watching her.

He remained in the antechamber, his back propped against the arch support, and listened to her speak the words he had crafted for her.

Bellona was the only woman in the known worlds who could demand that humanity turn its back upon a millennium-old way of life and find a better alternative. A simpler choice, one that was the right of every man, woman and child.

She painted a picture of what that life would look like, if everyone reached and plucked it for themselves. The fulfillment and purpose they would find if they choose their own path in the world.

The evils of tyranny which thought it was right.

The first time she paused, the applause and calls from the hall were thunderous in their intensity.

"Yes, yes, applaud!" Bellona encouraged them. "You who stand before me are applauding yourself, for you have already made that choice. You are living proof that liberty does not mean chaos. It is not something to be afraid of. Independence should be embraced. It is within the grasp of everyone who listens to me now. No matter where you are, or what your circumstances—you, too, can be free. It starts here in your mind, first. And it grows here, in your heart."

The cheering and shouting drowned the applause. Bellona had to shout to make herself heard, more than once, before they settled to listen to her once more. The energy pulsing from the audience would energize a village or more.

"True liberty comes with responsibility," Bellona continued. "It is joined at the hip with duty and purpose. You are free to find your purpose in life, whatever that purpose may be. They only work when *you* do. When you choose for yourself the values you will live by…and you abide by them, no matter what. If you live with your own internal compass to guide you, then you have no need of an authoritarian state tell you what direction to take!"

The reaction from the audience made the wall against Sang's back tremble. The sound washed through the archway, rolling like distant thunder.

It hid the crack of rattler fire.

The first warning for Sang was the screaming.

He threw himself around the arch, as the great waves of applause and shouting checked, as the screaming increased.

Bellona laid on the floor behind the podium.

Sang fell to his knees beside her, as Thecla's house guards formed a wall behind him. The captain spoke quick, sharp commands, ordering the arena be locked down, to search the highest tiers, to bring a medic.

Bellona's eyes were open and unmoving. The scorch mark on the front of her robe was tiny, barely a fingerwidth, the sign of a marksman.

Sang knew it was too late. Still, he formed a bridge to the hospital and picked her up and stepped through.

Staff coalesced around him, plucking Bellona from his arms and taking her away.

Sang waited.

Thecla found him there. She wore exoskeleton and a full array of weapons. "We have to empty the arena, Sang. We can't search when it's full of people."

"There's no need to search," Sang told her. "Find Retha. He's already made his way down to the main floor to mingle with them there. He would have broken up the rattler first. You'll find pieces of it spread across the control booth and the projector room beside it. He took the shot from the projector room."

"How do you know that?" Thecla breathed, her face pale.

"It's the best vantage point."

"How do you know it was Retha…?"

"Find him. Empty the hall and scan everyone as they leave. He'll be among them. He won't deny what he has done when you ask him. Then you will know, too. You have control of the military, now, Thecla. Use them to keep the city contained."

Thecla nodded and strode away. She was shaken, but she had been reminded of her responsibility.

Shortly after, the chief medical officer came to tell Sang that Bellona was dead.

SANG MOVED THROUGH THE NEXT twelve hours wishing he had Dyse's ability to withdraw from human reactions. Instead, he locked his focus upon what needed to be done.

One of the very first tasks was to give the news to everyone else. Sang told Chidi to hold open all the feeds that had been trained upon Bellona's assembly speech.

Then, for the first time in his life, Sang let the lenses focus upon him. It should have terrified him. It should have sent his programmed reticence into a fugue. Instead, all he felt was numb, as he spoke the simple words, which Chidi sent out across the galaxy.

"Twenty-three minutes ago, Bellona Cardenas Scordina de Deluca, formerly of the Scordinii clan of Erium, formerly known as Xenia, the hero of the Sodality, leader and captain of Demosthenes, and protector of free worlds and people everywhere, was shot and killed by an assassin who will be identified shortly.

"Demosthenes will go on. The liberty Bellona valued and has died for will be upheld in this city, and anywhere people choose to take autonomy for themselves."

SANG RETREATED TO THE COMMON room in the private wing for the silence and stillness he needed to do what must be done.

Dyse coordinated messages, pleas, threats, demands for information, submissions for a few minutes with someone in authority, calls for troops, and thousands of requests for bridges to step across to Demos. He juggled and delegated and in between swiping at screens, he wiped his cheeks, instead.

Hero found them there. She ducked under and around Dyse's forest of screens to move in front of Sang. "What can I do?" Her voice was calm. Her eyes were red.

"Help Thecla control the city. She has the troops. You calm the administrators and the people."

Hero nodded and went away.

Sometime later, Thecla returned. Her calm shell showed signs of cracking. "It *was* Retha."

"*Why*?" Hayes demanded, coming in behind her. Hecate Hult also stepped through a bridge, directly into the common room.

"Because Bellona took away his life, three times," Sang said. "As he reckons it, at least. She took it the first time when he was taken from Menali and put in the Ledan program, and his memory wiped. She took it a second time when she pulled him out of Ledan and he learned what he had lost. Then she took it the third time by defying the Alliance, who responded by destroying Menali."

Thecla's mouth opened. "That is almost exactly…Sang, how did you know that?"

"He said so, when Menali was destroyed. Just not in those words." Sang looked at Hayes. "Lynn Alberda will call for permission to enter the city in a while. Will you cross to Cerce and bring him over, please."

Hayes' heavy brows came together. "Now? Before he asks?"

"He is being polite and biding his time, but he wants… no, he *needs* to be here, to help, even if all he does is trip people up. He was Bellona's friend. He is also the spokesman for the free worlds. We must let him mourn the way he wants to."

"What do we do with Retha?" Dyse asked, his tone hard.

"He confessed, Thecla?"

She nodded. Her chin creased then smoothed out.

"We must get that confession on record and spread the record as far and as wide as we can," Sang said. "When you have it, give it to Chidi. He will make sure it does not get buried."

"I will," Chidi's disembodied voice agreed, from the screen he was using to monitor the common room.

Thecla nodded and hurried away.

"Why spread it around, Sang?" Hecate asked.

"Because without it, everyone will think the Alliance did this," Dyse said. "Even the Alliance will believe someone in their ranks did it. The Eriumans and Karassians will accuse each other."

"Let them tear each other apart," Hecate growled.

"That's only the politicians," Dyse said. "The military—both militaries—will prefer direct action and they will take it."

"Against each other?" Hecate asked, still sounding puzzled.

"Against Demos," Sang said. "A pre-emptive strike against the blow they think we will deliver them."

• • • • •

KHALIL PUT THE BOOK ASIDE when Woodrow returned. Two visits in two weeks—it was a break in the pattern. Wariness built in him. His muscles readied for action.

Woodrow nodded at Khalil, the expression on his bland round face sober. He put the screen projector on the table in front of Khalil.

The video was only a few minutes long, showing Bellona giving a speech in the assembly hall. Khalil's heart ached as he watched her speak. She had grown just in the weeks he had been gone, becoming an unstoppable force.

This was why Woodrow had looked worried, two weeks ago.

Was this Sang's solution?

"Watch," Woodrow warned him.

Khalil glanced at him, startled. The soft, distinct sound of a long-distance rattler bolt firing jerked his attention back to the screen, in time to see Bellona falling backward behind the podium.

Every corpuscle in Kahlil's body grew still.

Screams. From the dark archway behind the podium, Sang lunged, dropping out of sight behind the podium itself.

The screen shifted. Sang, facing the camera, speaking the terrible words.

"...Demosthenes will go on. The liberty Bellona valued and has died for will be upheld in this city, and anywhere people choose to take autonomy for themselves."

Woodrow turned off the projector. "You must go back to them," he said. "Tell them it was not us who did this. It was not Karassia. Do you understand?"

Khalil leapt, his fingers gripping Woodrow's throat. He squeezed, and squeezed, until bones cracked and flesh stretched. And still he squeezed.

When Woodrow was quite dead, Khalil picked up the

screen projector and tossed it in his palm, his expression implacable.

He got to work.

ONLY WHEN DYSE PULLED SANG around by the shoulder and told him to go and sleep, did Sang recognize the exhaustion pulling at him. He stood for another five minutes, making sure everything would hold for a few hours.

When he moved past Lynn Alberda's chair, he rested his hand on the man's shoulder, topped up his glass, and moved on.

Sang's quarters were still. Silent. He stood in the doorway and contemplated returning to the muffling frenzy of voices and screens and movement in the common room. Contemplation could be put aside, there.

Yet, even as he stood, his legs trembled. He was beyond exhaustion. Even if he laid down for just a few minutes…

He sat on the edge of the bed, then waited for the energy to accumulate so he could swing his legs up and lie down and let sleep take him. While he sat, he unfastened the robe and slid his arms out of it. His fingers brushed against the hard object in the inner pocket.

He pulled out the image projector and reached to put it on the shelf behind the bed. It dropped between the bed and the shelf and disappeared.

The first sob tore at his throat and his eyes. The agony induced more. Sang bent, shuddering.

When the worst of it tapered off, when he could see even a little bit, a hand held a cloth out to him. It was Hero's hand.

He took the cloth and used it. When he could see properly once more, he looked up.

Hero silently offered a glass filled with colorless liquid.

"It will help you sleep."

"I don't think I need the help. Not now."

Hero put the glass on the shelf. She bent to bring her eyes level with his. "Your freckles are all standing out."

"Your nose is red."

She nodded. "I took care of Retha for you, Sang." Her mouth turned down. "He knew why I was there. I think he was glad, in the end. At least he can sleep now."

Sang closed his eyes. "And the recording?"

"Recording?"

Then he remembered. She had not been in the common room when he had told Thecla to get Retha's confession on record.

21

Kachmar City, Kachmar. Karassian Sodality.

EVEN THOUGH THE SHELTERS WERE made of garbage and materials found in the street, or stripped from buildings, there was an orderliness about the rows that spoke of purpose.

Directly in front of the old broadcasting house doors and for thirty meters on either side, the road and sidewalk were clear of squats. Instead, the people who had found themselves drawn to the abandoned building stood watching the old, static screens mounted on the front walls.

In the last six weeks, the screens had come to life, drawing in Karassians with images not seen anywhere else in the Sodality, displayed side-by-side with their favorite host, Chidi—or the ghost of him, at least.

As the ghost was as charming and news-filled as the original version, everyone was happy to keep watching. They watched in larger and larger numbers, because the images and the stories Chidi told were compulsively *different.*

Tales about the worlds beyond the borders of the Sodality. Stories about people dying, their homes destroyed, their worlds disabled. People who didn't look all that different from proper Karassians, really.

And of course, their favorite hero, Xenia. Not Xenia as she was—a awe-inspiring Karassian warrior fiercely defending the Sodality. The new Xenia, unlike the new Chidi, didn't look the same at all. She *felt* the same, though. She was still defending the lives of others. And so they watched, drawn in to the narrative.

They had gathered on the sidewalk when Chidi died, and gradually, their numbers increased. In ones and twos, in small groups, the people who listened to Chidi found themselves thinking in odd ways. Wondering about fundamental subjects like truth and liberty.

They sought each other out, for the average Karassian still believed in the superiority of the Sodality, and the lawless worlds beyond who wanted to destroy Karassia just because. Those who listened to Chidi felt alone, until they came here.

Now the images and the language had shifted once more. There was an urgency to the news. Worlds destroyed…by *the Alliance!* How could this be?

The news continued and slowly, understanding arrived. The Alliance intended to destroy Xenia. Bellona. They watched as the pressure upon their darling increased.

The moment Bellona died was replicated upon every single screen, while the street below grew still with shock. The people on the street looked at each other, seeing their dismay and horror reflected in others' eyes.

The arrival of Karassian troop carriers at either end of the blocked street sent a ripple through the crowd.

"Stand together!" Chidi urged them, speaking from every giant screen. "The soldiers are here to arrest you, so you cannot speak the truth! Stand together, as Xenia did!"

Mumtaz, one of the forty-five raw recruits in the carriers, approached the silent people ranged across the street in front of him, his rattler leveled. Their implacable expressions shook the little confidence he had. He'd never pointed a gun at another Karassian before. It felt wrong to do so now. It went against every reason he had joined the military three weeks ago.

"Advance forward!" the sergeant screamed.

Only, there was nowhere to advance. The leading edge of the people they were here to disperse had not moved.

The muzzle of the rattler brushed their bellies.

Mumtaz swallowed. "Move," he whispered.

No response.

The troopers to either side of him were equally mired. They looked at each other, then at their sergeant for guidance.

The unarmed man in front of Mumtaz pushed forward, so the rattler buried itself in his belly. He reached for Mumtaz's neck.

Mumtaz reared back, his finger tightening. The rattler fired, blue death exploding from the muzzle, to flare in the man's middle. His skin and skeleton snared the bolt. Contained it.

Mumtaz dropped the rattler, horrified. He backed up a step. He could hear his sergeant screaming but couldn't process the words.

The man he had killed slid to the ground, his melted innards oozing onto the fused surface of the road. It spread like blood...and there was plenty of that in the milky cloud, streaking it and making it pink.

For a moment the tableau on the road held still, as everyone absorbed what had just happened.

The unarmed Karassians moved forward as one, as if a silent sergeant had screamed a command at *them*. They reached for the troopers with hands and elbows and fists...even teeth.

They used whatever they had at hand—pieces of carbonized building materials, grown furniture legs. Then the first Karassian picked up a dropped rattler and used it upon a soldier. More of them followed the first's example.

As another pair of hands gripped Mumtaz' neck and pulled him to the ground, he saw the big screens were monitoring the melee with dispassionate accuracy.

As he died, Mumtaz wondered who would watch the screens now.

ADMIRAL LOYOLA TORE HIS GAZE away from the carnage on the screens. "What fool put green recruits on the ground?" he demanded.

"You said we could not pull from the cadres," Captain Howse ground out. His white flesh looked gray. He stood in front of his tall command chair, while the balance of the ship's personnel bent over their screens, suddenly very busy.

"It was a simple arrest-and-clear operation," Loyola shot back. "They're *civilians!*"

The floor of the bridge shifted and dropped, making everyone on their feet stagger.

"We're under fire, sir!" a lieutenant called out.

"From *whom*?" Loyola asked, acid in his voice. "The Eriumans?" For that was a flat impossibility.

"There's nothing on any scanner anywhere!" the security chief shouted back.

The bridge heaved once more and this time, Loyola could feel the rumble of…something. It was far beneath this deck, transmitted along the ship's structure.

"What in the stars is going on?" he demanded, looking directly at Captain Howse.

Howse frowned. "Exo, internal station reports, now."

The exo was also frowning. "Multiple reports. From across the ship. Intrusions…dozens of them."

Light flared to Loyola's right, warning him. He snatched at the personal rattler sitting on his hip as the light turned into one of the alarming circular bridges used by Demosthenes.

The bridge formed. He saw a woman with short blonde hair and a blank, cruel face staring at him through the bridge. She had enhanced arms. Karassian. This was Thecla, then.

He braced himself for her attack.

Instead, she turned the long rattler in her hands toward him and fired.

Other key people on the bridge, including Howse and his exo, all dropped to the ground, their bodies smoking.

Loyola clutched at his destroyed chest, his very last thought one of surprise. Everything they had learned about the Demos bridges was that they *had* to be crossed. They were so unstable that if they were not used, they would implode.

As his legs weakened and he folded to the ground, Loyola experienced an electrifying *aha!* sensation.

The bolt from the rattler passing through the bridge *was* a crossing.

Why hadn't they anticipated that?

THE NEWS OF BELLONA'S DEATH was slow to spread across the Erium worlds, although no one understood why until much, much later.

Riz was the only other entity in the house permitted inside Iulia's private suite without express permission, so Iulia didn't look up when the outer door opened without announcing anyone.

Riz padded into the room as Iulia wound the last folds of the delicate lace mantle over and around her shoulders and minutely adjusted the hems around her face. She didn't want to obscure her features, after all. Especially her eyes. Although a solid edge to peer around often doubled the impact of one's gaze, she had learned.

Especially when sitting at a large table full of men with larger egos, like the family council table. The meeting had been called quickly, with some urgency and mystery to the summons. Her instincts told her she could not afford to miss this meeting.

"Is the car ready, Riz?"

The android failed to respond, which was only the first of the shocks Iulia was about to experience.

Iulia made an impatient sound and turned away from her reflection. "I said—"

The second shock was by far the worst.

There were tears upon the android's face. Its throat worked, as if it was choked.

"Riz, for the love of Erium, what is *wrong* with you?"

"Iulia! *Iulia!*" Raine was shouting from the atrium, his voice echoing against the stone and marble.

Only now did Iulia realize that something was very wrong. She was forced to step *around* Riz. It was another shock yet muted by the first two and by Raine's strident shouting.

She hurried out to the atrium. Riz followed. She could hear the thing's feet slapping the cold tiles as they moved up the tablinum to the main peristylum.

Raine threw out his hand when he saw Iulia enter. "There's news," he said grimly. He looked at his android, Blink. "Run it."

Blink didn't move. A standard-sized screen formed in front of it, hanging in the air.

The images were astonishing. People fighting in the street against armed soldiers. Karassians, she identified. Hundreds of them. The people were winning, too. The fierce notes in the screams and shouts proclaimed their victory.

"Not that," Raine snapped.

The screen flickered. The blackness of space this time. A fleet of the ugly Karassian navy vessels, with their chunky lack of esthetics. The fleet hung over a red and green ball Iulia didn't recognize at first glance. Like most ships which parked over a planet, they were laid out along an invisible plane, their positions level across it.

Only two of the ships were not holding to the artificial surface. They were drifting, dipping. As she watched, the ships lit up with huge fireballs and explosions, which quickly imploded as the vacuum of space sucked the energy out of them.

The ships were dropping, for they had been holding at the very edge of the planetary atmosphere, which helped provide stability. As weak as the gravity would be at that point, it was enough to suck the disabled ships down in a steadily accelerating dive.

Raine whirled to look at Blink. "I said, *the other one*, damn it! Are you deliberately misunderstanding me?"

Blink didn't move or respond.

The screen shifted again.

Iulia saw Riz move to one side of her, placing itself in a position to study the screen, too.

The assembly hall on Demos. Iulia had seen images of the hall many times, in the privacy of her suite. High above the people standing on the floor of the hall, and in the rising tiers all around the big circular area, stood Bellona upon the mildly pretentious dais with its podium carrying the emblem of Demosthenes—a bird rising from flames.

She wore the more-than-pretentious headdress and robe, which glittered and sparkled with every movement and was speaking—more words about hearts and minds and liberty—

Iulia jumped as a bright blue rattler bolt streaked across the hall. It moved horizontally, putting the shooter at the same level as Bellona's dais.

The bolt struck Bellona in the chest and threw her backward. She fell, disappearing behind the podium, as screams sounded on the screen.

Iulia clutched at her chest, as pain speared it and made her bones ache. "No…"

Riz lifted its hand and wiped its cheeks, which were sodden with even more tears.

"No, no, no…" Iulia moaned.

The screen dissolved.

"They killed her," Raine breathed. "The Karassians are insane. The reprisals…" He shook his head. "They *killed* her."

Iulia reached out for something, *anything*, to use to prop herself up. She found flesh. An arm. She gripped it desperately as the agony rolled through her. "They killed my baby, my darling…"

It hurt too much to cry. She thought she might explode with the pressure building in her if she did not, though. She shook with the power of it.

She was led across the atrium. A cold stone bench sat by a pillar, just where the force fields held off the deep winter chill and prevented the snow from drifting into the interior of the atrium. The bench had a spectacular view of the rolling farmlands to the south of the city, and the private family gardens between the house and the public lands.

Iulia saw none of it as she sank onto the bench.

She saw her feet in the slender house sandals, and the edges of the red gown she wore. She had worn mourning red every day since Max died. How stupid could she be? That left her with nothing to mark the death of her last child, her most precious child, the one who had been so wrongfully taken.

The flash of light on the other side of the atrium made her look up, at last. With some surprise, she saw that Riz stood beside her. It was Riz whose arm she had taken. Riz had guided her to this bench.

The light hung in the middle of the air like a screen, forming a circle which rapidly expanded. Iulia had seen bridges being formed before and recognized it now.

Sang stepped through the bridge. His expression was implacable, as he looked around the atrium. He spotted Raine and strode toward him.

Iulia gasped when she spotted the knife in Sang's

hand.

"You would not dare," Raine cried. "We know how to track your damned city, android. Kill me and your precious Demos dies!"

Sang didn't stop.

"Blink, defend me!" Raine cried out, shuffling backward.

Blink didn't move, not even when Sang almost brushed its shoulder as he passed.

Sang reached out for Raine with his free hand. Raine threw up his arms, trying to slap Sang's hand away.

Sang didn't make a sound. He merely shifted around Raine and grabbed a big fistful of his hair and yanked his head back, exposing his throat.

Iulia made no attempt to rise from the bench or protest as Sang slid the edge of the blade across Raine's throat, opening it up.

Raine scrabbled at Sang's arm with weak fingers and made gurgling noises. His eyes were very wide as he died.

Sang let the body drop and lowered the dripping knife. He studied Iulia.

She shivered. "You need me, now," she reminded him.

Sang considered that. "Then you know what you must do?"

"Yes."

He nodded and adjusted the belt at his waist. Another bridge formed. There were armed people on the other side, and their rattlers shifted to point at Iulia.

Sang tugged a hand-held rattler from the holster on his hip and tossed it to Riz. Riz caught it and armed it with competent movements.

"Check your targets," Sang told the android. He glanced at Blink. "You know who to find."

Blink nodded. So did Riz.

Sang stepped across the bridge, blood dripping across

the floor to where the bridge formed.

The bridge closed up behind him, leaving Iulia with the two androids and Raine's body.

The androids left, moving at a steady, inexorable pace, and then Iulia was alone with the body and the steadily spreading pool of blood around it.

She still couldn't cry.

22

IT WASN'T A MEETING THAT formed in the family council chamber, two hours later. The few survivors huddled in the room together, with blank expressions in their faces as Iulia swept into the room, Riz beside her.

"Why are you hiding here?" Iulia demanded of the four men standing in the far corner. She glanced at Riz. "I don't know how to turn on the lights. Do you?"

The lights came on.

The men stared at the heavy-gauge rattler in Riz's hands.

"Relax. She carries it to protect me, not kill you. If you were on the Demos hit list, you would be dead by now," Iulia told them. "You may as well sit at the table, gentlemen. You are the last of the family council and will be the first of the new order."

Their gazes shifted to her. Horror shone in their blank eyes.

Raine's murder had been replicated across all the families on all the Erium worlds. Riz had kept Iulia apprised as they traveled to the council chamber. Peru—darling, sensual Peru—had been one of the first to go. The others were all key people in the families. Their death hobbled Erium, for no decisions could be made without their quorum votes.

Sang had struck with surgical precision.

"Sit down!" Iulia railed at them.

They shifted. Moved apart. Slowly, they selected chairs and sat.

Iulia took the seat at the top of the table and dropped the lace mantle back around her shoulders, baring her head. "We do not have much time," she told them. "You will agree with me now, and quickly, that Erium must withdraw from all hostilities against Demos. *Now*, gentlemen."

Laronius of the Carosa family cleared his throat. "You mean, admit defeat?"

"We *are* defeated, fool!" Iulia raged.

"Withdrawing from hostilities will anger the Karassians," Salienus pointed out.

"Let them be angry. The Alliance is at an end. Demos has been stirred to battle and *they will win*. Whoever killed Bellona—" She drew in a breath. Let it out. "Whoever killed Bellona has unleashed a monster who will destroy us all, if we do not take immediate remedial steps to avert the danger to Erium. Do you understand?"

"What of this tool Traverse built, which can find Demos?" Laronius asked.

He had always been the negative one, the one who thought outside the box. Iulia gave him her best, dazzling smile. "What *they* have built is of no concern to us now."

"If it can find the invisible city…" Laronius protested.

"I *don't care*!" Iulia shouted. "Do you not understand? We are withdrawing from the conflict. The war. The whatever the hell this is. There is no way to win. Not now Bellona is dead. Not even if they destroy Demos itself. You cannot kill a martyr hero. You cannot defeat them once they are dead."

More blank looks.

"Riz, please show them the riots, and the Karassian navy."

A big screen formed in the center of the table, visible to all of them. The footage showing the rioting Karassians, and the imploding ships dropping to the planet ran silently.

The five men who remained of the family council—all

of them weak and easily influenced, and therefore not worth the effort of assassinating—looked even more ill than they had when she arrived.

"How do we withdraw?" Laronius said.

Iulia laughed. "We send out an announcement on every feed and channel we can access, and we pull every Eriuman ship back to local space. Now."

"No, I mean, *how* do we do that? Peru would have had to...I don't know...reach out to the other councils and reach an agreement. Then an order would be passed on to the military leaders. How do we do it now?"

"There *are* no other family councils left," Iulia told him.

They sank back in their seats, the news a weakening blow to them.

"*We* are all which remains of any government in Erium," Iulia informed them. "Get it through your heads, gentlemen. In the meantime, I happen to know two or three of the generals on a first name basis. I will speak to them and have them withdraw immediately."

Laronius licked his lips. "And the message on all channels?"

"Riz will help me."

They shot nervous glances at the android standing behind her, the rattler in their hands.

Riz smiled.

THE BEXENS AND BOTS HAD cleared the old command level of walls and furniture by the time Sang stepped through. The prisoners being held by the security cadre were moved to a different area of the city. He didn't know where. Thecla and Hero managed it.

Sang looked around the oval space. It was empty and echoed. When Demos had been just an abandoned

Karassian carrier called *Aarens*, this area had been filled with over-soft chairs, static screens and hard controls.

It seemed fitting that they return to this place now.

Sang connected with Dyse. "Ready?"

"As I will ever be," Dyse said sourly via Sang's aural feed.

"Chidi?"

"Recording and feeding. Every second of it, across two thousand and three feeds."

Sang nodded. Chidi would likely see the gesture. There were old lenses still buried in these walls he would have figured out how to access by now.

Sang generated screens, locking them to the original posts and positions of the bridge. While he worked, Thecla and Hayes came into the area. Hecate Halt followed them.

"Dyse?" Sang asked.

"Nearly there," Dyse said in his ear, sounding breathless.

"Hero?"

"I see her on the Ginza. She's coming."

Sang waited for everyone to arrive. He generated six screens around the old command chair, then patiently networked all the screens.

When Hero arrived just behind Dyse, Sang turned to them. "We've been a city for so long, we've forgotten how to be a ship. You must recall those skills now. We'll need them."

"What has happened?" Hero asked.

"Besides Erium collapsing?" Thecla asked grimly.

"It hasn't collapsed," Sang assured her. "Not altogether. A new structure will emerge from the old system. A democratic one."

"Democracy?" Thecla snorted. "Democracies don't work."

"As the Sodality is just finding out for itself," Sang replied.

"Is that why we're here?" Hayes asked.

"We're here, because Mesut Traverse, the third member of the triad controlling the Alliance, found a way to trace Demos and predict where we will be."

"Oh, shit…" Hero breathed.

"How did she do *that*?" Thecla demanded. "If they can track the city, we're…" She shook her head. "We're fucked."

"Not completely," Sang replied.

"How *did* she find us?" Hero said.

"Through Dyse," Sang said.

Dyse hung his head.

"You?" Thecla whirled on Dyse, her hand dropping to the butt of her rattler.

"He has not betrayed us," Sang said. "The opposite, in fact. He has spent years helping Demos hide in space. It was sensible to run strategy diagnostics, to learn if there were any weaknesses in our defenses and make adjustments. Dyse is essentially a database, and Traverse is… *was* Bureau."

"She hacked *you*, Dyse?" Hayes asked.

"There is a weakness, then?" Thecla added.

"Yes, to both," Dyse said. "Traverse accessed a core of mine that was once publicly accessible by the Bureau, using a backdoor she inserted in Bureau days. She found my theory that the forge belts the Alliance have stolen from us over the years—"

"They're useless to them!" Hero cried. "They're keyed to biometrics!"

"The navigation and coordinate setting software can be analyzed. With enough belts, a pattern could be found."

"A pattern which predicts where we will be," Sang finished.

"Then we don't jump there," Thecla said. "We change the pattern."

Sang shook his head. "There is a reason we've forgotten to think of ourselves as a ship in space. This city is thirty times larger than the *Aarens*. The null generator engines could no longer overcome inertia, even at full power. We've had velocity since the city began jumping constantly, though. The engines keep us moving, just enough for the city to jump to null space and emerge somewhere else. Changing the direction of the city is impossible. We would come to a dead stop…and then we couldn't jump again. We would be defenseless."

"If they can find us, we're already defenseless," Thecla said.

Hero crossed her arms and tilted her head at Sang. "You *knew* this would happen."

"Yes."

"How long have you known?"

"A while."

"And you did *nothing*?" Thecla cried.

Sang braced himself and prepared to answer.

"He did everything he should," Dyse said. "Everything he had to do, he did it without flinching. Sang has the courage I lacked."

"You knew about this, too?" Hecate demanded.

"I think you will find that even Chidi has sensed the shape of this, too," Dyse told her, his tone gentle. "In the end game, there are a limited number of moves. Most of them are fatal. Sang has navigated around every danger."

"You *let Bellona die*?" Hayes cried.

Sang let the sadness touch him. "I could not stop it. Not by then."

"You knew she would die…" Hero breathed, her face working.

"Then you might have stopped this, sometime earlier?"

Thecla asked.

"For nearly a year, I did nothing," Sang told her. "Only, doing nothing is also a choice, and the future it would bring us to was an abyss which humanity would never climb out of."

Hecate's cheeks were wet. "Did Bellona know what you were doing? What would happen to her?"

Sang sighed. "She made her choice. Freedom for everyone, no matter the cost."

"And this, where we are, this is freedom?" Thecla demanded, her face working. Her hand gripped the rattler with convulsive squeezes. "Erium destroyed by androids, Karassia in flames and fighting itself? And us, caught in the middle, a fat, lumbering target for the Alliance to take potshots at, as soon as they appear through their superbridges?"

"There is no more Alliance," Sang said gently.

"Then who is tracking us?" Hecate said.

"For the last decade…more than that, I suppose, the Karassian military has been inundated with patriotic recruits filled with rage against Bellona, driven to defend their precious Sodality via years of hate speech and propaganda. Chidi barely dented the conditioning, but the few hundred he turned will infect others. More will open their eyes when the Karassian military is defeated by the free worlds and bought to heel."

"Defeated…how?"

"I gave the free worlds the forge belt designs and the last of the carbyne," Sang told them. "And they also have the working designs for the neural networked superforges the Alliance built. And the city killer, too. They have it all."

"Where did they get the superforge design from?" Hecate demanded.

"Khalil," Hero breathed. She closed her eyes. "He's ex-

Bureau, too. He was being held in the heart of Karassia."

Sang nodded.

"How could he possibly escape from there?" Hayes breathed.

"He knew he wouldn't," Thecla replied. Her voice was hoarse.

Hero sighed.

"To answer your original question, Hecate, those who are about to attack us are the core of the Karassian military, who hate Demos and everything it stands for. They will know by now that the free worlds have the superforge and the city killer, and it will scare them and make them want to hit out. Only, it is too late. Equilibrium has been reached. A permanent balance, one which eluded Bellona all these years."

"And Demos has to die for that?" Thecla breathed.

"Demos is the last of the old power structure. Yes, it must die," Sang replied. "It is the end of the story. Bellona has died for her ideals. Now Demos must, too, so the ideal lives on. Only then will the story survive. The story is everything, Thecla. Stories are the means by which humans learn how to survive. It is how they remember what *must* be kept alive."

He stirred and waved around the oval room, at the screens which hung over work stations which no longer existed. "We still have a role to play, though."

Thecla crossed her arms. "Fight to the end," she said grimly.

THE END, WHEN IT CAME, was still a surprise, even though they were all braced for it.

"The trouble with predictive extrapolation is that it only tells the future in broad strokes," Dyse pointed out, after the thirty-seventh hour upon the old bridge.

"Couldn't we do this from the common room?" Hero asked, stretching her back and bending to touch her toes. "There's food there. Coffee."

Sang asked the bexens to bring both.

Hayes laid down upon the cold floor and slept with his face upon one arm. His snores were soft background sounds as they worked on the screens, growing accustomed once more to bridge commands and directing a large ship.

Chidi filtered the news from across the known worlds to their screens, reporting on events everywhere. They watched Karassia collapse, and Erium go dark and silent. The free worlds stirred and came to life, as the old structures crumbled. Wild speeches were made from city steps, announcing the end of the Alliance, the end of tyranny.

Spontaneous celebrations broke out on nearly every world. They listened to the music, the fireworks and the parties, while they worked on the bridge and braced themselves.

"Heads-up!" Hecate shouted, at the top of the thirty-eighth hour. "Port side…and damn, only five kilometers away!"

"Right on the dot," Thecla muttered, arming the weapons.

"Fire at will," Sang told them.

Chidi thoughtfully threw a super-large screen at the top of the room, high overhead so they could all see it just with a lift of their chins, if they dared glance away from their screens. Sang, at the command chair, could afford the time to look.

The tethered micro satellites gave a perfect vantage point. Demos was a cosmopolitan jumble of structures and towers, plateaus and crevasses. It had long ago lost any resemblance to an elongated carrier. That original structure, at the back and top of the city, had long ago been subsumed by more civilized components. Only the null generator engines were left fully exposed, for they were needed to drive the city forward. They gave the city the speed needed to make the endless jumps to null space, then back to normal space.

"Override the programming and jump now," Sang told Dyse.

Dyse shook his head. "There's not enough time. The generators need to reset and come back up to full. Forty seconds at least."

Sang nodded. It was the answer he had expected.

On the big screen, Sang saw the two Karassian frigates hurtling toward Demos. They were not braking. Their city killers were not glowing, ready to fire. They were throwing themselves at the city, like a soldier upon spears.

Thecla and Hero controlled the port and starboard weapons arrays, while Hayes protected the top of the city and Hecate guarded the lower levels.

"The engines!" Sang cried. "They're exposed! Don't let the frigates through!"

Thecla's *and* Hero's novo-gun turrets sprayed the path in front of the frigates with mines. Bolts of energy played over the shielded sides of the frigates, which returned fire, their energy beams flicking over the city.

"Dyse, warn everyone to hold on!" Sang cried, as the floor beneath his feet trembled.

"Done," Dyse said calmly.

"Six more bridges just opened," Hecate warned.

The first of the frigates reached the area strewn with mines. It didn't deviate from its course.

Sang had been ready for this stoic relentlessness. He had expected it.

The broad nose of the frigate bloomed into a red fireball, while more explosions peppered its flanks.

The second frigate continued on, the path cleared by the first. It slid passed the first, its upper decks almost scraping the belly of the first as it shot through the narrow aperture the first had opened for them.

Thecla and Hero sprayed the oncoming frigate with everything they had. Fires flared and died, explosions threw up splinters of fuselage all over the frigate. Still it came on.

Thecla ran her beams and bolts down the side of the ship, tearing a ragged seam along the length. Then she carefully picked out the repulsor engine cones on the rear and concentrated on the bulkhead right behind them. The micro satellites gave her a perfect view and let her correct her aim.

The bulkhead buckled and imploded. Then the entire rear of the ship blew out and backward, as the reactor overloaded.

"It's dead," Thecla declared happily.

"Six more frigates," Hecate warned.

The frigate continued at the same inexorable pace, inertia driving it now. Nothing would shunt it aside. It was dead, as Thecla had intended.

They all lifted their gazes up to the big screen, to watch the frigate slide toward Demos. The massive craft looked small against the size of the city, yet it shadowed the engine exhausts.

"Brace yourselves!" Sang cried.

The impact shoved the city through space and threw everyone to the floor. The critically injured engines roared and rumbled, making the floor vibrate. From here, they could hear the explosions.

The screens flickered and came back. Sang looked up at the large screen.

The dead frigate had cannoned off the engines and

now drifted in the opposite direction.

The engines exhausts were black and cold. They were dead.

"Null generators off line," Dyse told Sang.

Sang nodded, watching the second disabled frigate float past the end of the Demos.

"What do we do with the other six frigates?" Hero demanded, as she squeezed her elbow and winced.

"We do what we agreed to do," Sang told her.

"We fight to the end." Thecla cracked her knuckles. "Dyse, whatever you can spare for my turrets, please?"

"Coming up."

"And mine," Hero added, settling back behind her screen.

"How bad is it in the city?" Sang asked Dyse.

"Bad enough that you don't want to know right now," Dyse assured him.

Hecate tilted her head. "They're not firing."

Sang looked up at the screen showing the frigates as they hove into view. They were in a spear head formation, running close to each other. Close enough that their proximity alarms had to be screaming at them.

Understanding flashed through him, making him cold. "They're going to ram us..."

"They watched our engines die," Thecla added. "Hero, focus on the noses. Let's soften the impact as much as we can before they hit."

Hero swallowed. Her face was pale as she pulled her attention to the screen.

Both sets of gun arrays played over the front of the approaching frigates. They lobbed mines, and sliced off hull pieces, until the space directly in front of the spearhead became a junkyard of scrap metal moving just ahead of the ships.

"Too close! Out of range!" Thecla cried, as the guns fell silent.

It seemed to Sang that the entire city held its breath as the spearhead raced toward them. Chidi would make sure everyone near a screen would see what they were watching on the bridge. Or he would generate a screen and *make* them see. Just as he was force-feeding the channels going out across the known worlds. Everyone had a ringside view upon these last moments in the life of Demosthenes. Were they all holding their breath, too?

Sang hoped so. For Bellona's sake.

The impact shook and rattled the city. Alarms sounded. Explosions shattered the silence beyond the bridge. Sang could hear the roar of fire and screams and shouting, far away on the other side of the private wing. It echoed from the screens showing quick snapshots of various parts of the city. For less than a second, Sang saw the empty, dark assembly hall, with debris upon the floor.

"Ah…Sang?" Dyse pointed to his screen.

The screen showed the crescent of a blue-green planet. The edge of the crescent shimmered.

Atmosphere.

"Where is that?" Sang breathed.

"Directly beneath," Dyse said. "Or I should say, ahead of us. We're on a collision course, Sang. There's nothing we can do to shift out of its way, now the generator engines are dead."

Sang pulled up the diagnostics on his screen as everyone watched him. He scanned the readouts. Breathable atmosphere, nearly standard gravity. "Are the maneuvering thrusters working?" he asked Dyse.

Thecla snorted, as she held a torn away sleeve against the back of her head to staunch the cut there. The sleeve was Hayes'. "They're buried under city superstructure."

"Not anymore," Sang said. He nodded toward the big screen. "Look."

The top of the city had been sheared away. Debris and

flotsam was drifting up from the jagged wounds. The old outline of the *Aarens* could be seen among the fractures and gaping holes.

Behind the city, the six frigates drifted aimlessly. They were lifeless shells, now.

"Let me see what I can do," Dyse said, turning back to his screen.

"Hurry," Sang said. "We'll hit atmosphere in three minutes. I need them online by then."

"To do what?" Thecla demanded. "You can't pull Demos out of the atmosphere once we're in it, not with itty-bitty steering engines."

Sang shook his head. "We can't stop this now. Only, instead of nose-diving into the surface, we can *glide* in. All we have to do is keep the city as horizontal to the surface as we can. There's so much surface area on the lower levels, it will act like a hull in the air. The maneuvering jets will help keep us upright."

Everyone watched Dyse as he frowned and muttered and punched at his screens. "Damn, they're fighting back."

"They haven't been fired for over ten years. I'm surprised you can get them to even acknowledge you're there," Thecla said.

"I have my ways," Dyse shot back, with a lift of the corner of his mouth. "There. Control is yours, Sang."

The dashboard Dyse had thrown together while he muttered appeared on Sang's screen. Yaw, pitch and roll. A horizon gauge.

Sang touched the controls, a gentle nudge. He let his awareness out beyond his body, into the city networks, which ran through the walls and floors and the heart of the city itself. He *became* the city. When his fingers nudged the control to roll the ship to port, it was really the city dropping its flank to correct the yaw and bring the horizon back to steady.

Then a lift of its bow, to slow the descent against the drag of the atmosphere. Another flex to starboard as the port side dropped.

The bridge was silent, as the city vibrated around them, shaken by the thick atmosphere and the heat of entry against the hulls and exteriors which had never been designed with atmosphere in mind.

Sang could sense/feel the scorching of the exterior, the cracking and tearing of the interior at the extraordinary stresses, as if it was his bones fracturing and bending.

He gritted his teeth and fought to keep the city alive for a few moments more…just a little more.

"Ten thousand meters," Thecla intoned.

They had descended so far already? Time, which had always been a constant for him, had dilated the way it did for humans.

"Dyse, warn them," Sang gasped, as the elevation spun downward.

"They know," Dyse whispered back.

The false horizon became the real one. He saw landmass. Oceans. Mountain chains. The glint of an inland sea.

Open ocean was ahead, although it would be no softer than earth, not at this speed. He resisted the human temptation to drop the nose of the city and let it slap into the water. He straightened the city up one last time.

The bottom levels touched the surface. A fleeting scrape. The city lurched. Momentum checked. More scrapes and bounces. The speed was slowing.

Slowing…

Land ahead.

Green mass. Trees. They would be softer than the ocean. They would act as the brush of fingers beneath, slowing them even more.

The city staggered and checked. Slowed.

Sang could feel/sense structures tearing away beneath them. Sections…whole suburbs…ripped away.

Everyone but Sang had dropped to the heaving floor and laid with their hands thrust out to stop themselves from being flung across the room. Sang shifted his feet automatically, able to anticipate the movement of the floor by the out-flung extremities of his senses.

The city slowed, rumbling with death groans. The eyes providing the viewpoint at the front of the city, by which Sang had been watching, blanked out. His senses withdrew, as the city tore apart.

"Sang, watch out!" Hero slammed into his side, shoving him across the floor, as the room shrieked and groaned around them.

Sang landed on his back, as the ancient girder dropped where he had been standing.

The screens flickered and disappeared.

Darkness swallowed them as Demos died.

Epilogue

Two thousand, two hundred and six years later.

ROCHUS ASKES STEPPED THROUGH THE private bridge to the Secretary General's antechamber. He had been granted access privileges many years ago, when Yarrick Kader had first been elected to the chair position of the League of Sovereign States.

Even though this visit was a formal, official one, Yarrick wouldn't mind the informality of using the private bridge. It saved Askes from the clearance procedures surrounding the public gate.

Kader's assistant, the sweet little biobot, Hilargi, tilted her head as he stepped over. It was her version of a smile, as her face was still rigid metal fiber. She was working on earning her first body, she had confessed to Kader years ago. He hoped she was close to her ambition now. She was a good-natured woman.

"He's expecting you," she told Askes.

Askes went in.

Yarrick Kader turned away from the window. The view from up here was dizzying. The altitude, he'd told Askes, gave him perspective when he needed to reflect.

"You look cold, Rochus. Coffee?" Kader said.

"It's the environmental suit. They are never warm enough." He'd been glad to shrug out of the damn thing.

"Arriguci has a mean summer temperature of two hundred and twenty Kelvins," Kader pointed out, as he poured and handed Askes a big mug of coffee. "A chill is nothing. Returning with all your toes intact should be considered an achievement."

"You've been reading the dig prospective," Askes accused him.

Kader's expression sobered. "That's not all I've been reading. While I've been waiting for the bridge to be built and for you to cycle through a hot shower, I scanned the first rough translation of the records your exo cracked open."

"The Indigo files."

"Is that what we're calling them?"

"It's what the entity called himself." Askes paused. "Sang Indigo," he added.

Kader considered him, his thick gray brow lifted. "If it really is the Invisible City, Askes, then it is nothing like the myths you have been collecting all these years."

"No." Askes drew in a breath and let it out. "It is far, far more…*real*, than I ever hoped it might be."

"Only the record—the story this Indigo recorded—it doesn't match known facts, Askes. He talks about the planet he guided the city onto having an atmosphere and oceans."

Askes nodded. "If the city is the size he seems to imply, then its impact upon Arriguci could have been an extinction level event. There is a layer of dirt beneath the surface crust, sitting on top of the ship. It could be masses of earth which settled back on top of the ship once it landed. Crashed. That means it flung a *lot* of dust into the air. An endless winter, a leaching of the atmosphere, which would expose the surface water to unfiltered sunlight. Evaporation and drying after that." He shrugged. "We'll be years and years sorting out what really happened after it landed."

"And what happened before. We can't take these records as the truth, Askes."

"Why *not*?" Askes demanded. "Why would *anyone*, digital or otherwise, lie to themselves in a private journal?

Give me one good reason."

Kader grimaced. "Because he knew they would be found and read. He was planning upon it."

Askes blinked. "You don't know that."

"I read the reports, Askes. He anticipated this day. He knew it would arrive. His…epiphany, whatever it was he had…it was on a scale only the largest virtual minds can encompass even today. And he was just a digital human."

"One of the first," Askes added. "These records have to be made public, Yarrick."

"Must they?" Kader replied softly. "Think what the impact upon society would be if we told them their favorite childhood story was true…just not anywhere close to the way they thought it happened."

"They were all still heroes," Askes pointed out.

"Even C'leel the Traitor, apparently," Kader said, his tone sour. "I couldn't believe it when I read it. That's just it, Askes. I'm having trouble accepting this and I'm a grown adult."

"You're a skeptic of giant proportions," Askes replied. "Besides, I don't think you *can* hide this. Someone will talk about it. The truth will emerge. It always does. And this is about Bellona the Czarina! You can't suppress it, Kader. Not for long."

Kader grimaced. "That's what I'm afraid of." He pointed to the screen hovering over his desk. "Did you read the coda?"

Askes drew in a breath. "Yes."

"He updated the report one last time."

"*After* the crash," Askes added.

Kader met Askes' gaze. "He survived the crash. Long enough to update his records. Maybe longer."

"There is no trace of DNA on the wreckage," Askes pointed out. "Maybe he *did* get everyone off, the way he wanted to."

Kader snorted. "Then went off to stabilize the known worlds?"

"There are no bodies. Not even calcified fossils, Kader."

Kader sobered. "It's too fantastic to consider. *That's* my concern, Askes. If this must come out, and I agree with you that the truth has a way of emerging all by itself, then it must be handled properly. You don't want the entire quadrant laughing at you."

Askes shuddered and drank his coffee. "No," he murmured into the mug.

"The myth of Bellona the Czarina had given humanity a set of basic human principals we have lived by, more or less, for two thousand years. *You* wrote your thesis arguing the myth pulled humans out of the Age of Misrule! You really want to be the man responsible for dismantling those tenets?"

Askes considered. "Perhaps we have acquired enough stability as a civilization to withstand the truth."

Kader sighed. "This is not a question to be answered today. It will require careful thought."

Askes drained the coffee. "You have skirted around the other implication with neat precision, Yarrick."

"Oh?"

"Even back then, the androids were using DNA-generated bodies."

"The humans were not, back then."

"There were three digital people on that ship, at least," Askes pointed out. "During the chaos of Misrule, the technology advanced at a rapid pace because there were no controls. Terrible experiments and horrible accidents increased our understanding of digital minds exponentially. If Sang Indigo survived the crash and got himself and his digital friends off the planet somehow, then where did they go?"

"Into the chaos, one presumes," Kader said sourly. "You're the digital. You tell me."

Askes put the mug on the table with a soft thud. "Very well then. Consider this. What if Sang Indigo is still alive? A hundred bodies on from his original, but with his identity intact. What if he's still working to make Bellona's vision come true?"

Kader tried to laugh. Then he tried again.

He failed.

Coda

There were few people surrounding Bellona who understood that it was not another empire she sought to build. She wanted to tear down empires and alliances and let all free people go their own way.

Even I did not understand, at first. I had to become human before I could grasp such a concept. Bellona gave me the gift of freedom that she wanted for everyone. I am the embodiment of her ambitions.

Bellona and Khalil knew what they had asked me to put into place. They agreed, anyway. I knew they would, for I loved them and knew them too well. It is why I could clearly see the path ahead, when Dyse could not.

Their choice helped me make mine. History will prove if I am wrong.

We will see.

Did you enjoy this series? How to make a big difference!

Reviews are powerful.

Authors like me, without the financial muscle of a sleek New York publisher backing me, can't take advertisements out in the subways and billboards of the world.

On the other hand, New York publishers would *kill* to get what I have: A committed and loyal group of readers.

Honest reviews of my books help bring them to the attention of other readers. If you enjoyed this book I would be grateful if you could spend just a few minutes leaving a review (it can be as short as you like) on the book's page where you bought it.

Thank you so much!

Cameron

About the Author

Cameron Cooper is the author of The Indigo Reports science fiction series and the alter ego for an Amazon #1 bestselling author in an unrelated genre. The Indigo Reports was originally conceived as a one-off series, but readers demanded more. The Imperial Hammer series releases in early 2020.

Cameron tends to write space opera short stories and novels, but also roams across the science fiction landscape. Cameron was raised on a steady diet of Asimov, Heinlein, Herbert, McCaffrey, and others. Peter F. Hamilton and John Scalzi are contemporary heroes. An Australian Canadian, Cam lives near the Canadian Rockies.

Other books by Cameron Cooper

For reviews, excerpts, and more about each title, visit Cameron's site and click on the cover you are interested in: https://cameroncooperauthor.com/books-by-thumbnail/

Imperial Hammer

Hammer and Crucible
Star Forge
Long Live the Emperor
Severed
Destroyer of Worlds

The Indigo Reports

(Space Opera)
Flying Blind
New Star Rising
But Now I See
Suns Eclipsed
Worlds Beyond

Standalone Short SF

Resilience

www.ingramcontent.com/pod-product-compliance
Lightning Source LLC
LaVergne TN
LVHW010222110826
845148LV00022B/1227

* 9 7 8 1 7 7 4 3 8 1 8 5 4 *